Girls' Night In

Gentlemen by Invitation

To all the people who made the original
Girls' Night In such a fabulous success
and this wonderful sequel possible.
You know who you are! Thank you!

Girls' Night In

Gentlemen by Invitation

Edited by
Jessica Adams,
Chris Manby and
Fiona Walker

PENGUIN BOOKS

Further information about this book may be found at www.girlsnightin.org

Penguin Books Australia Ltd
487 Maroondah Highway, PO Box 257
Ringwood, Victoria 3134, Australia
Penguin Books Ltd
Harmondsworth, Middlesex, England
Penguin Putnam Inc.
375 Hudson Street, New York, New York 10014, USA
Penguin Books Canada Limited
10 Alcorn Avenue, Toronto, Ontario, Canada M4V 3B2
Penguin Books (NZ) Ltd
Cnr Rosedale and Airborne Roads, Albany, Auckland, New Zealand
Penguin Books (South Africa) (Pty) Ltd
24 Sturdee Avenue, Rosebank, Johannesburg 2196, South Africa
Penguin Books India (P) Ltd
11, Community Centre, Panchsheel Park, New Delhi 110 017, India

First published by Penguin Books Australia 2001

10 9 8 7 6 5 4 3

Text designed by Nikki Townsend, Penguin Design Studio
Typeset in Galliard by Midland Typesetters, Maryborough, Victoria
Printed and bound in Australia by McPherson's Printing Group, Maryborough, Victoria

National Library of Australia
Cataloguing-in-Publication data:

Girls' night in, gentlemen by invitation.

ISBN 0 14 300004 7.

1. Short stories, English. 2. Short stories, Australian.
I. Adams, Jessica

823.0108

www.penguin.com.au

Foreword

Many is the time I have heard parents, mothers, speak of their children with a love so strong they claim it threatens to overwhelm them, but I never really knew what that must be like.

I would sit in the comfort of my living room and watch television pictures of emaciated, desperate children, hope and laughter having long since disappeared from their eyes, and would feel sad, and guilty, and hope that somehow someone was doing something to make their lives better.

And now someone is. You.

By buying this book, you are helping to make someone's life infinitely better. You are helping to bring love and laughter into a child's life, a child who often hasn't had much experience of what is joyful, and positive and fun.

All you have to do is curl up and start turning the pages.

Some of the most popular young writers in Australia and the UK have gathered together to provide the stories for this book, not to mention a few of my personal favourites. Fiona Walker with her warmth and humour, Patrick Gale with his brilliance and emotive truths. You are not just doing a favour for charity, you are letting yourself in for a real treat.

I am a mother now. I fully understand what it is to have children, and how you would do anything to keep them safe from harm; to ensure they feel loved and secure. I have a year-old son who is the most amazing, extraordinary, wonderful thing to have ever happened to me. I watch him toddle around, holding onto furniture for balance, grinning at me as he claps his hands together clumsily, and my heart feels like it's going to burst with love and wonder.

I now know what every mother in the world talks about when she talks about her child.

And when I watch those same television clips, I am moved in a way I never was before. As a mother you want nothing but the absolute best for your children, to provide them with a safe, warm and loving environment, even when circumstances are beyond your control. Even when you are in the midst of a war zone and everyone else's priorities have changed.

The children served by War Child are often not lucky enough to have that safety and warmth, and without that, their laughter is not quite so loud, their tears fall that bit harder.

Which is why War Child exists. Every copy you buy will enrich these children's lives just a little bit more.

Thank you.

Jane Green

Contents

Chris Manby, Fiona Walker and Jessica Adams
Introduction xi

Neil Morrissey and Hugo Speer
A Thank You from War Child xvii

Kaz Cooke
Girls' Night Innaggin xix

Jessica Adams
Love is Science Fiction 1

Maggie Alderson
The Master Baker 13

Louise Bagshawe
What Goes Around . . . 40

Emily Barr
Revenge 49

Mark Barrowcliffe
Little Boots – An Unfairy Tale 63

Colin Bateman
Chapter & Verse 82

CONTENTS

Matt Beaumont
Boy's Night In   98

John Birmingham
Actually, Twenty-Three Beers Will Not Improve
Your Judgement   119

Marc Blake
Bighead   129

Yasmin Boland
She Came in Through the Open Window   145

Bruno Bouchet
Iron Lady, Ice Maiden   151

Colette Caddle
When the Fat Lady Sings   173

Anna Davis
Delivering Happyware   193

Martina Devlin
Home and Dry   211

Isla Dewar
The Alma Club   228

Neal Drinnan
Gentlemen Prefer Special K   247

Nick Earls
Cabin Baggage   260

Imogen Edwards-Jones
Weddings and Wonderbras   282

Tim Ferguson
Death of an Executive   299

Patrick Gale
Obedience   313

CONTENTS

Mike Gayle
Grumpus — 331

Sarah Harris
Mother Figure — 347

John Hegley
Ultimate Um — 364

Linda Jaivin
Iron Orchid — 379

Gretel Killeen
Bullet Point Bravery — 401

Sophie Kinsella
Changing People — 403

Kathy Lette
Been There; Licked That. Or – The Things
I Wish I'd Known at Twenty-Five — 422

Paul J. Livingston
Not a Rehearsal — 426

Robert Llewellyn
The Deck Hangers — 441

Josie Lloyd and Emlyn Rees
For a Few Dollars Whore I & II — 460

Hector Macdonald
Relative Madness — 479

Serena Mackesy
Stone Money — 498

Chris Manby
Art Lover — 514

Monica McInerney
Just Desserts — 525

CONTENTS

Santa Montefiore
The Fortune Teller 547

Alexandra Potter
No Strings Attached 559

Mark Powell
Forwards 576

Matthew Reilly
Altitude Rush 595

Allison Rushby
The Rat 621

David Smiedt
Hit and Myth 635

Michael Marshall Smith
Last Glance Back 652

Stephanie Theobald
The Masturbation Map 670

Helen Townsend
Behaving Badly 685

Fiona Walker
Red Letter Day 703

Matt Whyman
Enfemme 725

Notes on the Contributors 740

About War Child 759

Introduction
Chris Manby, Fiona Walker
and Jessica Adams

CHRIS MANBY:

With the lotto making a new millionaire every week, it's hard to believe that buying a book can make a difference. But when a few people get behind one small idea, they have the potential to change a world. Which is what the countless people who bought *Girls' Night In* – in both the UK and Australia – have done for kids in Kosovo and Rwanda.

The book was published in the UK in July 2000 and in Australia in October 2000, and by late that year, War Child were able to build the first *Girls' Night In* safe play area in Dardania, a grim inner-city estate in Pristina, Kosovo. Fiona Walker and I were lucky enough to be there for the opening (a tough choice for me – I had to shelve a romantic weekend to spend my birthday with the Marines!). We spent three days shadowing the War Child team as they went about their usual business in the war-torn province: putting the finishing touches to the playground built in conjunction with the Royal Marines, taking groceries to families unable to feed themselves through illness or poverty, translating prescriptions and sourcing vital medicines, liaising with UN officials to ensure that children living in the kind of portakabins you see on building sites here had somewhere warm to spend the winter . . . We soon learned that War Child do a lot more than build swings and seesaws.

My abiding image of that weekend is of a little girl called Yasmina. She lives in a mental hospital in a place called Shtime, though it's not clear how she came to be there. She was about eight years old, dressed as a boy, with her hair shaven in a brutal crew-cut. Somehow, using a mixture of pidgin English and Italian, she persuaded me to part with my digital watch. As soon as I got back into the War Child jeep, however, she was surrounded by other patients – all adults – and I realised how stupid I had been to give her something that would make her a target for bullies. But I wanted her to know that she deserved more than she had. War Child have already built a fabulous playground at that hospital, where the kids can forget about the grim Dickens-style institution they live in for a while. They drive a much-needed truckload of fruit and veg to the hospital twice a week to ensure that the children get proper nutrition. But isn't that just the minimum all children deserve?

I'm sure that Fiona will agree with me when I say that attending the opening of that War Child playground in Dardania was a far more gratifying experience than seeing your name in print for the very first time. But I came away from Pristina feeling very unsettled. Just as the first anthology has to be followed by a second, it was clear that War Child's work in Kosovo is far from over.

It was meeting Yasmina that convinced me that *Girls' Night In* needed a sequel.

FIONA WALKER:

The first safe play area that was funded by *Girls' Night In* is situated on a huge flat clearing in the centre of a dangerously overcrowded high-rise estate. Crime is rife – Dardania is a Mafia stronghold and there's a big drugs problem; the Marines keep 24-hour surveillance and there is now an anonymous help-line set up for residents to report aggravation. In the heart of so much trouble, you don't expect to hear laughter, but on that day Chris and I attended the playground's opening, it was almost deafening. We watched in wonder as the whole community turned out – pensioners sat on benches, mothers swapped news by prams and other residents leaned out from their balconies to witness at least 4000 children running riot on the swings, monkey bars, climbing frames and seesaws. The Marines put on a great show, with displays and games and hundreds of chocolate bars. There were speeches, a band struck up and a helicopter swooped down to land, sending up a cloud of dust.

The party was a triumph, but it's the children and their playground that really matter. Just a few hours later, the helicopter took off again and the tanks began rolling away, the Marines packed up their mini-assault course and started to dismantle the temporary stage. But the kids played on regardless. As darkness fell, they were still swinging and shrieking and running from one piece of equipment to another. They stayed out there until they were practically asleep on their feet, and then they were back as soon as it grew light the following morning. They would, we were told, play on throughout the bitter winter, even when their hands stick to the swing's frozen chains and half the wooden struts of the tower are looted for firewood.

Almost 70 per cent of the Kosovo population is under the age of twenty-one. As well as a constant pelt of traffic in Pristina, there are children everywhere. The two are a lethal combination. Immediately after the conflict, with nowhere safe from landmines to play and the schools in chaos, these children took to kicking balls around in the street. The road beside the once-beautiful Gdanski Park saw four children killed in as many weeks.

That has changed, thanks to War Child and the money this book is helping to raise. Painted in primary colours and situated beside schools or in the hearts of estates like Dardania, the War Child safe play areas stand out amidst the litter and rubble. And they are always teeming with children. There'll be four on each end of the seesaw, three on a swing and an unruly, laughing, fighting line waiting to get to the slides. And, perhaps surprisingly, it's almost as enjoyable to watch the scraps and squabbles as the shared laughter. Because these children were once subdued and terrified, have grieved and struggled to understand what's going on around them. Now they can be children again – loud, teasing, shrieking, quarrelling children. They may face an uncertain future, but as they swing from bar to bar on the climbing frames and load onto the seesaws to find the perfect balance, one can't help but feel hopeful. For now they are content just playing, letting their energy and imaginations run riot far from the threat of land-mines or the sound of gunfire. To have that freedom is unspeakably precious.

Chris and I visited Pristina for just a few days; we saw the merest glimpse of the devastation war wreaks on communities, families and children, and the amazing work that War Child does to help remedy this. All we can give you is a thumbnail sketch of one city in crisis and the charity striving to change that. But our short time in Kosovo left us without doubt that this very special book is as badly needed as the first. What you are holding in your hands isn't just a collection of enter-taining stories. It isn't just a coin in a rattling bucket. It's something that will make a difference – a huge difference – to thousands of lives. Thank you for being a part of it.

JESSICA ADAMS:
Girls' Night In was definitely *the* book to be seen clutching in airports from Heathrow to Sydney over the summer of 2000 – and why not? It's been a bestseller in England, Ireland and Australia and it's been translated into Dutch and French. It's paid for a girls' school in Kigali, wind-up radios in Africa, and the first of many safe play areas in the Balkans. In America, it's inspired a similar charity short-story anthology, involving everyone from Candace Bushnell to Karen Moline and Meera Syal.

Along the way, the original *GNI* authors (what an incredible bunch of women) compiled an extremely wobbly home video of War Child hard at work and female authors enthusiastically waving their handbags at the camera wherever possible. (There are more handbags in the *Girls' Night In* video than you normally find on the lower ground floor of London's Harvey Nichols.) We filmed authors at a Sydney bookshop reading to hundreds of people who'd turned up in the rain, and mad manicure events where you could get your book signed with one hand, and have your nails covered in Chanel on the other. From Bath to Brisbane, the original *GNI* women signed books, squeezed publicity out of local radio, and helped turn a vague idea into a publishing phenomenon. Thank you!

War Child famously keeps its office and staff costs low (you should taste their instant coffee) in order to make the projects the priority. If you'd like to know more about the story so far, please visit the website www.girlsnightin.org. You're funding theatre workshops for children in Montenegro with this book. Watch for photos on the website this summer – I'll try to hold the camera still.

A Thank You from War Child

Welcome to *Girls' Night In, Gentlemen By Invitation*. It's your excuse to turn the TV off, find yourself a drink and relax with a fantastic book! And remember, you and the many others who are reading this have already made a difference to the lives of thousands of children.

Since getting involved with War Child we have seen children living lives full of suffering and despair. Children in Rwanda who, having seen their parents and grandparents massacred in the genocide of 1994, have had to live, without adults, in desperate poverty ever since. Children like those in Southern Sudan who have never known anything but famine and brutal conflict. And children from Kosovo whose lives had been turned upside down, who had been forced to flee their homes without knowing when or if they would return.

But we have been lucky enough to be part of an organisation that can help. We have seen how giving children the chance to play safely – as War Child and *Girls' Night In* have done in Kosovo – allows them to regain some of their childhood. How a wind-up radio given to a child-headed household in Rwanda can not only give them access to education and health programming, but also a connection to the world outside their small commune. And we have seen how a child in Sudan who arrived at a feeding centre emaciated was transformed into a smiling, healthy little boy in just a month.

That is why this book is important – because without the money that you donated when you bought this, we couldn't help.

So thank you to all the authors for donating their stories, to HarperCollins and Penguin Books for their great support, and particularly to Chris, Fiona and Jessica for their commitment and hard work, for coming up with the idea in the first place, and for making it happen twice in so short a time.

And thanks to you for buying it. It's a damn good read. Enjoy.

Neil Morrissey, Trustee

Hugo Speer, Patron

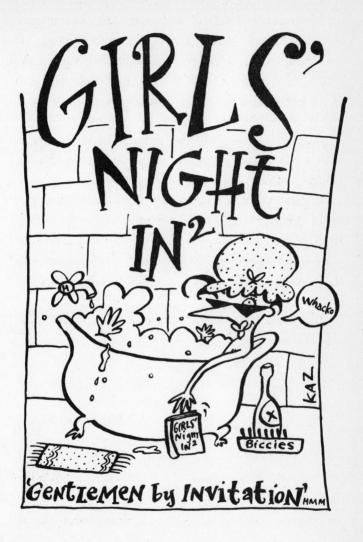

Love is Science Fiction

Jessica Adams

I decided to bring my transistor radio into work this morning. We're not supposed to. They're always saying the make-up van is for make-up, not entertainment. But anyway, I thought it might cheer things up a bit. It gets so boring in here – staring at other people in the mirror, staring at you.

Men always say to me, 'Oh it must be so exciting working in television.' I say, it depends on what sort of television you're working in. *Skippy,* I will admit, was a highlight. But this! We're not even in colour!

We got rained out yesterday, which means the final battle between the Dragors and the Vods for control of Bodaris 5 had to be postponed. Hector the Director came in and had a look at the quarry this morning – we're on a building site in Dubbo as per usual.

He said a rude word when he saw the mud, then he went off to catering and said another rude word because they'd forgotten the Vegemite. Then he accidentally put his clog through the side of the space capsule. So I don't know.

It's still raining out there. When I stuck my head round the side of the van to have a look just now it even rained in my tea. Of course it's gone cold now. The rain's always a lower temperature in Dubbo.

When I think of the trouble I went to doing the Dragors' eyebrows yesterday, I could spit. An hour trying to hold my hand straight, and even then I poked one of them in the eye. A rubbish bin full of mucky green cotton wool and nothing to show for it. Just as well I'm wearing my lucky headscarf today. It's got little laughing ducks on the inside. It's psychology. If you look good, you feel good, don't you?

I'm glad I brought the radio in. We've had The Hollies on this morning. And Procol Harum. Not that I can ever pronounce it. But at least it's not the Rolling Stones. Aren't you fed up with them? It's 1971! Someone should tell them to break up.

My ex-boyfriend was a big Rolling Stones fan. He had this record, *Their Satanic Majesties Request*. I used to say, I request you to turn it off. Of course we split up. It was my hi-fi. He went off with someone called Birgitte. She had plaits. She had a stall at the Copenhagen Sex Fair.

I like something I can sing along with. 'Let It Be'. Let it be! If the quarry's flooded in Dubbo, let it be. If you get rain in your tea, let it be. If there's no Vegemite in the catering caravan, let it be. You know what I mean. Less rude words, less bother, more love and peace. It's going to take ages to get the dent out of that space capsule and I bet he's ruined his clogs.

I had Terry in the van again this morning. He came

in early because he'd got a boil on his neck. He made the mistake of having two Choc-Top Woppas before he went to bed, and bingo – he woke up with one, right on his Adam's apple.

He was worried you'd see it in the close-ups. I said, 'What close-ups, Terry? I think you've got the wrong script. You're a Dragor in a corridor. As far as I know you're going to be obliterated.' He was annoyed about that.

He said he thought Hector had him down for a big love scene with a Vod. A sort of interracial harmony episode. Lucky for him I've been here since 5 a.m. to look after the boil. The rest of them were stuck in traffic again – apparently.

He calmed down in the end. Terry's what I call one of the repressed but overemotional ones. A lot of them from theatre are. It's too much of an adjustment for them. He was in *Hair*. Now he's about to suffer a fatal dose of radiation on Bodaris 5. Just when he'd got used to tribal love rock, as well. When he first got here he wanted to walk around in the nude, because of *Hair*. He said they'd all got used to it. I said, 'Please Terry, not here.'

People think this job's just about make-up. Well it's not. It's how you look after people. You've got to care. Sometimes I get extras in here, and I say, 'Do you feel like a good scream? Go on, give it all you've got. If you do a good enough job you might end up in Sound Effects.'

I will admit, I've got no qualifications as a psychol-ogist. Basically I'm here to make sure Terry looks like a Dragor and not some bloke from Footscray with a moustache, which of course he actually is. But what's the point unless you understand the man inside the monster?

Naturally, they've all had a go at me about Terry. But they don't know the half of it. His wife left him and his dog's got one kidney. Then she came back and took his beanbag, so he's been sitting on the floor all week. One good thing – if she takes the fridge as well he won't be having any more Choc-Top Woppas.

Still, at least he brushes his teeth. You know what gets me? People who come in – and I'm talking some very big names – stinking of spaghetti and garlic. And then they sit under the hairdryer for an hour reading the *Women's Weekly* fiddling with themselves. They think a terry towelling dressing gown is a cover-all, apparently. Well it's not. And you should smell the van afterwards. It's like going out for a cheap Italian without going out.

Terry's been under a lot of strain, which is why I think he got the boil in the first place, because it's not like him. Normally he's so professional. In the end I said, 'Be serious, Terry, who's going to notice a boil on your neck? You're a Dragor. You're bright green with a rotating eyeball on top of your head.'

I still had to get out the tweezers and the Dettol, though. 'Very nasty,' I said, 'don't you want Medical to do this boil?' He said, 'You are my Medical, darling.'

I think I'll have a quick lie-down. You can do that in here, you just need to draw the curtains so they don't know you're in here. Nobody's even offered me a fresh cup of tea yet. At the ABC we used to have a lamington run for elevenses. Everyone put in their five cents, Human Resources paid for the milk, and one teabag went round four of us. It was the best job I ever had.

Of course, I'm not allowed to mention the ABC here. And God forbid I should mention the BBC. That was the kiss of death, talking about *Doctor Who*. I said, 'It was a working holiday in London. It was fun. Don't you want to hear about it?' If looks could kill, I would have been exterminated on the spot. That's my make-up van joke. If you talk about *Doctor Who* round here, they'll exterminate you.

I wish we did have Daleks. At least they don't need their hair done. I've never heard of a Dalek wearing blusher. It takes me the best part of three hours to do a full Dragor body paint, and half the time they only show them from the knees up. They might as well be wearing their slippers.

I wonder if Terry's remembered about the five dollars? Because of the boil I didn't like to ask, but it's been a week and I've got a red corduroy trouser suit on lay-by at David Jones.

I thought I might wear it to this party on Saturday night. I've got my bandana, and my afro wig. So I thought I might go a bit wild. I'll be thirty soon. One of the girls said, you don't look thirty. Well, I suppose if there's one thing I can do, it's make-up.

Terry's a Scorpio. It's on his medallion. He caught me looking at it this morning, and said, 'So what are you?' I said, 'Guess.' He didn't say anything at first. Then he looked at me and said, 'Virgo the virgin.' I went bright red. I thought you were supposed to stop doing that when you were a teenager. It hasn't stopped me.

I'm a Libra actually, not a Virgo. Librans are very good listeners. My sister's got the book. It says, the typical Libra is destined to be a loving wife, a hairdresser, or a United Nations diplomat. I did start out as a hairdresser so it's very accurate. We don't get on with Scorpios though.

My sister's a Leo. She's married. They're very stubborn.

If I could lock the door, I would. I don't need any more Dragors in here this morning. Only Terry. It's funny, but when they're all standing there in a line with their eyeballs waving at you, you can still tell it's him. Just by the way he looks at you. I suppose he's forgotten about the five dollars.

MONDAY

In the end, the party turned out to be great. It was dead trendy. There was someone who was apparently related to Yoko Ono in the loo – he was there all night as a matter of fact, you couldn't get in. And we had Cheese Tasties, which if you're after the recipe is 4oz of hard cheese and self-raising, and 4oz of margarine. I don't care if we've gone decimal. No garlic.

And get this! Hector the Director asked me to dance. Admittedly it was to '2001: A Space Odyssey', but then, he's a very serious science fiction fan. I found out all about it on the fire escape.

First he said he was sorry about ignoring me for so long. Then he said I was a good little worker. Then he said he was going to lend me a copy of *The Muller-Fokker Effect*, one of the greatest science fiction novels ever written.

Then someone put on 'Sugar Sugar' so I got up with Terry. He was wearing Indian moccasins and he had his motorbike goggles on his head. He said, 'You look hot to trot, darling.' I said, 'So do you. Darling.'

We did 'Sugar Sugar', then we did 'Georgie Girl', and he said my hair looked a bit like Judith Durham's, and I went red again. I'm so embarrassed about blushing at my age! Someone said use green foundation, but how are you going to stop the forces of nature? Lucky the lights were off, or rather we did have one lightbulb, but it was red so you couldn't tell.

The toilet had a red lightbulb too, as we discovered when Yoko Ono's relative got out. And there was a mobile in the shape of an owl, and someone was burning incense. I've never seen that before.

I sat with Terry on the sofa for hours while this owl went round and round our heads – he kept banging into it – and Hector was next to us, eating Cheese Tasties. Then Terry put his head on my shoulder and said he felt tired.

I think I'm going to get some incense.

I made a joke about the Vegemite to Hector and he laughed. I thought that was a good sign. Maybe I'll get a pay rise if I keep making him laugh. Maybe I'll get a bigger caravan. I wouldn't mind one with a lock on it. Then Terry put on my afro wig and the owl got caught in it. We all laughed after that.

Then I fell asleep. Or, as someone said to me this

morning, I went into a coma with a copy of *19* magazine on my face. I wonder if you're still allowed to read *19* when you're about to turn thirty?

TWO WEEKS LATER

If you asked me to describe myself, I wouldn't say I'm a virgin. I mean, I thought it was about time when we got equal pay, but that doesn't make me a women's-libber, does it?

Not that we get equal pay round here. They got in someone new last week, he was on *The Six Wives of Henry VIII* – Hector knows him. Two years younger than me, and I heard he's getting five dollars more. I could go crazy in David Jones with that kind of money. I could probably buy myself some incense. But I'm not going to complain to Hector. He'd just say a rude word.

Getting into bed with Terry was nice. I'm glad I've done it now. Though I'm not sure what I was expecting. I didn't realise how hairy he was, I suppose.

No more evidence of boils though. He took off his Scorpio medallion because he said his wife gave it to him, plus it was digging into my head. He's like that, Terry. He thinks about things before you have to say them to him.

He said, the reason he liked me better than the others was because he could tell I cared. I said, of course I cared. He's going to send his dog in for an operation if he gets the part in *Play School*. Terry, not the dog.

I told him about the new make-up assistant. He said, he doesn't care as much as I do about people. He said it was just a case of Hector hiring someone he knew.

Terry was in my bath for an hour, with the Radox, after we made love. He's had the gas cut off at home so he said it was a luxury using mine. I said why don't you stay, but he had to go. He had to feed the dog.

MONDAY

I got told off about the transistor radio by him in the next caravan, so I didn't bring it in today. I said, didn't they listen to Procol Harum on *The Six Wives of Henry VIII*? Didn't they like a bit of pop music? He just looked at me. He wears dungarees and a flat cap. Never trust a man who wears dungarees and a flat cap if they've got a posh voice.

And then I'd just finished doing the last of the Vods when Hector knocked on the door. He was smiling, which made me nervous to tell you the truth, but then he went back to our little joke about the Vegemite, from the party, so I knew it was all right. He said, close the door. Then he tied up the latch with one of his boot-laces. He's gone off clogs.

He had a book he said he wanted to lend me. Not *The Muller-Fokker Effect*. It was still science fiction, though. Apparently. It was called *Do Androids Dream of Electric Sheep*. I said, I wouldn't know. He laughed. He said, he could tell I was committed to the pro-gramme, and he had more in mind for it than monsters with eyeballs coming out of their heads. He said true science fiction was actually a very sophisticated medium, and misunderstood by most people. He said he thought we were on the same wavelength and he'd like me to develop some ideas – in conjunction with the art department. I said, 'I didn't know we had an art department.' He said, 'It smells of garlic in here.' I said, 'I know.'

Then he brought up the subject of Terry. And what it all boiled down to was, had I spent the night with him, and did I know what I was getting myself into?

What it says in *19* magazine is, never cry at the office. Well this is a van, not an office, so I wonder if that lets me off? Hector was very good. He gave me his cravat. I always thought it was for show, to go with his tie, but it's actually the same as a hankie – in fact, even better. It's thicker material so you can really blow your nose on all four corners of it. He didn't want it back – which was nice.

Hector said he didn't want to pry into my private life, but he liked to take an avuncular role on set. I said, 'Does that mean you're like my uncle?' I never liked my uncle. He said he knew I was from the provinces. I said, what did that have to do with anything? Then he asked how I was getting on with the new chap and had I been an admirer of the beard and moustache work on *The Six Wives of Henry VIII*. I mentioned about the five dollars and he said he'd ask the producer.

I wish I lived in Israel. I bet Golda Meir makes sure you get equal pay over there. The only thing is, I don't think our show will ever get to Israel. Someone said the other day we'd be lucky if it got as far as North Adelaide.

Hector asked me did I think the women's-libbers would ever win? I said I didn't know what he meant. He said, 'Do you think we'll ever get a female Prime

10

Minister, like Golda Meir?' I said, 'You must be joking.'

Hector said he spends more time thinking about the future now that he's working on this programme. I said, 'What, the year 3030? That's a long way off.' He said no, maybe just 2020. He said he was looking forward to the day when we'd all have telephones in our handbags. I laughed.

He said he was looking forward to the day when men could be bold and free about their love for each other and walk down the street hand in hand, wearing shorts. I didn't know what to say then. And then he asked me if I'd heard of the Gay Liberation Front. I said 'No.' Then one of the Vods started moaning outside the door, wanting his ears put back on, so we left it there.

ONE MONTH LATER

It was my sister who put the complaint in eventually. Well, that's Leos for you. She said, if they couldn't provide a separate toilet for men and women on the set, she'd tell the union.

Hector said, 'What union?' She said, 'Take your pick.' Then I was sick. Well, I'm always sick now. Apparently it runs in our family. As soon as you know you're pregnant, that's it. Take one look at a sardine sandwich and all you want is a bucket.

I haven't heard from Terry. Someone said he had got taken on at *Play School*. They'd seen him walking around with Big Ted under his arm apparently. I don't know. I did ring. The phone had been cut off.

Things have changed round here, plot-wise. In the

next episode, they're sending all the Dragors back to the English countryside in the Middle Ages. One of the Vods has found a time tunnel and apparently it ends up at Hampton Court Palace. Well, I'm not doing the beards. Or the moustaches. It's too much like hard work.

Apparently it's all hands on deck for *Miss World* next week. It's a live broadcast. If you can tell a tube of lipstick from a tube of eyeliner, you're in. They say the women's-libbers are going to disrupt it, but I don't care. The girls have still got to look good on camera, don't they, even if Germaine Greer does mow them down with machine guns. I'm a Libra, you see. I see both sides.

Hector took me aside today. He said he was sorry about Terry. I said, all I ever wanted to do was understand the man inside the monster. He said 'No, sweetheart, you've got it the wrong way round.' He said women always do.

The Master Baker
Maggie Alderson

I had my first serious doubts about Ricky when I saw him crouched on the kitchen floor blowtorching cockroaches with the gas lighter.

'What *are* you doing?' I asked. 'I thought you were making another cake.'

'I am. It's in the oven. Now I'm having fun,' he said, blasting another spout of flame at the desperately wriggling insects. 'Take that, you filthy little bastards.'

'But can't you just squash them, or spray them?' I asked him. 'That's so cruel.'

He looked up at me with a maniacal gleam in his exquisite almond eyes.

'That's why it's fun, stupido. Anyway why would you care? They're only cockroaches.'

I left him to it and went back out onto the verandah, my desire for a glass of water totally vanished after witnessing the torture in the kitchen.

Closing my eyes, I surrendered myself to the late December sun, the smell of Ricky's sponge cake as he

13

took it from the oven, the sound of the waves on the beach just yards away, the occasional squawk from children playing untiringly on their Christmas boogie boards, until I sank into the opiate daze of summer.

I awoke suddenly to the sensation of something very cold being placed on my bare stomach. It was Ricky with a lavish cocktail, the rim of the glass crusted with pink sugar, with chunks of pineapple and maraschino cherries pushed onto a plastic stick shaped like a flamingo, the whole lot topped off with an umbrella and a couple of frangipanis.

'It's a cockroach daiquiri,' he said, flashing the white teeth that reminded me once again why my friend Dominic was so obsessed with him. 'Toasted.'

He placed his own cocktail on the table next to me and removed his sarong to reveal another cause of Nic's ardour. He wasn't wearing any swimmers and something that wouldn't look out of place on the David Jones small-goods counter was dangling about fifteen centimetres from my head, set off by a deeply tanned and perfectly taut abdomen.

'For God's sake, Ricky, have you no shame?' I asked him.

He flipped his hips at me and I clamped a hand over my eyes.

'With a body like mine? No, darling. Drink your cocktail and stop being such a convent-girl spinster.'

'But I am a convent-girl spinster.'

'Well, start praying to Saint Jude, sweetheart, because you're a lost cause trapped in a beach house with a bunch of drug-taking, alcohol-abusing perverts like us.

You know – your fabulous best friends?'

He had a point, I reflected, as he positioned the George Hamilton sun reflector we'd given him as a joke Christmas present, but which he adored far more than the Versace shirts, Gucci belts and Calvin Klein undies Dominic had heaped upon him. On Boxing Day I had seen him dry himself with one of the silk shirts rather than walk five paces to pick up a towel.

He was right, though, we were an odd crew, but apart from Ricky, we'd spent the last five Christmases together, on this beach, all fugitives from families we couldn't stand, or who couldn't understand us. We each had our reasons for spending Christmas in our orphans' colony, as we called it.

Dominic, thirty-five and the managing director of a large international advertising agency, could run a multi-million dollar budget and a staff of hundreds, but couldn't tell his Killara brahmin parents he was gay.

Sveta and Daniel – a model and a photographer respectively – were married, but found it easier to cop out of the holiday season entirely than face the all-out war between their families. Sveta's were Cabramatta Serbs, Daniel's Vaucluse Jews, and each believed their beloved only child was in the grip of the devil.

Sveta and Daniel had also never found a way to explain to their devoutly religious families that they could be perfectly happily married even though Daniel sometimes liked going to bed with other women and the occasional man, and Sveta had been seeing her girlfriend Lou once a week for over four years.

Sweet, gentle Tom ran a second-hand bookshop, largely funded by the guilt of a father who had hit him so hard as a child he had lost the sight in one eye. He couldn't go near the family's Bowral farm, Palm Beach house, or Bellevue Hill mansion, for the punishing memories they brought back. And he couldn't bear to see the powdered-over bruises on his elegant mother's face any more than he could ever talk to her about them.

And me? I just couldn't stand the strain of being surrounded by my five happily married brothers and sisters and all their gorgeous children, noting how carefully nobody brought up the subject of my own single, childless state, with my thirty-fifth birthday just weeks away. Their loving concern was more than I could stand.

We'd never talked about our reasons for being there, it had just happened, like everything in our lives, under the pretext of 'having fun'. So, for the past five years this funny old house on Hyam's Beach had been our sanctuary, where we could have our own kind of Christmas, without having to explain anything more complicated than why we had mixed sangria for afternoon drinks rather than the traditional Pimms.

'But we *always* have Pimms,' we would cry in unison, if anyone tried to introduce such a change. Refugees from family life as we were, we had created our own annual rituals, which we treasured as much as my nieces and nephews looked forward to putting out Santa's mince pie and Rudolph's carrot.

This year Ricky had introduced a new Christmas Colony tradition – afternoon tea with lavish cakes and biscuits he prepared every day, using the baking equipment he'd brought with him specially.

Moulds, tins, trays and patty pans of every shape and size filled the kitchen cupboards, along with piping bags, crystallised ginger, slabs of Valrhona chocolate, organic sultanas and other essentials he had figured he wouldn't be able to find anywhere near Jervis Bay. He had two kilos of Normandy butter in the fridge and great jars of castor sugar soaking up the aroma of fresh vanilla pods lining the benchtop.

The lavish tea made sense, he explained, because we always got up too late for a proper breakfast or lunch, and it stopped us getting so drunk on our post-nap cocktails that we couldn't make it through to dinner. He also said that five years as a pastry chef in some of Sydney's best restaurants had left him with a burning urge to create and baking was the only outlet he had for it.

Ricky had given up his promising cooking career to concentrate on his sideline as a male prostitute. I'd never knowingly met a hooker before and when Nic told me about Ricky I didn't know what to expect. But right from the start I had respected Ricky's honesty about it.

'My looks are God-given,' Ricky had told me the first time we met. 'And my Irish grandmother said it was a sin not to use God's gifts. "You have to share what you have, Richard," that's what she always told me. So I'm sharing.' He'd wagged his tongue at me suggestively.

He certainly was beautiful. As well as the Irish granny, his other grandparents were a crazy United Nations mix of something like Jamaican, Norwegian and Chinese, and the combination was extraordinary. He seemed to have the best of each race and his caramel skin, perfectly smooth body, sleek black hair, almond eyes and other attributes – like the one I had just witnessed up close – had put him in such demand with top-dollar clients that continuing to work all night in a hot kitchen had seemed madness.

He'd met Nic on a 'job' and realised immediately he had found himself a companionable meal ticket he could manipulate entirely to his own satisfaction. If he shacked up with Nic he'd never have to work again, apart from daily trips to the gym to keep himself 'pool perfect' as he called it, and his compulsive baking.

Since moving into Nic's designer Darlinghurst penthouse, Ricky had made him install an entire new kitchen with professional convection ovens and a huge industrial fridge. He baked every day when he got back from the gym and gave the results of his labours to the men's refuges in Woolloomooloo and Surry Hills, making deliveries in the open-top Merc that Nic had also bought him.

Down at the beach, Ricky baked every morning and afternoon, at times when he said contemptuously that the sun had no tanning power and was only for amateurs. As well as making all manner of sweetmeats for our high tea, he also baked a large iced cake each day for the general store, just a few metres along the sea shore, which they sold by the slice to hungry beachgoers, with polystyrene cups of tea and instant coffee. The $30 they paid for it gave him a little bit of 'drug money' of his own, he explained, so he didn't have to keep liberating it from Nic's wallet.

Drugs and other stimulants were another key part of our Christmas traditions. We all had our favourite escapes, which we brought with us to share around. Tom loved the numbing effect of dope, which suited his introspective nature. Sveta and Daniel loved ecstasy – it was the only way they could ever have sex with each other Nic said bitchily. His penchant was for cocaine. It was part of his job description, he would quip, to have a serious coke habit. Ricky partook of all of them, but never seemed affected by drugs as we were.

I wasn't particularly bothered about any of it, as long as I had lots of drink. And I mean *lots* of drink. I had filled the back of my four-wheel drive with cases of wine and champagne for our holiday fortnight and made almost daily trips into Huskisson to stock up on beers, spirits and mixers. I started drinking with a morning beer and didn't stop until I fell into bed with my last brandy. I was on holiday, wasn't I? And several of my PR clients were booze companies, so it was only right that I should partake of their products, so I knew what I was promoting. The discount was handy, too.

Ricky's cocktails were another reason I had grown to like him. He applied the same alchemy to mixing drinks that he put into patisserie and never served the same mixture twice. He had brought an armoury of exotic liqueurs with him along with the cake ingredients, many of them obscure European concoctions I'd never seen before, which he claimed were made by monks in remote abbeys. Some tasted odd, but Ricky said they contained mountain herbs that staved off the worst effects of hangovers and aided digestion. I slugged them back happily.

The cockroach daiquiri was deep brown with flecks of shaved chocolate through it and clearly contained large quantities of dark rum, which reminded me pleasantly of my early drinking days of Bundy and Coke. I'd started about age fourteen, slugging the remains out of empty glasses at my big brothers' parties.

Ricky topped my glass up from his cocktail jug and I was developing a pleasant buzz by the time the others came back pink, sweaty and laughing from their after-noon power walk – another Christmas Colony tradition.

'Hello beautiful,' said Nic, kissing Ricky wetly on the mouth and squeezing his bum. I noticed that Tom saw it and looked away quickly. Poor Tom, I thought. He was desperate to have a boyfriend of his own and it must be so hard for him seeing his best boy pal so happily ensconced after all their years on the prowl together.

I had felt the same when my best friend Annabel got married – so much more lonely without a bestie girl-friend to share single life with. From the moment she met hideous Peter she talked only in the Royal 'we' until I could hardly stand to see her any more. Now she lived in Queens Park with him and two ugly toddlers. I lived only a couple of kilometres away in Paddington, but she might as well have moved to Mars. I wished she had.

Tom followed Ricky inside, saying he was going to help him get the tea ready, but from my position near the screen door I could hear Ricky telling him to go away.

'Fuck off, Tom, you stink,' he said with his usual tact.

'Go and have a shower. I don't want a sweaty sous chef in my kitchen, thank you.'

Sveta sat down on the end of my banana lounge and took a big gulp out of my glass.

'Yuk,' she said, pulling a face. 'That tastes weird.'

'Well, don't drink it then,' I said, snatching the glass from her and settling down with it propped on my chest, the straw in my mouth.

'Look at you,' said Sveta, tweaking my big toe. 'You should have come on the walk, Emmo. We saw dolphins and found a new cove we've never seen before where we can go skinny-dipping.'

'You can show me another time, Svet. It's too humid for me to move today,' I said.

'You've just got too much of a bloody hangover,' said Nic. 'I saw you open that extra bottle of shampoo last night. And you drank the whole lot yourself, you greedy bitch.'

'So what? I'm on holiday. Pass me that jug.'

They all went off to have showers and Ricky called me from the kitchen to help him carry the tea out.

As well as a fresh jug of cockroach daiquiris, there was a plate of cheese scones, the Victoria sponge he'd been making earlier, and a plate of cookies, one each, made in the shape of our initials.

'E for Emily, you see?' he said proudly, indicating my biscuit, which had pink icing and silver balls on it.

'E's are good, e's are good,' sang Daniel.

'Oh shut up,' I said. 'It's so pretty. I love silver balls. Thank you so much, Mr Rickski.' I pecked him on the cheek, forgetting the earlier cockroach massacre. The youngest of six children, I was still a sucker for any special attention.

We took our afternoon tea outside, around the kitchen table that we had moved out there specially. Filling up my glass first, I ate two cheese scones and a slice of cake before reaching for my special biscuit. When I saw the T-shaped cookie next to it I realised Tom hadn't come down for tea, which was odd since he normally loved his cake. Just the day before Ricky had made a special plate of madeleines just for him, because he loved Proust so much and was re-reading *À la recherche du temps perdu* as his holiday treat. He'd scoffed the lot.

'Where's Tom?' I said. 'TOM!!' I called out. 'You're missing tea!'

'I think he has a headache,' said Ricky. 'He said he wasn't feeling hungry before.'

'Well that'll be a first,' said Nic, reaching for another slice of cake. 'I think this is a plot to make us all as fat as Tom, Ricky, just so you will look even more beautiful in comparison. I'm going to need liposuction when we get back.'

He arched his back, sucking in his stomach and cheeks theatrically. Ricky took another drag on his cigarette and raised a bored eyebrow. He never ate any of the lavish teas he prepared, saying he didn't fancy food he'd made himself. In fact, he never seemed to eat much of anything and he didn't sleep nearly as much as the rest of us either. He was always up early baking, and when we had our afternoon disco naps, he'd go for a run, or start making dinner.

I felt a bit dizzy as I lay down for my nap after tea and assumed it was the combination of dark rum and too much sugar in the heat of the afternoon. My heart was beating really fast and the room was going round a bit. I felt like the walls were coming in on me. Maybe I'd better start going on the walks for the rest of the week, I thought, instead of having my extra afternoon cocktails.

Eventually I managed to drop off and woke to the sound of loud dance music – the usual Orphans' Colony wake-up call. It was dark and by the time I'd showered and dressed, the others were putting the dinner on the table. I'd missed evening drinks altogether, but I still felt a bit light-headed. I'd been asleep for over four hours.

'That was a long nap, lazybum,' said Nic. 'But a smart move as we've made dinner and all you have to do is open the wine, which we know you hate. We're having prawns in honour of the fact that tonight is Wednesday, when Sveta normally sees Lou.'

I punched him playfully.

'Don't be disgusting, Nic. Your vaginaphobia is pathetic.'

As we sat down and I poured the first of the suite of light whites I had selected I noticed that once again Tom wasn't at the table.

'Where's Tom?' I asked. 'Surely he's not going to miss two meals in one day? That really would be a first.'

'I looked in on him just now,' said Ricky. 'He says he has a migraine and just wants to stay in bed.'

Dinner was the usual hysterical affair, with lots of wine and jokes. Afterwards I initiated a demolition disco in the sitting room, where each of us had to take it in turns to pick great dance tracks from the huge pile of CDs we'd brought with us. I forgot all about Tom and his headache. I just really felt like dancing.

Several hours and several bottles later, I was happily getting on down to 'What's New Pussycat?' when Nic and Ricky said they were crashing. Sveta and Daniel followed them up, but I still felt full of energy – must have been that long nap, I thought – so I carried on alone after they had all gone to bed, smoking most of Nic's packet of Silk Cut and finishing the wine. Eventually they started shouting at me to turn the music off and I was forced to call it a night.

I sloped off to bed reluctantly and lay staring at the ceiling until sleep finally took hold. What felt like hours later I awoke with a very unusual sensation between my legs. I wondered if I was dreaming, but I wasn't. There was something extraordinary going on down there. Something extraordinarily nice. As I regained consciousness I realised I was having the most intense orgasm of my life and the first assisted one in well over a year – the question was, who the hell was assisting it?

Was it Sveta, driven to lesbian distraction by missing her Wednesday night with Lou? Was it Daniel playing around with whoever was available? It certainly couldn't be Nic or Tom – they'd rather set fire to themselves than go anyway near a vagina, a body part they invested with all kinds of voodoo horror.

I sat up on my elbows and saw very white teeth

gleaming at me in the darkness.

'Ricky?' I said in amazement.

He said nothing, just carried on smiling as he threw off the bedcovers and moved up the bed like a giant python licking and nibbling my body all the way. Every touch felt electric. My brain was horrified by what was happening, but my body was so happy with the situation it seemed to take over. As Ricky's head hit the pillow next to me, my hands were all over that perfect bod, discovering that it felt every bit as good as it looked, especially the bit I'd seen for the first time earlier, which felt even better in this situation.

I'm not proud of what happened next, but like the initial interlude, I felt it was beyond my control. Nic's face crossed my mind for a milli-second, as I kissed Ricky, but immediately disappeared as I abandoned myself to sheer pleasure.

When I woke up he'd gone and the only way I knew I hadn't imagined the whole thing was a damp patch on the sheet and a cookie in the shape of the letter R on the pillow next to me. I also had an unmistakable throb between my legs, a simultaneous longing for more of what had caused it – and a dawning feeling of absolute horror as I thought of facing Nic.

What had I done?

For what felt like hours, I lay rigid on my damp bed contemplating how devastated my darling Nic, my very best boy pal, would be if he knew I'd just had a night of passion with the love of his life. Because although he knew all about Ricky's days as a working boy and what that involved – it was how they met after all – now they were living together, Nic guarded Ricky's virtue like a Greek father.

'I used to pay him to work, now I pay him not to,' was how he put it.

It was midday and the house was deathly quiet. I just lay there feeling dreadful and wondering how I was going to face either of them. As well as my agonisingly guilty conscience, I felt physically awful. My head was throbbing and I felt really sick. I had drunk quite a bit and smoked all those ciggies, but this was far worse than my customary morning blahs. I drifted in and out of consciousness, jerking awake every time I remembered what had happened.

An hour or so later there were stirrings in the house. It sounded like they were all heading off to the beach. In the stillness of the day I could clearly hear the sound of the fridge door opening and closing as someone got their water bottle out. I froze when there was a tap on my door.

'Em? Coming swimming, you lazy cow?'

It was Nic. I felt even sicker and lay completely still.

'Em?' he said again and then gave up.

I heard Sveta's voice from outside, shouting to Daniel to bring her hat out with him, and the swish-thud of the screen door. There was a pause, then I heard two voices whispering fiercely at the other end of the landing, followed by feet running downstairs. Then it all went quiet.

I lay there until I was completely sure they were gone

before tiptoeing out to the loo. I looked at my face in the mirror. The face of a treacherous, lecherous pig woman. My cheeks had blotches on them and my chin was bright pink. Beard rash. I groaned and checked my neck for bite marks. Feeling disgusting, I turned the shower on full to try and blast my guilt and nausea away.

As I was drying myself I heard a very loud crash downstairs. Wrapping the towel around my body I crept down to the hall. Tom was standing in the kitchen surrounded by the smashed remains of one of Ricky's jars of sugar. He had his back to me and jumped round when I said his name. He looked dreadful. He was unshaven, his eyes were red and had a mad look in them. Normally immaculately groomed, I had never seen him like that.

'Tom?' I said. 'Are you all right?'

I touched his arm and he flinched away from me.

'Yes, yes,' he said quickly. 'I . . . I just knocked it over. Better clean it up I suppose.'

He rushed to get the dustpan and brush and started sweeping it up in a frenzied way. Almost immediately he cut himself on one of the glass shards. Blood was pouring from the base of his thumb, turning the spilled sugar a ghastly pink, as he carried on scrabbling like a madman.

I pulled him up and grabbed a tea towel to bandage his hand.

'Tom,' I said, 'Cool it, will you? It's only sugar. I'll clean it up in a minute. This cut looks quite deep.'

As I spoke he burst into heaving sobs, tore his hand away from me and rushed from the room. He ran upstairs and slammed his bedroom door. I stood in the kitchen feeling stunned. First my own hideous situation and now Tom was clearly having some kind of flashback to his nightmare childhood.

Picking my way over the broken glass and gory sugar, I poured myself a long glass of cold beer and then another. Feeling less queasy I cleared up the mess and went and tapped on Tom's door.

'Go away,' he said, then after a pause he spoke again. 'Look Emily, I'm sorry, it's just I'm feeling so lousy.'

I opened the door a crack and peeped in at him. He was sitting on the edge of his bed looking down at something in his bandaged hand. When he saw me, he just shook his head.

'Just leave me alone, Em. I'll be better later. Don't worry, the bleeding's nearly stopped.'

As I closed the door, I realised the thing he was holding was one of his special madeleines.

The house was starting to feel claustrophobic, so I decided to go out for a walk. I went along the road by the beach, deliberately heading in the opposite direction to the place we always had our sunbaking HQ. Once I felt I was safely out of view I ran onto the sand and straight into Sveta, Daniel, Ricky and Nic, who were lying on beach towels in the full sun, as usual.

'Darling,' cried Nic. 'Where have you been? First you insist on dancing all night and then you won't get up to play. We've been here for hours and we've had lots of swims. The water's divine.'

'Oh, I just wasn't feeling very well. I'm better now.

Why are you sitting along here?'

'We felt like a change,' said Sveta. 'And so did you, apparently . . .'

She was looking at me with her eyes narrowed, a little frown line between them. Oh God, I thought, womanly intuition. She's probably taken one look at me and knows I've recently had a shagathon, although I didn't feel I had much of a post-coital glow. More like radioactive fallout.

'Oh, yeah,' I said lamely. 'Just felt like a walk, to clear my head. Think I will have a swim. Good idea, Nic.'

Ricky was lying on his front with his head turned away and hadn't stirred at all on my arrival, but as I ran down to the water I heard footsteps on the hard sand catching up with me. It was him. I thought I might throw up because, when I looked at him in daylight, his black hair slicked back, his body glistening with sweat and sun oil, that wicked smile in his eyes, my internal organs leapt for joy. I could have jumped on him there and then. I couldn't speak.

'Good morning, Emily,' he said, in his archest voice. 'Had a good night's sleep? You look a bit pink today.'

I just swallowed and looked at him stupidly. He bit his lip and put his head on one side. It was unbearable. I stopped at the water's edge hardly able to breathe and he grabbed my hand and pulled me into the surf. I plunged under the water, feeling delirious. When I came up for air he was there right next to me and somehow, under the pretence of two friends larking innocently in the surf, he had one hand down my bikini bottoms and the other inside the top. It had exactly the same effect as the previous night. Before I could protest I was gone, washed away on a wave of pleasure, suddenly coming to when a real wave caught me smartly round the head.

Collecting myself enough to turn my back to the beach, I steadied myself on the sand and put out my hand to stop him touching me.

'Ricky, what are you doing?'

'I'm giving you a good time. Reckon you haven't had one for a while, judging by your performance last night. You were like a bucking bronco.'

'Ricky, I shouldn't have done that with you, but you crept up on me. You took me by surprise and you've just done it again. You have to stop this. Nic's my best friend. He's mad about you. It would kill him if he knew and now I'm going to have to carry this guilt around for ever.'

'But you enjoyed it, didn't you?' He moved closer and took my hand, pressing it onto the front of his swimmers.

'Ricky, stop it.'

He started moving his hips, rotating them slowly and I snatched my hand away, realising I should have done so immediately. He had me and he knew it.

'Well, I'll stop if you really want me to, or else you can meet me behind the rocks over there,' he indicated down the beach. 'At six, when they're all asleep.'

Before I could say anything he took off, swimming a lazy crawl along the line of the beach. I swam as fast as I could in the opposite direction.

Well, I would love to be able to tell you that at six o'clock I was tucked up in bed having my nap like the others. But instead I was waiting for Ricky, who kept me dangling, quite deliberately, I'm sure, for ten minutes before he appeared around the corner of the rocks.

I won't go into details but, barely half an hour later, I was so disgustingly sated by his lascivious skills, my guilt was beginning to fade into the background. It was like being possessed, but one thought was nagging at me.

'Ricky,' I said, as he sat leaning against a rock smoking a cigarette. His jeans were still undone and the brown skin on his stomach was gathered in little folds over the muscle beneath. 'How come you are so skilled at giving a woman pleasure? Aren't you meant to be gay?'

'Whatever gave you that idea?' he said, flicking the cigarette end onto the sand as he got to his feet. 'I'm a professional, remember?'

And he ran off down the beach.

Tom finally appeared at dinner. He hadn't made it to tea again and had missed Sveta and Daniel's delight as Ricky brought out a plate of special pastries for them – *pita od jabuka* for her and *teiglach* for him. He'd arranged them on special plates, complete with doilies, with S in sesame seeds on Sveta's cakes and poppyseed Ds on Daniel's. There was a plate of undecorated ones for the rest of us.

'I haven't tasted these since my granny's house in Capetown,' said Daniel, reaching for another. 'They're superb.'

'Oh God,' said Nic. 'They're bringing out the

Afrikaans in you. I can't stand it. Don't make those again, Ricky. It's like having tea with Botha.'

'What's wrong with Botha?' said Daniel and they started one of their protracted political arguments.

I was glad of the distraction, which enabled me to get used to being around Nic again in the knowledge that I was sexually obsessed with his boyfriend. I was almost alarmed by how easily I was slipping into my new role of betrayer. Ricky was clearly a master. He never caught my eye, held a gaze, or brushed against me. He just acted as he always had, with amused indifference to all that was going on around him, as he smoked cigarette after cigarette, grinding the butts out on the wooden deck.

Between his liaison with me and Nic waking up, Ricky had prepared dinner. I cringed inside when Nic sat on his knee and stroked his hair, cooing about what a clever and resourceful boy he was. You don't know the half of it, I thought.

In a freshly ironed striped shirt and chinos, shaved and with his blond hair perfectly combed, Tom looked more himself. He had a large plaster on his thumb and made up some story about an avocado and a slipped knife. He looked at me as he said it and I kept my mouth shut. I had enough secrets of my own now to question anyone else's wish for discretion.

Dinner was the usual carry-on and I got through it without too much difficulty. Daniel and Sveta were in a party mood and I was more than happy to watch as they demonstrated dances from each of their cultures – to a disco soundtrack – which seemed remarkably similar to me, considering how much their parents hated each other. Ricky kept disappearing out to the kitchen to check on some major feat of patisserie he had on the go, until eventually I couldn't help myself and followed him in there.

'Get out,' he said quietly, his back to me as he took something from the fridge and stirred it. 'Get out and don't do it again. Ever.'

I stood speechless. He turned around and looked at me, not a trace of warmth in his face.

'I said, get out,' he said again, quietly, but with such menace in his voice I went back to the others feeling I had been slapped. Sveta and Daniel were still dancing. Tom and Nic were playing cards outside. I poured myself a large brandy and went to bed.

The next day followed a similar pattern. I forced myself not to follow Ricky around, literally, or with my eyes, and stoically went on the afternoon walk when I could have quite easily stayed behind with him as I used to, without anyone suspecting a thing. Unusually Sveta didn't join us on the walk, blaming a sick tummy.

I was rewarded for my stoicism when I was hanging my cossie on the clothes line before tea. Ricky came out of the kitchen and stood next to me to hang up a wet tea towel.

'The rocks – seven,' he said, grabbing my crotch with a sudden movement that sent sparks flying through my body, and went back inside.

Sveta was still feeling sick at tea time and didn't come down. Daniel said it had started in the night and he wasn't feeling great himself, so he thought he'd have his nap on the sofa downstairs where he had also slept the night before so as not to disturb her.

'I don't know what's wrong with all you people,' said Nic, reaching for a chocolate eclair. 'You've got no stamina. It's only me and darling Rick who haven't had some kind of lurgy on this holiday so far. A bunch of wusses, aren't they, darling?'

He put his hand over Ricky's and gazed adoringly at him. Ricky looked back at him with cold lizard eyes, a little smile curling the edges of his mouth. Tom stood up suddenly and said he was going upstairs to read. I said I was going to lie down too.

'Well, you lot are no fun,' said Nic. 'I suppose Ricky and I better go and have our rest as well then, eh?' he said, winking at him in a way that made me feel irrationally furious. I was actually jealous.

By six the house was silent as everyone napped and rested. I lay restlessly on my bed, checking the clock constantly to see if it was time to go to my rendezvous. Not wanting to be kept waiting like last time, I left at seven, skirting through the trees rather than walking along the beach. I got to the rocks about five past.

Sveta and Tom were already there. I was so surprised my mouth just gaped open. Sveta had red eyes and had clearly been crying, while Tom looked pale and grim. I had no idea what to say. Was it a coincidence? Had they both decided to go out for a walk and ended up at the rocks – Ricky's and my rocks, as I thought of them – by chance?

'You too, eh, Emily?' said Tom, his voice shaking

slightly. Sveta slumped down onto the sand.

'What do you mean?' I said, desperately hoping I had the wrong idea.

'Ricky,' said Tom, smiling his most polite antiquarian-bookseller smile.

I sat down next to Sveta with a thud and put my head in my hands. Then there was the distinct sound of feet running along the beach and we all snapped to attention. Daniel appeared around the end of the rocks. He was clearly just as surprised as I had been and looked at each of our faces, puzzled.

'Oh, you were just having a walk too . . .' he said feebly.

'No, Daniel,' said Sveta, getting shakily to her feet. 'We're all waiting for Ricky. Like you are.'

I think I was the first to start laughing. It was awful. I felt completely humiliated and, when I thought of Nic, physically ill, but it was such a ridiculous situation I just couldn't stop and the others soon joined in. It broke the tension and we sat on the sand and shared our sordid stories. Tom had been first, visited in the night as I had been. Then me, then Sveta while Daniel was sleeping on the sofa downstairs, where he subsequently had his own close encounter. All four of us, one by one.

'How does he do it?' said Tom. 'So many people at once.'

'He's a professional,' said Sveta and I in unison.

'He certainly is,' said Daniel wistfully. 'No wonder Nic's so mad about him.'

Remembering Nic, happily snoozing back at the

house, dreaming sweetly in the arms of his beloved partner, we all felt terrible again.

'What are we going to do?' I asked. 'Do you think we should tell Nic? I mean, if Ricky's capable of doing this with us, what else is he doing? We all know he takes money out of Nic's wallet.' Then I remembered the cockroaches and shuddered. 'I think he's capable of anything. Should we warn Nic?'

Daniel wanted to have a man-to-man talk with Nic, just the two of them. Sveta was all for a big showdown, all of us together, telling Nic in front of Ricky – a tough love challenge, she called it. Tom visibly shivered at the prospect.

'Oh God no,' he said. 'I can't bear scenes. Why don't we all just pretend nothing's happened. He never needs to know.'

I was so confused, I didn't know what I wanted. Apart from a drink. On the one hand I was relieved to find I wasn't the only faithless hound among us, on the other I was unbearably frustrated not to have my liaison with Ricky. I had been looking forward to it so much.

'God, he's an amazing lover,' I said, unconsciously voicing my thoughts. The others looked at me, surprised, and then sighed deeply.

'Out of this world,' said Tom.

'Incredible,' said Daniel.

'Even better than Lou,' said Sveta.

We sat there in silence for a while, then another thought occurred to me.

'Tom,' I said, 'did you say it was Tuesday night when

36

Ricky came to you?'

He nodded.

'Wasn't that the day he made you those madeleines?'

'Yes, it was. Why?'

'Well, he came to me on Wednesday, which is when I had my special biscuit. And he did you two yesterday, after your ethnic granny cakes . . .'

They all looked at me, puzzled.

'What do you mean?' said Daniel.

'Well, I think there's a connection. I felt really odd after tea on Wednesday. I thought it was that cocktail, but now I'm beginning to wonder. And he left his R-shaped cookie on the pillow.'

Tom looked up suddenly.

'He left a madeleine on mine.'

I nodded. I remembered him holding it.

Sveta and Daniel were looking at each other.

'Same,' said Sveta. 'And I felt really crook after tea too, then I wanted to dance all night. I reckon there was something in those cakes.'

'Eccies, at a guess,' said Daniel. 'I felt unbelievably horny after dinner. I remember I was really pissed off that Sveta felt sick and made me sleep downstairs.' He grinned. 'Then later, I was really glad I was alone down there. Ay yay yay.' He shook his head.

'So he drugged us and then had his evil way with us,' said Tom bitterly. 'God! And I thought he actually liked me.'

He slammed his hand down on the sand and I could see there were tears in his eyes.

'So what are we going to do?' I asked. 'He's had his

little joke with us. Shall we shop him to Nic to get revenge and break our best friend's heart, or shall we protect our friend's feelings and just let Ricky get away with it?'

We sat there going backwards and forwards over it until it began to grow dark. Eventually we decided we had to tell Nic the whole story, so he would know what kind of a guy Ricky really was, and we started walking back along the beach.

When we reached the house it was dark except for one light on the verandah, illuminating the tea table. On it was a large white Christmas cake complete with holly leaves and a plastic Santa pulling a sledge.

'That's odd,' said Tom. 'We've had tea.'

When we got up close we could see there was writing piped onto the top of the cake in pink icing.

Happy Christmas, darlings. Hope you enjoyed my little present to you all. Love Nic xxx

That was the last Orphans' Christmas Colony. After Nic's surprise present we felt too uncomfortable ever to be together as a group. Tom was so angry he never spoke to Nic again and I felt pretty humiliated myself. It was the embarrassment of thinking that Ricky had never actually been attracted to me that hurt so much. In fact I had meant no more to him than one of his murdered cockroaches.

Not long after Christmas, Daniel and Sveta split up – she ran away with another photographer, younger than Daniel, with caramel skin, shiny black hair and almond eyes. Then in March, Nic was promoted and moved to London, taking Ricky with him.

I've lost touch with all of them now, except Tom. I see him every week. At AA meetings.

What Goes Around…
Louise Bagshawe

'I know it's hard to believe, but eventually you're going to get over it.'

Emma McCloud looked at her husband and blinked. As if she were trying to take it in.

John McCloud looked nervously around Le Petit Coq, the fancy French restaurant he had booked them into for dinner. He had ordered cheese soufflé, partly because he liked cheese, and partly because it took half an hour to prepare, and that way the waitress wouldn't bother them. Ordinarily, he didn't mind being bothered by the waitresses here – all of them long-legged, bottle-tanned and under twenty-five – but tonight, he needed some privacy. For Emma, he thought nobly, as much as for him.

'Say something,' John said, his American accent low-pitched so that none of the neighbouring tables could hear. 'And don't start with the crying, okay? That's Mary-Beth Astor at table four.'

Emma turned round semi-automatically. Yes, she

registered in a small part of her brain. John was right; there was Mary-Beth, the fourth wife of Richard Astor, the famous TV producer. Mary-Beth was twenty-two, with pneumatic tits, a fountain of scarlet hair, and lips plumped up monthly with cow collagen. She had also had one of those Botox injections that paralysed the muscles in your forehead that let you frown, thus giving her a permanently surprised air. She looked like an inflatable sex doll, with her round, lazy, open lips always lined a shade darker than her lipstick. She was sitting there with a friend, a brunette version of herself. Salads – doubtless *sans* dressing – were being delivered to their table. And, of course, John was anxious that they not upset Mary-Beth. He *cared* about the opinion of Mary-Beth.

Emma smothered a small giggle. Wildly inappropriate for the occasion, of course, but it just came out. What was a Surrey girl to do?

John scowled at her. He thought, I hope she's not going to make a scene. He hated that about her, the sentimentality, always clinging, always fussing about the children. She had fought him for so many years on the most trivial things, and sometimes the waterworks had come out. He thought of them as her nuclear weapon. What busy executive wanted to see his wife crying in public? Goddamn limey broad. Weren't they supposed to have a stiff upper lip? Just because he'd wanted to send Brad and Sophia overseas to boarding school instead of educating them here in the US. He was the one that paid the bills, he should have had the final say. But Emma was always making things difficult.

'What do you want me to say?' Emma asked softly. A waiter hovered to refill her glass, and to his annoyance, she didn't wave him away. A splash of chilled Pouilly Fuissé swirled into her glass, and his wife lifted it, sipping at the pale gold liquid like she was enjoying it. Like this was just a regular dinner. Man, he hoped she wasn't going to cope with this by getting publicly smashed.

Emma looked presentable tonight. She had always dressed well, he couldn't deny that; neat Chanel suits, pearls, kitten heels. Tonight she wore a rose-coloured silk suit with the diamond studs he had given her last Christmas in her ears. Her hair was dark and neatly bobbed. She looked sophisticated and elegant, but hardly a babe. He knew that the trim body under that suit had stretch marks, and then there were the laugh lines around her mouth and eyes. All of his friends' wives – first wives, anyway – had popped off to see the dermatologist and then the plastic surgeon when those first appeared. But not Emma. She seemed unaccountably happy with herself; never went on a diet, and, unimaginable in LA, was content to look her age. Of course, she had good skin and stayed out of the sun, but that, in his opinion, was no substitute for the surgeon's knife. Emma had good humour and good home-making skills. Even before he had gotten on the Hollywood studio gravy train, before he had given up his foolish screenwriting dreams to become a studio executive, Emma had kept a great house. On a tiny budget, she had managed to cook delicious meals, to always have fresh flowers around the place, and to keep the kids happy without parking them in front of the TV all day long. And later, he was the only husband he knew that hadn't had to hire an interior decorator.

But Emma refused to adapt to her surroundings. That was her problem, he told himself righteously. Imagine not caring about going to premieres, not caring about wrinkles, and not caring about getting on in the Hollywood social scene. Emma had turned down countless opportunities to co-chair one of those all-important, $2000-a-plate charity balls. She said her 'job' mattered to her too much to take time off. Her stupid little book company. As if she needed to work! It embarrassed him. He thought she did it deliberately. Just like that business with the children's schools.

It would be better for him and better for her to end it now. He had been cheating on her for years, anyway. Not that she'd ever suspected a thing. Now Shelby was pressuring him for a ring, and he thought it was the right thing. Sophia had left for college exactly one week ago. The city wouldn't demonise him; on the contrary, they'd see he'd stayed in his marriage for the sake of his children, and now they had both flown the nest he was taking a little time to pursue his own happiness. They'd applaud him for waiting the way he applauded himself.

Twenty years of marriage. John couldn't say when it had gone wrong, exactly, when he'd started looking at other women, because when he was twenty-four and Emma was twenty-five, she had been his everything, working a night job to support him while he cranked out those screenplays that never sold. Ah, back then she had been so young and beautiful. Even Shelby was not so beautiful as Emma had been. But the years had stolen the elasticity from her skin, and the two children had left marks on her belly, and, besides, he'd gotten a high-paying job; and with that came more options. Men weren't made to be monogamous anyway. Thank heavens he'd eloped with her and married in Las Vegas. Nevada was not a community-property state, and she had signed no pre-nup. Even though his salary was astronomical, he liked to live above his means . . . to take first-class everywhere. This restaurant, French cuisine with outrageous prices, was just another symptom of that.

But hell. John McCloud stretched his legs under the table and stole a glance at the barmaid. She was new, fresh in from Texas, and his buddy Sam Goldfarb, in Business Affairs, swore that he'd had her last week, and that she was sensational. *And* that her tits were real. Mmm, McCloud thought, big Southern titties and a tiny little waist, and an obliging disposition towards powerful studio players. Not sure if he believed Sam had actually laid her, though, because Business Affairs wasn't glamorous enough. But he might have better luck. He could get her a part. He imagined a flat little butt. Maybe he'd try it, later.

After he had dissolved matters with Emma.

They had large credit debts, as a couple. Once his lawyers had gone through the paperwork, she'd be left with barely a quarter mill. Maybe even less. But after the divorce, with the joint debts paid off, he could earn more money. This time he'd keep straight. And she would get none of the future wealth he'd generate.

The main thing was to get her to sign the papers.

'How long has it been going on? And who is it?' she finally managed.

'Not long,' he lied. 'And it's Shelby Harris.'

'Shelby.' He could see Emma's mind working, trying to place her. 'Shelby the yoga girl? The twenty-two-year-old?'

Shelby had instructed their daughter in yoga. He remembered that first sight of her out by the pool, in that outrageous thonged leotard over flesh-coloured tights, all firm young blondeness and large silicone boobs.

'Yes. She's a very spiritual person.'

'I'm sure she is,' Emma said dryly, with that English accent of hers his friends thought was so smart-sounding. Well, she hadn't been that smart when it came to keeping him. 'John, she's less than half your age.'

'We have a mental connection. Look, I'm sorry to cause you this hurt. But I think it's better to be honest. Honest as to what I need. I'm at that kind of a place in my life right now.'

'Did you realise it was our wedding anniversary?' she asked softly.

Damn. 'Yes,' he lied. 'I thought it brought a period to this passage in our lives. Like closing the circle. With honesty, the way we started out.'

Emma took a large, fortifying sip of her white wine. She wanted to make sure that John couldn't read her. A part of her brain that was detached, a bit like the part that informed you you were drunk when you were, wanted to videotape this moment and keep it before her

45

for ever. 'Closing the circle'! She almost felt pity for him, but not quite. What a miserable little shit he was, and he didn't even seem to know it.

Shelby wasn't the first. She might not even have been the twenty-first. Emma had buried herself in her children and her job, and tried to forget all about the loser she was married to. And now, thank God, he wanted an 'amicable' divorce. The head-rush of relief she experienced was rather like being back in the 70s in the front row of a Who concert. Emma quickly made a plan to call Father Freddy, her local parish priest. She could get an annulment without any trouble; John had never meant any of their marriage vows. And then, there would be Paolo.

John was like all the other miserable, stressed-out, moneygrubbing executives here; only interested in a rolling line of bimbos with nothing to say except 'divorce settlement'. He would wind up with four or five Mary-Beth clones, and divorce one after the other until he had nothing left. Young girls that would be out screwing the pool hand and spending his money on blow. She thought about Paolo, his dark eyes and intelligence and Italian appreciation of her still-firm but nicely rounded butt. Emma forced herself to look serious.

He fished hastily in his pocket. Better get her ink on his documents before she started to cry. Wedding anniversary. Who knew? What a nightmare. 'These are some papers my lawyers drew up. I hope you'll sign, because I think it'll be better for the kids if we do this amicably.'

'I totally agree,' Emma said quietly.

'Okay. Good. So what I'm proposing is that we sell the house and stocks and pay off our balances, and split the rest, not that there's much, but we'd be debt-free.'

'Fine with me,' she said.

He couldn't believe his luck. 'You know that this gives you an opportunity to start over. It could be the best thing that ever happened to you.'

She was silent.

'Your future and my future will be split.' Would she realise that she'd have no claims on his future earnings? He hoped not. He'd need it all. Shelby had picked out a four-carat flawless Tiffany diamond. 'A fresh start for both of us, including financially. You have . . . your books, after all.' He could pretend her little hobby, her independent press, meant something.

'So your company and mine would be separate . . . ?'

'It's still a good deal, Emma. I'm being generous, because that's what you deserve,' he said warmly. 'You get half of what we have now, and yes, we separate our jobs out, which is only fair.'

He pushed the papers across to her. 'One copy is for you to keep. I signed both already. Please Emma, for the children's sake, won't you do the civilised thing?'

She nodded and signed both, folded one up neatly and put it in her crocodile purse, then handed the other across to him.

The waitress sidled up to them with the wine list.

'We'll have champagne,' Emma said.

'You're taking it pretty good. It's the best thing.'

'I absolutely agree. I wasn't going to tell you to-night, but I've met someone, too. I was waiting for the children to go off to college before I told you. You've made it so much easier for me.'

'You?'

Emma grinned at the stupefied look on his face.

'Yes, me. It's Paolo Forza,' she said.

'Paolo?' he spluttered. The man they met at the Cannes Film Festival? Paolo, the urbane, charming Italian count with the huge, ancient villa outside of Rome he'd envied so much? Emma would be a contessa.

'And it's excellent that we're splitting up our interests. I received an order to buy me out from St Martin's Press in New York. I think I'm going to clear about eight million dollars.'

The waitress reappeared and filled their champagne flutes. He picked his up, but set it back down because his hand was trembling. Suddenly his wife looked so beautiful to him.

'I have to warn you though, John. I heard a rumour that you're on the outs at the studio. That they were going to fire you for expense-account fraud. Even something about a prosecution.' She smiled reassuringly. 'Of course, my information might not be reliable, because the same person told me that you'd been sleeping with Shelby for years, and of course it hasn't been going on long. But perhaps you'd better check it out all the same.'

Emma lifted her glass and toasted him.

'To fresh beginnings, my dear.'

Revenge

Emily Barr

As I hold the binoculars to my eyes, the wind whips through my hair, and I see the thing I have been waiting for, and dreading. On the mainland, heading in my direction, is a white car. I follow its progress for a few seconds. In a couple of minutes, it will cross the causeway and stop while the passenger gets out and opens the gate. It will move forward a couple of metres, and wait for the passenger to close it again.

I know the men who are inside. I met them both in the pub last week. In fact I knew the younger one years ago, when I used to come to the island as a child. Then he was skinny, with permanently scabby knees. Now, he's quite handsome. They were both friendly to me last week, but they won't be friendly now. Usually I like having visitors. It's a rare event, and it breaks the solitude. It stops me thinking about what I've done. I do not, however, plan to welcome these guests. They are the police, and they have come to arrest me.

I knew it would happen sooner or later. In a way,

I am almost relieved. I have no chance of getting away, but my instincts still urge me to try. I've got this far. I have hung onto my freedom, and I won't give it up without a struggle. I'll be in trouble for the rest of my life. I rush inside and wrap myself up in coats and scarves.

I give myself a quick glance in the hall mirror, as if anyone here cares what I look like. I never wear make-up now, but I seem to look better without it than I did when I was dolled up for work in London. I examine my messy hair and pasty face. I look young, and innocent. I am neither.

'Floppy!' I call, as I run down the stone steps, two at a time. 'Skip!' I add, just in case.

Normally my dog comes running as soon as he hears either of his names. I don't know where he's gone. I shout a few more times, and then set off on my own, half running to get away in time. I rush downhill to the edge of the island, staying where I can't be seen from the road. I am aware, all the time, that my flight is futile. I can't get the image of what I did out of my head. She looks at me. She is horrific. I never saw her, but I can imagine it.

I make myself concentrate on my surroundings. This island is spectacular. The grass is mossy and green. The sky is invariably cloudy, and the soft light heightens everything. I breathe the cold, fresh air and appreciate it. I might not be breathing it for long. Dry stone walls criss-cross the fields. The sheep get up and walk away, with dignity, whenever I lurch in their direction. Flop, wherever he is, is always kind to the sheep. I wonder whether a London dog, abruptly relocated, thinks he's died and gone to heaven. There are no scrawny poodles rushing up to smell his bottom, and he has the run of the entire island. Sometimes I watch him leaping around on the hillside, going crazy. Once he tried to swim in the loch, but it was too cold for him. It will, however, be spring next month.

It will be spring on the island, but that will make no difference to me. I notice I am shaking. By spring I'll be in Holloway Prison, and Flop will presumably be back with Stuart and Alison. I wince as her name comes into my head. I can hear the car driving faster than advisable over the stones. I should have got a boat for when this happened. I wonder idly where the dog is. As I scramble down to sit at the water's edge, I realise that it was probably Skipper's new name that led to my downfall.

When Stuart dumped me, we both wanted the dog. We each thought we had a claim. I'd adopted him from the shelter, but Stuart had housed him. I'd walked him, but Stu had paid for his food. I kidnapped him from Stuart's house, without leaving a note. Stuart and Ally turned up on my doorstep the following weekend, and demanded him back. They came together just to taunt me. She was looking rangy and elegant. If I'd known she was coming, I'd have brushed my hair, but I knew I couldn't compete. I hated her. I couldn't believe she had the nerve to come to my flat.

We all stood awkwardly in the kitchen, and I showed them the way the dog answered to his new name. Stuart looked at me with something like pity, and said, 'My God! You're a psycho!' They both laughed, shook their heads, and left. I suppose I'd shown them my true colours. I'd been the doormat for years. If I'd kept it up a little bit longer, I might not, now, be running away from the law. I should have sacrificed the dog.

My stomach is scrunched into a ball. I didn't mean to do it. This has been my mantra for the past ten days. I don't know whether that makes it better or worse. I didn't mean to do it; but I meant to do something. I wanted revenge, and I suppose I have got it. A life is ruined, and I should be glad.

I don't know how my relationship with Stuart led to this. I used to think our biggest problem was the fact that we worked together. Our colleagues loved him and hated me, but we didn't care. We loved each other. We had happy Sunday mornings, reading the papers and eating toast in bed, while Skipper (Floppy) lay across our legs. Stuart could talk for hours about Crystal Palace's hopes of promotion (lack thereof) or about rare plants. He was a horticulturist, by training. A horticulturist stuck in an office job. We would stand by his front window and look at his hedge. It was his pride and joy. He adored his rare shrubbery. He would talk, and I would listen, because that's the kind of woman I am. I am quiet. I'm a good listener.

I'm boring. That's what they used to say in the office, because I could never be bothered to talk to them. They'd sneer at me, and talk about me, and because I was so quiet, they'd forget they were within earshot. I've always held myself back. People have overlooked me since my first day at nursery school. The mistake people make is to assume that just because someone's quiet, they are necessarily good. The world at large sends quiet people to the bottom of the heap, assuming that they are lacking in confidence, that they are shy, that they want to be liked, that they are eager to please and therefore easily dismissed with contempt. No one would think to feel threatened by me.

I sit beside a rock. It's a big rock and I hope it might screen me. The air is bitterly cold, and I huddle into myself. By now they will be inside the house. I never lock the door. No one does. The police are in my house, looking for me. They are ready to arrest me. If the dog comes home, they'll ask him where I am. He might help them look for me. He'll be able to smell me. He'll help them find me. I throw a stone into the water. Treacherous Mr Floppy.

I disliked Ally from her first day at work, but it took me a while to notice that she was stealing my boyfriend. I knew she was taller, slimmer and prettier than me, but I despised her because she was self-consciously bubbly. I could see through her, so I imagined Stuart could too. She was desperate to be liked. I could see how insincere she was.

'I'm going to the canteen,' she simpered to Stuart, in her second week. 'I need a chocolate boost. Not to mention a packet of fags. Can I get you anything?'

'Oh, no, cheers,' he said. 'I'm not a chocolate fan. I prefer savoury things myself. And I definitely don't smoke.'

'Oh, me neither,' she said, performing an inept U-turn. 'At least, I'm quitting.'

And off she skipped. When she came back, she'd bought them each a packet of salt and vinegar crisps.

Then Stuart started dropping her name into the conversation, on almost any pretext.

'Shall we go to France at Easter?' I asked him, about a month ago.

'Okay. You know, Ally was saying she grew up in France. She speaks perfect French. I got her to say something for me, and she really did sound like a French person.'

'Well you don't speak French, so it's easy for her to impress you.'

'No, she went to school there and everything. She even has that weird curly handwriting they have abroad. Really, you should ask her to say something. Being bilingual is such a blessing. I'd love my children to be bilingual.' He hastily corrected himself. 'Our children.'

I told myself that he was just infatuated, that she probably had a boyfriend, that it didn't mean anything. I knew I was wrong on all counts. He fancied her, and she fancied him. It was staring me in the face. I noticed it and everyone else noticed it too. They loved it. It had all the ingredients of the perfect office scandal: boyfriend of unpopular girl goes off with gorgeous, lithe, friendly girl. Unpopular girl is humiliated. Friendly girl is triumphant. Office is bitchily happy.

I became tense. I didn't want to be dumped. I started asking him about her, pestering him, demanding answers.

'Of course I fancy her,' he admitted, warily. 'Everyone does. She's gorgeous. That doesn't mean I don't love you. Everybody looks at other women. It doesn't mean anything.'

'Well, what would you do if she came on to you?'

'I'd never cheat on you, if that's what you mean.'

'What if she was persistent?'

His eyes lit up. 'I suppose I'd just be flattered and walk away.'

He was lying. I knew he was lying. He knew that I knew he was lying.

I throw another stone into the water, and stare out to sea. There is no way I can escape now. When it happened, it came in an irresistible whirlwind. It was almost comically predictable. I came to Scotland to visit my parents one weekend. It's not something I particularly enjoy, but it has to be done from time to time. Leaving Stuart for two days felt wrong, but I knew I couldn't stay by his side for ever, just to ensure his fidelity.

As I left the office on Friday afternoon, I watched Stuart and Ally flirting. I'd brought my weekend bag with me, and by the looks of things, one of them should have done the same. He was standing by her desk, talking to her, leaning forward, being overly attentive. She was looking into his eyes and giggling. They both looked as though their next logical step was to rip each other's clothes off. I seethed, and didn't say goodbye.

Sometime during the weekend, he'd pushed a note through my door. I had expected to be asked out for a drink or something else ominous. I hadn't expected to be given my marching orders on a scrappy piece of paper torn from his filofax. He didn't mention her name, either out of a misguided attempt to avoid hurting me, or, more likely, through cowardice. It was not a friendly letter. Three years, and that was all I got.

It still pains me, although I know I've cancelled my entitlement to feel wronged. At the time, I was in agony. I'd been half expecting it for weeks, but I still wasn't prepared for losing Stuart.

I sat down in my kitchen, and crumpled the note. I poured myself half a pint of whisky. I straightened the note out again, and smoothed it down. I read it. It hadn't changed. I knocked back the whisky. I hated him. I hated her. I realised I had to be at work in twelve hours, and that they would both be there. Everyone would know. I decided to resign.

So I went to the office, just to check that the obvious was, indeed, the case. I put on my best, red suit, and more make-up than usual. I kept my chin up, and applied a fixed grin to my face. When I walked over to my corner, everyone went quiet. They looked at me, and I caught a few sniggers. They were so predictable. I looked around. Stuart was at his desk, head down. He knew I was there, but he wasn't making eye contact. Ally was there too – of course she was; they must have come in together. She caught my eye, and looked away quickly with a small smile.

'Good morning, Alison,' I said loudly. She mumbled something.

'Morning, Stuart,' I added. 'Thanks for your scrap of paper. Very gentlemanly. I'll have the dog.'

I got a laugh, and for a few seconds I was triumphant. Then I was wretched. I didn't want him back, but I was humiliated.

I left work at lunchtime, and I never went back. I knew they weren't going to bother to take me to court. I wasn't important enough. I stayed at home for a while, fuming. I wondered why he had said he loved me, if he didn't mean it. I wondered why I'd let myself get so involved. I'd never done it before. I might not do it again.

As the days went by, I disgusted myself by acting like a parody of a woman scorned. I sat around in my pyjamas, writing him furious letters and throwing them into the bin, while Richard and Judy murmured platitudes on TV in the background. I went to his house while he was at work, and took the dog. Some piece of faulty wiring in my brain made me decide that if I renamed Skip, everything would be all right. Mr Floppy kept me company, but he didn't make me feel any better. I came to realise that I would only be able to overcome my rage by unleashing it. The more I thought about it, the more logical it seemed. All I needed was to exact some fleeting revenge on them. They wouldn't know it was me, but I'd know that I'd caused them anguish of some sort, and that would be enough. Then I'd be able to get on with my life, such as it is. My jobless, friendless life. That was when I decided to come to Scotland. I'd cause Stuart some misery, and immediately afterwards, I'd drive north. I ascertained that my great-aunt's cottage was available, and that the key was under the stone.

I made a plan. I would set Stuart's precious hedge

ablaze while he was in his house with Alison. They'd be scared, they'd call the fire brigade, they'd be fine, and the rare and wonderful hedge would be ruined, by which time I'd be miles away.

I drove out of town, so no one would remember me, and bought a small container of petrol. At ten-thirty one night, I poured it generously over the leaves. They were drenched. I was excited. I had a box of matches in my pocket, but the house was empty. I knew Ally lived in a shared house, so I was banking on them staying at Stuart's. They'd come home soon – they'd have to – and then all I had to do was walk past, toss a lighted match over, and move swiftly away. I knew that I could cut through the alleyway two houses along, and be on the main road within seconds. Normally I would have avoided the passage, in case I met anyone dodgy, but in this instance I was the evil one, and I calculated that the chances of there being two of us about were remote. I was hugging myself in anticipation. I wanted to bring Floppy with me, but I feared he'd give me away, so I made him wait in the car, with all my possessions.

Soon, I saw them coming down the street. He was holding her hand. This sent a hot wave through me. He never, ever used to hold my hand in public. He just didn't want to.

'Hey, don't think it's because of you,' he once told me, when I complained.

'Why is it, then?'

'Public displays of affection just aren't my thing. That's all. Never have been. Nothing personal.' He rumpled my hair. And now here he was, with Ally's skinny hand in his. She was tottering along on high heels. I caught a good glimpse of her pretty face in the light of a street lamp. I knew she smoked, but I never gave it a moment's thought. I knew that Stuart was bitterly opposed to anyone smoking in his house. I should have realised what might happen. It came as a complete shock. I was hidden in the shadows across the road, wearing black. I was waiting for them to go in so I could make a pretty conflagration, and get into my car, which I'd parked at the top of the alley.

It happened quickly. She said something to him, and stopped. He walked on, and put his key in the door. She took out a packet of fags, and leaned into the hedge to get out of the wind. A second later, she went up in flames.

I ran.

I woke up in a nondescript hotel at some motorway services near Leicester, with Floppy curled up in a corner, and I turned on the radio. I hoped it would be a dramatic enough story to make the national news, and it was. She was alive, but she'd lost her lovely face. She was covered in burns. She was in intensive care. I got in my car, and drove as fast as I could towards my new life, as she began to come to terms with hers. I reflected that this would test their great so-called love, and then I remembered that they'd never claimed to be in love at all. I tried to tell myself she deserved it for stealing my boyfriend, but I knew she didn't. I tried to banish the knowledge that it was entirely my fault. I thought I might get away with it. My trump card was the fact that I was so meek. No one would even remember that I used to go out with him.

I cannot feel triumphant, however hard I try. When I close my eyes, I see her lovely face, lost for ever. I try to picture it covered in burns. I cannot believe I did that to someone. It's funny how fine is the line between good and evil. You go through life with yourself firmly marked down as good and law abiding and sinned against. With one easy act, you shift yourself straight into the other column. You become a criminal. I am an accidental perpetrator of grievous bodily harm.

I've known all along that the police would come for me. I have been dwelling on the miracles of forensic science. It's not easy to get away with things. They know someone poured petrol on the hedge. The consensus seemed to be that it was random vandalism, but I can't assume it's going to stay that way. There must be ways that I've never even thought of for them to identify me. You always leave a trace. Apart from anything else, I had a motive.

It could be the fact that I changed the dog's name. Where is that bloody dog? It could be that I left a hair at the scene. It could be that someone saw a short woman in black running down the alleyway and leaping into a car. It could be anything. The chances are, however, that they don't actually *know* it was me. I'm going to have to be clever with my answers. They'll make me go to London. I'll be back in the city, breathing the foul air. I'll go to prison. People will only want to talk to me in the same way they want to talk to Myra Hindley, so that they can tell people they met me. No one will want to be my friend, except the sick people who fall in love with people in prison, and that only works when it's the man who's incarcerated. Men are too practical to kid themselves that they're in love with an evil witch like me.

I am crouched at the water's edge, in a futile attempt to be invisible. I hear their footsteps, and I know I'm doomed.

'There you are!' says the younger policeman, Robbie. He seems to be smiling. I wonder how he'll tell the story of the day he discovered the village had a psychopath on its outskirts.

'Hi,' I tell him, weakly.

The older one speaks.

'We've looked all over for you,' he says. 'I'm afraid we've got some bad news.'

I force myself to look at him. 'What?'

'It's your wee doggie. He's been run down.'

'It was an accident,' adds Robbie. 'The postman's terribly sorry.'

'My wee doggie? Mr Floppy?' Poor Floppy. He'd never deserved that name, and now he's dead. 'Is that why you came?'

I live in a village where the police solemnly inform you that your dog is dead. In London he'd have been scraped off the tarmac by unscrupulous restaurateurs by now.

'That's terrible news,' I add. Mr Floppy has been sacrificed so that I may walk free. I am not going to prison. Not yet, at least. I can't take it in.

I look at the police, trying to remove all traces of

61

guilt from my features. Robbie smiles sympathetically. I realise that he's not exactly spoilt for choice round here when it comes to the ladies. I think I've known all along that the best revenge I could ever exact on Stuart would be to have a happy life without him. Perhaps I am beyond revenge now, but I might try to do it anyway. It might ensure my continued freedom.

'I'm going to have to pour myself a drink,' I say loudly, startling myself. 'Will either of you join me? And, um, do you have the . . . body?'

Two hours later, a slightly drunk young policeman is digging a grave outside my cottage. Floppy has gone, and now I have Robbie. He's grown up well, since he was a scabby-kneed boy. He's going to get me a puppy. He and I seem to get on well. I vow to give it my best attempt.

If any other woman looks at him, I think I'll be able to sort her out.

Little Boots – An Unfairy Tale

Mark Barrowcliffe

With thanks to Ben Marshall, who told me about the dog.

The shed was where Henry went to be alone, technically.

Henry was a man who chose his words carefully and when he said technically he meant it in two senses.

First that he went to be alone with his craft, his labour. That kind of technically.

Then the other sense. Obviously he was alone in the house too but the presence of his wife and the children meant that, technically, he was in company. That's what he meant by technically.

He enjoyed this sort of fine distinction, the sort of distinction that caused his wife of fifteen years, Sue, to call him things like 'a stupid smart arse'. In fact, she went further. She said that his pedantry and his pickiness and his one-upmanship over the tiniest things at home were direct products of his failure to achieve any sort of success or sense of self-worth in the rest of his life.

Fair point, Henry had thought, setting out once again for a day at the design agency where he worked 'colouring in', as Sue put it, under the demanding eye of Trent, his twenty-four-year-old pierced boss.

So Henry had long since learned to keep his observations to himself at home, particularly as his children had now transferred their affections from him. His son Kai – Sue had wanted something unusual, ironic as there had been five Kais at his junior school alone, along with four Jordans and a brace of Leonardos – was obsessed with rapstars. The child seemed to be operating the aesthetics of obscenity, the more vile the song the more he seemed to like it. Mind you, he did play one very encouraging and relatively tuneful ditty (Henry liked the word ditty) about a child murdering his mother, so there was always hope.

The daughter – she who had been inseparable from his side for the best part of thirteen years, she who had sought his comfort in the night and made him promise that he'd never leave her and they'd both live for ever – was now too concerned with her status as a respected and precocious neighbourhood slut to pay him any attention.

Mix all this in with his wife's preoccupation with everything but him and, at the dinner table, Henry couldn't have been more alone in the middle of the Gobi.

The shed, however, was his sanctuary. Here he indulged his transitory enthusiasms, usually for something conspicuously crafty, painstaking and above all centred, projecting a vision of inner calm. He'd tried model soldiers (boring), remote controlled aircraft (too depressing when they kept smashing), wood carving (he was more of a two-dimensions man) and Spirograph (very good results). At least, even during the highly costly and abortive antiques restoration phase, he was out from under her feet in his shed. As Sue said, he was always under her feet and quite often she'd tread on him to illustrate it. But when the best thing that ever happened to him happened to him, it was from under his feet that it came.

He was in the shed stitching the tunic of a life-sized figure of the the Emperor Caligula that he'd been asked, after some persuasion and a donation to the woggle fund on his part, to put together for a scout tableau. He'd become quite a student of Roman History recently. Since he'd seen the film *Gladiator* he'd also rented *Spartacus* and the fantastic *Caligula* itself, which had given him the idea for the dummy. He'd tried the toga on in front of the mirror one day and been impressed. He looked quite imperious as he'd put his thumb into the 'no mercy' position.

What had worried him, as he'd placed on a silver cccclaurel crown he'd made from KitKat foil, was that he'd forgotten to eat breakfast. It seemed that, as the rest of the world was operating a policy of ignoring him, he'd opted for the 'if you can't beat them join them' policy and started ignoring himself.

He was about to sneak in and grab a bowl of Sugar Puffs when he'd heard a scratching from beneath the floorboards.

'Rats,' he thought, as usual in two senses. Rats like

'Oh dear I'll have to put off my Sugar Puffs' and 'Rats' like 'Oh dear disease-carrying vermin below my shed'.

On the bright side, he thought it'd give him something to do. He took a machete from the shed wall. Curiously he felt like seeing something suffer that morning.

It was only when he was about to crouch to look beneath the shed that he gave a little pause for thought. Rats, he thought, bite. That would be his luck, to start off attempting to vent his spleen on something and end up with a septic wound. He then remembered, giving himself a mental pat on the back, that rodents are dazzled by bright light. He fetched his torch from the shed.

He flicked it on and knelt down, shining it into the gap that had proved such an excellent insulation against damp and frost and had been well worth splashing out the extra cash above the price of a floor-standing shed, just the way he'd told Sue it would be.

He could see nothing there but then, a movement. He put his arm up to his neck to protect his throat in case it sprang. Then he flicked the torch around again. Reflected in the beam were two luminous discs, bigger than any rat's, or at least he hoped so.

Henry peered into the void. He'd lost the discs. Then a sudden sharp feeling on his torch hand and he drew it back. He'd been bitten, only lightly, only playfully, but bitten. He shone the torch into the dark once more. Right in front of his hand, an inch from the front of the torch, he could see what had been making the noise. About the size of a Scottie dog, but much rangier, with fur of steel wool.

'Good God,' said Henry, 'a puppy, come on boy, come on.'

And out it came, nuzzling and biting at his hand. 'Gosh,' said Henry, 'you're really lovely aren't you.' Three things struck him about the dog. One, it had blue eyes, quite unlike any other dog that he'd seen, enchanting eyes like he understood huskies had, eyes that he imagined had taken the cold of the snow and the wastes and reflected it back on the world. You're allowed to think things like that when you're on your own. Then of course, the paws. He'd never seen such large paws, even on an adult dog. They looked, on his small form, comic, like a cartoon figure. And then there was the biting.

'I'll have to get a glove or stop him doing that,' thought Henry. Even at that point there was no thought in his head to get rid of the dog or take it to a pound, even though it had nearly drawn blood.

He picked it up. It stopped biting and nuzzled into his breast. Henry felt something he hadn't felt in years – the uncritical presence of another being, warm, comforting and cosy.

'Oh there,' said Henry, 'there he is,' it was a he, 'just a little scrap of fur in the world, aren't you? A piece of warmth among all those cold stars.'

He looked back into the shed to where the toga of the emperor hung. Little Boots, that had been the emperor's nickname. An outsized paw padded his chest. Little Boots. What a great name for the dog. Ironic too, the dog's paws being big. That sort of subtlety always appealed.

'You're going to need feeding, my chap,' said Henry looking into the pale blue eyes. The dog panted back at him. He almost appeared to be laughing. 'Come on Boots, let's go in.'

He'd taken the dog out of the mild summer night and into the house. This, of course, had been a mistake. Sue wasn't at all pleased.

'What in the name of God have you got there?' she'd asked.

'Dog,' said Henry. Missing the indefinite article gave his reply just the sort of double meaning of which he was so fond.

'I can see that, why have you got it?'

'I found it under the shed,' said Henry.

'Call the dog's home then,' said Sue, 'someone'll be missing it. And get it out of the house, we've enough mess in here with you.'

'I'm not calling any home,' said Henry, 'if people are missing it they'll put up notices. Otherwise I'm looking after it.'

'Not in my house,' said Sue with a curt smile. She was a bugger for cleanliness and, had he considered for a second, he'd have known he would have met resistance.

'Fair enough,' said Henry, 'I'll keep him in the shed.'

'You do that,' said Sue, 'now.' The curt smile came back onto the face, the smile he never saw when she was with her friends, when she was leaving or returning from her 'social life', the smile she kept only for him.

'And Henry,' said Sue, 'I know you. What are you thinking of calling it?'

'What's it to you, you clearly don't want to have anything to do with the poor thing?'

'If you keep it then presumably you'll walk it, and if you walk it you'll meet the neighbours. I don't want you calling it Darth Vader or Elric of Melnibone or anything else stupid.' She'd never got science fiction or fantasy, no matter how he'd tried to explain it to her in their early days.

'It's called Boots,' said Henry defiantly.

Sue looked impressed. 'Oh that's nice,' she said, 'after the Chemists. Gratifyingly normal. Off you go.' She gave a little wave of dismissal. 'And remember. It sleeps in the shed.'

Again the smile, the smile that suggested, were it not for the meddlesome bureaucracy of the European Human Rights Act, not only the dog would be sleeping in the shed.

As it was, Henry decided to sleep in the shed anyway after a couple of days. He'd lain next to Sue, back to back, listening to her guttural clearings and hackings in the night and thought, with a fart, 'I don't need this any more.'

So after a day of labour, during which the son pronounced the dog 'dope' (a good or a bad reaction, who can tell?) and the daughter confided to her friend that 'Donovan Bradshaw (a popstar) has a dog' and asked if she could take it out when its paws were harder, the shed was clear.

'See,' said Henry, to Boots, who was growling away on his third cowbone of the day, 'this is our little palace.

You and me son, in here. It'll be great.' Come the winter, thought Henry, I'll insulate it and stick one of those Frontiersman stoves in. The selection, Frontiersman One, Two or Three, would of course all be part of the fun.

'Why are you sleeping in there?' Sue asked.

'I think he's missing his mother,' said Henry.

'I know how he feels,' said Sue.

Lying with the peace of the summer nights about him, Henry took Boots to his bosom. The dog had, after some nose smacking, a bit of retaliatory snapping and finally a reward regimen Henry had read about in *How Your Dog Thinks* by Barbara Woodhouse, stopped the biting. Instead it pushed its muzzle into his neck and, though its increasing weight made breathing slightly uncomfortable, Henry had never felt so loved.

At the weekends and during the week's 'Paternity leave' he took to go walking with Boots after he'd had his injections, he saw places he'd never seen.

The Rec, for instance, normally a forbidding place where children loitered and marked out their territories in spraypaint and broken glass, seemed welcoming with Boots by his side. The dog got him out of himself, gave him something to talk about. He became a citizen again.

He spoke to a reasonably attractive woman outside the shops about the size of Boots's paws. A man in a car stopped one day in August, about six weeks after Boots had first come into his life, and said, 'Look at its paws, it's never still a pup?'

True, the dog was becoming large. Bloody large. In early November, five months after the day they'd met, Mrs Greerson at the shops had said, 'Look at the size of him, if he keeps growing you won't know whether to walk him or ride him.'

He'd related that story to the daughter's latest boyfriend. Both daughter and youth had burst out laughing at the 'ride him'.

Henry had ignored it. He felt pride in the dog, even when it had pulled his shoulder out when it strained against the lead for a cat one day and he'd had to go to casualty.

The dog even taught him about humans. If you want to be liked, he observed, just be friendly and say nothing.

The dog didn't have a witty line in double meanings but everyone wanted to pat him, everyone wanted to know him. A wag of the tail and a cheerful growl and everyone was entranced.

In fact, the only person who didn't seem to like him was Sue, and that was a definite plus.

He told the dog all his secrets, how he'd like to give his boss Trent and his eyebrow ring, his nose stud, his unguessable mutilations, a piercing he wouldn't forget. How he'd like to get what was his due in life. Even if it wasn't strictly his due.

It wasn't all bile, though. The dog taught him to be calm, to live in the moment. They'd step from the insulated shed, out of the warmth of the Frontiersman Three and into the winter cold.

Loading up into the cheap car he'd bought because Sue wouldn't let him take the dog in the Peugeot, he'd have a sense of adventure.

'Where today, mate?' he'd ask, studying the book of walks he'd bought and worrying if he was one day going to have to trade the estate for a Transit, if Boots was going to be comfortable.

All anxieties disappeared, though, when he and Boots were in nature. The dog returning after a run, Henry running his hands through the cool fur and feeling the heat beneath, the muscle rippling under the skin. What would it be like, he thought, to be like the dog, immersed in the moment like a molecule in the surf, like the chill on the wind, like something that meant something and didn't know it.

Back in the day-to-day there were problems. Sue had become angry when he'd revealed to her friend Fat Janet, she who he supposed had her make-up delivered by hod, that he slept in the shed.

She'd raised her voice to him and followed him out into the yard as he retreated to the shed. 'Do you think I want her thinking we're freaks?' she'd said.

Boots, though, had simply slid a tooth from beneath his massive lip and given Sue the sort of look that suggested silence was the best plan for a long and generally unmaimed life. Sue had gone deathly white. As the dog had lowered his lip Henry raised an eyebrow. Things, it seemed, were going to be different.

There had been hints of trouble, of course. The dog really didn't like anyone coming near his food. Really, really, really, really, really, really. At all. Henry had taken to persuading Boots into the shed by throwing a cowbone in from the garage roof. He'd bolt the door while the dog munched the bone. Then he'd put out the bowls of Pedigree Chum into the back yard and open the shed from the house with a string. But Boots was fine, as long as you didn't have any food on you.

He'd felt sure Boots wouldn't hurt him but the neighbours had complained about the level of canine cursing and threats issued from deep within the throat that would ensue should he stand within twenty yards of the beast at feeding time.

Apart from that Boots was fine. Henry was glad he'd been obliged to forego his night-time mints after the dog had torn them from his hand one night and nipped him badly. It had hurt his hand but saved his teeth, he thought.

We all live with idiosyncrasies, we all put up with things. If he thought of the level of shite he'd suffered from Sue over the years, the dog's food thing appeared to be no more than a charming caprice.

On the positive side, friendships had evolved with dog people. Dave Higgins, the Labrador man, while rather boring on the subject of Fulham FC and in his constant requests for details of Henry's drinking – having surrendered his former alcohol addiction he now seemed determined to pursue it vicariously – was more than willing to hear Henry run Sue down and to join in with a few comments about his own wife.

And dark Mona, with the Whippet, she with the smile, the nice smile, not like Sue's. Obviously her name wasn't Mona, it was Lisa, but he'd called her that and she seemed to like it. She was in his situation too, he'd discovered as he'd watched Boots chasing the Whippet which was mercifully fast on its toes.

'My wife doesn't understand me,' he'd said.

'My husband neither,' she'd replied.

They'd joked, they'd laughed, she'd said Boots should have a muzzle. Was it love? He didn't know, but it was relief.

The incident that had made him see Mona's point of view about the muzzle had occurred on a sunny day in November. He'd been up on the common walking Boots near the big ponds. The leaves were lovely at that time of year, russets and browns, pinks and yellows, and Boots was beautiful against them, bounding across the autumn like a sliver of steel on a field of rust. Henry had been lost in the golden light, sucking in the chill, deepening himself in his overcoat and feeling alive. For a second he'd lost Boots and wondered where he was. He'd descended to the pond which was carpeted in leaves, indistinguishable almost from the ground like the treacherous terrain of Faerie Land (*Dungeons and Dragons* had been another passing fad).

Anyway, it appeared that Boots had noticed Dr Baker's dog Bruno's habit of drinking from the pond. So Boots had, very cleverly, it had to be admitted, secreted himself in the pond, only his eyes and nose above the water and obscured by leaves.

When Bruno had come down to take his eleven o'clock refreshment Boots had emerged primeval-style from the pond to drag it thrashing to its death. 'Macabre' the local paper had called it but as Henry had pointed out, Boots had never done it before and the Baker's Bruno had been no saint itself, often bullying smaller dogs.

Luckily the Dangerous Dogs Act only covers people and livestock and a German Shepherd is no one's idea of livestock, so the coppers couldn't touch them.

So the muzzle had been purchased, which was just as well, as the dog now insisted on being allowed in the house. Even with the muzzle on, it was best to keep food away from him as he could cause an awful mess, tearing at boxes of cornflakes, soap powder or even bottles of bleach with his claws. You have to look at things positively, though, and it at least encouraged people to be tidy.

The dog psychologist had been called at Sue's insistence. She had been unusually quiet since Boots had taken up residence on the sofa, his great shaggy head on one arm, his legs poking over the other.

Boots was feeding in the back yard and, as everyone knew, it was best to keep the door locked at that time. The son, however, had forgotten this and foolishly gone to retrieve his bicycle to cycle to school.

Boots had rightly conjectured that the child's obscenity-daubed pack had contained food. So it was natural that he should pin the child to the floor and tear open the bag.

The teacher had, of course, called to confirm that the dog had indeed eaten Kai's homework, along with his ruler, calculator and sandwich box and that the boy hadn't, as normal, faked the letter explaining the state of his exercise books.

Anyway, the incident had wiped the smirk from the boy's face and replaced it with a much preferable cowed expression. Also on the positive side, when Henry had finally got to the boy, by throwing a packet of Sugar Puffs down the garden, the child's whimpered 'Please help me Dad,' had been his first sentence that hadn't contained the words 'Bitch' or 'Ho' since his twelfth birthday.

So the dog psychologist, all charm and fee, had been called, assuring him that 'Ninety-nine per cent of cases' are solvable.

'He's in the garden, is he?' the psychologist had said, with a wink; 'it's just a matter of reward and denial,' he'd said from beneath his friendly baseball cap.

'I shouldn't go out there with those bits of cheese in your hand if I were you.' Well, Henry had warned him.

The rate at which the psychologist had retreated on seeing Boots had been quite impressive. Luckily he'd thrown the baseball cap, which had distracted the dog and he'd managed to get the door shut before serious harm could ensue.

'That,' he'd said, looking around him like a peasant in a Dracula movie, 'is a Czech Wolfhound, and you need to have it shot. Now. You'd be safer keeping a tiger out there. It's a man-killer.'

He'd explained how the Wolfhound is a cross between an Irish Wolfhound and the Caucasian Timber Wolf. The CTW (his acronym, not Henry's) is the only dog that hunts alone. It has no pack instinct, it won't bond. You can raise dogs like 'Boots' up to adolescence, about a year old, but after that the CTW will assert itself he'd said. It'll view its owner as competition for food, 'That's my Winalot!' it'll cry. It will begin to want to roam. Crucially it will go for anything with a limp. It's programmed to select the weakest as the easiest prey. A 400 pound mass of muscle attached to a face full of teeth the size of hunting knives.

'And, he won't stand the muzzle for long,' the psychologist had warned, shaking. He'd been about to present his invoice when Henry had gone to open the back door and he'd decided to make himself scarce.

Henry had gone out into the yard, after first dusting himself for crumbs, and taken Boots's head in his hands. 'Oh my poor boy, my poor boy, what are we going to do with you?' he'd said.

The dog looked back, not understanding, but his eyes were soft, like they'd been when he was small enough to sleep on Henry's chest. He put his arms around Boots and absorbed himself in his warmth. 'My poor boy,' said Henry, 'I wish I could make you understand. I wish my love could change you.' The dog's great tongue caressed Henry's ear.

'All right Dad? Sure he's not tasting you?'

It was the daughter's latest beau – Lee. He who had been loudly pleasuring the girl in her room for the best part of three weeks and who called Henry 'Dad'. Lee was a footballer who, Henry recalled, had been pleasantly hobbled in a staff vs school game the week before, the penalty for skipping round the fat games teacher once too often.

Henry looked down at Lee's leg. It was encased, from the ankle to the knee, in white plaster. He'd always suspected him of a weakness for melodrama. Disturbingly, the plaster bore the legend 'Shag machine', in what looked suspiciously like his daughter's handwriting, all the way down its length.

He'd told Lee not to move and he, being Lee, had moved, backwards in his uneven, uncomfortable gait. In short, he'd limped. He'd been told, it was his fault, you couldn't blame the dog.

A flash of seething fur shot towards the door and the dog was upon the leg, Lee screaming as the huge teeth lacerated the plaster.

'Oh stop, Boots,' said Henry, somewhat half-heartedly.

'Get him off, get him off,' screamed Lee.

Luckily the daughter had the presence of mind to snatch some chops from the fridge and throw them behind the dog. Distracted – magnificent, though, in his anger Henry thought, the dog looked to see where they fell. Henry seized the moment to bundle the boy out of the way and slam the door behind them.

'You bloody little fool!' he shouted. 'What have you done? What have you done?' It was then that he noticed the boy had fainted and his plaster, which now read 'hag chin' owing to the damage of the teeth, was seeping blood.

Of course, after that there was no stopping Sue. The dog had delivered himself into the hands of his enemy. Conspiring with Lee's father she made it very clear that unless he had the animal destroyed they'd invoke the law and have it taken away.

'I want it dead by tea time,' she'd said, pushing her little smile into his face.

'Why don't you tell him yourself?' said Henry, going to open the back door. That had shut her up.

There is no longer journey than that to say goodbye to a friend. Henry was in the car, Boots in the back, on his way to the vet's and the needles of death. The dog rested his head on Henry's shoulder as they drove.

'You're still a pup really, aren't you?' Henry asked the dog. He just licked back in reply through the muzzle.

It was outside the vet's that Henry realised he couldn't do it. So he put the ageing Estate into gear, riding the clutch (problems with the synchromesh the mechanic had said), stopped off at home to pick up his passport and credit cards and headed out towards Kent.

Fuel stops were hard. There's a slovenly habit of eating on the way back to your car nowadays but Henry put a T-shirt over the dog's head to blindfold him when they stopped and the worst that happened were some funny looks.

The Shuttle gave them time together, speeding under the English Channel, both asleep in the back, brothers in oppression. Then there was Belgium and a route map. Other countries came and went in a blur of credit card transactions and petrol stations, the clutch protesting through the low countries, relaxing on the Autobahn. Finally, after days, South West Russia. The Caucasus mountains. The dog seemed to sense it, its genes stirring with the call of home.

It was a beautiful country, unbelievable. The mountains like something from *Heidi*. 'I'll take my holidays here in future,' thought Henry, 'just to be near him.' Mount Elbrus, the giant, according to a guide book he'd bought in a service station, was where he wanted to go but the car was making an unpleasant noise so he pointed it into the mountains almost at random, following the one in ten elevation signs, taking the smaller routes. Finally he was in the high country, the road just a track among rolling fields and wild forests. Far off he could see a herd of something, deer maybe. As if it knew that this was the spot the car gave a cough of smoke from beneath the engine and would go no further.

Henry wept. He thought of Sue and the children and his work and he looked at the country before him, the country that seemed to ask him what he wanted, not tell him what to do.

'You'll be all right here,' said Henry with a brave smile. He didn't want Boots to see him crying. The dog wagged his mighty tail excitedly as he opened the back of the estate.

Boots sprang out, dancing about, full of life, and Henry felt glad he had spared him. The dog would survive and if he didn't, well he would have known freedom.

'Go 'ay, go 'ay,' said Henry, waving his arms.

Boots just looked at him. He was waiting for him to throw him a ball to eat.

'Oh Boots,' said Henry, 'I'm going to miss you.' He put his arms around the dog one last time and kissed him. Then he shooed him away. Boots retreated down the stony track, still watching Henry.

Henry addressed himself to the practicality of the matter in front of him. To get home, or at least back to his house. If he could turn the car around he felt sure he could roll down the hill for a fair way, at least until a village. He got in and let the handbrake off. The car rolled backwards more violently than he'd anticipated and slammed into the verge. Henry got out. 'Great,' he thought, 'I'm stuck.' Boots was still watching him, but also scenting the air. He was going to be fine. Nothing for it but to push the thing out, he thought.

From somewhere he found the strength, ghoul-eyed and knackered from the journey, to shove the thing. From across the valley he heard howling. Boots stiffened, heeding the call.

The second that Henry slipped he knew he'd done something wrong to his ankle. He got out of the way of the backsliding car but his foot found a crack between two rocks and he practically heard the tendons snap. Boots looked at him. All Henry's pain seemed distilled into his ankle and he cried out, cursing his wife, his children, his job, his luck.

Henry looked at Boots. 'Come on, boy,' he said, limping towards the dog.

Chapter & Verse
Colin Bateman

Dolly's voice is nicotine.

'She doesn't see me comin'. I have her by the hair, pull the head straight back, then slit her throat.'

The woman who put the dead in deadpan.

'I use a knife, the knife she bought me on our first anniversary. She doesn't even make a noise, the blood just burbles out.'

'Burbles?' Ivan glances up from his fingernails. Michelle, right at the back.

'Burbles, yeah, okay?' says Dolly, her voice caught between embarrassment and threat.

'Let her finish, Michelle,' Ivan says, 'it's not easy.'

Dolly nods curtly at him, then returns her attention to the page. Her fingers follow the words. 'The blood just *burbles* out . . .' She tosses a defiant look back at Michelle. Michelle tosses it back. '. . . and then she collapses in my arms. She's dead. I kiss her once . . .'

There's a chorus of *ooooooohs!* from the rest of the class. Dolly waits for them to settle again before continuing. 'I kiss her once on the lips, then I bury her in her own garden, just where we used to sit in the summer.' She nods to herself for a moment, then adds a quiet, 'The end.'

They applaud politely. They enjoyed it, but they're nervous about being asked next.

'Ahm, yes, very, uhm, descriptive. Dolly.' Ivan gets off his desk and taps his chalk on the blackboard. 'Of course, the title of our essay assignment was actually, *What I Will Do On My First Day Home From Prison*. I, ahm, wouldn't show that to the parole board.'

They laugh. He likes to make them laugh. Dolly gives him a limp-wristed bog-off wave, 'Oh Mr Connor,' she says, 'what would you know about writing fiction?'

Ivan smiles. 'Okay, who's next?' Eyes are averted. 'Come on, we're all friends here. Eileen?' A shake of the head. 'Betty?' Not even a shake, just a stare at the floor. A small, elfin-featured girl slowly raises her hand. 'Donna? Okay, off you go.'

Donna licks her lips, pushes hair from her brow. 'The . . .'

'Stand up so we can see you, Donna.'

She gets up. Her voice is soft. 'The light of the ark surrounds me, the dark of the night astounds me . . .'

'Is that a poem, Donna?' Ivan asks.

'Yes, Mr Connor.'

'It *was* an essay I specifically . . .' He trails off. He glances at his watch. He sighs. 'Okay, let's hear it.'

'Will I start again?'

'Come on, girl!' Michelle shouts. 'Get it out!'

'All right, Michelle. Yes Donna, from the top.'

She nods slightly. 'The . . .'

'Shit!'

Donna looks up sharply to see Mr Connor with his foot on a chair, and the broken end of a shoe-lace held up as evidence of a legitimate excuse. 'Sorry, Donna. Please . . .'

Donna swallows, takes a deep breath. 'The . . .'

At that moment the bell rings and class is over. They're up out of their chairs like they're back at school, then they remember they're volunteers for this class, they aren't going anywhere. They slow down. Ivan scoops up his own books and joins the exodus. He doesn't notice Donna, still standing with her poem in her hand.

Ivan is forty years old, he wears an old raincoat, his hair is long and straggled. He has been teaching this class in the women's prison for eight weeks. It pays reasonably well, enough to tide him over until the new contract is sorted out. He looks at his watch. He's caught in heavy traffic, going nowhere. Ben Elton would get a novel and a million out of it. Ivan's Metro is decrepit. He's listening to Dvorjak on a tape. His most recent novel, *Chapter & Verse*, sits open on the passenger seat. The passages he will shortly read at Waterstones are highlighted in yellow. Beside the book there's a half-eaten packet of Starburst, although he will call them Opal Fruits until he goes to his grave.

He lifts the book and reads aloud, his voice strong, confident. 'But it was not only by playing backgammon with the Baronet, that the little governess rendered herself agreeable to her employer. She found many different ways of being useful to him. She read over, with indefatigable patience, all those law papers . . .'

He stops because he's aware of being watched. He looks out, and then *up*, at the cab of a lorry, facing in the other direction, and the bearded driver laughing at him. Ivan closes his book, sets it back on the passenger seat, then grips his steering wheel with both hands. A moment later music booms out from the truck. Someone with at least a fingernail on the pulse of popular music would recognise it as rap, but to Ivan it is noise. And noise annoys.

Ivan scratches suddenly at his head. He thinks he may have picked up nits in the prison.

Ivan hurries across the busy road, freezing rain slicing into his face. Halfway across he steps out of the shoe with the broken lace, and before he can go back for it a car drags it along the road for a hundred yards and he has to hop after it. Look at the great author! Stepping off his lofty pedestal to pursue an Oxford brogue along the tarmac! He picks it up and hugs it against his chest.

Campbell is watching him from the Waterstones doorway. His agent gets ten per cent of everything he earns. Ivan's coat is ancient, but at least he has one. Campbell is damp and cold. Ivan hurries up, full of apologies.

Ivan isn't nervous until he sets a damp foot in the bookshop, but the moment he crosses the threshold, the weight of literature and competition is suddenly upon him. Thousands and thousands and thousands of books. Half of them appear to be about a young boy called Harry Potter. Ivan admires anyone who can make that much money, and hates Her with a vengeance. He wonders if She will ever write *Harry Potter and the Provisional IRA*, or *Harry Potter and the Palestinian Question*. He loves corrupting popular titles and idles away many hours of his writing life at this very pursuit. His favourites are *Love In The Time of a Really Bad Flu*, *The Day of the Jack Russell* and *A Quarter To Three in the Garden of Good and Evil*.

As he moves through the shop Ivan becomes aware that the aisles are actually very crowded. This is a good sign. Campbell pushes ahead of him, then comes to a halt at the edge of a seated area; a hundred seats and they are *all filled*. Butterflies flap in his stomach. This is better than he could ever have hoped. At previous readings he has been lucky to scrape a dozen hardy souls. He glows. Word of mouth. He has never quite been popular enough to be considered a cult, but perhaps this is the beginning of something. He is ready to be acclaimed. He observes the microphone, the small lectern, the table with the bottle of Evian water, the glass, the chair, the pen for signing books afterwards.

The manager of the shop steps up to the microphone and taps it once. 'Ladies and gentlemen, sorry to keep you waiting, but our author has at last emerged from the nightmare that is our traffic.' They laugh. 'Our guest tonight is quite simply an author who needs no introduction. Universally acclaimed, a master of the English language . . .' Ivan swallows nervously, takes a first step forward, 'put your hands together for . . . Francesca Brady!'

Ivan freezes. Applause erupts around him. Posters curl suddenly down from the ceiling. A mile-wide smile, expansive hair, red-red lipstick, the cover of a book, but the spitting image of the author now stepping forward from the audience not six feet away from him. His heart is racing. His first impulse is to dive on her, force her to the ground, and then batter her to death with a copy of *Insanity Fair*, her latest 'novel'. Ivan always makes that little quotation marks sign with his fingers when anyone mentions *Insanity Fair*, or even Francesca Brady. She writes fat romantic books for fat romantic people. She dresses them up with smart one-liners so that she can appear hip, but she's really *ugh!* Mills and Boon for the e-generation, and every time he thinks of her he suffers a vowel problem. Francesca Brady takes the stage with a modest wave, pretends to look surprised at the posters.

Ivan jumps as he's tapped on the shoulder. There's a boy of about twelve, wearing acne and a Waterstones identity badge around his neck like a Marine with dog-tags, and why not, bookselling is war, and the enemy never stops coming.

'Mr Connor . . . ? We've been looking everywhere for you. You're in the basement. Follow me.'

BEN, it says on the dogtags. BEN turns and leads Ivan back through the crowds of people still arriving to hear Francesca Brady. She's still milking the applause –

'Thank you, thank you, I keep looking behind me thinking a real author must be standing there' and they're all bloody laughing – as Ivan, Campbell and BEN hurry down the stairs into the basement.

BEN charges ahead. Ivan glances back at Campbell, who shrugs helplessly. Signs for *Astrology*, *Military History*, *School Texts*, *Gay & Lesbian*, *Erotica*, flash past like inter-city stations of the cross. Finally they emerge into a small circular area in which there are set about thirty chairs. Ivan quickly calculates that seventy-seven per cent of the chairs are filled. Something salvaged, at least. There is already a small, balding, middle-aged man standing at the microphone, the literary equivalent of a warm-up man, a no-hoper, a glorified typist who's stumbled into a book deal because he's slept with someone famous or been held hostage in an obscure country for several years. No problem.

There is a lectern. A table with a bottle of Evian water. A chair. A pen. The man is saying 'For me, philately is not so much a passion as a way of . . .'

Ivan becomes aware of BEN waving urgently at him from three aisles across, under a sign that says *True Crime*. Campbell gives him a gentle push and Ivan skirts the outer ring of chairs; BEN turns and hurries away. Ivan passes through *Science Fiction*, *Science Fantasy*, *Terry Pratchett* and then finally emerges in a tiny rectangular area set out with a dozen chairs. Seven of them are filled. There is a lectern. A microphone. A table, chair, bottle of Evian water and a pen for signing copies of his books, which sit in several tremulously high columns on another table.

BEN taps the microphone. He squints at the folded piece of paper he has removed from the back pocket of his black jeans. He glances up at the giant air-conditioning system which whirrs and blows above him, then speaks into the microphone.

'Ladies and gentlemen, sorry to keep you waiting, but our author has at last emerged from the nightmare that is our traffic.' He pauses for laughter, but it is not forthcoming. 'Our guest tonight is quite simply an author who needs no introduction. Universally acclaimed, a master of the English language . . . put your hands together for . . . Ian Connor!'

Campbell hisses, 'Ivan!'

'Ivan Connor!' BEN shoots back quickly, but he has already stepped away from the microphone. His voice is not drowned out by the applause, which is on the dead side of restrained, but by the air-conditioning.

Ivan approaches the stage. He sets the hardback edition of *Chapter & Verse* down on the table and pours himself a glass of Evian. His heart is racing again. There is no reason for him to be nervous, but he is. He always is. He lifts the glass and sets it down somewhat pre-cariously on the narrow base of the lectern.

'Th-thank you, all, very much for coming,' Ivan says into the microphone, 'I, ahm, gonna . . . *going to* . . . read from my new novel . . .' He holds it up for them to admire, but the book slips out of the dust jacket and crashes down onto the glass of water, which immediately cracks. Ivan makes a desperate attempt to retrieve the situation, although it looks to the audience as if he is indulging in some kind of bizarre performance art, juggling broken glass, damp novel and handfuls of water. Meanwhile, the dust jacket floats gently away on the breeze from the air-conditioner.

Ivan smiles foolishly while BEN removes the broken glass and soaks up what he can of the water with a Kleenex. Ivan tries to peel apart the damp pages of *Chapter & Verse* in order to find the section he intends to read. Campbell hides himself in *Graphic Novels*.

When they are ready to start again, Ivan decides to ignore the water incident. 'The, uhm, new novel . . . which is set in England in the eighteenth century . . . an era which I'm sure you're all . . .' He blinks at them. 'Anyway, this is from Chapter Three.' He clears his throat. 'He took Rebecca . . .' *Do I sound pompous? Slow down. They're here because they want to be.* '. . . to task once or twice about the propriety of playing backgammon . . .'

'Speak up!'

He glances up at a gnarled, elderly man sitting at the back.

'Y-yes, of course . . . He took Rebecca to task once or twice . . .'

'Louder!'

'HE TOOK REBECCA TO TASK ONCE OR . . .'

'Philately!'

Another man, in the second row, is on his feet, waving a finger at him.

'I'm sorry . . . ?'

'Stamps, man! We're here for the stamps!'

BEN bounds up to the microphone. 'B2,' he says, 'the stamps lecture is in B2. Third down on the right.'

As the man shuffles along the row of seats Ivan is aghast to see five other members of his audience, including the deaf man, get to their feet and shuffle after him, leaving only an old lady in the front row.

Campbell retreats into *Occult*.

Ivan waits until some strength returns to his legs, then smiles weakly down at the old lady. 'Mother,' he says, 'I can read to you when I get home.'

'You can read to me now, Ivan. I didn't come all this way not to be read to.'

He shakes his head. He laughs. He does love her. 'Well,' he says, reaching up to move the microphone, 'at least I won't be needing this . . .'

Except the spilled water has soaked into the wires, and the moment he touches it there's a crack and flash and the author of *Chapter & Verse* is hurled into the air.

He is not seriously injured. His eyebrows are singed and his hair stands on end. The paramedics, nevertheless, insist on taking him to the hospital for a check-up. They also insist that he leaves on a stretcher. Regulations. He feels foolish, once again. His mother holds his hand and tells him he's going to be okay. The paramedics heave and blow as they carry him back through *Science Fiction*, *Science Fantasy*, *Terry Pratchett*, then *Astrology*, *Military History*, *School Texts*, *Gay & Lesbian*, and *Erotica*. When they reach the ground floor their exit is blocked by a crowd surrounding Francesca Brady, who has called a halt to her signing session, suffering from cramp, and has been pursued to the front door by adoring fans. She notices Ivan on his stretcher and immediately goes to him. She places a hand on his chest and purrs, 'I'm so glad you could come.' An assistant hands her a copy of *Insanity Fair*. 'Please have this as a gift and I hope you'll be feeling better soon,' she says, handing it to Ivan, but making sure the cover is turned towards the camera which takes their picture.

As she strides out of the door, Francesca Brady scratches suddenly at her head.

The hospital wants nothing to do with him. Campbell takes him to a pub and they get very drunk and rail against the state of the world, and publishing. Then he's in a taxi, and he can't remember where Campbell went . . . but here he is, home again, except the key won't fit in the door. He hammers on the wood, he presses the bell. A window slides up high above him and two kids look out.

'Daddy . . . what are you doing here?' Michael calls down.

'I sleep . . . perchance . . . Michael, open the door, there's a good chap.'

Michael is pulled away by his mother. She glares down at Ivan.

'Avril . . . darlin' . . .'

'Go away. You're drunk.'

'And you are ugly, but in the morning I will be sober.' He cackles. Avril slams the window down while Ivan struts around in front of the house. 'We will . . . fight them . . . on the . . . beaches . . . nevuh, evuh, in the . . . field . . . of human, conflic . . . AVRIL FOR CHRIST'S SAKE OPEN THE DOOR.'

There is no movement on the door front. Ivan is dizzy and giddy and operating on a high voltage. He bangs on the door again. He staggers back. He sees shadows moving behind curtains. He yells through the letterbox.

'I am forty years old! I have created two widely respected children and eight beautiful novels! My publisher does not care about me! I am represented by an estate agent! I was electric tonight! Nobody cares! AND I THINK I HAVE NITS IN MY HAIR!'

The door opens suddenly and a man he does not recognise punches his lights out.

He is in a bathroom he once decorated, or at least paid a man to decorate. He sits on the toilet seat while Avril, in nightie and dressing gown, sponges the blood from his face. She is saying, 'If you apologise again, *I'll* punch you on the nose.'

'Sorry,' he says. 'He didn't have to hit me.'

'Yes he did.'

'What sort of a name is Norman anyway? Did he conquer you?'

On cue, Norman calls from the hall. Avril shouts, 'No, go to bed, I'll be fine!' He won't go to bed. He'll linger in the hall, trying to hear.

Ivan's nose is fine now, but there's a small gash just above his hairline where he hit his head on the pavement. Avril leans forward to examine it. Ivan puts a hand on her breast.

'Don't,' she says, and slaps it away.

He puts his hand back on her breast.

'Stop it,' she says. She slaps it away again. 'Oh Ivan, when are you ever going to grow up?'

'We must have made love, what, a thousand times? And now you won't let me touch your tit.'

'Don't call it that. And we're divorced.'

He looks wistfully at her. 'Oh Avril, where did we go wrong?'

'*We?* I don't think so.'

'Avril, darling, I'm a writer.'

'Stop it. I don't want to hear this shit.'

'Is everything okay in there?' Norman calls from the hall.

'Yes! Go to bed!'

'A writer has to grow, experience, live . . . inhabit the spirit, create the legend . . .'

'It's crap, Ivan. You spend half your life sitting in a little room making up little stories nobody reads, and then you spend the other half of your life FECK-ING AROUND making everyone else miserable and you have a perfect excuse because it's all in the name of LIT-ER-AT-URE! Well it's all *crap*, Ivan! Then you come round here to moan at us because your publisher's so crap and you expect us to be interested? Well, why don't you write something that somebody wants to read instead of trying to bore everyone to death?'

He blinks at her for several moments, then gives a childish shrug. 'I only wanted to feel your booby.'

She rolls her eyes. She comes towards him again

and opens her dressing gown. He puts his hand on her breast.

'This Norman, do you love him?'

'He's good and he's straight and he loves me. And yes, I'm starting to love him.'

'That's good.'

'I do like your books.'

'I know.'

She smiles down at him, then frowns and leans forward to examine his hair. She pulls her dressing gown across, then hurries to the door and opens it. 'NORMAN! THE NIT COMB!'

When the prison officer leads the girls into the classroom, they find Ivan Connor stamping his feet on a newspaper. He has read this headline: *Francesca Brady Short Listed for Booker.*

The world is not a just place.

The reading of the previous week's assignments continues. Mairaid, Ann-Marie, Bethany, some of the Albanian names he cannot pronounce. He stares out of the window and fumes. Francesca Brady. That it should come to this. She has the Holy Trinity: money, fame, and now respect. He seethes.

'The light of the ark surrounds me, the dark of the night astounds me . . .'

He's up out of his chair. 'Christ almighty, Donna! What's your problem?! Essay! I said essay! Why's it always poetry?!'

'I like . . . poetry . . .'

'Like . . . like . . . it's not about like! Poetry is an art, it's a technical wonder. What the hell could you possibly know about poetry?'

'I just . . . you know . . . like . . .'

'And I like opera, but I don't delude myself I'm Pava-*bloody*-rotti! Do you even know the first thing about poetry? Do you even *know* what a sonnet is? Do you? Or iambic pentameter? Can you tell me about that? Iambic . . . ? Anyone? Anyone?' They're looking at the floor, at the ceiling, at their books. 'Is it, is it perhaps an Olympic event?'

He moves swiftly up the aisle and makes a grab for Donna's exercise book, she tries to hold onto it, but he pulls it free. 'Don't be shy now, Donna! Let me read it for you!'

She's on the verge of tears as he begins to read it, but not like a poem, he gives it the rhythm of the rap he has heard spewing out of the radio. 'The light of the ark . . . *surrounds me* . . . the dark of the night . . . *astounds me* . . . you make me smile like Jesus . . . *and fight like* . . .' He closes the book, shakes his head, then slaps it back down on her desk. 'This isn't poetry, Donna, these are *lyrics*.'

Donna lowers her eyes. There are tears rolling down her cheeks.

Nicotine Dolly raises her hand. 'Mr Connor?'

'Dolly?'

'Can I ask a question, Mr Connor?'

'Yes, Dolly.'

'When exactly did you turn into an asshole? Cause we got enough assholes in here without having to bring one in from outside.'

He looks at her, and he looks at the class, and it seems to be the consensus of opinion that he is, indeed, an asshole.

Later he wonders if he could sell a book about lesbians in prison.

Boy's Night In
Matt Beaumont

The idea came to me in bed on the night my parents had been to my place for dinner.

I generally try to give them a call once a week. I visit them once a fortnight or so. Dinner at mine is a much rarer occurrence – twice a year, three times tops.

They're usually pretty uncomfortable when they're round. My dad can't bring himself to sit on my futon and, as it happens, I'm glad. Seeing him ease his sixty-something arse into a low-slung slab of Jap minimalism would be like watching him get up and dance to Apollo 440. Just plain wrong. Bereft of anything he can define as comfy, he stands with his hands behind his back next to the window. Occasionally he looks at my CDs and says something like, 'Foo Fighters? What kind of a name is that then?' When I give him a tired glare he says, 'No, go on, I'm curious'.

I can always tell that my mum is doing a mental spring clean even though, believe me, I do not live like a slob. She smuggles in Glade air fresheners in her handbag and hides them behind the cistern.

They're like a lot of parents. Superficially concerned but profoundly deaf. Fuck all goes in. For instance:

Mum: 'How's work, Mark?'

Me: 'Pretty good actually. The Swedish company that took us over is really great. They're letting us vote two non-management representatives onto the board. I'm one of the nominees.'

Mum (staring at something over my shoulder): 'I'm sure that's a damp patch on the wall but your dad swears it's only a shadow. Remember that girl Jill Peacock? You went out with her when you were fifteen. She's engaged to DS Reid from *A Touch of Frost*.'

I'm not a bad cook for a man. That must surely put me in the minority. Okay, I know that Jamie Oliver is giving the impression that it's 'wicked', 'sorted' and, very probably, 'lovely-jubbly' to bomb around town on a Vespa with a pannier filled with over-ripe Brie and Belgian cooking chocolate. But every bloke I know, me included, would rather endure half an hour of *Vets in Practice* on the off-chance of seeing Trude with her hand up a horse than sit through a single minute of *The Naked Chef*. For a start the title is highly misleading – not, you understand, that I want to see our Jamie sauté anything *au naturel*.

Jamie Oliver is a twat first, a chef second. He is not making it cool to cook. It'll be a while before Britain's chippies go out of business because blokes are frying their own cod in beer batter.

Having said all that, I can cook, cool or not. I can gut and fillet a fish. I can poach an egg (not as easy as you'd think). I can make a green chicken curry that tastes almost as good as the one at the deli counter in Waitrose. And not only can I pronounce *bouillabaisse*, I also know what it is.

I do draw the line at soufflés. It's not that I can't. It's just that they're so fucking wanky.

However accomplished I reckon I am, I always get a bit tense when I'm cooking for company, even my parents. No, *especially* my parents. They may not pay attention when I tell them how well I'm doing at work but the one sure way I know of reassuring them that their son is all right is to present them with, say, a first-class *boeuf en daube*.

'Mmm,' my mum will say, 'is this one of Delia's?'

'No,' I'll reply, 'it's from an old French recipe book I found at Camden Lock.'

(I'll be lying, of course. It is one of Delia's.)

My dad won't compliment me. He'll be far too busy moaning about women/gay/black priests ('If Jesus had wanted women/queers/coloureds to offer the sacrament, wouldn't he have said something?' – this from a man who hasn't been inside a church since my christening) or how Vauxhall don't build cars like they used to ('The Viva. Now *that* was a car'). But he'll be moaning with his mouth full while he's helping himself to seconds, so I'll know he's impressed too.

Whoever you're cooking for, you want it to be right. That takes the two Ps, planning and preparation. You have to make sure the flat is clean and tidy. Plan the menu. Shop. Cook. *Time* the cooking. Choose the wine. Uncork the wine. Fill a few bowls with peanuts and hand-cooked (as if!) kettle chips. Empty the ash-trays. Hide/display the spliff, depending on who's coming. Not least, you have to get yourself out of the oil/flour/offal-splattered T-shirt and into something clean so you look as if you've actually breezed through the entire cooking part of the deal.

Quite hard work, all in all.

The point is that the effort usually leaves me feeling shagged. That evening with my parents was no exception. Not only from the work I put in but also because I'd had a row with my dad about asylum seekers. I get as pissed off as the next man at the eleven-year-old Romanians who try to clean my windscreen at the Hanger Lane Gyratory but something about my dad's slightly unforgiving, toss-em-back-into-the-sea-at-Dover approach made me come over all *Guardian* reader.

As soon as I'd seen them off I went straight to bed.

And had a wank.

This is the best tension reliever I know. Usually. That night it didn't pan out the way I'd hoped.

Having a wank, a top-quality wank, all comes down to timing. Or, rather, timing the come. This particular wank didn't work out because it got buggered up by circumstances beyond my control. I was so very nearly there when the phone rang.

I'm perfectly capable of ignoring a ringing phone. I do it all the time, especially at work. But this was at 11.15 p.m. No one phones then unless it's important. It could have been my boss wanting me to get the next flight to LA to head up a new office there. Or Jill Peacock saying she had to see me right away because she couldn't bear the thought of spending the rest of her life with DS Reid from *A Touch of Frost*.

It was neither of the above. It was my mum phoning from the car. She'd bought a Virgin pay-as-you-go and she couldn't stop playing with it.

'Your dad thinks he left his lighter in your living room. It's only a little blue disposable but would you mind having a look for it when you've a moment?'

After I'd hung up I lay down and started again but it wasn't the same. The moment had been destroyed. The images I'd been playing through my mind only minutes ago were now reruns. I'd already seen what the slender brunette from the Clarins counter in Selfridges did to the Estée Lauder girl with the unreasonably large breasts. I wanted to change the script but I was tired and my imagination just couldn't be arsed. I still came but it wasn't the blast that it would have, should have been.

Fucking telephone.

That's when the idea came. As I lay there in bed afterwards having a post-non-coital fag it struck me that, actually, I'd never had the perfect wank. I'd had hundreds, no, thousands of them and, sure, some of them had been so blindingly good that I could actually remember them. (What were *you* doing when you heard the terrible news about Lady Di?) Even so, all of them were missing something. Not one of them was *perfect*.

It dawned on me then that getting a wank right was surely like everything else. A case of the two Ps.

Why don't we plan our wanks with the same meticulous attention to detail as we do our dinner parties?

Surely that was the way to achieve orgasmic excellence. To consider every single detail, plan every aspect before we actually fish our cocks out of our pants and get down to business. Planning and preparation would definitely, I was almost certain, result in the most stunning and powerful climax a bloke could have.

In the words of the mighty Gillette, 'the best a man can get'.

I'm one of life's finishers. I don't have that many ideas but when I do I see them through. They might be crap and I might realise as much halfway through the execution but that never deters me from ploughing on to the bitter end.

I've always been like that. When I was ten I had the brainwave (or so it seemed at the time) of hanging all my Airfix models from my bedroom ceiling. I spent an entire Saturday with a roll of string and a box of drawing-pins recreating the Farnborough Air Show. I realised after an hour or so that it was a folly, the weight of painted plastic kit being too much for a drawing-pin shoved clumsily into plaster to bear. Nevertheless I soldiered on, supplementing the pins with small balls of Blu-Tack until the ceiling was busier than Heathrow's eastern approach. That night my worst-case scenario was played out. It was like the fucking Battle of Midway up there, with doomed aircraft plummeting into the carpet every five minutes or so. I finally admitted defeat when a 1/48th scale Grumman Hellcat dive-bombed into my skull as I lay in bed. It's only tiny but you can still just make out the scar.

I blame my dad. The only nugget of wisdom he ever gave me that I've always adhered to was 'never start a job unless you know you can finish it'. It isn't necessarily good advice. Too often it leads to stubbornly wasting your time on futile tasks that should have been abandoned at the earliest opportunity.

I knew that my quest for wanking nirvana would be carried out to the letter of my dad's maxim. The experiment might turn out to be a disappointment, a blow for the planning ethic and a hearty endorsement for 'hey, kids, let's have the wank right here' spontaneity. But I was on a mission that could only end in a precision-engineered ejaculation. I was not to be deflected.

I felt I had the grounding to put in place the ideal conditions. I had discovered my right hand's God-given purpose when I was eleven and I was so excited that I spent the remainder of my adolescence pummelling my poor cock up to six times a day. My wrist suffered what would now be diagnosed as repetitive strain injury, probably earning its owner disability benefit.

I slowed down once I found out that female sexuality wasn't mere wishful thinking on my part but was something real, palpable and tangible (Jill Peacock's breasts were very bloody tangible). Even so, while my right hand had its hours cut dramatically, it didn't go into retirement. It has kept up a steady, more or less one toss a day since. Even those days that I do manage to have sex (not as frequent as I'd like but have you ever met a bloke who gets enough?) aren't necessarily wank-free. A good fuck can be an inspirational thing and a couple of hours later I often feel ripe for a mental action replay.

My last but one girlfriend caught me one night but there was no way in the world that I could persuade her to see it as a tribute to her obvious gifts. God knows I tried and, if I'd succeeded, she might not be my last but one girlfriend.

Appointing the right time for what soon became code-named Operation Etna was critical. Too soon and I wouldn't be sufficiently desperate for it to be truly spectacular. But if I left it too long I knew that my bollocks would be so backed-up that it would all be over in a couple of unsatisfying minutes. I settled on Friday, 8.00 p.m., three days away.

I spent those days executing Step One of my master-plan, making deposits into what my best mate at work, Steve, calls the wank bank. This entailed committing to memory every detail of every vaguely attractive girl who crossed my path. I say only vaguely attractive because even my average imagination has some excellent cosmetic surgeons on call. They are well capable of transforming Miss Piggy into Jennifer Lopez (a version, I might add, without the outsize arse).

No girl was safe. All of them were mentally undressed before being put into a fresh wardrobe of something flimsy, boned and offering only scant protection from the winter's chills. Then they were set to work in the boudoir of my mind doing stuff that no girl I've met would ever agree to even if I had the nerve to ask.

By Friday morning I was psyched and in a more or less permanent state of tumescence. That lunch time

I turned down an offer of beer from Steve. He was not best pleased.

'What the fuck do you mean, no? It's Friday.'

'Sorry, mate, I've got to go shopping.'

'For what?'

'My mum's birthday,' I lied.

I was going shopping but my mum would have been less than chuffed with my intended purchase, however prettily gift-wrapped. She's strictly a Crabtree & Evelyn Lavender Bath Salts kind of girl.

I was about to enact Step Two: tooling up. For this I made the short trip into Soho. This part of London has changed a lot in the last few years. It has become fashionable, gay and almost respectable (though if you asked my dad, he'd tell you that the words gay and respectable have no business residing in the same sentence). There are many who lament the demise of Soho's traditional retailers: the butchers, the delis, the haberdashers and, of course, the pornographers. They haven't all disappeared though. You can still find its pustulant underbelly. You just have to know where to look.

There was one particular shop on Old Compton Street that hadn't let me down in the past, so being a loyal sort of bloke, it was my first stop. It was a while since I'd been so I wasn't greeted with cries of 'Mr Gregg, how nice to see you. What can we interest you with today?' Actually, even for their hardened regulars such familiarity would have been distinctly, embarrassingly out of place. The far-too-old-to-be-that-spotty bloke who was slouched behind the counter barely looked up from his *Sun* as I approached him. At the best of times it's slightly humiliating having to cough to get someone's attention; 1.15 on a Friday in a sleazy sex shop was not the best of times. Spotty bloke registered me and so did the other three punters who were looking at magazines, surreptitiously trying to tear away a bit of the shrink-wrap to get at least a gist of the contents.

'Yeah?' asked spotty bloke in a voice that they don't teach you on customer care programmes.

'Fuck it,' I thought, 'we all know what I'm here for,' and I dived in.

'Hi, I'd like a video,' I said, doing a plausible impersonation of confidence.

'What of?' he asked, looking back down at 'Dear Deirdre'.

Did I have to fucking well spell it out?

'Er, hard core,' I said, spelling it out.

'I know that. What of?' He stopped short of adding, 'you stupid twat', saving it for his body language.

My absence from London's swinging porn scene had been longer than I thought. I was rusty. I now recalled that you had to be very specific unless you wanted to run the risk of walking out with, say, something gay set in a farmyard (not a risk, of course, if you happen to be a homosexual zoophile). But I was unprepared and he was impatient. Well, he did have 'Dear Deirdre' to finish – I'd read it at work and it was a particularly juicy one. As I tried to assemble a mental wish list he reached under the counter (yes, that is exactly where they keep them) and pulled out an unmarked VHS.

'Try this,' he said. 'Straight, group, lesbian, bit of anal. All right?'

'Terrific,' I replied with a touch more enthusiasm than was required before adding, 'Is it American or German?'

'What, you want to follow the plot?' he sneered.

'Um, not really.'

'It's German and it's thirty-five quid.'

I handed him the money and he gave me the tape, now wrapped in an incriminating brown paper bag.

Your average sex shop operates on trust, in as much as you trust them not to completely fleece you. Like drug dealers and the blokes selling fake perfume out of suitcases, these people have not been reading up on consumer rights. Why should they? No one's going to shop them to *Watchdog*, are they? As a result you never quite know what you're walking out with. Experience has taught me that you have to go into this with the attitude of a kid going into Santa's grotto. You might come out with a deeply satisfying Tonka toy or you could end up with the made-in-Hong-Kong plastic elephant (small, green and not particularly elephantine). The not knowing is part of the thrill.

On the way back to work I called in at a newsagent and pulled *Mayfair*, *Fiesta* and *Razzle* from the top shelf. They'd provide a lively warm-up act for the main event.

That afternoon I had work to do. Namely Step Three: ensure disturbance-free evening. I'd only seen her a few days ago and she'd called me the previous evening but

I decided to give my mum a bell. This would minimise the risk of my plans being scuppered by an untimely call or, worse still, a visit. This being our third contact in a week, she was alarmed.

'Are you sure everything's all right, dear? Is it work? Nothing you want to tell me? Jean's coming over for tea. They didn't have anything nice in at the bakery, so I'm going to M&S in a mo. Isn't it chilly today? I must get the winter duvet out . . .'

She may have been alarmed but she doesn't change.

Next I wandered by Steve's desk. It was his birthday the next day and I had sort of very casually, totally loosely said I might be up for a beer after work. We were going out on the Saturday as well but he saw the Friday session as an entirely necessary rehearsal. I cried off, using my mum again and hoping he wouldn't twig that their birthdays hadn't seemed to clash a year ago.

I think he understood. 'Call yourself a mate? You're a sad fucking tosser,' was what he said. What he meant was, 'That's fine. Have a great time with your folks and give your mum a kiss from me.'

I'm sure of it.

Shortly after that I suffered my first major hiccup. Helen from admin.

Helen is gorgeous. Helen is sensational. Helen is the only woman I know who can turn the simple act of collating photocopies into an erotic spectacle. She'd been at the firm for five months and there wasn't a single day that I hadn't been down to her office on some pretence or another. My desk was heaving with headed paper, staples, manila envelopes in four different sizes and fat pads of forms, the purpose of which remain a mystery (D420 anyone?). All of it had been requisitioned from Helen in the fond hope that it might be handed over with an offer of a coffee, a sandwich, anything.

It never had been.

Now she was perched on my desk talking about nothing in particular. The corner of my PC was making a tantalising indentation in her buttock (which, I needn't add, was totting up credit in the wank bank). After twenty minutes of inconsequential gossip she produced a grenade.

'So, you are coming to Steve's drink tonight, aren't you?'

After a beat she added, 'It'll be fun.'

She'd just pulled the pin and lobbed it into my lap, where it was threatening to blow my plans to smithereens. I didn't know what to say so I stalled for time by looking in a drawer. It was full of bottles of White Out, staples, rolls of parcel tape and a pad of D420s, booty from past visits to Helen. I slammed it shut, nervously hoping she hadn't spotted it.

'Well? Are you coming or not?' she chivvied.

I was under pressure now and the words just came out. 'Sorry, tonight's not good but maybe . . .'

'Forget it, Mark, your loss.'

She was off.

Fuck, fuck, fuck!

Why today? Of all the days to come through, why this one?

This wasn't the first time that Helen had stopped by

for a chat and, not unreasonably, I'd wondered whether her visits to me were for the same reason as mine to her. However, this was the first time she'd made what constituted a clear-ish proposition. Okay, I know it was only for beer in the pub round the corner but these things have got to start somewhere.

You might wonder why I hadn't simply asked her out already. After all, I'd had plenty of opportunity and I had the stationery supplies to prove it. I remember watching some courtroom drama where a barrister said that he never asked a witness a question unless he already knew the answer. I'm the same when it comes to asking girls out. If I'm absolutely, positively sure that she's going to say yes, I'm in like Flynn. Otherwise wild horses won't drag the question out of me. You probably think I'm a coward and you're probably right.

I'd talked to Steve about her and he'd said on more than one occasion, 'Are you fucking mad? Course she fancies you. What do you want, a written invitation?'

As it happens, Steve, yes I do.

Now I'd just had the closest I was ever going to get to one and I'd passed it up.

For an evening alone at home.

Wanking.

What can I say? I'm a finisher.

Thanks, Dad.

As I sat on the tube home I tried to console myself by thinking that, if Helen was really up for it, she would surely wait a day or two. And, anyway, when she said 'You are coming for a drink' she probably meant precisely that – a drink, no more, no less. Neither thought provided any comfort. Then I felt the video in my coat pocket. I mused that, however minxy Helen might be, she was an administrative assistant, not a porn star. She couldn't possibly be capable of the wonderful, unspeakable acts of depravity that were on the tape.

Now I felt better. Everything was going to be just fine.

No one, not Helen, not anyone, knew my needs as well as my right hand. It had stood by loyally since age eleven, watching girlfriends come and go. It had never complained and it had always been there for me. Now would be its finest hour. This wasn't going to be any old wank, no sir. It was going to be profound, Wagnerian in its intensity and very probably life-changing. It was going to stand as a monument to Onan. And I was going to produce enough bloody jiz to put Solvite out of business.

This wank was going to be perfect.

I arrived at my flat at 7.22. It was time for Step Four: ambience and atmosphere, creation of.

First I listened to my messages.

Steve: 'You total moron. You don't deserve Helen. See you at the Roundhouse tomorrow.'

Mum: 'Are you sure you're okay? Can't talk long. I'm on the mobile. Jean sends love. I'll call you in the morning.'

Wrong Number: 'Robert, we really do need to get things moving, so I'm going to need the papers first thing Monday and I'll be catching an earlier flight. If there's any problem, make sure you call me back. It's imperative that we make the . . . Beeep.'

Wrong Number was out of time. If I'd been a nice person, which I usually am, I'd have dialled 1471 and called Wrong Number back. I almost did but I was on a mission and there was work to be done.

I drew the curtains in my bedroom, the living room and, just to be sure, the spare room. Then I art directed *Mayfair*, *Fiesta* and *Razzle* in an attractive fan at the foot of my bed, resisting the temptation to flick through them while I was at it. Next I unplugged the TV and video in my living room and wheeled them into my bedroom, setting them up at the end of the bed. I put the tape into the slot, again resisting the urge to press play and sneak a look. The remote control went next to the magazines and a box of man-size tissues on my bedside table – as I said, I'm not a slob and I hate mess.

Everything was now in place. During the planning phase I'd ruled out artificial aids such as baby oil. I'm a bloke who prefers the firm grip of a dry hand. I have to say there's something distinctly unmanly about those who have a predilection for oils, soap-based lubricants and, God forbid, hollowed-out fruit.

I went to the fridge and got myself a beer. The anticipation was incredible. It was making me tense. A beer, I felt, would restore some necessary calm and perhaps have the beneficial side effect of preventing me from firing off too hastily.

As I drank I thought for the first time about music. Some of my best fucks had played with a soundtrack, which, even if they hadn't heightened the mood at the time, had certainly enhanced the memory. I thought back to Kim and 'Papa Don't Preach', Claudia and 'Unfinished Sympathy', and, inexplicably, Paula accompanied by 'Lord of the Dance'. In the end I decided against it because it would mean spending upwards of an hour trawling through my CDs ('Bizarre Love Triangle', original or Armand Van Helden remix? I know only too well what I'm like). I also figured that tunes would mean muting the TV and missing out on the all-important cries of fake orgasm.

'*Ja, ja, fuck me, baby, ich kommen.*'

Or something like that.

The clock on the microwave read 8:02. It was time. I drained my beer and headed for the bedroom. The corridor that runs down the middle of my flat felt longer than usual. I was nervous, my hands just a little clammy, my legs a touch weak. Was this how Prince Naseem, the magnificent Lennox or even Rocky Balboa felt as they headed for the ring? Fuck, I thought, at that moment I needed music.

'Eye of the Tiger'.

I reached the arena and dropped my trousers, followed by my boxers and laid them carefully over the chair. Then I took off my socks. I'm not someone who can have sex, accompanied or solo, with socks on. I plumped up the pillows against the bed-head and sank back into them. Then I flexed my fingers in a carefully rehearsed routine. I'd once watched a Michael Owen coaching video and knew the importance of warming up. Finally I checked the time on the radio alarm. If this wank was to go down in history, it went without saying that it should be clocked.

It was 8.05.

I felt a twitch and looked down at my groin. My cock was stirring. It had started without me, the eager little sod. Weren't we supposed to be a team?

I picked up *Mayfair* and took a leisurely stroll through its pages. There was Linda looking very fetching in only her spike heels and a wet-look thong as she stretched her long limbs on a Kawasaki Ninja. Next up was Fiona wearing an alluring yet practical uniform that whoever dresses our NHS nurses would do well to take note of. I skipped past Jody – fishnets have never lit my fire. I also missed out the article on TVR's frisky new runabout. I've always found these non-tits-and-arse features an irritating aspect of some men's mags. I mean, you don't find *Performance Car* dropping a nudey spread into its layout for those readers who fancy a quick toss in between motor reviews. Stick to what you know, *Mayfair*. Mind you, they more than made amends with that old faithful, Joanne Guest, on page 144. That girl can do no wrong for me, even dressed as she was as a mechanic (dirty overalls with seamed stockings and filigree lingerie underneath – not at any Kwikfit I've ever been to).

After fifteen minutes or so I hadn't even touched myself but it was granite down there. I moved on to *Fiesta*. It fell open at 'Readers' Wives'. No, no, no, I thought. I was seeking perfection, a quest that would not be aided by a size-sixteen wearing her bifocals and something she'd bought at a lingerie party.

The doting husband who'd immortalised her on film with his trusty Canon Sure Shot was welcome to her but he had no business inflicting her upon the rest of us. I picked up *Razzle* and flicked through its pages. It contained some excellent stuff that any other night would have led to a wet and highly satisfactory conclusion. But the mags were no longer doing it for me. They were just the trailers and I was ready for the main feature.

I picked up the remote with my left hand and my cock with my right. Years of masturbation have given me a rudimentary sort of ambidexterity. I can carry out simple tasks with my left hand, such as manipulate a remote, while my right is focused on important business. I pressed play and waited. My cock was pulsing but I resisted the temptation to accelerate my strokes. This was a marathon not a sprint.

Production company logos were followed by the title, *Foxy Lady IV*. I figured that, if numbers one to three had been successful enough to lead to a fourth *Foxy Lady*, I was in for a treat. You know what? I was right. The opening scenario had two businessmen in a hotel room. They were in tie-loosening mode, clearly exhausted after a hard day of doing whatever it was they did. One of them picked up the phone. Who was he calling? Room service? Head office? His mum? I had no fucking idea because, apart from *Ja, ja, fuck me, baby, ich kommen*, the only other German I'd picked up had been from Commando Comics (and neither *achtung Englischer schweinhund* nor *Gott in himmel* had ever proved useful in my few encounters with our

Frankfurt office). It turned out to be room service because moments later one of them opened the door to not one but two charming waitresses bearing coffee. You know what happened next, don't you? Living up to the motto of Holiday Inns the world over ('What the customer wants, the customer gets') the waitresses undressed and relieved executive stress the only way they knew how. They started with a cabaret. What the pair of them did to each other on the bed with the complimentary fruit basket really doesn't bear repeating. Suffice it to say that I was enjoying it enormously. Three days of starvation meant that my cock was showing the temperament of a rodeo bronco but the control I was exercising over it almost made me weep with pride.

Destination Perfection.

After a few minutes the two executives stripped and joined the girls on the bed. It seemed that things were about to move up a gear.

They very probably did but I'll never know. The perfect images of love, German style, flickered and faded to snow, which in turn was replaced by . . .

I'm not sure I can bring myself to tell you.

No, it's been four months now and it's about time I faced up to it.

The porn was replaced by a dinosaur. The fact that the beast was big, bloated and purple served only to rub salt into the wound. It was flanked by two kids and they were singing a song.

If you're happy and you know it, clap your hands,
If you're happy and you know it, clap your hands,
If you're happy and you know it,
And you really want to show it,
If you're happy and you know it, clap your hands.

Well, Barney, I have to say I've had cheerier moments.

I did finish my wank. Silly not to really. It fell well short of vintage, even though my prick exploded with the muzzle velocity of an 88mm howitzer. I still haven't managed to remove the stain from the wall behind my bed.

Did I tell you that I can't abide mess?

I spent the next night at the Roundhouse watching Steve push his tongue so far down Helen's throat he could probably tell whether she'd had Shreddies or Cheerios for breakfast. As I stood at the bar and looked on, it dawned on me that there was no such thing as the perfect wank.

Only the perfect wanker.

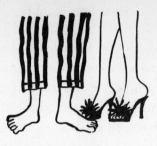

Actually, Twenty-Three Beers Will Not Improve Your Judgement

John Birmingham

In my youth I was a mad drinker and known for arriving at the most civilised of parties up to five hours before the other guests. I would come through the door lugging a carton of beer under one arm and clutching a plastic bag full of those dangerous little bottles of spirits you find in hotel room bar fridges. Emergency bottles were also stowed about my person in shirt and jacket pockets. I've never liked to be tardy about these things. By the time most of the other invitees had arrived I would likely have knocked off that carton and most of the mini-bar before devolving into a horrible, drooling grease spot in the corner which everyone, particularly the womenfolk, were keen to avoid. Such was the figure I cut at my best friend's eighteenth birthday party.

I passed out mid-afternoon and came to with the other party-goers having circled the wagons around the barbecue in the back garden. They were all sitting, chatting politely and attempting to balance soggy paper plates full of chops and sausages and homemade coleslaw on their knees. I slowly blinked and licked my lips and dragged my stinking carcass from the floor and out into the light. There was a moment, which I infer rather than remember, when everyone saw me and went into a panic attack, all praying I wouldn't collapse next to them. Or on top of them. I fished about in a cooler for someone else's beer to drink, cursing and muttering darkly to myself about the shards of broken mini-bar bottles digging into my chest. I shambled unsteadily over to the barbecue to scoop up the scraps of burned onion and meat refuse. I slowly turned to examine the talent, started shovelling this garbage into my face, and tried to wash it down with an icy-cold beer, most of which I just poured all over myself like an action guy from an old Foreign Legion film.

When people realised I'd probably be content to leave them alone, the conversation slowly restarted and climbed back from a murmur to a noisy buzz. They spoke too soon though. My targeting radar had settled on some poor medical student called Karen, a fresh-faced little babe with curly cute bangs which, sadly for her, set lights a-flashing and sirens a-wailing inside my head. I narrowed my eyes and stared at her, trying to nut out an approach which would be certain to move her, with all dispatch, from an uncomfortable perch on a kiddie-sized folding stool into the arms of a stinking drunk with a whole lotta lovin' to give. I knew that she knew I was scoping her out because she studiously avoided looking anywhere even vaguely in my direction. I thought, *Fantastic! She knows I'm interested*. Then came my moment. From way across that garden, through a haze of twenty-three cans of full-strength lager, I spied, with my little eye, something beginning with 'S'.

A spider. A spider crawling across the top of Karen's shoe. A spider which might soon make a dash up her lovely leg. A spider which had to die that I might love.

A momentary shiver passed over my body, a physical intimation of the knowledge of what I was about to do. I closed my mind to any doubts. Took one last swig of fortifying ale, stiffened the sinews, summoned up the blood and launched myself through the thin circle of garden chairs, into the air, across the expanse and onto the foot of the girl I intended to make mine for ever.

Unfortunately, Karen did not see herself as the life mate of a drunken baboon with a half-chewed arachnid sticking out of his mouth, and nothing ever came of it. Except that three or four other guys beat the crap out of me and threw me into the back of somebody's farm vehicle where I landed on top of some old bricks and rusty machinery.

I could have made her so happy.

We did not meet again for many years. But when that moment came I had at least learned enough not to stuff the nearest insect into my gob. I had not learned much more though.

I discovered her on the organising committee of a ball, a formidable black-tie affair, and I rushed to offer my services so that I might get in her good graces. And of course, there's something about a guy in a dinner suit which drives the babes wild. But it didn't happen for me, not with Karen anyway.

You see she was a very popular girl by then. There must have been about thirty other guys trailing along in her wake, and compared with most of them I had nothing going for me. I had no job, no money, no future, no nothing. The other guys were these impossibly glamorous, totally connected, well-heeled types. Guys who could afford to hire limos to pick her up and take her to restaurants where they didn't ask if you wanted fries with your main course. I didn't even drive, still don't, and as for fries? Well, I used to dream about having fries with my meal.

I tried all sorts of desperate ploys with this woman. Even cultivated alliances with all of her girlfriends. Had them running interference for me on the football jocks and junior captains of industry. And they did look after me, those girls. Even took up a collection so I could invite Karen out to an actual restaurant. The Black Duck. Man, this place was classy with a capital K. It had all the trappings of synthetic French snottiness: a maître d', lotsa candles, no beer list, and scary waiters with napkins draped over their forearms. Of course I couldn't just ask her out. She might have knocked me back and then I would have had to curl up into a tight little ball and sit in a corner for two or three years. No, I had to be certain of getting her into that restaurant. So I used one of my faves. An oldie but a goodie: told her my best friend had just been killed in a horrible service station explosion in the Outback. And I just couldn't be alone that night.

Whether she fell for it and took pity on me because of my recently immolated best buddy, or whether she took pity on me because it was just about the lamest, most pathetic pick-up line she'd ever heard in her life, fact was she took pity on something and agreed to come out. Went pretty well, too.

The food was way too rich for me, after living on rice and fish fingers for so long, and I was nearly sick a couple of times. But by the end of the meal I was cruising. I'd figured out the cutlery and the wine ordering business and as the sticky, syrupy golden dessert stuff was slipped in front of us I relaxed for the first time that night. Leaned back in my chair. Crossed my legs. Got a cramp. And knee jerked the table and everything on it all over my date.

I guess I was her date from Hell. Yet all this was still in the future when we got to this Ball, which was crawling with smarmy dudes looking to snack down on the girl of my dreams. I decided I wasn't going to make a fool of myself moping around her all night. I'd put so much work into this bash I figured I might as well enjoy myself at it. So I started putting away jugs of beer and pints of whisky and lots of joints in the toilets and more beers and more joints and more whiskies and so on until I was this totally fucked-up drooling excuse for a boy.

When I got to that point where one more Scotch would have pushed me over the line into a long-term vegetative state, this woman came up, stone cold sober, and introduced herself to me. Her name was Sondra Johannson, or Villalobos, or something. I forgot it about a half a million times on the night, too. I vaguely recognised her from somewhere but she seemed to know all about me. So we talked for a bit. Or rather she talked and I sort of swayed about and bumped into the furniture a lot, until I got bored and wandered off to have another joint in the toilets. I vaguely recall tackling maybe another jug of beer, and I definitely remember sucking half a litre of warm champagne out of some drunken trollop's filthy stiletto before turning around to find this sober woman at my elbow again.

Oh yes, they called me Mr Smooth in those days.

This went on all night. Now, my threat detectors hadn't shut down completely and somewhere through the fug of alcohol and marijuana a little red warning light kept blinking frantically at me. I dimly remembered seeing this Sondra woman turn up with some huge bearded guy, about seven feet tall and two axe handles across the shoulders. I'd said something about this guy and she'd gone, 'Oh, he's my lover'. So you can see I had good reason to be running away and hiding in the toilets all the time.

Trouble was, whenever I came back she was waiting for me. Finally, she asked if I wanted to dance. I'm thinking fuck, I can hardly stand up, let alone dance, and there is the issue of this gigantic jealous man lurking around somewhere. Old Redbeard looked as if he could have snapped my spine like a chopstick. On the other hand, she's a pretty good-looking babe, and I'm horribly drunk, and there is the bitter frustration of the unreachable Karen to deal with, so yeah, okay we'll have a dance.

Big mistake.

We got out on that dance floor and I got that pneumatic body pressed up against my filthy, beer-stained dinner jacket and my little red warning light blinked out for ever, swallowed up by this hot, sludgy lust which welled up from my groin and smothered whatever was left of my rational mind. I'm thinking, *Yeah, this is good, I'm gonna put the Move on her, that's right, the Move.* And the thing is she's cool for the Move. She likes the Move. She wants the Move. And even now, years later, all I can think is, why? What did she see in me? I was sweating, I was drunk, I was stoned, I was just about the worst catch in the world. And it got worse.

Friends kept wandering over, wanting to know who she was. Wanting to be introduced. And I kept forgetting her name. I must have done that about six times in a row. And she just patiently introduced herself to this procession of drunken yahoos.

The ball started to wind down about two in the morning. Redbeard was gone, disappeared without trace, leaving me with his girlfriend. Even then though, hanging off this girl's arm like some drunken retard, I was still scanning the room for Karen, still trying to track the thirty competitors who were also after her. Most of all I was wondering what Karen was going to make of this overly forward and completely sober woman leading me into the night. Wondering if maybe I shouldn't just give this woman the Flick right now. Because the Flick was coming, we all knew that, I guess. So why not just jump to the Flick? Save us all a shitload of hassles. In the end it would have been better if I had.

Sondra knew I had a room at the Sheraton. Each of the ball organisers received a complimentary room. And she suggested we go back there. But by now I had the Fear. I was so confused by this woman's interest in me, and by what I was going to do about Karen, and by the location of the big spine-snapping jealous dude with the red beard, I was so unbalanced by all of these things and by the massive amounts of alcohol and marijuana in my bloodstream, that the Fear took over. We were walking back to the hotel room because I couldn't think of anything else to do. I was probably calm enough on the outside, or so wasted you couldn't tell, but inside I was freaking.

Luckily we made it to the room and found it full of people, maybe twenty or thirty had turned up there for drinks and it was like a reprieve from the gallows. I'm thinking, *Whew!* I had enough drinks and cones to finish me off and I passed out on the floor.

When I woke up the next morning my friends had cleared out and I was alone. In a hotel room. With Her. The scenario quickly degenerated into one of those really bad 1950s Ealing comedies. Sondra lay on the bed, slowly drawing her ball gown up over her legs while I was tearing around the room in a frenzy, *Oh gee check-out's soon and this room's a fucking pigsty I think*

I'd better clean this room d'you think they've got a vacuum cleaner here I bet room service does I'll call down and get a vacuum cleaner from them that's the trick! But the ball gown kept whispering and creeping up and revealing ever more leg as Sondra crooked a finger and motioned for me to come hither.

I felt like a dead man as I trod over to her and climbed onto the bed. I just didn't want to be there. I couldn't believe this was happening. I'd started to go through the motions when the phone rang. It was Karen, spidergirl, the girl I'd actually wanted to go out with. She asked if I wanted to have breakfast with her, and inside me this little cartoon guy jumped about ten feet in the air, punched the sky and went Yes!

I clambered off Sondra and told her we had to go to breakfast. I think that was the first time I really upset her. But I just changed and dragged her to breakfast and pretty much behaved as though we'd bumped into each other on the way down. She kept giving me this strange look as if to say, you know, what the fuck's wrong with you, I've just spent the last eight hours throwing myself at you, I could have thrown myself at any of two hundred worthless, drunken bastards and I picked you, you sick joke. Like, what part of the word 'Yes' don't you understand?

I didn't know how to cope with it. All my reproductive urges were still locked in on this other babe and I just couldn't come at the idea of abandoning that hopeless quest. So I did a bad thing. I ignored Sondra from then on. Cut her dead for the next three days until she eventually pissed off. I look back now and I think, what a shameful fucking episode that was. And a real waste too. As I said, I never really got anywhere with spidergirl and as far as I know she married a druid.

To think I ate a spider as big as your fist for that woman.

Bighead

Marc Blake

It was on the Friday when I first noticed. Had a bit of a thick head as Jez and I'd got lashed at Oriel's the night before. Vicks was off with her coven so it was babe alert, code red. Anyway, crack of dawn and I'm ready for the off when I find I can't get the old shirt collar to do up. It's a fresh one from Pink's as well, so when I got in I had the grunt take it back and swap it for the next size up.

NASDAQ had done well overnight. The ten mill Ford oh-five's I bought at 120 were trading at one-ten so that was me in for ten beeps. Solly's great for traders. Digsy, our trading manager, isn't too much of a prick and the bonuses are sweet: just love seeing the faces of those CFSB tossers at The Sanderson when I flash the old platinum.

Off at six and the Porky – the nine eleven in metallic silver if you must know – made mincemeat out of the traffic until I hit the Embankment. Back in SW10 I did the old shit, shave, shower then hooked up with Vicks at The Bluebird. She was late too thank God, waggling her feet at me and banging on about new shoes. Shopping's a religion with that girl. I reckon at dusk she faces east and prays to South Molton Street – except it's not Allah, it's Prada . . . That one always goes down a storm, although Vicks usually pulls a face.

'So. Vicks,' I say.

'Yes, Guy?'

'D'you think I'm getting a bit . . . lardy?'

She wrinkles up her nose. Nice nose. Nice bod too, right side of scrawny. Big tits as well. Obviously.

'Why d'you ask?'

'It's just that –'

'Are you trying to say that *I'm* fat?'

'God no, you're like a hat stand. My shirt's a bit tight that's all – so?'

'Guy, you had two pints before we ate and you spend half your life in Nobu and The Pharmacy. What d'you expect?'

'Right. That's it. Gym in the morning.'

'You don't belong to a gym.'

'I do. Joined up ages ago. Still charging me every bloody month. Time I made some use out of it.'

'Good for you. You are getting a bit of a gut. And a chin.'

'Thank you, Victoria.'

'You did ask.'

She went off to the little girls' room and I finished off her plate. I mean God I'm only twenty-eight. Years in me yet. I play footy every Sunday, between fags. There isn't time to make a decent wedge and keep yourself trim, who am I – Superman? The weird thing was I was just knocking back the rest of the Merlot when I got the headspins. It must've been the knock-on effect from last night's sesh.

Can't say the gym was a total success. I started jogging down there but I only got as far as the paper shop before needing mouth-to-Mars-Bar resuscitation. Drove in the end. The place had changed what with all the cardio-vascular torture racks and the new people. Half of them had no right to be in there in the first place. Advert for bloody bulimia if you ask me. I flipped through some women's magazine on the exercise bike and figured out that height-to-weight ratio thing. I'm slightly above the borderline but then all our family is short so it doesn't really count. And anyhow I'm way off obese, which is disgusting. Ever noticed how fat people stink? I did – in the sauna. I got out sharpish. I was short of breath anyway.

Decided I'd go on another day.

It took it out of me, actually. Vicks blamed me for overdoing it and nookie was on the bench for the night. She works over at Morgan's now, though we met at Solly's when she was just a group secretary. The only one I hadn't pulled actually, so it was a matter of pride. You know how it is. We've sort of settled into a routine nowadays. We match diaries when we can midweek and she stays over most weekends. I like surprising her by showing up for a quickie after a night out on the lash but mostly it's Saturday nights. Though, I must admit she's started campaigning for Sunday mornings.

I suppose you can see her point. No alarm clock, I'm almost sober and she says she's more in the mood. It's a match of two halves. Footie was out on Sunday due to injuries so I popped her back over to Earl's Court. Then I got this splitting headache so I necked down some Nurofen.

I was shaving on the Tuesday when I noticed I was getting jowly. Worse still, there wasn't one of my shirts that'd do up properly at the neck. We're all casual at work but there's casual and there's casual if you get my drift. Sent the grunt off to Hackett's for some new ones with a fourteen-and-a-half-inch collar, only when I tried one on in the loo it still pinched. The arms were fine so it must've been a faulty batch. Told him to get his arse in gear and get back over there. The fifteen-inch did it. A good snug fit though the sleeves padded up a bit inside my jacket.

Busy week what with being dined by the new Eurobond salesman and various clients. Tried out some new Hoxton restaurant that night – usual barn where you can't hear yourself think. Big plates. Tiny food. Totally gorgeous waitresses. One little Doris in particular wearing a black miniskirt and leggings. I said to her, you can gob in my food after this but I absolutely *have* to slap that little arse of yours. Everyone thought it was hysterical until she got the manager. Thirty notes shut him up and off we went to China White.

I was feeling worse for wear the next day. The old headache was back and I didn't like what I saw in the mirror. My head was all swollen and puffy. I rang work and said it was food poisoning, which is endemic among bond traders, especially those of us who work and play hard. Jez buzzed a bit later.

'Wasssuppp? Work says you're ill. Nothing trivial, I hope.'

'Got a migraine.'

'Oh. You coming to see Chelsea thrash some northerners tonight?'

'Not up for it, mate.'

'You is a big girl's blouse, innit.'

'Cheers.'

I rang off and called Vicky, see if she'd come over.

'Not until later. After work.'

'But I'm *ill*.'

'No, you're bored. If you're really ill, call a doctor.'

'I don't need a bloody doctor.'

She went quiet.

'Viickks. Come over. There's some Chablis in the fridge I think.'

'Sorry, look I'm out tonight.'

'You can go out any night. What about me?'

She did that thing where she puffs out her cheeks then slowly lets out the air. 'Guy, the reason I make these arrangements is you're never around. Six months we've been together and we ought to be, I dunno, going somewhere with this . . .'

'Vicks. Just bloody well get over here, will you?'

'God, you are swollen. You allergic, do you think?'

'Could be, I suppose.'

'What're all these tissues doing on the . . . euww, they're all wet.'

'I was trying to get the swelling down.'

I wasn't feeling so bad at that moment so I put my hand up her blouse and grabbed her tit. 'There's some other swelling I'd like you to help with, wink, wink.'

She pulled away. 'You're meant to be ill. I just lost half a day's pay coming here.'

'I am ill.'

'God. Be consistent, will you?'

'C'mon, Vicks. We missed out at the weekend.'

'Is that all this is for you?'

'No – what about the holiday?'

'A chalet in Chamonix with five of your mates. How intimate is that?'

I got angry. 'Bloody hell, Vicks, I've paid for it up front. We'll have a brilliant time with Jez and the lads.'

'He's your broker. You're just bringing your work with us.'

'They're my mates.' Suddenly my head was splitting and stars were swimming about. Don't know what I said but by the time the pain had settled down Vicks had gone. I had the Chablis anyway.

Next morning I decided not to take the car in. On the trading floor there was this weird atmosphere like you get when it's someone's birthday and some joker's got something planned. I throttled one of the grunts but he wouldn't give. Fine. Sod them then. And the looks I was getting? I put that down to the poloneck sweater. It isn't my taste but it was all that'd fit me except for my tracky top but you can't get away with that in here. Made some good trades and Digsy seemed happy with my estimate price for tomorrow.

On the tube home I'd given up my seat for this bird before realising she had a kid with her. I was feeling the weight of the world on my shoulders and sort of lolling off standing up when I noticed the brat staring at me. I glared at him like, hasn't your mum taught you *anything* you snotty little git?

Kids are something that's come up once or twice with Vicks. Usual story. She wants the whole shebang and I say walk before you run. Let's wait until we're settled. She says, you're on a six-figure salary, how much more settled d'you want? I say, two words. Mortgage and crippling. Anyway, so we're passing South Ken and the kid, who is still staring, suddenly comes out with this.

'Mum, why's that man got such a big head?'

Well, she shuts him up pronto but of course I've gone red as a beetroot and now they're all bloody looking. I was feeling woozy so I staggered off at the next stop and climbed into a cab. At home I got my metal tape measure out of the toolbox and had a proper look. My neck was seventeen inches and my head twenty-six! It's off to the bloody quack.

Despite having BUPA cover I got a locum: little Asian bloke by the name of Rajneesh who kept flicking the top of his biro with his finger.

'Could be an allergy, but I'd expect you to have suffered some kind of anaphylactic shock. You're having no difficulty breathing?'

'No.'

'Are you particularly under stress?'

'Thrive on it. Come on, Doc – what is it?'

He flicked at his biro. 'Too early to say . . . possibly fluid retention.'

'You mean I've got water on the brain?'

'I'd like to run you over to the hospital for some tests.'

'Stopped doing tests at school, old son.'

'Just a CAT scan. And we'll let the ENT people take a look at you.'

'So I'm a guinea pig now, am I?'

'All perfectly normal. I'll set up the appointments for you.' He sat back, worked out on the old biro for a bit, then pulled out this pad.

'Are you experiencing any discomfort apart from these headaches?'

'Yeah. I'm not sleeping. Hurts when I try and turn over.'

He scrawled something. 'I'll give you a mild sedative. Don't take any more aspirin unless you really need to.'

I took the sheet. 'What's this?'

'Valium. It's a low dose but try to avoid mixing it with alcohol.'

Bollocks to that, I thought.

Had to play phone tag for a bit before I nailed Vicks down.

'Where've you been – and don't say shopping.'

'Alison had a crisis, something to do with her work permit.'

'Typical Aussies. Steal a loaf of bread and their grand-children come back and nick all our jobs. Well, bar jobs.'

'She doesn't work in a bar. She's a pediatrician. How's the head?'

'Like a pumpkin. Daren't go to a funfair in case I get mistaken for the coconut shy.'

'Are you tiddly?'

'No.'

'You sound tiddly.'

'Tiddly, darling Vicky, was an hour ago. I'm trollied, hammered, mullered. So would you be if you had my problem.'

'Mr Self-pity's arrived a little early this evening.'

'Come over – I'm bored, I want to see you.'

'Go out with your mates.'

'No one around.'

'What about Jez?'

'We did a trade this morning. He's busy till next week.'

'So I'm just the fall-back.'

I waited for her to get whatever it was out of her system. '*Vii-icks*,' I said eventually.

'*Wha-at?*'

'You know.'

'No, I don't know.' She didn't give me a chance to speak. 'Look, I'm not your Florence Nightingale, Guy. If you were treating me a bit better right now then of course I'd want to see you but the thing is the way things are going, I think a bit of a break's probably a good thing. Best all round. Listen, give me a call and let me know how it goes at the hospital. Kay, yah?'

I was going to give her an earful but she'd bloody hung up hadn't she.

What a fiasco. BUPA's bad enough but I'd better not ever end up relying on the NHS. First thing was I woke up with a bonce as heavy as a medicine ball. Couldn't even walk without holding onto the walls for support. It hurt to brush my teeth so I gave up on that. I couldn't shave as my vision had gone all blurry and it was impossible to stand up to have a pee so I sat on the loo and leaned my head back on the cistern. Eating toast was a nightmare as inside my head it sounded like I was chewing on a brick.

And have you seen the crap they put on telly in the day? It's subnormal. Shining mongs with only one name patronising even stupider spasmos who've got nothing better to do than sit round nattering on about nothing. I mean how empty can their lives be? I zapped over to Cable and thank God there was sport on. Okay it was only dirt biking and bobsleigh but it was sport none the less.

I took a minicab to the hospital. Didn't talk to the driver, never do. It turns out that I'm a medical miracle or a conundrum as they put it. They did the usual nonsense, blood pressure, urine (you taking the piss? I said), heart, all that. The ENT people stuck things in my ears and down my throat and hummed and hawed a lot. Then they attached all these wires to me and got me up on this machine and then – and this is the last straw – clunk! My head's only too big for the CAT scan machine. Instead, they X-rayed me and I had to wait around in a hospital gown freezing in a corridor for hours.

I wasn't going to stick that so I went through to the X-ray room only to find the consultant there with a bunch of medical students. They were shocked I could tell. I said, 'Well, what is it then?' First one offers up gigantism? I said, 'Do I look like I'm jolly and green and live on sweetcorn? I think not.' Another wants to send me over to the Institute of Tropical Diseases. The third says my bones are normal except that they're enlarged. I said, 'You haven't the foggiest. Maybe you should spend a bit less time dressing up like twats begging for money down the shopping precinct and a bit more time doctoring.'

Can't say it got a result.

They wanted to keep me in but you know, once you're in there you can catch anything. Got the tape measure out at home. I could only fit into a T-shirt, and even then I had to scissor it open at the neck. I was twenty-seven inches round the nape and nearly thirty from the top of my skull – which I could only just reach – to my chins. I put it all down in a notebook, started a progress report. Got knackered walking round and had to hold onto my ears for balance like they were jug handles.

I buzzed Adrian and Steve who were in the bar at The Sanderson. They said Digsy's been asking when I'm coming back in. Apparently the grunt's been given permission to use the Bloomberg while I'm off. I nearly went over to Canary Wharf to kick his arse but it was too much hassle. To be honest, by then the top of the stairs was too much hassle.

I had a hell of a time calling Rajneesh as my mouth and ears were too far away from each other to use the mobile properly. I had to speak, then move the receiver up across to my ear. He got the message in the end. Said he'll fax the sick note over to Solly's. They owe me sick pay. All I've made them over the years . . .

. . . Jez's gone quiet, which is odd since he's my best mate. I can't use the mobile now but that's no excuse for him not belling me. Always did when he was making shedloads on my portfolio. Hold on, I'll just plump up the pillows . . . I'm out of step, that's all. Treading water. It's like being on holiday, slowing the pace . . . reminds me, that skiing trip's coming up with Vicks and the lads. She's not rung either. Or come round. Well, to be honest the place is a bit of a tip. I'm living off takeaway pizzas and striking up quite a rapport with the pizza-boy through the letterbox. This keeps up I'll ring Mum and Dad.

Bloody Hell, I'm out on my ear. Turns out there was a cockup in personnel and they never got the sick note. Work did try to call or so they said. How would I know? I unplugged the phones and dumped the mobile ages ago. Well, they're no use, are they? Not when your head's the size of a planet. They've just written to me. Blah, blah, no contact, informal hearing, severance pay, cheque enclosed, wish you well. What as, the Elephant Man's ugly brother? That's gratitude for you. Six years

I've given that bank. What am I going to do now? Okay, so the redundancy should cover the mortgage, but in my condition I'm hardly going to get head-hunted.

Ha bloody ha.

Maybe I'll go over to Morgan's. Vicks will get me in there, no probs. She came over last Saturday. I'd had a postcard from her and Alison. Seems they had ten days in South Africa. Anyway, I'm keeping the curtains drawn, which I do all the time now, as I can't stand the light. She rang the bell a lot then peered through the letterbox. I saw her between the piles of pizza boxes. I didn't answer so she went away. Must have thought I was out or moved or dead. Serve her right if I was, the silly cow.

Later on she sent Jez over. Didn't want to talk to him either. I've seen neither hide nor hair of anyone these past weeks, least of all mister fine weather so-called mate Jezza Thompson. Amazing how fast they drop you. It's like I'm invisible or something, which is ironic since if I actually did step outside everyone would think a barrage balloon was loose in SW10.

Come to think of it, I haven't seen the pizza-boy either, not since I gave him the last of my credit cards. Sort of my last link to the world, really. I'm coming to terms with it now – the disability. I'm not dying, the swelling's eased off and the headaches aren't so bad. I broke most of the mirrors so I can't give an accurate picture of what I look like. I lost that metal tape measure, well I say lost; more lobbed it through the window in disgust. I measure my head daily by hands, then write it down in the book. What's happened is my nose is still dead centre but all my other features have sort of spread out. So it's two hands from nose to mouth and five from mouth to ears. My earlobes, which I can just about still reach, are enormous flappy things. Eating is a bit hit and miss, truth be told. Luckily I've given up on washing.

I've not got much of an appetite and I try to make it to the loo when I can. I have to sleep on my back otherwise the blood pools forwards and sets off the migraine. I'm using an eye patch now, which makes it a lot easier to see the telly. You'd be surprised at how little there is on, even with upwards of fifty channels.

Hang on. Something's happening. It's a tingling in my nose. And I'm getting a sort of tickle in my throat. Hold on. Ah, ah, choooooo. This dudn't bode well. Sniiffff.

The stupid thing is I hate people who are ill. They go on and on about their symptoms all the time as if they were some kind of medical marvel. I've just raided what's left in the medicine cabinet. Not a lot there besides cough linctus and Beecham's powders, but I've taken the lot anyway. It got worse when my nose started to stream and I had to use a towel to stem the flow. Every time I sneeze it really hurts. Feels like my head's going to explode. It's not on, having a cold as well as all this. I'm like Humpty Dumpty all full of yolk.

Crawling through to the kitchen I found the last of the booze stashed away at the back of the cupboard. It's the leftovers, liqueurs and Advocaat and all that gooey Christmassy muck. I've polished off the lot now in order to sleep off this bloody virus. Seems I've been sick all over my jim-jams, only I can't remember when that happened. And I'm crying which is a bit pathetic. There're tears dripping off either side of my balloon face into the pools of wee all around me. It's a wonder I hadn't thought to hunt out this stash of drink before because I have been getting increasingly desperate.

Still, you have to keep your dignity, don't you?

It was 4:36 on the LED display on the cooker clock when I came to. I was drenched in sweat and the top of my head felt like a construction team of woodpeckers were going at it full whack. Bloody agony. Like molten lava up there. Somehow I got to my feet, turned on the tap in the sink and threw water over myself. Suddenly, there was this searing pain and a blinding light and next thing I knew I was slap bang on the floor again. I wish Vicks were here. Then before I could do anything there was this awful tearing, stretching sound. It felt like my head was actually splitting open. Never had it this bad. Then something started dripping down past my nose and I stuck my finger in it and there was all this pus. I hate pus. There came this deafening noise and before I fainted my vision went and each of my eyes floated away as my head came apart.

It's eleven a.m. and I can see properly. The pain's gone, too. The house stinks and I stink but who cares. I'm fine. Bloody brilliant. Light-headed even. I'm just patting my head and it seems okay. It's really okay. Got to check this out in a mirror.

'You're a real beauty.'

'What? Who's that?'

'Come on – get a move on. Chop chop.'

I looked round but I couldn't see anyone so I stormed through to the bedroom. I'd busted the wardrobe mirror ages ago but there are plenty of broken bits on the floor. I held one up to my face and here I am. Me. Guy. A bit beardy, a few spots, but otherwise right as rain. Shit, shave and a shower and I'll be a new person. Start all over again.

'Oy – to your left – tosser.'

I tilted the mirror slightly and there he was.

'Lovely ain't I?'

It was my head, only all twisted and sort of evil-looking.

'You want to watch who you're calling evil.'

I started to cry again. 'But I don't understand.'

'What's the problem? Two heads are better than one aren't they?'

She Came in Through the Open Window

Yasmin Boland

Tony was knackered. His shoulders felt so heavy he thought they might tip him forward. His eyes were so tired they threatened to close before he hit the bed. Half-seeing, he plodded from the bathroom in a towel, showing a body that while bowed, was still strong. Just outside his bedroom door, he stopped. He could swear that was Linda's perfume. He'd smelled it in here before. He often dreamed of her and her fragrant body, and wondered how she was. Contact between them was now legally forbidden. Tony dropped his towel to the floor and slipped between the bedsheets, the bed creaking under his weight. He switched off his bedside light and hit the pillow in one manoeuvre.

Linda pressed herself against a wall in the shadows of the spare room, breathing through an open mouth to make no sound as she listened to Tony's night-time ritual. Hearing the bedsprings creaking – with pleasure, she thought, just as they'd always done when she and

Tony made love – she crept to the door of the bedroom, and pressed one eye to its crack. She could almost feel Tony's sinewy body against hers as she scanned his outline under the covers. Best of all, she could see his crowning glory silhouetted by a diagonal sliver of moonlight; the part of Tony that made him a man; the part of Tony which had cheated on her.

Linda allowed Tony time to settle into bed. Into *their* bed. Fifteen, twenty, then thirty minutes passed. Finally he was ready, and so was she. In one hand she held the sedative, in the other a handkerchief, her duffel bag over her shoulder. She squeezed the solution onto the hanky, then used one finger to push open the bedroom door. She made no sound crossing the carpet, knowing, after seventeen years, where to tread to avoid the squeaky floorboards. Her silence didn't save her, though. The acrid chemical scent of the sedative roused Tony before she reached him, and his eyes shot open just as Linda pushed the sodden handkerchief over his nose and mouth, relishing his panic as he inhaled.

Maybe he recognised her, maybe he didn't. Either way, Tony passed out.

Trembling, Linda drew four pairs of handcuffs from her bag. They were the novelty type, trimmed with faux fur, but made of steel, and strong. Tony had given them to her as a fifteenth wedding anniversary present.

Lifting his muscular arms above his head, Linda clicked one set of cuffs around his wrists and then linked a second set around the first, locking them to the slats on the head of their marital bed. She suspected it was a bed Tony had shared with dozens of other women, before and since their separation.

Tony stirred so Linda clasped the hanky to his mouth again, before repeating the procedure with the cuffs around his feet, clamping his ankles together and then imprisoning him by securing them to the foot of the bed.

Finally, she drew back the covers.

Tony was on his back. He liked it on his back. He always wanted to lie under Linda so she did all the work on top of him. In hindsight Linda realised Tony could probably only do it from this position because he was too worn out from the whores he'd had earlier in the day.

With his arms stretched out above his head, the soft white flesh underneath exposed, Tony's torso reminded Linda of a beefcake spread on one of the www.cum.com sites she'd frequented since their separation. His pecs looked almost pumped, his chest puffed out. He looked so gentle asleep. She traced a finger over one eyebrow, down over his whiskers, the length of his throat and to his left nipple, which hardened to her touch. She leant over and sucked it. Tony always said women didn't pay enough attention to men's nipples, that women wanted their body sucked and kissed and licked, but didn't realise that men wanted that, too. As she sucked and blew, the nipple stayed hard and the other started its journey.

She looked down. Of course, it didn't take much to get Tony going. That was the problem that ended their marriage. One pathetic suck on his nipple and he was iron-rod hard. He denied cheating, but Linda wasn't fooled. For example, at his agency's last Christmas bash, before their separation, Linda had watched Tony interacting with the rest of the staff. Call it female intuition, but she knew instantly that he'd not only had Stacey, the 24-year-old blonde trainee accountant, but her older boss Cheryl, too, and Linda sensed he had designs on at least three of his clients' wives as well.

Instinct assured her Tony was as incapable of keeping his privates in his pants as she was at leaving them there. Linda and Tony had shagged furiously in the bathroom at that last Christmas party, while the rest of the guests made merry upstairs. Tony couldn't get enough of her that night, pushing her up against the cold tiles, lifting her skirt, and groaning when he saw she was wearing suspenders and stockings with no knickers. Just for him. She knew what she had to do to keep him interested.

And now she was aching all over again, seeing her once-beloved spread-eagled and naked. Linda placed both her hands on his stomach, leaning into him, enjoying his familiar warmth and scent. She allowed her hands to glide around his navel, skimming the line of hair leading downwards. She touched him, up and down, with her lips, just as he loved it. Just as he'd directed her and God only knew how many other women to do for him.

She put her duffel bag on the bed where she could reach it, and clambered on top of him, lifting her skirt. No knickers. A final gift. She straddled him, resting half on his thighs and half on her heels. She licked her fingers and massaged him, for old times' sake. He loved that, too. Stroking and licking were Tony's raisons d'être, and his demise. He was moaning in his sleep now. He wanted her, though awake he'd never have admitted it.

But she knew.

One night, post-separation, Linda called Tony late and found him drunk. He confessed he missed her and actually cried as he told her why she couldn't come home. Threatening him, shoving him and punching him when she accused him of 'doing' Stacey, had been a forgivable relapse. Going around to Stacey's flat and belting the girl until her nose bled and her teeth were broken had changed everything.

Tony blubbered like a child when they went to court. In the hallway afterwards, under their lawyers' observation, he held Linda and choked out that he was sorry he couldn't love her properly any more. He swore he was innocent of the infidelities she accused him of. He hoped she would work with – not against – the treatment the court had ordered. Maybe after that they could talk, he said. Then his bitch of a mother had dragged Tony away from her. Just another woman tearing them apart.

With one more application of the handkerchief, Linda raised herself to kneeling, then slid down on top of her husband, letting out a cry as she enveloped him as perfectly as ever. She started a rhythm which Tony's drugged body rose to meet, his torso twisting and his arms and feet pulling at their shackles. Linda closed her eyes and forgot she'd drugged him. She squeezed her breasts, imagining Tony's strong fingers cupping and caressing them while he kissed her.

He was moaning louder now, his head starting to thrash.

Her eyes never leaving Tony's face, Linda reached into her duffel bag for the piece he'd given her the first time he went away on business all those years ago. She wondered how many women he'd had on that business trip. Probably as many as every other trip. What mattered now was that Tony had shown Linda how to use the gun. She cocked it, then straightened up, light-headed with lust. Still on top of him, she pressed the cold gun to her cleavage as she willed him on, moaning as tears splashed down her cheeks, onto her breasts and onto his body. Tony's breath quickened and his back arched. Linda rested the gun on his forehead as he grimaced in ecstasy. The exquisiteness of it pushed Linda over the edge, as it always did. His eyelids flickered at her. The last thing he ever said was her name.

Iron Lady, Ice Maiden
Bruno Bouchet

The first time I saw Catherine there was a war on – well almost, the 1987 British General Election. Having rejuvenated half of the country, Margaret Thatcher was sweeping towards another victory. We were in Manchester, the economic recovery hadn't reached the city and we were determined to do our bit to oust the Tory bastard in our constituency by canvassing for the Labour Party.

We were the Labour Club from Manchester University Student Union, or at least my faction, the Dem Left*. As we worked our way down the street from door to door a different group worked their way up the other side.

'It's the Tories!' someone cried, and we ran across the road to confront them with the fascist nature of their government. Turning away from a door, with her smile still intact, was Catherine. She was wearing a dress, but

---

* The Democratic Left: a faction within the University Labour Club whose only identity was 'non-Trotskyite'. The name was a misnomer – we were neither democratic nor left-wing.

not well, less like a dress and more like a disguise. I could tell she wasn't used to smart clothes. Her hair, a thousand different shades of blonde, was forced back by a brutal navy velvet ribbon. She looked too nice to be a Tory, I told myself, refusing to believe that I could be transfixed by anyone with such evil politics.

Her smile vanished when she saw us bearing down for a confrontation and she walked discreetly away, breaking into a run when she reached the corner. By the time I got there she had gone.

The next time I saw her she was transformed. In the library I was researching an essay on Rosa Luxemburg (we all loved Rosa, founder of the Communist Party of Germany – if the revolution had been down to her, the entire world would be living in socialist bliss). In the men's toilet I was splashing water on my face to wake myself up. Last night there had been a selection meeting for Labour Club delegates to the National Union of Students' national conference. It had been a complete wipe-out. Socialist Organiser* trounced us and we had to drown our sorrows.

As I looked up in the mirror, a toilet door opened and she marched out, waving a tampon applicator. No smart dress and tidy hair this time. Jeans, a combat jacket and loose hair – its thousand shades of blonde had revolted against the velvet ribbon and flew in every direction.

* Socialist Organiser (otherwise known as S.O.): far-left Trotskyite faction of the Labour Party. They had a newspaper (imaginatively titled *Socialist Organiser*), which promised to use every elected position as a 'campaigning post', whatever that meant. They didn't wash very much.

'I'm bleeding and I've just changed my tampon – deal with it,' she announced, and headed for the door.

She was on a crusade to liberate men's toilets and raise awareness of female bodily functions. She always changed her tampon in the men's toilet. It was only by exposure to the process of menstruation that men could become comfortable with the concept and address the issue.

She told me this in the corridor as I shot out after her. I was thrilled. It was brave, confrontational and would not impress her Tory MP.

'Hardly seems the behaviour of an aspiring Margaret Thatcher,' I challenged.

She smiled brilliantly, sweetly, contemptuously, wryly and mysteriously.

'It's not,' she replied and marched into the library, leaving me transfixed.

I had fallen in love as soon as she emerged from the cubicle, but the reasoned argument, the complete contradiction and the smile locked it down – it was pure worship.

That night I lay in bed thinking of the moment she appeared. The feeling of powerlessness as she invaded male territory was delicious. I decided she had to be the radical daughter of the Tory MP, forced to canvass or lose income support from him. I plotted schemes to rescue her from patriarchal tyranny. Sleepless nights were a regular feature of life with Catherine.

The next sighting was in a second-year political science lecture. The lecturer, having droned us into a stupor, announced that 'In 1873 the political landscape was barren'. Catherine shot out of her seat and demanded that the lecturer rephrase this term.

'The word "barren" is offensive to women who cannot bear children, rendering them useless members of society because they cannot reproduce to maintain the patriarchy. In a revolutionary state, such offensive terminology will no longer be acceptable.' She stormed out to thunderous applause. Half the audience were delighted that something interesting had happened, the other half were impressed that she had found a new word to add to the 'unacceptable' list. Anyone who could put a new word on that list had kudos.

I followed, determined to speak to her again. I had to find out why she canvassed for the Tories but had great sexual politics. There was something terrifying and yet alluring. She would probably hate me on principle. As a man, sexism had been instilled in me at birth. My every action and thought was based on the social advantage of being male. And my family was wealthy. My father ran his own business. I stank of privilege which she would smell.

I knew pursuing her would change me, I just hoped it was for the better. Finding her was easy. For all politically minded students the only place to go to after storming out of a lecture was the Union cafeteria.

She was sitting alone.

'Can I join you?' I asked. She looked me hard in the eye and then looked down at the cup of coffee in my hand, her attention attracted by the slight shake.

'What coffee is it?'

'Nicaraguan,' I lied. The Union general meeting had voted that the cafeteria should offer coffee bought from the Sandinista government in Nicaragua. The Sandinistas were the last hope for socialism. In Nicaragua class and gender oppression had been banished and the workers smiled as they grew coffee safe in the knowledge that they were feeding themselves and not corporations. At least they would have been smiling if they were not being brought to their knees by American-backed, proto-fascist rebels. The coffee was expensive, politically pure and disgusting.

Catherine dipped her finger in my cup, tasted the brew and rolled her eyes at me. The first question she asked me and I had lied.

Five minutes later I was back with a virtuous cup.

'It really is this time. Can I sit down?' She shrugged her shoulders which I took as a yes.

'I thought what you said in the lecture was great. These lecturers have no idea, they're dinosaurs.'

'Yes, but they still rule the planet.' She didn't look up from her book.

'Why were you canvassing for the Tories?' I asked, unable to hold my curiosity any longer.

'Oh,' she shifted uncomfortably, 'that was you chasing me.'

'Is your dad the sitting MP?'

She didn't answer. I pressed the point, determined to find a good reason, any reason. I was so thrilled to be actually sitting with her I was prepared to accept an evil-twin story.

'Isn't it obvious?' She pointed to the WRCP* badge on her combat jacket.

From my blank look, she realised it wasn't.

'You're one of those vanilla boys from the Labour Club, aren't you? You still think the Labour Party can do something for the masses. It's crap. There's only one salvation and that's revolution. A Labour government only fools the working class into thinking they have some power and so prevents them from rising. Conservative governments expose the reality of the power oligarchy and so hasten the inevitable collapse of the capitalist system. The interests of working people in the long run are best served by supporting the Tories because under them the revolution will come sooner.'

I was dazzled. Sitting with my head in my hands, I gazed at the revolutionary fire which was shining so passionately in her eyes. I drank every word she said. Enlightenment cascaded around me. Her passion caused the tiniest drop of spit to leap from her mouth into my coffee. I drank it quickly to ensure I swallowed that drop. The Sandinista coffee was transformed into nectar. I would never drink anything else again.

I asked another question and listened. Political theory, analysis and passion came forth. It was like she opened my head and poured golden light into the void.

---

* Workers' Revolutionary Communist Party: a non-Trotskyite Marxist–Leninist group advocating revolution. Gave impassioned speeches, got elected to nothing, sold newspapers. They washed more than Socialist Organiser. Generally, you couldn't find a nicer bunch of revolutionary extremists – especially Catherine.

I suggested we grab the next flight to Nicaragua. She smiled patiently.

'It wouldn't be fair to feed off the hard work of others while neglecting our own revolution here. We owe it to ourselves, to our sisters and brothers in this country to create revolution here.'

'Can I see you again?' She analysed my request. Had I been genuine in my interest or had I been feigning it to seduce her? Would being asked out compromise her or could she use the situation to recruit me into the WRCP?

'Meet me in the Student Union foyer on Saturday, 8.00 a.m. We'll spend the day together,' she decided.

I skipped home, stopping only in the Union shop to buy a pack of that delicious coffee.

Saturday came and I panicked over clothing. If she was going to take me canvassing for the Tories to hasten the collapse of the capitalist system I had to dress smart, but if it was a more direct revolutionary action I needed politically credible clothes. The 'Free Nelson Mandela' T-shirt came out – good cause, but a bit too safe, too middle-class. It went. The 'Ronald Reagan's brain's missing' T-shirt – too schoolboy. 'Radioactivity fades your genes' – too cute. I needed something to say I was not afraid of confrontation. I found it. Karl Marx rogering Magaret Thatcher from behind with the words 'Fuck the patriarchy'. She would appreciate the humour, given it was exactly what she was doing by canvassing for the Tories. Perfect.

Disaster. The Student Union foyer was packed. Our

date was a demo against Nottinghamshire County Council. They had refused to put sexual orientation in their equal-opportunities policy. The Gay & Lesbian Society and the Lesbian Society (two separate but mutually supportive groups) had organised coaches to add voices to the protest march. We were going on a gay-rights march and I was wearing an image of hetero-sexual sex. Catherine laughed and told me to turn it inside out.

Clive, one of the leaders of the Dem Left faction in the Labour Club and the male co-chair of the Gay & Lesbian Society, drew me aside.

'Good to see you supporting us, even if you do feel the need to publicly state your heterosexuality. Hope you're not being recruited?' He indicated Catherine, who had just jumped into an argument with a closet member of Militant* about whether a man could adequately fill the post of Women's Officer in the Union.

'We're on a date,' I answered Clive.

'With the Ice Maiden, congratulations! Finally someone might melt the ice . . . perhaps *you* could recruit *her*,' he said.

Clive explained that Catherine was a strong feminist and keen supporter of gay and lesbian rights, however, the official WRCP line on homosexuality was that it was a bourgeois deviation. Come the revolution there would be no gay men or lesbians.

'She doesn't believe that, and it's a great wedge

---

* Militant: another Trotskyite organisation. Banned from the Labour Party, they always denied they were members, even when caught selling their paper, imaginatively titled *Militant*.

between her and the party. If they're wrong on that, they could be wrong on other issues, too. We could use it to prise her away. She's brilliant – fantastic analysis and good-looking. She could get elected to any position in the Union if she was with us. You could be just the man to do it.'

'Isn't that dodgy sexual politics?' I asked.

'All in a good cause.' He nudged me and charged off to throw the male SWP* members off the women-only bus. They didn't believe in positive discrimination.

The Dem Left had sanctioned my pursuit through the words of Clive. I was not just pursuing my own desires, I was following the cause. On the coach, I raised the WRCP policy of 'bourgeois deviation'. Catherine felt sure the line would change soon. It was a question of education and policy evolution. That was what she loved about the party. It continually examined its policies to ensure that they were for the here and now.

'Some of the issues of oppression are fundamental and will not change, but we have to move to ensure relevance to the working class. Homosexuality is one issue. Just wait, the new line will come through any day. I was half expecting it today, the national committee were meeting Thursday night. I've been campaigning hard on the issue.'

'What if it doesn't?' I asked.

'You have to believe,' she said smiling, and I did.

---

* Socialist Workers' Party: a Trotskyite group much the same as S.O., only outside the Labour Party. Sold a paper, imaginatively titled *Socialist Worker*. Always got their placards in front of the cameras at every demo – macho boys of the far Left.

As we headed for Nottingham, our hearts full of political virtue, I thought I was doing the wooing by listening carefully to her analysis of Union politics. Clive had been right, she was brilliant. Ideas didn't pour out, they were clearly expressed with a logic that made the world make sense. The low sun shone through the coach window, setting fire to the thousand shades of blonde. It was me that was being wooed. If she had had a membership form, I would have signed up on the spot.

We didn't march together. Catherine thought it was important that we both identify as gay and lesbian for the day and experience any abuse from passers-by to further our understanding of the issues. She marched in the women-only section. I followed Clive, who plastered me in stickers with pink triangles and the words 'Faggots Ignite'.

'I'm not getting too far on prising her away from the WRCP,' I reported to Clive.

'I'm sure you'll do whatever it takes.' He smiled ruefully. 'Have you tackled her on all the mandating that goes on?'

Clive explained that the party's ruling committee decreed what must be done on certain issues and everyone had to follow.

'She'll have been canvassing for the Tories because the branch secretary told her to. It's very hierarchical and I know from the History of Women in Politics course we both do that she's got a streak of individualism – always admires women who struck out on their own.'

'I'll do my best.' I resolved to double my efforts.

They did not work. More ideas poured out in the coach on the way back. Decrees from the committee were not dictates but expressions of the collective view. No one had to do anything, but everyone was so committed they wanted more tasks, not less. She had even guessed that Clive had planted the question.

Back at the Student Union, everyone retired to the bar to analyse the day's events. The SWP managed to get off the coach first and hog the best booths closest to the bar – very aggressive. Afterwards, I offered to walk Catherine home. The next women's bus was not for another forty-five minutes and so she agreed.

I timed our conversation brilliantly. She had just begun her explanation as to why the revolution would resolve the Northern Ireland conflict by removing dated concepts such as nationalism, when we turned into her street. She had no choice but to invite me in to finish the discussion.

The discussion finished at 4 a.m. It was a very complex issue and I needed several concepts repeatedly explained. I was staring at her mouth, watching it move and losing my hearing. The pinkness looked so soft, I longed to feel it with my lips. I realised she had stopped talking, more because her lips were not moving rather than by not hearing words.

'I want to kiss you,' I said. 'I'm not trying to get you into bed and I've been totally absorbed by your words, but I want to be honest so you can make a decision about what you want without any gender oppression from me.'

'I respect your honesty,' she said. 'There's nothing wrong with being sexually attracted to someone as long as you don't use it to take away their power.'

We moved closer.

'I believe that, too. However, given the hundreds of years of sexual attraction being used as an instrument of oppression by men, I think it's appropriate for you to take the lead and communicate what you believe are the acceptable expressions of mutually respectful affection. You are in control.'

She moved her lips onto mine for a few seconds and pulled back. The gentle power was overwhelming. She smiled.

'It's nice that you don't revert to type at this point. Most guys give you the talk and then go in for the kill.'

Was that a warning? I wanted to go in for the kill – take her in my arms, kiss her passionately and be carried away without a thought for politics, but Catherine demanded self-control. There would be no running away with desire. I kissed her back, not daring to part her lips too far and penetrate with my tongue. It would have ruined the moment. Restraint was every-thing. We were living our sexual politics. Consistency between words and deeds. It had a delicious purity.

I stayed the night. We did not have sex but slept head to toe. I was allowed to kiss the soles of her feet. I could not believe how little they smelled after a day's hard protesting. Not wanting to impose my manly odours on her, I had washed my feet when I went to the toilet.

I said that we slept, but only Catherine did. I lay awake in ecstasy. This woman was a goddess, taking me to a higher level of consciousness. I could believe in any revolution that she was part of. I dozed off eventually and dreamed of Catherine as Joan of Arc, returning during the French Revolution to lead the people to victory. Whenever she mounted her horse, she kissed me for good luck. The imprint burned on my forehead like a badge of honour.

A week later and we were officially 'going out'. We were not a couple (too married), we were not partners (it was a relationship not a business venture). We liked the childlike innocence of 'going out' and, try as we did, we could not find a political objection. The word 'out' hinted at solidarity with our lesbian and gay friends.

Clive was not impressed with my recruiting progress. It had got back to him that I had attended the weekly WRCP meeting with Catherine. His sources were so good he challenged me at the bar while the meeting was still on. I had left for the members-only communication from the national committee, and was waiting for Catherine in the bar when Clive tackled me.

'You can't be a member of the WRCP and the Labour Party. It could ruin your career with the party.'

'I was just supporting Catherine. We agreed to attend each other's political meetings to ensure fairness,' I lied. Catherine had agreed to no such thing.

'You might have to resort to withholding sex.'

'I can't,' I said.

'That good, eh?'

'Actually, I'm declaring myself politically celibate. In the current climate, it's impossible to separate the sexual act from sexual oppression, and until we feel we can, there'll be no sex.'

'Politically celibate – I love it!' cried Clive. 'You've coined a new phrase. It's great, all the straight male candidates at the next Union election will declare themselves politically celibate. Creating a new political position, it's what we all aspire to and you've done it!'

I smiled. I had just made the position up on the spot as an excuse for us not having sex. Clive suddenly cackled even louder,

'It's fantastic, there'll be so much sexual frustration it'll be just like being at a boys' boarding school. Thanks!'

It turned out to be gay night all round. Catherine came out of her meeting and ran up and kissed me, then Clive too, beaming with delight.

'It's happened, the line's changed. The committee decreed that homosexuality is a natural expression of sexuality and come the revolution discrimination, homophobia and heterosexism will no longer exist.'

She was thrilled. The satisfaction of achieving an outcome was obvious. Clive was pleased for her, but knew it meant our chances of recruiting her were slim. The one policy she really objected to was gone.

Everyone was happy. Catherine's party had dragged itself into the twentieth century, I was starting a new political trend and the gays were looking forward to lots of sex. But there was something at the back of Catherine's joy. Something she was not telling me. I waited to hear what else the revolutionary committee had decided.

That night, we lay in bed head to head and I only had to wear my underpants. Not only that but she was comfortable enough with me to sleep topless. I tried hard not to look at her breasts but still glimpsed them as they passed by me from her bra to under the sheets.

We lay in bed and confronted our isms. I racked my brains for acts of sexism I had carried out that day. I bit the bullet and went for total honesty, citing my lustful glimpse of Catherine's breasts just a few moments before. She thought for a moment, blushed slightly (I yearned to know if her breasts had blushed too) and then thanked me for my honesty. It had confronted her but also empowered her with knowledge. She absolved my sexism. She then wondered if she had been heterosexist in pushing hard for change in the WRCP policy on homosexuality. She did not want to take ownership of their campaign away from lesbian and gay men. Perhaps she should have supported them in their struggle for change rather than doing it for them.

She lay talking to the ceiling, worried that she might have been disempowering, the anguish genuine as she scrutinised her day's actions for errors.

'How many gays do you know in the WRCP?' I asked.

'You mean lesbians and gay men,' she corrected. '. . . None.'

I suggested that she had created a space for them within the party to fight their own battle. They could not have done this from outside.

'The gay and lesbian floodgates will now open and it'll all be thanks to you.'

She looked at me suddenly, as if shocked by what I had said, and then stopped.

'Thanks for your analysis. Good night.' She leaned over and kissed me. I felt her nipples touch my body as she put the light out, scuppering any chance of sleep.

Two days later in the union bar, Clive held an informal panel to investigate my defection. I had been spotted selling papers for the WRCP. I argued that I was only accompanying Catherine, but Clive's spy had actually handed me money for one of the papers while Catherine had been arguing with the SWP paper seller over the two-state solution for Israel/Palestine. Caught red-handed.

I tried to argue that buying the paper was worse than selling as it was contributing funds. However, Clive's spy had 'liberated' the money from a Socialist Organiser's collection tin and thus had used Trotskyite money to fund revolutionary communism. Something they all found hilarious.

I was unofficially reprimanded by the informal panel and made to get the next round in. But they were right. I was being seduced by the Ice Maiden's politics. She hadn't melted – there were no puddles of soft socialism or sexual heat. The Labour Party now seemed weak and ineffectual to me. Parliamentary democracy was just a tool of capitalism. In one sleepless night I had formulated a theory that sex might be a secret prize for joining the WRCP. Catherine might have decided she could only have sex with someone from within the party. It could even be a rule from the committee. She would not tell me so my conversion would be genuine, not just to get sex.

The following week, Catherine was supposed to be joining me in the bar after Women's Group but it was not a fixed date. She was free to spend the entire evening with women if she wanted. I was happy to be the fallback position, until she didn't turn up. I told myself it was important for her to spend time with her sisters, but there was no avoiding the fact she chose not to spend the night with me. Nothing could have made me choose not to be with Catherine. Every second without her was wasted.

Clive saw me looking glum and invited me to a demonstration in one of the city's gay clubs. The drag queen on that night had been telling racist jokes. A group of them were going to stand at the front and chant 'Oppressor! Oppressor!' if he started up again.

I thanked him for the invitation, but said that given I was only going because my girlfriend had stood me up, my support would be tokenistic at best.

That night I dreamed she was hovering above my bed, surrounded by a dazzling pink light. She held her hand out to me but every time I reached up to touch her, she moved further away. She lured me out of bed and I was running hard through the university campus as she disappeared over the library building, when I woke up.

We met at morning break in the Union cafeteria. Catherine was sitting alone, with two coffees – one was for me. My dream had been worrying. The fact she had bought coffee for me was bad (it was a traditional woman's 'task' and so I always had to buy my own), but my dread set in completely when the coffee tasted good. It was not Sandinista. Alarm bells rang so loud I expected a building evacuation. I looked around in panic. Clive and the others were keeping a safe distance. Normally we would be surrounded by arguments, shouting and political gossip, but this time Catherine had achieved the impossible: she'd found a quiet spot in the Union cafeteria. Was there anything she could not do?

'I'm sorry if it's something I've done. If I've oppressed you, I'm sorry. I'll confront my sexism. Just let me know.' It was a desperate pre-emptive gesture.

'You've done nothing wrong. I don't know a man with more genuine politics. I trust you more than any other man, even the national committee chair.'

'So why the decent coffee?'

'This is the hardest thing I've ever had to do. And I want you to know it's tested my loyalty to the party more than anything else. Part of me wanted to say it was wrong, but it's not. The end justifies the means and I want you to understand my reasons and why I have to do this.'

For a split second I thought my mission to recruit her for the Dem Left of the Labour Club had come far closer to success than I had ever realised. Then the truth spilled out.

The WRCP national committee had communicated directly with the branch concerning the new line on homosexuality. The recruitment of homosexuals into the party ranks was now a priority. This aim could only be achieved by lesbians and gay men within the party seeking out new members. As there were currently none, certain members throughout the country were being mandated to come out as lesbian or gay in order to recruit others. Catherine was one. She was being called on to play an essential role in hastening the collapse of the capitalist system.

I was speechless. I wanted to shout out, 'We're not even having sex – what needs to change?' I wanted to beg her to reconsider, to refuse the mandate, to not let her sexuality be decided by a committee in London. How could she take up the yoke of oppression like that? Instead I just bleated for the first time, 'But I love you!'

'I know and I'm enriched by that,' she answered. She drank some coffee, winced and continued. 'I want to do this. I have to. I could recruit the one person that tips the scale, that brings the revolution forward by just one day. I could create one day less oppression for the workers. How can I refuse that call?'

How could I argue? I recognised the zeal lighting up her face. Sex would never be her passion. The good of the workers was her passion and everything else was secondary.

'We have to break up,' she continued, 'but you know it's for a good reason don't you? You know it's not because of you or anything you've done. You are the only man I've ever slept with and I am delighted about that.'

I drank some coffee. My taste buds were relieved that I didn't have to drink revolutionary coffee any more. That was my positive. That was my only bright side, not having to drink crap coffee.

'So what now? Do you come out straight away? Does everyone know about the directive?'

'I think everyone's expecting me to come out. I raised it at Women's Group, but they don't know about the directive.'

'And I suppose I have to keep my mouth shut about you not really being a lesbian, so you can seduce some women.'

'I am a lesbian,' she said loudly. 'You'll have to deal with that.'

I closed my eyes and tried not to cry.

'Don't use me to establish your credentials. Can't this moment be just us?'

'I'm sorry,' she said. It was the first time she had ever apologised to me.

'That was wrong, but I *am* a lesbian. I define myself. You can't do it. If I say I am, I am.'

'I'll go now,' I said. 'It'll look better if I rush out and then I don't have to face anyone. Goodbye.'

I wanted to grab her for one moment and force a kiss on her, push my tongue in her mouth and make her realise she was being ridiculous, but I didn't. There was something that told me to keep my distance. There always had been. Her space was sacrosanct, there was no invading it.

'Goodbye then.' We both stood up and I fooled myself into thinking I stole a kiss on her cheek. I didn't.

She offered her cheek and I took it with a gratitude more bitter than Sandinista coffee.

After that I only saw her denouncing lecturers, exhorting general meetings and marching loud and proud in the women's section at demos. I retreated to the safety of the Dem Left. Clive kindly admitted to conflicting feelings. He was politically jubilant at Catherine's coming out but personally felt sorry for me.

The ranks of the WRCP did swell with one or two gay and lesbian revolutionaries. Catherine was their inspiration, but she was working on a bigger prize. The Union Women's Officer, elected by the women in the Student Union, was a political giant. Unaligned to any political grouping, she commanded the support of everyone on the Left. I started seeing her and Catherine together. They laughed a lot and were always touching. I saw the need to be in physical contact with a person whose very skin made you feel alive. I knew that need but had seldom dared seek the contact. This woman could not resist. Catherine could not resist.

I had decided to torture myself with a silent cup of Sandinista coffee and was walking around the cafeteria trying to find a seat. I spotted them, but they didn't see me. They didn't see anyone. If it had been a public display, it would have been easier. I saw them kiss, tongues locked within the not-so-discreet shield of their lips. When they stopped they were lost in their own magic, as I stood holding my plastic tray. The Ice Maiden had melted.

The following Thursday, the Iron Lady was re-elected. In our constituency, the Tory candidate scraped in by two votes. The revolution was a day closer.

When the Fat Lady Sings
Colette Caddle

1981

Ellie let herself into the big old house and headed for the sitting room where her aunt – resplendent in a pink jogging suit – pedalled furiously on her exercise bike, *Coronation Street* blaring in the background.

'Hi Darling,' Marilyn said breathlessly. 'Just give me a minute and I'll make us some tea. Forty-eight, forty-nine –'

'No rush.' Ellie wandered back out to the grand-father clock in the hall, climbed on a chair, corrected the time and started to wind.

'Eighty!' Marilyn came out to join her, mopping her brow with a towel.

'Aren't you supposed to do a hundred?' Ellie winced as a splinter went into her thumb. 'Bloody clock,' she muttered as she clambered down off the chair.

Marilyn sighed. 'Eighty, a hundred, I doubt if it makes much difference. Oh, thanks for winding Cyril.'

Ellie sucked her thumb as she followed Marilyn into

the kitchen. 'I don't know why you don't get rid of the damn thing.'

'Get rid of it? Oh, I could never do that! Cyril is part of the family! Now let's have that tea.'

Ellie gasped at the array of cream cakes and biscuits set out on the table. 'You know, you'd save a fortune on classes, tapes and equipment if you stopped eating this stuff.'

'Yes, dear,' Marilyn said with exaggerated patience. 'But life would be very dull if we always did the right thing.' She filled the large pink teapot and fetched milk and sugar before seating her ample bottom on the chair opposite Ellie. 'So how are things?'

Ellie started to pick the chocolate off her éclair. She would love to be able to answer that question honestly but Ben would murder her if she did. 'I didn't go into business on my own in order for your aunt to rescue me every time things got tough,' he'd stormed the first time she'd told him that Marilyn had offered them a loan.

'Everything's fine,' Ellie said now, flashing Marilyn a reassuring smile.

'That's good,' Marilyn said, not believing her for a minute. 'Ben's such a hard worker.'

'Tell me about it,' Ellie said miserably. 'I hardly see him these days.'

'I'm afraid that's the penalty of going into business on your own. My poor Tommy used to put in some very long hours in the early days. Now, you would ask if you needed my help, wouldn't you Ellie?'

'Of course, stop worrying.'

Marilyn patted her hand. 'I can't help worrying about you. You're the only one I've got.'

'Me, two brothers *and* two noisy nephews,' Ellie pointed out.

'Don't remind me.'

'Marilyn Connor! You should be ashamed of yourself!'

'Sorry. I'm afraid that I'm turning into a cranky old woman.'

'Hah! That's a good one! You've *always* been cranky and you're no spring chicken either –'

'You can stop right there, young lady!'

Ellie laughed as a tea cloth came flying through the air. 'Sorry, Aunty. Didn't mean it, Aunty.'

'That's more like it. I prefer it when you grovel. So if you don't want to talk about Ben's business tell me about the exciting world of law.' Marilyn lit a cigarette and sat back.

Ellie happily complied, supplementing and embellishing to satisfy Marilyn's love of a good story.

Marilyn gazed affectionately at her niece as she talked. Ellie could really do with putting on a few pounds – way too thin. Still, her mother had been the same. Marilyn sighed as she thought of her beloved sister. Everyone was always amazed when they found out that she and Joanna were twins. She, short, plump and a real chatterbox and Joanna, tall, slim and quiet – they made an unlikely pair. But they were as close as two sisters could be. When Joanna died of breast cancer at the ridiculously young age of forty-eight, Marilyn felt as if her right arm had been torn off. The only thing that kept her going – apart from her darling Tommy, of course – was Ellie. Poor Joe had never really recovered from Joanna's death and needed all the help he could get raising a teenager and Marilyn threw herself into the task. Not that it had been difficult. Ellie had made Joanna's death bearable and soon became like the daughter Marilyn and Tommy never had. When Tommy died three years ago it was Ellie who had got Marilyn through that terrible time, bringing them even closer than before.

'You're miles away.' Ellie's voice brought her back to the present. 'What are you thinking about? Or, more's the point, what are you plotting? If it's how to bump off Aunty Brenda I don't want anything to do with it.'

Marilyn glowered at the mention of her sister-in-law. 'Don't even get me started on that one.'

Ellie laughed. 'So what is it then?'

'I want to make a will.'

Ellie's cup clattered into the saucer. 'But why?'

Marilyn looked at her from under raised eyebrows. 'You're the lawyer, dear. You work it out.'

'But you're still young. There's plenty of time.'

Marilyn sighed at the worried look on Ellie's face. 'Oh, don't worry, I'm not planning to keel over just yet. I just want to make sure that the likes of Brenda Clarke doesn't get her grubby little paws on my money.' Marilyn bit viciously into a cream dough-nut. 'Isn't it bad enough that she trapped my poor brother into marriage and has made his life a misery ever since?'

'You don't *know* he's miserable. Just because we

don't like her doesn't mean he feels the same way.'

Marilyn snorted. 'Rubbish! Paul only married her because she said she was pregnant.'

Ellie gaped at her. 'You're kidding! I never knew that.'

'Well, your grandparents didn't exactly like to broadcast the fact. They were shocked that their darling son had got a girl into trouble. They couldn't get him up the aisle fast enough!'

'So what happened to the baby?' Ellie looked puzzled. Paul and Brenda didn't have any children. At least none she knew about.

Marilyn scowled. 'Well, she *said* she had a miscarriage but my mother never believed she was pregnant in the first place. It seemed very convenient that she lost it the moment there was a wedding band on her finger.'

'How come they never had any more?'

'I don't know. For whatever reason Brenda never got pregnant again. I wouldn't be surprised if she was using contraceptives on the side.'

'Oh, Marilyn, she wouldn't . . . would she?' The skeletons tumbling out of the Clarke closet had Ellie enthralled.

'I wouldn't put anything past Brenda,' Marilyn was saying bitterly. 'She was never interested in children and having a bunch of lively babies to look after would have been too much like hard work to her.'

'And you resented that because you wanted children so much,' Ellie's eyes were full of sympathy.

Marilyn shook her head impatiently. 'Oh, that's all in the past and it should be left there. Now let's get back to my will. I know I should have made one when Tommy died. Still, better late than never. How complicated is it?'

Ellie shrugged. 'As complicated as you want to make it.'

'Well, if I leave something to Paul, can I make sure that Brenda can't touch it? And what about poor Karen? Could I leave money to her and not to Robert?'

'But he's your brother,' Ellie protested half-heartedly. She didn't particularly like Uncle Robert. He was a cold man with little or no sense of humour. In fact he was nothing like his three siblings.

'I don't care,' Marilyn was saying, her mouth set in a determined line. 'He wouldn't bother keeping in touch at all if he didn't think I was worth a few bob. But I *would* like to leave something to Karen. She deserves a bloody medal for staying with him. And as for those boys of his. Lord, they're only kids and already they treat her like dirt. Talk about chips off the old block.'

'How on earth did Aunt Karen marry him in the first place?' Ellie asked, mystified. 'They're so very different.'

'I suppose she must have loved him. There's no accounting for taste. Mother was thrilled with the match. She thought Karen might be able to soften Robert up a bit. Hah! Some hope!'

'Well, it's your money and you can leave it to whomever you want but Robert could still contest the will after –'

'After I've kicked the bucket,' Marilyn finished the sentence. 'But he wouldn't win, would he?'

'Maybe not, but he could tie up the estate for

months, maybe even years.'

'Oh no, I'm not having that!'

'There's not much you can do about it. Of course it will be harder to contest if the will has been drawn up properly and it's proven that you were of sound mind when you signed it.'

'Now that *could* be a problem!' Marilyn chuckled. 'Oh, but seriously, love. I don't want any fighting after I'm gone. That would be terrible.'

Ellie chewed thoughtfully on a gingernut. 'You could divide up your estate *before* –'

'What was that?'

'I'm not sure but maybe you could divide up your estate *before* you died instead. That would save on death duties and inheritance tax too.'

'Lord, I'd forgotten all about them. Bloody ridiculous! You try and do something nice for the people you love and you end up costing them money.'

Ellie grinned. 'That's the trouble with being a wealthy woman!'

Marilyn laughed. 'Who'd have thought there'd be so much money in disposable bedpans! My Tommy was way ahead of his time. So what do you think I should do, love?'

Ellie stood up. 'Nothing. You must think long and hard about all this. It's a big decision. I'll talk to my boss and see if he has any ideas. The gift idea probably isn't realistic. You can't afford to give all your worldly goods away now. You could live for another thirty years.'

Marilyn shuddered. 'God forbid!'

'Look, sleep on it and phone me if you've any questions.'

'I will love, thanks. Oh, by the way, I won't be using your firm.'

'Oh.'

Marilyn laughed. 'Don't look at me like that! Obviously you're going to be one of the beneficiaries and Robert would immediately be suspicious if your firm had handled everything.'

'Of course, you're right. Well, I can recommend someone else if you like.'

'Grand.'

'Okay then. See you on Saturday.' She dropped a kiss on Marilyn's forehead.

'Oh, I'm not sure about Saturday,' Marilyn called after her. 'The girls are arranging a poker night.'

Ellie shook her head. 'The girls' – not one of them under sixty – always seemed to be organising something. Marilyn's hectic social life made hers seem terribly dull sometimes! 'Well, if your exciting plans fall through, dinner will be at seven as usual.'

2000

'So the old girl's finally popped her clogs.' Robbie Clarke leaned over his mother's shoulder and helped himself from the joint she was carving.

'Robbie! Have some respect,' Karen admonished, slapping his hand away automatically.

'Oh, come on, Mum. She must have been nearly ninety –'

'Only seventy-eight,' she protested.

'Only! That's ancient!'

'She was the funniest, cleverest woman I've ever known,' Karen said with a tremor in her voice. 'Nothing got past Marilyn.'

'She certainly managed to keep a tight hold of her money.'

'Robbie!'

'Well, she could have helped out with our college tuitions,' Robbie complained. 'And Dad would have been able to retire sooner if she'd slipped him a few bob.'

'Your dad never wanted to retire.' Karen said wearily, adding *Thank God* to herself. The thought of having her husband at home all day under her feet filled her with dread. But he would be sixty-five in August and that day was fast approaching. *Don't think about that now.* 'Go and get your suit, Robbie. I'll have it dry-cleaned for the funeral.'

'Oh, do I have to go? Aidan isn't.'

'Aidan is in France,' Karen said sharply, 'and yes, you most definitely have to go.'

'Dad?' Robbie appealed to his father, who was sitting at the table reading the paper.

'Of course you must go,' Robert said abruptly. 'Anyway, don't you want to know what's in the will?'

Robbie scowled. 'I already do. You can bet that my darling cousin Ellie will get the lot.'

'She deserves every penny,' Karen said angrily. 'She's been like a daughter to Marilyn.' She slammed down the carving knife and ran out of the room. When she was in the privacy of the bathroom she burst into tears.

Tears for Marilyn and tears for herself. She was going to miss her. She had liked all the Clarke women but Marilyn has become a dear and close friend over the last few years. Probably her only friend, Karen realised and the tears bubbled up again. She splashed some water on her face and blew her nose. 'You're being a silly old woman,' she muttered, brushing back the iron-grey hair from her tired, worn face. 'Yes, you're an old woman and it's time you stopped dreaming. This is as good as it gets. You're healthy and your family is healthy. You've a lot to be grateful for.' And after taking a few deep, if shaky, breaths she went back downstairs and finished making dinner for her family.

'Are you okay, Mum?'

Ellie looked up to see her daughter looking down at her, big brown eyes full of concern. Christened Joanna after her grandmother, her three-year-old brother, Billy, hadn't been able to manage such a big word and had called her Jo. And Jo she'd remained ever since. It had always amused Ellie and Ben that the child they had named after the quiet twin had turned out to be a miniature version of her great-aunt – much to Marilyn's delight.

Ellie smiled. 'I'm fine. Do I look okay?'

Jo looked doubtfully at the charcoal-grey suit and the sensible, low-heeled black shoes. 'Honestly, Mum? No. You'd look great in that outfit if you were about sixty. Wait there a sec.' She disappeared into her own room and appeared moments later with a fluorescent orange chiffon scarf. 'Try this.'

Ellie stared. 'Oh, I don't know.'

Jo rolled her eyes. 'Mum!'

'Oh, all right then. Give it here. And get my suede shoes out of the wardrobe. I may as well go the whole hog.'

'Nice one!' Jo said approvingly and ran to fetch the stilettos.

Ellie tied the scarf around her neck, put on the shoes and did a twirl. 'Well?'

'Excellent! You look amazing, Mum.'

'Well, thank you, darling. Now what are you going to wear?'

'How about my purple mini-dress and my knee-high black boots?'

'Perfect. Marilyn always loved purple.'

Jo giggled. 'Aunty Brenda will have a seizure!'

'All the more reason to wear it,' her mother said drily. 'Now, hurry up, love. We don't want to be late.'

'Should I wear the navy suit or my black coat?' Brenda held up the two for Paul's inspection.

Paul didn't look up. 'Whatever you like.'

'The navy suit looks better but I suppose black is more suitable.'

Paul's lips twitched. 'Marilyn would probably prefer red.'

Brenda tossed her head impatiently. 'Don't be ridiculous, Paul. That would be very disrespectful.'

Paul raised an eyebrow. Brenda had never shown Marilyn any respect when she was alive, why start now? But of course he knew the answer. Brenda believed in keeping up appearances. She would talk to the priest and the neighbours. Tell everyone what a wonderful woman Marilyn was. And all the time she'd be wondering how long it would be before the will was read and how much Marilyn had left them. Lord, she was in for a shock. Paul smiled. At least some good would come of this sad day. Brenda would get her comeuppance.

It was nearly twenty years since Marilyn had told him her plan.

'Good idea, love,' he'd told her. 'Go for it.'

'You don't mind then?' Marilyn had asked anxiously.

'Of course I don't bloody mind. As if you need to ask.'

'Brenda may not agree,' she'd said tentatively.

Paul had thrown back his head and laughed. 'Since when did you care what Brenda thinks?'

Marilyn gave him a lop-sided grin. 'Sorry.'

'Don't be. She's never been very nice to you. She hasn't been very nice to me either, now that I come to think about it.'

Marilyn's eyes had filled up. 'Oh, Paul, are you very miserable?'

He'd patted her hand. 'Of course not, silly, you know me. Once I've got my golf I'm happy.'

And that had been that. They'd never discussed the matter again. Paul watched as his wife struggled with the zip of her skirt. Yes, the best part about today would be seeing the look on her face when the will was read out. It was a pity Marilyn wouldn't be there to enjoy it.

Brenda stood outside the church, counting the attendees and checking to see if she'd missed greeting anyone important.

'Hello, Brenda.' Ellie joined her aunt after thanking the priest for a lovely ceremony. It had actually been quite boring but she couldn't say that. Although she knew that Marilyn would have loved her to!

'Oh, hello, Ellie.' Brenda frowned at Ellie's scarf fluttering in the breeze. 'You look very . . . colourful.'

Ellie sighed. The woman just couldn't resist a dig. 'Thank you, Brenda, you look very nice too. Oh, hello, Paul.' Ellie smiled as her uncle joined them. 'How are you?'

Paul bent to kiss her cheek. 'I'm fine, my dear. You?'

'Oh, you know.' Ellie shrugged.

'Poor you. Losing your mum so young, then your dad last year and now Marilyn.'

'Oh, I don't know, Paul. I think it's a minor miracle that Marilyn lasted this long. Between the cakes, cigarettes and her nights out with "the girls", I expected her to croak years ago!'

'That's not a very nice thing to say at the woman's funeral Ellie,' Brenda said piously.

Paul chuckled. 'It's true though. And I can't believe that she just slipped away in her sleep. Not her style at all.'

Brenda was about to remonstrate with her husband for his equally disrespectful comments when she caught sight of Jo coming out of the church. 'Oh, my goodness! What on earth is Jo wearing?'

'Doesn't she look lovely?' Paul said smoothly and

took his wife firmly by the arm. 'Come along dear. We should be going. See you back at the house Ellie.'

'My name is Charles Gray, of Gray, Reilly, O'Mahoney and Associates,' the solicitor began. 'Firstly I would like to offer my condolences to you all. Mrs Connor was quite a character.'

'Get on with it,' Robbie muttered and received a sharp nudge from his mother.

'This won't take long,' Mr Gray continued, looking at the papers in front of him. 'Mrs Connor left very clear instructions and while her will was drawn up in 1981, she met with me every year since to re-evaluate the situation. This is addressed to you all in Mrs Connor's own words.'

'*To my dear friends in the ladies' club, I leave one thousand pounds. Have a few drinks on me, girls.*'

Ellie smiled. She'd no doubt that despite arthritic hips, enlarged livers and dodgy kidneys 'the girls' would comply quite happily with Marilyn's wishes.

'*To my great-niece and nephew, Joanna and William Summers, I leave the sum of five thousand pounds each.*'

Jo and Billy gaped at each other in delight.

Ben smiled at his wife. 'Trust Marilyn to think of the kids.'

'*And to my nephews Aidan and Robert Clarke, I leave the sum of ten thousand pounds each.*'

Robbie scowled. 'Is that all?'

'Shut up Robbie,' Karen said through gritted teeth.

'*To my niece, Elizabeth Summers, I leave the sum of ten thousand pounds along with my beloved grandfather clock.*'

You always looked after it for me over the years, Ellie, so it seems only fair that you should have it now.'

Ellie sighed and bent her head. Marilyn had always had a sick sense of humour.

Robbie smirked over at her. Well, that was a turn-up for the books! Dear cousin Ellie only getting ten grand and that battered old clock. It almost made up for his own disappointment.

'To my sister-in-law, Brenda Clarke –'

Brenda sat up straight in her chair. She hadn't expected an individual bequest. Still, she'd been a good sister-in-law to Marilyn.

'– I leave all my gym equipment. I know you will appreciate it, Brenda, and use it to good effect.'

Brenda's mouth fell open.

Jo and Billy sniggered as they eyed the large round frame of their great aunt.

'She'll have a heart attack if she climbs up on that bike!' Billy whispered.

'Shush,' Ben admonished his children, trying to keep a straight face.

'And to my other sister-in-law, Karen Clarke, I leave my car –'

Karen gasped. 'Oh my!'

'But she can't even drive!' Robbie protested. He'd had his eye on Marilyn's good-as-new BMW for a while now.

Mr Gray stared coldly at him over his glasses. *'– I've already organised and paid for driving lessons. Please use them, Karen, it would mean so much to me. You know, it's never too late.'*

187

Robert calculated that was forty-five thousand at least. Together with his portion of the house.

'*To my dearest brother Paul: I know you don't need or want my money and if I left you anything it would just end up sitting in a bank . . . so instead –*'

'What on earth –' Brenda started but Paul stopped her with a look.

'*– I have organised life membership of your golf club and a new set of clubs. Play a few rounds for me, brother.*' Mr Gray looked over his glasses at Paul and smiled. 'Such a thoughtful lady. I have already organised the membership, Mr Clarke, and your new clubs will be delivered next week.'

Paul beamed at him, though his eyes were bright with tears.

'*To my brother Robert,*' Mr Gray continued, '*I leave twenty thousand pounds. I'm sorry it's not more imaginative, Robert, but I couldn't think of anything you would prefer to money.*'

Robert permitted himself a small smile. Between the sale of the car, his twenty thousand pounds and his cut from the sale of the house . . .

'*And finally you are all welcome to look around the house and help yourself to any keepsakes. I hope they will give you as much pleasure as they did me. God bless you all.*'

Robbie looked scornfully around the room cluttered with ornaments and furniture. 'Load of junk,' he muttered to his father, but Robert wasn't listening.

'But what about the house?' he exploded. 'You haven't said anything about the house.'

'Ah, yes, the house . . .' Mr Gray shifted uneasily and looked at Paul.

'It's already sold, Robert.' Paul's voice was clear and calm.

'What the hell are you talking about?' Robert said angrily. Paul was even more senile than he thought.

Mr Gray nodded. 'Mr Clarke is correct, Mr Clarke. Mrs Connor made an arrangement with a financial institution in 1982. She sold them the house on the understanding that she could continue to reside here until she died.'

Robert paled. 'But what did she do with the money? This place must have been worth a couple of hundred grand.'

'Not in those days, Mr Clarke. The property market wasn't quite as buoyant as it is today. As to what she did with the proceeds, I can only assume she spent them.'

'In Barbados, and that month in Africa and the summer in Canada,' Brenda muttered bitterly. She'd assumed when Marilyn was going on all her lavish holidays that there must be plenty of money in the bank. How could she have been so selfish spending it all on herself? What about her family?

Paul glared at his wife. 'It was her money, why shouldn't she spend it? She was bloody right. And she's right about me too. I leave my money sitting in a bank account – well not any more. I'm going to take a leaf out of my sister's book and start to enjoy life.'

Ellie smiled brightly around the room. 'Right then, shall I make some tea? Good. Okay. Won't be a minute.'

She escaped to the kitchen and was filling the kettle when Paul appeared by her side. 'Well, well, well, that was quite a speech, Uncle!'

Paul looked shamefaced. 'A bit over the top, eh?'

'Not at all. Marilyn would have been proud of you.'

He took her hand and kissed it. 'You know she was very proud of you too, don't you? She was always talking about the way you used to climb up and wind that old clock. From the time you were a child, you'd be huffing and puffing with the effort. It gave her a great laugh.'

Ellie smiled but her eyes were full of tears. 'I think it was very mean of her to leave me Cyril. She knew how much I hated the bloody thing. And where am I going to put it in my little house?'

Paul looked slightly shocked. 'But you're not going to keep it, surely?'

'What else can I do? Who'd want to buy that monstrosity?'

Paul smiled enigmatically, led her out to the hall and stopped in front of the clock. 'Quite a lot of people actually. You see, Ellie, "that monstrosity" is an antique and worth more than the rest of Marilyn's estate put together. You can't really believe you were only getting ten thousand?'

Ellie looked away, embarrassed. She had been a little disappointed in her inheritance. Ben's business was doing much better these days but what with Jo's school fees and Billy starting college . . . She stared up at the clock that had stood in this hallway for as long as she could remember. 'I don't believe it.'

Paul smiled. 'It's true. You see Tommy wasn't very keen on tying his money up in bonds and shares. He didn't trust them. So instead he bought Cyril. And he told Marilyn: "Whatever happens, love, hold onto Cyril. He'll look after you".'

'But why didn't she ever tell anyone?'

Paul nodded towards the living room. 'She thought life might be a lot easier for you if that lot thought you'd only been left a keepsake. She was adamant there were to be no arguments over her estate.'

Ellie's mind flashed back to that day sitting at the kitchen table all those years ago.

'Ellie? There you are!' Karen rushed out to hug her. 'Are you all right?'

'Fine, Karen. Just admiring my . . . inheritance.'

Karen looked doubtfully at the clock. 'Well, as long as you're happy, love, that's all that matters. Can you believe Marilyn left me her beautiful car? I can't wait to learn to drive it.'

Robert appeared at her side. 'Don't be ridiculous, woman. We'll be selling the car.'

Karen glared at him. 'Let's get one thing straight, Robert. Marilyn left her car to me, not us, and I have absolutely no intention of selling it.' She winked at Paul and Ellie and stalked off leaving Robert with his mouth open.

'She'll see sense,' he said nervously. 'It's just the shock. She'll come around.'

And he hurried after her. 'Karen? Darling?'

Paul and Ellie looked at each other and burst out laughing.

'What's the joke?' Ben asked curiously as he and the kids joined them.

Ellie slipped into his arms and hugged him. 'I'll tell you later.'

Jo frowned up at the clock. 'I don't know why Marilyn left you that ugly old thing, Mum. I think maybe it was a joke. Are you going to dump it?'

'Dump it?' Ellie looked at her daughter in horror but there was a twinkle in her eye as she leaned across and kissed the clock affectionately. 'Oh, I could never do that, love! Cyril is part of the family!'

Delivering Happyware
Anna Davis

I have written a plaintive love song called 'Twenty-Six, Divorced and Jewish'. The title has to be a secret one, known only to me, because the song tells the story of the way I feel about Sean Prosser. Nobody must know that this is what it's about because I am only sixteen and because Sean isn't quite divorced yet. I don't even want to tell my friend Louise.

The first lines of the song go:

Time after time I sit alone waiting for you.
Time after time, staring at the phone,
I never call you.

That first line is about me, sitting in my room, thinking about Sean, waiting for something to happen between us. The second line is also about me but it doesn't quite work because I do call Sean very frequently to find out when his band, Citizen Duane (the best band in Cardiff), are playing gigs, and to chat with him and check on how he is. It's him who doesn't call me, but I had to put it the other way around so it would fit into the song properly.

The chord sequence has lots of minors in it – especially A minor and D minor. These minor chords contribute to the song's plaintive quality. I've also made up a chord which is a bit like D minor but in which you move the third finger of your left hand (the hand that holds down the strings) from second string on the third fret to third string on the third fret. This gives the chord an edgy, ominous quality. I don't suppose I really invented it – it must already exist and have some stupid elongated name like D minor seventh add four, or something. But I don't really care what anybody else calls that chord. As far as I'm concerned it's the special Sean chord.

I am thinking about the special Sean chord as the bus twists its way into St Mellons, and I'm wondering what Louise will say when I get home and ring her up to tell her where I've been. Louise and I have been out to St Mellons on the bus before, to see what Sean's house looks like. But we've never been inside it. We got the address out of the phone book and went over there on a day when we knew Citizen Duane were up at the recording studio so Sean would be out. We didn't want him to know we'd been snooping around. The house is actually a very ordinary two-up-two-down semi on a bland estate full of cul-de-sacs and grass verges. My theory is that Sean and his wife Carol chose that house because they were trying to be a normal couple so they wanted their home to be as boring and mundane as possible to make them *feel* normal. But that would never have worked for Sean, not in the long run – he's too special, too talented, and Carol just couldn't understand that. So now he lives there on his own.

Today I'm not just going out there to visit the house. I'm going to visit Sean. And I know he's at home because I phoned him to ask if I could come over.

'Jane! Hi.' He sounds surprised to see me. He shouldn't be – it was only two hours ago that I phoned him.

'Hello, Sean.' Actually, *I* should be the surprised one. When I last saw Sean at the gig on Wednesday his hair was short. But today it's long – comes right down over his shoulders.

He sees me looking. 'Extensions.' He gestures at the hair. 'Do you like them?'

'Yes. They're cool.' He looks like a lion. He looks beautiful.

'Come on in.' He opens the front door wider for me to walk past him. Stepping into the hall, I notice his feet are bare. I've never seen his bare feet before.

I wander through to the lounge. Previously I've only glimpsed this room through the net curtains. It's smaller than I'd have expected. And it's immaculate, which is something of a surprise. I'd thought it might be full of takeaway packaging and dirty ashtrays now that Carol's gone, but it seems that Sean knows how to take care of himself. Either that or he's cleared up for *me* . . .

'Do you want some coffee?' He's standing in the doorway behind me. I turn around and find myself staring at his neck. He has the *best* neck . . .

'Yes, please.'

He goes out to the kitchen and I sit down on the brown leather couch, placing my guitar on the floor beside me. I'm suddenly painfully aware of the Wham! stickers all over the case. My Wham! days are *so* over, but I'd never bothered to remove those bloody stickers. I have a go at the edge of one of them now but it's really stubborn so I give up – it would be more embarrassing to be caught trying to get rid of the stickers than it would be for him to see them. Sean's battered acoustic guitar is propped up against the wall next to the TV. I've never heard him play the guitar – when he's on stage he just sings. But I know he uses the guitar for writing songs. Sometimes when I'm in my bedroom playing *my* guitar and writing *my* songs, I've imagined what it would be like for the two of us to sit around having a jam together, drinking beer and jamming around, trying riffs out. It's always seemed to me that this would be heaven. And then I've imagined other things too . . . Things I wouldn't care to admit to and which could never really happen, because I'm sixteen and a schoolgirl, and he's twenty-six and talented and the most beautiful man in Cardiff.

'Here you go.' Sean is back, passing me a yellow mug of instant coffee with the milk already in. 'Hope you don't take sugar. I don't have any.'

'No, no sugar for me.' Our hands touch as I take the mug. I'm blushing now – *why* do I always blush . . . He sits down in the armchair opposite me and crosses his legs. I like the smell of his house. It smells of him.

'So,' he says, raising one eyebrow. 'Where's this Happyware catalogue, then? I want to hear your pitch. I want to see what you have for sale.'

Selling Happyware is our summer holiday job – mine and Louise's. A Happyware seller in Rhiwbina (the part of Cardiff where Louise lives), sold a broom to Louise's mum, and it occurred to us that this might be the sort of job that we could get into. We really need to make some money while we're waiting for our O-level results, and as the summer of '87 has turned out to be a shiny, golden, vest-top sort of season we thought it would be so much nicer to be wandering about with a bunch of catalogues knocking on doors than to be stuck in some sweaty shop in town. We decided to do this from my house in Pontcanna – partly because there are already Happyware sellers in Rhiwbina, and partly because Louise's mum is a gorgon and will go apeshit if she finds out that her daughter is selling household equipment door-to-door. My mum, on the other hand, is an intellectual liberal-thinking sort of person (except on Sunday mornings when she goes mad about me and my brother not doing any housework) and said she thought it was an 'admirable entrepreneurial venture which should be encouraged'.

We phoned the number on the back of the catalogue and this stumpy man called Selwyn came round in his van with a pile of catalogues. As it turns out, Selwyn is a sort of emperor of Happyware selling. He told us at great length how he's been doing it for thirty years and how when he started he was just a humble schoolboy, 'rather like yourselves, girls', but that now he has risen to the lofty heights of being 'area manager'. He took himself so seriously that it was all we could do not to laugh in his face. He kept saying 'There's an indefinable something which makes a good Happyware salesman. I can't tell you what the something is but I know it when I see it, girls, and I can see it in your eyes . . . You've got all the right ingredients.' He got very close to me when he said this and I could see all the blackheads on his nose and the dirt on the inside rim of his shirt collar. His breath didn't smell too great either, so you can be sure I was quick to jump off the couch on the pretext of offering him another cup of tea. When I got back from the kitchen, he had a street map out on the floor and was showing Louise our 'patch' – basically most of Canton and Pontcanna, and the Pontcanna end of Llandaff. Then he started acting like this was a job interview, and he said, 'So, girls, when you go out to sell the Happyware, what do you think is the first thing you'll do?'

'Well, Selwyn . . .' I put on this mock-serious voice, kind of taking the piss out of the way he had been talking, and I could see Louise was trying not to crease up. 'I suppose we walk around the streets and stick the catalogues through the letterboxes –'

'Wrong!' Selwyn sounded absolutely delighted that I'd got it wrong; I guess because it gave him the opportunity to deliver another lecture. 'What you do, girls, is you ring on the doorbells and you say, "Good morning, madam" – or "sir". "I have here the answer to all your household needs in the form of this Happyware catalogue. Our products have *value and verve*" – that's the key catchphrase. And then here comes the skilful bit: you have to evaluate your customer, *psychologically*, and you give a specific plug to a few appropriate products. For example, if you can hear a dog barking you might show them the pet toys on page fourteen; if the lady looks a little hard-up you might stick to the hand-brushes at the front; your more sophisticated housewife might go for the freezer boxes and pepper grinder – you shouldn't bother that sort of lady with cleaning products, they probably have a little woman come in to take care of all that anyway . . . Then at the back of the catalogue there's our new jewellery line which is proving very popular . . .' I think he noticed at this point that his audience was not exactly rapt, because he stopped and cleared his throat: 'Anyway, girls, you get my drift. Ask them if they would like to keep the catalogue to peruse at their leisure for a few days. Then when you go back to collect the orders, make sure you retrieve the catalogue – oh yes, girls, you don't think I'll be giving you a fresh set every week, do you? Every catalogue must be collected or the cost will be docked from your commission.'

We started with Palace Road in Llandaff, thinking it would be good for selling Happyware because it's all big detached houses where the wives are quite churchy and stay at home out of choice, baking their own bread and stuff like that. But these women all turned their noses up at us. Before we could begin our pitch they'd be closing the door with one of those politely pained smiles that means fuck off. Some of them even said,

'Not today, thank you.' Can you *believe* that anyone really says that these days? I hadn't realised how horrible doorstep selling could be. When Pencisely Road was no better we decided to give up on Llandaff and head down to Canton. Canton is more working class – people there are more likely to be in need of the odd mop and bucket.

This proved a good decision. Wyndham Road was the best road of all. Lots of people placed orders right there on the spot and others agreed to take the catalogue and look through it. An old lady asked us in for a cup of tea but we said no because she clearly didn't have the dosh for much more than a dustpan and brush and we had to crack on. A completely tasteless woman with peroxide hair went through the whole catalogue and ordered the entire jewellery line! It's hard to believe that anyone would really wear that stuff. A forty-ish bloke with receding hair bought a load of gardening equipment and a toast greeting – oh yes, we sell toast greetings: they look like plastic pastry cutters and you're supposed to press them into your slice of bread before you toast it so that when the toast pops up it tells you to have a nice day. They're magnetised so you can stick them to the fridge.

Severn Grove wasn't as good as Wyndham Road but it wasn't bad. By the time we'd done Kings Road we'd got rid of all the catalogues and taken a fair few orders. We got some chips from Iannos the Greek and ate them as we walked back to my house in the sunshine. We were looking good, Louise and me. I was wearing my black cropped top and my denim cut-offs. She was wearing my white jeans. She still hasn't given them back actually – I hope she hasn't stretched them. We were singing – we sing all the time because music is the most important thing in our lives. We sang 'Break Out' by Swing Out Sister, doing an impression of the way the lead singer can't say her 'r's. Then we sang the new song we'd heard on the radio that morning which cracked us up for its sheer crapness, called 'Wang Chung'. Then we got more serious and sang 'Slap Your Head', our favourite Citizen Duane song. When we stopped singing, we talked about the perfect boyfriend. She said he'd have to be a Happyware area manager, and we both laughed. Then I said my ideal man would be twenty-six, divorced and Jewish – and we gave each other a meaningful look because we both knew that I was talking about Sean. And that's when I got the idea for the secret title of my song.

Later, alone in my room, I wrote the final lyric:

This is the way to move it on.

Sean is flicking through the catalogue while I sip my coffee. 'Christ, who buys this shit?'

'Lots of people, actually.' I don't know why I'm getting defensive about Happyware. I guess because it was my excuse for coming to see him and now the excuse is crumbling. I usually like the way he raises one eyebrow at a time in that quizzical manner of his, but at this moment I'm feeling like a dumb kid and I know he's taking the piss out of me.

'So, what's in here for me, then?'

'Well . . .' I struggle for a Selwyn-type psychological analysis. 'On page thirty-five there's a special zip-up carrying case for brushes and combs. Could be handy now you've got your hair long.'

He shrugs (how I love his broad shoulders . . .). 'I'm not really supposed to brush this too hard or the extensions will fall out.'

'How about the shoe cleaning stuff on page twenty-three, then?'

But he's spotted something else. 'I like the slogan underneath the picture,' he says. '"The happy toast greeting makes breakfast a friendlier meal!" I'll take it!' He smiles at me in a friendly sort of way. 'Now, Jane, what is it that you're going to play for me?'

'Play for you?' A new panic. 'What do you mean?'

He nods at the guitar. 'You wouldn't drag that all the way here unless you intended to play me something, would you?'

I'm terrified. Absolutely bloody terrified. What was I *thinking* of? Well, it's obvious what I was thinking of, but now it seems like the stupidest idea in the world. I open my mouth to speak. 'I . . .'

He leans forward. 'Yes?'

And then the phone rings from the kitchen, making me jump, and he's leaping out of his chair and striding over. (His legs look so good in those stone-washed jeans.)

'Yeah?'

What a stylish way he has of answering the phone. Straight to the point. I've heard that 'yeah' so many times.

'I've told you, Carol, I'm not prepared to discuss that. You'll have to do it through your solicitor . . . Yeah, that's right. No, you stay away from my dad.'

Sean's dad is filthy rich. Smelly Chris, the Citizen Duane PA-man, told me that's how Sean can afford a house and a car. His dad helps him out.

'I'm warning you, Carol, stay away from Dad or things will get much harder for you . . . Yeah, good. Bye.'

He slams the phone down and I hear him mutter, 'Fucking bitch.' Then there's the sound of the fridge opening and closing, and he comes back in carrying two cans of Stella. 'Here you go.' He lobs one over to me. I just about manage to catch it. 'Where's your friend Louise today, then? I thought you two were joined at the hip.'

'Us? No. She had to go out shopping with her mother.' I snap the ringpull and take a big gulp.

He flops back down in the armchair and runs a hand through his mane. (He has such elegant hands . . .) 'Her mother's pretty strict, isn't she,' he muses. 'It's a mistake to be like that. She's going to lose Louise if she's not careful.'

'Yeah . . . Actually, Sean, I do have something to play for you. There's this song I've written. The tune's okay but I could do with a second opinion on the lyrics . . .'

Tuesday was the day for collecting the Happyware orders. The air over Pontcanna Street was rippling with heat and the Coke in our cans went flat and warm almost before we could raise them to our lips. On the way to Wyndham Road we sang 'Digging Your Scene' by the Blow Monkeys. Also we tried to work out why some of the men who chat us up at Citizen Duane gigs go for Louise and why others go for me, and we decided that it's to do with our facial features. She's got a big face, high cheekbones and full lips – so the men who like soft features go for her, while the men who like small, sharp, elfin features fancy me. Not that we do anything with those losers anyway. It's just that we're trying to understand how men think.

The old woman on Wyndham Road ordered a dustpan and brush. Lots of women bought disinfectant and air-fresheners of various kinds but our most popular produce was the 'speedy mop' featured on the front of the catalogue. Iannos the Greek bought some freezer pots and tried to persuade us to come back in the evening and help him cook the chips. We asked him how much he'd pay us and he just winked and laughed his horrible laugh.

We thought we'd done really well, but afterwards, when we totted up the totals in my bedroom, we found we'd barely sold three hundred quid's worth of Happyware. That would only produce thirty quid commission for us, and we'd have to split that 50–50! In addition to the two afternoons' work we'd already done for this thirty measly quid, we still had to deliver the goods. Not only that but lots of people were out today, so we hadn't been able to get their orders or retrieve the catalogues. This could drag on and on . . . Shop work was starting to look appealing in comparison.

I played my song to Louise and she said she liked it,

but then she started up this really stupid conversation, saying that she wanted to be a musician more than anything else and more than I could possibly imagine. This got on my nerves, as she knows full well how much I want to be a musician. It was me who first discovered Citizen Duane and it's *me* that's learning the guitar and writing songs, not her. She told me she's going to save up the money to buy a bass guitar, and that bass players are in short supply, so she stands a real chance of getting into a good band – a better chance than I would as a singer/guitarist. And all this in spite of our plans to form a band *together* and play my songs.

Selwyn turned up at five to take the orders and he was pleased with our three hundred quid's worth until we told him we don't want to sell Happyware any more after we've delivered the stuff. He tried to persuade us otherwise, saying it takes a while to 'warm up your patch' and 'hone your sales-pitch'. When we stuck to our guns, he said, 'You know, girls, if just *one* of you gave up and the other one carried on selling the Happyware alone, you wouldn't have to split the commission 50–50 . . .' This hit a raw nerve after the conversation we were having before he arrived, but he wasn't to know that.

Louise went home not long after Selwyn left, and I went upstairs and played my song over and over until the fingertips on my left hand were red and sore, etched through with deep grooves where I'd been pressing the strings down.

I know Sean is watching me as I start playing my song,

but I don't dare look up at him. I hug my guitar close and keep my eyes on my left hand as it moves over the fretboard. Somehow my fingers are finding the right places. Somehow this is really happening. I'm really sitting in Sean's living room, in front of Sean, playing the special Sean chord. My voice is really singing those words which are so full of longing – it's maybe a little thin and wobbly on the first line or two, but it's gathering strength. My right hand is plucking away for all it's worth and so far I haven't hit a single wrong string. Somehow I am coasting along through my song, playing and singing it with even more feeling then I've ever been able to give it when alone in my room. I feel as though I'm about to cry. I feel as though my heart is about to explode.

This is the way to move it on.

Wednesday. Louise turned up so early that I was still in bed. Selwyn knocked on the door while we were eating our toast and asked us to come out and give him a hand getting the merchandise in from the van. He was obviously pissed off that we were jacking in the Happyware and he had another go at trying to get us to change our minds, but to no avail. He said he was clearly wrong about what sort of girls we were, and that he had no time for wasters. Then he told us he'd be back tomorrow to collect the money and drove off with a big sniff. I'll be glad to see the back of him – smelly old git.

After he left we began to realise the full extent of the

nightmare it was going to be, delivering all this stuff without any form of transport – things like the jewellery and the toast greeting were small and easy to carry but the brooms and mops with their long handles were hell. We walked to Tesco's in Canton to nick a trolley, and even with the trolley it was impossible to carry everything. Back and forth we went between Canton and my house as the day began to steam and boil.

Happyware is shit. Never buy it. It was all we could do to make sure the heads didn't fall off those brooms before we could take the money. And the speedymops looked as though they would disintegrate in two seconds flat. We were so knackered and thirsty by the end of Wyndham Road that we were tempted to accept the old lady's offer of tea. To cheer ourselves up, we sang 'Lips like Sugar' by Echo and the Bunnymen and Citizen Duane's 'In That Light', but things were not right between us.

We left Iannos the Greek until last but when we got to his shop we were still carrying a load of stuff for people who were out. Iannos seemed to have forgotten that he'd ordered some freezer boxes, and grumbled about having to pay for them, so that we had to threaten him by saying that if he didn't cough up the cash we'd start buying our chips elsewhere.

All morning I had managed to keep my feelings to myself, but finally, when we were eating our chips on a bench under a conker tree on Llandaff fields with the unclaimed Happyware items parked beside us in the trolley, I just had to ask her.

'Louise, what is going on with you? You're being

really funny with me and I don't know why.'

And then she said it. Just said it. 'I think Sean fancies me.'

I'm shaking as I lift my right hand, let it rest on top of the guitar. I've never felt so naked. I try to steady my breathing and I wait . . .

'Hey, that's not bad,' says Sean. 'Not bad at all. You've got all the right ingredients there.'

'I have?'

'Yeah, sure you have. All you need to do is . . .'

'What? What do I need to do?'

'Hang on, what are the first couple of lines again?'

I have to swallow but I can't. 'Time after time I sit alone waiting for you. Time after time, staring at the phone, I never call you.'

He scratches his head. My face is hot. Slowly, he stretches out his arms towards me . . . Gently, he extracts my guitar, leans back with it.

'Nice,' he says, adjusting the tuning. 'Nylon strings wouldn't be loud enough for gigging, though. You want to get a steel string guitar. Easier to amplify.'

'Yes?'

'Hmm.' He scratches his head again. 'What you need to do, Jane, is to take the lyrics you've got and obscure the meaning a little. You don't want to be too obvious. Keep it subtle.'

'You think so?'

'Sure. How's about:

Time after time I watch the walls waiting for you . . .

Wade through wine, stepping on the mines until I call you.'

He raises one eyebrow and smiles at me.

'Wade . . . through wine? Stepping on the . . . mines?'

'Yeah. You have what they call an *internal rhyme* there.'

'I have?'

'Want another lager?'

I haven't drunk my first yet, but he's up and off to the kitchen. He's humming my song to himself as he goes. I should be happy that he's helping me. Why can't I feel happy?

'So do you think Louise's mum is going to let her buy that bass guitar she's after?' he calls from the kitchen. 'I've got this old amp kicking around, and she can have it if she wants.'

I looked hard at Louise to try to work out if she was kidding me. '*What?*'

'I do. I think he fancies me.'

'He doesn't!'

She took the biggest chip and ate it whole. 'You can think what you like. But I've noticed him looking at me lately. He was doing it at the gig last Wednesday when he was singing "Bumpy Ride".'

'Oh, come on, Louise. We're just a couple of kids to him. He could have anyone in Cardiff – *anyone* – so why should he want *you* of all people!'

'I don't know why he wants me – but he wants me.'

'You're wrong. *I* saw him first and *I'm* the one who

phones him all the time and I know him better than you do. If anyone's going to do anything with Sean then it's going to be *me*. But it won't be me because he's not interested in me – not like that. And he's not interested in you either so you'd better just forget it or we're going to have a big falling out, you and me. Got it?'

She was smiling a nightmare of a smile. 'I can't help the way he looks at me,' she said.

Sean tosses me another can of Stella and this time I miss it and have to scrabble about under the coffee table to find it.

'So when do your O-level results come out?' he says.

'Not till August.'

'Long time to wait.' He fetches a pack of Silk Cut from the mantlepiece and offers one to me.

I decline and watch him take one for himself.

'Who's going to get the highest marks then? You or Louise?'

'Me,' I say. I take no joy in saying it. It's just a fact. 'I'm the one with the brains and she's the one with the looks, or hadn't you noticed?'

'That's not very fair, now, is it?' He lights the fag.

'On me? Or on her?'

He raises one eyebrow. And a whole phase of my life is over.

Home and Dry
Martina Devlin

Save. He stopped typing and pressed the Control plus Home keys to return to the beginning. Yes, that captured it succinctly. Ben stretched his taut shoulder muscles with an extravagant sweep of limbs and read over what he'd written.

Dublin-based single man (39) seeks woman with view to marriage. Home-owners only need apply – house preferred but not essential, please specify location.

Just two sentences, but he felt he'd distilled his life essence into them. Ben allowed a needle of resentment to jag as he doubled the typeface size so the engorged words swallowed the screen. If that gnarled-toed-teaser Adele hadn't led him up the garden path and then treated him like a packet of slug pellets he'd be home and dry by now instead of posting an electronic 'come and get me girls' on a lonely hearts' website.

He needed a home. He couldn't live in his sister's spare room indefinitely and there was no way he could afford to buy a house in Dublin on his wages. Renting wasn't an option either; Ben hadn't been impressed by the flats he'd viewed which were either too cramped, too squalid or too expensive. Especially too expensive.

Shortchanged, he mooched out to the kitchen to boil the kettle, where a doubt assailed him about the brevity of his prose. Shouldn't he have included some personal details, maybe build or temperament? He abandoned the kettle to assess his appearance in the mirror studded with seashells his sister had hanging in her hall. Dipping his head he peered among the shadows caused by a jostling coat rack at a planed-down face, all right angles and triangles. Nothing to complain about in that department.

Ben carried his coffee through to the living room where his laptop computer was plugged in. He rehearsed the two sentences he knew already by rote, still pondering whether they were too bald. And speaking of bald, maybe he should mention he wasn't. Or was that too pathetic, own teeth and hair territory; would a woman want something more – he winced at the word – dynamic? Surely she'd prefer the unvarnished truth of a trade-off, women were always insisting on being treated as equals and what could be more egalitarian than to tell it straight.

Ben understood what he wanted and he was fairly confident he'd grasped what women wanted. His stipulations were simple: someone with a house; he required a home. In return she could wear a wedding band, describe herself as his wife, take his name or keep her own as she liked. Quid pro quo, life was all about bartering. Men and women swapped what they needed from each other and called it a relationship.

Ben realised such a pared-down view was best not expressed, women took exception to his deconstruction of the exchange system. Overly simplistic they termed it. Mono-dimensional. Even oafish.

He did not consider himself an oaf. Not at all. He had a degree in English, ergo he'd read Chaucer with the help of translation notes and managed half of *Finnegans Wake* before deciding life was too short for books without punctuation. And women were drawn to him, there had been a seamless succession since the age of eighteen. Never married any of them but never hurt any of them permanently either, he'd enriched their lives and moved on. Although not before visiting art galleries with Barbara, discussing poetry with Birgit, attending the ballet with Adele. Nobody could accuse him of failing to appreciate culture.

He'd even toyed with the idea of working in the arts but somehow it never slotted into place. For now he had a part-time job framing pictures – it wasn't the most challenging position but it suited Ben's checklist of minimal stress in return for slightly above subsistence level remuneration. And absolutely no responsibility.

Verging on two decades ago when he left college, Ben had never envisaged himself framing Mucha prints and living in Kitty's spare room. He imagined he'd either become a rock god who composed lyrics of universal potency or the author of a seminal sci-fi novel. In the meantime he'd travel.

This was the longest time he'd spent in Ireland since himself and Mia (horseshoe scar on her forehead, legacy of a driving accident) graduated and set sail in 1980-something. He preferred not to compute the exact date, it sounded too long ago. He wasn't even sure how he'd wound up in Dublin, his intention had been to spend a fortnight belatedly attending to family duties and then jet off for Cairo.

But somehow he'd lost the heart for travelling. He was so settled with his last girlfriend, Adele (a ballerina, Utopia had been glimpsed), it came as a jolt when she complained he wasn't dynamic enough for her. Unambitious. A drifter.

'Babe,' he explained, 'ambition is for dwarf intellects. True achievers know nothing of value can be attained by effort, it must be arrived at through osmosis. From contemplation and from being at ease with your essential oneness.' He transfixed her with the eyes Barbara (perpetual minty scent) had once compared to Michelangelo's Sistine Chapel sky and expanded his theory. 'Consider the flowers, they don't jockey for position or fawn on the boss for a raise, they're content to be.'

It was Ben's stock answer when people occasionally commented on his lack of drive. It had silenced critics in the past; Adele simply packed his bags for him.

'So long, petal,' she snorted.

Which is how he came to be in Dublin. Never was he so unprepared – no girlfriend, no home, no airline

ticket in the zipped inner pocket of his rucksack. His
sister was plugging the gap in the roof department but
he suspected her hospitality was finite. His misgivings
were confirmed the previous evening when she remarked, her back to him as she washed their dinner
dishes, 'Lisa at work was asking after you.'

'Do I know her?' He did not lift his head from the
daily paper he'd liberated from her briefcase.

'No, but she knows you. "The brother still with
you?" she asked. "He is," I answered, "it's been five
months now." "Makes sense," said Lisa, "a spare room
is like a mad dog. A liability."'

Ben waited, expression wary, no longer scanning the
newspaper. But Kitty continued her methodical stroking
and rinsing of suds. The conversation was concluded.

Ben watched the infinitesimal movements of his
sister's narrow back with its twin outcrops of bone.
A memory of their mother washing dishes in a corres-
pondingly systematic fashion contracted his stomach
and he thought, with an emotion vacillating between
guilt and resentment, that he should find time to visit
her in Clonmacdove. He'd only been there once since
his return and it wasn't a success. He blamed it on the
aunt with whom his mother lived; she clucked over
him, urging milky tea and slices of Swiss roll, moving
him to an armchair by the fire where he battled against
a debilitating sense of drowsiness. His mother was in
vacant attendance throughout the charade.

'Seeing you has bucked her up no end,' whispered
Aunt Breda as he left – his customary bonhomie cloud-
ed over from spending time with a mother who didn't

betray, by so much as a lone facial flicker, that she recognised him. She had Alzheimer's disease. Breda took her in when she left a shepherd's pie in the oven and went to Cork for a day's shopping, fitting on winter coats as fire engines roared towards her smouldering home.

Ben noted the twisted bra strap traversing Kitty's right shoulder blade and acknowledged she was tiring of supporting him. His sister turned and smiled, their father's crinkling eyes in their mother's clotted cream face. Embarrassed by her oblique notice to quit, she opened a bottle of Merlot and they sat in front of the television set. Together apart.

Kitty had already started work as a teacher in the school where she was now a head of department when Ben bought his backpack and caught the boat from Dun Laoghaire. Mia nestled against his shoulder during the train journey from Holyhead to London. He swapped her for Sandy (her body undulated like her initial), whom he met in the Brixton pub where he worked. After Sandy's abortion – it cost them their holiday in Corfu and their relationship in rapid succession – he strapped on his backpack and relocated to Germany.

In Munich he found work in a hotel laundry. He also found Birgit (inexplicable predilection for Irish Mist liqueur), who had an apartment in the suburbs. That's when he realised the benefit of women with vacant possession of a roof to cover their heads – and his.

He took the train to Naples when Birgit's latent hygiene obsession spilled over into a daily blitzkrieg on germs, clutching the address of Rosa. She had waitressed for a summer in the Munich hotel where he worked. Rosa, it emerged, was only seventeen and a schoolgirl so he abandoned the notion of crashing with her, not least because her roof was shared by two brothers and a set of parents.

Retreating as far as Rome, Ben was diverted from his intention to push on to Trieste and then into Eastern Europe by Jackie (she had a porn star's taste in underwear), a student of art history. She shared a flat with Barbara, also an American, but Barbara liked to wander around the Roman galleries so for much of the time it felt to Jackie and Ben as though they were alone in the apartment. The scaffolding of their days constructed itself into a modus vivendi: Ben distracted Jackie and Rome distracted Barbara.

This arrangement collapsed when Barbara returned to New Jersey to continue her education and Jackie's allowance failed to cover the rent. Ben couldn't contribute, he was working as an artist's model and while it paid minimally, he regarded himself as subsidising the arts. But he wasn't subsidising the relationship, so Jackie moved out of her airy apartment with its cherubim-festooned fountain in the forecourt and into a noisier, more crowded one. She lost her allure for Ben.

It didn't matter because by this stage he had saved the air fare to JFK, thrown the rucksack into an overhead rack on a Greyhound bus and been driven through upstate New York into New Jersey. Where he attached himself to Barbara. She was the sole occupant of a clapboard house in a row of identikits. It had a porch with twin rockers and he yearned for that porch and the catatonic state he could lull himself into on the white painted rocker when Barbara was replaced by Betty (she had so many moles on her body that touching her was like handling a braille route map).

There were other women and although they never overlapped there was rarely more than a few weeks' hiatus. Nancy, who joked he only dated women named after America's First Ladies; Donna, who disproved the theory; Susan, whose blue-black skin was the sleekest he'd ever caressed . . . So many names, shapes, hues, temperaments. They shared one attribute in common: from Birgit onwards they each had their own place.

Now here he was in Dublin with a heart which, although not quite broken, had been bounced off the ground somewhat carelessly, he felt. In his newfound fragility, Ben lost the urge to travel. He equated his battered rucksack with his slightly dented heart and packed it out of sight in his sister's wardrobe.

Ben's eyes were on the television screen, one of Kitty's interminable murder mysteries, but his brain was whirring. His sister wanted him out of her house, she preferred a semi-detached brother to an en-suite one. Perhaps he should move on, it's not as if he were particularly fond of Terenure. To-Be-Endured, it should be renamed. But he needed a breather, time to regroup.

Just as the fishmonger's delivery boy was denounced as the poisoner, the solution slammed into Ben with such force he could only conclude it was inspired. He'd advertise for a wife on the Net.

'Of course,' he said.

His sister's fingers halted their mechanical stroking of the sofa nap. 'You knew it was the fishmonger's assistant?'

Ben twiddled an imaginary moustache. 'Of course,' he purred. 'The clue lay in the rainbow trout.'

'I don't remember any rainbow trout.' Kitty's frown was rooted in disbelief as she ransacked her memory banks; she prided herself on her powers of observation.

'Only codding.' Ben ducked from the cushion that was lobbed in his direction. 'Why don't you have the bathroom first while I clear up in here? You're looking a little wan tonight, Kitty-cat, nothing a sound night's sleep won't set right and you'll be your usual vibrant self in the morning.'

There was a wine bottle and two empty glasses to dispose of but he presented it as a marathon mop-up. Kitty was touched by his consideration and by her brother's use of the nickname all but consigned to childhood years – their mother certainly never remembered it. In addition she had the uneasy sense she might have been a little too forthright with Ben, he was her only sibling and she should prize the opportunity to reacquaint herself with him.

She hovered by the door. 'Need a sub until payday?'

He considered; some socialising was inevitable with the women who responded to his advertisement.

'Perhaps a few pounds for bus fares if you can spare it, just to tide me over.'

'I'll leave something on the hall table for you, Ben.'

He waited until he heard the bathroom lock slide and click. Good woman Kitty, three notes. That should take care of the first date or two at least. Ben whistled as he dropped the dark green bottle into the bin instead of following Kitty's procedure of standing it to one side of the kitchen door for recycling. It was a tune from *My Fair Lady*; he'd taken Adele to see the musical for their second anniversary shortly before she flailed him for his lack of ambition.

'Wait and see, Miss Tippy Toes,' he muttered. 'I can be as dynamic as any of your Sydney media types.'

It rankled that she'd replaced him with a radio station executive; Ben was the one who'd always upgraded in the past. What he lacked in material assets he compensated for with his beguiling ways. It was effortless in him. He discovered some inkling of his capacity when he was eight and a shopkeeper caught him sneaking out with a comic tucked down the leg of his jeans. Ben slipped into supplication mode, teardrops trembling, and promised he'd never steal so much as a glance again. His career as a serial charmer was unleashed. But a charmer implies artifice and for Ben it was never contrived, it was as natural as breathing.

He called up his advertisement on the screen before bed and inserted another word at the start so it read, *Charming Dublin-based single man (39) seeks woman with view to marriage.* Satisfied, he pressed Send and the website posted up his lonely-heart pitch together with his own email address, charming@ireland.com. Ben sank into the sleep of the just.

Three women responded on the first day.

There was one discounted immediately because the

address was in Longford, too far away. Now that he was back in Dublin he might as well stay in the city environs instead of allowing himself to be lured out to the midlands. There was another from Stoneybatter which intrigued him because the woman demanded he define *charming*.

The third was from Malahide, which he favoured because everybody knew you needed a wad to live there. If he were prepared to offer a woman his name in return for a home, he'd prefer the premises to be comfortable.

Ben deleted the email from Longford, snapped back 'meet me and puzzle no longer over definitions' to Stoneybatter and arranged a date for the following evening with the Malahide favourite. They would meet at the film centre where you could linger over a glass of wine or coffee, scan the bulletin of forthcoming attractions, browse in the bookshop and – although only as a last resort – take in a film.

He borrowed one of Kitty's disposable razors to shave, congratulating himself on how well his tan was surviving the dearth of sunshine, and checked the inbox on his laptop before setting off. Mail from Stoneybatter again.

'I like puzzling over definitions, it defines my life,' she wrote.

He cracked his knuckles, composing a riposte.

'I've discussed definitions over gin in London, Heineken in Munich, espresso in Rome, Pepsi in New Jersey and Foster's in Sydney. In Dublin I won't do it without a pint of Guinness to hand. Meet me in The Palace Bar on Fleet Street at 8 p.m. tomorrow.

I'll be the one with the foam moustache.'

This business of being witty on screen was less demanding than he'd anticipated.

Malahide and he were connecting swimmingly until he lobbed in a question about her property. She admitted she didn't own her apartment overlooking the estuary, it was rented.

'I thought you were joking about home-owners only need apply,' she stuttered, matching ovals of disbelief flaring on her cheeks.

Ben was astonished. 'What gave you that idea?' Maybe he'd need to re-jig the ad.

Malahide was still spluttering. 'The reference to marriage – nobody bothers with electronic dating because they want to get married, they do it to meet people for sex.'

Ben reflected he'd been too long out of Ireland as he spent some of Kitty's loan on a taxi home. Gloomily he decided to pack some condoms for his date with Stoneybatter in case she expected to inspect the merchandise.

His spirits soared when he signed onto his laptop and saw there was new mail from a fourth contender. She was from Greystones and responded with a question. No wonder women never answered questions, they were too busy asking them.

'Why do you want to get married?' she queried.

He flirted with the idea of the truth, abandoned it as something to be left in storage for absolute emergencies and delayed replying while he brushed his teeth and raided the fridge, thereby cancelling out the benefits of fluoride.

'I'm just a genuine guy,' he tapped. 'I'm at a place in my life now where I'm ready to commit to someone, not play silly games. I want a woman to know exactly where she stands, to show her she's a cherished object. She can feel safe with me.'

Ben read it back, hesitated over the word 'object', clicked onto delete and keyed in 'individual'. If that didn't have her clamouring for him he was no judge of women. He despatched his electronic emissary and wandered into the living room to watch television, taking advantage of Kitty's Spanish language course which kept her out until after midnight on Wednesdays. He trawled channels until he stumbled on a 1960s episode of *Star Trek* and settled back.

Ben dawdled over his pint in The Palace Bar for forty minutes, ordered another and finally acknowledged at 9.07 p.m. that he'd been stood up. In a fury he slammed home and sent an astringent email storming its way into Stoneybatter's postbox.

'Definitions of time and place clearly aren't your strong suit. Remind me to define common courtesy for you.'

He was mollified to note Greystones had messaged him suggesting a rendezvous in the bar of The Morrison, a designer hotel he'd never visited but was theoretically familiar with because he read newspapers and magazines assiduously these days with so much time on his hands.

Greystones would be an agreeable place to live, he mused, pouring Kitty's lavender bath oil into the tub and climbing in after it. He'd always considered himself a shower man until Adele effected a conversion. Granted he may have been influenced by her predilection to share the tub with him . . . ah, good luck to her, she could discover how it felt squashed into the bubbles with an overweight Aussie radio-head instead of with a man whose body, if he said so himself, was in grand shape. He admired his concave stomach and then twisted the hot tap with his toe, raising the temperature.

He didn't hear Kitty's key in the door before he turned in for the night. Surely she wasn't avoiding him?

Tonight, thought Ben, would be the night. He had a positive feeling about Greystones. He could imagine himself with an attractive flirtysomething living in one of those bungalows on the hill above the sea. He'd commute by DART into work until he found a more convenient job locally, she'd listen worshipfully as he regaled her with stories about his travels, they might even invite Kitty over for Sunday dinner once in a while.

He checked his email before setting off in case Greystones had messaged him to reschedule. There was an email from Stoneybatter.

'Sorry, classic case of arrested development. Never managed to progress beyond screen conversations.'

He digested that, running a comb through his thick black hair still without a single grey strand, and cringing as a clump detached itself and curled around tortoise-shell teeth. He couldn't be thinning already, his father hadn't so much as a bald patch when he died. Of course, he was only forty-four.

Curiosity overcame Ben. He tapped out a reply to Stoneybatter.

'You mean you do this regularly, send men emails and never meet up with them?' He was still patrolling his scalp with tenderly inquisitive fingers when the new mail box flashed.

'Guilty as charged. I find the combination of anonymity and intimacy intoxicating.'

Morals outraged, Ben switched off his computer and stomped out to meet Greystones. It passed like a dream. She had her own house, not with a sea view but he could live with that, his backpacking tales enthralled her and she was really rather fetching if you disregarded the misshapen teeth. Which he was fully prepared to; he'd simply persuade her to register amusement without allowing her lips to separate. In such a discreet way she'd never realise he was realigning her smile, naturally.

'I could tell you were a sincere person from the emails, you've no idea how many men are only out for what they can get,' she breathed, curving towards him.

He nodded regretfully.

Escorting her to her car – last year's model, he noted – Ben permitted himself a peck on the cheek, although he knew she was angling for a clinch, and arranged to meet her in two days' time.

Kitty was at home and flicking through a magazine when he arrived back.

'Haven't seen much of you,' she remarked.

'Been out flat-hunting all week,' he fibbed. It didn't count as a lie, he was looking for a new home in a roundabout way. 'Anyway, you've been conspicuous by your absence, too.'

'Summoned to Clonmacdove by Aunt Breda,' said Kitty. 'She has a proposition she asked me to sound you out about.' Her blue-grey eyes were cautious as she faced Ben. 'She can't manage Mammy any longer, she wondered how you'd feel about moving in and taking over. She's weary of Irish rain, she wants to see something of the world, maybe test-drive her sister's invitation to live with her in California.'

Indignation suffused Ben. 'That's the height of selfishness, turning your back on your own flesh and blood.'

Kitty was impassive. 'She's had our mother for four years, cared for her well when neither of us were willing to do it. As you know, the house belongs to Aunt Breda, she'll have it transferred to your name if you agree to live with Mammy. She's not' – her composure faltered momentarily – 'difficult to handle but she can't be left alone. Think about it Ben, it would be a home of your own.'

He lay awake through the night deliberating on his options. Maybe he was finally home and dry, for even with conditions attached this represented independence. But to wind up in Clonmacdove after he'd travelled halfway across the globe to escape his home town – it scraped like a fishbone in his gullet. Then again, he'd led a selfish life floating where the wind wafted him: time to shoulder a few responsibilities. There was always the Greystones fall-back position but she was a chain smoker and that would be even less agreeable to live with than crooked teeth.

Ben thought of his mother. First he envisaged the stranger who drank five consecutive cups of tea dense with sugar during the visit to his aunt's house, then he remembered the woman who used to bake fairy cakes iced with a B for him. This could be exactly what he wanted. He'd shut down his email address and the serial charmer would devote himself to one woman: his mother.

Shortly after dawn, without realising what he intended to do, his legs carried him from bed to wardrobe and he rooted out the rucksack. The stitching was peeling away on the flap but it could be repaired; a tailor in Bangkok had re-sewn it once already.

Ben's fingers held the memory of his packing routine. He started with his hiking boots at the bottom, added sweaters, jeans and T-shirts, squeezing in underwear around the sides. The laptop would travel separately. He extricated a bank book from the backpack's inner pocket and checked the balance – there should be just enough. He left a note for Kitty propped against a pillow and felt a laugh bubble up through his diaphragm as he swung out of the gate and along the street to the bus stop.

All those years in the United States and he'd never made it to California; his Swiss roll aunt wasn't going to reach it ahead of him.

The Alma Club

Isla Dewar

I suppose, if I was to be honest with myself – and I rarely am – I'd have to admit I always envied Alma. There was a lot to covet – the lips, full, wide and always a smile quivering on the corners of the mouth. Cheekbones to die for. The leather jeans, crotch-hugging tight, pink, Alma could get away with sugary pink. A colour I'd given up at sixteen. Long, fast fingers, perfect nails. The hair was ever fabulous. Well it would be. Alma was a hairdresser. He did my hair for over twenty years.

Only the special people in his life got to call him Alma. And I was his special client. That was after my third visit to his salon. We'd got really chatting, conversation beyond the normal salon banter – holidays, weather, holidays, holidays, holidays. I told him about me, Tillie Betts. About Christopher, my partner. We were lawyers. I was into corporate law. Not as exciting as criminal stuff. But, if I worked at it, made the right moves, to the right companies, I could make big money.

And, I was good at it. I had an eye for the small print. Nit-picking, if you want to be brutal. I often am – though I didn't tell him that.

Suddenly, he stopped. Ruffled my hair. 'No,' he said. 'No. This isn't right. We need something special.' He took a breath, and set to. He cropped my hair. Bringing soft frondy bits onto my face. 'There, takes years off you.'

I told him I wasn't old enough to need years taken off me. I was twenty-five at the time. But I was thrilled with the look. Elfin. I loved that. And I knew Christopher would, too. He was into boyish-looking women. As I was paying, giving him my usual extravagant tip (good hairdressers have to be nurtured), the phone rang. He answered it. 'Hello, Robert Blythe Salon.' Very efficient. Then his face lit up, he cooed into the receiver, 'Darling, hello. How are you? The flu? When did this happen? Are you tucked up in bed?'

I lingered. I wanted to make another appointment. I hadn't meant to eavesdrop. But I did. He fussed and fretted over the flu victim. 'Listen, Darling, let me come round after work. I'll bring grapes and champagne and Lemsip. You let Alma spoil you.' He put the phone down.

I paid. Made my next appointment. As I was leaving – I just couldn't resist – 'Alma?' I said. Smiling. One eyebrow raised. But only slightly.

'Alma,' he said. He was so gracious. 'All my special people call me Alma.'

'Ah,' I said. 'Well, see you next time, Robert.'

He reached out, took my hand. He could do that. Take people's hands. Stroke their shoulders, put his arm round their waists. He could touch with ease. I have never been able to do that. If I try, my movements become clumsy. I embarrass people.

But Alma's touch was light and gentle and lovely. He made you feel wanted, part of his world. Important to him. He looked me in the eyes, fondled me with that gaze of his. 'Call me Alma,' he told me.

I was thrilled. My God, it made my day. My week. My life. Only his special people called him that. I was special. His special client. And he was a hairdresser to die for. He had the gift of the scissors. He could snip with the gods. My Alma.

I had the cropped look for three years. It wasn't hugely fashionable at the time. But I suited it. People noticed. Made comments. Christopher adored it. I often wonder if my decision to grow it longer (well, Alma's decision really, 'Time for a change, Darling') had something to do with us splitting up.

'What are you doing with your hair?' Christopher asked.

'Growing it.'

'Why?'

'I'll be thirty soon. I think sultry would be more the thing.'

'Sultry,' he snorted. A nasal explosion. Like he was holding one nostril and thrusting the word in a pile of snot onto the carpet. 'Sultry.' He stamped out of the room.

We'd a lovely flat. At first I paid most of the rent. I earned more than him. Then he'd overtaken me. Moved higher than I had. He'd bought most of our things. I took the Paul Simon CDs, the Annie Lennox and the Aretha Franklin. He took the Clash and the Pogues (I always regretted that). We fought over the sofa. He won.

I found the flat I live in to this day. Alma helped.

Working my hair, discussing what action he'd take with it, he said, 'Girl, what's up with you? This hair's dry and dry hair is not you. There's no life in it at all.' He turned, clicked his fingers at his junior. 'Conditioner. We need conditioner.'

It was lovely. Warm water over my head. A massage, enveloped in scents of jasmine, geranium and lavender with a slight under-bouquet of tea tree. I loosened up. Shoulders eased, eyes shut.

I told him about Christopher. Everything. How we'd been together since university. How it had all gone wrong. How I was looking for a new place to live. And finding a place wasn't easy. Furthermore, I had all the Eurythmics records. And we were fighting over the sofa. It was black leather and stainless steel, very chic.

He snipped. Lifting my hair, working at the ends, holding the layers, busy blades cutting into the ends. I asked what he was doing.

'Revamping, Darling. You need a new look. New haircut, new life, new Tillie.'

I do believe that was the only time he called me by name. I was always Darling, or Sweetie, or Girl. Darling was a kind of mean – when I was Darling, I was fine. In the good books. Sweetie when he was extra pleased with me. Girl when I was getting a ticking off for letting myself, and my hair, go.

As I was leaving, Alma said, 'Actually, if you're stuck, I have a friend, Judy, who's selling up. You might do a deal. Cut out the middle man. Estate agents take such a bundle.'

I never met Judy. Man or woman? I'll never know. I didn't like to ask. The flat was lovely. Small, but perhaps, right then, at that point in my life, I needed that. Somewhere snug, safe, womb-like. I have since bought the flat below and put in a flight of stairs. But those three upper rooms remain my sanctum. Where I go to find calm.

I snapped it up, even though it was plain the sofa wouldn't fit. I don't think I'd have got it up the stairs. I was on the third floor. But Bloomsbury. Christopher was green. Even the sofa triumph couldn't appease him. I gloated.

Not long after that I went blonde. It was masterly. Alma waltzed round me. The other assistants gathered to admire, fondle the tresses. 'Gorgeous,' they murmured.

I floated from the salon. I noticed a few sidelong glances as I walked along the street. I'll admit it, I was smirking.

I had two glorious blonde years. If I have my figures right, and I don't always, I had ten lovers in that time, not including a somewhat excessive number of one-night stands. I went clubbing. I went to gigs. I met new people. My answering machine was hot with messages. I was never in.

Alma calmed me down. 'Girl, this hair is tired.' Lifting a strand in disgust to his nose. 'Smoke.' He glared at me in the mirror. 'Are you smoking?'

'Yes.'

'Well stop. It's ruining my cut.' He sighed. Flounced a bit.

I felt just awful. I'd been smoking a lot. I was going for a job interview in a couple of days. I wanted a change. I wanted to move up. But I felt I had no chance of securing the position. And I just hate failure.

'Time for a change, Girl. We need something a little more sophisticated.'

I went ash. The subtlest of colours. Not grey. Absolutely not grey. Not blonde. A kind of smoky white. Cut straight at the bottom, all one length. When I moved my head, the hair fell perfectly, immaculately back into place. He leaned over me, pulling my hair down at the cheeks, showing me the cut, the length. I was amazed. I didn't look like me any more. I looked – not really older – just more together. I looked, suddenly it seemed, like the sort of person who knew what she was about, where she was going. Who knew what she wanted, and how to get it. I do believe I sat there for a full five minutes, breathing in this new persona. I was a different person.

'See you tomorrow, Darling. One o'clock. Here. Don't you dare be late.'

'Tomorrow?'

'We're going shopping.'

Alma was like that. He called the shots. And you always did what you were told. I never dared get on the wrong side of him. Where would I find another hair-dresser as talented as him?

We bought a black linen suit. Tapered trousers, long black jacket. White silk shirt. And high-heel boots. And a grey suit. Shorter jacket. My first really sophisticated black dress. And shoes with higher heels than I had ever worn. A handbag that I thought I might have to remortgage to pay for.

'Your clubbing days are over, Girl.' He told me. 'I don't want to see you in jeans in my salon again. Save them for your cottage in the country.'

I pointed out that I didn't have a cottage in the country.

'You will,' he said. 'Give it time. And wear the grey for the interview. And lose the clumsy watch and the soap-opera earrings.'

I got the job. I could hardly fail. With Alma's haircut, Alma's selection of clothes I felt so poised. I almost broke down and confessed that this wasn't the real me they were seeing.

But I didn't.

Mr Bannerman, my new boss, stretched out his hand. 'Welcome to Bannerman, Wardrope and Smythe. We're proud to have you aboard.'

I near as dammit wept. But I kept myself together. I smiled and said it was an honour.

I was a junior partner. They did some criminal work, but I handled their corporate accounts. I had an office.

My name on the front, in gold letters. I got my first PA.
I met James.

It still hurts to think about James. I think it always
will. I suppose for all of us there is one real love. James
was mine. My mother told me that if, just once in your
life, you found one true love, then you were blessed.
I cherish that thought.

James was already well-known when I met him. He
handled the big cases. If a pop star was suing a tabloid,
it was always a race to get to James first. He never lost a
case. He was so arrogant in court. He'd curl his lip, turn
his back on the dock. I'd seen him reduce grown men
to tears. I remember thinking, God I hope never to get
on the wrong side of that man.

We got together after the office Christmas party at
the end of my first year with Bannerman, Wardrope
and Smythe. I was wearing the black dress Alma picked out for me. I'd had my hair done that afternoon.
And my nails. Alma had advised me on the choice of
manicurist. By now, at Alma's suggestion, my make-up
was more muted than it had been in my blonde
years.

James walked straight across the room, and led me to
the dance floor. No asking, 'Will you dance?' As if he'd
only come that night to waltz with me. I had only gone
because I'd heard he was going.

The funniest thing happened when he touched me.
A thrill shot through me. I have never before, or since,
felt anything like it. He told me he loved my dress. He
said I had style. He was often to tell me that. Of course,

by then Alma would take me shopping every few months. And, just by way of saying thank you, I always bought him a little something, or a large something. I never told James about that. I never told him about Alma. Somehow, I just couldn't.

James saw me home. But wouldn't come in. Just a polite, but very pleasant, peck on the cheek. And an invitation to dinner after New Year.

Two dinners later we slept together. The sex was fantastic. I'd never known anything like it. I didn't know it could be like that. That bonding when you love, really love, is sweet, magical, thrilling, exquisite. I cried.

James was made for me. I was made for him. We fitted. Our bodies moving together in perfect time. Sleeping entwined. Waking still meshed together. That sticky sweat, annoying with anyone else, made me laugh. And James and I laughed a lot. Nights in bed, telling jokes, singing silly songs. We drank gallons of wine. We danced. Our holidays return to me – sun-drenched memories. We went to Egypt, Peru, cycled across Cuba once. That was fun. Well, mostly it was fun. I get a bit grumpy if I'm far removed from Harrods Food Hall for too long.

We saw one another most days. Though we never moved in together. James was recovering from a messy divorce, and needed space. I was happy enough about that. I'd no intention of letting my flat go. Prices these days. The flat had tripled in value.

I was in heaven. It lasted three years, and the sex did wonders for my hair.

'James is very good for you,' said Alma. 'You haven't

needed conditioner in months. It's so glossy, Darling.' Lifting my hair, letting it fall.

I had heard the whisper that Smythe was retiring. Someone would move up. I wanted that someone to be me. I'd been working on promotion. Making moves. Lunching. Networking. I knew that there would never be another chance like this.

James went to America for a month. And that gave me a chance to do some serious moving and shaking. But my real chance fell into my lap.

Bannerman was entertaining some German clients. He usually did this at home. He has a beautiful house in Kensington. His wife, a cook whose books sell out almost as soon as they hit the shelves, does the catering. I was invited. Wonderful, I thought. I made an appointment with Alma for the afternoon, planned my outfit. This was my moment. I knew how to make an impression. Alma had taught me well.

On the morning of the dinner party, Bannerman burst into my office in a dreadful state. His wife had fallen down the stairs and was at that very moment in hospital having her leg put in plaster. The maid was on holiday. There wasn't a catering firm in London available to provide a meal. And, two weeks before Christmas, the restaurants were all booked. Not a hope in hell of getting a table for ten.

'Don't worry,' I said. 'Bring them to me. We'll eat at my flat.'

The words hung between us. They were out before I thought about them. Why did I say that? Was I insane?

I can barely boil an aubergine. Well, I know you don't boil them. But what do you do with aubergines?

'Oh would you?' said Bannerman. 'You're a gem. A lifesaver. Thank you. Thank you so much.'

'It's nothing,' I lied. 'It's a pleasure.'

I took the rest of the day off. I shopped. I bought anything, everything I could think of. Then I went to Alma's. 'What am I going to do?'

'Panic,' he advised. 'Works for me.' Then he sighed. 'Tell you what. I'll come. I'll be wicked.'

He was like that. Nobody ever invited him, he invited himself. And, woe betide anyone who refused him. I didn't know what to say. I hadn't told anybody at work about Alma. But how could I turn him down? It was a choice, my job or Alma. Alma won. After all, I could always get another job. There wasn't another Alma.

He turned up at my place just after five. Took a cursory look round and sighed. 'We'll have to do something about this flat.'

I rather liked what I'd done. White walls, stripped wood, a few plants and herringbone coir on the floor.

'What's wrong with it?' I needed to know.

'It's banal, Girl. It says nothing other than you're afraid to make a statement. That, or you haven't discovered where your taste really lies. Don't worry. We'll fix it. But first, the meal.'

We went into the kitchen. There are two kinds of culinary chaos. The chaos of the enthusiastic amateur cook, and the steamy sodden peelings, the inedible disarray of the utterly inept. Mine was the latter.

He put his hands on his hips, and turned to me. 'Girl, now we find you out. You don't know a ragout from a ramekin.'

'A what?' The only thing I knew about food was I liked to eat it.

He sat me down by the fire, told me to get my face back in order. I'd gone into shock. He disappeared into the kitchen. The smells started drifting out.

I hadn't known he could cook. He made tiny crab tartlets in the most delicate cheese pastry. Then citrus sorbet. Roast beef, he thought for the main course, classic British fare. The meat was crisp at the edges, melted in the mouth. He rounded it all off with a daringly alcoholic Bavarian cream. He used Amaretto.

Then he considered my record collection. 'The Eurythmics? When did you last buy a CD?'

I couldn't remember. I'd been so busy, I'd let that side of things go. He disappeared. Returned half an hour later with a selection of music – a little rap, some reggae, cajun, Mozart and Schubert. He spread some books about. One in the bathroom, a couple by my bed. He told me I had to appear cultured. 'Terribly important, darling. You *have* to appear interested in the now.'

I introduced him as Robert, one of my oldest friends. Which, now I think of it, was true. He held the party together. At first it was flat, boring. I could see Alma twitching. Dreaded what he might say. I was right. Suddenly, out of the blue (as it were) he told a filthy joke about a prostitute with one leg. There was a silence. It was horrible. Then one of the Germans started to laugh. And how. He roared. He held his sides. So we all laughed. And that was that. We didn't discuss business. We spoke about art, books, music, life – the importance of love. It was wonderful – a triumph.

Next day Bannerman came into my office. He was aglow. 'My dear, I didn't know you could cook.'

I didn't confess.

'And you know so much about art, music. Terribly important, I think. I get so tired of these people who work endlessly and let culture slip by.'

I agreed.

'And you have such interesting friends.'

Actually, I only had one. But that was enough. And at the time, the way Alma spoke, it seemed like I had so many more. I got the promotion.

Alma celebrated by redecorating my flat. He chose pastels, and persuaded me to buy the red velvet sofa. It's a deep claret. And I love it. Though at the time, I had my doubts. I'd wanted leather, to replace the one I lost to Christopher.

When James came back from America, my life had changed. I was now earning more than him. He made a show of not minding. He was deeply impressed by my taste in furnishings. Said I was quite the homemaker. And asked me to marry him.

I wasn't sure. James was a catch, and I was tempted. But he wanted children. Theoretically, so did I. But not then. Not when I'd just moved up. I had a full work-load. 'No children,' I said. 'Not yet.'

It was my undoing. Over the next year, as we planned

the wedding, we fought. I hadn't known he had such an urge to reproduce. The fighting was hell. The making-up fabulous. But in time there was more fighting than making-up.

Three weeks before the big day, he broke my heart. There was someone else. This is painful – she was younger than me. Until that moment, I hadn't considered there was anyone – or, at least, anyone interesting – younger than me. I'd thought I was young. She was thinner than me. She wanted marriage, a home, children. He said he loved me. But he wanted to spend his life with her. And he left.

My life went bleak. Silence. I'd been so wrapped up in James, I'd let my friends go. My red-hot answering machine had one tale to tell, that horrible digital voice, 'You have no messages.'

I stopped eating. Took to Chardonnay. Then vodka with cranberry juice at lunch times. Then a little gin of an evening after the Chardonnay, well a lot of gin after the Chardonnay. Or perhaps a little whisky. Looking back on that time is hard. It's blank. A dark hole where my life once had been. I remember little.

Alma visited me in detox several times. And when I emerged back into society, he bought me evening primrose oil, vitamins A and D. He made sure I was eating. And once even went with me to my AA meeting.

He fixed my hair. It had been months. And it was, for the first time in my life, really long. He braided it. Pinned it up. The style was soft. It was the gentlest hair-do ever. He said I looked like a sexy mistress. A French siren. A woman of wit and wisdom. He leaned against the wall, and coughed. I'd noticed that cough. Didn't like the sound of it. I tipped him my usual huge amount. By now, my tips were larger than the cost of the haircut. And that was pricey enough. Alma was in demand. Non-regulars had to wait as long as four months for an appointment.

He was moving premises. Invited me to the bash in his new salon. And I met Peter. He was married, of course. Fifteen years older than me. We spent evenings together when his wife thought he was working late. And we met for lunch twice a week.

It was through Peter that I got the Japanese deal. He recommended me. It was a scoop. Actually, it was a fluke. I've always been meticulous. I nit-pick the fine print. And that's what I did with the Japanese contracts, studied, bullied, fussed over the points and didn't really look at the big print. I'd skipped that. Missed a couple of noughts. The deal that I'd thought was for five hundred thousand, was in fact for millions. If I'd known, I'd never have been such a bully. I'd never have said that if Mr Yang wanted to have a lesser company deal with his affairs then there were plenty of them, but we were the best and for that you had to pay. At that point, I shoved the contracts back into my case, and made to walk out. He called me back. Shook my hand, and told me he liked assertive women.

I bought the cottage with my bonus. Three months later, Alma spent Christmas with me. It was the best time. I hold it like a jewel in my memory. Every now and then, in my car, sitting at my desk, sitting on my sofa at home, I visit it in my head, and sigh.

He drove down with me. He even approved my decor. I'd been thinking about him with every stick of furniture I'd bought.

He was a joy. At that time I hadn't known any of the locals. But he changed that. By the time he left I was on first-name terms with everybody. Now I sing in the church choir and sit on the community council. We won the pub quiz. He had such knowledge.

After we'd exchanged gifts, I couldn't help noticing the cashmere I'd bought him was too large (though it was his usual size, the watch hung on his wrist). We sat by the fire and sang Nat King Cole songs. He was too weak to chop the logs. 'Just a touch of flu, Sweetie.'

I did it. I was enthused. My cheeks winter pink. 'I feel so in touch with things,' I told him. 'It's so much more rewarding than just clicking on the central heating.'

Next time I visited the salon, Alma wasn't there. He was sick. Marcia did my hair. It was fine. But it lacked that special Alma touch. And after that, I never knew if Alma would be there or not. Often he wasn't. He was sick a lot.

In summer he phoned me. Asked me round to his flat. I was excited. I'd never visited him at home before.

It was amazing. Filled with original paintings. Shelves lined with books. The floor in the hallway was marble. The whole thing must have cost millions. Absolute millions.

He was lying on a huge sofa, looking frail and tiny. He must have been down to about seven stone. Was wearing thermals, though it was August and a heatwave.

Of course, by then I'd guessed what was wrong. He had AIDS.

'Your hair,' he said. 'Who has been at it?'

I told him Marcia. And let him fix it. He was too ill. It was the worst cut I've ever had. The fringe was lop-sided, the ends raggy. I didn't say. After all he'd done for me – how could I?

That was the last time I saw him. He died three days later.

I was nervous about the funeral. Where to sit. Not right at the front, I wasn't family. But near the front. I was, after all, his special client. He'd told me often. 'You, Sweetie, are special.'

When I got to the crematorium, I knew exactly where to place myself. With all the other bad haircuts. About thirty of them. Occupying the two back pews. Squint fringes, ragged ends, miffed expressions.

We looked at one another, and knew. We'd all been special. We'd all had our flats decorated, our music selected, our lovers vetted, our lives set out for us by Alma. And no doubt all of us had been tipping vast amounts. It was a shock.

At the gathering afterwards, trying to be polite, we could scarcely take our eyes off each other's hair. Finally, all reserves melted. We pointed at the appalling cut, 'Alma?' We nodded.

We had a meeting at the bar. (I noticed quite a few of us were on the Diet Cokes.) At first we were furious. We'd all been suckered. Those huge tips. The shopping-trip gifts. But it dawned. I mean, where would I be now without Alma? I'd be an ageing, down-at-the-heel solicitor with bitten nails, bad hair and soap-opera earrings. I took a breath and admitted it – out loud. Others looked shocked. But I could see I was hitting a communal nerve. We all owed the man.

We exchanged cards. We networked. We formed the Alma Club.

There are twenty-five of us. There is only one way to join. You must have been styled, inside and out by Alma.

Margaret is big in the Stock Exchange. Miranda, MD of one of the country's biggest publishers. Jean edits a tabloid. Rachael's job is hush-hush, MI6, no need to say more. Maxine has one of the country's most influential PR firms. Clare is on the board of one of the world's biggest chemical companies. And I'd place bets on us having another woman prime minister, Amanda has got herself placed very sweetly in the Cabinet. We keep in touch, we phone, we fax, email, we get things done. The Alma Club is powerful.

Every now and then someone asks about us. How can they join? I always deny it exists. Once *The Times* wanted to run a story. A journalist phoned. It was some kind of female masonic thing, he hinted. I laughed, said he was being absurd.

He said, 'It's the Alma Club, isn't it?'

I refused to comment.

He asked if it was some sort of university thing. We'd all been students at the same provincial redbrick. I said this was nonsense. He got nowhere. None of us would talk. We are dedicated. We have plans. We are turning the tide in our favour. Smashing glass ceilings. There is one thing we are resolute about. The hunt for another Alma. But it's hard. You know what they say about hair-dressers – a good one nowadays is hard to find. And as I say at all the Alma Club meetings – if just once in your life you have known, and been styled by, a good hair-dresser then you have been truly blessed.

Gentlemen Prefer Special K
Neal Drinnan

'Feminism or no feminism, I still think it's gentlemanly to hold a door open for a lady.' My mother's words stop me dead in my tracks; they always have. It's so like her to parrot that sort of platitude, especially at a time like this, at the dawn of a new century. Her comments come to me in waves at the most inopportune moments. They travel to the inner sanctum of my mind and arrest me in the midst of a fashionable life she could never have hoped to be involved in.

'Half these feminists don't know what they want. *Vive la différence*,' she says from some place else in the ideological cosmos. And so I stand, with an idiot grin plastered on my face, holding open a huge glass door at the entrance to a popular nightclub, listening to an inner tirade of banal and fatuous things I've heard a thousand times before. I am steadily letting younger and more conceited people go in until eventually a visiting American adds to my humiliation by offering me a dollar tip.

'A gentleman is the rarest thing of all,' says my mother, who is certifiably insane. In my mind's eye she sits in her rocking chair, mad as a snake and drunk as a bitch from sherry, reciting a pastiche of lines she remembers from her various starring roles in the Edithvale Amateur Dramatic Society. She calls it the Edithvale Repertory Theatre, but its real name *was* Edithvale Amateur Dramatic Society – it says so on the programmes she hoarded. I guess she never liked the A-word.

It's so long ago now it scarcely matters what it was actually called. Suffice to say, she refers to the period simply as 'when I was in the theatre . . .' She has a way of glamorising the past, and I say to myself, Here we go again, as it all comes out like pus from a lanced boil for the umpteenth time . . .

'"Don't let your daughter on the stage, Mrs Worthington." Oh, how I remember that!' she'd say to me – her only patient, listening son – when reminiscences got the better of her. She loved her precious moment of bohemian rebellion.

'Mother was horrified, *horrified*. She had no idea how fortunate I was to have been invited to train under Dame Cora Sumersby shortly after she'd returned from a breathtakingly successful theatrical season in London. *Whhhere, whhhen, whhhy, whhhat* – so few people enunciate those words properly any more. Our language is being murdered, *murdered*, I tell you. I would have travelled to London myself but Mother wouldn't have it. A woman travelling on her own! Not on your Nelly. I tried to enlist your Aunt Marjorie in the struggle, but she was never as spirited as I and she already had her heart set on that wretched doomed marriage to your Uncle Gus. Your father, now he was *almost* a gentleman . . .'

Two blocks from my mother's house was the church hall where Edithvale Amateur Dramatic Society used to perform some years before my birth. Edithvale is not a well-to-do suburb, but nor is it a ghetto of violence and desperation. Its inhabitants would call it 'respectable', and it's by the sea, which adds a certain shabby, summer lustre to it. My mother, in true Blanche DuBois style, liked to fantasise that cruel circumstances and disappointing men led her to these less-than-auspicious circumstances, when in fact she only ever had one man – and seldom had cause to rely on the kindness of strangers.

'Men die or leave you – either way you learn to do without,' she mutters despondently. And I nod in resigned sympathy.

Edithvale is the sort of beachside suburb where retired men collect concrete gnomes and paint the rocks in their gardens bright colours. Behind clean lace curtains, women furnish model dolls' houses with 'authentic' reproduction furniture. The lounge rooms are cluttered with doilies, well-dusted antique doll displays, and dolefully curated souvenir teaspoons purchased from gift shops and caravan parks in popular Australian beauty spots. The homes have names like Weona, Thistledoo, Didjabringyagrogalong or Dunroamin and they all seem to have nasty little yapping dogs behind their gaily painted tra-la-la fences. My mother's own usually murderous miniature terrier, Li'l Sheeba, sits as quietly in her lap as it would if it had visited the taxidermist.

In my mind I'm looking around her house. It contains a profusion of fine china ornaments, including her prized Wedgwood miniatures and a dozen shelves filled with Venetian glass pieces. 'All this will be mine,' I say to a passing punter who looks at me strangely. With a mother like that, small wonder I came out homosexual. I was weaned on Noël Coward, and Tennessee Williams was my teething ring. It's amazing my siblings turned out straight.

'Your sister's like your Auntie Norma, pretty as a picture but not much going on upstairs. Heavenly hijinks I call it. A God who makes girls pretty and dumb at the same time would have to be a man. You only have to look at what becomes of them to see He's got one sick sense of humour. Your brother's got the worst of your father and the worst of me, poor sod, but he works hard – which is more than could be said of someone else! I suppose you inherited my gift for the arts, but you've never stuck at anything, never made anything of yourself.' I shift on the spot. I am at least *trying* to be a gentleman.

'Children can be a disappointment as well as a joy, you know . . .' And if you needed proof, look no further than the family itself. For every sin and human failing there is a ready-made parable or personification in the shape of an aunt, uncle or cousin. Who needs a Bible for their moral guidelines when every crime and punishment, every sin and an occasional redemption can be found amongst your kin.

'You could write a book about my life!' I can hear my mother saying, before she lists all the failings I know so well.

'God, your Auntie Norma. An idiot for love and a fool with the purse strings. Your Uncle Roger was a drinker and I know for a fact he raised his hand to his wife on more than one occasion. Your Aunt Marjorie never learned to put her foot down so she ended up a doormat to those kids and that husband of hers. Your Uncle Syd was far too keen on the gee gees – always picking the ones that were ready for the glue factory. It was the filthy cigarettes we can thank for the death of your Uncle Ed, and his wife Irene would have lasted a good deal longer if she hadn't carried all that weight she kept after the children were born.'

The aunts, it seemed, with the exception of Ida, could all have married far better than they did. Trophy wife material every one of them if you believed Mother, but somehow they threw themselves away on the first man who came calling.

'Now, look at your Aunt Ida, married that waste-of-space Arthur, though God knows they weren't exactly queuing round the block for her. She had four sons; and what for, you ask? No-hopers every one of them. Thank heavens she had Sarah. Worth more than the lot of them put together, if you ask me. Not a beauty, I know, but she's got her head screwed on. In my day "pretty" was all that really mattered, men weren't interested in brains and university degrees. You couldn't scrub the floor with a degree or serve a baked doctorate to your husband's boss, so what was the point? Girls these days have lost the art of playing a man and reeling him in like we had to – and it's a shame, a downright shame . . .'

I feel hot and a little nauseated. I know where this is headed. Straight for the home paddock. Once we've done the aunts it'll be Dad, my sister and brother, then me. I hate that part – *Please don't go there!* – but she can't hear me. Not a word. And the clubbers wonder what I'm on about with my feeble protests. People are staring at me like I've lost my mind, and perhaps I have.

'Of course, you can bet there wasn't a cent left lying around Norma's house that hadn't been through a dozen poker machines or squandered down the bingo hall. Not that that husband of hers ever had a pot to pee in or a window to throw it out of. At least with your father I knew there'd be food on the table. Yes, there were finer-looking fellas around with better prospects, and I could have taken my pick, believe you me, but he was that sweet on me it would have broken his heart if I'd turned him down. I had a young doctor quite keen on me for a while. I didn't have Norma's lovely hair and eyes but I had a prettier little figure than her and didn't she know it . . .'

I feel bile rush into my throat but I swallow it back down and it mixes with the nasty chemical taste from the back of my nostrils. If I list the sins of the fathers and aunts, perhaps I'll be all right. I'd rather she went right back. The memories from fifty years ago are safer, even when she tints them. If I know her, she'll tint them in those lurid shades used to colourise old movies: *Singin'*

*in the Rain, Easter Parade, A Star is Born, Carousel,
April in Paris, The Wizard of Oz.* There's no place like
home, there's no place like home, I chant – but I see it
still: hordes of smiling, tapdancing movie stars around
me. And I can hear them singing it now up on stage
under the bright lights. *This was a real nice clambake* . . .

Poor Ida was the one you had to pity – plain, plain,
plain, though she never seemed to mind. Norma and
I tried to get her to make something of herself, because
you *can* do something with plain. Ugly! – well, you're
just *plain* stuck with that!' She laughs at the pun while
I retch again. I'm picking off the layers of skin that she's
putting onto me, layer upon layer of rotting historic
residue: Norma, Ida, Roger, Marjorie, Syd, Ed.
I chant their names like a mantra, and that's just her
side. All of them mating and reproducing in some
distant hand-coloured pornographic postcard from
the past. Trains hooting and powering their way across
the land, newspaper headlines spinning into view, calendar dates flipping past, red lips and white teeth flashing,
flannel suits and Craven A cigarettes. *All aboard the
future* hollers the newsboy from a street corner, but on
she goes, relentlessly picking up on my thoughts, parading the past in front of me, reading through a tortured
litany of nostalgia. It is her yearbook of destinies – my
genetic past gathered up like my great-grandmother's
skirts as she disembarked from an English ship.

'At least your father was prepared to pay the extra to
have our wedding photos tinted. That was quite an expense then – the other girls had to make do with black
and white. Harry Burleigh-West was the photographer.

He had a lovely studio just over in Frankston – of course, it's not there any more, it's all out with the old and in with the new these days. And he threw in that portrait on the mantelpiece for free.'

And isn't the mantle a struggle! I daren't look. Dozens of pictures competing to be noticed: the aunts, uncles, my sister Rhonda and brother Keith. Me, smiling like a chimp. Perhaps if I don't look at those photos she won't start on us. I've kept her away from it so far.

'You know when I was in the theatre there was an odd bod.' Oh no, no, no. Here she goes. 'Odd bod' was Mother's term for a homosexual. I don't care for it at all, no sirree, and I don't want to hear this story. I heard it as a child and I didn't like it then, but she'd trot it out whenever she was feeling wicked and drunk. Do Auntie Norma's affair, I willed her. Do the time Roger was so drunk he drove into the creek or do when Uncle Syd had the house repossessed by bailiffs. Anything but the odd-bod story. Do 'Let me compare thee to a summer's day', or Ophelia's madness speech from *Hamlet*, Chekhov's *Seagull*, Ibsen's bloody *Doll's House* if needs be, but not the odd-bod story.

I'm so disorientated now I no longer know how old I am or what year it is. I could barely tell you which country we inhabit, but on she forges like a train through the Nullarbor, while I politely hold the door open for an endless parade of thankless strangers.

'Oh, he was a strange one that odd bod, Cyril Lister was his name. Five foot nothing, a balding redhead with a toupee, and didn't we girls used to snigger about that! As if that wasn't bad enough, he used to colour in his moustache with an eye pencil if you can believe it, and the lispy simpering voice would put you right off. Old Lispy Lister – that's what we used to call him.'

She cackles at the memory. 'Jean Elsmere used to be a right old stirrer and was always up for a prank. She told him he looked like Danny Kaye. Well, he believed her, didn't he, even though he looked more like Mickey Rooney on a bad day. He said he'd acted here, there and every-bally-where. Always wanted the male leads, which was absurd given his height – a man has to be taller than a woman onstage, it goes without saying . . .'

I'm dying inside, there can be no mistaking it. 'Stop the story now, I want to get off!' but she hears me not. She never listens, no one ever does. I hum 'Singin' in the Rain' to myself, trying to do a few of the steps while holding the door. My feet feel like lead and still her tirade continues.

'We all thought it was very strange when he stopped turning up for rehearsals and then next thing you know, there he was in the local paper without his toupee, arrested for doing something most peculiar in the Mornington public lavs. The other girls had no idea what the article was about but I was a little more worldly than them. I knew what indecency was when it was paraded before me on the front page of the *Edithvale and District Times* . . .'

At least she hadn't kept the clipping from that. She'd kept everything else: the Coronation, the Melbourne Olympics, the first man on the moon. There were endless yellowing, cheesy little snippets from the *Edithvale Times* about the plays she performed in: 'Will The Real

Mrs De Winter Step Forward,' 'No Coward, Noel', 'What Light From Yonder Church Hall Breaks', and 'The Importance Of Being Edithvale Players'. I read them slavishly as a child, convinced they were badges of courage and glory.

The new Mrs de Winter might appear for all the world as a cultured English lady on stage, but you'll probably know her as Miss Dorothy Gorse from the Edithvale Postal Office. Never short of a cheery smile and a friendly greeting, Dorothy is soon to become the new Mrs Richard Weston. The wedding will take place at Saint John's Anglican Church, Edithvale, on Saturday April 10th, 1955. The bridesmaid attending her will be Miss Marjorie Gorse, and the Matron of Honour will be Mrs Norma Johnson.

I seem to have led my mother in another direction. I still feel a little ill and I'd like to sit down, but being a gentleman is important – and if I don't hold the door, goodness knows who will.

'Of course, with an April wedding you can never be sure what to wear. In Melbourne it could just as easy be warm or cold. I had a cape made out of the fabric just in case and was considered quite risqué for not wearing a full-length gown. Still, there were about twenty petticoats and the whole ensemble cost me nearly four pounds, which was a fortune on my wages then . . .'

My foot is going to sleep and I can see that over on the dance floor another show is about to start. Someone comes out with a microphone, then two more follow. I can't believe it, it's Mum, Auntie Norma and Auntie

Ida. Mum of course is the one with the mike, and she's heading towards me.

'I do so love the kindness of strangers, don't you?' She's talking to everyone in the whole club. The spotlight is on my mother and she is walking over to me.

'And I think there's one very special stranger we'd all like to thank tonight. What's your name, Darling?' She holds the microphone to my mouth and I have to think for a moment until a name comes. She's trying to humiliate me in front of all these people. 'I'm, I can't, Lis . . .' I say.

'And where are you from, Love?' I look into her eyes and they're caked with theatrical make-up. 'Mutton dressed as lamb,' she'd say, 'Winter parading as spring,' so many things she might say. But I remember where I'm from and I tell her because I won't let her ridicule me like this. 'Edithvale,' I say with subdued pride.

'Well, I think we owe Lispy Lister from Edithvale a big round of applause because for the last two hours he's been holding the door open without any encouragement from the management. He's been a gentleman, which is the rarest thing of all!'

I want to speak, I want to say 'What about Tasmanian tigers, dodo birds, the yeti, white rhinos and peace in our time?' but I'm stuck, unable to speak and hearing nothing but the applause. I feel only the lacerations of that name, Lispy Lister. They're laughing with her, at me. She's waving her hands in the air, loving every minute of it – but she hasn't finished yet. 'Now, I think Mr Lister from Edithvale might have taken something nasty tonight, don't you?' She's not asking me, she's asking *them*. She's playing them, presumably the same way she liked to play men. She turns back to me. 'Now Darl, I think you've been a bit naughty and had a touch too much Special K.' She turns to the audience, tapping her nose and oinking like a pig. 'That's ketamine, a horse tranquilliser to you bush pigs from places even more remote than Edithvale.' She leads me away from the door and my head clears a little. My foot is regaining its circulation. 'Now let's just sit Lispy Lister down here by the stage where we can keep an eye on him while we turn back the hands of time with a number you'll all remember . . .'

I look up at the stage – it's not my mother and aunts, it couldn't be, they've been dead for years. It's just three ugly drag queens done up to the nines. People are staring at me, wondering how it must feel to look such a fool. 'Hey Lispy Lister, got any more of that K?' asks a guy from the next table who looks remarkably like a young Uncle Roger. 'Sure,' I say, still numb to the total humiliation of it all. 'Have some. Have it all if you want.'

I watch him vanish eagerly into the toilets and shake my head. 'These kids nowadays don't know what they're getting into. You only have to look at young Evan if you want to know what drugs can do to you,' I can hear my mother say. 'EVAN,' I shout at the drag queen who is now doing the Chattanooga Choo Choo. 'My name's not Lispy Lister, it's Evan.' But of course it's too late and no one cares anyway. I feel all the history come to a jarring halt like a train finally reaching New York or Chicago or wherever it was they always seemed to be going. I don't know what I'm doing here and I don't even like drag shows, but at least at my journey's end I know who I am and that I have a name and it is not Lispy Lister. It's Evan – the child for her old age, the one who forgot to grow up. The gentleman on K.

Cabin Baggage

Nick Earls

Claudia was the one with the big ideas about cabin baggage. The big ideas and the dare. Which is fine by me. Not that I'm much for dares, but chances are I'll never see her again.

'Sure, I'll do that,' I said when the dare came into the conversation. 'On my way home. With a plank, a fence paling, something like that.'

I'm in her city now, London, and I get my first look at it as the train slips out of the darkness of the long tunnel and into the suburbs just inbound from Heathrow. It's early here, but Claudia's in Singapore where it's already well into morning or perhaps even afternoon.

Why am I measuring by Claudia time, even thinking that way? I might as well, I suppose. There's no other time that makes sense to my body right now.

Twenty-four hours and nine or ten time zones ago, I flew out of Brisbane. I had the window seat and I thought I'd have all three. Then Claudia turned up and took the aisle. She had that deep brown English-tourist tan, and shiny black hair and blue eyes. I noticed all that as she sat down, so obviously I must have gawked at her the moment she arrived.

She ignored me for several minutes, and fair enough. We ignored each other, as good plane passengers should. Then someone clocked her with an enormous Sambuca bottle on their way past her, and as she turned her head and winced I might have been gawking again, and she caught my eye. No, it was the sound of bottle hitting skull – that's what made me turn. That's my story now anyway.

She rubbed her head – the Sambuca owner didn't even notice – and she said, 'Fucking cabin baggage. That bottle was at least four feet long.'

And that was the beginning. She was off – oversized cabin baggage and people's bizarre and selfish carry-on expectations were obviously some pet hate of hers. And one of mine too as it happens, partly because of the thoughtlessness involved, partly because I'd never have the guts to try it.

On she went, telling me about a flight out of Nairobi a couple of years ago when someone got on with a wooden giraffe that was 'practically bloody lifesize – any bigger and they would have kept it downstairs and fed it hay.'

Either Claudia had been bottling it up, or she's got a routine going with this stuff. Would a giraffe eat hay? Could that possibly matter?

'Next time you fly,' she said, 'you have to promise me you'll carry the largest piece of timber you can. Wrapped up specially, like a gift. And you should tell me how you go. Email me or something.'

I remember thinking, My God, what's going on? Isn't my frequent flyer number supposed to be linked to the numbers of enormous people who snore and snuffle and have all kinds of problems with gas and odours and personal space? What can have gone wrong? Last time I visited Tash in London, I'd swear I turned up smelling of another person's BO, having lived in the cradle of their huge armpit for the best part of a day.

An hour or so of conversation later, when we were far over western Queensland, Claudia said, 'I don't normally talk to people on planes, of course,' and I said, 'Neither do I.'

I told her my story about smelling of another person's BO and she laughed and said, 'That is absolutely disgusting.' So I came up with all kinds of stories about huge grim travel experiences in these small seats; some true, some embellished, some that came up because it just seemed to be where my act was going. And we got on well.

'This is amazing,' she said. 'I really never talk to people on planes. Really.'

And I said, 'Neither do I.'

We exchanged some details. 'Now that we're talking we probably have to contextualise ourselves,' Claudia said, and rolled her eyes. She told me her name and held her hand out for shaking.

I told her my name and I told her about Tash and her wedding somewhere near Cambridge the weekend after next. How we'd done a kind of bridal-party sibling-swap deal that made me Toby's groomsman and his sister one of Tash's bridesmaids. I told her, 'I am about to be bossed around from one end of the day to the other, but that's family for you.'

And she said, 'Why do you think I'm a travel writer? Well, not really. Well, partly. You haven't met my mother.'

Claudia travels a lot with work, but she has a set of permanent arrangements in place in London, from the sound of it. A downstairs flat at Hammersmith that terrifies her because she actually owns it now and she used to just rent, a cat called Butch, a guy called Glenn.

In her back pocket she carries a battered old men's wallet – it turns out it's her father's, and I think there's a story there somewhere – and in the wallet she has a photo of Butch. When she pulled it out and showed it to me I said something like, 'To be honest, he doesn't look very butch,' and she said, 'Oh, no, he's a complete nancy boy. It's after the Bruce Willis character in *Pulp Fiction*.'

And I said, 'Was his name Butch?'

And she said, 'I hope so. I could look pretty stupid otherwise.'

I asked her if she had a picture of Glenn, too, but she doesn't. I showed her me on my driver's licence. It was the only picture I had but always good for a laugh, as those things tend to be.

The train glides through row after row of red-brick houses at a height just above their second storeys. There's rain on the window next to me but the sky is mostly clear and the sun is out on the wet roads and roofs.

Tash is at the tube station to meet me and she asks how the flight was, and I say, 'Fine, the usual, long.'

She shows me where things are in the house – coffee, tea, anything I might need.

'You'll be okay wandering round if we go to work?' she asks, and I give her a look that's meant to tell her, very clearly, 'I may be your little brother but fuck you, I'm twenty-eight.'

'Got it,' she says, and she knows she should have got it long ago.

Jet lag is rocking sludgily through me by the time they get home. They've fought on the tube – that's how they seem anyway – but they do that. And it works for them. Toby's not much of a fighter.

'Elope, mate,' he tells me when Tash is upstairs. 'That's my advice.'

'Chicks, man,' I say, as if restating an ancient tribal mystery.

'Yeah.' He shakes his head. 'Chicks. Can't live with 'em, but sometimes they make you.'

We go into the kitchen and he opens a couple of beers and hands me one.

'Met one on the plane,' I tell him.

'One what?'

'Chick.'

'On the plane? People don't meet people on planes, do they? I'm really getting out of touch.'

'No, they don't. You're right. She was the exception

to the rule. We talked all the way to Singapore.'

'That's a bloody long way.'

'I know. I tried it again on the flight from Singapore to here – after she'd got off – and it was the usual disaster. A strange-smelling Swiss guy who really, really wanted to talk me through the rise of the new Right in Austrian politics.'

'That's more like it. That's the class I usually travel. So, um, where's she from?'

'Here.'

'Pity.'

'Here and in a relationship. But that was what was good about it. It meant we were free to talk, once we'd established that kind of stuff early.'

'And would there be a third beer?' Tash says as she comes in. 'Or have the remaining beers been divvied up between the boys?'

'Always a beer for you, my love,' Toby says, but he says it in the way that Tash calls 'so bloody laconic.'

They tell me more about the wedding, the plans for the day itself. They're risking a marquee and I say, 'Sorry, but isn't this England?' before I realise it's a touchy topic.

It's in the grounds of Toby's parents' house near Cambridge. 'Grounds' makes it sound so much grander and bigger than a garden, and perhaps it is.

'You haven't been there, have you?' Tash says. 'It's a nice place, particularly in spring. They've got some lovely big old oak trees. And peacocks.'

Toby shakes his head wearily. 'The peacocks aren't even supposed to be there. They just turned up one day.

And they're awful anyway. A nuisance. Prancing around like . . . like bloody peacocks. Like they own the place. And they aren't nice.'

'Toby's afraid of the peacocks,' Tash says.

'I'm not afraid of the peacocks.'

'He is.'

'One of them pecked my wing mirror, remember.'

'So he had to wait till his mother had shooed it away before he got out of the car.'

'What's that got to do with being afraid? That's just clever. Why get pecked when your mother can get pecked for you?' Tash laughs at that and he adds, 'Anyway, she likes to feel useful.'

Toby's eyelids are low most of the time, as though he's tired of us all. He is physically, as well as verbally, laconic. He says 'useful' as though it's a particularly useless thing to want to feel. He's good at feigning a lordly indifference, just to amuse. Underneath it, though, he's not indifferent at all.

There's more to talk about, but that's weddings for you. Tash says Toby's grandmother's cousin in Scotland has broken her hip, 'otherwise the guest list is looking reasonably intact so far.' There's plenty to do over the next week – my suit, final dress fittings, the flowers, picking up the cake – but that's why I'm here. I'm the family's designated gopher in the lead-up to Tash's Big Day.

Toby gets bored with wedding talk soon enough and says, 'Hey, tell Tash about the bird you pulled on the flight over. Well, almost pulled.'

'Oh, no,' she says. 'This is so like school.'

And that's when I notice how English, how this-part-of-London, her vowels are becoming.

I try to explain, but her mind's already made up. Of course.

'Oh, Bradley,' she says. 'Most people pick up duty-free, but all you got was a crush.'

'It's not a crush. It was a diversion. The Brisbane to Singapore leg's not a sleeping sector, remember. And that new Bette Midler movie . . .'

I told Claudia about you, I want to say, like a big dobber. I told her about you and how you were two years older at school and now you think you always will be. And don't get smart with the maths, sister. You never were smart with the maths, so don't go starting now.

I'm twenty-eight and you're thirty and that's two years older only on paper, so quit big-sistering me right away.

She's lived here too long. She should have forgotten school. She moved out of home in the middle of her degree, then moved over here five years ago, and in her mind my development arrested the day she first packed her bags. I should have come here in short pants and a blazer, with my tie loose and my white shirt hanging out at the back, ready for the standard telling-off about sloppiness.

Bugger you, Tash, I'm tidy now. Reasonably tidy. One look should tell you that. School was more than a decade ago, my tidiness hasn't figured in conversations with Mum for years and this isn't a crush.

Claudia only had two or three days in Singapore, so I call her on Saturday when she's back just to say hello and tell her about the moves I made on the Swiss guy on the next leg, and how well that worked out. I get put through to her voice mail, but I was expecting her to answer and I don't know what my message should be, so I just hang up.

I call back a little later. Still the voice mail, but I leave Tash and Toby's number and address. I think I gave them to her on the plane, but . . . I *did* give them to her on the plane, but slips of paper get lost so easily in transit.

We go to Wagamama for lunch – Tash, Toby, me and the entire bridal party, sitting there along the steel benches with bowls of noodles. This is our chance to meet and bond, and we all give it our best shot even though it can't help but feel pretend. I tell a couple of appalling stories about Tash, and that breaks the ice.

Later I have to tell her it was 'a strategy', even though I only really did it for personal pleasure. Still, it worked both ways. She should thank me. And I'm sure it's been years since she wet her pants, so what's the problem? It's a school story. She usually likes school stories.

On Sunday I sneak in another call to Claudia from the upstairs phone. Still the voice mail. I mention the Swiss guy, as though he's just sprung to mind. What do I think that'll do? Tantalise her?

Then it's on to further bonding, this time with Toby and the best man and a few of their mates in a pub.

Huge English beers at a wooden outside table in only slightly warm British spring sun. By mid-afternoon I think the jet lag's kicking lazily back in, but the number of toilet visits should tell me that's not it.

There was a buck's night a week ago, and I couldn't get away from work to be there, so this is when I hear about it. Tash's only mention of it was last Sunday, in an email: 'Well, it's done, thank God.'

It's a source of some tension now, apparently, the best man tells me when Toby's in the loo. 'Just boozing and strippers,' he says, and shrugs his shoulders. 'Dunno what she was expecting. I mean, we felt a certain obligation to give his bachelorhood some kind of send-off.'

On Monday, I stop calling Claudia. After just one more try. Face it, that's four times now, possibly six. She hasn't returned one call, her plane hasn't crashed and she's almost certainly back in the country.

I don't want to look like I'm stalking her. And, on those occasions when my mind does drift to the first leg of my journey here, it's best to remind myself that there is, after all, a man involved in the life of my fellow traveller. Even if he was the one who suggested to Claudia that there were problems, and that's why she was cutting the Australian leg of her trip short.

'I'm not sure about these problems,' she told me. 'It could be just my rising damp getting worse, but I'm getting a sneaking suspicion that my time may be up . . .'

So she did put that idea out there – she did tell me that she wondered what was on Glenn's mind, that he was sick of her being away, that it was an issue, that his tone of voice had changed on the phone, that there were things he wasn't saying.

'But why the hell am I telling you this?' she said, shutting the door and laughing at the line she'd crossed.

And I looked at her then, after hours of listening to her, and I thought, How could anyone, ever, think of dumping you? I nearly said it, too. Can I blame it on the mood of the Bette Midler movie? I'd like to.

On Monday afternoon, there's a dress disaster – Tash, the bridesmaids and me there in the shop, and they're all trying on their dresses and Tash's doesn't fit.

'I wouldn't care so much if it was one of theirs!' she screams at the dressmaker, the last of her good judgement slipping away unnoticed. 'But I'm the bloody bride. You had to get this one right.'

I extract her from the scene. We go for coffee, just us, and I insist that we talk about other things. Two hours later the buttons do up, frown lines smooth again.

'Thanks,' Tash says to me after apologising to the dressmaker. 'I nearly lost it there.'

None of us knows where to look. I just say, 'Nearly,' in the most brotherly way possible.

I will be so glad when our parents get here on Thursday.

Claudia said, 'What is it with men? More to the point, what is it with Daniel Day Lewis? All these years and he still doesn't know he loves me . . .' That's what I'm thinking on Tuesday as Tash moves into the advanced stages of a debate about flowers with Toby and the florist.

Claudia said, Claudia said. Claudia should have said, 'Snap out of it, loser. We're killing time and lots of it, but I won't be returning your calls.'

Be a sensible person with a chosen single status, that's what I tell myself. It has worked, and it does work. Life is good and I'm not the one replacing my whole face with today's frown lines while talking about flowers. I'm the one with the benign smile and the calm private joke about not being able to forget a fellow plane passenger days after we flew together.

Be a sensible person, even though her stories were beguiling. That's the advice I'm giving myself and the word I've settled for. Seriously bloody beguiling. I am beguiled by this, and that's a reasonable and adult and nonsexual non-loser thing. Okay?

This is not a crush. It's not. I don't know what I'd call it, but that's what it isn't. It would be better not to think of her, that much I know. Her and that flat at Hammersmith. And her cat and the rising damp and the man she's with. I hope he appreciates her, that's all. How very stoic and grown-up of me.

Daffodils, Tash? You can't be serious.

But, really, you can be whatever you want to be. Toby won't fight and I won't say a word against you and even the florist will give in if he has to, though he does seem set in his ways.

Wednesday's worse. Wednesday's the family dinner with Toby's side and everyone's tension just gets wound up tighter.

'That was completely horrible,' my now very British-sounding sister says to me later through the wall.

Says it to me through the wall, says it loudly and directly to Toby, who's in the same room as her. Then there's some more, but it doesn't quite get to my side.

It's the vowels. That woman from Hammersmith whose name begins with C – the woman I've stopped thinking about – has them, too. 'Unbelievably homosexual,' she said, with at least six e's in the middle of 'unbelievably', and not a one that could be deleted.

That was about Nathan Lane's performance with Bette Midler in *Isn't She Great*.

'It's absolutely dreadful,' she said as the opening credits flickered on the screen. 'I had to watch it between Singapore and Melbourne and it's awful, the whole thing, but you simply can't believe him. Maybe it's just that it's atrociously miscast.'

Claudia comes with the whole set of adverbs. I learned that quickly. You can't just describe something if you're Claudia, you have to go all the way.

'So here's what we'll do,' she said. And she made us revoice the whole film, from start to finish, like bad dubbing, even though I had no idea what was happening with the plot. Claudia's helpful summary: 'Lots of histrionics, then she dies.'

She plays the Nathan Lane part, I play Bette Midler as Jacqueline Susann, we split the rest.

She plays the Voice of God, and I don't even know if

272

there was one of those in the original but, in Claudia's version of the film, God has a lot to say and most of it isn't nice. Culminating in 'Drown, bitch' when Bette Midler walks into the lake. And I did query that line, but Claudia said, 'I'm God from the Old Testament. There was no mucking about in the Old Testament.'

Thursday's counselling, tag-team. I'm the counsellor with no one to tag, Tash and Toby are the team and definitely the enemy trying to wear me down in turns.

My parents arrive early in the morning. They should save me from this but instead they sit on the sofa drifting in and out of a jet-lag haze, no use to anyone.

'Jesus, old people,' I say to them. 'Snap out of it. Get with the programme. All of that.'

My mother makes more cups of tea and says they should go for a walk to clear their heads. Useless.

So, for me there's shopping with Tash, some close-up shouting – *to* me but not *about* me, so I can nod and be brotherly and supportive. And say things like, 'Yes, I know you might think he's a prick right now, but most days we call that laconic and we like it a lot, remember? Not that I'm saying he's not a prick right now, an absolute prick. But he is a laconic one, who's nice at heart.'

Then a break from her and a quiet beer over lunch with Toby who keeps going, 'What the fuck . . . what the fuck,' like someone whose every next step expects a bear trap, and who will be right about that often enough.

Then Tash again, and my reassuring, 'No, of course

he's looking forward to Saturday,' when doubt surfaces mid-afternoon. 'It's all he talks about. You know that.'

Pizzas at home, I tell them. That's the Thursday night plan. Pizzas or some kind of takeaway, a video, a quiet night at home of pretending we haven't descended into madness. And the olds will let the coma take hold before they should, they'll be out of action by seven and awake at three, clattering around in the kitchen making tea, but that's just the way it goes.

'Well, all right,' Tash says snappily, as if to tell me in some stupid wordless way that my pizza plan's pretty damn far from all right. 'But I'm not drinking. I'm not drinking and Toby's not drinking. We have to keep our wits about us.'

'And I s'pose a really grubby porn video's out of the question, too?' I say to her, and she looks horrified and shakes her head, as though I've gone over to the other side, the buck's night side, and I'm now the guy who used to be her brother.

There's no levity to be had this evening, none at all.

The olds, as predicted, are long gone and the Chinese food is gone, and we're temporarily close to a state of calm later as the kettle boils in the kitchen.

'I'll make a pot,' Tash says. 'I'm sick of bags.'

And Toby says, 'Lovely,' but he doesn't stop re-arranging the magnets on the fridge and he doesn't turn around.

There's a knock at the door. I don't move since it's

not my house. Toby doesn't move since there's something compelling about the fridge magnets and he's being rather annoyingly laconic tonight, and Tash says, 'Well, my turn, obviously.'

Toby shrugs, as if the fight's out of him for ever now, and Tash strides from the room. At what point do I get to scream, Snap out of it you two?

The front door opens and there's the sound of talk, just audible in here with the kitchen door swung most of the way shut.

Tash comes back in and looks at me as if I've come up with a new problem for her. That's not what we need.

'There's someone here to see you,' she says. 'I've left her at the door because she seems to be carrying a piece of wood. I would have shut the door on her but it's sort of wrapped in bubble wrap, and before I knew that it was a piece of wood I'd invited her in.'

I'm already on my feet straight after the first 'wood', passing her in the doorway as she waffles on with her meeting-Claudia story that I'm not at all interested in.

'Claudia,' I tell her. 'My friend Claudia from the plane.' Meaning: shut up – I am being terse so you will shut up and behave. This is my evening now. My turn. Snap out of it you two. Any time round about exactly now would do.

Claudia's in the hall with the door closed behind her and her hair is glistening and flattened by rain that I didn't even know was falling. She smiles.

'Hello,' she says.

'Hi. Good to see you.' Generic, damnit, but how specific can I be? Pretty specific, it turns out as a pause threatens. My next line goes: 'So, did he dump you?'

Clearly as a joke, and that's how it's taken. She's smiling, still smiling and I'm thinking, Of course, of course it was safe ground, how could anyone ever . . . et cetera. She is clearly not a dumped person. I've seen one, been one, it's not her. Next he'll knock on the door having just parked the car.

'Yeah,' she says, still smiling, 'he dumped me. You're such a direct nation, aren't you? Any more direct and you'd be an American.'

She looks at Tash – who is now behind me – as though they can be English together and have a laugh at us all, the excessively direct of other nations.

Tash, by now mostly English in many respects and certainly going to take Claudia's side, gives a sigh and punches me on the shoulder and says, 'Dickhead.'

'Oh, sorry,' Claudia says, 'you're Australian, too. I forgot you might be, um . . . Brad's sister?'

'Sure, I try to forget it myself,' Tash says, and they like each other from the start. 'Now, you should come and have a cup of tea. We might be awfully rude, some of us, but we aren't inhospitable.'

That's when Claudia remembers what she's carrying and holds it out to me, horizontal and in both hands, and I feel like a Roman general being presented with a ceremonial sword.

'We have some common issues with cabin baggage,' she says to Tash on the way to the kitchen, as though that explains it.

'It's lovely,' I tell her. 'It'll go with me everywhere. It's probably my favourite fence paling already, and so thoughtfully packaged.'

'Well, it is Georgian, I think. Been in the family for some time.'

'Really?'

Okay, instant regret at falling for that one as both of them laugh. Tash calls me a dickhead again and Claudia says, 'I tripped over it a couple of days ago. It was lying on the pavement near the end of my street.'

Tash makes us sit, and she makes us tea. I am all totally tea'd out by my last few days in this country, but who cares?

There's a conversation right away, as if all four of us have known each other for ages – cabin baggage, long-haul flights, the one or two people they might have in common.

Claudia says, 'I don't usually say this, but your house smells really nice. Maybe my rising damp is a bit of an issue after all. Some of the walls are a bit mouldy. Maybe he was right to want to move.' She shrugs. 'But that's no reason to tell me that it's the cat making the smell by peeing inside. Right?'

'Absolutely,' Toby says. 'Rising damp and cat's piss? Nothing alike.'

We talk about the wedding. She says it's not a touchy subject, don't be silly. I mention the peacocks, just because the idea of them still seems bizarre.

'Not the bloody peacocks again,' Toby says. 'They just turned up one day. I don't even like them. They're so . . . rough. And big. Do you know how bloody big an angry peacock is?' Tash looks at him and doesn't make much of an attempt to stop a laughing noise working its way out. 'All right. They are a bit of an issue. If they could come up with a special word for a phobia for peacocks, I'd be their man.'

Claudia tells us about her life – some things I know, some things I don't, some things about the last few days. It had to end, she says. Really, it did. There was a lot about ending it that was mutual, but still. Still, there's a lot of fallout, isn't there?

Is it rude to keep looking at her, even when one of the others is talking? I'm tired, and far too lazy to move my head. Or eyes.

Tash takes me out of the room, saying, 'I've just remembered something I have to show Brad.' I'm expecting a telling-off for staring, but instead she takes me to the stairs and says, 'Do you want to invite her? To the wedding? Instead of Toby's granny's cousin with the hip?'

'Invite her? But it's on Saturday.'

'Oh, seize the bloody day for once. There's a dare going on here, boy. And it's not just to do with a Georgian fence paling.' I don't know what to say to that, so Tash says, 'Right, that's it. She's invited.'

She drags me back into the kitchen and I'm feeling stupid and younger-brotherish but also dangerously happy. There's probably some Latin phrase that means 'Let your big sister seize the day.'

Claudia's insisting to Toby that she's never talked to anyone on a plane before and Toby's saying, 'Yes, but they all say that, all the big plane talkers.'

And she says, 'No, really, and I tried it again on the way home from Singapore and got a frightful man who thought I wanted to have sex with him or something. The number of times I had to tell him we wouldn't actually be sharing his blanket . . . but I'd give it another shot, I suppose. Maybe I am a plane talker now. You've got nothing to lose. Not too much, anyway.'

Tash, who has absolutely nothing to lose, gets straight to inviting her to the wedding. Why can't she seize the day for me just a little more gently?

'If you don't have anything on, of course,' she says, and Claudia says, 'Well, nothing that can't move around a bit.'

'It's just up the M11,' Toby says. 'You turn off at Royston. We've got a map drawn. So that's it then. You're coming. Great. Now, there should be no more tea tonight. Our empty wedding chair is filled, and we shall drink wine.'

He opens a magnum of something cheap and red and Italian, and when it's done he opens another.

Tash says, 'I'm so happy,' and it's the first time she's said that.

We all have our moments, happy and otherwise. Claudia goes from being the raconteur to being a bit drunk and rather sad, and Tash offers to make up a bed on the sofa.

'It folds out,' she says, but Claudia says she has to go home to the cat.

'Probably soon,' she says. 'Actually, probably ages ago.'

It's another half hour before she gets Tash to call her

a cab, and the four of us go and wait near the door. Outside it's raining softly, and stupidly cold for an evening that's allegedly happening in spring. A big fat black London cab pulls up.

'Back to reality,' Claudia says, and that's what I'm thinking, too.

Don't go, don't go, that's what I'm thinking. So what if the cat's stuck inside and weeing all over the place? It already stinks because of the rising damp. And I've seen Butch's photo. He's kind of on the fat side. You wouldn't have to feed him till Tuesday at least.

Claudia stands on the top step with the rain drizzling down onto her hair and she says, 'Now, I have to be fair,' with a tone that says fairness is everything. 'So I'm going to have to kiss you all.'

She goes to Toby first, and he gets a peck on the cheek. Then to Tash, who gets that plus a hug. Me last, more of a hug and she kisses my neck and whispers, 'Thank you.'

And I'm drunk now, too, I have to admit it, and her ear's right in front of me and I should reply so I whisper, 'That's okay. Just between you and me, my life's sort of quietly fucked at the moment as well.'

And she goes, 'Ha,' a laugh that's just between the two of us, and she moves her head back, then closes in and kisses me on the mouth. Possibly for several seconds, but I know enough to realise that drunk people's estimations of time are bad.

'I'll call you,' she says. 'Maybe tomorrow morning. To sort out the arrangements for Saturday.'

And then she stumbles down a step, clangs against

the railings, rights herself and sets off for the cab.

'No tongues,' Tash says. 'How merciful of the two of you. That was hardly like school at all.'

'No, I told you.'

I turn to go inside, and I'm feeling weary. I turn right into the front room and slump onto the nearest sofa.

'Well,' I say, giving the issue a little more thought, 'not entirely like school. But it is sort of crush-ish I suppose. More smitten, though. Smitten's nice. Sweetly smitten. A smitting not a crush, and that's as it should be.' My eyes are closed – I realise that rather abruptly, but it doesn't seem to open them. 'I'm older now and, as you can see, far wiser for it.'

Tash laughs. I feel my shoes coming off.

'Good man,' Toby says. 'There's not always enough wisdom around here.'

There's a slapping sound, a single slap of hand hitting trousered thigh.

'My fault, of course,' he says. 'I'm nothing more than the sum of my shortcomings, most days.'

And Tash says, 'Just as long as you know that.'

And he says, 'Always.'

Weddings and Wonderbras

Imogen Edwards-Jones

'So what do you think?' asks Claire standing on my doorstep, sporting a huge, faux fun fur hat and a long red jacket, looking like Sophie Rhys Jones. She smiles keenly. 'Rubbish, isn't it?' she sighs answering her own question, as she corkscrews a cigarette butt into my doormat. 'I just don't know how to dress for a wedding any more, now I no longer need to pull,' she sighs again. 'There are huge disadvantages of having a boyfriend, you know,' she insists. 'Not least not being able to underwire your breasts when going to a wedding . . . Anyway,' she adds, 'come to think of it, you look pretty rubbish, too.'

Irritatingly enough Claire is right. I am certainly not at my most attractive, in fact, I am probably at my most unattractive – which is unfortunate – as today is rather a big day. Today is the day that Claire and I have been looking forward to since the minute the robust invitation forced its way through the front door. For today is the day that Jemma and Alex have finally decided to get married.

Not that Claire and I particularly care about the 'finally' part. Jemma and Alex have, after all, known each other since the first year of university, which is going on twelve years now. And they have, as so many modern couples do, been living together for the majority of that time. So, truth be known, the wedding has hardly come as any great gobsmacking surprise.

No, the thing that Claire and I are particularly excited about is the university reunion bit of today. '*The Big Chill* aspect of it all', as Claire pointed out over seven vodka and tonics last week. Not strikingly popular at Bristol, we were both dropped as speedily as a prostitute's pants as soon as the rest of the group entered the real world. So today will be the day, the first time in over a decade, that either of us will have seen any of them. The first time, since we shared those life-changing moments together – smoking pot (all of us), hennaing our hair (Claire and me), cultivating our armpits (um . . . me), but most importantly of all, having sex (me and Mark . . . and possibly Rachel).

Claire and I have, of course, hired a car. It was Claire's idea. If she wasn't allowed to 'score' at this wedding, she explained, she was certainly going to 'swank', show them all how well she was doing selling advertising space on a top-shelf men's magazine. They are all going to be so impressed, so her logic went, that they would all be really sorry they hadn't tried to suck up to her more all those years ago.

'So what do you think?' she asks, arm extended in the

general direction of what looks like an extremely fast car.

'Great,' I smile, trying to keep my head as still as possible. 'What is it?'

'Something red with fuel injection, because it did over 120 mph just now on the Westway,' she announces proudly, as she swans into my one-up, one-down house and throws herself onto my just-puffed, pale pink sofa.

'Gosh,' I say, unable to contain my lack of enthusiasm.

'Exactly how bad is your hangover?' quizzes Claire, with the familiarity gleaned from two years living together.

'Quite bad,' I smile weakly.

'Quite bad?'

'Oh, okay. Shocking,' I admit.

'How late?'

'Four in the morning,' I moan.

'Why?'

'Oh, I don't know,' I reply with more irritation than I intend. 'It seemed appropriate and interesting at the time.'

'Who were you with?'

'D'you know?' I confess. 'I'm not sure I can really remember.'

'Très groovy,' she says, lighting up another cigarette. 'Hurry up and get ready,' she chivvies. 'We should leave in about ten minutes.'

'But I am ready,' I protest.

'You are?' she says, sitting up and exhaling all at the same time. 'But I thought you'd just come straight from a nightclub.'

'Oh,' I reply, looking down at my pink strappy sandals with stratospherically high heels, my fluoro fishnet stockings and my raspberry plunge-neck top, black side-split skirt, and Wonderbra with straps so short I could lick my own cleavage. 'I was just trying to make an impression.'

'Well, that should certainly do the trick,' smiles Claire, swinging her feet off the sofa. 'There'll be no mistaking you . . . Shall we make a move?'

It is one of those clear, balmy, blue mornings that the English summer occasionally manages to pull off when it puts its mind to it. A lone fast-food-choked bird breaks into song, while clouds like fluffy cleansing pads drift along in the sky. Claire floors the Audi Quattro, with optional sunroof extra, and generously awards random one- or two-fingered gestures, as she weaves her way through the traffic, heading towards the M4.

'What a wonderful day.' Claire inhales so deeply she nearly bursts the brass buttons off her military-style jacket. Her faux fun fur hat flaps around in the breeze on the back seat, while she leans over the radio in the front, searching for anything but Capital FM.

'Feeling better?' she smiles as she turns towards me, her blonde highlights sailing perpendicular to her head, waving like ears of corn through the sunroof.

'Not too bad,' I reply, kicking aside the two empty crisp packets already cluttering up the passenger foot well.

'So? Who are you most looking forward to seeing?'

'Sara,' I say, barely without a pause.

'No-o-o?' replies Claire, sounding shocked. 'Why he-e-r?'

'Oh,' I say. 'In the vain hope that her peach-perfect backside might have slid halfway towards her suitably fat knees by now.'

'Know what you mean, I have always hated that sort of quiet confidence she had about her. The way she was always assured of her own marvellousness. The way she minced around in those Lycra cycling shorts like they were invented for her tight little arse.'

'Yeah,' I agree. 'Talking of smug, I bet you anything smug Rachel will be there, smugly pregnant, smoothing her shiny smug hair.'

'Oh God, smug Rachel, she is so bloody . . . smug,' Claire shivers at the wheel.

'Horrible.'

'Who else do I hate?' I say.

'Hairy Penny with her moustache?'

'Oh God, she was damned worthy, all she ever made me feel was that I was light, trite, shallow and really rather stupid. God, worthy people,' I shudder. 'I wonder what's worse, worthiness or smugness?'

'Penny-tache,' muses Claire. 'I wonder what has happened to her? D'you know, I don't think I ever really hated her as much as you did?'

'She's probably some bloody human bloody rights lawyer, or a bloody UNESCO consultant,' I mutter, edging my nose through the window like an Afghan hound. 'Which of course are a helluva lot more marvellous than a bloody cinema manager.'

'Well, at least it's a bloody art house cinema, Alice,'

enthuses Claire. 'You could be doing the Odeon in Leicester Square which would be a whole lot more . . .'

'Lucrative?' I suggest.

'Sad,' she grins, and leans in to light another cigarette. 'Which reminds me. I hear Mark is one of the ushers?' she exhales with exaggerated nonchalance.

Mark. My heart starts to race. My cheeks burn. The palms of my hands sweat. I feel really rather sick. That's the dreadful thing about being chucked. Somehow, no matter how cool and smashing you now think you are, it still hurts. As the chucker, things are simple enough, done and dusted and confined to the annals of history, something to be screamed uproariously over in the company of tequila slammers in a bar. 'Chri-ist and I was in love with him!' We all laugh. 'I gave him my Mexican silver ring with turquoise inlays!' We all laugh again. 'And we had sex!' A couple now weep with hysteria. Someone falls off their stool, becomes alcoholically incontinent and protests very loudly that they have to pee. The whole thing is so amusing. It is what's known as a chucker's top night out, tripping up memory lane.

But as the chucked, things are dramatically different. No matter how hard you try, no matter how many special brave faces you put on, the bastards remain in your system. You dream about them in your sleep. You think about them on long train journeys, staring out of the window at passing cows. You still talk about them when extremely drunk at parties. And we all have our favourite story. 'There he was in the bed, a post-coital roll-up smoking between his fingers,' is how mine always begins, 'when I decided to nymph naked across the room in search of something suitably ethnic and diaphanous to wear. I felt wonderful and gorgeous until he opened his mouth. "Christ," he snarled, his top lip curling with contempt, the ashtray balanced on his chest. "Christ," he repeated. "You've got a wide . . . flat . . . arse." Needless to say (I am normally in tears at this point) my confidence is so in tatters that I have never walked around naked again.'

'Mark, you say? Interesting, I can't say I have thought about him much recently . . . really,' I lie.

'Oh,' says Claire. 'You surprise me.'

She knows I'm lying. I know I'm lying. The whole reason why I'm in this hungover state in the first place is because of him. Instead of a sensible night in, depilating in the company of *Friends*, I had numbed my nervous tension by downing more shorts and chasers in one night than a stag weekend with Oliver Reed. As a consequence, instead of looking calm, confident, preened and manicured, I exude sweaty open-pored glamour infused with the gentle heady aroma of a slops-soaked carpet. But Claire good-naturedly elects to accept my lie and breezily changes the subject. With a flick of her ash, she regales me with anecdotes of the marvellousness of her own new relationship almost as far as Membry Services. In fact by the time that we stop for full-fat Cokes, Skips, and mechanically recovered egg sandwiches, to line our stomachs against future alcohol attack, I know exactly how much fun her life has become since I moved out, and Tim moved in.

For not only does the man flip and flick her around like Olga Korbutt between the sheets, he is kind and sensitive and a total dream around the house. He, apparently, has none of the bad habits that I have. He spits cleanly down the basin and puts the lid on the toothpaste. He cooks *and* washes up. He changes the loo roll. He loves Chunky Monkey ice-cream and doesn't moan at the sentimentality of *When Harry Met Sally*. He takes videos back to Blockbuster and doesn't complain at the idea of doing a weekly shop. He doesn't make Pot Noodles at four in the morning when he comes home inebriated, nor does he leave his bra over the back of the sofa at the end of a long hard day counting the ice-cream and popcorn takings. So as we speed up the long tree-lined avenue towards the village of Threpford, near Bath, any hope that Claire might have regretted asking me to move out three weeks ago so her assistant on *Something For The Weekend* or *SFTW* could move in, is dashed. As is any idea of a *rapprochement* with Mark.

'Jesus, there he is!' I squeal, sliding down in the leather seat, trying to hide.

'Where . . .? Where . . .?' replies Claire, spinning her head like the girl in *The Exorcist*.

'There!' I say, cowering and jabbing the air frantically with my finger. 'Fag, chatting up a thin blonde girl, leaning against the graveyard wall.'

'What the hell are you doing down there?' says Claire, looking down at me kneeling amongst the cans, crisps and sandwich boxes in the foot-well.

'I don't know!' I hiss, not knowing.

'Get up,' she hisses right back. 'I have hired this car for a reason . . . so for Christ's sake sit up and pose,' she says through her grinning, gritted teeth. 'Hi!' she waves to two fat-ankled girls in transparent floral dresses, clutching pastel pashminas. 'Hi everyone,' she repeats as she slowly spins the car round the tight driveway, before realising there is nowhere to park. She stalls it as she attempts to pose just that bit more and then spins it right back out again, only to be directed into the lane.

Three minutes later, we are crunching back up the drive towards the diminutive grey-stone chapel, happy faces firmly in place.

'Try not to make a total arse of yourself,' smiles Claire as we approach the mêlée of fluttering frocks, floral hats and striped trousers. 'I'm glad I left my hat in the car,' she continues, looking at a large girl in something faux and furry and really quite similar.

'How do I look?' I mutter, as my right ankle gives way on the uneven ground. I recover well.

'Gorgeous, lovely, head up, swing the hips,' grins Claire some more.

'Is he looking? Is he looking? I can't look.'

'Hang on a sec,' she scours the crowd.

'Look, I can't cope, the tension is killing me.'

'Wait . . . wait . . . there he is,' hisses Claire out of the side of her mouth. 'Yup . . . yup . . . he's looking . . . you have been clocked, girl.'

'Oh . . . HA, HA, ha, ha!' I laugh loudly and

expansively, flicking my hair like I've just stepped out of a salon.

'What . . . the hell . . . are . . . you . . . doing?' whispers Claire, incredulity forcing her voice whole octaves higher.

'Looking popular,' I reply, grinning away. 'Looking very popular.'

'More like certifiable . . . just act natural,' she smiles broadly. 'Hi,' she says turning towards a slim, glossy, dark-haired girl in a navy knee length number that plunges at the front and the back and looks expensive.

'Ahhhh!' the girl screams.

'Ahh!' Claire screams back.

'Ahhh!' so do I.

'Look at you-u-u!' she says.

'Look at you-u-u!' Claire and I reply.

'Claire Hollands and Alice Irvine! Ahhhh!' she repeats, hopping from one slim leg to the other, opening her arms and group hugging the space in front of her.

'Sa-ra Hey-wo-od!' says Claire very slowly, as we both undress her, going over every single angle, curve and well-placed bit of adipose. It is an entirely disheartening move. For not only does her figure-hugging dress have something worth clinging to, but her peach-perfect behind has not moved south but apparently further north.

'Actually,' she smiles. 'It's Lauri di Castello . . . now,' she adds with a blinding flash of a rock the size of Gibraltar that weighs heavily on her left hand. 'You?' she asks with a glossy flick of her hair.

'Any day now,' assures Claire.

'Good for you . . .!' replies Sara, tapping her on the shoulder with a square-tipped shiny nail. 'Well done . . .! Alice?'

She says my name in such a way that what I want to say is I am a lesbian, just to see her grope – hard and fast – for a liberal face to replace the patronising one she is now wearing, but instead I say the same.

'Oh, any day now, too,' I smile.

'Good for you too,' she smiles, turning to slip her arm through that of a plump-lipped, affluent-looking Italian with a manner as oiled as his hair. 'Are the lucky men here?'

'No,' we both say together.

'Shame,' she smiles.

'Mmm,' we say.

'Well . . . see you later!' she adds before trotting along behind her husband.

Claire and I are left standing outside the church.

'What did you say that for?' she asks.

'I don't know,' I reply, thinking I could quite easily have asked the same question. 'There is just something about her . . .'

'We should hurry up, the bride will be here in a sec.'

Inside the church is packed. The dark wooden pews, each sporting a jaunty wreath of pink and white flowers tied on with a white satin bow, are all full. On the ushers' instructions the women, in big hats and best dresses, huddle in twos or threes on the benches, their backs to the door. At each of the stone pillars that form a colonnade either side of the short church, stand groups of men in smart morning suits, ill-fitting morning suits and just plain old suits. Some of them are losing their hair. Others, rotund on early success, have developed expense-account paunches and loose taxi buttocks. There are few who have aged well. The sun pours through the colourless diamond-shape leaded windows. The air is chilled and the previously dormant dust hangs in the air like some moorland mist.

Claire and I walk into the back of the church and are lucky enough to find two wicker chairs lined up next to a pillar on the far right of the aisle. Our view of the altar is restricted, but the one of the ushers all seated together at the opposite end of the church, is not.

Even from this distance Mark is handsome. Tall, slim, a white rose in his buttonhole, his dark curly hair is shining in the sunlight. He is hunched over, leafing through the Order of Service, checking how long he has to wait before the drinks. He shares a joke with the bloke sitting next to him who looks like Alex's brother and then sits back to check out the church. I watch his eyes scan the pews for people he knows, a smile curls his lips as he waves and nods to various heads. He takes an age to see me. While my heart leaps and performs unfeasible feats in my chest, he just stares. I grin, it's wide and manic like a serial killer with a knife in the toaster. He is not impressed. He simply nods and goes back to reading his Order of Service.

The organ suddenly strikes up and Jemma appears at the door in something simple and white, strappy and cut on the cross, holding a huge bunch of lilies. As the overweight organist with fingers like a butcher's window belts out the bride's entrance, Claire suddenly grabs my arm.

'She's pregnant,' she whispers.

'No she isn't.'

'She is,' Claire insists, leaning along the line for a closer look. 'She never had tits before and now look, she's built like a Playmate centrefold.'

'Maybe they're saline,' I reply behind my hand. I can't argue they are not there, because two zeppelins in white headscarves entered the church a whole chord before the rest of her.

'No I've seen fake, and take it from me those aren't fake,' announces Claire, boasting her superior knowledge again.

The bride kissed and the register signed, Claire and I cut the crap and head straight for the canapés. In fact I'm four tinned asparagus tips wrapped in brown bread down, by the time Claire's fixed her lip-gloss in the Portaloo cabin mirror, and made it back into the marquee.

'Seen anyone we know yet?' she asks.

'Not yet,' I mumble.

'Well, she is four and a half months gone,' declares Claire, reaching for a Rider on Horseback as it goes past.

'Really?' I say, finishing off a Pinky in a Blanket.

'One of the bridesmaids was gossiping on the loo,' she says before following along after a tray of flutes as they circuit the room.

I stand and smoke, keeping busy, smiling at the various guests as one by one they trip over the coconut matting on the way to the toilets. A group of music students is murdering 'Greensleeves', while the pink and white motif-ed marquee fills up.

'Hello?' comes a voice. 'It is Alice, isn't it?'

'Yes,' I smile.

'Paul,' he says. 'We did French together.'

'Oh right. Yes. Hi,' I say, trying not to stare at the rather large spot on his cheek.

'So what are you up to?' he asks, taking a sip of his champagne.

'Oh, I am really well, running this arts cinema in Hampstead,' I smile.

'You!' he says. 'Arts,' he adds. 'But you know nothing about the arts.'

'I know,' I laugh. 'And you've lost most of your hair.'

It would honestly have been quicker to flick Vs at each other from the other side of the room and be done with it, I think, as he walks off, leaving me near the toilets again. I never liked him. Anyway, Claire is still here somewhere because I can hear her laugh, and I have seen Mark over the other side of the marquee seemingly avoiding me at all costs. I don't know why everyone always says that weddings are great fun. I have always found them depressing. I finish off my fourth flute and start to circulate somewhat unsteadily on my heels. Near a flower-festooned pillar in the middle of the room, nursing a flute, on her own, is Penny Adams.

'Hello,' I say. 'How are you?'

'Just terrific,' she replies, her reassuringly hirsute top lip catching the light. 'You?'

'Oh, just terrific,' I reply. 'Got this really highly paid job running this multiplex cinema, have a lovely boyfriend, we live together in a big house in North Kensington, you know, the usual sort of thing . . . you?'

'I have just come back from counselling flood victims in Mozambique,' she replies, draining her glass.

'Great,' I say. 'That sounds . . . um . . . rewarding.'

'Surely not as rewarding as seeing me?' says this smooth voice as a pair of hands finger their way around my waist.

'Mark?' I say trying not to sound too much like a breathy damsel in a 50s movie.

'Hi, Al,' he smiles. 'You look underwired,' he adds, biting his lips as he stares at my cleavage.

'God, not really,' I giggle, flicking my hair. 'Just a little something I . . .'

'I was wondering when you two would finally have a chat,' slurs Sara, who has somehow managed to squeeze her pert backside between the two of us. 'Bit late though, Marky,' she adds, borrowing his shoulder while she taps the side of her nose. 'It seems that our little Alice has got herself a boyfriend and a source tells me that wedding bells are imminent.'

'Well . . . no. Well . . . yes . . . well,' I smile.

'Good for you!' says Mark, kissing me just above the ear. 'I'm not far off myself, am I, darling?' he adds, turning to squeeze the smug behind of a smug-backed, smug girl. Rachel Smug, who simply turns round

296

smugly and lets off a smug smile.

'It's only a matter of months, isn't it, da-a-arling,' smiles Rachel, smugly flicking her hair.

Deflating like a popped party balloon, I keep it together enough to retire to the corner with a bottle of champagne. I listen to some bloke called Walter talk about how much fun we had doing the Spanish play. I struggle through my plate of coronation chicken listening to some fat and florid uncle talk about the wonderful and fabulous charms of his niece. I cheer as they cut the cake. I laugh at the turgid best man's speech, and then I disgrace myself a bit dancing to 'Come On Eileen'. I sit back down at an almost empty table covered in greenery and empty bottles and realise I haven't seen Claire for a long time. I light another cigarette, develop a mild form of marquee spin and I feel that I need some air.

It's a blissfully warm night, as I walk through the garden under the stars. The strains of 'Hi Ho Silver Lining' float across the flare-lit lawn. I walk to the bottom of the garden and turn back to look at the golden light of the marquee. There's a noise off to my left. The bushes are bouncing and grinding with the regular monotony of sex. I approach on tiptoe, tickled at the prospect of sharing the gossip with Claire. There's one long loud and appreciative moan and then the noise stops. I stand at the entrance to the bushes, hands on my hips, smile at the ready, awaiting the bust. Suddenly Claire appears, buttoning up her Sophie Rhys Jones jacket, pulling down her skirt.

'Oh my God, Alice,' she says, looking up adjusting her Wonderbra. There is a rustle behind her. 'Um, Alice – this is Mark. I believe you two have already met.'

Death of an Executive

Tim Ferguson

Norman Renquist was lord of all he surveyed, captain of his ship, mayor of his tidy town, Grand High Poobah of the Order, and General Manager of the divine realm that was known simply as The Network. Always immaculately dressed in suits that were five years behind the fashion but twenty years ahead of Renquist, the General Manager was the Last Word – the place where bucks didn't just stop, they froze in fright and watched with dumb fascination as the headlights approached. With a squirt too much l'Egoiste Pour Homme on his cheek, and that new bint from Publicity's lipstick on his balls, there was no greater man than this regal lord who sat on his throne, glaring darkly down the boardroom table at his assembled minions. The Board, The Owner and Shareholders aside, Renquist was king.

Which was why it came as a shock to all attending when, mid-speech, Norman lurched from his chair and fell shuddering to the carpet in the throes of a heart attack.

The meeting had been going so well. Since entering the halls of power, Norman had refined the art of entering a room. He knew well that proximity to power is guarded more jealously than power itself. So he never entered alone – he'd barge in laughing and slapping the back of someone, anyone, so long as the other execs saw it. They'd stew on it for the rest of the meeting, wondering what they were missing out on. And he always entered at full speed or, to use a footy expression, 'on the full'. The momentum would stick· with him for a minute or so.

He had also learned to give an emphatic, irritable, exasperated 'No' to whatever was first on the meeting's agenda. This gave everyone notice that he was in full executive mode, able to cast aside the dreams, toil and aspirations of his respected colleagues without skipping a heartbeat. If the matter was something he wanted to give an emphatic, irritable, exasperated 'Yes' to, he simply employed one of his many original hybrid expletives and shifted it to the back of the pile.

Thus, on this day Norman Renquist had entered the boardroom of the Network in grand style, Dunhill smoke chuffing from his nostrils, mobile phone in his jacket pocket bleeping 'Waltzing Matilda', goblet of claret appearing from nowhere and sploshing everywhere. His shock of white hair glistened with gunk after his visit to the make-up lady. It felt greasy, clammy, like woven rats' tails. But it looked, according to the make-up lady, absolutely magnificent, no really. For today, the lord of the manor had chosen one of his most lurid bow ties – a hot pink number adorned with fluorescent yellow racehorses galloping every which way. He wore no wedding ring, just to keep his bastard wife on notice.

Renquist, plunging into the boardroom at full speed, was guffawing at some half-baked innuendo made by Godfrey Buchanan, Head of Production. Renquist gripped Godfrey's flimsy shoulder like he was a true mate of the highest order and not a lying cunt with a limited future. Godfrey smiled his shoelace-thin smile, surprised that his innuendo had found such good soil with the boss. But before Godfrey could lay another one on him, the chief was steaming on to the head of the table, clicking his free fingers and speaking with his cigarette still in his mouth, 'Let's go, people, fuck, come on, let's go, Suzie how are ya darl, love the skirt, let's go, let's fucking go, the hell is Jock, ah, there you are y'bastard, did y'get me those tickets, let's go, switch off those mobiles, your master's voice is about to speak, I swear I love that skirt, Sooz, love it to pieces . . .'

Everyone called everyone else 'mate' and sloshed vino into their glasses. All except Jock Newton, Head of Sport, who quaffed the last of his coffee and poured some Margaret River red into his mug. 'Robbo's in Japan, Normie. Sends his love.'

'Fuck's he doing in Japan?'

'Working his guts out, mate, rest assured.'

'Remind me to become Head of News. The bastard's a bigger traveller than the one I used to get on the school bus.'

Dutiful laughter from all, even the new bint from Publicity. She was sharp enough to laugh at Renquist's jokes, particularly the ones that weren't funny. *Watch out, Suzie, this one's a killer.*

Renquist affected a need to adjust the Roman blinds that looked over the car park, giving the others time to sit. There were six of them, the Heads of Sport, Production, Programming, Drama, Sales and Publicity. Seven if you counted the new bint who'd managed to sneak in as note-taker. Renquist took note. She dutifully made no eye contact with him, lest the others discovered their dirty secret, but if Renquist knew anything about television, the bastards knew already. Idly, he wondered how many other eyes she was avoiding.

The others shuffled to their positions, slow enough to seem unhurried to their colleagues, fast enough to seem respectful to the chief. 'Suck up and spit down,' as Norman often said.

Once the group had settled themselves, lit their ciggies and clicked their pens, the chief turned from the blinds and commenced his opening salvo.

'Good news, bad news, I'll give them together. *Plastic Surgeon* rated its tits off. Thirty-two points. Bugger me if reality isn't the next big escapism. But the fuckers who made it want to sue us for playing it outside of the agreed timeslot which was – Wazza?'

Warren Garret, Programmer, golfer, golfer and Programmer, woke in fright from his reverie at the end of the table. 'Eight-thirty Tuesday, like it's any of their business . . .'

'Eight-thirty Tuesday, thank you Wazza.' Renquist strode to the head of the table and took his seat, a large, black executive number that did everything but give head. He pressed a silver button on the armrest and the chair reclined an inch with an electric hum. 'Sadly, it *is* their business because to get them signed before the other mob poached 'em, *someone* put a timeslot into the deal. I've looked this act up in the *Oxford Concise* and found the term "monstrous breach of every fucking thing we hold dear". The Legal Department's been strung up by the testicles, even the girls. Blood will be spilt, heads will roll, et cetera, et cetera. But we won't be showing plastic surgeons carving up the tits of the rich and ugly next week. Kiss thirty-two points goodbye.'

Wazza gave a deep sigh.

'I know how you feel, Wazza, I really do,' said Renquist as though Wazza had lost a family member. 'So, people, we need something to fill up eight-thirty Tuesdays until further notice. Suggestions?'

Toby Fulham, Head of Drama, peered dimly through his twee lemon-tinted Lennon glasses. Toby was once a sports director – footy matches, cricket, the Olympic swimmers. Two years back he made a doco for The Network called *Aussie Cricket Legends*. It rated a forty. In the same month, the then Head of Drama commissioned a gutsy, hard-edged mini-series with a top-notch cast, ground-breaking director and fresh, incisive script. While it didn't rate so well, the Head of Drama was pleased that the series won high critical acclaim and got sold to the BBC and Germany. Renquist took great pleasure in sacking the deluded fuck. Toby was the ideal replacement – he took orders, made a high-rating mini-series on the life of Saint Donald Bradman, dreamt up a beachside soapie all by himself and slavishly agreed with every word Renquist uttered. 'Suck up and swallow,' as Renquist often said.

Toby cleared his throat. 'Eight-thirty Tuesday. There's that sitcom thing we shot over Christmas. I'd like to give it a go.'

'The thing with the talking cat?'

'Yes. It's got legs, I reckon.'

'The cat or the show?'

'Both.'

Renquist made a show of giving the idea absolutely no thought before delivering an emphatic, irritable, exasperated 'No.'

Yes, it was all going nicely to plan. As the Heads bickered about what could fill the prized Tuesday slot, the General Manager swished down some claret and snuck a peek at Head of Publicity Suzie Carter's fabulous breasts which were on show as usual. In Norman's estimation, Suzie was enjoying the last days of her beauty. Her sun-dried skin was already beginning to sag on her scaffolding.

He didn't bank on Suzie being around much longer. Forty was the prime breeding age for publicists. Renquist had seen it again and again. He could hear a publicist's body-clock alarm bell ringing before she heard it herself. One day she'd be happy in her work, the next she'd experience a belated desire to leave something behind – something more than a pile of *TV Week* covers and an *Animal Surgeon* photo feature. Renquist knew the signs and had lately seen them in Suzie.

In his view, babies shouldn't cause a problem. Four

weeks off for birthing and recovery, then the little darling treasure could be palmed off to a child-care centre. Mum would be back on board in six weeks tops, weary, a little guilty for the trouble she'd caused, but ready to publicise. Suzie, however, was a loyal, old-fashioned sort. Lots of strong Catholic family values. She wouldn't surrender the baby to child care for at least three months and that was too long. A younger, firmer, sharper girl would have taken her place in three months. Someone like this new bint – she was a killer. It was a shame, really. If Suzie had been born a man, Renquist reckoned she could have succeeded him as General Manager. She had the nous, the guts, the will and those terrific tits. But the good Lord had made her a woman and there was only so far a woman could rise at The Network, nothing personal.

It was just that if they let a woman in the top chair, they'd never get her out of it. Someone like Suzie would be too good at it, undistracted as she was by male pursuits and drives. Renquist had always said there was no nice way to cut a man's throat. As he looked at her now, he knew Suzie would find a nice way, a smart way that would keep everyone happy – a way to slice and stitch at the same time. Thank God she was a woman.

Renquist first realised the survival skills of Suzie when she'd let him come onto her in his office during a station Christmas party. They'd kissed, Suzie with a delicate flicking tongue that seemed to be searching for a place in Renquist's gob that didn't taste of French onion dip and Dunhills, Renquist's tongue groping and shoving like a front-row forward who's lost his shorts in a scrum. To use a footy expression.

He'd wanted to fuck there and then and had pulled out the Little General Manager. Suzie ruefully declined, pleading that if they started something, she knew she'd fall in love with him. Renquist saw her point – he was an attractive, powerful man. But the next thing he knew, Suzie had become best buddies with his bastard wife. They swapped gossip, cuddled, went out on girls' nights. At first Renquist thought there might be some dyke thing going on, which was fine by him. It took him a whole month to realise Suzie was stitching him up. After a meeting that hadn't gone Suzie's way, he came home to find his wife in one of her lathers, cursing him for hurting poor Suzie's feelings. The message was simple – fuck with me and I'll fuck with your marriage. It was the act of a true executive. Thank God she was a woman.

A bullbar hit Renquist in the chest and he grunted in pain. His heart was going to burst out of his chest, he knew it. Struggling for breath, he looked up through a red, clouding mist at the others.

To Renquist, they all seemed to be moving in slow motion. Then, through his agony, he realised this was not due to a distorted perception on his part – the fuckers were moving in slow motion.

'Jeez,' murmured the bald and lanky Dalgleish, Head of Sales, 'What do we, uh . . . do?' As a sign of his great distress at his master's dire predicament, Dalgleish went so far as to extend a wiry arm and dab his cigarette in the ashtray, extinguishing the tip while saving the rest for later. Ascension in the upper halls of a network are based strictly on a 'what have you done for us lately' principle. As Head of Sales and mastermind of the new Mitsubishi deal, Dalgleish was next in line for the top post.

Wazza Garret, golfer, Programmer, Programmer and golfer, attempted a heroic leap across the table to save his master, but barked his shin on the edge of it. He began rolling around the floor, gripping his knee as though he too was having some kind of attack. 'Shit, shit, oh Christ, shit!'

Godfrey Buchanan did what Heads of Production do in emergencies and ran off in search of someone who knew what to do. The others gathered around, staring helplessly down at their contorting master.

Renquist heard a high-pitched squawk and wondered if it was coming from him. Then Suzie barked at the new bint from Publicity, 'That's enough of your squealing, thank you,' unknowingly echoing Renquist's words to the girl only ten minutes previously. The new bint, who had done a marketing degree, a business degree and a desktop publishing something-or-other, stopped squealing. *Too quickly*, thought Renquist. *Ten minutes ago she was licking m' lollypop, now she's stopped squealing in two seconds flat. Bitch, this is probably her fault. I told her, don't work it once I've shot, sends me into a spin. Fuck, this hurts.*

The man of action in all the frenzied shuffling and eyebrow-raising was, of course, Head of Sport Jock Newton. Jock was flame-haired and built like a brick shithouse. He'd been the top rower in Renquist's last year at Scots. Throwing aside his double-breasted jacket to reveal his new Network golf shirt complete with gold-plaid station logo, the muscular Newton leapt upon Renquist's cramped form and wrestled him onto his back.

Newton gave Renquist a manly wink. 'Don't worry, Normie, Jock's gotcha.' Renquist's reaction was to struggle like his life depended on it. And well it may. Newton was always telling people he'd been in Vietnam. Everyone assumed the war trauma he'd suffered there explained why Newton was a fucking lunatic. Only Renquist knew that Jock hadn't been in Vietnam during the War at all – he'd merely holidayed there in 1986, suffering a nasty case of food poisoning from some Saigon Hilton yum-cha. But Newton thought his Vietnam Experience was just as traumatic as any war. This was because he was a fucking lunatic.

Jock Newton carried for ever a certainty that his Vietnam Experience endowed him with the right to take command in any crisis. For this particular situation, he chose to sit on Renquist like an emergency doctor, clasp his own enormous fists together, heave his buffalo torso back and slam down on Renquist's flabby chest with full force.

'I heard a cracking sound,' said Suzie, in distress or satisfaction Renquist couldn't tell.

'Ribs – that'll give his heart more room.' Newton spoke with battlefield urgency. 'Stand back. He needs air.'

What Renquist needed was for the Head of Sport to stop splintering his ribs, but his heart attack kept him from saying it. Besides, maybe Newton knew what he was talking about. After all, he'd been in Vietnam where people have heart attacks all the time.

'Hit him harder, Jock,' barracked Toby Fulham. 'I've seen this on *Emergency Surgeon*. You've gotta whack them hard or there's no point.'

Dalgleish gazed upon Renquist with a scientist's detachment. 'Has, uh, anyone told anyone?'

There was an uncomfortable pause. In television networks this question is always accompanied by an uncomfortable pause. Even Renquist seemed between gasps.

Toby piped up. 'Godfrey ran off to get the nurse.'

'Fuck, I think my leg's broken,' said Wazza, still rolling on the carpet. 'Are you sure he's getting the nurse?'

Suzie Carter snapped orders at the new bint, who scrambled for the phone on the trophy shelf that lined the west wall. The girl dialled the wrong number and got through to the Drama Department.

She turned back to Suzie. 'I'm sorry, but who am I supposed to call?'

Renquist's head was ringing like the lunch bell at Scots. *So this is the way the world ends. And I can't even make a whimper.* He stared through the mist at Jock Newton, who was pounding at his chest with enough force to kill him outright. The proximity of death inspired in Renquist a rare moment of self-pity. He wanted to ask Newton if he believed Renquist had been a good man, a fair man. *I know I've been a bastard but it came with the job. Did you know, could you tell it was just part of the job? I was obeying television's natural law.*

I'm not so bad, really, am I? You can't make an omelette without fucking a few chickens, can you? Even a good man has to fuck chickens every once in a while. I tried to do good. In between the things that were necessary, I did some good. And when I was bad, Jock, don't blame me. The chook made me do it.

But even Renquist in his diminishing awareness knew that Jock Newton would be the last person on earth to know what a good man looked like. He was all fucked up from 'Nam.

'It's broken, oh Jesus, I'm sure it's broken,' moaned Wazza, still writhing on the carpet.

'Medic!' shouted Jock between chest thumps. 'Medic! Medic!'

As he felt another rib splinter under Jock's hammering, Renquist looked to Dalgleish for comfort. He'd have had better luck looking for candy-flavoured condoms in a Mormon's wallet. Dalgleish, the slimy pigfuck, was standing above him *with his hands in his pockets.* He was already planning what to put into the eight-thirty Tuesday slot, Renquist just knew it. Some poncy British detective drama, not bad but no thirty-two rating, that was certain. Rancid cuntfuck asslicking piece of –

Renquist came back from wherever the blackness had taken him. He had no idea how long he'd passed out for but it couldn't have been long. Dalgleish was still standing there with his hands in his pockets and Jock was pounding away like there was no tomorrow, which there wasn't. Suzie was there, beautiful Suzie with those marvellous tits, thank God she was a woman, thank *God* she was a woman. Suzie gazed upon him like an angel, her brow furrowed in deep concern. Renquist was about to use his last breath to tell her he loved her, that she should have fucked him at the Christmas party, that he would have loved to have seen her with his bastard wife, in the shower maybe. But just as his lips formed the words, Suzie looked askance at Dalgleish. Jesus Christ, she was sizing him up already. Renquist was dying before her eyes and she was already planning her move on Dalgleish, already gearing up for the succession she'd never win. This is how a pope feels before he dies, thought Renquist. I'm not a man, I'm not a leader, I'm an imminent vacancy.

The thought of the Pope brought an issue to mind. He had to repent of his sins! Fuck! Did he have enough time?

'I think that's enough, Jock,' said Dalgleish and Renquist knew what he meant.

Dear God, oh God, I'm sorry for . . . if I did anything wrong. I should never have . . . done what I did when I was . . . doing . . . wrong . . . things . . . Whatever they may have been . . . I can't think of anything right now because I can't breathe and my blood's stopping in my guts . . . but I hope you don't think things like that blowjob from the new bint in Publicity are a sin because if you do . . . I'm fucked . . . oh, Suzie I love you . . . truly . . . sort of . . .

'This is terrible, terrible,' whispered Toby Fulham, proving Renquist had been wrong about promoting him to the big table. The prick was too dumb to realise he'd be moving up by a parking space tomorrow.

Still, Renquist was touched that Toby realised the utter tragedy, the incomparable loss to the world that he was witnessing. Good old Toby. Perhaps he'd commission a mini-series on Renquist's life, *Boardroom Surgeon*. It'd fill eight-thirty Tuesdays nicely.

Suzie, God love her, told Wazza to shut the fuck up or she'd break his other leg for him. *Atta girl, Sooz. Ah, what you could've been if you'd gone to Scots. I love you and not just because I'm dying . . . God, I wish I'd been born a woman . . . No, I don't.*

Jock was near tears. 'Goddamnit, soldier boy. You can make it. Do it for Jock, son.' One last chest thump for luck. But Renquist was leaving the field of play, going out of bounds, completely arsefucked, to use a footy expression.

The last thing Norman Renquist heard in his life was the voice of that ratpiss cuntfart Dalgleish saying, 'Hold his tongue, someone hold his tongue.'

But Renquist didn't have anything to say.

He never had.

Obedience

Patrick Gale

Perran was slightly late arriving because the puppy was still unused to car travel and first vomited then shat in the Land Rover on the way over. Classes took place in a barn on a remote farm a few miles inland from Zennor. Evidently used for pony classes at other times, the old building was deeply carpeted with sawdust and its inside walls were marked out with whitewashed numbers at intervals.

As always, Chris greeted the dog not the owner.

'Evening, Toffee.'

He pulled Toffee to heel and joined the other pupils walking in a large clockwise circle around her. The dogs varied from a ball of fluff, too young yet to do much more than follow its owner in a childish panic, to a magnificent Belgian Shepherd, forty times its size. There was a handful of clever mongrels, a Border Collie rejected for sheepdog training on account of a 'hysterical tail', an ancient, unexpectedly spiteful Labrador and two white lapdogs he could not place but suspected were French. The owners were as varied as the breeds. There were children dutifully attending with bewildered Christmas presents and two women, well into their sixties, who always wore gaudy fleeces and hats as though to suggest they were warmer than their wintry expressions suggested. These two had dogs who were exceptionally obedient, clearly veterans of many classes, so perhaps they only attended as a favour to Chris, to inspire and encourage.

'Toffee, heel. Good boy,' he said, remembering to keep his tone light and playful because apparently that was what puppies responded to best.

Toffee did not look like a puppy any more. Although only five months old, he was already well over twenty-five kilos and tall enough to rest his head on the kitchen table. He was a source of some guilt. Perran had always wanted a Deerhound, had been fascinated by them ever since he was old enough to pore over guides to different breeds, doubly fascinated because there seemed to be none in the county, only Lurchers of all shapes and coats and the occasional Greyhound, retired from racing and rescued by a charity. He had watched them on the television – at Crufts or in period dramas – and had once been allowed to pet one as it waited obediently outside the beer tent at the Royal Cornwall Show. But owning one of his own had never been possible. First his father vetoed it, buying the family a Golden Retriever instead, precisely, bewilderingly, because it was what other people had. Then there was Val, his wife. Val liked dogs well enough, she maintained, but they should get children out of the way first because a farmhouse was cluttered enough without both. But then children had never come along, first because money was too short and then because of his technical difficulty.

When he saw Deerhound puppies advertised in *Farmer's Weekly*, he became like a man possessed. He twice found pretexts to drive out to Dartmoor to view the litter, each time feeling as guilty as he imagined a man must feel meeting a mistress. The third time he was unable to resist buying one. It cost a crazy amount, enough to pay a broccoli cutter's wages for over twenty days, but he had some cash put by in a building society from when he got lucky on a horse, money Val knew nothing about. He introduced the puppy as a charming mongrel bought for a tenner from a man at the slaughterhouse, somewhere Val never went.

'Ten quid, for *that*?' she complained.

'He says it's nearly a Deerhound,' he told her. 'At least half. Maybe more. You only have to look at him. We can call him Toffee, 'cause he's so soft.'

She fought it for a while but softened when Toffee licked her hand and fell heavily asleep against her feet, exhausted by the terrors of a first car journey. She was adamant, however, that the dog eat nothing more expensive than scraps, that it come no further into the house than the kitchen, that clearing up after it until it was housetrained was entirely his responsibility and that should it fail to be housetrained in six weeks, it was to live in the old milking parlour.

He agreed readily to all conditions in his excitement; the greatest triumph was still his, after all. He hid the pedigree documentation when it arrived from the Kennel Club (Toffee's real name, his secret name, was Glencoe McTavish, of which Toffee had seemed a reasonable and plausible diminutive) and took care to *lose* his various dog encyclopaedias in a bale of things for the parish jumble sale, to lower the chances of Val making comparisons between the breed ideal illustrated and the dramatically emerging lines of their so-called mongrel. Toffee was like a disguised prince in a fairytale; sooner or later his breeding would out.

The deadline for housetraining was two weeks gone. Perran always woke first anyway, trained to farming hours since boyhood, so it was easy enough to slip down to the kitchen, mop up any accidents, plead with Toffee to try to be good next time, then slip back upstairs with a large enough mug of tea to keep Val sweet and in bed while the tell-tale taint of disinfectant floor cleaner had time to disperse. Obedience classes met with no objection; he knew she was glad to have one night a week to herself.

'And halt.' All the owners halted. Half the dogs sat obediently. The other half had to be pushed down. A puppy yelped. You could always spot the puppies who would be a handful if they grew up unchecked, the monsters-in-making. It was the same with children. Everyone watched Chris expectantly. Half the fun of these classes was that you never knew what she would have you do next; jump little pony jumps, weave your dog in and out of poles, have it sit and stay while you walked to the fullest extent of the lead or even let go of the lead altogether and crossed the room, if you were showing off and your dog could do it.

He knew she was a lesbian, that she lived with a driving instructor who had cornered the market in teaching car-shy wives and widows, but that didn't mean he couldn't admire her. She was a good-looking woman, very neat, not like Val, who dressed for warmth and had a horror of revealing herself. Chris showed off her trim figure by wearing jodhpurs and a tailored suede jacket. She carried a little riding crop for pointing with and tapped it against her thigh when they were performing tasks with a pattern to them.

'And weave,' tap, 'and through the tunnel,' tap, 'and halt,' tap. He liked that. She did this for love, since the tiny fee charged could barely cover the cost of barn-hire and training treats, but there was a nice mystery to her because although she plainly loved dogs, she was here without one and you had no way of knowing what breed she favoured.

'So ask her,' Val said, typically, Val who could ask anyone anything. It took a woman without mystery to assume another had nothing to keep to themselves.

Chris waited until she had everyone's attention and a rescue Greyhound called Misty had stopped yodelling.

'Now,' she said. 'Now that we're all here . . .' That was meant for him and Perran looked suitably crestfallen, only no one was laughing. 'I think you'll all agree,' Chris went on, 'it's only right we should have a minute's silence to think about Janice.' He looked around. Everyone was hanging their heads. One of the children was even dutifully mouthing what could have been a prayer. He hung his head too, so that Toffee looked up at him and produced one of his curious cries of uncertainty and impatience that was half yawn, half whimper.

He wanted to crouch down and give him a hug only Chris was always telling off the men in the class for leaning over their dogs too much. He supposed it was love he felt for him. Because of the lack of speech, love for animals was an odd affair, doomed to frustration. You couldn't hug them as hard as you wanted or they'd be frightened. What you really wanted, he supposed, was to *become* them. You wanted to see out of their eyes and have them see out of yours. There was a bit of particularly soft fur, just behind Toffee's huge black ears, that gave out a marvellous scent, a warm, brown biscuity smell, a bit like horse sweat, which brought on this feeling in a rush. He had heard Val talk with friends about babies often enough, heard, with an alien's fascination, how often women were filled with a hot desire to eat them, had once even seen a woman thrust one of her baby's feet entirely into her mouth and suck it.

'So long, Janice,' Chris said at last. 'We'll miss you, girl.' Someone blew their nose. 'Now,' Chris went on, having cleared her throat. 'The police have asked if they can have a brief word with each of us afterwards. Don't worry if you're in a hurry. The sergeant can just take your details and pay a house call tomorrow or whatever. Otherwise they'll want statements tonight.'

'But I thought she was on holiday,' one of the elderly fleece ladies said.

'Were we the last to see her alive, then?' asked her friend.

'Looks like it.'

The Greyhound yodelled again, breaking the gloomy spell.

'Right,' said Chris. 'Misty's getting bored. Let's practise our downs. In a big circle now. That's it. You first, Bessie. Off you go. Not too slow. That's it. I'll tell you when. Now.'

'Down!' said Bessie's owner and Bessie dropped from her trot to flatten herself most impressively in the sawdust. It looked slick but somehow insincere and you sensed she'd never do it so well without an audience.

So Janice was dead. Unthinkable. Janice Thomas. Haulage princess. *Brassica Tsarina* they had called her in The Cornishman once. Her father had begun the business in a small way, running three lorries that collected produce from the farms and took it to a wholesaler in the east. But Janice, hard-faced Janice, who nobody liked much in school, had been away to business college and made some changes when she came home. She wasn't proud. She drove one of the lorries herself for a while until she got to know all the growers, however small. Then she used her knowledge of them to persuade them to sell through her instead of merely using her as haulier, so Proveg was born, sprawling across an industrial estate outside Camborne. She was no fool. She chose the site because there was high unemployment thanks to all the closed mines and retrenching china clay works and labour was cheap. Soon everyone had a son or daughter or wife who had done time in the packing lines or quality-control shed.

The pay wasn't brilliant but she was still regarded as something of a saviour. 'She doesn't *have* to do it,' people said. 'She could have worked anywhere. She could have worked in London for big money.'

Then she began to show her sharper side, bailing out farmers and truck owners in trouble so that she seemed their rescuer until their fortunes took enough of an upturn for them to realise that she now owned their truck or most of their farm. Or rather, that Proveg did. Janice always played a clever game of making out she was just one of the workers and speaking of Proveg as though it owned her, too, and she was merely another employee, paid enough to stay loyal but never quite enough to break away.

She put her father in a home when he went peculiar – a home substantially refurbished by Proveg's charity. She drove several growers to the wall. There was a suicide or two, nothing compared to what BSE caused, but enough to register as a local outrage. Women in their cups joked that some lucky bloke would get his hands on the money soon enough but no man tamed Janice in matrimony. No woman either, for all the mutinous gossip. She lived alone in the hacienda-style estate that had sprouted from the paternal bungalow. She went to church; her pretence of worker solidarity didn't extend to attending Chapel. She smoked with defiant satisfaction. She took one holiday a year – in the brief interval between the end of the winter cauliflowers and the start of the early potatoes – always somewhere fiercely hot from where she would return with a leathery tan that showed off the gold chains that were her only visible finery. She kept a horse and bred Dobermans. She had been bringing the latest puppy to classes for several weeks now. She favoured the lean, houndlike bitches over the heavily muscular males.

When he had mentioned this, Val said, 'Lean or no, she'll never get a husband with those around the house. Devil dogs, they are.'

'Maybe she doesn't want one,' he said. 'A husband, I mean. Maybe she's happy as she is.'

'Happy? Her?' Val asked and snorted in the way she did when she wanted to imply that there were some things only a woman could understand.

'Toffee, heel. Good boy. That's it. Down. *Down!*'

'Don't repeat your order,' Chris said, as he knew she would. 'He'll just learn to ignore you.' But Toffee went down after a fashion, largely because he was tired.

'Good boy,' Perran said, then tugged him back onto his feet. 'Toffee, heel. Good boy.'

Val set great store by marriage. She thought he couldn't understand or wasn't interested, but he could tell. He saw how she divided women into sheep and goats, with marriage the fiery divide between them. Women who lived with a man without marrying him first she thought not loose but foolish. She did not despise spinsters or think them sad, not out loud at least, but it was plain she thought of them as lesser beings. Childlessness, her childlessness, was thus a great wound in her self-esteem. He could tell from the way she huffed and puffed over the young mothers in the village who sometimes blocked its one stretch of pavement with their double-occupancy pushchairs.

'As if they're something really special,' she snorted, but her glare would have a kind of hunger to it.

He did not mind staying on to give a statement. He was collecting Val from the First and Last and she wouldn't thank him for appearing early and cramping her style. He gave his name and recognised the sergeant from schooldays. Garth Tresawle. A mate's younger brother, for ever trailing behind them as they skived off, whining 'wait for me'. And they'd had to wait because even then he had a tendency to take notes and bear witness.

'And when did you last see Ms Thomas?'

'Here,' Perran said. 'Last time we had a class. We talked a bit about boarding kennels because she was about to go on holiday to Morocco. The next day, she said.'

'You drove straight home afterwards?'

'Not exactly. I stopped off at the pub to pick up my wife.'

'What time was that?'

'Nearly closing time. Only she wasn't there. Found out later some friends had taken her on to theirs. Someone's birthday. I went back on my own.'

'Talk to anyone at the pub?'

'Er . . .' he cast his mind back to smoke, music, turned backs around the television. 'No.'

'Did anyone see you get back?'

'No. There's just the two of us and I was asleep when Val got back.' He remembered her drunken curses as she stubbed a toe on one of the bed's sticking-out legs.

'What time was that?'

'I was asleep. Past midnight.'

'How well did you know Ms Thomas?'

'We were at school together. You remember that, Garth. You were there too.'

'Sorry, Perran,' Garth sighed. 'We have to do this by the book.'

'Okay. Sorry.' Toffee whined and Perran settled him back on the sawdust. The wind was rising again, whistling round the barn roof and flapping a loosened tab of corrugated steel. 'I was at school with her so you could say I'd known her all my life, but we weren't friends. Of course, I had dealings with her later, through Proveg. She buys . . . I mean she bought our broccoli and crispers. Pushed a hard bargain. Did with everyone. She won't have many friends, I reckon.'

'You harvest your own broccoli?'

'Yeah.'

'What with?'

'Knives. Same as everyone else.'

'Stainless steel?'

'No. Proveg have been on at us to change. New rules. Supermarkets don't want rust on their precious broccoli stalks. But there's nothing wrong with the old ones if you look after them. Dry and oil them. Keep them sharp with an angle grinder.'

He had been cutting broccoli since he was twelve, and in that time had seen the move from boxing them up in hessian-lined wooden crates that were taken to

Penzance Station on a trailer to bagging them individually and arranging them in supermarket crates on the spot. There were health and safety regulations now. Knives had to be signed out and in by the cutters and so did any (regulation blue) sticking plasters, for fear someone get a nasty shock on finding a blood-encrusted bandage in their cauliflower cheese. Other Proveg rules forbidding smoking, eating or dogs and insisting that *'in the absence of a chemical toilet, allowable where teams number five or less, antiseptic wet wipes are to be handed out to workers needing to relieve themselves in the field'* he and Val blithely ignored. They had even discovered that, once the tractor had driven down a row once or twice so that tracks were well cut into the mud, it was possible to send the tractor slowly through the field without a driver, thus freeing up an extra pair of hands to cut while Val rode in the makeshift rig at the back trimming, bagging and packing. Health and safety regs would surely have outlawed this but Val kept a weather eye open and if she saw a Proveg four-wheel drive in the distance she could tip him the wink to down knife and drive for a while.

Garth Tresawle made an extra note and underlined it. He looked up. 'How many knives do you have?' he asked.

'Four.'

'Where d'you keep them?'

'In a shed. And no, it isn't locked.'

'How many men work for you?'

'On the broccoli?' Garth nodded. 'Two. Ernest Penrose and Peter Newson.' He gave their addresses, as best as he could remember them, and his own, and that was all.

They would have a hard time pinning charges on the mere basis of a knife. West Penwith was bristling with knives at this time of year. The daffodil and broccoli harvests brought crowds of itinerant workers into the area in search of hard labour and tax-free bundles of earthy notes. There was some resentment among the local hands, jobs being scarce, but Poles and Serbs would always be prepared to work for that little bit less than Cornishmen, especially with the threat of deportation hanging over them. Every winter there was a flurry of lightning raids by customs officers and police, tipped off about the latest troupe of illegal immigrants slaving in the eerily weedless bulb fields or in stinking acres of vegetables but every spring brought fresh vanloads. Many of them slept rough in barns and hedges to save money. Perran had found them in his sheds occasionally, or evidence of their passing through.

It was said that many of the home-grown cutters were fresh out of prison or dodging parole. He had seen the way Val discreetly clicked down the locks on the car doors when she rounded a corner at dusk to find a gang spilling across a lane, their shapes bulked out with extra clothing, their muddy knives flashing as the headlamps swept across them. There was no lack of suspicious and appropriately armed strangers to pin a local murder on.

As always, Toffee was too exhausted by the class even to remember to be carsick on the way home. Perran left him in the Land Rover while he went inside the pub.

It was a ladies' darts match night – Val played on the pub team – so there was a scattering of unfamiliar faces, though not half as many as during the tourist season. Then everyone staying on the windswept campsite would take refuge in here until closing time forced them back to caravan and canvas. There was, however, an unmistakable holiday atmosphere tonight. He would have expected to find the women in one room, garrulous around a table, the men hunched, wordless, around Sky Sports in the other. Instead, he found the outsize television neglected and almost everyone squeezed around two long tables beside the fire, a jumble of glasses, exploded crisp packets and overflowing ashtrays in their midst. The landlady was with them, sure sign of a rare celebration, like the occasions – cup finals, the odd wake – when she locked the doors and declared the gathering a perfectly legal private party. Ordinarily, sat amongst her cronies, women she had known since childhood, Val would only have acknowledged him to demand he bought the next round or a packet of cigarettes. She certainly would not have asked him to join them but would expect him to wait with the men until she was ready to leave.

Tonight was quite different. She spotted him at once and called out 'Here he is,' with something like eagerness. A drink was bought him and space made on the settle beside her. It was quite as though they had all been waiting for him. Someone asked how the puppy classes were going and he told her but quickly realised no one was really interested.

Then Val said, 'Well?' and it transpired that they had heard the police were questioning everyone at the class because Garth and a couple of detectives had been in the pub at the beginning of the evening and one of the detectives, the younger one with the funny eye, was a cousin by marriage of the landlady's. It was not like on television, where the facts of a murder were kept under wraps so as not to influence key witnesses. Correct police procedure was near impossible in a community this small and inter-related. They might have thought they were withholding crucial details but the women who had found the body, or most of it, Proveg employees on the night shift, were cousins of a woman on the visiting darts team and, in any case, had been far too traumatised by their discovery not to phone at least two people each before the police arrived on the scene.

Janice had been stabbed in the stomach repeatedly with a cauliflower knife. This last detail was a fair guess, given the width of the wounds the less squeamish of the witnesses had glimpsed on lifting Janice's shirt. There was no blood on the floor, so presumably she had been killed elsewhere. Her mouth had been stuffed to over-flowing with cauliflower florets and a Proveg Cornish Giant Cauliflower bag strapped over her head. Her hands and arms had been hacked off. The girls could find no trace of them but, hours later, there were horrified phone calls from branches of Tesco's, Sainsbury's,

Safeway's and the Co-Op where they had arrived, neatly tucked into trays of Proveg quality-assured produce. And the body was said not to be *fresh* so the landlady, something of an expert on serial murder, was backing the theory that Janice had never been on holiday at all. No one knew what had become of the Dobermans or the horse but Perran asking that gave rise to a small wave of horror-struck and morbidly inventive suggestions.

'Still,' Val put in, barely keeping the relish from her voice, 'at least it looks as though they didn't suffocate her. She must have been dead already when they put the stuff in her mouth because there was no sign of a struggle. Judy said the florets weren't broken at all. Still fit to cook, she said. So what did they ask you?'

'Oh.' Perran shrugged. 'How long I'd known her. If we talked at the class that night – which we did, of course. What time I got home. What kind of knives we use.'

'Reckon Garth thinks you did it, boy,' someone put in. Laughter faded quickly into uneasiness.

'Well,' Perran admitted. 'I don't have a whatsit. An alibi.'

'You do!' Val insisted.

'Hardly,' he told her. 'You were out when I got home and drunk when you finally made it in.'

There was uproarious laughter at that, then one of the women said, 'Maybe Val did it. She always had it in for that bitch.'

'Val had an alibi. She was with us.'

'Not like Perran. Who'd have thought it!'

'Ooh, Perran! Here, Val. You sure you're safe going home with him and everything?'

'Good on you, boy. She had it coming.'

There was teasing and laughter and, amazingly, Val clutched his thigh under the table as she laughed back and faked girlish terror. Perran felt an unfamiliar sensation as the teasing and backslapping continued and the conversation turned to Proveg and how the growers might now join forces to buy it and run it as a co-operative, which is what they should have done all along. It took a minute or two for him to identify it as pride. He had not felt like this since their wedding day.

'She'll stop,' he thought, 'once we're alone. Once we're back outside.'

And certainly Val seemed sobered by the night chill and the silence in the Land Rover. But as he drove her back to the farm, she slipped her hand over his where it rested on the gear stick.

'Poor Janice, though,' she said. 'I mean, I know she was a cow but the thought of her all alone . . . Things like that don't happen to married women. Not so often, anyway. I'm glad there's you. You too, Muttface,' she added because Toffee had woken and was leaning over from the back, sniffing the smoke in her hair. 'I'm glad there's you too. You'll keep us safe, won't you, boy?'

'Reckon he'd just wag his tail and lick the blood off the mad axeman's fingers,' he said.

'Don't!' she squeaked and shuddered.

They drove the few minutes home in silence but

when he pulled up inside the garage and cut the engine she turned to him in the darkness and asked, 'You didn't do it. Did you?'

And from something in her voice he sensed the distinct possibility of sex.

Grumpus

Mike Gayle

It's Sunday, a balmy night in August, and Sally and I have just arrived home from our honeymoon in Antigua. Home is Shepherd's Bush in The Flat of Mysterious Stains (so-called because there are these bizarre patches of soiled wallpaper. Neither of us can work out what they are and neither of us saw them when we rented the flat). Sally hates this place. The hot water tap in the bathroom won't work, the cooker's on its last legs and just before the wedding some drunken weird guy flashed Sally from across the road. 'I want us to get our own place,' she says to me when we're in bed. 'Somewhere nice that we own, somewhere without stains and somewhere without flashers. Is that too much to ask?'

'No,' I say. 'Of course not.'

'So what are you going to do about it?'

I shrug. In answer to my silence, Sally turns over, facing her back towards me. Not spooning. Not touching feet. She is sulking. Angry at the world and everything in it. Grumpus is out.

People who don't know Sally think that she can be a bit of a misery. It's not true. It's just the way that she is. Sometimes she's in a bad mood for no reason and that's when I know that Grumpus is out. Grumpus is my pet name for Sally when she's in a bad mood. As I don't tend to get bad moods I find her bad moods quite entertaining especially because I know she doesn't mean it. Now, after two-and-a-half years together, I like the idea of Grumpus being a separate person to Sally. That way I don't get the two confused. Grumpus doesn't come out very often – usually when Sally's really knack-ered or stressed at work. She always apologises once Grumpus has done a runner. In a lot of ways, Sally's a lot like the TV series *The Incredible Hulk*: someone rubs Dr Bruce Banner up the wrong way, he turns green, grows these huge muscles and then smashes things up a bit. Once his anger has subsided the Hulk disappears, leaving poor old Dr Banner with tattered clothing and a headache. Honestly, the similarities between Sally and the Hulk are amazing. When Grumpus has gone she'll cry and tell me that she's sorry and all that and I'll say it's okay, honestly, it's okay. It wasn't you. And it wasn't because . . . well . . . it was Grumpus, wasn't it? The golden rule of course is that I would never, ever, even on pain of death tell Sally that I call her Grumpus. Why? Because I know what's good for me.

Sally and I met at a house party in Didsbury, Manchester. I'd gone back home for the weekend to see my folks and catch up with some old mates and on the

Saturday night I'd ended up at a party. I spotted Sally the moment I walked in the door. There was something about her that made me melt inside. Right there and then, I wanted to take her in my arms and squash her so that she could fit in my pocket and I could take her around everywhere. We started seeing each other in that boyfriend/girlfriend kind of way almost immediately but we were hampered by that all-important location, location, location. She worked at BBC North West as a radio producer and shared a three-bedroomed house in lovely, lovely, Chorlton. What's more she didn't like London. She hated it in fact.

In spite of this the relationship blossomed and we alternated weekends in London and Manchester. Friday nights would be spent sitting in traffic, Sunday nights would be spent sitting in traffic. Sally/Grumpus would be pretty unbearable to be around for the first three hours of our seeing each other and as she mellowed she'd remember that Grumpus was wasting precious time and she'd apologise and for the time that remained she'd be the perfect girlfriend. Laughing at my jokes, looking at me like I was the centre of her universe, making me feel like I was King of the World. Then all too soon Sunday would arrive and Sally would cry and tell me that she didn't want us to part. And I'd always tell her that if I could I would squish her up in my pocket and take her with me. This went on, the going up, the coming down, for over two years until six months ago out of the blue, Sally told me she'd applied for a job in London. And I said, 'Are you sure?' And she said, 'Well, I love you don't I?' And I said, 'Well, while we're

all making big decisions, would you like to marry me?'
And she said, 'Yes.' She moved down two months later,
into the flat I shared with my friends Niall and Gwen
and soon after we rented a place on our own – The Flat
of Mysterious Stains – in Shepherd's Bush. We got married three weeks ago at Lewisham registry office. Best
day of my life.

It's 7.30 p.m. on the last Tuesday in September and the
honeymoon period is definitely over. It's my own fault.
I have disturbed Grumpus. I know this because I am on
the loo having a shouty conversation with Sally who, if
I'm hearing correctly, is in the living room watching her
favourite episode of *Oprah* again. It's the one where Dr
Phil McGraw is telling a bunch of women how to take
control of their lives.

'Sally!' I yell loud enough for my voice to be carried
through the loo door, along the hallway and into the
living room.

'What?' she yells back.

'Sally!' I yell again.

'What?' she yells back again.

'Sally!' I yell again.

Sally, although resistant to the idea of having a shouty
conversation with me, will, I believe, at some point give
up and come to my assistance in the bathroom if I keep
on shouting. I want her to come to the bathroom only
I won't say this because it is pointing out the obvious.
And it categorically states in section 2.3 of the Book of
Bloke that a man should never point out anything that's
obvious for fear of looking 'a bit girly'.

'Where are you?' she calls, even though she knows I know that she knows where I am.

'I'm in the bathroom!' I yell.

'What do you want?' she yells.

I can tell she is still in the living room. Probably still watching *Oprah*.

'There's no loo roll!' I yell.

'I know there's no loo roll!' she yells.

I couldn't believe this one. 'You know? You know? If you know then why's there no bloody loo roll in here?'

'Because I wanted you to appreciate the fact that they don't appear in there as if by magic. That there aren't little loo roll fairies that wake up every time they hear the last sheet being torn off and replace them. No loo roll fairies, Adam! Only me and I'm fed up with it, okay?'

Silence.

'So you'll replace the loo roll when it runs out instead of leaving it for me?' she yells (at a guess) from her position in the living room.

Silence.

'And you'll do the washing-up tonight, too?'

I can no longer remain silent. 'What?'

'If you want the loo roll you're going to have to give in to all my demands. Now, the washing-up?'

'That's blackmail!'

'You call it blackmail. I call it negotiating from a strong position. Anyway, do you want the loo roll or not? Because if you don't I'm going out in a minute and I *will* leave you there.'

'You would, wouldn't you?'

'In a second,' says Sally.

I listen to Sally locating the loo rolls that I know full well live in the airing cupboard by the stairs. I hear her take one out and she pushes the bathroom door ajar and then pauses.

'Anything else?' I ask sarcastically.

'No,' she snaps as she hands me the Andrex. 'That's all I want.'

Later that night, as we're silently getting into bed still fuming with each other, she apologises.

'Adam?' says Sally.

'Hmm?' I mutter non-commitally.

'Are you talking to me?'

I say nothing because I'm not talking to her – or rather not talking to Grumpus.

There's a long pause. 'So you're not talking to me?'

I allow myself to shrug because it's not really talking.

'Well listen,' she says quietly. 'I'm sorry.'

'That's okay,' I say. 'I'm sorry too.'

'Friends?' she says, opening her arms to hug me.

'Friends,' I reply.

It's a Friday night in late November and Grumpus is out again. I'm lying on the sofa watching *Weekend Watchdog* having been knocked sideways with a bout of the flu. Sally is sitting in the brown armchair that she hates for its very brownness. To be truthful I am acting like a child over this flu thing but I reason that I've earned the right, what with being up all night coughing. But Grumpus is having none of it. Grumpus doesn't like it when I'm ill. I think it distorts Grumpus's view of the world.

'Do you have to do that?' asks Sally.

'What?' I protest.

'You know,' she says, 'that whole being there thing that you're doing now?'

'What whole thing?'

'Just sitting there like a . . . like a . . . like a lump of lard. Can't you just do something?'

'Like what? I'm ill? Ill people tend to lie down when they're ill, it helps them to keep from falling over.' I then force a massive coughing, phlegm gurgling and wheezing fit guaranteed to make me sound like I'm only seconds from dying. It's excellent. I sound like I've got TB.

Sally sighs and switches channels.

'I was watching that!'

'You weren't,' she snaps. 'You were coughing and spluttering. Coughing and spluttering. Coughing and spluttering!'

She gets up and walks out. For a moment I think she has left the room for good, maybe to have a bath or something, but then she pops her head around the door and says evilly, 'How long are you going to be like this?'

'What?' I reply somewhat astonished. 'Are you asking me the question: How long do I think I'm going to be ill?'

She nods.

'I think about four years,' I snap back. 'I was actually thinking about lying here with snot coming out of every orifice for the next four years. You can Hoover round me, surely?'

'You're being sarcastic now.'

'No I'm not being sarcastic, I'm being ill. This,' I point to myself, 'is what ill people do.' I sigh heavily. 'Sometimes you're merciless, do you know that?'

Later that night, as we're silently getting into bed still fuming with each other, she apologises.

'Adam?' says Sally.

'Hmm?' I mutter non-commitally.

'Are you talking to me?'

I say nothing because I'm not talking to her – or rather not talking to Grumpus.

There's a long pause. 'So you're not talking to me?'

I allow myself to shrug because it's not really talking.

'Well listen,' she says quietly. 'I'm sorry.'

'That's okay,' I say. 'I'm sorry too.'

'Friends?' she says, opening her arms to hug me.

'Friends,' I reply.

It's late on a Saturday night in early January and Sally and I have been to a wedding in Wolverhampton, Spencer's and Alison's. It's all over now and we are in the car driving back to London.

'What did you think?' asks Sally, as we begin our usual debriefing session.

'It was nice.'

'Hmmm,' says Sally keeping her eyes firmly on the road ahead.

'Hmmm what?'

'Well, you know,' she replies. She looks across at me briefly and then looks away. 'It was a bit . . .'

I know exactly what she's going to say but only because of her preamble. Sally always does her preamble mumbling pantomime when she wants to say something a bit bitchy but doesn't like to say it aloud. I on the other hand have no problem with a few catty comments. My motto being if you can't bitch about your friends then get some better friends. I try to guess what it is she wants to let loose about. Alison's dress? The venue? The food? Sally continues to 'Ummm' and 'Ahhhh' like a game-show contestant pondering the million-dollar question. Finally I come up with the answer.

'You didn't like anything about it did you?'

'No,' says Sally sharply. 'That's a terrible thing to say.' Then there's a long silence and then she adds a barely audible 'Yes. Does this make me a terrible person?'

'Not at all,' I reassure. 'I'm quite sure our friends talk about us behind our backs, too. It's sort of expected. Anyway, we're here in our car alone, so we can bitch away to our hearts' content. Especially as we are married.'

'What do you mean?'

'Well, we're one aren't we. We're spliced together. You plus me equals us. Therefore you're not so much bitching as vocalising your thoughts to another part of your brain.'

'Namely you.'

'Namely me.'

'Which side of the brain are you?' she asks, smiling.

'The smallest part, of course. Come, come now.

339

Which part of everything didn't you like?'

'I don't know, Adam. I didn't like any of it. I hated Alison's dress especially. She should have gone for something simpler, something with . . . well, with more flattering lines.'

'What, like a tent?'

'No, Adam that's awful. Too far.'

'And what else?'

'I didn't like the food either.'

'I thought it was okay.'

'You think so?'

'Yeah.'

And that's it. That's all I say. One simple 'Yeah', and Grumpus is out and is giving me the cold shoulder. Sally doesn't speak another word to me for the rest of the journey even when we stop at the service station for something to eat.

'Do you want a Mars Bar?' I ask Sally as we wander around the shop bit of the motorway services. She says nothing. 'Oh, look Sal,' I say, pointing to the magazine racks, 'the new issue of *Cosmopolitan* is out. You like *Cosmo*, don't you?' She says nothing. 'I'm going to the car if you're going to be like that!' I retort. I turn and walk away and finally she says her first words to me since Junction 5 of the M1 – a single sentence (delivered at maximum volume) containing a world-record-breaking number of Anglo-Saxon expletives.

Later that night, as we're silently getting into bed still fuming with each other, she apologises.

'Adam?' says Sally.

'Hmm?' I mutter non-commitally.

'Are you talking to me?'

I say nothing because I'm not talking to her – or rather not talking to Grumpus.

There's a long pause. 'So you're not talking to me?'

I allow myself to shrug because it's not really talking.

'Well listen,' she says quietly. 'I'm sorry.'

'That's okay,' I say. 'I'm sorry too.'

'Friends?' she says, opening her arms to hug me.

'Friends,' I reply.

It's a year later. The day after our first wedding anniversary. We're in our bed in our new flat. A flat that has no bizarre stains. No knackered cookers. No flashers. Just a lovely new sofa from Habitat that cost the price of a relatively old but sound second-hand car.

'Adam?' says Sally who is reading a magazine.

'Yeah?' I reply.

'Do you think we have enough sex?'

'Pardon?'

'I said do you think we have enough sex?' she says. 'It's just that I've just read this article . . .' she stopped and waved the magazine in front of my eyes, '. . . and according to this chart . . .' she pointed to the page on the magazine which she was still waving, '. . . we're above average.'

'So what are you worrying about?'

'Well, I know this is going to sound paranoid but that's the average, yeah?'

I nod.

'So that means there are people out there who are

having less than the national average?'

I nod again.

'And there are people having more than their fair share.'

'True.'

'In which case there are people out there who are having more sex than we are.'

'So?'

'So, don't you wonder who they are? I mean, okay, say you discount people in the sex industry – who I suppose must have their own separate survey – that means that there are average people like you and me having more sex than we are.'

'But Sally, it's not like they're having our fair share, is it? It's not like the very fact that these people are having sex means that we can't have more sex. In fact it's the opposite. It means that we can have less sex – not that that is a desirable thing,' I add hastily. 'But it's like this. They have more, which means there's more in the pot – so to speak – for the rest of us to share.'

Sally is suddenly outraged by this statement. I fear Grumpus may be emerging. 'I don't want somebody else's sex. That's horrible. A complete stranger's sex life is making up for our own. No,' she says, slamming down the magazine. 'If I'm going to have sex I at least want it to be our own.'

'Look, Sally, don't you think this is a little ridiculous?' I begin, which is perhaps not the best way to keep Grumpus at bay. 'You're going to give yourself a heart attack at this rate.'

'At this rate? What rate? Aren't you worried that

we're not normal?' I look at her blankly. I don't really have an answer to that one. 'Okay,' she says determinedly. 'Name three of our friends that you think have less sex than we do and I'll let you go back to sleep. Agreed?'

'You are joking?'

'I think we should shake on it.'

'What, don't you trust me?'

'Only as far as I can throw you. Remember that last bet we had?'

'No,' I lie.

'Yes you do.'

I nod reluctantly. We'd been arguing over some of the details of our first date. She'd bet me a whole month of cleaning the bathroom that on our first date we'd gone to see a revival of *Seven Brides for Seven Brothers* while I'd insisted it had been a Spanish film about a guy who was in love with his mother. It turned out that she was right because she took me to a suitcase under the bed and showed me the very ticket stub from that night. What made matters worse was the fact that I hadn't seen the Spanish film with her at all but rather with my previous girlfriend, Anne. I compounded my shame by refusing to honour the bet on the grounds that the game was 'stupid'.

'Okay,' I say. 'What are we betting?'

'Full breakfast in bed.'

'You're on.'

We shake hands.

'Right,' I begin. 'We've got to have more sex than Tina and Alex.'

'Not from what Tina tells me,' says Sally.

'Okay, what about John and Lydia? John's always going on about how exhausted he is from work.'

Sally nods in agreement. 'Okay, you can have them.'

'Helen and Jay. Word on the grapevine is that Helen's not even that keen on it.'

'So we beat Helen and Jay,' she says, laughing. 'The Pope beats Helen and Jay – hands down, no contest.'

'Gary and Penny?'

'At it like rabbits.'

'Bill and Pavi?'

'Can't keep their hands off each other.'

'Your sister and whatshisface?'

'She's split up with whatshisface and if you'd been listening when I told you that last night you'd know!'

And once again Grumpus is out. Sally storms out of the bedroom, slamming the door. I get out of bed, open the door and watch as she heads to the spare bedroom we use as a dressing room and slams the door. She then leaves that room and heads to the bathroom and slams the door. After a few moments she leaves the bathroom, goes to the spare bedroom again and slams the door. I go back to bed. There is a brief respite from door slamming which I assume is a sign that Grumpus has gone. Getting out of bed, I put my head around the door to check if the coast is clear. Sally is standing in the hallway with her bags packed.

'Where are you going?' I ask.

'To my mum's,' she says.

'Why?' I ask rather stupidly.

'I just need some space,' she says.

'Space?' I repeat, resisting the temptation to add 'the final frontier'.

'Yes, space.'

'But I thought you loved me,' I say rather pathetically (I do pathetic very well). 'I love you. You love me. That's what we do.'

Sally shakes her head. 'I do love you. I do. It's just that sometimes, Adam, you get in these useless bloody moods and I don't know what to do. It's weird, like Jekyll and Hyde – like you're somebody else. One moment you're the sweetest guy in all the world. And the next it's like your entire reason for existing is to rub me up the wrong way.' There's a brief silence and then she laughs but not in a 'funny ha ha' kind of way, more of a 'Damian from *Omen III* wins again' kind of way. 'Your mood change happens so often now that I even have a pet name for it – Nigel.'

'Nigel?' I repeat.

'Yeah, Nigel,' she laughs, and her whole face lights up for a moment.

And for some reason I begin laughing uncontrollably and together our laughter is so infectious that clutching each other we collapse on the floor of the hallway and we kiss.

And kiss.

And kiss.

And then she stops suddenly.

'Have you got a pet name for my bad moods?' she asks playfully.

I think hard. I want to tell her. I even need to tell her. But my lips remain sealed. After all, I know what's good for me. And so I take her in my arms again and kiss her lips, secure in the knowledge that Grumpus has left the building.

For now.

Mother Figure
Sarah Harris

I need a man in: that is what my mother says. She tuts at the blistered paint on my kitchen wall; the frozen pipes; the smell of rotting eggs behind the fridge; and the dead wires hanging above my door, like mistletoe.

She hands me my spineless copy of the *Yellow Pages,* and says that if I don't phone a plumber, she will. But Mum is not here to talk about taps. She is here to Tell Me So.

Naturally, she wants me to be fulfilled. But a child needs a father. Yes; and she was surprised it was so simple for a single woman to buy sperm. *Oh, that word.* Surely one has to first spend years under investigation by social workers? Undergoing counselling? Convincing the council?

'I'm not adopting; I'm having a baby of my own,' I say. 'And I did see a counsellor.'

My mother says that when I announced I was going to go and get pregnant, she thought it another of my silly whims – like the tap-dancing, the glass-blowing, and the life-drawing. *Naked people, sitting there for people to paint.* Frankly, she did not believe me. Or she would have said her piece sooner. I would not go through with it; that is what she assumed. Being inseminated. Artificially. Not when push came to shove, and I was lying there, cold, in the clinic.

'Oh Tamsin,' she says, and the lines under her eyes look like tears.

'Mum, try and understand. Please. This wasn't a whim. It had become a need. If I'd have been with someone I loved . . . If I'd been *married*, I'd have preferred that. Don't you think I would? I'm *twenty-eight*; and I could just as easily have become pregnant by Mike. But that wouldn't have been fair on him. This way, it's my decision, and no one's hurt.'

'Except the child.'

'Can't you even be the tiniest bit pleased?'

I want to share with her my excitement. According to my pregnancy manual, today is something of a landmark date for my developing baby. 'I'm ten weeks, you know.'

'I didn't think it would be like this. I thought . . . I thought at least you'd be with a man – even if he was a do-nothing, like your dad. Better the devil you know, Tamsin. I mean, what d'you know about this *donor* person? This father of your child?'

'More than I've known about some of my boyfriends. He's a medical student, six-foot . . .'

'I really don't want to hear. I just wish . . . Oh Tam, I wish you'd done this differently. Then, I could have had such fun, buying you . . .'

'Unnecessary accessories?'

'*Yes.*'

'Mum, I'm a grown-up. I'm earning well. I didn't want your money; I wanted a baby.' I think of the foetus, and his separating fingers.

His fully developed heart.

I was proud of my weight gain during pregnancy. Three stones from organic health-store food. I thought that the fat would come out with the foetus in one clean drainage operation.

Only, the ventouse suctioned out merely Billy, and a measly portion of placenta.

My hips are still in need of siphoning; and I can see the pity, sometimes, in Harriet's eyes. Of course, all mothers are fat. This, despite the fact that they eat nothing but bananas and puréed carrot. This, even though they spend their time at playgrounds and babygyms, exercising.

Harriet does not know that I have a baby. So she cannot understand why I am overweight, when my hand never, ever strays towards that bowl of Twiglets.

None of the women in this room knows that I am a mother. It would feel somehow inappropriate, amongst such determined singletons, for me to mention this fact. It would be like bringing a one-year-old into a wine bar. Besides, Billy is an easy secret for me to keep. The reading group meets only once a month, and always here, at Harriet's flat in Clapham. On these evenings, my mum comes to my flat in Kentish Town to look after her only grandchild. Well, she comes to sit and watch the TV soaps. *EastEnders* is turned up loud enough to drown out the desperate screams of my colicky baby.

Screams that I can hear across the river.

My son's yells punch through the north–south divide. But here, I am determined not to feel like a mother. Despite the baby stains covering my clothes, I am intent on appearing carefree, like Harriet, Paula, Rhianna, and Bryony.

This place helps me to recall what life was like before motherhood. For only a childless woman could live in Harriet's fourth-floor flat. Concertina files gape open in front of the fake gas fire. There are cashmere throws placed, just so, to cover the brown leather couch. Valuable space is taken up, not by baby swings and soft bricks, but by a filthy sweep of purple, velvety rug.

The stains are all from rich red wine and cheap cigarettes. The smells, from the night before. In the kitchenette, a juicer is out and proud, ready to squeeze vegetables. Jars of beautiful food prevail. Here, the pasta twirls. The tomatoes are sun-dried. The bread is fresh, and French. Stuffed into my larder at home are ugly tins of powdered milk. Fruit lies useless in a wire bowl, like elderly breasts; and the jars are all Baby Organix.

Boxes of breadsticks commandeer my cupboards.

There would be no room in my flat to seat these untidy, beautiful women. They would not fit in around the baby furniture. I doubt I could accommodate Harriet, standing, as she is, in that fourth ballet position. Rhianna and Bryony could not sprawl about like that, lighting Marlboro after Marlboro. Not on my

Lilliputian sofa. Paula would not have space to lie on the floor, simply to show off a stomach exercise.

'You have to imagine a penis going through your belly button.'

'Ugh. That is so disgusting.'

'But it works.'

'What use are stomach muscles anyway? It's just another way of diverting women's attention away from what really matters.'

'Chocolate?'

'Dialectical materialism?'

Harriet's flat feels like a refuge. With these women, I am not judged as a mother. None of them cares about Billy's paternity, the amount of pain relief I need, or the state of my pelvic floor. It does not matter that I become clumsy around baby accessories. In Harriet's world, I do not have to be superwoman, able to turn a pram, fast, into a pushchair. I do not have to juggle fifteen feelings at once.

'Right. Carol Shields. What did we all think?' asks Harriet.

'I loved it,' I say, hugging my knees.

'I haven't finished hearing about *Tim*,' says Paula, handing Bryony her lighter, shaped as a fire extinguisher.

'I just need to know what to do about him.' Bryony smiles, lighting the cigarette. 'Bloody hell, where did you buy this *lighter*? I want one.'

'I want your *shoes*,' wails Rhianna, who brings all of

our conversations back to the subject of shoes. Like a Chinese woman, at the turn of the last century, she is excessively proud of her tiny feet. 'Where d'you get 'em, Bry? Not that they'd make them in size three,' she sighs. 'It's as if we don't exist.'

'I think I've got those stilettos. Are they from Bertie's?' This is Harriet, who collects footwear.

'Tim bought them for me, to wear in bed.'

'What a waste of good shoes.'

How I admire Harriet and her round cheese of a face, like a child's drawing of a full moon. She reminds me of myself, before Billy came. I too wore awkward dresses, bargain-binned from antique stalls. Dresses fashioned out of unforgiving materials such as hard silk. The corsetry left pink marks on my breasts. Marks which have still not faded.

I too had the patience for shoes.

I met Harriet Prentice at an audition, four months ago. We were both up for the part of Postman Pat's cat. Neither of us was considered suitable. After our humiliation, I suggested we go for a coffee at Starbucks. There, we discovered that we were both reading Wilkie Collins. *The Moonstone*. Harriet's book fell out of a Muji rucksack I too had used. Before Billy. (Now I need a roomier bag, with plenty of pockets.) She, like me, left the froth on her cappuccino to liquefy, as we discussed literature, and lecherous directors. Flea markets, and lap dancers. I told her about Mike, and his refusal to commit. She talked about her common-law marriage to Mark. We tore up serviettes. Harriet rolled hers into couscous-sized balls as she sighed about Mark, back-packing around northern Africa. I twisted my serviette into strings, and told her where I lost my virginity. *Morocco: 1984.* She laughed, and said that her own was abandoned long before that, on a corduroy sofa in her headmaster's office. So I confessed to cheating in my O-levels. That was nothing, according to Harriet. She had stolen almost half of her one hundred and thirty-two pairs of shoes.

I wanted her to see that we were the same, so I did not tell her that I had a baby. Before I became pregnant with Billy, I too drank until I wet myself, and woke up in strange sleeping positions. It is only now that I am closed-up, and feel embarrassed discussing sex.

'Does Tim insist you *only* wear shoes in bed?' Paula asks Bryony, curiously.

'He does have a shoe fetish.'

'Sounds like Harriet.'

'They'd be a perfect match,' grins Bryony.

'I bet he's just being cautious,' says Rhianna. 'He doesn't want to catch anything horrible, like a verruca.'

Every time Harriet moves, she shines. This is because her cheekbones are crayoned with silver highlighter. Her dress collar is diamante. When, on the day we met, she suggested I join her reading group, a thrill shot through me. I felt superior to the mothers at the neighbouring table, beset as they were by buggies.

I was being invited to join an exclusive club. Adults only. Even the address sounded glamorous. Harriet lived in the sort of built-up area that would not allow out children's sounds, after seven.

The reading group needed new blood, said Harriet. Different women. In the last six months, the group had stagnated; and there were now only four members – all of them a gang of old schoolfriends.

'Can you open the wine I brought, Aitch?' asks Rhianna, now. 'Or were you saving that for when we'd gone? To drink on your own?'

'Piss *off*! I supply the food.'

'For God's sake, Harriet. I was only joking. Get a sense of humour.'

I used to quite like myself, until I met Rhianna, who is the type of woman to wink at someone mid-sentence. Now I see myself through her eyes; and, oh, am I unattractive? For I appear much older than my twenty-nine years; I have red wine stains on my teeth; I wear too much mascara for the size of my eyes; I do not look like a serious actress; I do not sound sophisticated, as a Tamsin should.

I have man-sized feet.

My appearance is softened only because I make an effort with it. I clearly buy my shoes from specialist shops; my mascara seems designer; I have obviously tried to change my common accent; I am prepared to risk losing the enamel on my teeth, by brushing with 'American' tooth whitener. I do not try to appear young by dressing fashionably.

I am at least not mutton dressed as lamb. Merely mutton.

'You're always implying I'm an alcoholic or something, Rhianna.'

'What's the "something"?' asks Bryony, trying to lighten the conversation; because that is what she does with every conversation.

'Oh Harriet, you're so defensive. Of the eighty-five nice things I say to you, you take one thing, and wring it out, looking for nastiness. I didn't say you were an alcoholic; I said you seemed to drink all of your week's unit ration in one evening.'

'And how else am I supposed to interpret that?'

Harriet glances at me, and raises an eyebrow. When I accepted her invitation to join this reading group, she said that, of course, I might not like her 'best' friends.

She said the word *best* using her fingers to illustrate quotation marks.

As the Starbucks counter assistant cleared away her mug, grinning at me, Harriet admitted that the three of them did have their faults. *Paula*, for example, resented the fact that Harriet had her life, and she her own. It was as if Harriet having a boyfriend automatically prevented Paula from having one. *Bryony* was vain. She thought she resembled Audrey Hepburn when it was clear to everyone else that she looked more like Una Stubbs. On a good-face-day, Sinead O'Connor.

Rhianna had a chip on her shoulder about being the only one of her schoolfriends to have gone to Oxbridge. She exaggerated the difference between herself and Harriet by making a point of knowing nothing about popular culture, and was especially proud of her inability to name a single Spice Girl.

Harriet rolled her serviette balls towards me, saying that she could not be responsible for her cronies. I laughed, although I felt as if she was saying she could not answer for her bank's unethical investments.

I would judge my own gang on the small number who show up for my birthday parties, but most of them are agoraphobics.

Frankly, I liked the sound of her friends. Their characters were so fixed, whereas I resemble the narrator in a crime novel. I can change my personality at a whim; perhaps that is why I am an actress. Well, a demonstrator on an electrical-goods counter.

'*So*,' says Bryony, flicking on and off the fire-extinguisher lighter. 'Should I finish with Tim?'

'I do think he should change his name,' says Harriet, irritably.

'What's wrong with the name?'

'A Tim's just trying to be strong, like a Tom.'

'Mike changed his name,' I say, missing my mouth with the wine glass. I am quickly tipsy these days. 'He was born Norman.'

'Oh dear.'

'Oh *no*,' laughs Harriet; and she briefly leans her head on my shoulder, in sympathy.

I am pleased. I want so much to be a part of this group. For it feels as if I am with old friends. This is how my own gang behaved, before motherhood changed them. Now, no matter how hard my old college housemates and I try to drag our conversations back to the basics (life, loves, haircare products), we stay stuck on subjects such as six-month-olds learning to sit up, and vaginal secretions.

My childless friends see me simply as Mother-of-Billy. I cannot be sympathetic, even during their bouts of post-relationship depression. I pay for every second with them, in child care.

'Is Mike the one who left you to walk home alone from that New Year's Eve party?' asks Paula; and I nod.

'Yeah, we don't like him,' says Bryony.

Girls need to share secrets, to be accepted. This is something we learned in the playground. I could hold hands with Samantha Raven in the school dinner queue because I confessed to a liking for Matthew Long. Tracy Hicks ate my carrots after I shared with her where I had hidden them. *Underneath the mashed potatoes.*

We became best friends when I told Tracy that, secretly, I hated Samantha Raven.

'Mike sounds like that bloke I slept with after Mark,' says Harriet, plaiting a piece of her hennaed hair. 'Roger.'

'Self-obsessed, you mean?' I ask, wishing I had kept my red hair long.

'You mean Reading group Roger? *I* invited him.'

'Those were the days,' smiles Rhianna. 'When we actually discussed books.'

I laugh, remembering Harriet's description of the reading group before it was made women-only. The men were crudely competitive. How many Thomas Hardys had they read? How many themes could they count in *Tess of the D'Urbevilles*? Why did Hardy write *Far from the Madding Crowd*? Boys need to swap facts to be accepted. This is something they learned in the playground. There they exchanged football cards and *Star Wars* memorabilia.

'Talking of which?' says Harriet, patting *The Stone Diaries*.

'Oh, wait. First, tell me what to do about Tim?'

'Timmy, who has an odd thing with his Mummy,' says Paula.

'An odd thing?' I feel able to ask, because these women know so much about me. After a mere four meetings, they know how I felt, at twelve, when my father left home. How Mike hurt me. Why I live north of the river, and do not eat beef. They know about my bad trip in India, and my allergy to cats. They know that I used to live in Leytonstone. 21B, Oates Block, Severill Estate. They know that I was nearly raped one New Year's Eve.

'She sleeps on his floor, in a sleeping bag, when she's up from Manchester,' says Bryony about Tim's mother.

'*Down* in London,' corrects Rhianna.

'I'm in bed with Tim, and the woman creeps in at three in the morning and sleeps on his floor. I feel like saying: "Do you know what time it is? I've been worried sick about you".'

We all laugh, and Bryony re-fills our wine glasses.

'His Mum sleeps on a cold, bare floor?' I ask.

'A sleeping bag Tim's set up *specially*.'

'So, where's she been?'

'Oh, on a date. She goes on these singles supper

evenings. Tim really worries about her. She drinks like a fish, and smokes naughty cigarettes. She goes to *Glastonbury*, for God's sake. And she's always trying to get me to talk about sex with her son. It's repulsive.'

'A mother shouldn't *be* like that,' says Harriet, and Rhianna nods. Paula lights her last remaining cigarette.

I wonder what a mother should be like. The truth is, I probably have more in common with Tim's Mum than I do with these women. I too return from dates at 3 a.m., giggling, and tripping over my son's sleeping body. Sixteen-year-old babysitters look at me in disgust.

I am a parent, and should not still be having sex.

Of course, every woman instinctively thinks she'd make a saintly mother. These women probably do. I certainly did. Yet, I should have been able to predict that, in practice, I would be inept. I am selfish. Plus, I was never able to craft the objects on *Blue Peter*. My mother never had sticky-backed plastic. Only Sellotape.

'Anyway. Carol Shields,' says Harriet, loftily. 'What did we all think?'

'Good choice for once, Bryony,' teases Paula.

'Did *I* choose it?'

'Didn't you?'

'Can't you even remember?' asks Rhianna. She picks up her battered copy of *The Stone Diaries*. 'Yes; it was you. I didn't want to read it again.'

'*Did* you read it again?' asks Harriet.

'No, I'll remember it. It was about a woman's life,

wasn't it? There's lots of kitchen-sink stuff. I didn't like it. Overblown rubbish.'

'I loved it,' says Harriet, pouring herself another glass of wine. 'It was beautifully written, and really, hmm, womanly.'

'Soapy, you mean,' sneers Rhianna.

'Well, if it was like a soap, no wonder *I* liked it,' says Paula. 'I think it's the first book we've ever done where . . .'

'*Done?*' laughs Harriet. 'God, it's like having the men back.'

'*Read* then. It's the first book we've read that I actually enjoyed rather than thinking: "Oh, I should be enjoying this".'

'But how can it be soapy?' asks Bryony, reading the blurb on the back of her copy. 'Didn't it win the Booker?'

'Is that why you chose it?' says Paula, smiling indulgently.

'*Yes*,' says Bryony, laughing.

'But it was only nominated.'

'Oh,' says Bryony, still laughing. 'Oh well.'

'We were still impressed with your choice, Bry,' says Rhianna, patting Bryony's arm.

'I thought you didn't like it?' says Harriet, biting her lip until I can see blood.

'I didn't.'

'But didn't you see the point at the end? When Daisy Flett died, there was so much she hadn't done.'

'Oh yes, I remember. She listed it all, yeah?' Rhianna opens the book at the last few pages, and reads aloud.

'Oil painting, skiing, sailing, nude bathing, emerald jewelry, cigarettes, oral sex . . .'

'Poor thing.'

'It made me want to go straight out and oil-paint,' says Bryony.

'Well, that was the point. She'd wasted her life.'

'Bit obvious. Live every day as if it's your last. That's all she's saying.'

'I think Daisy had a really full life,' I say, starting to slur my words. Since Billy, I have a much reduced capacity for alcohol.

'How? She hardly made her *mark* on the world,' says Harriet.

'Not like we're doing, you mean?' says Paula, pulling out the foil innards of her box of Marlboros.

'She left a recipe for lemon pudding,' jokes Bryony.

'At least we have ambition. I mean, I'm not always going to be working at the Millennium Dome.'

'Too right you're not. It's coming down in a few months.'

'I *mean*, I'm going to make it as an actress.'

'*Fame*,' sings Rhianna. 'You're going to live for ever.'

'None of us would be satisfied with Daisy's life. You're not going to be happy until you publish your PhD. Tam's going to win an Oscar. Paula'll end up as Director General of the BBC. Bryony'll . . .' She stops.

'Thanks. You can't think of anything for me.'

'Well, you don't just want to be *married*, with *children*. The point about Daisy was she didn't travel, or read many books . . .'

I say, 'She didn't have time, she was doing something far more important.'

'There was no point to Daisy. That was the only idea in the book,' says Rhianna, sighing, and closing the novel. 'Wowie.'

'Hang on. She had children. Isn't that an achievement?' I say, furiously. But I am met by blank faces. For a moment, I think I will tell them about Billy. Then I realise that these faces would still peer at me, emptily.

'No, anyone can do that. Single women on council est . . .'

'She never heard the words: "I love you",' says Paula, sadly. 'That really stuck with me. D'you think I'll go through my whole life, and not hear . . . ?'

'But children don't necessarily *say* "I love you" to their mothers,' I say, almost crying with frustration. Suddenly, I wonder what I am doing here. It as if I am starring in a time-travel movie. *Tamsin Robinson gets pregnant.* 'It's not that sort of relationship.'

'I *love* babies,' says Bryony, trying to end my tantrum.

'I think we've done Daisy anyway.' Harriet snaps shut *The Stone Diaries.*

'Yeah. Next.'

'She was born, she reproduced, she died. What more is there to say?'

'Oh, come on,' says Rhianna, her voice bloated with sarcasm. 'She did have a gardening column.'

I was standing in a park yesterday, watching Billy run to the swings, when I saw Harriet Prentice walking past.

Although it was one o'clock on a Wednesday, she was wearing a tight-bodiced dress, and I was reminded of the marks left by that type of corsetry on my breasts. Marks which have all now faded into pale, silvery lines, like jewellery. I could not help it, I gazed at her, through the wire fencing. She was looking around, with a childfree woman's curiosity in everything. Birds; trees; eligible partners. For a moment, even the playground was within Harriet's gunsight; and I could see her contempt for the way we mothers, all of us with the empty faces of security guards, stood vigil over our children.

She did not see me, behind Billy's buggy.

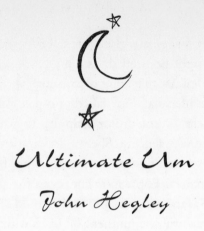

Ultimate Um
John Hegley

ROME
The Empire's fall some lifetimes away.
A middle ranking citizen, at a table
in the ground floor tenement café.
Before him his freshly ordered beverage.
And the day.

The arrival of his best and only friend.
The brief and initial exchange.
'Hail Antonius. Sit, please.'
'Tritus, hail, thank you.'
At this time the Christian, Tritus, is particularly keen
to love a particular neighbour, inhabitant of rooms in
a similar tenement a sling-stone's throw distant.
His desire is of considerable size.
'She is much to my liking,' he tells his companion.
'And you to hers?'
'Ah, there's the rub, or the lack of it. I offered her out
to the amphitheatre, but it was no-go to the going.'

'So what was on at the amphitheatre?'

'Gladiators.'

'Perhaps she is not much entertained by barbarism,' observed the pagan.

'Mm,' said the other consideringly.

At which point the café proprietor appeared through the dangling strips of beads

which kept the flies out of his kitchen – what he called his *dags*.

The love-troubled one considered his newly arrived companion.

'Antonius, what will you have? And I'm buying.'

'I'll have the soup, what is it?'

'Rancid fish.'

'Lovely.'

Antonius sorted, Harrius checked on his other customer.

'And are you all right there, Tritus?'

'No, I'm not. But that aside, I have no wish to supplement my initial order, which I made before the unexpected but pleasing arrival of my friend.'

Antonius took up on what was making Tritus not feel all right:

the woman . . .

'Perhaps you should be buying *her* a bowl of rancid soup?

Or perhaps a visit to the new soothsayer might go down well,

apparently she knows the future like it was born yesterday.'

Harrius rattled his dags once again.

'Here you are boys. One fish soup and a couple of
  beverages,
on the house. Sorry, I meant on the table.'

The next morning Tritus was sat at the same table
  but this time, opposite the object of his big desir-
  ing. He'd dropped off a note at her tenement. He
  wanted to say how very, very glad he was she'd
  responded, but instead he just told her he was
  glad, without the verys.
'So, what do you say to a soothsayer visit, *at my
  expense*, Cleotorius?'
'Yes, that would be nice.'
'Really?'
'Hopefully. It sounds worth a sling-shot anyway.'
'So why would you not come to the amphitheatre?'
'I am not much entertained by barbarism.'
'Antonius, my friend, thought that might be the
  case.'
'Mm, with the indigenous eye it isn't always easy to
  see that
for which history will condemn us.
And I have a woman's aversion to violence.'
Tritus suppressed the urge to pick his nose . . .
'Do you think the Empire would be different if it was
  to be run by women?'
'I think the senses would play a larger part, it would
  be an . . .'
'. . . Empire of the senses?'
'I was going to say it would be an improvement.
  I don't need you to finish my . . .'

'Sentences?'

'Rancid fish soup. I don't need you to finish my rancid fish soup,' clarified Cleotorius. 'Come on, let's go.'

Harrius, on hearing the sounds of departure from the café's interior, was back through his dags like a sling-shot.

'You've not finished your . . .'

'Rancid fish soup,' said Cleo, finishing.

'Can you put this on my tab, Harrius?' Tritus loved his tab.

'Your tablet is full, Tritus,' answered the owner.

'I'll pay,' suggested Cleo.

'The woman usually does in the end,' quipped Harrius.

And the woman replied,

'Shut your . . .'

'Face,' finished Tritus.

'To whom are you talking?' enquired the café's owner.

In unison the two customers answered 'The fish.'

They were talking to the fish.

And so they left the tenement tiles, stepped out onto the cobbles,

already ancient, and headed South to satisfy the soothache.

Some halfway into the promenade, they hit upon the hard bargainers

clustered in Monday morning market mode.

'Candles, get your scented candles, here.'

'Scandals, get your more than mere hearsay, here.'

'Best quality toga material, get your toga rags here.'

Tritus went for the grapes. 'Can I have them in a bag,
    please?'
'We don't do bags, mate. In your basket!'
'Shall we take a taxi?' Cleo asked, a grape in her well
    womanicured grip.
'It's only a sling-stone,' replied Tritus . . . 'But I'll
    hail one anyway.'

Wobbling over the cobbles in the hand drawn
    contraption;
'So, Tritus, how long have you been a Christian?'
'Ever since I heard one of his followers preaching.
She was amazing.'
'Yes, but how long?'
'Three years. Loving your enemies was the most
    revolutionary idea I'd ever heard.'
'I didn't get the impression you were a revolutionary
    kind of guy. You like gladiators!'
'I'm full of contradictions, me.'
The taxi veered; Cleo continued regardless, musing
    upon the nature of their respective religions.
'Worshipping one God's so much less hassle isn't it?
But I do prefer a female God myself.'
'But ours is father/mother, God the parent . . .'
    Tritus explained, spitting forth grape-pip.
'Yes, but I prefer a female God.'
'Oh well, we don't say ours is the only way . . .
anyway, what do you *believe* in, Cleo?'
'Desire.'

'Really?' asked Tritus, really interested.

Getting out, or rather off, the taxi, his friend Antonius happened to be on the street, just come out of the library.

'Cleo, this is Antonius. Antonius, vice versa.

He's the friend who thought you wouldn't like the gladiators.

'Hello, perceptive friend,' fraternised Cleo.

'Hail,' regaled Antonius.

Inside the Soothsayer's, Tritus got 'the London' on the future of his belief-system.

Or the 'low down', if you like, but you may well prefer 'the London'.

'It will go right up the spout,' said soothsaying Ruth. 'An all-male God.

An almost all-mole priesthood.' (All-male, that should be, sorry.)

'And this, they will say, is the only way!'

'The blinkers will be on?' asked the Christian.

'Right on,' confirmed the sayer.

'And this Empire is going to go the way of all things.

The Roman way is going to come to an end.

Too much concentration on trivia,

not enough on the well-being of the organism . . .'

'But can you tell us who's going to win in the

4.30 chariot race?' said Tritus,

concerning himself with trivia rather than the organism's well-being.

'Just a joke, Cleo.'

'And how do you think Tritus and I will fare in our relationship?' Cleo enquired.

How shocked was Tritus at her question. Firstly there was the suggestion that something was to be between them, for which he thanked his God. But secondly if it was to begin, he didn't want to know how it would go, especially if the way of his Empire and his religion was anything to go by. Or if his past relationships were anything to go by. Great at the start, bad at the end and mediocre thereafter, *if* they managed to keep going. But this time, maybe it would be different. Maybe he could change it. Or maybe *they* could. It wasn't just him. He realised that now. It had been some time since his last liaison. He now knew that you had to think about the other. His Christianity had helped him with that. That was part of loving your neighbour as yourself. And you had to be very particular with sex. His Christianity hadn't helped him with that. That he'd learned from experience. What began as pure magic would turn so slyly into mere sleight of hand. But he'd always *let* it. *They'd* always let it . . .

Anyway the soothsayer was honest. 'There seems to be a veil in front of how it will be for you two. I think perhaps, this is in *your* hands and *your* hearts, and *your* genitals. And that will be three hundred thousand, plus tax.'

'But you've hardly told us anything,' complained Tritus.

'That's why it's so cheap.'

In the café under the soothsayer's tenement, they sat
with beverages twice the price as the same under
Tritus's. They shared the resentment for this small
extortion, but also shared a thirst and a need for a
sit down. The soothsayer had kept them standing.
There had been a queue.
'So what do *you* do, Cleo?'
'Work? Or sex?' . . . She answered in playful mode . . .
'I'm an administrator of civic arts monies.'
'And work?' Tritus jested.
As a sometime civic artist, he felt a little intimidated
by Cleo being in such a position of authority. A lit-
tle more than a little.
And also, taken aback that she had such a position of
power anyway.
The only power position a woman usually managed
was priestess.
Tritus didn't want to show too much surprise, how-
ever.
Why shouldn't women have big jobs?
Votes obviously not,
but if they could do the job, then they should be
allowed to do it.
Especially as they would obviously come cheaper.
Cleo asked Tritus as to his own employ.
'And what about you?'
'Sculpt. Hammer and chisel. Specialist pillar work
mainly.'
'But I thought it was all just scrolls and crenellations.'

'It is, usually. But not always. I did the stuff on the
front of the public library.'
'That's been around a while, how old are you then?'
'Guess?'
'Sixty?'
'Forty.'
'Yes, I thought you were about forty.'
'So why did you say sixty?'
Tritus was confused and enchanted, both. Cleo
eradicated the confusion.
'Because you wanted me to say thirty, and
I want to give you twice as much as you want.'
And with that, the man wept.

The next morning, a similar beverage sat before him,
but at a more familiar and acceptable price.
He was below his own apartment once again and
once again he was in the company of his usual
friend.
'She had me weeping, Tony.
There was all this non-committal chat, and then
suddenly she said something that meant she
wanted in with me, big time.'
'Why, what did she say . . .'
'She said she wanted to give me twice what I wanted
. . . I'm so sick . . .'
'What did you say back?'
'I didn't say anything, hardly; I cried and she asked
why, and instead of saying I was crying because she
was so beautiful, I said I didn't know why I was
crying and then I said I did, I said I was crying

because I'd just thought about my pet tortoise that died when I was a kid.'

Tritus gave his nose a quick picking and continued.

'Will you tell her what I feel, will you be my go-between? I can't face rejection.'

'It doesn't sound as though she wants to reject you.'

'Look, I just think I might have blown it. And if I have, it'll be less embarrassing for her if she tells *you*, not me. I've written a poem, will you show it to her?'

'Yes – for a hundred thousand.'

'Without tax?'

'You drive a hard bargain, Tritus. Have you the poetry about your person?'

'It's in my satchel. I'll read it to you. Ready . . . It's called Living Longing.'

The piece was heavy. It was chiselled in stone.

I want another chance.

I want to dance

with you.

Baby.

Antonius said that it was a bit short and he wasn't sure if it needed the 'Baby'.

Tony wrote a note to Cleo reminding her of their brief bumping into each other, requesting a further meeting. The note suggested an important document and was favourably answered with a time when she would be in at her tenement home.

As he enters the building, he sees that it must be nearly two hundred years old. The craftsmanship feels so much more loving than that of Tritus's modern place, round the corner. Through the café, up to the top floor. Antonius notes it's always best to have no one above you – one less orgy-possibility with which to contend. A ring of the bell, the door open, the come on in, the low couch, the offer of wine. Accepted.

'Nice rug, where did you get it?'

'An heirloom.'

'Nice.'

'So you said. To business then. The document.'

'Well, a poem.' Antonius pulls out the weighty words.

'It's not business, then?' she observes lightly.

'You can't do business with poetry?'

Antonius seems so young and alive at this moment.

'It's not that you can't, just that people don't.' Cleo is almost humbled.

'They should,' says Antonius

'They should,' says Cleo.

They are in agreement.

Cleo continues the dialogue.

Captured.

'So, what do you do for a living?'

'Teach.'

'You look fit for a teacher . . . What do you teach?'

'History.'

'Just history?'

'Well I teach everything in syllabus, but it's history

I have a passion for. And the Punic wars are my *big* passion.'

'How about me?'

'Sorry, I was getting very egocentric, going into transmission mode . . . yes, what do *you* do . . . ?'

'No, I meant how about a passion for me, have you got one of those?'

'I came to show you this,' said Antonius. He did have desire, but no desire to betray his friend.

He expanded upon the nature of his visit.

Cleo took the poem. She smiled.

'I'm not sure about the "Baby".'

They said in unison.

They laughed at their like-speaking.

They kissed.

Cleo climbed onto the couch with Tony.

Tony pushed her off onto the heirloom. He knew the rug would break her fall.

'It's lucky it's very thick,' commented Cleo, keeping the humour good.

She knew he didn't intend humiliation.

She listened to his reasoning understandingly.

'I'm sorry, but I don't want to betray my old friend.'

'Is it betrayal?'

They kiss.

Cleo climbs onto the couch with Tony.

It is mid-morning. It's a Saturday. Or the equivalent. The sunlight is upon them.

There is no school and no office today. Today they stay together indoors. And tonight – they get no sleep. Their passion sees to that – and the orgy overhead on the sun roof.

Ruth the soothsayer has just popped round to the history bookshop. The owner is her friend. She has brought her friend a takeaway beverage from her ground floor café.

The proprietor makes a small reduction if purchases are not premises-consumed. The vessel is a return-able item.

'So how's business?'

'Good. Troubled times mean troubled minds and the need for reassurance,' says the woman in the business of books.

'Have you just farted??' asks Ruth.

'No, but funnily enough I was just about to. There it is, that's better.'

'Mm, very nice,' comments the odour's recipient.

'I thought a man likes only the smell of his own farts,' observes the other.

'Yes, but I'm a woman,' the soothsayer asserts.

'Oh yes. So how much does he knock off for a take-away, Ruth?'

'Only five per cent, but it all helps.'

'No deposit on the cup?'

'No, he trusts me.'

And Tritus trusts Antonius.

Antonius was not looking forward to visiting his friend.

But he had to go.

And he had to tell him.

The night he rang the bell, part of him hoped

the betrayed one was out. But his heart craved
hastening of the inevitable.

Tritus was at home.

The come on in, the low couch, the offer of wine
reluctantly accepted.

'Come on in, I'll get out some rancid nibbles, we can
have a game of dicing for each other's clothing.'

But first the need to know whether the going-
between had been a goer.

'What did she say about the poem?'

'She said she wasn't sure about the *Baby*.'

'Like *you* weren't,' observed the author . . . 'Any
hope for me?'

'No. Look, Tritus, you need an explanation.'

'No it's not. I just wanted to be sure I blew it, and
that's that; I don't need to know the details.

Thanks for trying, that's it. Let's dice!'

Of course, that wasn't it. Outside, Antonius sees

the pulling moon's face, full and unchanging.

He knows that the face of his friend will not be the
face of his friend for much longer.

He continues gravely.

'You shouldn't be thanking me. And you need to
know the details.

'Look, it's not your fault that it's ended. You've done
me a favour by letting me know.'

'I've done you no favours. I've been with her for the

past two days. We are lovers . . . I'm sorry.'

Tritus's enthusiasm for an evening spent with his
   guest suddenly waned:
'Antonius,
you have not only hurt my heart,
you have un-haved my having
you have scuppered my basking
you have dirtied my diamond
you have ruined my rainbow
you have busted my beauty
you have carnaged celebration
you have hampered halleluiah
you have crucified salvation
you have over-stepped your station
you have over-ruled my passion
you have under-mined my person
you have charged a chariot through my craft-shop
you have shafted my hope
you have cleaned out my bee-hive
you have until I count Five to get out of here.'

Iron Orchid

Linda Jaivin

'Shush!' Precious Jade raised a slender finger to her lips. Her companions immediately stopped talking and looked up, alert, their hands moving to their swords. A burst of wind rustled the foliage of the dense bamboo forest and fanned the leaping flames of their campfire, which sounded to her now like a battle flag snapping and fluttering in the breeze. The prospect of combat stirring her blood, Precious Jade gripped the handle of her Monkey-Blade Sword . . .

Absorbed in her novel, May didn't notice the man in the tuxedo jacket, top hat, frilled shirt, cummerbund and board shorts get on the bus at the stop near the Bondi Pavilion until he began to speak. 'Ladies and gentlemen,' he pronounced in a voice full of theatrical timbre, 'welcome to Playhouse 380, North Bondi to Circular Quay.' Startled, May looked up from her book, and the man caught her eye and grinned.

She quickly looked away again, flustered, and pretended to look out of the window at the ocean.

Hearing snorts of laughter, she cautiously returned her gaze to the man. He had raised his top hat, releasing a tumble of shiny auburn curls. As May watched, he extracted from the hat a tiny toy violin, felt around inside for something else and, not finding it, finally held up the hat and shook it, catching the small bow which fell out. Raising the toy violin to his chin, he played it wildly and dramatically, making no sound whatsoever. He then mimed tuning it, and tried again. Now, suddenly, he sounded like Isaac Stern playing Stravinsky on one of her favourite recordings – no coincidence as it was actually Stern playing Stravinsky on the pocket tape player he'd somehow managed to turn on at the same time.

A few people giggled. One or two applauded. Everyone who'd shared the initial thought 'who is this nut and is he going to hurt or embarrass us?' relaxed – except May, for the violinist was once again looking at her, this time as though the performance was meant for her alone. Flushing, May lowered her head and stared at the open novel in her lap. She shook her head slightly so that some of her thick shoulder-length hair fell forward, curtaining her moon-shaped face.

May was not, to put it mildly, an extrovert. When she had arrived in Australia from Taiwan ten years earlier to study medical pathology, she threw herself into her studies. She rarely socialised with her classmates, whose taste for loud rock bands, getting 'hammered' and falling into bed with people they scarcely knew she found culturally alien. She attended some of the Asian students' parties, but didn't find much in common with them either – most of the other Chinese students were Cantonese and she didn't understand their brash dialect or care for the greasy yum cha brunches of which they were so fond.

She'd have returned home after graduation, but that was the year China chose to launch missiles in Taiwan's direction, one of which landed only about sixty clicks from the island's north coast. Her nervous parents urged her to stay on if she could; it was safer in Australia. She said she wasn't scared. Her parents replied that they were and that it comforted them to think they could follow her to Australia if they needed to. They'd lived through one civil war, were old and tired and didn't want to live through another.

Staying on didn't prove as difficult as it sometimes was made out to be, especially for someone with two feet already on Australian soil and a useful degree. May found a job in a pathology lab in the city, and a flat in North Bondi. Her colleagues liked May and invited her to Friday night drinks and Sunday afternoon barbies. She went just often enough that they wouldn't think she didn't like them, but preferred to spend her leisure time quietly, reading her beloved kungfu novels, walking along the cliffs by the sea and going by herself to the café by the beach where the waiters made beautiful, swirling patterns with the milk in the cappuccinos. The familiar way in which the waiters greeted her made her feel at home and, while she occasionally missed Taipei, her parents, old friends, oyster omelettes and crushed ice with mung beans, she had no real complaints about her life in Sydney.

The bus stopped again and more people crammed on. It was early autumn and the fresh wool smell of new jumpers mingled with perfume, deodorant and someone's cinnamon doughnuts. The bus doors closed with a sigh and those standing did a little shuffle to absorb the newcomers. The violin-player was swallowed up in the crush. Relieved, May returned to the world of her novel . . .

At last. The White Flower Society had fallen into their trap – just as her beloved father had fallen into theirs more than five years earlier. The head of the White Flowers, the notorious Two-Face, named for the diagonal knife scar which cleaved his face into two distinct halves, had framed her father over the theft of a priceless gold Buddha. Her mother wailed inconsolably as the bailiffs dragged him off. When he protested his innocence, they struck him and the careless blow killed him. The following morning, Precious Jade discovered her mother's body hanging from a tree in the garden. Though only thirteen, she vowed through her tears to avenge her parents' death. For five years she'd trained under Master Flying Crane in the Daoist monastery on Black Phoenix Mountain, honing her skills with the Monkey-Blade Sword, and gathering around her a faithful band of men, many of whom had been her father's loyal retainers. Now, at last, was her chance . . .

The woman who'd been sitting next to May got off at Bondi Junction. May took no notice of the person sliding into the vacated seat until he spoke. 'That Japanese?'

May looked up. 'Sorry?' She could make this word of apology sound as rude as any other Australian when disturbed.

It was the man with the resonant voice and the tiny violin. He was smiling and pointing at her kungfu novel.

'Chinese,' she said flatly. Why couldn't people tell the difference?

'I see,' he responded, oblivious to any annoyance on her part. 'Are you from China, then?'

'Taiwan.' Her tone did not invite further conversation.

'Of course. The Land of Smiles.'

May sighed and treated him to her most withering look. 'Taiwan. Not Thailand.' Australian politicians could prattle on all they liked about Australia being part of Asia. Most Australians didn't have a clue as to what was what in their own neighbourhood.

'Oh, right, Taiwan,' he repeated, nodding and rolling his eyes as if to say, 'stupid me.' He searched for something else to say. 'So that makes you Taiwanese?'

'No, Chinese, actually.' May briefly considered whether it was worth explaining the difference. She decided it wasn't. Although his manner was pleasant, he remained a lairy and intrusive stranger in a tux and board shorts. She'd been brought up not to talk to strangers.

'But –'

'My parents,' she stated, pre-empting his question, 'came from Beijing.'

'Oh. Right. Beijing duck and all that?'

'All that.' She sighed again. 'Any more questions, or may I get back to my book?'

He blew up his cheeks in a comic rendering of dismay. 'Of course. Sorry.'

'No worries.' May forced a little smile before returning to her book.

He thought how cute she sounded saying 'no worries' in her light Chinese accent.

She could just make out Two-Face himself, heading towards them at the head of his men, lured by a message sent from his deputy, Hunchback Li, whom they'd taken captive two days earlier. Precious Jade's sword slid out of her scabbard with a zing. And not a moment too soon – a whistling sound alerted her to danger. She whipped her sword above her head. Clang! A wolf-tooth-blade spinning wheel shattered against her sword and fell in shards onto the ground.

'So what's the book about?'

Swivelling her head, she looked at him closely for the first time. He was probably a little older than her, maybe thirty, though it was hard to tell with Australians. The sun they worshipped treated them cruelly. Faint smile lines were etched around his large, green eyes with their thick lashes. His reddish brown curls were thick and shiny, his nose large like those of most Caucasians, but well-formed, and he had a nice smile. Good teeth. She registered his features without any particular emotion, much as she might study tissue under her microscope and declare the results of a biopsy benign, not malignant.

'Kungfu,' she answered. 'It's a kungfu novel.'

'Kungfu?' Grinning, he raised his hands in front of his face and chopped at the air, making sound effects with his mouth: *whoot, whoot, whoot*. 'Like *Crouching Tiger, Hidden Dragon*? Did you love that movie or what?!'

May saw her opportunity. The enemy had unknowingly exposed his vulnerability and she was going to move in with a small, precise move known as *dian xue*, in which by striking certain points on the body with one's bare hand, it is possible to immobilise one's opponent. 'Put it like this,' she said, pausing to organise her words to maximise their deadly effect. 'That movie is like a fashionable Chinese restaurant in the CBD. Trendy Westerners like to go there. Chinese people think it's okay, but overpriced. They prefer little places in Chinatown where the décor's not so flash but the food's more authentic.'

'Okay,' he agreed cheerfully, apparently unaware that he had just been paralysed by her put-down. 'Let's do it then.'

'Do what?' she asked cautiously, cocking her head to one side, confused. Her English was quite good, but sometimes she missed nuances.

'Go to one of those little places in Chinatown.'

May shook her head. Her expression was composed of equal parts disbelief and refusal. 'Excuse me. This is my stop,' she lied. She didn't care if she had to walk an extra couple of blocks to get to work.

He swung his long, semi-bare legs out into the aisle and stood up so that she could get out. As she made her way to the side door, he called out, 'Hey, Taiwan girl! What's your name?'

May stared at the doors, willing them to open. He was embarrassing her. Thankfully, at that moment the bus jerked to a halt and the doors hissed open. As she stepped onto the pavement, she heard him shout, 'Mine's Lionel!' She didn't look back. Her sensible heels clicked on the pavement as May strode towards the hospital on Macquarie Street where she worked.

What's my name? Depends who's asking. May to my Australian friends. Meilan, Beautiful Orchid, to my parents. Me, I like to think of myself as Tielan, Iron Orchid, warrior maiden, righteous outlaw.

She checked her watch. Quarter to eight. May liked getting in to work early. There were always important problems and puzzles to be solved, new ones every day, little mysteries of the human organism behaving badly, acting violently towards itself for no apparent reason. Drawing on her knowledge of molecular biology, genetics and other scientific disciplines, she was able to tell the doctors what was wrong and they told the patient. She was very glad that the last bit was their job, not hers. If her alter ego Iron Orchid loved a battle, the thought of any sort of confrontation made May nervous. She recalled her conversation with her mother over the phone several nights before. 'You know,' her mother had ventured, 'Mrs Huang's son is living in Sydney. You remember Huang Jian-hsiu? He's a very nice boy. He's got a good job, too.'

'Ma.'

'So I've given Mrs Huang your phone number to give to him.'

'Ma.'

'Just meet him. You know, Lan-lan, it would be good for you to have a man around. I'd feel better knowing you had someone looking after you in a foreign city.'

'I can look after myself.'

'And you're not getting any younger, you know.'

May rolled her eyes at the phone.

'Lan-lan? You there?'

'Yes, Ma.'

May and her colleague, Sarah, often took their lunches to the Domain, where they sat under the trees and breathed air that didn't reek of antiseptic. May thought of Sarah as a typical big Aussie girl – big by comparison with her small-boned self, certainly, but big too in personality. She had a loud, contagious laugh, a face rampant with freckles, and a passion for living life to the full, even if that meant that on Monday mornings she was usually still hungover from Saturday night and Thursdays often saw her wiping away tears for the bloke who left on Sunday morning and still hadn't called. Her love life was very complicated, and May couldn't always remember the names of the males who populated it, or whether they were good guys or bad guys, but she enjoyed listening to Sarah's tales of adventure and con-quest set in the clubs and pubs and parties of Sydney.

That lunchtime, the big kookaburra who always sat on the same branch of the same tree, facing the art gallery, turned to May and Sarah and let out a great long belly laugh, and it occurred to May to tell Sarah all about the strange man on the bus. But Sarah had already launched into a complex saga involving two ex-boyfriends, her flatmate, a cute bartender and a borrowed Blaxploitation soundtrack, whatever that was. By the time she'd finished, their lunch hour was nearly over. May decided her story would keep.

The following day, after getting onto the bus, May opened her novel, but found it difficult to concentrate. As they approached the Bondi Pavilion, she looked to see if Lionel was waiting at the stop, telling herself that this was only because she didn't want him to catch her unawares.

He wasn't at the stop, or the one after. She picked up her novel again and was soon lost in a world of deadly feuds, inventive weaponry, good-looking heroes, and feisty heroines.

That lunchtime, Sarah suggested they vary their routine and head for Circular Quay. They could sit on the lawn of the Museum of Contemporary Art and watch the ferries chug in and out. It was a Thursday.

'What are you up to this weekend?' Sarah asked as they waited to cross Macquarie Street.

'Nothing much. Maybe a swim if it's warm enough. Reading.'

'What are you reading?'

'A kungfu novel.'

'Huh. Is that like kungfu movies?'

'Yeah, well, lots of those are based on the novels.'

'It's funny, May, but I'd never have pegged you for the type to be reading kungfu novels – not that I even knew they existed.' Sarah guffawed and pretended to perform karate chops at the air, much as Lionel had.

'I'm not going to tangle with you, that's for sure. You actually practise the stuff?'

'Only in my head,' May confessed. 'I've got another May in here.' She tapped her skull.

'What do you mean?'

May blushed. She'd never admitted this to anyone before. 'She's called Iron Orchid. Her special weapon is a deadly dart in the shape of an orchid, whose petals are sharp as knives.'

Sarah shook her head appreciatively. 'That's seriously wacky. The closest thing I've got to that is my rock-'n'-roll wrestling alter ego, "The Pre-Menstruator". Actually, that's just what my last boyfriend used to call me.'

'Iron Orchid doesn't have boyfriends.' They were walking down Bridge Street now, weaving among the suits towards the Quay.

'Is she, you know, gay then?' Sarah asked, fascinated.

'No. But she's vowed never to marry.' Once May started talking about Iron Orchid, she found she couldn't stop. 'She'll always be independent and free. She obeys no rules but those of justice, righteousness and loyalty. She lives in the world of *jianghu* . . . hmm, I'm not sure how to translate. It's literally "rivers and lakes" but kind of means the world of the outlaw.'

'Outlaw? Like criminals?' Sarah giggled. The notion of May as a criminal, even in her fantasy life, was too funny. So far as she could tell, May didn't even jaywalk.

'Some are criminals. Not all, though they're definitely on the outside of the law in many ways. I suppose you could say *jianghu* is the world of people on the margins of society, who live by their wits and don't have proper jobs or even homes.'

'Renters not owners?'

'Are you, how do you say, taking my piss?'

'Taking *the* piss.' Sarah grinned. 'Not at all. I'm just trying to get a handle.'

May squinted at her friend. It really was hard to explain. 'Okay. They don't rent or own. They might sleep in the desert, or the woods, or in a small inn they pass along the way . . .'

They reached the Quay. 'Okay, I think I get it,' Sarah replied, motioning towards the performers spread out by the wharfs. 'In Australian terms, these buskers would be part of the, how do you say it?'

'*Jianghu.*'

'Yeah, the jyang hoo.' May silently marvelled at the Australian's ability to mangle any phrase in a foreign language, as they observed a woman in front of them covered in gold paint and standing as still as a statue. A tourist dropped a coin into the hat at her feet and, as May and Sarah watched, the golden lady launched into a cheerful mime.

'I suppose –' May's voice caught in her throat.

'What? What's wrong?' Sarah looked curiously in the direction in which May was staring. She saw a tall, spunky bloke in a tux and board shorts, bowing a tiny violin.

May paled. 'Let's go.'

'Why don't we watch for a while?' Sarah lingered. 'That guy's eye candy. And I daresay he's looking straight at us, too. Mad. I'm sure he just winked at us.'

May slipped her arm through Sarah's and yanked

her in the direction of the Botanic Gardens.

'What's with you?' Sarah asked, sneaking one last glimpse over her shoulder. 'What's wrong? Do you know him?'

'Yes. No.'

'You've had a fling! You haven't told me, either, you sly little fox,' she squealed.

Now May looked over her shoulder, nervous that he might have heard, though they were nearly at the Opera House forecourt. 'I have not had a fling,' she asserted.

Over sandwiches by the pond, May told Sarah about Lionel and his 'outrageous' behaviour on the bus the day before.

Meanwhile, Lionel, bowing his violin and playing up for the tourists, held onto the vision of May's lovely round face, her intelligent black eyes, luminous skin and small plum of a mouth. He'd been smitten the moment he spotted her on the bus the day before. And she read kungfu novels. How cool was that? Anxiously, he watched her and her friend disappear in the direction of the Botanic Gardens. He wanted to run after them but a group of enthusiastic Americans replaced the Japanese honeymooners who'd been watching him earlier. The Yanks didn't tire of him for a good fifteen minutes. The moment they left, he clicked off his tape recorder, picked up his hat from the ground, tipped the coins without counting them into the little cloth sack he tied to his waist, stuffed the violin and bow back into the hat, and strode towards the Botanic Gardens.

He looked everywhere, finally spotting her at a

distance just as she and her friend rose from their bench and walked off in the direction of Macquarie Street.

He hurried after them, feeling a little like a dog chasing a car and not sure what it would do if it finally caught it. He intercepted the pair just at the entrance to the hospital.

'G'day,' he greeted Sarah. Then, to May, 'Remember me?' It was a fairly silly question for a man wearing a top hat and board shorts.

'Sorry,' May replied, poker-faced. 'You all look alike.'

'I'm Sarah.' Sarah smiled charmingly. 'I take it you know May?'

'May I know May?' he asked playfully.

May pursed her lips.

'What are you doing at the hospital? Are you . . .' His voice trailed off.

'Yes, I'm terminally ill.'

Lionel reeled, shocked. 'But you look great, I mean, you don't look . . .' He blinked.

May observed him coolly. Sarah stared at her friend, speechless for once. 'Don't look what?' May persisted. She glanced at her watch. 'I'll be late. I've got tests. I've got to go.' She turned and strode purposefully through the gate. Sarah gave Lionel a sympathetic look and opened her mouth as though to say something. Then, deciding against it, she turned and caught up with her friend.

Lionel stood for a moment on the street. His eyes watered. He briefly imagined holding May's hand as she lay on her deathbed. Their love would be brief and tragic, but intense. She just had to get over her antipathy towards him first. He turned and walked with a heavy heart back to the Quay.

'What the fuck was that all about?' Sarah demanded. 'He's a quirk, but he seems really sweet. And he's gorgeous.'

May shrugged. 'In Chinese kungfu, it's called Digging a Trench to Divert a Stream".'

Sarah waited for May to explain. When she didn't, Sarah shook her head. 'Very bloody mystery-of-the-Orient if you ask me. I've heard of Digging a Hole and Burying Yourself in It. What the hell does that mean, though?'

'Think about it.' May walked over to a rack of test tubes and selected one.

Sarah shrugged, sat down at her desk and picked up a file. After a few moments, she looked up and nodded vigorously. 'Right. Of course. Why didn't I realise?'

'What are you talking about?'

'Oh, look, that's cool. I should've known. You know,' Sarah added in a low voice. 'I've had fantasies myself, just never followed through. One of those things.' Why hadn't she realised that May was a lesbian? What an idiot she was! Sarah silently berated herself for her insensitivity.

May looked up. She had no idea what Sarah was on about. But if it meant she'd let the subject of Lionel rest, that was fine with her.

On the following Saturday morning, walking down Campbell Parade in an ordinary T-shirt and jeans with the weekend paper under his arm, Lionel's heart went thump in his chest when he passed the café with the designer cappuccinos and noticed May there reading her novel. He'd already had a coffee somewhere else and was going home to change and head out to Circular Quay. Saturday was always good. Lots of tourists. He wasn't sure what compelled him instead to take a table near to hers and order another coffee. He watched her out of the corner of his eyes while pretending to read the weekend paper.

'You're not a bad-looking girl.' As he spoke, Two-Face leered down at Precious Jade, whom he'd pinned to the ground with his lance. She lifted her head and spat in his ugly face. He sneered as he wiped off her spittle with the back of his hand. 'Feisty little thing, too. Maybe I should take you as a wife.'

With a Flying Chariot Wheel movement of her legs, Precious Jade knocked the lance out of Two-Face's hands and rendered him temporarily incapable of taking anyone as a wife. Back on her feet, she retrieved her sword and was driving it towards his neck when she sensed a presence behind her and whirled around just in time to block an attack by Two-Face's deputy. Her Monkey-Blade Sword flashed. She'd take on the lot of them . . .

May sensed she was being observed and looked up.

At that moment, Lionel raised his head from his paper and feigned surprise. 'What a coincidence!' he exclaimed.

'Are you following me?' she demanded.

'I would if you'd allow me to,' he replied, a disarming

smile on his handsome face. He pointed at the empty chair at her table. 'May I? I mean, I don't want to intrude, and you're perfectly free to say no, and if you say no, I'll never approach you again. But if you say yes, I'll . . . I'll . . . I dunno, I'll stand on the table and sing my joy to the world.'

'You may sit with me,' May replied. 'But only if you promise not to do anything of the kind.' The corners of her mouth twitched upwards.

'Agreed.' He sat down looking concerned. 'So, how are you feeling?'

'Great.'

'That's a relief. So you're okay, you know, for the moment?'

'Yeah, why wouldn't I be? Oh.' May suddenly recalled their last conversation and grimaced. Taking a deep breath, she confessed that she'd made up the terminal illness thing. He looked completely taken aback, but then roared with laughter. Finally, cringing, he asked, 'Am I really so horrible that you had to make up a disease to get rid of me?'

'No, you're not,' she answered, suddenly appalled at her own behaviour, and realised that she meant it.

May never expected that she and Lionel could find so much to talk about. He had a way of drawing her out and making her laugh. She found herself telling him all about Taipei, medicine and her family, and asked him about his life, too. He told her how he travelled around performing his little acts – the violin shtick was just one of them – and had lived a fairly nomadic life, travelling through Europe, South America and the United States, though he liked Bondi and planned to stay in Sydney indefinitely. Later, when they were ambling along the cliff between Bondi and Bronte, he admitted to a degree in computer science.

Watching the sun set and sharing their fish and chips with the seagulls, she told him about Iron Orchid. He asked her if she actually knew any kungfu. She giggled and said no. He'd just started learning tai-chi and proposed that they do a class together. 'Why not?' she said.

He walked her home but didn't kiss her, though they each privately considered the possibility and each went to bed that night with a tight but delicious feeling in their chests.

After the Tuesday night tai-chi lesson, Lionel started to put his arm around her shoulder but pulled back, uncertain of her response. 'So when are you going to take me to a restaurant for some authentic Chinese food?' he ventured.

May considered. 'Are you free on Saturday night?'

'I'm all yours.'

The way he said that caused a tingle in her tummy. When they got to her flat, they kissed cheeks briefly on the pavement before she turned to go inside. 'See you on Saturday, then.'

Sarah, hearing this story, was almost more excited than May, although she warned May that if he 'pulled a no-show', or did something else equally 'arseholic', not to be too broken-hearted about it. Men simply had those tendencies, she warned.

'Lionel isn't like that,' May stated.

Sarah smiled. 'Oh, Woman of the World, I guess you'd know, wouldn't you?' Observing May's dismayed expression, she quickly added, 'I just don't want you to get hurt. He sounds almost too good to be true. He is a babe, though, and seems keen enough. You just never know.'

May made a booking at a Sichuan restaurant in Chinatown. She thought about what she was going to order for them: some crunchy jellyfish and blue 'thousand-year-old eggs' to start, perhaps, then a Chongqing hotpot with bits of rubbery cow's stomach and slippery eel cooking in a lip-numbing chilli broth. He said he wanted authentic food and that's what he'd get. She smiled to herself.

She'd taken the train from Bondi Junction to Town Hall. It wasn't too long a walk from there down George Street to Chinatown. Originally, they were going to go to the restaurant together, but Lionel had promised to help a friend build a website that afternoon and said they'd be better off meeting at the restaurant itself. Daylight savings had just ended. Though only seven, it was already dark by the time May strolled down George Street, thinking about Lionel.

'Whachyoo smilin' at, bitch?' May snapped out of her reverie. She was facing five teenage boys in hooded sweatshirts with cut-off sleeves that exposed their massive arms. Although she guessed that, like her, they belonged to some kind of ethnic minority or immigrant community, May did not think they were the sort who watched SBS.

'Chink chink chinagirl,' one taunted. Before she knew

what was happening, they'd surrounded her and manoeuvred her into an alleyway just off George Street. The leader stepped up close and grabbed his crotch. 'You likee this, chinagirl?' he sneered.

Though George Street with its bustling crowds was just metres away, the alley was deserted and dark. For a moment May nearly blacked out with fear. Her heart pounding in her chest, she asked herself what Iron Orchid would do. Not even knowing where her strength was coming from, she curled back the fingers of her right hand, bent the whole hand back at the wrist like a tiger's paw and drove it straight up into the nose of the leader. He clearly wasn't expecting that and staggered backwards, yelping. The others muttered angrily but kept their distance from her.

Her fear drained away, replaced by fury. 'Yeah, I likee a bit of that,' she screamed, turning tiger's paw into eagle's claw and, driving upwards this time, grabbed hold of the leader's testicles and twisted them hard. She'd have pulled them straight off if she could. He went down howling. Grabbing the strap of her purse, heavy with the kungfu novel inside, she swung it around as if it were a mace, clipping another one of the gang in the temple. Then, she ran like buggery.

When she stopped and leaned against the gilded 'money tree' that marked one of Chinatown's busiest intersections, panting for breath, her head pounding with the adrenalin, she looked back but could see no sign that they'd even attempted to follow her. Shakily, she made her way to the restaurant. She was a bit early and Lionel hadn't arrived yet. She went to the ladies and splashed her face with water until she calmed down. Once her hands stopped trembling, she brushed her hair and applied some lipstick. There were some terrible men in the world. Lionel was not one of them. May really, really wanted to see him. She wanted him to wrap her in his arms and kiss her. She might even sleep with him if he asked her and, perhaps, if he didn't ask her she'd ask him.

May sat down at the table and the waiter brought her some tea. She decided they should just have the fish-flavoured pork, chicken with cashew nuts, and other dishes that he'd probably like and which were, in fact, every bit as 'authentic' as the jellyfish and cow belly.

May looked at her watch. He was five minutes late, then ten. Where was he?

Fifteen minutes. She felt tears forming and blinked them away. She pulled out her novel, her reddening eyes flicking up hopefully to the door every time someone else came in.

Precious Jade, using her teeth and her good hand, ripped a strip of cloth from her sleeve and tied it around her wounded arm for a bandage, breathing as evenly as she could to overcome the pain. She'd comported herself well in battle. And she'd managed to kill both Two-Face and his deputy. Raising her wineskin, she turned her face to the sky.

Lionel looked up and blinked at the medic. His vision was blurry. He wasn't sure why he was lying on the pavement. There were people standing over him. He turned his head painfully and saw the ambulance. He vaguely remembered walking past an alleyway and someone calling him a poofter. That's right. He'd been walking past, thinking about dinner with May, when he felt a hard punch to the side of his head. Instantly nauseous and confused, he'd turned to look at his attackers and copped another punch to his face. There were four of them. Four or five. Hooded sweatshirts with the arms ripped off. The leader had had a freshly bloodied nose and was a mean, angry bastard. Shit. May. How long had he been lying there on the ground? She was waiting in the restaurant. He struggled to rise, but his head swam sickeningly, and he passed out again. The medics lifted him carefully onto the stretcher, and then into the back of the ambulance.

May, hearing the siren, looked up from her book. She picked at the pickled cabbage and cold mung-bean noodles she'd ordered to placate the waiters. The siren grew loud and then faded into the distance. He was now half an hour late. For a moment, she wondered if something had happened to him, if he'd been in an accident or something. She told herself not to be ridiculous. She remembered Sarah's words and, dabbing furiously at her eyes, smiled grimly to herself.

The fierce sorghum liquor warmed her and dulled the pain. Wiping her mouth with the back of her hand, and tucking her hair under her cap, Precious Jade mounted her bay charger and galloped away, determined to reach Shamaness Mountain by sunset. Her horse's hooves echoed in the mountains like thunder . . .

Bullet Point Bravery

Gretel Killeen

. . . or 'shortcuts to super-dooper-superwomandom when you're tired and lonely and have breasts the size of sultanas'

- wear a cape
- put shoulder pads in it
- put shoulder pads in your bra
- wear a push-up bra at all times . . . especially on your bum
- don't slouch
- don't feel guilty
- don't befriend your gynaecologist
- do befriend your car mechanic
- find a job you absolutely love
- never plan to retire
- stop waiting
- keep moving
- don't do aerobics in a G-string
- tell the world when you've got PMT . . . wear a PMT hat and matching T-shirt
- laugh when you fail
- laugh when you succeed

- laugh when your boyfriend breaks up with you
- don't laugh when you're eating carrot
- always eat your greens
- avoid beige food
- feng shui your brain
- feng shui your friends
- every morning take a moment to pretend you're Maria from *The Sound of Music*
- show off . . . when you're by yourself
- take up ballet . . . when you're seventy-five
- tell the truth, because lying's exhausting
- floss like a demon
- take gas at the dentist's
- start the gas in the waiting room
- smile at strangers (you'll find it unnerves them)
- don't look inwardly
- give outwardly instead
- skip . . . while wearing no undies
- act like a bubble . . . float, bring joy . . . pop
- never have sex on the first date . . . unless he's good looking . . . but boring
- never do anything that makes you feel bad, just to make a man feel good
- actually . . . never do anything that makes you feel bad
- know that the only thing worth suffering for is shoes
- let your friends love you
- if your friends don't love you then find new ones
- understand that no one will ever love you as much as you want them to
- don't be desperate for a bloke
- have a million affairs of the heart
- be your own love of your life

Changing People

Sophie Kinsella

So we're sitting in front of *Changing Rooms*, eating pizza, and Fizz my flatmate is deciding what she might do with her life. Fizz is what you would describe as 'between jobs', if she'd ever had one. She's got a sheet of paper and a list of 'possibles' which so far consists of 'corporate trouble-shooter' and 'taste-tester for Cadburys', both crossed out.

'Okay, what about . . . aromatherapist?' she exclaims. 'I love all that kind of stuff. Massage, facials . . .'

'That would be good,' I say. 'You'd have to train, though. And buy all the oils.'

'Really?' She pulls a face. 'How much are they?'

'About . . . three quid each? Four, maybe?'

I'm not really concentrating on her – I'm looking at some people from Sevenoaks whose living room has just been transformed from chintzy blue into sleek, pale minimalism.

Their faces remind me of my parents when they came to meet me at the airport, after it had happened. They had the same wary eyes; the same mixture of anxiety and relief; the same initial shock, which they tried to mask beneath welcoming smiles. They gazed at me, searching for signs of the old Emma – as these owners are peering disorientedly around their room, wondering where their curtains have gone.

'I can't believe the transformation!' someone is exclaiming. 'In such a short time!'

I was away for ten months in all. Plus the two months in hospital. A year to change a person. Linda Barker would do it quicker.

I open my mouth to say something about this to Fizz. Something about change, about growing up. But she's gesticulating wildly, her mouth full of pizza. She often does this, Fizz. Monopolises airtime. *I'm thinking – therefore no one else may speak.*

'I've got it!' she says at last. 'I'll be an interior designer!'

'An interior designer!' I echo, trying to hit the right note of support. 'Do you know anything about interior design?'

'You don't have to know anything!' She gestures to the screen. 'Look at that. It's easy!'

'I wouldn't say "easy", exactly . . .'

'All you need is loads of pots of lilac paint and some MDF . . .'

'Oh really?' I raise my eyebrows. 'So what does MDF stand for, then?' Fizz shoots me a cross look.

'It stands for . . . micro . . . dynamic . . . federal . . . Anyway, that's not the point. I won't be bloody Handy Andy, will I? I'll be the person with creative vision and flair.'

I roll my eyes and take a swig of wine. I know I should be more supportive. But the thing is, I *have* been more supportive. I was supportive all through the writing-a-film-script phase, the opening-a-dancing-school phase and 'Dial-A-Dessert – we'll deliver a freshly made pudding to your door!' That last one might actually have been a winner if we hadn't ended up buying ingredients worth about two hundred pounds in order to deliver one small trifle to West Norwood.

I say 'we', by the way, because somehow I always end up getting dragged into Fizz's little schemes.

'Fizz – listen – why does it always have to be some great entrepreneurial plan? Why don't you get a job?'

'Get a job?' she says, as though I'm mad. 'Everyone knows it's impossible to get jobs these days.'

'It's not impossible. You get a paper, look through the adverts –'

'Oh right. Easy. So I'll just apply for . . .' she grabs the *Evening Standard*. 'For . . . Product Unit Manager (retail), shall I? Look, I get a company car, and a pension. Ooh, goody.'

'Not that sort of job . . .'

'It's all right for you! You're still a student!'

'Yes,' I say patiently, 'and when I finish my thesis, I'll get a job.'

'Yeah, well . . .' She sighs. 'God, it's all such bloody hard work, isn't it? I mean look at her.' She gestures at Mrs Sevenoaks. 'I wish I could just get married and do nothing.' She takes a thoughtful bite of pizza. 'Hey, Emma, when you were engaged, were you going to give up work?'

'No,' I say after a pause. 'No I wasn't.' And before she can ask anything else, I change the subject.

There's a lot of things I don't talk about to Fizz. In fact, there's a lot of things I don't talk about to anyone. Part of me is afraid that if I once started talking, I'd never stop.

I was twenty-two and thought I owned the world. The first time he asked me to marry him, I laughed in his face. The second time I shrugged, the third time I agreed. We bought a ring; he talked to my parents. But I couldn't take it seriously. Even when he was telling me he loved me, I barely listened. I used to act like a spoilt kid around him. It was like the time my parents gave me a watch for my seventh birthday. They wrapped it up in layers and layers of paper, and I got so impatient, ripping it all off, I cried, 'There's nothing in here, is there?' and threw the whole lot in the bin.

My parents should have just left it there. If my father hadn't screwed up his sleeve and reached, grimacing, into the mess of tealeaves and eggshells, maybe I would have learned a lesson. That sometimes you throw things away and no one, not even your dad, can get them back for you.

When Fizz tells me three weeks later that she's got her first appointment with a client, I nearly drop down dead with astonishment.

'It's an Arabella Lennox, in Kensington. She saw my insert in *Homes & Gardens*!'

'You put an insert in *Homes & Gardens*? My God,

Fizz, how much does that cost?'

'I didn't pay, you moron. I went to Smiths on the King's Road and when they weren't looking, I slipped a load of leaflets into all the posh magazines. Felicity Silton, Interior Consultant. Our appointment's at two.'

'*Our* appointment?' I echo suspiciously.

'You're my assistant.' She looks up and sees my face. 'Oh, go on, Em, I need an assistant, otherwise they'll think I'm crap.'

'I don't want to be your crummy assistant! I'll be your partner.'

'You can't be my partner. It's not a partnership.'

'All right then . . . your creative design consultant.'

There's a pause while Fizz thinks about this.

'Okay,' she says grudgingly. 'You can be my creative design consultant. But don't say anything.'

'What if I have some really good ideas?'

'I don't need ideas. I already know what I'm going to do. Designer's Guild wallpaper and huge candles everywhere. I've found a rather wonderful local source for those, actually,' she adds smugly.

'Where?' I ask, intrigued in spite of myself.

'The pound shop! And we can charge her a tenner for each one.'

Arabella Lennox has short blonde hair and widely mascaraed eyes, and sits on an old piano stool while Fizz and I sit side by side on the sofa.

'As you can see,' she says, gesturing around, 'the whole place needs an overhaul.'

I look around at the fading paintwork, the wooden shutters, the battered leather chair by the fireplace. There's a bookshelf by the fire and I run my eyes over the spines of the books. I've read most of them. Or I'm intending to.

'It's not my style at all,' she adds, adjusting her pearls on her cashmere cardigan.

No, really?

'My . . .' I see her weighing up a choice of words. 'My . . . chap has handed over the job to me to do. Or rather, I insisted!' Arabella gives a little tinkly laugh. 'I mean, if I'm going to live here one day . . . It's hardly the lap of luxury, is it? And all these awful old books everywhere.'

'So you're moving in here?' says Fizz. She's writing on her notepad and doesn't see Arabella's face tighten.

'Well. I mean, it's the next obvious step, isn't it? And when he sees what a fabulous job I've done with the place . . . I'm sure he'll come round.' She leans forward earnestly. 'I want to transform it. Bring in bright colours, and some lovely gilt mirrors, and lots of chandeliers . . . My favourite colour is pink, by the way.'

'Pink . . . chandeliers,' says Fizz, scribbling on her notepad with a serious expression. I look over, see that she's written *Barbie's Fairy Palace*, and try to conceal a giggle. 'I really must say, you've got some fantastic ideas there, Arabella.'

'Thank you!' she dimples. 'So – did you have any initial ideas for this room?'

'I was thinking . . .' Fizz pauses consideringly. 'Off the top of my head . . . Designer's Guild wallpaper – in pink, of course – and candles. Candles everywhere.'

'Ooh, I love candles!' trills Arabella. 'They're so romantic.'

'Good!' says Fizz, scribbling again. 'I'm afraid they *are* rather expensive . . .'

'That's okay.' Arabella gives a coy smile. 'Dee-Dee has given me a very generous budget.'

'Your boyfriend is called Dee-Dee?' I say dis-believingly.

'It's what I call him,' says Arabella. 'I love pet-names. Don't you?'

'Well,' I say. 'For a pet, perhaps.'

Arabella stares at me, eyes narrowed.

'What's your role, exactly?' she says.

'I'm the creative design consultant,' I reply pleasantly. 'Plus, I'm a qualified specialist in mantlepiece adornment.'

Arabella gives me a puzzled look.

'So you advise on . . . ?'

'Which *objet* to place where,' I say, nodding. 'It's a very underrated skill.'

We all turn our heads to look at the mantlepiece in this room, which is bare apart from a box of matches.

'If you like,' I say generously, 'I'll throw in a mantle-piece consultation for free.'

'Really?' Arabella's eyes widen. 'That would be great!' She peers more closely at me. 'You don't mind me mentioning it – but is there something wrong with your face? Under your chin. Is it psoriasis? Because my beautician says –'

'No,' I say, cutting her off. 'It's not psoriasis.' I smile at her. 'But thank you for drawing my attention to it.'

'Let's look at the rest of the flat,' says Fizz firmly. 'Okay?' And as she gets up she gives my hand a sympathetic squeeze.

We walk through the spacious hall, and I can hear Fizz blathering on quite impressively about proportions and colour palettes. Then we turn down a little corridor towards the bedroom. There's an abstract painting hanging up above the door, which sends an unpleasant little twinge to my chest as I glance at it. Because it looks very like . . .

It looks almost exactly like . . .

As I get near, my heart starts to thump. I run my eyes quickly over the canvas, looking for discrepancies. It can't be the same. It can't. But it is. I know every square inch; every brush stroke of this painting. Of course I know it. I helped to choose it.

I stare up at it, transfixed; unable to breathe.

'Oh, the painting,' says Arabella, turning back. 'Yes, it's quite nice, isn't it? Not really my thing, but apparently the painter is quite up-and-coming. He's –'

'Spanish,' I hear myself saying.

'Yes!' she says, and eyes me in surprise. 'Goodness, you do know your stuff, don't you?'

'Where did you get it?' My voice is too urgent; too clumsy.

'It's not mine,' she says. 'It belongs to my chap. So this is the bedroom . . .'

I follow her numbly into the room. And now, of course, I'm seeing the signs everywhere, like fingerprints appearing under dust. The old leather trunk. The books in the living room.

I glance at myself in the mirror – and my face has drained of colour.

'Ooh, look!' says Fizz, spying a photograph by the bed. 'Is that him? Is that your chap?'

'Yes, that's him!' beams Arabella. 'That's Dee-Dee. Of course, his real name is David –'

I saw it coming; I had the four-minute warning. But hearing his name again is like being hammered in the stomach.

'Excuse me,' I say. 'I . . . I don't feel well. I think I'll go and wait outside.'

'Are you okay, Em?' says Fizz, and puts a hand on my arm.

'I'll be fine,' I manage. 'Really. I just need to sit in the fresh air for a bit.'

As I walk blindly back down the corridor, towards the front door, I can hear Fizz explaining: 'She was in this car crash in Peru a couple of years ago . . .'

We used to tease each other about sleeping with other people. I used to pretend I fancied his friend, Jon. I used to flirt outrageously. It was all a big joke. Even when I found myself letting Jon slip his hand inside my shirt; even when I agreed to meet him for secret lunches, it was still supposed to be a joke. A kind of a game. Look, your friend fancies me! Look, I've been to bed with him! I still prefer you, though. Of course I do. I was just playing around, silly! When he found out, I felt a thud of fear – but still I thought I was invincible. I thought he would forgive everything, if I explained properly. I practised my kittenish

411

phrases; put on my most charming smile.

Somehow it didn't work. I couldn't make him understand; couldn't get past the betrayal in his face. When I tried to touch him, he flinched. When I tried to laugh, it was a shrill, grating noise, like nails on a blackboard. He called me very young and said that I would grow up. That was the worst bit of all. The disappointment in his voice as he said it.

Can you believe, Arabella fell for Fizz's spiel? And to my amazement, Fizz seems to be doing a pretty good job of it. She's found a friendly local decorator named Danny, and she seems to spend most days over there, drinking coffee with Arabella and flicking through magazines and wallpaper books. They go out for lunch, too – which Fizz can afford, because of the enormous down-payment she's managed to extract from Arabella, her New Best Friend.

To be fair, she's invited me along a few times, but I've always managed to invent excuses. Not that I don't listen to all the details of Arabella's life with a kind of masochistic fascination.

'What's "the chap" like?' I ask casually one day. I cannot bring myself to say 'Dee-Dee'.

'Dunno,' says Fizz vaguely. 'He's abroad all the time.' She starts giggling. 'God knows what he's going to think of his flat when he gets back. You know Arabella's latest idea?'

'What?'

'Gold tassels on all the light switches. For that luxury touch.'

'As creative design consultant,' I say, 'I'm afraid I veto that.'

'Too late, I've bought them! Six quid each, I'm charging her.'

'Where from?'

'The pound shop.'

Then, overnight, the New Best Friendship disintegrates. Fizz has a huge row with Arabella over the placement of a curtain tie-back (something like that, anyway), and Arabella threatens to sack her. She complains that Fizz's taking far too long and she wants the sitting room finished now.

'Stupid cow,' says Fizz, when she's finished telling me. 'Stupid stuck-up cow! We're supposed to be friends.' She takes a swig of wine and eyes me wildly. 'Listen, Emma, you have to help me.'

'What?' I say apprehensively. 'What do you mean, help you?'

'I told her I'd get the sitting room finished by to-morrow. Danny's buggered off, leaving one wall unpapered.'

'Why did he bugger off?' I say suspiciously.

'He always wants cash up-front. And I've kind of . . .' She bites her lip. 'Run out of money.'

'Oh, Fizz!'

'Look, Em, you know how to paper walls. I've seen you.'

Unfortunately, this is true.

'Please, Em,' she wheedles. 'Just this once. I'll owe you for ever. Otherwise, Arabella's going to sue me!'

Oh God, I always fall for her blarney.

'Will anyone be there?'

'No!' says Fizz confidently. 'It'll be completely empty.'

We arrive at the flat just as dusk is falling. As Fizz lets us in, I can't help gasping. The place is transformed from when I saw it last – all pastel paint colours and stencils of grapes.

'Where's that abstract painting gone?' I ask as we walk down the corridor. 'It was up there.'

'Dunno,' says Fizz vaguely. 'Arabella never liked it, apparently. And it doesn't go with the stencilling, so . . . okay.' She opens the door of the sitting room. 'Here's your paper . . . and here's your ladder.'

'What do you mean, *my* ladder?'

'Oh, I can't stay,' says Fizz in surprise. 'I've got a meeting with another client.'

'*What?*' I exclaim. 'What other bloody client? You're expecting me to do this alone?'

'I'll be back as soon as I can, I promise,' she says, blowing me a kiss. 'Look, there's hardly anything left to do. Take you five minutes.'

She disappears out of the room and I hear the front door slam. I know I should feel furious with her. I should walk out and leave her in her own mess. But I'm feeling too confused to move, or even feel angry. I'm in David's flat, alone.

I look slowly around, trying to see some clues of his life amid the pinkness. It's been three years since I saw him. What's happened in that time? What kind of person is he now?

I sidle over to a side table and am cautiously opening a drawer, when there's a sound at the door. Quickly, I close the drawer and hurry back to the ladder.

'Hello!' says Arabella from the doorway. 'Just popped back for my umbrella. Fizz told me you were coming. Doesn't it look good?'

'Lovely,' I say politely. 'It's very smart. Except . . .'

'Except what?'

I rub my face, not sure how to say it.

'Arabella, are you sure your . . . chap is going to like it?'

'Of course he is!' she says. 'It was a horrible hotch-potch before. This is a finished look.'

'But don't you think . . . wouldn't he prefer . . .'

'I think I know my own boyfriend,' snaps Arabella defensively. 'He's going to love it.'

'But –'

'Do you have a boyfriend, Emma?'

'No,' I say after a pause. 'No, I don't.'

Arabella's eyes run dismissively over my face and I can see the words 'no wonder' forming above her head in a thought-bubble. Then she taps out of the room – and a moment later I hear the front door closing.

I stare at the empty wall in front of me. Clean and prepared, ready to be papered. The wallpaper is ready, all cut into lengths. Fizz is right – it'll take no time.

But something is building up inside me; something hot and heavy, like a scream.

Before I can stop myself, I'm reaching for a paint-brush and a pot. I'm opening the pot and dipping the brush in, and writing on the blank, empty wall.

Things you don't know about David.

1. He hates pink.

I breathe out, feeling a small satisfaction. And then, almost at once, I'm dipping the brush in again, and scrawling some more.

2. If he says he likes being called Dee-Dee, he's lying.

3. He used to kiss my hair goodnight.

I write and write, feverishly dragging the ladder to the wall, using up nearly a whole pot of paint. Soon I'm not just writing about David, I'm writing about me – about all the mistakes I made, all the regrets I've had.

About my months abroad, about South America, about the crash. The way the plastic surgeons skilfully rebuilt my face afterwards. How although I recognised myself, it was a different me.

Like a junkie, I just can't stop. Words and words; everything I've wanted to say for years and never have.

When I've finished, the whole wall is covered in writing and I'm exhausted. I lie on the floor for a long while, staring up at the ceiling rose. At last, calmly, I get up. I have a drink of water, and take a deep breath. Then I mix my paste, climb up the ladder again and begin to paste length after length of fuschia pink paper to the wall.

Just as I'm on the last length I hear a key in the lock of the front door.

'If you're here to help, you're too late,' I call out cheerfully. I'm feeling happier than I have for months. It's an effort, putting up wallpaper by yourself, and I know my bad leg will throb tomorrow. But even so,

I feel as though months of tension have drained away, leaving me light and optimistic. As I turn to greet Fizz, I'm actually smiling.

Except it's not Fizz.

We stare at each other in a shocked silence. The air seems to be prickling at my face.

'Hi,' I say at last in a strangled voice.

'Hi.' David puts his hand to his head. 'What – what are you –'

'I'm helping out. It's a . . . it's a long story . . .' My voice doesn't seem to be working properly. Suddenly I remember I haven't pasted down the last length of paper. I turn back to the wall and quickly smooth it flat. When I look back, he's watching me with that look.

'Are you all right? You look . . . different. Your face . . .'

I duck my head down and lift my hands defensively to my chin, feeling the familiar scar line; the rough scar tissue which will never go away.

'I'm fine,' I say, running my eyes over the papered wall, searching for bubbles. But it's perfect. A flawless finish. 'I . . . I have to go. It should dry all right if you just leave it.'

As I gather my things, my hands are trembling. I look up, and see that he's finally noticed the wallpaper.

'I didn't choose it,' I mutter as I pass him. 'Don't blame me.'

A few weeks go by, and Fizz has somehow snaffled two new clients, who occupy all her waking thoughts.

I don't hear an awful lot more about David or Arabella – until Fizz tells me I've been invited to the 'new-look flat christening party'. Fizz is determined to use it as a promotional event and equally determined I should come too. She dismisses all my excuses and keeps demanding, 'Why not?' And after a while I start to think, 'Why not?' myself. I'm strong enough to face him. I can do it.

Besides which I have a secret desire to see him being called 'Dee-Dee' in public.

When we arrive, people are milling around in the hall, gazing at all the stencils and gold tassels and pound-shop candles with shell-shocked expressions on their faces.

'What do you think?' says Fizz to me. 'It's frightful, isn't it?' She giggles. 'But it's what Arabella wanted. She thought it was fabulous.' She takes a sip of wine. 'Quite ironic they split up, really.'

I freeze, glass halfway to my lips.

'Split up? What do you mean, split up?'

'Didn't I tell you? They had some huge row. About the wallpaper, apparently! I did recommend something more subtle, but she just wouldn't listen . . .'

I take a sip of wine, trying to stay calm.

'Fizz, you know, I think I might leave.'

'You can't go! We've only just – David! Hello!'

'Fizz,' I hear him saying behind me. 'You made it.'

'Absolutely! And this is Emma, my creative design consultant.' She pulls at my shoulder and I find myself forced to turn round.

I've prepared a formal, polite expression – but at the

sight of his warm, brown gaze, I feel it starting to slip.

'We've met,' says David. 'Haven't we, Emma?'

'So!' says Fizz, swigging back her wine and pouring another one. 'Doesn't it all look fab? Let's go and look at the sitting room! The *pièce de résistance*!'

'Yes,' says David, and shoots me a swift glance. 'I think you might be quite interested to see that.'

'So sorry to hear about you and Arabella,' I can hear Fizz saying as we walk across the hall. 'Was it really the wallpaper?'

'Not the wallpaper, exactly –' he replies, and opens the door to the sitting room with a flourish.

And my heart stops still.

The facing wall is completely blank. All that fuschia-pink paper I put up has gone – and it's been repainted in a light, string-like colour.

'Hang on!' says Fizz, peering puzzledly ahead. 'What's happened to the wallpaper? Who pulled it off?'

'I did,' says David.

'But why?'

'Good question,' says David. 'I had a hunch I might like to see it uncovered.' He shoots me a deadpan look. 'And I'm pleased I did. It was very . . . illuminating.'

My heart's thudding. I can't meet his eye. All those things I wrote. Things about him, about me, about Arabella. In huge painted letters, from ceiling to floor.

'But what did Arabella say?' Fizz is demanding. 'Wasn't she furious?'

'Arabella?' He pauses thoughtfully. 'I have to admit –

she wasn't too pleased. Especially when she saw the evidence.'

'Well, I'm not surprised!' says Fizz. 'I mean, that wallpaper wasn't cheap! Designer's Guild, twenty-eight quid a roll. I mean . . . thirty-eight quid,' she hastily amends, 'including unavoidable surcharges. It's all perfectly clear on the invoice . . .'

'What do you think, Emma?' says David lightly. 'Do you think I made the right choice? Or should I have left it as it was?'

I can feel the blood pulsing in my ears. My fingers are slippery around my glass.

'I think you made the right choice.' I say at last. 'Because now at least you know.'

He's staring straight at me, and very slowly I tilt my face upwards. I see his eyes running over the scar line along my chin. The place where they made a new me.

'So listen, David,' says Fizz, leaning forward confidentially. 'Tell me honestly, I won't be hurt. Do you *like* this decor?'

'Truthfully?' He takes a swig of wine. 'I loathe it.'

'Me too!' says Fizz. 'Isn't it awful? But it's what Arabella wanted. A Barbie palace. Barbie and Dee-Dee.'

'I miss what I used to have,' says David, and his brown eyes meet mine with a sudden affection. 'Whether it's ever possible to go back . . . What do you think, Emma?'

There's a long silence.

'Not go back, exactly,' I say. 'But maybe . . . start over?'

'Well!' Fizz's voice rings out triumphantly. 'You're in luck, because my new venture offers exactly that service. "Restore-a-room. Has a designer wrecked your house? We'll put things back the way you always liked them – but better!" Honestly, this one is going to be a complete winner . . .'

Been There; Licked That.
Or – The Things I Wish I'd
Known at Twenty-Five

Kathy Lette

Nostalgia is that weird emotion which makes things seem a hundred times more wonderful now than they really were then. But when I truthfully analyse my twenty-fifth year, my predominant wish is that I'd known that Lycra hotpants give a whole new meaning to the expression 'read my lips'. Topped with a tie-dyed boob tube, it was a look which didn't quite come off – but gave the impression that it definitely would later, probably for the whole band.

There are other things I wish I'd known at twenty-five, like the fact that the differences between men and women are not, as the 1980s feminist doctrine dictated, down to nurture, but nature. Then I wouldn't have wasted so much time trying to convince men that it wasn't the Toilet Fairy who changed the roll on the spindle. I would have understood that men are genetically geared to think reading in the loo is a leisure activity; to play air guitar; to fiddle with the fridge thermostat just for fun; to prefer to die rather than ask directions (which is why they now always include a token female on the space shuttle); and to think that 'sex drive' means doing it in the car (probably because of that little sign on the rear vision mirror which reads 'Objects in this mirror may appear larger than they are'). Then I would have known that a male's DNA structure demands that he approach commitment the same way he'd negotiate a barbed wire fence whilst naked.

Not that there was a lot of commitment about when I was twenty-five because at the time we girls thought that promiscuity was Feminism. In the 80s it wasn't socially acceptable to be a virgin, monogamous or celibate. Ignoring pangs of guilt, young women felt beholden to prove our newly won sexual freedom. Dutifully my girlfriends and I roamed Sydney's meat markets in high-heeled packs, skewering bronzed hunks on the ends of our stilettos. I was an FBI agent's wet dream – I had fingerprints all over me. Only lab rabbits had more sex than we did. We had phone sex – but in the booth. We did it while listening to music – but in the back row of Duran Duran concerts. Like men, we tried to be below-navel geared and blasé about carnal encounters. After all, it was only a bodily function. You wanted it as much as he did. Besides, what would he think of you if you *didn't*? You'd get a bad name. People would presume you were a prude, or a protes-tant . . . But then, what was that empty ache afterwards? Lying there watching the luminous minutes blink by on his digital clock, the awful question gnawed away at you – *am I liberated or an easy lay?*

I wish I'd known that men were taking full advantage of our confused situation. With their Coq Sportif track-suits, smooth talk and vasectomies, the blokes of the day thought they had it all sewn up. They preyed on liberated girls, insisting that they were all for 'free love'. When they didn't ring or write or smile at you again, you couldn't help thinking that all that meant was they didn't have to pay for it. Beneath the 'male feminist' veneer, these blokes' views on women dated back to the Jurassic Period. It would have looked much more natural if they'd just squatted on their haunches and groomed each other's back hair for nits.

But the most embarrassing aspect was not the act, but the encore. When the puff and pant had passed, there had to be pillow talk. 'Ummm.' Although coupled with him so closely on top of the doona that you covered your character from neck to knee, mentally you were painfully modest. To expose a bare minimum, words were kept serene and pretty and preferably witty. Desperately censoring anything too revealing, safe topics included EST, vegans, herpes and of course, his next 'male-consciousness-raising' meeting. So much for sex relieving stress. Sex in the 80s was about as relaxing as amateur ovarian cyst removal.

If only I'd been liberated enough not to be liberated. A girl should never really have sex if her heart isn't in it. Otherwise it's as though a party is being thrown on your body to which you haven't been invited. I wish I'd listened to my conscience occasionally (although really one should never ever take advice from strangers), then I would have realised that a woman should only spend her spare time with a married man if they're both kidnapped by Osmara bin Laden terrorists. I wish I'd known that word-play is foreplay for females. (Hey, how else does Woody Allen get laid?) Then I would have understood that it's good to find a man with a strong libido, but even better if he can spell it. And even more fulfilling if he knows it doesn't refer to the words in an opera. Although, on second thoughts, the word 'opera' wouldn't have been in my boyfriends' vocabularies either, except perhaps next to the word 'soap'.

At twenty-five we were so busy being laid, we somehow mislaid the essential ingredients of romance, passion, adoration and devotion. And it's loving emotion, not an all-night performance and a well-read penis, that makes sex sensational. I wouldn't return to the genital dictatorship of those days for anything. Hell, I'd rather remove my own IUD with garden shears. Rather master the Kama Sutra for One. Wish I'd known at twenty-five that being liberated . . . well, it can be very oppressive.

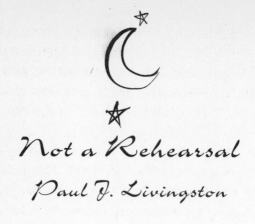

Not a Rehearsal
Paul J. Livingston

SUDDENLY, ONE DARK SATURDAY
A Screenplay By Wayne Long

EXT. SHOPPING MALL DAY.
Camera arcs over a shopping mall. Down. Down. Across a swirling sea of suburban streetlife. We stop on a WOMAN burdened with groceries lumbering heroically towards a pram. She stops several paces from the pram. A look of horror crosses her youthful face.

CUT TO – INT. PRAM. DAY.
The pram is empty!!!

OPENING TITLES over distraught woman in the mall. We wonder, who took the baby? ...

We wonder. Yes we do wonder. We wonder how Wayne Long, graduate mind you, of the Australian Film, Television and Radio School, had the gall to send me this script, *Suddenly, One Dark Saturday*. That's rich. It's got a comma. The title's got a fucking comma in it. Well Wayne, Wayne Long, why don't we just put your script over here with these other 'scripts', for want of a better word. For want of better words. Absolute crap. Crap. Absolutely.

Let's get this clear. I can't write. That's no crime. Not my business. I'm not a writer. I'm a director. A damn good director. Paul Sheath, film director. No. You don't recognise the name. But what if I say *Jupiter Rising* or *La Femme Nadine*. That's right. Directed by me. Written by people you will never hear of. No doubt you've heard of Val Dittman, James Richtor, Alyce Phesher. Oh yeah. Actors. Well those people work for *us*. We hire *them*. We can do that. We director/producers. I love having that slash in my title. I would prefer writer/director/producer but as I have said, I can't write for shit.

Good writers are rare. Great writers don't exist. Good writers achieve greatness through people like me. We make them work. Writers are fucking lazy. Not just screenwriters. Novelists. We director/producers hate novelists. Indulgent crap. Impossible to adapt to the screen. But when we do manage to filter the tedious drivel from their seventy-thousand-odd words to reveal an actual story in there somewhere, it becomes a hit. Then the writer accuses us of demeaning the integrity of the work. Fuck me. The prick is pulling in monster royalties. From the sweat of a hundred guys like me. Writers are fucked. I'm having a bad day. Fucked day. Sorry about all this swearing. I don't pretend to be eloquent. Eloquent. That's a big word for me. No. My medium is visual. Interior dialogues are useless in my game. Action. Actions speak louder than words. Now that's good writing.

I need a hit, I need one now. Michael Caine said it. Every fourth film has to be a hit. I've had three stinkers. You'll never see them. Two are unsaleable. The other, well, you might see it on late-night telly sometime. If we can get a cheap sale. Salvage something. Two things can kill a film. Shit writing and public indifference. You can't pick it. The public will embrace crap. Who knows why. It's my job to know why, but it's a lottery. Bad writing, though. I can pick that. Easy.

Presentation. Gives the game away. Look at Wayne Long's script. Title page. Fancy fonts and, God help us, a picture of a naked child wandering on a highway. Images are my business. Not the writer's. One look at the cover and I can tell if it's got legs. Take this one over here for example. Simple, clear title. *Not a Rehearsal.* Doesn't really grab me, but then we can always change the title. I'm looking for a professional attitude, see. Nothing fancy. And this one looks promising. Hang on. Where's the author's name? It's not written by anyone. Shit. Can you believe it? No return address, phone, agent, nothing. Normally I'd just toss this aside, but for your sake I'll proceed. Just to show you how it's done. Just to prove to you that an author who forgets to acknowledge himself can't possibly produce the goods. It only takes a minute. If you're not hooked by page three, out you go brother. Out there with Wayne Long. Let's see.

INT. MATERNITY WARD. NIGHT.

A woman, IRENE, mid-thirties, lying on a bed. Giving
birth.

[Giving birth! The first image of the film? There goes
three-quarters of the audience. Bad start Mr Nobody.
The only positive thing so far is the name, Irene, a solid
normal name, not Aisha or Sade or Sinead. Irene, that
was my mother's name]

JUMP CUT TO:

[Oh great. He's telling me how I should cut the thing.
Cut to, pan across, slow fade, extreme close-up. That's
my job. All I require is a story]

EXT. HOUSE. EVENING.

A quiet suburb. Summer evening. A modest weather-
board house. The year is 1955.

[Stop right there. Mid-fifties. Massive production
design job. This had better be a brilliant idea]

IRENE cradles her newborn son, PAUL.

[Another fine name, if I say so myself]

Irene, on the verandah, blows cool breath onto the
child's forehead. Young Paul giggles. Irene softly sings.

IRENE: Go to sleep, my little jackeroo.

As the stars are shining bright tonight
Above you.
Go to sleep my little jackeroo.

[I haven't heard that song in years. Sentimental crap]

Irene looks to the stars, and then to the sleeping child.
A tear glistens on her cheek.

[We're really pushing it now. Let's see what's on page two]

INT. CLASSROOM. DAY.

In an early 60s classroom, PAUL, now aged six [fast grower] sits at a desk, uncomfortable, flushed. We see beneath the desk.

[We see. I hate that 'we see'. Of course 'we see'. It's a fucking film. So. What do 'we see' Mr Nobody?]

We see that Paul has wet himself.

[Happened to me once, about that age, only in my case the piss ran across the floor and all over old Denning's boots. Didn't I get a caning for that]

The urine trails across the floor towards a school-teacher, FATHER DENNING, pooling around his boots.

CUT TO:

INT. OFFICE. DAY.

PAUL with trousers down in the office of FATHER DENNING who wields a cane, lashing the boy's buttocks.

   FATHER DENNING: For your own good, Sheath.

CUT TO:

A montage which takes us through Paul's childhood to adulthood:

PAUL in the schoolyard, playing marbles in an air-raid shelter.

PAUL breaking a collarbone in the quarry.

PAUL watching St George win the premiership for the eleventh consecutive year.

PAUL winning the fifty-metre sprint.

PAUL solving Rubik's cube.

PAUL'S nose being broken by Dave Calpis.

PAUL'S first beer.

PAUL'S fifteenth beer, later that day.

PAUL'S hair getting longer.

PAUL'S hair falling out.

PAUL leaves home.

PAUL moves back home.

PAUL leaves home.

PAUL moves back home.

PAUL leaves home.

PAUL'S parents leave home.

PAUL leaves Australia.

PAUL returns to Australia.

PAUL directs first film.

PAUL produces/directs next film.

PAUL wins AFI award for second film.

PAUL gets fat.

PAUL gets bitter.

PAUL gets drunk.

PAUL blames writers for his own shortcomings.

SLOW DISSOLVE TO:

INT. PAUL'S APARTMENT. NIGHT.

The year is 2001. PAUL SHEATH slouches on a couch. Before him a sea of scripts. The walls are covered with film posters: *La Femme Nadine*, *Jupiter Rising* etc. Paul looks much older than his forty-five years. His belly pokes over his shorts, cigarette butts everywhere, a foam mattress with no sheets on the floor. Nearby an AFI award gathers dust in a corner.

Paul sits, intent on a script which bears a title, *Not a Rehearsal*, but no author. He is some way into the script. He devours each page, unaware of the traffic outside, the flashing neon lights of the city, the fighting in the flat below, the couple having loud raucous sex across the alley. He is unaware of a cockroach rummaging through a plastic bowl of stale vinegar chips.

Paul barely breathes as he holds the script close to his eyes, his brow clenched in a frown. Sweat beading on his bare scalp.

PAUL: (reading from the script) Paul reads from the script. It seems that every word he thinks appears on the page as he speaks it. His heart races faster as he reads on. The words falling before him as if belched from his own mind. He stops. Throws the script down.

Paul throws the script down, holds his head in his hands. He stands, takes a breath, and paces a few steps towards the bathroom.

INT. BATHROOM. NIGHT.

PAUL throws water on his face. Stares at his reflection.

PAUL: I am Paul Sheath. And this is not a rehearsal.

INT. APARTMENT. NIGHT.

The script askew on the floor. PAUL darts towards it, grabs it, steels himself and reads.

PAUL: I am Paul Sheath. And this is not a rehearsal.

Paul turns a page. Reads on.

PAUL: Paul turns a page. Moves tentatively around the apartment holding his life in his own hands. The beating of his heart is so intense he imagines he will soon read of his own demise as his heart explodes. But this could not be. For Paul was well aware that he was only up to page fifty-eight. He dared not turn to the last page of the script. He did not care to know in advance the end of his story. As he read on he flinched at the dialogue knowing full well that this monologue was much too long for film. That the action had halted and the only thing on screen was a man staring into a script sweating. It reminded him of those goddamned European art flicks with all their tedious four-minute monologues shot over expressionless faces. So well lit, so beautifully shot, so fucking boring. And now he was the star of such a film. This bleak, independent, low-budget, badly acted tale of surreal alienation. Paul has always hated art films, revelling in his popularity with the real people. But now he was smack in the middle of a film that would delight that elite minority of middle-class academic self-congratulators. This was bad filmmaking. And excrutiatingly bad writing. Yet he could not escape this interior monologue. Again he threw the script.

Across the room. He screamed at the pages.

PAUL: (screaming) I am an individual. I have free will.

Paul could not believe the bad dialogue and appalling delivery. Let alone the chronic overacting. But it appeared he had no control over his speech.

PAUL: It appears I have no control over my speech.

DISSOLVE TO:

INT. APARTMENT. NIGHT.

The apartment is dark. It is the early hours of the morning. No lights on. PAUL slumped, exhausted by the door. Extreme close-up on script as we read the current page:

> The apartment is dark. It is the early hours of the morning. No lights on. Paul slumped, exhausted by the door.

We see that he is more than halfway through the script. We see that Paul sees that 'we see' is written on the script. Paul grabs a pencil from his desk, lunges at the script. He tears into it. Crossing out sections which command him to cross out sections of the script.

> **PAUL:** 'We see' do we. Who are we then who sees? Who is the see-er and who is the scene? What am I saying? This script is shit. Where is the hook! Where is the initiating incident! Where is the act-one turning point? Where is the alsatian in the tartan coat?

Paul pauses.

> **PAUL (CONT):** The what?

Paul scans the apartment. He begins to laugh.

PAUL: Well. Where is it? Come on out. Where are you? Here boy.

He turns to the script accusingly.

PAUL: There is no alsatian in this scene. You are wrong. This is not my life. You piece of hack crap, there is no dog here. Ever heard of research? Lazy fuck.

SLOW DISSOLVE TO:

INT. APARTMENT. DAWN.

Thin first light bathes PAUL, script in hand, only a few pages left.

PAUL: Paul is curled over the script. His shirt soaked with sweat. He is not reading the script. He is merely staring. Trying not to think. Trying not to think? (hitting the script)
How the fuck do you film someone trying not to think. This is not a film, it's more like some quirky short story. That's another thing I fucking hate. The short story. Probably for the casual reader. Imagine making a film for the casual looker. What crap.

Paul glares at the script.

PASUL (CONT): PASUL (CONT)? Who the fuck is PASUL (CONT)? Doesn't this guy have speell check? All right. Enough. Cut to the chase.

Paul tears the last page from the script.

PAUL (CONT): Let's do it. What have we got here. A happy ending? Do I ride off into the sunset? Or is it one of those bullshit arty endings where the conclusion is left to the viewer? That anti-narrative crap. Too fucking lazy to think of an ending. Or perhaps we just leave on some symbolic image laden with deep psychological overtones?

Paul stands.

PAUL (CONT): Okay, Mr Nobody. What happens if I just decide to throw this fucking piece of paper out the window? Where does that leave your audience? Or don't you give a damn about them. You arty wanker. You'd love that wouldn't you. Get right off the hook. Oh it wasn't the writer's fault, the lead actor bailed. We don't know how it ended. Well I'm not about to do that, arsehole. You're going to have to satisfy the audience. Leave them laughing, crying or preferably both. Nobody is going anywhere until we resolve this to everyone's satisfaction.

Paul moves to the window.

PAUL: Moving to the window isn't going to help.

He stares into the glowing dawn.

PAUL: That's very original.

Camera moves past him dissolving the image to golden –

   PAUL: Oh no you don't.

Paul slams down the blind. The room goes dark.

   PAUL: Credits up on sunrise? Get fucked. They'll lynch
   you for that.

Minutes pass where nothing happens.

   PAUL: Come on. Take it to them. Resolve the conflict!

More minutes pass.

   PAUL: I've got all the time in the world. We're well
   under budget. Plenty of stock.

Pause.

   PAUL: What's wrong? Writer's block? Poor thing.
   Better head down to the café for four hours, see if
   that inspires you.

Pause.

   PAUL: This is not a play. It's a feature film. You've held
   them this far. How you've done that is beyond me. As
   I said, you can't account for public taste, but to your

credit, I admit that some of them are still with you. All you need is that final twist.

Long pause.

Hello? Hello? So it's like that is it. Back to reality. You just want me to toss the script onto the pile with the others. Is that it? Fine by me. I've got better things to do with my time than try to rescue bad scripts. I've done that all my life. Made shit like you look good. Made you popular. Made you money. I'm screwing the page up. See. That's an action. I'm throwing the page out the window. More action. Get the picture? The page is falling to the pavement. Catching the first light of the sun as it drifts to the ground. Growing smaller. It rushes on banks of air, questioning then deciding which slipstream, whisking upwards, then down, unsure of its fate, unsure of its content, unsure who it is.

What is its role? Does it have a purpose? Is it suicide? The last page has leapt to its death. Unable to decide its future, it chose none. A glorious golden light bathes its last moments before touching at last, the tree, its mother, its roots – IT'S CRAP!

EXT. PARK. DAY.

The final crumpled page of the script gently touches the earth, nestles against a park bench. We see the final page of the script.

PAUL: IT'S CRAP!

EXT. PARK. DAY.

Pull out to aerial view of the park. As end credits roll, an alsatian in a tartan coat* sniffs before urinating on the last page of *Not a Rehearsal*.

FADE TO BLACK

---

* This is a symbolic image laden with deep psychological overtones.

The Deck Hangers
Robert Llewellyn

'Come on Greg, we've only got twenty minutes.'

I had to shout because Greg is an idiot. He's an Australian, nothing unusual there. Over 250 000 of them living inside the M25. Of course I'm not saying that's why he's an idiot. He would have been an idiot wherever he came from. He's forty-two and he has a unique haircut which is apparently referred to as a 'mullet'. I say unique because it is uniquely unattractive. Cut short on top with long whispy bits at the back, if it had ever been fashionable it would only have been so in the mid-1970s and then for a very limited period. I'm talking months. Not only that, Greg squeezes lemon into his hair each morning to bleach it. He hasn't been near a beach in years, he lives in Bayswater.

It was a Friday evening when I shouted at Greg and I'd had enough. Friday evenings are special because it's the time I always go for a curry. True, I go with Greg which is a bit worrying, far more worrying is the fact that I also go with Julian.

Alice is fine about the Friday night arrangement, slightly patronising but then I'm used to that, I can see past it. There was, I have to observe, a hint of bitterness in her tone when I first suggested it. Everything got a little tight between the two of us after Josh was born. But it's only one night a week and we've kind of built it into our routine. Monday night she does yoga, Tuesday evening is her reading group, Wednesday she plays tennis with Frank, Thursday she goes to see her mum, so I have Friday.

That may sound like it's loaded in her favour, but then I'm working five days a week. Leave on my bike at 6.45 in the morning. Cycle to Old Street. I usually get back about 7.00, just as Alice is rushing out of the door.

She looks after Josh far more than I do.

Greg and I were building a deck on the back of my house which is on Biggelow Road in Hornsey. It's on a steep hill; when you stepped out of the back door there was a flight of crumbling concrete steps leading down to the small patch of dirt we like to believe is our garden.

'You need a bloody deck, mate, out here, mate,' said Greg when he first came to see the new place. That was a year earlier when we had just moved in and I was feeling pretty depressed. Josh was only six months old and I wanted to die. I had a hundred thousand pound mortgage, a baby who never slept and a wife who wouldn't come near me. I loved Alice very much, as much as it was possible for me to love anyone. I come from an English family, we are hard wired to be emotionally blocked, slightly constipated and unable to touch outside a sexual context. Actually loving people in a healthy, expressive, open way is very hard for me.

After Josh was born Alice suffered from a string of minor physical ailments which overlapped each other. I described them as serial annoyances once when we had people around for dinner. Alice told me that wasn't funny and she told me in front of the friends and she told me in a loud voice.

Greg was right of course, a deck was a great idea. We had watched people build decking on home improvement shows on the telly. It looked pretty straightforward, but then the decking on telly was usually a couple of inches above a flat garden. We lived on a hill, but when Greg showed us pictures of his parental home in Queensland, we were won over immediately. A huge expanse of sun-kissed wood sitting high up on tall wooden struts. Their house was also built on a hill, the deck was sprung out over a jungle precipice so that when his parents dined al fresco, they were sitting at treetop level.

Wonderful.

Our deck in Hornsey, we liked to believe, had all that potential, except it looked over the row of red brick houses opposite and, unfortunately, directly into the bedsit of a man with ginger hair and a fearsome facial blemish who did nothing all day but view downloaded pornography on a very large computer screen.

'Here you go,' said Greg. He passed me a long length of timber from somewhere below. I pulled it up and felt myself wobble a little, I didn't want to look down. We had sunk eight long poles into huge concrete-filled holes in the garden and started to construct the deck's structure high in the air. When the poles had been delivered on a large truck, it was a very exciting moment.

Manoeuvring the giant poles through the house was very difficult and caused higher than normal levels of marital stress.

Standing on the three crossbeams we had coach-bolted into position was, in theory, quite safe. If I looked one way I could see into our kitchen and I felt safe. If I looked the other I looked over the rows of small gardens which seemed to be a very long way beneath me.

'Hi there, sorry I'm late.' It was Julian. He wasn't late, he was early as usual, but he has to say sorry whatever is happening. 'The front door was open, someone's left a load of wood sticking out into the street. Sorry, you probably knew that, sorry.'

He walked down the concrete steps from the kitchen door, his old leather bag firmly clutched before him as always. As he descended I couldn't really look, but I could still hear him.

'Yeah, that's for the decking, mate,' said Greg cheerily. 'We'll need a hand getting it inside.'

'It's sticking out in the street and you can't close the door, anyone could come in.'

Julian was staying in his mental hermit cave. He didn't like change. I had known him since I was six and he seemed to resent any change I went through as if it was a direct threat to our friendship.

'What d'you think of the deck?' I asked without looking down.

'I missed the 14, so I had to get the tube.'

'Julian, what d'you think of the deck?' I repeated.

I knew how it went, Julian had his things to say, he liked to explain things to people so they'd understand. He'd obviously felt misunderstood for a lot of his life.

'I'm supposed to be at a meeting about the new intake, but I said I couldn't go. I normally do go but I explained to Michael that I couldn't go. The meeting is normally on a Thursday but because Michael has been in Alabama we had to move it. I had told them time and again. They know I'm busy on Fridays.'

Greg clambered up the ladder carrying a toolbox, the deck's timbers shook rather disconcertingly as he joined me on the narrow beams. He lay down on the one piece of board we had dragged up and dropped his head over the edge. Just knowing he was doing that made me feel mildly nauseous.

'Julian, will you shut up and put him out of his bloody misery,' Greg shouted. 'Tell him his deck looks great and then we can all fuck off and get a curry.'

'Is that what you call it?' asked Julian. 'I thought it was a fence.'

'He's coming up,' said Greg, and he leaned yet further over the newly joined timbers. Greg is a man who has no fear of heights, in fact he's a man who has no fear of anything, which has made him uniquely vulnerable. His list of personal injuries through sporting activities could fill a book.

Julian's sad, long face eventually appeared at my feet. I couldn't bend down to help him up, there was just too little to stand on. We were at the very furthest point from the house and we still hadn't tied the whole structure together. With the three of us clambering around it swayed way too much for my comfort.

'Is this what you've been talking about?' he said as he stood next to me. He was in theory a good four inches taller than me, but because life had crushed Julian steadily since he was about fourteen, I always felt I looked down to him.

'Yes, what d'you think?'

'You know I can't think about things like this. Sorry, I just can't think about it. You know that.'

'Mate,' said Greg, as he stood up suddenly, 'all you've got to say is, "Well done Rupert, well done Greg." That's all we're asking, some basic acknowledgement of our efforts. It's like a fundamental boy thing, it's not that hard.'

'Sorry,' said Julian. 'I'd better go back down. I'm not going to be able to help.'

Julian's feet are big but that still doesn't justify the stupidity of what he did. Although his face and speech patterns say 'depressed individual with a lot of unsorted issues' his body movements have always said 'highly angry male with barely controlled violent tendencies.'

Julian's big foot kicked the ladder. It was a large and heavy aluminium extendable job I had got from the tool hire place in Tottenham. It wouldn't have been easy to kick over, but Julian did it.

It crashed to the ground, sending bits of sawn timber flying into the air. The three of us stood on top of what had to be at least twenty-five feet of rickety wooden structure in utter silence. I clearly heard the trains going through the station at the bottom of Hornsey Lane.

'That'll be the ladder,' said Greg dryly. I believe this

very dry humour is a Queensland thing, although I've never been there to check.

'What was that?' asked Julian. Only he could be so disconnected.

I know I shouldn't have said it. 'You, you stupid prick!'

It just came out. 'What are we going to do now!'

I was angry. In the presence of physical danger Julian was a liability.

'Don't call me a prick, sorry, but you know I get upset. I've told you that before.' Julian stared at me. I don't know if you could call it aggression, but he clearly wasn't happy.

'Sorry sorry sorry,' I blurted. 'But really Julian, we've been up and down that ladder all day.'

'Well, let's use a little pinch of accuracy here, guys,' Greg said. 'I have been up and down the ladder.' It was true. Somehow, once I'd got up the great wobbly thing, I suggested I stay up and do whatever needed to be done from up top.

'Anyway, we haven't kicked the ladder away, we've been really careful,' I said. I felt annoyed. How could he do something so dumb-footed and then top it off by not letting me criticise him for it. Only Julian could get away with something like that. I looked at him as accusingly as I could.

'It's only a ladder,' he said eventually.

'I know it's only a ladder,' I snapped. 'I know that, it's just that it isn't a lot of use to us lying sideways on the ground fifty feet below us.'

'It's nowhere near fifty feet,' said Julian. 'Sorry, but you always exaggerate. Always. It's a real issue with you, you have to exaggerate. It's like the thing you do about the number of students I've slept with. "Oh, Julian sleeps with all his students." Sorry, but it's really annoying when I hear things like that come back to me. I've asked you not to say stuff like that. I've asked you.'

'What are you talking about?' asked Greg with, I was pleased to notice, a little more anger in his voice than was normal. 'We're stuck up here and you're talking about all the students you've rooted.'

'No, sorry, that's just it, Greg. I haven't rooted. I haven't done anything. It's him.' He pointed at me. 'I'm just saying that he always exaggerates. He said we were fifty feet off the ground, which is pitiful. Sorry, but we're not half that.' Julian held his chin as if he was in pain. He wasn't, I'd learned that. It was a habit he had when he wanted to explain something clearly.

'Okay, yes, I have slept with some of my students over the past twenty years. Twenty years of teaching the same course at the same art school, and yes I have slept with some of them. Probably one or two per thousand if you were to work out the statistics.'

'Julian,' I said, 'I'm really not interested in you and your student shagging statistics.'

'You're always going on about it,' he said accusingly. I couldn't believe my ears. Why did I put up with him, why do I? It can't be because he listens to me, because he doesn't. Whatever you say to Julian, he interrupts and tells you something you don't want to hear about his own miserable life.

'Well, anyway, sorry, maybe one student per year

would be more accurate, but that's not the point. Look,' he said, then after a long silence, '. . . just use the other one.'

I stared at him. What bloody planet did he live on?

'Other one what?' I asked.

'Other ladder.'

As he said this, he didn't look around for another ladder, he just stared at me, sort of accusingly, but also with his own special dead eyes.

'Julian, you slap-headed dag, there isn't another ladder.' Greg spoke close to Julian's face, which was bound to upset him.

'Don't get that close, Greg. Sorry, but you know I don't like it.'

'Oh Jesus!'

Seeing Greg lose it was actually quite educational. He was so mister easy-going. So not a problem mate, not an issue, to see him facing a real issue was a good thing.

'What d'you mean,' said Julian. 'You're working up here with only one ladder!'

He'd made it our fault again.

'We've only got one ladder! You just kicked it off. We're stuffed now.'

I looked at my watch, it was ten-past seven.

'Oh poo heads!' I shouted. I was attempting not to swear because I didn't want Josh using bad language as his first words. He was just starting to pick things up and the thought of my little angel boy 'effing' and 'bollocking' really didn't bear imagining.

I clearly remember hearing one of Wendy's children,

Puntara I think she's called, something like that anyway, she was barely able to walk, she threw her juice at the wall and was mildly scolded by her mother. Without hesitation the child told her mother to 'piss off'. Of course, the coven loved it, they all screamed laughing.

'Diwana's will let our table go unless we get there in a couple of minutes,' said Julian. 'You know what they're like. I've told you what they're like, and you've only got one ladder.'

'We only need one ladder,' I said.

'Well, how stupid. How am I going to get down?'

'How are any of us going to get down?'

'No,' said Julian flatly, his hand now seeming to be welded to his chin. 'You're forgetting I don't care about you. Sorry, but you know I've had to stop caring about other people, I've told you that. It's part of my healing. I want to know how I'm going to get down.'

'You're going to be going down head first with my boot in your arse if you don't shut the fucking fuck up,' said Greg through gritted teeth, and Greg had a lot of teeth to grit. He stood up and looked around. Julian held his chin and didn't move but his eyes darted around a bit.

Although on our regular visits to Diwana's Bel Pouri House, a vegetarian curry place that had become our favourite, Julian and Greg got on tolerably well, there was no point pretending there was a friendship there.

They both knew me, I knew I had been the catalyst in the weekly jaunt, what was happening now was no big surprise. It would have been easy to predict the result, put these two individuals under pressure and the dislike would soon emerge.

Greg stared at Julian, then shook his head in that special male, 'resigned to live with fools' way and looked over towards the back door of the house.

'No,' I said at once. I just didn't want to get Alice involved in any way. She had gone three doors down the street to Wendy's, to 'the coven' as she laughingly called it. Wendy and three other unspeakable women spent any spare time they could find getting drunk together and laughing about, well, I have no idea what, but laughing a great deal. Actually, I do know what they spent some of the time laughing about. Men, me included. Alice told me. I did everything I could not to react, I just shrugged and walked away. Under the openness of my modern relationship with Alice it is essentially war.

I did on one occasion try to laugh back at them with equal piss and vinegar when I was with Julian and Greg, but it never really worked. Especially with Julian as he had slept with Wendy.

Just the once.

I had warned him, I told him it was a very, very major life error on his part. It was not often Julian agreed with me, but he did that time.

'I feel castrated,' he said when he finally emerged from a six-week depression. 'She denied my very right to life, to basic humanity. She animalised me.'

'I've heard she does that,' I'd said.

'It's not that I want a woman to have a heart, or to have any feelings about me at all, but that was mental cruelty delivered in enormous portions. What man could live under such a regime?'

'None we've ever met,' I said, and I listed the men she had consumed. From some of the toughest hard ass ragamuffins to some of the most sensitive emotion men in town. All had so bitten dust, some had left the country never to return.

Alice of course was in awe of Wendy, everyone was. I had only survived by resolutely finding her physically repugnant, which wasn't easy. Wendy was gorgeous, but I found if you work at it, you can put yourself off anyone.

As I stood on top of a very tall pole in my back garden with no clear way of getting down, I found I was going off Julian with very little effort.

'I didn't really want to go for a curry anyway. Sorry, I had sushi for lunch,' Julian said, standing still and waiting for either me or Greg to sort out the dilemma he was in.

'Look, I've got my mobile,' said Greg.

'No,' I said.

'Where is she, anyway?'

'She's down the street. At the coven.'

'Oh my God. Don't ring!' said Julian.

'What is it with you two!' said Greg. 'They are a bunch of women, that's all. What's the bloody issue, mate?'

'No, they're beyond women,' said Julian. 'You know I can't deal with talking about them. Sorry, but I cannot allow them to see me, especially in a compromising male position.'

'What are you talking about? We're stuck up a pole, not sitting in the dunny having a group pull.'

'What?' said Julian, hand still fixed to face, face looking angry.

'He means we're not sitting in a toilet taking part in a mutual masturbation session,' I explained.

'Oh. I don't do that. You know I don't do that sort of thing, sorry.'

'I don't think Greg was suggesting it.'

'I didn't know you were gay, Greg,' said Julian.

'I'm not. Jeez, let's just push him off and be done with it.'

I moved my foot and felt something tug on it. It was the rope we had attempted to pull wood up onto the deck with but had failed, mainly due to the reduced amount of effort I could put into pulling the rope on account of the trapped nerve in my neck.

It's not actually trapped any more, I had it fixed by a really expensive chiropractor, but I didn't want to strain it and revisit the whole difficult issue of my upper back.

'What about the rope, what about the rope!' I blurted.

'Yeah, even better idea,' said Greg. 'Tie that round his neck and push him off.'

'Sorry, I really don't respond to that sort of male aggression,' said Julian. 'I really think we should have moved beyond that.'

'Oh please, Julian, I'm trying to work out how to get down from here without dying, without involving Alice and the coven and without going completely raving mad. Now, help me pull this rope up.'

'I don't have any gloves with me.'

'Just use your hands.'

'I can't, you know I can't use my hands for that sort of thing.'

'What are you on about? What's so special about your hands?' asked Greg. I half wished he hadn't because I knew what was coming.

'I'm a potter,' said Julian.

'Yeah yeah, I know that,' said Greg, who had already taken the rope from me and started pulling it up with great ease even though there were four long pieces of wood tied to it.

Julian was still in mid-explanation of his pottery and the need for his hands to be in good shape and the need to stand near his students when he was showing them how to control clay on a wheel and that his physical proximity to young women wasn't for any of the perverse reasons I had implied.

I helped Greg haul the wood up, carefully laying it down on the structure we had already built. I felt good doing something fairly physical in front of Julian. He was always criticising me for being so out of touch with my body, I went to a Pilates class with him once and I couldn't walk for a week.

Greg spun the small steel hook which was on the end of the rope around his head.

'Let's fish for ladders,' he said with a toothy grin, the only sort he had. He dropped the rope off the side and started swinging it around. It sort of rested on the ladder, but never seemed to get caught around one of the rungs.

'Reckon the hook's too small,' said Greg.

'Give us a go,' I said, now all fear of heights a thing of the past. Greg handed me the rope and I swung it gently, it caught on the side of the ladder and I thought for a moment I had reached the zenith of my physical abilities. The hook had sort of caught in a hole at the side of the ladder, the rope went taut as I pulled it.

'Got the little baby,' I said, the slightly macho terminology feeling good in my mouth. Too soon, the hook immediately slipped out and the ladder clanked back down on the ground.

'I'll do it,' said Julian.

Greg and I turned and looked at him.

'But you haven't got any gloves,' said Greg with a spoilt-kid voice.

'Just give it to me. I'm bored of being stuck up here.'

I passed the rope to Julian, who then started to, rather expertly I have to say, wind it into a big loop. He then held the hook in his right hand and with one deft movement threw the rope with enormous force towards the ladder. We watched in amazement as the hook spun around one of the rungs on the ladder and latched back onto itself. This image of pure skill was then obliterated as the remainder of the rope obscured the view. Great long lengths of rope tumbled down, finally joined by the other end.

Greg and I turned to look at Julian, the ropeless man.

'Sorry, but why didn't you hold onto the other end?' asked Julian.

'What?' Greg was clearly close to doing something quite ugly.

'I was applying all my concentration to getting the hook to attach itself to the ladder, which I did. I cannot be held responsible for what happened to the other end of the rope.'

Greg slowly bent down and picked up the nail gun which, apart from a rather rusty saw of mine, was the only tool on the structure.

'Greg, please,' I said, feeling rather nervous. I like watching confrontation, but I like to be able to move to a safe distance. On top of the poles I was very limited as to where I could go.

'I'm gonna make a fucking ladder,' said Greg, his teeth gritting business becoming more convincing. 'Okay?'

'Sure, sure, good idea,' I said. This is what we needed, jobs to do, things to keep us occupied. 'Tell me what I can do to help.'

I knew that men need stuff to do. There's nothing wrong with it, in fact it was a good thing. I'd just taken a while working it out. People like Greg knew all along, men need things to do with their hands, and it's better if they can build and make things rather than destroy them.

'Saw up that strip of flooring timber into twenty-inch lengths,' said Greg.

'Sure thing,' I said. He passed me the strip of wood he was referring to, which was just as well as I would not have had a clue how to tell a bit of flooring timber from any other. I got the tape measure off my belt and measured twenty inches and tried to mark it with my thumbnail. I didn't have a pen.

'Julian, have you got a pen on you?'

'What d'you want it for?'

Of course, as if he could just help.

'Forget it,' I said and made a little mark with the saw roughly where the twenty-inch mark was. Once I had sawn it, which took quite a while, Greg used the nail gun to attach it to the two long lengths of timber we had hauled up on the rope.

Five minutes later we had a ladder. Admittedly the rungs were slightly further apart than in a standard ladder but it was perfectly serviceable. Greg and I slowly lowered the ladder to the ground, it wobbled a little but once Greg had used his weight to sink the feet into the ground it seemed firm enough.

'I am not going to climb down that contraption,' said Julian with a slight chuckle.

'Suit yourself,' said Greg as he stepped onto the first rung. 'Solid as a rock, mate. Curry anyone?'

'Yes indeed,' I said. I checked my watch. It was a little before eight, we could still find somewhere, all was not lost. I watched Greg climb down rung by rung.

'Yeah, take it easy when you come down.' Greg shouted back up to me. 'The nail gun only had twenty-mill nails.'

'Sure, sure,' I said, not having any idea what he meant, 'Only twenty-mill nails, Julian,' I said. 'Take it easy, yeah.'

I put my foot on the first rung and it felt good.

'You two are not leaving me up here like a fool, for the coven to find,' said Julian. 'Sorry, but I'll go next.'

'Be my guest,' I said. I was feeling good, Julian had

a lot to give the world, if you gave him the chance. He made lovely pottery and his students adored him. I stood to one side and let Julian clamber awkwardly onto the first rung.

'Let me get down first,' Greg shouted up.

'It's fine,' said Julian, his violent movements making the makeshift ladder wave around alarmingly.

'Take it easy,' Greg and I said almost in unison.

Julian moved down the ladder at great speed.

Greg had been taking it easy, then suddenly, 'You're treading on my hand!'

I could see it was Greg, I could see Julian's great big boot treading on his hand.

'Get out of the way!'

That was Julian, that was Julian crossing the line. That was Julian treading on another human being's hand and telling him to get his foot out of the way. Something inside me snapped.

'Get your fucking foot off his hand!' I shouted down. I started to climb down, I wanted to grab Julian's hair and wrench it upwards so that he had to take his stupid foot off. Of course, he didn't have any hair, I could use his nose!

'Get off him you ignorant, selfish bastard,' I screamed.

'He left his hand there to cause trouble,' said Julian. It was too late for him, I was on him, but then something happened I wasn't expecting.

The rung I was treading on, the rung I had sawn myself, suddenly gave way. I dropped violently and the drop resulted in a scream of fairly deep unpleasantness.

I had landed, full weight, on Julian's hands that were holding the rung beneath the one I was treading on. I had trapped both his special potter's hands in a kind of homemade vice, and this caused Julian to scream, quite understandably really. As I tried to scramble up and relieve the weight the next rung above me came away too, in fact I ripped my thumb open on one of the nails that had stayed in the long timbers that made up the legs of our 'ladder'.

And all the time, beneath Julian, Greg was still shouting. 'Just get off my fucking hands you bald asshole!'

It was just then that, between Julian's screams, I heard the kitchen door open above me.

'What's up?' asked Alice. 'What the hell are you lot doing?'

I looked up. She looked beautiful.

She was holding little Josh, my golden-haired boy. Wendy was behind her, smiling. We had just managed to utterly reassure them that everything was well with their world view. Men were incompetent children who had to be looked after and laughed at. I pursed my lips.

'Better call an ambulance,' said Alice to Wendy, which she did.

For a Few Dollars
Whore I & II
Josie Lloyd and Emlyn Rees

FOR A FEW DOLLARS WHORE I: THE MADAM

I'm gonna quit this town, I swear it. Just as soon as I get enough money to buy me a plot of land. Somewhere so far away only the sky will know my business. I gotta. I ain't getting any younger. Not like these new girls.

Eliza's dark: high cheekbones, scared eyes. She'll lose those soon enough. Good skin, though. I'm thinking five bucks a time, to start.

The other, Mary Ann, stands rigid by the aspidistra, staring at the new red carpet in my back parlour. Blue eyes indignant, fresh blonde ringlets all quivering. Make the diggers round these parts remember their sweethearts back home, for sure. And they'll pay for the memory. I'll get eight dollars for this one, easy.

Ain't nobody more thorough than me when it comes to my girls. They all call me strict, but they don't have to answer to a certain Edgar G. Winterton. He's the Yankee bastard who owns this place (and all the ass in it). It makes him feel important to come in here, calling us his ladies. But he sure ain't so gentlemanly when it comes to counting all the money. He's over in El Paso tonight, but whether he's here or not, I never take any risks.

I walk round the girls, assessing, then tear off the lace from Mary Ann's dress. She flinches.

'You gotta advertise, girl . . . show them what's on offer.'

'Yes, Luella,' she mumbles, fluttering hand to pale, plump cleavage.

'Stand up straight. Be proud. I don't care where you came from. In this town, there's twelve men to every woman. That makes any old spinster a princess. But, you . . . you work for Luella Duane now. And that makes you a goddamned queen.'

I prod her in the back, feeling her corset through the thin cotton dress. Just as I thought.

'Can you do that thing yourself?'

She shakes her head. I roll my eyes to the ceiling.

'Honey! What's your thinking?' I lean in, arms akimbo, voice up like a hillbilly. '"Oh Sir, since we've finished our business . . . kindly lace me up"?'

I turn, sweeping aside my taffeta skirt and pull open the carved wooden doors of my closet. Eliza's snigger turns to a gasp. Piled up is the finest ladies' apparel you've ever seen. From as far away as Paris, some of it. Grateful customers.

I select a whalebone corset, before burying through the drift of lace handkerchiefs.

'This ain't the best bordello in the whole of Downieville by accident. I'm relying on you girls to

461

keep up the standard,' I continue, turning to face the girls, a small garter pistol in each hand. They take a step back.

'No, no,' I tut. 'First rule. Don't show your fear. The gold makes these men crazy. You gotta be controlled.'

I toss a pistol to each of them, fix them with a stare and put my hand on my chest. 'And never, ever show what's underneath.'

They fumble with their new weapons. I reckon they'd both shoot themselves if I hollered 'boo' loud enough. I take pity.

'It's simple. Promise them anything they want. That's all you gotta remember. Then you'll make a fortune.

Through the wall the music changes and I pull across the panel. Immediately, it's noisy with clinking glasses and men's voices. Murray's at the piano, the faithful old fool. Wire spectacles perched on the end of his crooked nose and a white bushy moustache that twitches as he nods back over his shoulder. New boys in town.

'Ready, girls?' I say. 'Let's go to work.'

It's crowded out front, shouting over the honky-tonk and fiddles, the air thick with smoke, but I spot them straight away. There's the leader: cowhide hat pulled low over his brow, one foot on his knee showing off his pistol to whoever cares to look. Dirty spurs and dark stubble. On the road for a week, at a guess.

I don't turn round, but they're looking. And looking good.

'Who are they, Lou?' I ask my barman.

He polishes a glass on the front of his striped waistcoat.

'Henry Van Sickle,' he replies, pouring me a shot of brandy. 'Him and his boys are just in from Frisco. He's a ranger, so they say. Looking for a poker game. And . . .'

His watery eyes lock with mine for a second and I nod.

Eliza's doing her hair in the new mirror glass. Roughly I pull her hand down.

'No fussin'. Act like a lady,' I hiss.

'Make 'em wait,' I say, holding Eliza and Mary Ann back. 'And *smile*, goddamnit.'

I down the shot. Slam the glass back on the bar. 'Thanks, Lou.'

Raised hats as we glide towards the table. Van Sickle flicks a match in the corner of his mouth. He ain't stirrin' yet. But he will.

I go through the motions.

'Mind if we join you, gentlemen?'

One is just a boy. Blond, eager. He ogles at Mary Ann like a salivating dog as he pulls out her chair. The other, a Spaniard, is shy, tip-twisting his moustache. He can't look at either girl for longing. Eliza will snare him. Easy.

Van Sickle's eyeballing me, but I'm not rising. Instead I order drinks, tell a few jokes, make them comfortable. The usual. Then, 'What brings you to Downieville?'

'This and that,' Van Sickle shrugs. His voice is rough. Dutch twang.

'Well, you've found the this, what's the that?' Straight back.

He's warming up. Can't help himself.

'You heard of William A. Terry? Wild Billy T?' he asks, shuffling forward in his chair. He leans on the table, cupping his beaker of whisky.

I raise an eyebrow. Say nothing.

'Me and the boys, we've chased him all the way from San Francisco.'

He takes out a cigarette and I pull matches from my sleeve. I look into his eyes over the flame. Mean brown. Hungry.

The Spaniard's found his tongue. He pulls out a paper from his jacket.

'This is him,' he says, blushing to Eliza.

The Wanted poster. I've seen it countless times. Actual fact, got one myself. I take the paper and hold it.

'Wild Billy T, you say? My, what a handsome specimen he is. What's he wanted for?'

'A bank robbery up in Frisco,' says the boy.

'He's a dead man,' adds Van Sickle, his voice cutting through the others like an axe. 'Shot a girl up. Killed her dead.'

'Oh my,' I gasp, impressed sounding. I hand the paper to Mary Ann. Flick open my fan.

'The Sheriff's offered a reward to bring him in dead,' says Van Sickle. 'But the girl's father, he wants Wild Billy T alive. Wants the pleasure of seeing him strung up. Wants to see him squirm. Says he'll pay five times the reward when we bring him in.'

When, not if.

He sits back in the chair. Pleased with himself.

'Five times,' I whistle. 'Why, you boys are sure gonna be rich.'

I smile at Van Sickle, giving him the Luella special. Never fails.

His eyes flicker. He knows he'll have me, but I'll make him pay.

He wins at poker. Cleans out the Craven brothers, fresh prospectors from the camp. He plays dirty. There's a brawl when the boys try to win it back. Van Sickle pistol-whips them outside.

When I get him to my bedroom, I figure he's got two thousand dollars in bagged gold nuggets, weighing down his trousers. And that ain't all that's weighing them down.

He's fuelled up with the whisky and gold. He wants it rough, so I play along. He wrestles me on the bed, ripping at my clothes, before flinging me away. I crash into my dressing screen.

Van Sickle wipes the back of his hand across his mouth. He gets up, leering, swaying. A slick of sweat makes his forehead look like snakeskin.

'Stand there naked, like the whore you are,' he growls.

I cock a hip at him, like I don't care. Look towards the purple-tasselled scarf draped round the ceiling.

'You got no dignity,' he hisses, slapping me hard across the face.

I turn my cheek away, hands down, keeping still. Seen it all before. Silence for a moment. He wants to hurt me, but he wants me more. I won't look at him, even when he grabs me.

After, he's calm. I stroke his chest like a cat. It's thick

with hair, parted by a long scar. Bowie knife, I reckon.

'You are some woman,' he muses.

My fingers stop by his nipple. Let him know I have a thought.

'I could help you.' Softly.

He crooks one arm behind his head. Armpit is close to my face. Sweat, greed and other men's blood.

'I wasn't going to tell you in front of the others, but –'

I stop.

'What?' he asks. Alert now.

'It'll cost you.'

He's tense, interested. His face turns to mine. Up close, his skin is pock-marked.

'I know Wild Billy T,' I whisper.

He grabs me by the throat.

'Where is he?'

His eyes dance with mine, but I don't flinch until the pressure goes. Then I set myself straight.

'As I said, it'll cost you.'

'How much?'

'Thirty dollars.'

'Twenty.'

I nod. 'Deal.'

He pulls on dirty breeches, then reaches for his vest. Folds the notes down on the counterpane.

'Wild Billy T. Oh yes, I sure can tell you a whole hell of a lot about him.' Run my finger over the bills.

'Start talking.'

I gesture for one more bill. He throws it down.

'He pays me to take him supplies. Supplies and . . .'

Van Sickle sneers.

'Where is he?'

'Up in the woods by Whisky Gulch. Camping out –'

He's racing now, pulling on his pants and boots.

I laugh. Like I'm so amused. Fold my arms. Watch him hurrying.

'You gonna go, just like that?' I shake my head. 'He's seen the posters, he knows men are after him. He'll be waiting. Believe me, you ain't the first.'

I watch him pace, angry he can't button his shirt up fast enough.

'They say he's the fastest shot in California. He'll shoot you before you've even got near. I suppose if you got real lucky, you might shoot him first.' I study my fingernails. 'But then you wouldn't get five times the reward. No, you won't catch him alive . . .'

He stops. Looks over his shoulder at me. 'And you got a plan?'

He's listening now. I tease him more before I tell him.

'I'll go to him as usual. Relax him.' I smile coyly, play with the silk brocade on the pillow. 'And when he knows it's me, he'll drop his guard. You could take him quiet as a baby. For the right price . . .'

He knows it'll work. He'll pay.

'What do you want?'

'Everything you won from poker. All that gold. Up front.'

A heartbeat. Then a nod.

'I'll raise the men,' he says.

'You scared to go alone with me? Don't tell me you're yella?'

'Won't have no two-bit whore saying I'm yella,' he spits.

'Do me a favour. Leave your boys for my girls. And think. If you do, Henry, you'll get that reward money all for yourself.'

He holds up his hand against me.

'Don't call me Henry. Only my wife calls me Henry.'

I smile, reaching for my gown. I tease his temper, wagging my finger at him, but he can't stay cross. He's got himself a deal and he needs me. Still he pauses, looking for the catch. He shields his eyes as I stand and tie my robe.

Then he turns.

'When we get up there, I'll be in the woods. I'll be watching all the time. I'll see and hear everything. One false move and I'll shoot you both.'

I shrug. 'He won't suspect.'

Behind my screen, I pull on silk stockings, then fix my pistol in my holster, a knife from a generous Colonel in my leather boot. Riding dress to cover the lot.

'Now, Sir. How about that gold?' Casual sounding.

A sneer. 'You think I'm crazy? I'll give it when you hand Wild Billy T over.'

I look over the screen. 'Half now.'

'All on delivery.'

He's agitating. No point in pushing it. I walk back out and scoop the bills from the bed, counting them deliberately. He's added the extra for the service.

He shakes his head, disgusted. 'You'll do anything, won't you? For money.'

I smile at him.

'Like you said, I'm just a whore. I ain't got no dignity.' I stuff the notes into the front of my dress and drop my smile. 'Be ready to leave at daybreak.'

FOR A FEW DOLLARS WHORE II:
THE GUNSLINGER

There's a chill in the air this morning and it's real tempting to climb up there on that big old hunk of rock that the sun's just settled on, and lie back with the lizards and bask a while. But I don't. I stay put down here instead, hidden amongst the junipers and the sweet-smelling pine, just the same as I have done for these past five days, and just the same as I will till enough time's passed for me to move on.

I gotta be careful, even at times like now, when the day ain't barely five minutes old and not even the rabbits are out of their holes sniffing the air. Truth is, no matter how peaceful and lonesome this forest looks, there could be any number of folks out there, sneaking up on me, looking to cut my throat. Or maybe they're just watching, as still as stones and as patient as Indians, waiting for me to make my move, so as they can shoot me dead.

God knows, they got reason enough. Five thousand dollars of reason, if that there piece of paper that Luella brought me is telling the truth. That's for taking me in alive, Luella told me. It's a whole lot less if they carry me back to Frisco in a wooden box. Alive ain't gonna happen, though, and, chances are, anyone that knows anything about me, ain't gonna try. I've killed eight men in the last two years and a whole lot more Mexies during the war. My name, some say, fills folks with fear.

Reaching down into my coat pocket, I pull the piece of paper out and unfold it. There I am: Wild Billy T, a lawless and evil man, with a wild head of dark hair and a mean glint in my eye. They got my scar on the wrong cheek, but that scar's only a month old, and the fact that they got it at all means that one of Solomon's boys talked and gave away my particulars. And if they talked, then they been caught. And if they been caught, then they been hung. And after what they done to that woman, I ain't sorry either way. I just wish folks didn't figure I had a part of it, an' all.

Money and death. That's what this country's all about. It makes you greedy, knowing there's all that gold in these hills, and not enough to go round. And it makes you brave, an' all, knowing you can just as soon die of hunger round these parts as you can at the end of a noose.

I tried looking for nuggets, of course, living by my muscles instead of my gun. I was there that day in San Francisco, when that Mormon fellah came riding into town, yelling, 'Gold, gold, gold!' just as hard as he could, and the whole place went paydirt crazy. I was still in the army, garrisoned there as part of Jonathan D. Stevenson's Regiment of New York Volunteers. But the Mexican war was as good as over and, along with a whole lot of other boys, I deserted my post and set off with the rest of the Argonauts for the new El Dorado.

That's how I teamed up with Sam Beattie. We claimed us a sluice box together over in Auburn Ravine, but got nothing out of it but busted backs and empty bellies. Wasn't long before we'd switched from sluicing for gold to bushwhacking those who'd already done the good work for us. It was easy and that's how come we stuck with it, I guess.

The killing came later, once we joined up with Solomon Pico's boys down south and started working over the *rancheros*, stealing their herds and driving them on up to the San Francisco slaughteryards, passing them off as our own. In all the time I ran with that blood-thirsty bunch of Californios and Mexies, though, I never killed a man for pleasure. The men I've shot, I've shot to stop them from shooting me. I wouldn't even call it murdering. And I never killed a woman, no matter what they say. That was Sam and the others, and that was why I left them and ran on my own to here.

Ain't nobody born bad. And that's the truth, so help me God. The same goes for Luella and me both. We done some things, for certain, that ain't exactly what a preacher might call decent, but what we done we done to survive. We done it because we *had* to, not because we wanted it that way. And we want it done with now. We want to be away from here, never having to come back.

I glance at the paper again. That's what I was trying to do up at that bank in Frisco, get me a stake big enough for us to disappear down south to the Nacimiento River and buy us some good land I got spied out and build us a *rancho*. But all I got was a bullet in the leg and a price on my head. Just goes to show that any which way you turn can lead you into strife.

Hungry now, I take another look over the smooth top of the fallen birch I've been sleeping against, but the old track leading down the mountain slope to the north is still clear. She'll be here soon, Luella, the woman I love and the woman I'm gonna marry.

Luella's more handsome than any girl I ever seen. She's smart, different to other women, maybe, I reckon, even as smart as a man. Some folks might think that wanting to be with a whore's plain crazy, but I love her all the same. I don't like it, of course, thinking about what she does and the men she does it with. But she tells me not to fret none. All they are is dollars to her, she says. I have her heart and when we're gone from here none of this will matter. We'll leave the people we are today far behind and won't think about them no more. That's what she says and what she says, I believe.

A noise in the trees to the east: a twig snapping, maybe twenty, thirty paces distant.

I move quickly and silently, twisting round to face that way, my Colt already in my hand. Could be a fox, I'm figuring, but could just as easy be a man. Either way, I'm certain sure it ain't Luella; she always takes the track.

Making myself just as small a target as I can, I hunch up close against the barricade of dead wood I've built up around me these last few days, and I keep my head real low. What with my leg being the way it is, I ain't up for running none, and if that *is* some vigilante or marshal out there and he's coming for me, then I'm gonna have to make mighty sure I get him first. All I pray is that he ain't got a posse by his side. I wait, count my way up to fifty in my head, but don't hear a thing. Slowly, I raise my head and chance a look, searching the trees for movement, my muscles already slackening up. There ain't nothing out there, nothing at all.

But then comes a voice – a woman's voice – and I'm twisting again, this time to the north, my finger closing on the trigger of my Colt.

'Billy?' the voice cries.

'Luella?' I call, seeing her as I do, a flash of white dress in all that green, walking towards me with a carpetbag by her side.

She waves and, in that instant, I find myself relaxing, forgetting about whatever rabbit or fox was worrying me over in the forest, knowing that all in the world is good again. Slipping my Colt back into my belt, I stand. She keeps on coming and then I see her face, and it knocks the breath out of me, just like it always does whenever I lay eyes on her after an absence.

'What you doing sneaking up on me like that for?' I ask her as she draws closer. My voice is stern, but I can't keep this big wide smile from spreading across my face. 'You nearly gone and got yourself killed, girl.'

'I'm sorry, Billy,' she starts to apologise, 'I –'

I hush her up with the raised palm of my hand, not wanting to talk now, just hold her. I lift my busted leg up over the fallen tree and haul myself on over, out into the open. I look to her face, close enough to touch now, and it's then that I see it – a twitch in her eyes, a darkening at their centres – and I know that something's gone bad.

'What?' I ask, stopping dead still where I am.

She says nothing and the possibilities run through my mind. I picture for an instant the posse that was waiting in ambush for me and Solomon's boys in Frisco and the tall man with the long coat and the dirty spurs who ran Sam Beattie down, and shot him twice in the back, and then once in the face for good measure on the ground where he fell. Men like that don't give up easy, I'm thinking. And I'm just praying he hasn't tracked me all the way to Downieville, and that's what bad news Luella's here to tell me all about. Running again . . . I'm too beat for that. My chances of making it through another chase without a whole lot of lead in my body ain't so good.

'What?' I ask her again, growing fretful now, wanting to hear what she's got to say, and knowing what a difference a head start can make to a man in a situation like mine.

Finally, she speaks: 'Trust me,' she says. 'I had no other choice.'

Again her eyes darken and again I see them shift, this time to the east and, suddenly, I understand. Only even as I do, I know it's already too late.

'I got a rifle on you, Wild Billy T,' comes the shout; something foreign about the way he speaks. 'And if you move so much as one pretty hair on your pretty head, I'm going to blow your brains clear across the county.'

I don't take my eyes off Luella for so much as one instant. Her gaze drops, down to the ground, further maybe, right on down to the place that she'll end up for treating me this way. I hear footsteps coming towards me from the east, twigs snapping and leaves rustling, and I curse myself for my own stupidity in ever trusting anybody but myself. *How can she still be beautiful?* I find myself asking. *How can I feel so much pain over her after what she's done?* The man covering me stops close by my side, so close as I can hear him breathing; soft and easy, like he don't have a care in the world.

'Gently, now,' he tells me. 'Take the revolver out and lay it on the ground.'

I do as he says; ain't no point in doing otherwise: the man wouldn't be standing where he was if he wasn't ready to shoot. There's a noise of him fumbling with something and I think about taking a chance, hitting the floor and rolling, coming up with my gun blazing. But before I can make a move, a rope lands at Luella's feet and I know the man's got me covered again.

'Turn round to face me,' he says. 'And you, whore,' he adds, 'get to tying him up, good and tight. If I find that rope's loose when you're done, I'll shoot you both where you stand.'

The barrel of the Henry rifle he's holding is pointing at my chest and he's wearing a low-slung cartridge belt and a holstered six-shooter. A dirty hat sits slumped on his head and below its brow is a face I've seen before. To tell the truth, I'm not surprised it's him: the man who did for Eddie back in Frisco. He's wearing the same look he wore then, kind of like he's enjoying it. Even as I feel Luella doing what he told her behind my back, I'm glad I didn't try drawing on him. He's a mean one, no mistake. He's got the eyes of a killer, same as me.

'Where your friends at?' I ask him.

He smiles, his thin lips drawing back over his cracked

teeth. 'You've got some big expectations of yourself, Wild Billy T,' he says, watching me close. 'I don't need friends of my own to bring you in, not when you got friends like her to help me along . . .'

Behind me, Luella finishes the knot off real tight, just like the man said.

'She's a whore,' I tell him, for her benefit. 'She don't mean nothing to me.'

He shrugs, the smile still there. 'A good whore, though,' he says. 'You gotta admit that.' He glances over my shoulder. 'A right *dirty* whore,' he adds, spitting on the ground. 'Best I've had this side of Mississippi.'

I flinch, thinking of them together, thinking as to how it must have been between them. But then I don't think of her no more. I won't let myself, not ever again in this short life she's left me.

'The gold,' Luella says, stepping away so that she's a couple of paces to my side. 'What you promised me. I done what I said I would. You got it with you?'

Again, I try not to think of her, but instead I see her standing by me looking out across the Nacimiento River at the land that might one day have been ours.

Supporting the Henry with one arm, the man digs into his dusty coat pocket and produces a small buckskin pouch – a miner's *poke* – which he then tosses over to Luella, so that it lands by her feet.

'Turn round,' he orders me.

'You're right about one thing,' I tell him as I start to do as he says.

'And what's that?'

I stare hard into Luella's eyes for an instant, before

spitting into her face. 'She is a *dirty* whore.'

I turn full round and hear the man approach, before feeling his hands checking on Luella's knots. He grunts, seemingly satisfied. And then I hear him cry out, before his weight falls hard against my back and we both drop to the ground.

I don't speak as Luella unties me and helps me to my feet. I don't speak because there's too many questions a-whirring round my head and I can't seem to find an answer to one of them. Instead, I watch her, as she sets to rolling the man over and going through his pockets, pulling out another couple of *pokes* and a whole lot of dollars, an' all. Then I look to his head, at the glistening red patch of hair at the back of his skull, and then across to the rock by his side, wet with his blood. I kneel down and pick up his rifle, before pressing its barrel up against his still-breathing chest and starting to pull the trigger.

'Don't,' Luella says, and I feel her hand on my arm.

'Why not?' I ask.

'Because I got a better idea,' she replies. I turn to her, uncertain. 'Trust me,' she tells me, and I nod my head, knowing for certain that, from here on in, I ain't gonna do anything but.

Some time past noon, and we're leaving the forest, coming down the ridge on the other side. We're heading south. In a few days we'll make Jackson, where we'll rest up a while. And then it's on to Nacimiento.

Luella's sitting up front on the saddle before me. My arms are round her little waist and my hands rest easy on the reins of what was once Henry Van Sickle's horse. His gun lies tight against my good leg and his hat sits proud on my head.

I don't know why Luella wanted to leave him that way, stripped buck naked and cursing, tied up back there on the road to Downieville. I don't know why she wanted him to live, worse, wanted him to be found, trussed up in her corset with his face all painted and pretty. Something to do with dignity, she said, whatever the hell that means.

Women: I'll never understand them, not for as long as I live. I spur the horse on a little as the track starts to flatten out, and then I smile. Shit, I think to myself, but he sure did look funny.

Relative Madness
Hector Macdonald

The designers of the new airport had chosen tangerine orange and imperial purple to coat every surface, wall, pillar, pot-plant pot and piece of paper. The colours wound in disciplined stripes around the peaked caps of Immigration officials and hung in snaking tassels from the berets of the military. They were the colours of the flag – the personal colours of the President – and it would have been commercial suicide for the contractors to challenge the choice. Nevertheless, decided the young Dane-Brit-Swede in the queue, it did make it difficult to write clearly on the Immigration forms. He was trying not to worry about the cost yet. A new airport with thirty aircraft gates to accommodate twelve planes a day? Assume fifty thousand dollars per gate . . . no, a hundred . . . And this bank of forty Immigration booths . . . at perhaps two thousand dollars a booth . . . add fifty per cent for African overspend . . .

The Immigration officer had removed his orange/

purple-banded cap by the time the Dane-Brit-Swede reached the front of the queue. Sweat beads formed a necklace around his crown. He studied the form for a few seconds, apparently couldn't read through the imperial purple, and raised his eyes to the suited foreigner.

'What is your name?'

'Peter Jacobsen.'

He handed over his passport. The officer left it unopened. He was squinting again at the pigmental battle in progress on the form.

'You were born in 1924?'

'No. 1972.'

He received an aggrieved look for the contradiction. 'Where are you from?'

'I'm resident in France. I have British and Danish citizenship, and a lifelong honorary citizenship for Sweden. Today I have travelled from New York.'

'So you are American?'

Peter Jacobsen glanced at the queue behind him. None of the other thirty-nine booths were functioning. The returning locals seemed perfectly resigned to the delay, but the non-natives were getting restless. 'No,' he said.

'Ah.' The officer seemed to notice the passport for the first time and flicked it open as if it might offer some passing interest. 'This says you are a Danish.'

'Yes.'

'Then you cannot be American.'

'No.'

The officer sighed, looked at his watch. He pulled the

lid off a fountain pen. Ink had leaked all over the nib and lower barrel. Seemingly oblivious, he wiped the pen clean on his hair. He made a single, illegible annotation on an orange fragment of the form.

'What is the purpose of your visit?'

'I've come to run the country.'

The officer lowered his pen, looked at the Dane-Brit-Swede, looked at the passport, looked back at the Dane-Brit-Swede. He opened his mouth, changed his mind, looked down, looked up. Confused, he sought refuge in bureaucratic process.

'Business or pleasure?'

Peter wasn't quite sure how to reply. He glanced a second time at the queue behind him. Even the returning locals seemed to be turning sour. He summoned up a smile: his for-middle-ranking-and-likely-to-stay-that-way-clients smile. 'It will be my pleasure,' he said.

Orange and purple bougainvillea ran the length of the Presidential Palace – or State House as it had been known the year before, or The Royal Residence as it was absolutely not allowed to be called any more – and orange and purple flags hung from each column. When Peter first saw it, he had to turn round in the limousine to remind himself how bad were the slums that led to it. On Presidential outing days, his driver helpfully explained, thousands of tall saplings were cut from the surrounding forests and arranged on human stands to form a screen hiding the worst of them from His Excellency's – 'please remember, He is no longer His Majesty, now that we are a democratic socialist

Republic' – sensitive but caring eyes.

Peter received a lot of impromptu advice like that: from the footman who led him to his suite; from the overwhelming chambermaid in starched linen who unpacked his case with great mirth while he bathed; and from the Special Adviser to the President, who sat on the edge of his bed and issued information at machine-gun pace while Peter Jacobsen tried to decide which pair of Calvin Klein boxers to wear.

When the Special Adviser decided that he was appropriately dressed, he led the Dane-Brit-Swede through the marble and mahogany halls of the Presidential Palace to the great doors of the Third Dining Room.

The President of the Republic was dressed in a sumptuous purple gown, with a token orange ribbon at the neck. He was seated at the end of a vast empty table, staring straight at Peter.

The Special Adviser had simply pushed him forward and pulled the door shut. Peter could hear his steps retreating rapidly down the hall. He stood stock still, waiting for the President to say something.

The President, however, declined to say something.

'Hello,' tried Peter in a small voice, moving one step forward across the great room.

Immediately, the President burst out laughing. Peter took a step back.

'It's me, Peter Jacobsen,' he said. 'We met in Paris. You asked me to –'

'You see?' interrupted the President, in his magnificently sonorous voice. 'You see?' He leapt to his feet, throwing his arms out, as if to embrace the room. 'You see?'

'See . . . what?'

The President was a tall man, rapidly acquiring fat around the waist and the cheeks. His enthusiastic smile sent his mouth burrowing deep into his jowls. Peter's research, after he'd moved on from balances of payments and international debts, had turned up the disconcerting fact that this man had once eaten a rebel commander's eyeballs for breakfast.

'You see? I really am the President.'

The Dane-Brit-Swede wasn't quite sure of the correct protocol in response to such a claim. 'I . . . er . . . never doubted it.'

'Of course you did. And you were quite right to. All rich black men who stay at the *Georges V* claim they're African presidents. Everyone knows that.'

'W-w-well,' stuttered Peter, moving tentatively towards him. 'I suppose all the young businessmen who stay there claim they're running Renault –'

The smile disappeared. 'You mean you were lying?' demanded the President in an icy voice. Peter shivered.

'No, no! I really was – at least . . . in an advisory capacity. As a consultant, building their corporate strategy.'

Fully recovered, the President was moving forward to embrace him. 'And as a consultant I welcome you to our modest little country. Are you hungry?'

Turning, he let out a great yell and instantly the doors on the far side of the room flew open. Six waiters rushed in, carrying place settings, bottles, vases of orange and purple flowers and two golden plates. The President gave Peter a shove towards the table and returned to his chair as the waiters flurried around them. In a matter of seconds, they were alone.

'I prefer to eat what my people eat,' said the President. 'It is of an incomparable importance to show solidarity with the populace, do you not agree?'

'Yes.'

'You do not agree?' The President frowned.

'Er . . . no . . . I mean, I think you're right.'

Mentally, Peter tried to reconstruct the conversation to see where he had gone wrong. It occurred to him that it might be important to listen more carefully to the literal grammar of his host's almost perfect English. He vaguely remembered from his research that the British had put the man through Sandhurst before Independence.

Glancing down, he was disappointed to find only a tiny morsel of unrecognisable fowl, all alone in the centre of his golden plate.

'What is it?' he asked, prodding gingerly with his fork.

'Sunbird. Captured in my home village.'

'Oh.' It was gone in two small mouthfuls. Peter wondered how far into his four-month contract it would be polite to ask for more European-sized rations.

'What is the speciality of your home village?' asked the President.

'I don't have any single home. My father lived in Denmark and my mother in England, while my step-mother – who was my real mother in all but biology –

moved us to Sweden after the divorce. So I have a bit of all three countries in me.' Years of explaining the complexities of what had been a thoroughly traumatic childhood had enabled Peter to develop a patter that was both straightforward and hygienic. He even felt comfortable using it with clients once they got to that crucial team-building stage. Nothing like a little sanitised family history in amongst the forced go-karting and alcoholic dinners to help bond.

But the President was staring at him, perplexed. 'How can you know who you are if you don't know where you're from?'

'I identify myself by the work I do.'

'Really?' said the President dubiously, dabbing his lips with his sleeve. 'Then perhaps you'd tell me what work you intend to do here, to turn around my country?'

Peter Jacobsen swallowed nervously. 'Well,' he said slowly, 'you understand I can't guarantee that kind of result.' Quite what had induced him to claim anything of the sort, late at night at the bar of the *Georges V*, had slipped his memory. Something to do with the relative size of the country's GDP (small) next to the annual revenue of his smallest client company (very large). 'But I think if we treat the country strictly as a business, with cost centres, profit centres and a large workforce, it should be possible to make big improvements in the state of the economy. Really you should think of it simply as a machine for making money.'

'Oh, I already do,' said the President with a wry smile. 'My cousin Albert, the Minister for Finance, has very clear instructions on that point.' Then he turned towards the kitchen. 'Next!' he suddenly yelled.

The doors flew open and four of the waiters returned. The first pair removed the sunbird plates, and the second pair replaced them with another course. New cutlery appeared, as if by magic. Peter's spirits rose immediately. So that had been the starter! The main course, while still small, at least looked like providing a reasonable level of nutrition.

'Smoked hartebeest tongues,' declared the President as the waiters vanished.

Peter wilted a little at that. He tried a piece. It had a smoky taste and rubbery texture, but at least it was edible.

'And what do we do with this machine,' asked the President, his own tongue struggling to move among the remains of five others, 'to fine-tune it?'

'Well, Your Excellency, the important thing is to identify the assets and strengths of the country –'

'Minister for State Affairs!' roared the President. 'My uncle Theo,' he smiled indulgently to Peter as a bent-over figure entered the room a moment later, breathless from running. 'Minister! What are our assets?' he demanded.

Uncle Theo stumbled across the room and leaned a heavy hand on the table. He was wearing a three-piece pinstripe suit and gumboots.

'I believe you have about four hundred and eighty million dollars in Switzerland. The rest of the family –'

'Not that kind of assets,' interrupted the President without any sign of embarrassment. 'The country's natural assets.'

'Oh.' Uncle Theo's face fell. 'Not so good. There are the game parks, the copper mines, the coffee plantations in the highlands, and one scenic mountain.'

'Plenty,' said Peter confidently. 'Game parks and mountains bring tourist revenue. Copper and coffee are always desired commodities . . .'

'Not really,' said Uncle Theo mournfully. 'We've poached all our animals; Zambia can mine copper for a third of our cost; our coffee is so bitter, even we don't like drinking it; and the mountain is . . . well . . . not very much more than a sandy hill, if I'm honest.'

'Our strengths, then, Minister,' said the President, before calling out to the waiters again. 'What are our strengths?'

'Oh, my boy,' said Uncle Theo, his eyes twinkling, 'we have many strengths.'

The four waiters had whipped away the tongue plates and – to Peter's amazement – were replacing them with great platters of shellfish: a lobster between two crabs, surrounded by a ring of oysters and prawns. Whole lemons were placed beside each platter. The President picked one up, ripped off an end with his teeth, and squeezed its juice all over the platter. He was just grabbing the second lemon when he noticed Peter's bewildered expression.

'What's wrong? Didn't you see lobster at the *Georges V*?'

Peter had been brought up in a good, conventional household and was now living – when work permitted – with a good, conventional girlfriend, so he was fully expecting the dessert course to consist of something sweet. The British members of his genes would normally have prevented him commenting on it, but this was a direct question, after all.

'I . . . well I thought we'd more or less finished the meal.'

The President stared at him in silence for a moment, then burst out laughing. 'Very good. Very humorous. Minister, hurry up.'

'Pardon, Your Excellency,' said the chastened Uncle Theo. 'As I was saying, our strengths are many: courage, fortitude, fertility, devotion, loyalty –'

'I'm sorry,' interrupted Peter. 'I really meant commercial strengths: manufacturing skills, for example.'

'Oh.' Uncle Theo looked crestfallen.

'Get out of here, Minister!' shouted the President. 'Worthless reptile.' He turned back to Peter as the old man shuffled away. 'You see my problem? This is why I hired you. How am I supposed to suck a decent fortune out of this country when none of my People have any useful talent?'

'Uh . . .' Peter wasn't prepared for that one. He was used to senior executives doing questionable things involving share options and pension plans, but most of them had the decency to keep such things under the table. 'Uh, Your Excellency . . . I'm not sure I understand. You want me to help your country become richer so you can . . . bank it all yourself?'

'Of course,' said the President, a crab gripped in each hand. 'What did you think?'

'Well, I . . . it's just in Europe our leaders tend not to *reward* themselves in quite the same way.'

'That is why none of them stay at the *Georges V.*'

'But . . . but don't you feel a bit uncomfortable, er, *stealing* from your own People?'

'Of course I do. It pains me grievously to have to take the money of good people living in mud huts, dying of starvation. Why aren't you eating?'

Quickly Peter grabbed an oyster shell, tipping the contents down his throat before his taste buds would notice it. He wasn't at all sure of the wisdom of pursuing this conversation. On the other hand, the overall goal of his assignment was a little hazy. And if he'd learned anything from experience, it was the importance of full and frank discussion of objectives before work began.

'Then why do you do it?'

The President sighed, as if faced with a particularly obtuse student. 'Let me ask you this: what would my People say if I had the chance to take their money and didn't?' Before Peter could reply, he had raised a demonstrative finger and launched into the answer. 'He is weak! That is what they would say. The President has the chance to enrich himself, but he is scared to do it. He is weak, weak, weak!' Suddenly he'd dropped his voice to a whisper and brought his face within inches of Peter's. 'And do you know what happens to leaders in Africa when the People think they have grown weak?'

'What?' croaked Peter.

'They are overthrown! Overthrown and replaced with an unstable regime run by a tyrannical despot.'

Then he was back to the shellfish, chewing softly on a lobster claw.

'So,' said Peter, swallowing uncomfortably, 'you

mean you steal from your People, even though you don't want to, in order to prevent civil war?'

'It is my sovereign duty,' smiled the President. 'And the People love me for it. You can get the polling figures from my brother Rudolph.'

'Rudolph?'

'Yes. You met him earlier. My Special Adviser. My Vizier . . .' he suggested, trying out the word. 'Yes, my Vizier.'

Another platter arrived, larger still, this time groaning under the weight of several cuts of game meat, swimming in gravy. Peter was already stuffed to the limit. He stared at the great hunks of flesh and felt ill. It was too late to invoke vegetarianism as a way out – he'd eaten the hartebeest tongues without complaint. Desperately he wondered how much of the meat he could transfer under the table in his napkin. Then he remembered neither of them had napkins.

Trying not to think of the imminent assault on his stomach, Peter raised a question that had been worrying him. 'Your ministers . . . a lot of them seem to be family members.'

'A lot of them?' said the President, half a slice of wildebeest fillet stuck between his teeth. 'All of them, you mean.'

The pile of meat was growing to surreal proportions in Peter's mind. Any moment, he was expecting a hunk of zebra to stand up and start grazing quietly on the orange bougainvillea. He tried to visualise a space in his stomach large enough to accommodate even a small sliver of fillet.

'Doesn't that look a bit like nepot . . . a bit like you're favouring the people you love?'

'Love?' He leaned in close to Peter and whispered, 'Actually, I can't stand any of them. I had two of them executed for incompetence last year. But if my ministers weren't all related to me, I'd spend most of the time I should be devoting to my People watching my back.'

'I see,' said Peter slowly, forcing himself to eat a tiny morsel.

'Look, don't concern yourself with the government. They're not a big wheel in this machine anyway. What I want to know is this: without any useful assets or strengths, is there any way to make more money?'

Nodding weakly, Peter prepared to spear a piece of Grant's Gazelle. It took all his strength to do it.

'Well, Your Excellency,' he started. 'There is a theory that could help. It's called Comparative Advantage and it's about the only thing economists really agree –'

'I want nothing to do with economists,' scowled the President. 'They're all spies for the World Bank: coming here, telling me I have to reduce the value of the currency. As if any sane man would voluntarily destroy his own country's wealth.'

'Yes . . . well . . .' Peter caught himself before he could get trapped in the dangerous waters of exchange rate theory. 'Forget the economists. Suppose you want a new house built,' he said. 'You have two choices: build it yourself or hire someone else to do it.'

'Build it myself?' The President looked bemused.

'Yes. Let's say you are an expert builder and you can

build a house in five days, while a boy in the street would take ten days.'

'You're comparing me to a boy in the street?'

From his experience presenting to the senior executives of some of the world's largest corporations, Peter knew the best way to deal with an irrelevant objection was to smile politely and then ignore it. 'You might think it better for you to build the house yourself as you can do it more efficiently than the boy. But because you have other, more valuable skills, like running the country, it's actually better to pay the boy to do it.'

He could see the President staring at him with a look of deep suspicion.

'Are you suggesting I should just ask some street kid to build my palaces for me? Is that what you're suggesting?' The frown across the President's forehead was intensifying.

'No!' cried Peter. 'I'm simply trying to say that even though the boy isn't as good as you at anything – he can't build as well as you and he can't run the country as well as you – he can still make a living by providing the less valuable of those two services. In fact, for building – because he can do it with less sacrifice of other opportunities than you can – he has a comparative advantage over you.'

As he said it, he knew it was the wrong way to express the paradox. The President was completely still, hardly breathing. Behind them, the kitchen door opened and a questioning face appeared. When he saw the rigidity of his master's posture, the waiter quickly withdrew.

'I do believe you just said a street kid is better than

me,' declared the President tonelessly. 'Is that not what you said?'

'No, your Exc . . . I mean: yes, it is not!' Now Peter was more than nervous; he was getting scared. 'Look. Let me give a real example that we might be able to use. Let's compare this country and Germany. Everyone knows the Germans make great cars, right?'

The President nodded slowly.

'Right! Now I guarantee one thing: this country has a comparative advantage over Germany in assembling cars.'

For a full five seconds, the President just stared at him. Then he burst into hysterical laughter.

'No, really!' urged Peter. 'It's because – no offence – Germans are much better than your own People at almost everything commercially valuable: engineering, software development, the arts, media, law . . . all kinds of professions. There's so much else an average German can do that's more valuable than car assembly: meaning he has many more opportunity costs if he chooses to spend a day assembling cars. So your People are comparatively better at assembling cars – because they have fewer opportunity costs – than the Germans!'

Now the President's laughter was in full flood. 'Very good!' he cried. 'Now I understand. How stupid of me not to realise.'

'But it's so simple,' Peter said, hearing the troubling tone in the other man's voice. 'The Indonesians have done it with sneaker assembly; the Chinese with textiles. Just set up a car assembly plant here in conjunction with the big corporations and there's no way any Western factory could compete with you on price.'

'We're better than the Germans!' cried the President with tears running down his cheeks. 'We're better than the Germans! How . . . ludicrous!'

Hearing the laughter, the waiters had grown more courageous and now re-emerged with a beef casserole.

'How could I not see it? And running Renault – to think I swallowed that as well. A little kid advising the head of a car giant . . . ha ha!'

Peter frowned. 'But . . .'

'If I didn't know better,' cried the President between torrents of laughter, 'I'd say you were an actor.'

'An actor?' Peter was mystified. 'But you know I'm not.'

'I do, I do,' the President assured him. 'No actor is that convincing – that convinced! No, there is only one thing you can be . . .'

The following morning, the British High Commissioner spent five minutes with the tearful Dane-Brit-Swede before returning to the Presidential Palace. His driver's name was Burton – after Richard Burton – and he had been working for the British ever since his uncle, the President, decided that he really was too simple to take a Ministerial post. His employment was one of many informal favours that the government and their former colonial masters extended each other as a matter of gentlemanly understanding. Whenever he was spoken to, he simply grinned widely and gave the same positive reply.

'Extraordinary,' muttered the High Commissioner.

'Yes, Sir!' The glass partition between the driver and the passengers had been broken for years, so the full effect of his enthusiasm carried back to the diplomat.

'Of course, the Special Adv . . . the *Vizier* warned me. But I must say he was worse than I could have imagined.'

'Yes, Sir!'

'Do you know,' continued the High Commissioner, 'he actually claimed the President personally invited him out here to run the country? A mere babe in arms! Have you ever heard of anything so ridiculous?'

'Yes, Sir!'

As they pulled up in front of the Palace, the High Commissioner glanced at his watch and saw with a shudder that it was lunch time. Quickly he rehearsed a plausible line.

'Well, that's awfully kind, Your Excellency,' he was saying a few minutes later, 'but I've actually just had lunch with my opposite number in the American compound.'

The white lie was accepted with easy grace. 'What a shame,' said the President, his fork halfway to his mouth. 'The guinea fowl tart is quite perfectly lovely.'

'I'm sure it is. I'm sure it is.' The High Commissioner paused for the requisite number of diplomatic seconds, then turned to the business at hand. 'This, er, Jacobsen,' he said, emphasising the non-Britishness of the surname. 'I've been to see him. Quite mad. Really quite as mad as your Sp . . . *Vizier* implied.'

'So sad,' murmured the President, plucking a whole thigh from the tart and chewing on the meat. 'I am correct in thinking that proper etiquette allows for the eating of fowl with one's fingers?'

'Quite correct, Your Excellency.' Again, the requisite pause. 'This, er, Jacobsen . . . bit of an issue with him, though.' The High Commissioner gave a resigned smile, as if to ease the weight of the world on his tired shoulders. He'd long ago discovered the secret to successful diplomacy was to give the other chap the impression that he was enjoying life more than you. 'Rather hard trying to decide which of us should be looking after him. The Danish ambassador says he's British, the Swedish consul says he's Danish, and . . . well, we're not sure quite what position to take.'

'Are you certain you wouldn't like some guinea fowl, Excellency?'

'Yes thank you, Your Excellency.' This time, he looked down, silently counting to five. 'And, of course, none of us can think what to do with him if we do repatriate him. We don't really have lunatic asylums any more – at least not with the kind of security that your fine facility can boast.'

'You have a problem,' nodded the President sagely.

'We do rather,' agreed the High Commissioner.

'It is a fine facility, isn't it?'

'Certainly.'

'It is nice to think there is something my country does better than yours.'

'Much better, Your Excellency.'

'It puts us in a comparatively advantageous position, I suppose.'

That was a new one. 'My thoughts entirely,' agreed

the High Commissioner, making a mental note to include the expression in his memoirs.

The President thought for a while, unconsciously licking pastry crumbs from his fingers. His big brows drawn together in concentration, his eyes remained fixed on the bouquets of orange and purple flowers on the table.

'In that case,' he said eventually, 'perhaps you would accept my offer to accommodate the patient indefinitely?'

Sighing with relief the High Commissioner smiled his gratitude. 'We'll take care of any inquiries from the family, of course.'

'A climbing accident, one might say?' suggested the President.

'I do hear the upper reaches of the mountain can be terribly treacherous.'

'A tragedy,' smiled the President. 'Please give my love to your wife.'

'I will,' said the High Commissioner, standing. 'Thank you so much, Your Excellency.'

Stone Money

Serena Mackesy

On the fourth day, the giant clam gets me. Well, not me, but the toe of my sandal, purchased at Palau International Airport (a very nice shed, with benches and everything), at truly an international price because, as the Texan 'C'cola' salesman with whom I shared a curled ham sandwich on the Air Micronesia (slogan: 'So much a part of you') flight informed me 'Y'all maht thaynk it lurks purdy lahk a swum'n pewl, but thur's thayngs in thayut lug*ewn*'s got *spahks* awn they ayuhssus'.

Funny how many cultures across the world have contrived to add a second syllable to the word 'arse'. It's as though it's just too small a word in its own right.

So one moment I'm ankle-deep, a hundred yards from the shoreline because the tide's out, and the next I'm knees-down on the coral sand and mouthing that time-honoured expression of surprise and hurt, 'Wha' the faa'?' as the water stains brown with my blood. For a moment I kick out in panic, then, feeling my foot move within the sandal webbing, remember that all I need to do is undo the ankle buckle. So I reach back, slip tongue from hole and collapse back onto my 'ayuhss', rubbing my thigh where it's twisted and stretched, and peer at the water where the sandal hangs, oddly static in the maelstrom.

The water settles, and I see that the leading centimetre or so of sole has slotted itself into a space that is, if anything, narrower than it is itself. Some optical illusion. I blink, lean closer. Yes. No doubt about it. The rubber sole is being *squeezed* by whatever has it. I take hold of the heel, try to pull. The grip tightens. I try hauling, and something moves, ever so slightly, under the sand, shifts upward, then comes to a full and rigid stop.

Ooh. I'm not sure if I like this. This is one of those situations you come across in *Dune* just before the entire surface of the planet erupts and swallows someone whole. I release my grip on the sandal and try to be very, very quiet while I wait to see what's going to happen next.

Nothing.

I wait.

Nothing.

Five minutes later, I'm feeling increasingly foolish, sitting here staring at the water, despite the fact that there's no one in the entire lagoon to witness my timidity. The diving boats crossed the reef with the dawn tide, and won't reappear until there's enough water to stop them holing themselves. The remaining staff at the centre – Concepcion, a tiny, grey-haired Filipina with a biltong complexion, whose gold teeth glint maniacally at you through the steam rising from the vats of miso and rice she prepares for our evening meal, and two local blokes, one long and thin and dressed in knock-off designer gear, the other a narwhal wrapped in a tent, whose prime function, aside from very slowly sweeping palm fronds about with the help of other palm fronds, seems to be to illustrate the infinite variety of Micronesian manhood – will have taken to their hammocks for a well-earned rest. I came here for solitude, and there are few places better suited to furnishing it than a Pacific dive centre in the daytime.

The lagoon drowses, a vast expanse of quiet sand where jungle-covered tippy-tops of a thousand great sandstone mountains stand like topiary on legs carved out by the endless shush of waves. At this time of day you can walk from island to island across the silver floor, slap a hand against the grey, rusting sides of Hirohito's sunken fleet. At high tide, only their gun towers show above the water. Palau, handy for Yap, over the horizon from Guam, a string of emerald dots in the blue Pacific desert, furthest possible point from Pinner.

I summon my courage and bend closer. The sand seems to have a neatly serrated mouth, zig-zags half an inch wide extending six inches or so along a crack in the rock bottom before they curve inward to form a lippy smile. I remove my other sandal, gingerly draw it through the water over the area until the dusting of sand moves, swirls and reveals my first sight of a giant clam.

'Oh, wow,' I hear myself say out loud to the puffer fish and the tiny blue-clawed crabs that lurk in the shallows. 'Oh, wow.'

This is a big thing for me. I know such things exist, because you see them in hammy 1950s movies where people like Victor Mature take off their shirts and get wet on the thinnest of pretexts, but reality is far more breathtaking than celluloid fantasy. And anyway, they're sea creatures, things that skulk in the reach of an aqualung. You don't find them in six inches of water when you're out paddling.

'Good God,' I say out loud again.

It's not exactly a blueprint for clamdom. It's more of a sand-kicked-in-your-face kind of clam. But it clings to my sandal with determination, if a lump of muscle can be allowed to possess such a quality, and, as I study it, I see that it is exquisite, as a shark is exquisite.

It is more than nine inches long from edge to edge, two sets of contiguous teeth arming and protecting a probing tongue and a digestive system. But oh, it's more than that. It's perfect. It's pink and white and powerful, the shell built up over decades like salt deposits on copper piping, and, though it remains clamped around the sandal, I catch glimpses of rainbow nacre within. A perfect, silent killing machine, and God's sweet joke to make it so unnecessarily beautiful.

And disfigured. Now I see why it's in here rather than out in the buffet of the ocean. In its infancy, washed over the reef by a storm, perhaps, or because the lagoon plays safe harbour to whatever microscopic form these creatures come into being as, it has lodged in a crack in the rock bed, settled where the tide cannot affect it, grown and formed its shell, layer upon layer, moulding itself around the contours of its sanctuary, building its own walls to fit the walls around it.

Studying it, I find myself caught up in a slightly shameful burst of fellow-feeling. Because the fissure in which it's found its sanctuary has a bit of a lip at the top, my giant of the ocean is effectively trapped. Safe and well-fed, yes, and protected from the buffets of the wider world, but nonetheless trapped.

I know how you feel, mate, I think. I'm in the same boat. Got my nice safe qualifications and my nice safe career and my nice safe not-too-stretching mortgage and my nice safe Charlie who wants to get married in due course and have two nice safe straight-haired children before I'm too old, whatever that is, but not before we're old enough to be properly established, properly equipped with all the toasters-wardrobes-wellingtons-summerhouses he deems necessary for survival. I know how it works, I find myself muttering out loud to no one. You think you're protecting your-self, and before you know it, your timidity means that you'll never know what it could have been like if you'd taken a risk or two. That's why I'm here in this stupid lagoon, all alone and talking out loud, instead of the two weeks of all-inclusive that Charlie thinks we should be aspiring to. I need – I need . . .

Charlie's voice in my head brings me back to the world. 'For heaven's sake, woman,' he says, because he talks like that, 'it's a mollusc. It feeds, it rests, it grows weeds. It really is time you grew up and faced reality. Besides, the tide's coming in. You're going to get soaked.'

I concede defeat and, leaving my sandal firmly

wedged in its prison, limp back to land, feeling my way gingerly lest I land an unfortunate digit on a marine arse-spike.

Stupid. I can't get the thought of that clam out of my head. Too much time in my own company. I know that this was what I wanted, that I thought that time alone in this demi-paradise would help me think clearly, but it's turning out that my brain is proving to be more muddied than I'd thought. So far, this island odyssey seems only to be teaching me about the things I can't do, not the things I can.

The Real Desert Island Experience, for instance. When I got here, I truly believed that I was going to take a knapsack and a sleeping bag and stroll the quarter mile across the bay to the hammock of sand, palm and mangrove that floats on the other side like a painted canvas backdrop. I would build a fire of coconut husk and dried leaves on the foreshore, feast on delicacies fished out with my bare hands from the rising waters, smoke a pack of Luckies gazing at the stars, fall asleep in the sand and be woken at dawn by the shriek of exotic birds celebrating another night survived, the thunder of great waves breaking on the reef.

I was going to do it, honestly. But when I was coming back from the toilet block in the middle of my first night here, one of the coconuts lying in the moonlit path suddenly moved, reared up and revealed itself to be a land-crab with claws bigger than my head, and, after ten minutes of trying to sneak round the side of him without stepping in the undergrowth and disturbing any companions he might have, I realised that I'm not the sort of person who's meant to spend a night alone in the tropical wilderness. I'm too accustomed to flush-lavatories and running water, mosquito screens and burglar alarms, to let it all go.

But as I say, I get plenty of time alone. I share my space with three dozen clean-clean, bobble-headed Japanese of the sporty persuasion, a couple of sincere American women with practical haircuts and a tendency to think that jokes are the product of misconceptions on the part of the teller, and a gang of broken-nosed Australian boys who drink themselves to oblivion by an hour past sunset. They rise with the dawn, make a ritual of dropping heavy metal objects on the wooden walkway outside my room and depart, clutching waterproof bags containing a day's supply of sushi and soft drinks, on the flood tide, come back in time to clean their gear and replenish their air tanks, take to their bunk beds by eight. Which means that I have roughly eighteen hours a day to pretend that this island is my sole domain.

Apart from the Aussies, they're a strangely silent lot, even in the dining hut, where everyone gathers at around six to wolf Concepcion's soup-and-starch dinners. The Japanese men seem to have perfected the art of grunting and gesturing to the foods they want without actually engaging in conversation, while the girls are so consumed by shyness that they merely emanate goodwill and hide under their fringes. Once the last morsel has been chased round the bowls, they rise as one like starlings and disappear without even pausing to watch the lunatic beauty of the sunset.

I'll read for a bit lying on the lower bunk in my spartan little room, and, once the cries of 'I'm a toilet? *You're* the fucking toilet, mate!' have died away in the Australian encampment, emerge onto my boardwalk with my duty-free whisky, rest my feet on the handrail and light my first Lucky Strike of the day. Charlie doesn't like me smoking, so I've trained myself not to do it during daylight, or when I'm in company, but I've never got over the romance of blowing smoke rings when lost in self-reflection.

I wake before dawn, and am momentarily gripped by panic. I've been dreaming that Charlie and I were looking round a nice, clean, executive house in Pinner. I'm wandering round featureless rooms – powder-blue carpets designed to show the dirt and keep your hoovering up to scratch, marble-effect laminate kitchen tops, and Charlie is asking sensible questions about guarantees on boilers. He turns to me, says, 'Well, what do you think?' and I try to say, Charlie, I hate it, it's got no life, I'll never find a way to give it a personality, warm it up, make it cosy. Instead, I hear myself say, 'Where am I going to put my seashells?' and Charlie laughs, pats me on the shoulder and says, 'I think it's time we threw all that old junk out, isn't it? Can't live like students for ever.'

But as I lie in my bunk bed, one thought overpowers me, makes me sick with panic. *It will keep growing until it dies.*

I can't believe I didn't see it before. I was so busy

with my admiration that the truth evaded me though it was staring me in the face. The lip on the fissure, the fact that its resident must already only be able to get its mouth open a couple of inches at most. With each meal it snares, the clam will continue to grow. And as it grows, it will force its own mouth closed. What has seemed like a safe harbour is, in fact, a tomb. The clam is, effectively, walled up alive.

Late morning, I paddle back across the lagoon with my Swiss Army Knife and a pair of flippers to act as a protective mat for my grazed knees. I don't know what I think I'm going to do once I've dug the clam out – shout 'Fly free, little mollusc!' and fling it through the air towards the open sea on the other side of the reef, hand it to a member of the diving party to plant it in the protected clam beds when they're out, or just remove the constriction and leave it room to grow – but I know I've got to do something. And it shouldn't, I reason, take long; the sandstone bed can't be hard to chip away.

Some time in the night, my clam has found my sandal inedible, and relinquished its hold. There's no sign of the sandal; no doubt it will be marring the ecology of Western Samoa in a few months. I kneel beside my clam, yank my hair back off my face and, with the big blade of the knife, begin to dig.

An hour later, I've got nowhere; the sandstone proves to be steel-hard, water-weathered coral and my puny blade has hardly succeeded in scratching its surface. I'm pouring sweat, and have discovered that a peculiar trick of the southern light means that, despite my pathetic green eyes, I have no need of sunglasses, even at high noon. The eighth time they slipped off my nose, I laid them to one side in a rock pool, and a grey-ish sea slug is currently exploring them with vile lemon tentacles.

The clam seems blissfully unaware of my attempts to liberate it. The side of my left hand is bruised and scratched from various attempts to use it as a hammer, and an ugly red gash decorates my palm.

And Charlie is talking in my ear. 'What exactly are you hoping to achieve by this?' he asks. 'Do you know what you look like? What would people think if they could see you?'

I shrug the thought away irritably, scrape on with the knife.

My father's voice. 'What are you wasting time for? You can't afford to waste time in this world, Maeve. You have no sense of responsibility. Do you think I made all those sacrifices so you could go swanning off round the world making sandcastles? Do you think your mother and I got you where you are by playing at hippies?'

Scrape, scrape, scrape. The back of my neck stings where I forgot the sunblock, and still the rock stub-bornly refuses even to scar.

More voices crowding in. 'You'll be forty before you know it, Maeve. You're a tax accountant, not an eco-warrior. You've only one day left here. What are you doing? You're making a fool of yourself. You're always making a fool of yourself. Act your age. Remember who you are.'

The finely crafted, precision steel blade snaps off in

my hand, and I realise that I've been muttering for the past ten minutes. 'Screw you. Screw you all. I have to do this, can't you see? It's important.' This is a matter of honour, now. I can't have wasted an entire day without getting somewhere. Wavelets lick my feet as the water level begins to rise. Soon the divers will be back and another long sleepless night will begin. I stride over the sand to the nearest rock outcrop, cast around beneath the overhang for something to drive the chisel blade with, come back with a lump of rock and squat down once more.

The clam just sits there. I know it's watching me. I'm going crazy. It doesn't have eyes, for God's sake. It doesn't have a brain. What does it care that I'm trying to save it?

I smash the rock down over the knife. The blade slips, snaps shut over my little finger, the rock smashing down on my wrist. I yelp with shock and pain, fall back on my haunches and rock there, clutching my injuries and moaning out my frustration.

You have to forget about it. You *have* to forget about it. It doesn't matter. Tomorrow you'll be on a plane to Manila and then to Hong Kong, three days shopping and adjusting to the real world, then back to your desk and wedding plans and tax returns and school-fee funds. You're crazy, lying awake shaking with rage because you couldn't smash your way through a bit of rock.

My last day, and the sky is an unnatural blue, a warm wind blowing from the typhoon that is building a thousand miles off the coast of Japan. I deliberately avoid the beach on my way to the dining shack for a handful of fruit and a bottle of water, and once I'm done, head immediately, without a backward glance, for the mangrove forest behind the camp. Anything to keep away from the sea.

Round the back of the shower block, a path leads over impacted sand into the dark. Coconut palms edge the forest, low, scrubby, sand-stained shrubs hugging their roots. The wood itself, loamy black peat from hundreds of years of leaf-shed underfoot, is full of rustles and cracks: land-crabs scuttle for the cover of holes in the ground at the low scrape of my espadrilles, clouds of insects rise from bushes, rattle irritatedly, settle back again as I brush past.

Above my head, the foliage of the mangroves hushes in the wind, obscured by mats of what looks like Spanish moss, great swaths of Tarzan-vines that I suppose to be lianas. Not that I'd know. I've only ever seen a liana in a crossword before. The mangrove trunks resemble candles left too close to a gas fire: twisted roots rising in rivulets as though they've melted and run down from above. I touch each one as I pass, as though I can partake in their antiquity, marvelling at the fact that these giants have been here since this island was just a stretch of shallow water.

I walk for ten, fifteen minutes, aiming for the far side of the island, passing a sweaty old dugout where one set of post-Pearl Harbor troops spent months lying in wait for another. The wind is rough, now, battering the invisible treetops, leaves and insect pods drifting from above to settle on my shoulders. And I'm thinking: this is it,

Maeve. This is what you get. Once you leave, it's back to a life of waiting and hoping, of pension contributions and monthly dinners-à-deux. Get used to it, girl. You've got to make a living.

In a small clearing, deep in seagrass, I stumble across the sculpture. Or at least, that's what I think it is. It's roughly cut; a perfectly symmetrical circle of what looks like granite, its surface decorated with hieroglyphs, a circular hole three feet across gouged into the centre. I gaze in awe, step forward, run a hand over the carvings, wonder how it got here, what it means.

'Stone money,' says a voice behind me, making me jump. I turn and find Marcel, the fat boat boy, standing barefoot behind me in his back-turned baseball cap, arms folded across his belly, regarding me with sad black eyes. 'You found the stone money.'

I shake my head. 'I don't understand.'

'It's what they used for money, back when,' he informs me.

'Who?'

'The people here. Over there.' Marcel unfolds an arm and waves it expansively around him. 'Before you came. Before,' he says with faint irony, 'civilisation.'

'But where does it come from? Who made it?'

He shrugs. 'It's all over, about here,' as though he was talking about a couple of close-lying hamlets rather than islands thousands of miles apart. 'On Guam, and Yap, and here. Whole villages would spend a lifetime carving it, making it, then they'd build rafts and the young men would take it across the ocean. Paddle it across the water to leave on other islands.'

We pause as I imagine the youth of Micronesia setting out from the safety of their atolls into the open sea, paddling a burden too great for any wooden raft.

'It's the most valuable thing hereabouts,' continues Marcel. 'They were happy to die for it. Most of the money never reached the islands. They overturned in the ocean, went to the bottom.'

'Why did they do it?'

Another shrug. 'It's what they did. It was what the stone money was made for.'

He continues. 'Stupid thing. It was so valuable, there was nothing anywhere you could buy with it. Every-thing, the whole of Palau, the whole Pacific: not brides, not food, not people. Nothing was worth as much as stone money.'

He makes a chucking noise with his lips and teeth, refolds his arms. 'All those young men,' he says. 'All at the bottom of the ocean. You're going today, yeah?'

I nod.

'You like it here? You gonna come back to Palau? Long way from England, huh?'

'Yes,' I reply. But my mind is a long way from England, too.

A gust catches the canopy, and the forest groans above us. 'I must go, Marcel,' I say. 'I must go.'

'Yeah,' says Marcel, and walks across to look down at the wealth of the Pacific.

I run back through the wood, pound along the path with hardly a thought for crab-holes. I suddenly know that I must have one last try, that if I don't succeed, life is over. A tyre-wrench leans against a tree-stump outside the generator house. I snatch it up as I pelt past, tuck it under my arm and canter across the lagoon.

The water has changed. The tide is earlier, and it's already calf-deep, choppy. Huge rollers crash on the reef like diesel trains, the palm trees on the foreshores already bent like feathers under the azure sky. I reach the place where my clam lies safe and warm and dying, collapse and start to pound at the rock. Over and over I raise my arm full height above my head, bring it down, splash into the cushioning water. It hits with a force that hurts my wrist, clangs, slips off.

I'm shouting out loud above the wind, saturated hair whipping into my mouth, shorts and T-shirt clinging. 'Oh for God's sake! Please! Please, just break! Please. For God's sake!'

A wave comes from nowhere, from out by the reef, grabs me, sends me rolling in a welter of sand and surf and screaming skin, snatches the wrench from my hand, leaves me coughing on my knees. It feels like seconds, but the sky has blackened, the rollers have breached the reef and the trees behind me are bent like jackstraws.

I crawl back, snatch huge breaths, duck below the surface, scrabble at the sand, but I can't see even the fissure any more.

Another wave picks me up, flings me landward, hauls me back out towards the edge of the world. I scrabble to my feet, and find that the water is waist-deep, a raging tyrant grabbing angrily at my clothes, biting, roaring. A wave slaps at my chest, slaps my face, tries to pull my feet from under me.

I turn to land, run, swim, flounder towards the huts,

where lights on strings dance and flicker in the sudden dusk. Gradually I emerge from the suck, chest-high, waist-high, thigh muscles yelling with the strain. And as I gain my foothold, lope for shelter, the rain hits: huge, stinging shards of water, like rice thrown by an angry wedding guest. Fresh, warm droplets, stabbing, bursting, wash the salt from my eyes.

Art Lover
Chris Manby

When it comes to compatibility, I believe there are three vital questions a girl can ask to save herself a lot of trouble later on. The first is, what's your favourite painting? The second, if you could hijack a plane and fly anywhere in the world, where would you go this afternoon? The third (and possibly the clincher), if you knew that you wouldn't get caught, how would you dispose of your least favourite ex? The latter question is something you probably don't want to have someone answer on your very first date. But you can ask a man what his favourite painting is pretty much as soon as you know his name and as general rule, I have found myself to be hopelessly incompatible with men who like Van Gogh. Perfect art for place mats, if you ask me. Lose ten points. Lose twenty if they tell me they love Da Vinci's *Mona Lisa*. I mean, come on! That's the answer of someone who got his art education in the birthday card section of WH Smith, not The Louvre.

My personal favourite is *Country Dog Gentlemen*,

painted by Californian artist Roy De Forest in 1972, the year that I was born. Imagine the final line-up at Crufts viewed through the bottom of an absinthe bottle – though being the 70s, there are no points for guessing the real drug of choice that might have inspired the artist to paint a Chihuahua breathing fire. The painting has a quality of traditional Aboriginal art about it. Giant stemmed flowers with blooms that look like jellyfish, or the kind of bacteria you don't want to believe live in your digestive system, loom behind the wild-eyed, bloody-tongued hounds. Blobs of bright polymer dot the canvas all over like slightly melted m&m's. But the best part is the blue-nosed, red-eyed collie to the right of the picture. He was disqualified from those sheepdog Olympics, *One Man and His Dog*, for taking perform- ance enhancing drugs. It's terrifying, compelling and completely incomprehensible. The man who tells me he loves *Country Dog Gentlemen* can have my virginity on the spot . . . Ha ha.

Anyway, the painting is part of the permanent collection at the San Francisco Museum of Modern Art, so when I had twenty-four hours to kill there (before creating some psychedelic installation work of my own in the loos of a United Airlines flight to Sydney – the result of a dodgy Chinese takeaway), a visit to the MOMA seemed like the perfect way to spend an un- accountable hour.

It was January. A Monday afternoon. Perfect gallery time. Not too busy. Just a few off-season tourists milling about the lobby, self-consciously trying to tick off all the San Fran boxes on their itinerary and secretly preferring the headset-guided tour of Alcatraz. In a room on the third floor, a bunch of fidgety schoolchildren were being kept far too long cross-legged in front of a Hockney. The fantasy azure swimming pool with its diving board shadow was painted on sheets of thick rough paper that reminded me of the sugar paper we were given to draw on at school. Later that afternoon, I bet those kids were asked to paint what they saw during their museum visit for an art class and they probably wouldn't be far off the quality of the original if they chose to copy the Hockney daub.

Each air-conned room was presided over by a diminutive curator. It was as though the largely Asian staff had been chosen so that they wouldn't block any visitor's eye line. Like funerary statues at the entrance to a tomb, they stood by the door frames and gazed ahead impassively. But as I passed, I was sure that they hissed into their headsets 'Watch out for the girl in the jeans and the red shirt. She didn't spend anywhere near long enough looking at the exhibition of black and white photographs of car parts shot from unusual angles.' Not like a proper tourist, trying to give even the least interesting exhibit the right amount of attention to avoid being taken for a Philistine. I've long given up on the idea that there is a 'right' way to look at art. Some pieces take seconds. Others, like my *Country Dog Gentlemen*, need to be regarded for years. On an 'on and off' basis, of course.

In fact, I've been to galleries where the building itself requires closer study than the exhibits it houses, where the quality of the blond wood floors fills me with a yen not unlike the urge I get to run my hands over a Henry Moore sculpture like I'm discovering an exciting new lover. The Getty Museum in Los Angeles, for example. I wonder how many people have experienced what for me is the whole point of JP Getty's self-glorifying edifice? Forget the formal gardens and the water features. Forget the specially imported Travertine marble cladding, hung so that it can sway in an earthquake. The best part of the Getty Museum is an empty corridor, on the way from the tedious mock seventeenth-century French château rooms to the loos. The curved external wall is all window there, floor to ceiling, shaded to block out the So-Cal sun. You can just see the canyons of Bel Air and Beverly Hills through the mesh of the blinds but you can't hear the traffic. And it feels to me like the true heart of the whole building. Empty, not flashy, and quiet. It's the moment of silence between two beats.

The MOMA in San Francisco has a place that feels almost exactly the same. On the top floor, a metal bridge connects the stairs to the gallery. It crosses a bright white atrium with two gigantic circular windows to each side. It's the kind of bridge that turns even the most happy-go-lucky guy into a tentative jumper. To stand on the middle of that bridge is to put yourself into suspended animation. And attract a worried look from one of the midget guards.

That Monday afternoon, I didn't linger on the bridge as long as I wanted to. Two of the school kids came up the stairs behind me, breaking my precious silence, excited to be away from their teacher's censorious eyes.

I stepped quickly into the fifth-floor gallery. Two

middle-aged men (Gay? Definitely. First date? Perhaps.) were peering closely at a picture assembled from newspaper cuttings. I don't suppose either of them were really that interested in the date on the cutting in the right hand bottom corner but it gave them the opportunity to bring their heads a little closer together. The tall one made a comment. The small one laughed almost twitteringly. A classic Rules Girl laugh from a man. They straightened up and looked at each other. How long before he kisses me, each of them thought.

Probably in the next room, I decided. Nathan Oliviera's *Stage No. 2 with bed* was drawing quite a crowd. An almost entirely black canvas at first. But in the middle, you see the bed, like a prop left behind at the end of the play's run. Deep blue-purple sheets tucked in tightly. Hospital corners. The only light in the picture comes from the door which is slightly ajar and a partially open window. Everyone's gone home except the leading lady and the lighting guy. There's a sense that something is about to happen.

That afternoon, a woman standing in front of the painting with her husband pulled her cardigan together at the neckline as though she found herself looking at a nude. Except that nudes are just too obvious, don't you think? Most of them? There's nothing erotic about Lucien Freud's hulking nudes like slabs of meat on a mortuary table. By contrast, *Stage No. 2* worked for that woman because it left everything to the imagination. And she wasn't imagining her husband.

I didn't stop long in front of the Oliviera but I picked up the sense that something was about to happen, too. They move the permanent collection around quite a bit at the MOMA. I wasn't sure where my *Country Dog Gentlemen* would be hanging. As luck would have it, I found my painting in the very next room.

And him.

There was a man standing right in front of my favourite painting. He was dressed in a suit, which seemed odd because he was also scribbling in a notebook that way art students do and I've never seen a student in Armani.

Sensing my presence, he moved from his position centre square in front of the picture to the side to accommodate me and I joined him at the black line on the floor that you cross on pain of death.

He looked at the painting and I looked at him. I took in the profile. Like Michelangelo's David, wouldn't you know it. All heavy, concentrated brow and long straight nose and a jaw line that seemed to be inviting my fingers to check for stubble. His blond hair was cropped short but you could still see the beginnings of a curl. His suit was expensive. Well-cut. Though he clearly had the kind of body that could make off-the-peg look made-to-measure.

I wanted to be able to see into his notebook but it was a very small notebook and he was holding it close to his chest as he scribbled. At one point, his pen strokes became frenetic and I knew he was sketching. Which aspect of the painting, I wondered. I got a little too close in my desperation to find out. He flinched slightly and glanced at me sidelong from beneath his too-long eyelashes. I had to speak to him now. Didn't want him to think I was just some ordinary nosey girl.

'Beautiful, isn't it?' I said.

Oh God, how very original.

He nodded. 'Yes. It is.'

'Is it,' I ventured. Nothing to lose here. 'Is it your favourite painting in the whole wide world?'

For the first time, he turned towards me and gave me the benefit of his full and perfect face. He didn't say anything, but his eyes were already starting to smile. His lips parted slowly to reveal his perfect teeth (why is it so much easier to describe something made in canvas and polymer, than a man in flesh and bone?) and he nodded. He nodded slowly, then he nodded emphatically. 'You know what,' he said. 'I think it is!'

'Amazing!' I said. How the power of eloquent speech had deserted me.

Then I nodded and he nodded and I nodded and he asked, 'It's your favourite too?'

'Of everything. It's just so . . . So . . .'

'I know,' he said.

And I knew that he did.

'You're writing about it,' I observed observantly.

He waved the closed notebook at me as though he was surprised to find it in his hand. 'Just a few notes, a quick sketch,' he said shyly. 'I'm doing an art history class. In my spare time,' he added. 'I'm in health food actually. Doing a convention at the exhibition centre across the road.'

'That's nice.'

'Pays the bills,' he shrugged.

'I'm a writer,' I told him quickly, in case he didn't get round to asking me what I did.

'That must be nice.'

'Sometimes. When I'm not writing brochure copy for health food manufacturers.'

He laughed. Bull's eye. I'd got him with a 'we have so much in common' line. I'd never written brochure copy for a health food manufacturer in my life but I did know how to start a conversation.

'You in San Francisco long?' I followed up.

'Just tonight,' he said. 'I fly back to Denver tomorrow.'

'I'm flying to Sydney in the morning,' I told him. 'Australia,' I added, before he could ask me 'which state' and confirm all those horrible preconceptions about the average American's world view.

'Long way.'

'Fourteen hours,' I nodded at him.

'You'll need to get a good night's rest,' he said.

'I don't know,' I replied a little slyly. 'Might be better to stay up all night.'

'This is a good town to stay up all night in.'

He smiled again, but this time a little wolfishly.

Bingo.

He said he knew a good place for dim sum and five hours later we were still there. He might have had a wife. I did neglect to mention my boyfriend. I ignored the disapproving look from the concierge and took him to my hotel room. We were still talking about art history when we sat down on the king bed. He used his finger to trace a Miro on my bare forearm. When I kicked off my blue trainers he said my toenails were Rothko red.

When he said I had the curves of a Matisse, I knew I had to kiss him. It was a soft kiss to say 'thank you' but he wrapped his arms around me and would not relinquish my mouth. He was as good at kissing as he had been at small-talking. He tasted of green tea and a low tar cigarette shared on the doorstep of the bar.

I liked the way he just took charge of things and tipped me back onto the pillows, like I wasn't nearly as tall as him with shoulders almost as broad. He slid his hand beneath my red shirt and was too impatient to undo the buttons. He made me pull it off over my head and laughed when it got stuck beneath my chin. He lost his jacket as soon as he got into my room and I made him take his tie off. His hair was already all over the place, like the tufts on a lemon meringue.

'You look like a Greek god,' I told him when he took his shirt off.

'Bet you say that to all the boys,' he laughed.

'If only it were always true.'

I ran my hands over his pectoral muscles. Not covered with a caveman rug but not hairless either, thank God. He chewed my neck, like some kind of animal getting hold of its mate's scruff before penetration. It sent an electric shock straight through the heart of me. A good one, though. I groaned.

I grabbed his buttocks in their smart grey slacks and suddenly he was on top of me. Between my legs. His pelvis pressing hard against the buttons on my jeans.

'This is uncomfortable,' I said. The buttons were digging into me.

'Take them off,' he said, wickedly.

I told him, 'I don't know . . .'

I wasn't going to do it, I swear. I have a Clinton-esque approach to fidelity. If he didn't see my knickers then . . . If I could just keep my trousers on . . .

How often would I meet a De Forest fan from heaven?

'You'll have to get off me so that I can get out of them,' I said.

He raised himself up on his arms so that I could wriggle free of my waistband. I got the jeans as far as my thighs. His legs between mine were blocking me from pulling them down further. We did a peculiar horizontal dance and my jeans found their way to the floor.

After that, it didn't seem fair that he got to keep his trousers on while I didn't. We were naked seconds later on top of the cool white sheets. My knickers hung from the bedside lamp. One of his socks ended up in the waste-bin. He made a growling noise into my collar bone that made me quiver and feel weak.

He stopped mauling me for a moment and touched my body much more tenderly. He dipped his head to my nipples reverently. I wrapped my hand around his cock.

We did everything I wasn't going to. I let him put his fingers inside me. I took his long shaft into my mouth and sucked him till he was hard as seaside rock. I had to stop sucking when he started licking me though. When he eased himself inside me, I felt like I wanted to melt.

I've never come like that. Not the first time. Must have been all that foreplay. The mental foreplay. Not just the kissing. Not the way he touched me like he had Grade 8 Making Love. I told him that he was my *Country Dog Gentleman.*

'Dog or gentleman?' He smiled at me. 'I don't know which is worse.'

Afterwards, we lay side by side and watched the ceiling in companionable silence. It was the perfect moment to ask him how he would have disposed of that troublesome ex. Except I didn't ask him anything. I really didn't ask him anything. I didn't even ask him if *Country Dog Gentlemen* was his favourite painting in the world.

That afternoon in San Francisco, I merely stood at the other side of the gallery. While the man in the suit finished sketching. I watched his blond head and his shoulders and the square curve of his butt. I didn't talk to him. Maybe I should have done. But when he walked away from the canvas, I don't think he even noticed me at all.

Just Desserts
Monica McInerney

'Oh Libby, listen to this one: *I'm planning to propose to my girlfriend after dinner, please give me all the help you can!* Oh, how sweet. Can I put his hamper together?'

Libby looked across the large kitchen at her cousin. 'Sure. What's he asked for?'

Sasha read the order form, murmuring under her breath. 'He wants an easy-to-heat soup to start, followed by an easy-to-heat casserole and then an easy-to-heat dessert. God, what's with the easy-to-heat business? Does he live in an igloo?'

'No, he probably means something he can microwave.'

'Well, that's not exactly romantic, is it? Imagine, you're in his arms, he's whispering sweet nothings in your ear, the delicious smell of cooking is wafting through the living room, then *ping*, the microwave goes. Dinner is served.'

Libby grinned. 'Sash, we're caterers not cooking police. He can heat it up with a blow-torch if he wants to.'

'I just think it's a shame. We supply him with the whole package: fantastic food, mood music, coffee table books as conversation starters,' Sasha waved her arms around the room, pointing at the library of books and CDs, 'even real linen serviettes, and he ruins it all with one ping of the microwave.'

Libby was openly laughing at her cousin now. 'Leave that poor man alone. He's obviously so nervous about proposing he can't bear to do the cooking as well. He doesn't need you shouting at him from the sidelines.'

'Well, I just hope his girlfriend knows what she's getting herself into. She might think he's a good cook. What happens when she realises, after she's said yes and it's too late to back out, that he can't cook anything more elaborate than baked beans on toast and he's a big fraud? What does that make us? Accessories after the fact?'

'No, with any luck he'll become completely reliant on us smuggling wonderful meals in to him and become our number one customer.'

Losing interest in that fax, Sasha picked up the next one on the pile. 'Now, what about this one: *My husband has invited his boss over for dinner and, quite frankly, I couldn't cook my way out of a brown paper bag from McDonald's. Help!!!* You're more like a Good Samaritan than a chef, aren't you, Libby? You should change the name of the company, I reckon. From Big Night In to Big Rescue. But then you'd get all sorts of calls from people – cats stuck up trees, kids down drainpipes, wouldn't you? And you'd have to explain that it's actually a catering company, not an emergency rescue outfit.'

Libby stared at her cousin in amazement. Sasha really needed to cut back on the coffee.

'That's right, Sash,' she said carefully. 'Now, how about we start putting the orders together? Can you choose the books and the CDs while I do the shopping lists?'

That worked. For the next fifteen minutes Sasha stood in front of the wall-to-wall library, trying to select coffee table books and CDs to suit each order.

Revelling in the quiet, Libby looked down once again at the food orders in front of her.

She was catering for six formal dinners, one children's party and one Sunday brunch, all for delivery by six o'clock Saturday evening. She cast a quick eye over the dishes her customers had chosen. Nothing too out-landish or out of the ordinary, she was relieved to see. Most people had stuck to the suggested menus she'd supplied, with just one or two exceptions. Gooseberry fool? She wasn't sure if she'd be able to do that one.

Sasha's voice floated over. 'Libby, what does roman-tic music mean, exactly? I mean, it depends on your taste really, doesn't it? Teenagers would find S Club 7 romantic, wouldn't they, but they would scare the willies out of an oldie. And I can't imagine a couple of eighteen-years-olds smooching away to Val Doonican or Nana Mouskouri. Should I ring this bloke and ask him to be a bit more specific, do you think?'

'No!' Libby nearly shouted. It was a good thing her cousin was such a sensational pastrycook, she thought, or she would worry she'd lost all reason hiring her in the first place. 'No, we'll take a punt. What age is he?'

Sasha looked at the form again. 'Oh, he's ancient. Over fifty. Euch! And he's trying to be all romantic. Isn't that the most disgusting thought? Two old people –'

'Sasha! What should he be doing? Ironing his lawn bowls outfit and watching black and white movies?' And fifty isn't so old, Libby didn't say out loud. She was only fifteen years off it herself. Oh my God, she thought, realising how true that was.

Sasha laughed. 'Sorry, I'm terrible, aren't I? Just as well you're here to curb my excesses. So let me think. Romantic music. How about a bit of Bach? And then a bit of Burt Bacharach. Bach and Bacharach, geddit? As a kind of theme? Bach-ground for a Bach-analian feast.'

Libby just put her head on the counter and groaned. 'Sasha, isn't it time you went to the market?'

Sasha looked at her watch.

'It's a bit early, isn't it?'

'No. Goodbye.'

After Sasha had gone, Libby took a moment to relax and have a cup of coffee.

She picked up the order form from the man who wanted to propose to his girlfriend. How sweet. And how heartening. Romance was alive and well for a lucky fifty-year-old.

Maybe there was hope for this single thirty-five-year-old yet, she thought.

Libby came in early the next day. Friday was Big Night In's most frantic day. There were usually a couple of last-minute orders waiting on the fax machine, despite the plea on their promotional brochure that Thursday was the deadline.

Sure enough, there were two faxes waiting. She'd look through them before Sasha had the chance to grab them and give her running commentary.

The first one was easy – an order for everything need-ed for a barbecue. *Can you please send us fish, chicken, sausages and lots of salads – don't need the books or the CDs, thanks!* Great. She liked that sort of order.

Libby picked up the second fax. Her heart nearly stopped.

It was from Hayley Kemp.

Hayley Kemp. She couldn't believe it. Hayley Kemp was daring to order a meal from her.

She read it quickly. It was definitely the same Hayley Kemp she used to know. Libby even recognised the handwriting. She was surprised Hayley had managed to fill out the order herself. Didn't she have slaves to do this sort of thing these days?

It was a very specific order. Hayley wanted the most up-to-date and innovative Australian cuisine possible. Asian fusion. Bush tucker. All and everything. She want-ed two different entrées. Three different main courses. Four – four! – desserts. The latest CDs, all by Australian artists. The latest books, all from Australian authors. There was even a long list of the newspapers and mag-azines she would like Big Night In to supply.

Libby couldn't believe her eyes. What did Hayley Kemp think she was? A caterer or a set decorator?

She heard the door open behind her. It was Sasha.

'Hi there, Lib. More orders? Gee, people can be thoughtless, can't they? Don't they realise we can't just magic their orders out of nowhere? Anything too complicated?'

Libby just handed her Hayley Kemp's order.

Sasha looked down and gave a low whistle. 'Hayley Kemp? *The* Hayley Kemp?'

Libby nodded. The Hayley Kemp indeed. Socialite. Author. Snob. Idea-snatcher. Client-snatcher. Boyfriend-snatcher.

Yes, that Hayley Kemp.

'You used to work with her, didn't you?' Sasha asked. 'Up in Sydney? Wasn't she that old cow that nicked all your ideas?'

That was putting it mildly, Libby thought. 'Yes, Sasha, *that* old cow. That old schemer. You know the whole story?'

Sasha shook her head. 'Only bits of it. Come on, spill the beans.' She sat down opposite Libby and waited, bright-eyed. She loved a good gossip.

Libby sat down too. 'Hayley and I met at catering school, twelve years ago. We went into business together, running a corporate catering company. It went fine for the first year. Until I realised she was stealing all my ideas and passing them off as her own, to private clients she was working for, outside our company. And then she went further – she started contacting our clients on the sly and undercutting our prices, offering to do it on her own, more cheaply. Turned out she'd been planning to open her own company, using all my contacts and recipes.'

Sasha was wide-eyed. 'How dare she!'

'How dare she is right. She was quite ruthless about it. And then I discovered she wanted my boyfriend as part of the package, too.'

'That's *awful*,' Sasha breathed. 'She took your clients *and* your boyfriend?'

Libby nodded. She should have guessed much earlier than she did. All the flirting. On both sides. But it had been an awful shock to come home to the flat one night after catering for a corporate function and find her boyfriend in bed already. With Hayley.

'And that's why you haven't had a boyfriend since? You've never got over him?'

Libby was a little stung. 'I have had the occasional boyfriend, Sasha. You make it sound like I've been living in purdah for ten years. No, actually, I did get over him. That night, in fact. I got over a lot that night.'

Libby had dissolved the company there and then. In her bedroom. She'd practically thrown her boyfriend and Hayley out of the house. She'd considered legal action to get her clients back and copyright action to get her recipes credited. Then she'd realised that neither action was worth the bother. The legal fees would bankrupt her.

So she'd decided to just cut her losses and start over.

She'd moved to Melbourne and started up her own business again. Hundreds of kilometres from Ms Sneaky Trousers Kemp.

But now Ms Sneaky Trousers had come visiting.

Sasha was reading through her order form. 'Wow,

she's really got a big evening planned, hasn't she? And look at the address.'

Libby looked over her shoulder. Oh, please don't say Hayley had moved to Melbourne. Please let her just be visiting. This city wasn't big enough for the two of them. No city was big enough for Hayley Kemp.

Sasha whistled. 'The Riverview Hotel Apartments. They're the sensational ones right in the city centre. With all the penthouses. I saw a full-page ad in the paper on the weekend. They've only just opened.'

That would be Hayley, Libby thought. Staying in the trendiest spot in town before anyone else. She wondered who she'd conned to get into there. She was probably staying in the show apartment. It wouldn't be the first time she'd done that.

Hayley was obviously trying to impress someone. Who? Libby wondered.

Hayley had written a mobile number on the fax. Libby couldn't help herself. 'Sasha, can you do me a favour? Ring that number and say you're just looking for some more details about her order. Find out as much as you can, will you? I can't do it, she'll recognise my voice.'

Sasha leapt at the idea. She picked up the phone, cleared her throat and dialled the number.

'Ms Kemp? Good morning. Sasha Delahunty here, from Big Night In caterers. Thank you so much for your order, it is clear you appreciate quality and excellence.'

Libby had to stop herself laughing. Sasha sounded like she'd spent the past twenty years at a Swiss finishing school.

'No, no, there's no problem at all with your order. It will be our utmost pleasure to meet your every need. But perhaps you can just give me a little more detail about the evening, so we can be sure we have the complete picture and can fulfil your every request.'

Sasha wandered over to the other side of the room. Libby could hear snatches of the conversation.

'Mmm. Yes. Is that right? What a marvellous compliment. Oh yes, indeed, I can think of no finer ambassador for our country's cuisine than you. Yes, of course. By six o'clock. Yes, of course. Thank you, Ms Kemp. Yes, goodbye now.'

She hung up and spun around, grinning at Libby. 'Gee, what a blabbermouth. It's all for an interview she's doing. For a big colour feature in some international magazine. *Foresee* or something, have you heard of it?'

Libby nodded. Of course she'd heard of *4C* magazine. She even bought it occasionally. It was the trendsetter's bible, its articles highlighting ideas and fashions months – or sometimes years – in advance. How in God's name had Hayley Kemp managed to pull off an interview with that magazine? And why was she doing it in Melbourne, she asked aloud.

Sasha shrugged. 'She said something about Sydney being so yesterday. Everyone's sick of it since the Olympics, she said. So she's doing the interview here. She said that Melbourne is the new Sydney.'

'Melbourne is the new Sydney? So where does that leave the old Sydney? The real Sydney?'

Sasha shrugged again. 'Dunno. So, anyway, they're

doing a feature on her. Dinner with Hayley Kemp. Food for the new century or some such thing, she said.'

Libby felt her blood begin to simmer. Then boil. Sasha watched, quite amazed, as mild-mannered Libby blew her top.

'No way, Sasha! Absolutely no way! She did it to me ten years ago, she's not doing it again. Nicking my ideas. Passing them off as her own. To hell with her order. I won't do it.'

Sasha looked a little uncomfortable. 'Um, actually, Libby, she didn't mention you. At all. She probably doesn't even realise it's your company.'

That stopped Libby in her tracks.

'She didn't mention me? At all? Really?'

'No, she just said she'd heard Big Night In was the most innovative of Melbourne's caterers.'

'Did she?'

'She also said money was no object. And she was happy to pay in advance if necessary.'

'By cheque?' Libby didn't trust her. That woman had bounced more cheques than Libby had made hot dinners.

'She didn't say.' Sasha was watching her very closely. 'But we can insist on cash. Was she that bad, Lib?'

'She was that bad.'

Sasha beamed. 'So. Have your revenge. Give her an awful meal. Show her up in front of this journalist.'

Libby gave a slow smile. She was tempted. What could Hayley do? If she was going to attempt to pass it off as her own cooking, there'd be no one she could blame, either . . .

She thought about it. She was more than tempted. She was really tempted.

Sasha was watching her, all eager-eyed, ready to burst into action.

Then Libby came to her senses and shook her head. It was nearly ten years ago. She'd put it all behind her, surely. She had a very successful business now. It was time she got over Hayley.

'No, Sasha, I don't think so. We won't do anything.' She was glad to hear herself sound like the grown-up voice of reason. 'That's the thing about running a business. You have to learn how to keep your personal feelings separate. Be professional.'

'Oh, Libby, come on. It'd be funny.'

'No, Sasha, I can't do it.'

'Even though she was such a bitch to you in Sydney?'

'Even so.'

'That's your final word?'

'That's my final word.'

'Rats,' Sasha said.

By five o'clock on Saturday, the Big Night In kitchen was an absolute hive of activity.

Libby and Sasha had been joined by Alan, the other apprentice chef. The hampers were laid out in long rows. The food was being assembled on the stainless-steel counters, all in the distinctive Big Night In foil containers.

Sasha had just finished putting the last of the CDs, books and magazines into one of the hampers.

'Are you sure the barbecue people didn't want any

CDs, Libby?' she called across to her cousin. 'I could put in Cheap Trick's "The Flame", or "Burn for You" by INXS.'

Alan joined in. 'Or what's that old song by Paul Young? You know, that ballad. He burst into song: "Every time you go away, you take a piece of meat with you".'

'It's "piece of me", not meat,' Sasha said, snorting with laughter.

Libby grinned. 'Thanks, Sasha, thanks, Alan, that'll be fine. Are we all done? Can I ring the courier?'

They both nodded. The hampers were all lined up, ready to go.

Libby dialled the number. 'Tim? Ready to go when you are. Two loads tonight, okay? See you soon.'

A little while later, Sasha and Libby sat down to enjoy a glass of wine. Alan had gone home for the night, after helping them to load the first lot of hampers into the back of Tim's van.

'You sure you're okay to help Tim with the other four?' he'd checked with Libby before he left. 'It's a filthy night, with that wind and rain.'

Libby had waved him away. 'No worries, Alan. See you next week.'

Libby had just taken a sip of wine when her mobile rang. 'Big Night In, good evening.'

She listened for a few minutes. 'Oh, Tim, that's awful. Are you okay? The van's okay? And the hampers? You'd already delivered them? No, of course you can't. No, don't worry. Sasha and I are here. We can do them ourselves. Really. Go home, Tim. And don't worry, really.'

She finished the call and turned to Sasha. 'Tim's had an accident. He says the roads are really slippery and the wind has brought some trees down. He didn't see them till it was too late. Nothing serious, but his van's off the road. There's no time to organise another courier. We'll have to deliver the last four hampers ourselves. Do you mind?'

Sasha shook her head. 'No, I'm not going out till nine anyway. Which ones will I do?'

Libby checked the addresses. One in south Melbourne. One in west Melbourne. And two in the inner city.

Including the one to Hayley Kemp.

Well, there was no way she was going to deliver that one.

'Will you do Hayley, Sasha? And the other inner-city one? Do you mind?'

'Mind? I'd love to. I can slip a little broken glass into her soup at the last minute. A couple of lizards into her salad. She wanted authentic Australian cuisine, didn't she? And you won't mind, will you?'

Libby wasn't sure if her cousin was joking. 'Sasha,' she warned, 'you won't, will you? Promise me?'

Sasha laughed. 'Of course I won't touch her food. I promise. Cross my heart.'

Libby checked her watch. She'd have to get going to make her deliveries to the outer suburbs in time.

'Can you lock up, Sasha, and manage those two hampers?'

'Trust me, dear cousin. Trust me. What is friendship without trust?'

Libby rolled her eyes. Friendship without trust. That was a summary of her friendship with Hayley Kemp, actually. She ruffled her cousin's hair. 'Thanks, Sash. See you Monday.'

Not long after Libby had driven off, Sasha turned off the lights and locked the front door.

She had just climbed into her car and was about to start the engine when she remembered she'd left her street directory in the boot with her two hampers.

She jumped out and opened the hatch. A gust of wind swept in, nearly tearing the door off its hinges. Two pieces of paper started flapping around. Sasha caught them just in time. And just as well, she thought. The delivery addresses were written on them. She secured them back onto the hampers and shut the hatch again.

As she got back into the car and started the engine, she looked back at the hampers. She had put the right addresses on the right hampers, hadn't she?

After all, she wouldn't want to make a mistake, would she? Like accidentally deliver Hayley Kemp's hamper to the other address. And the other hamper to Hayley Kemp.

Not when their contents were so drastically different.

That would never do, would it? she thought, a smile starting to form. She would hate to ruin Hayley Kemp's night. Ms Hayley Old Cow Kemp. Who had been so mean to her lovely cousin Libby all those years ago.

Who was so obviously still trying to pass off Libby's ideas as her own.

Sasha stopped the car suddenly. She couldn't think and drive at the same time.

She had promised Libby, hand on heart, that she wouldn't touch the food in the hampers.

But she hadn't promised she wouldn't make a simple mistake and deliver the hampers to the wrong address, now, had she?

She looked at her watch. Made her decision. Grinned and started the car.

She'd have to drive fast or she'd be late.

Good. She *loved* driving fast.

On the other side of Melbourne, Libby had just delivered the second of her hampers.

She was still smiling from the conversation. The fifty-year-old man was a true romantic. His house had looked lovely, the fire flickering in the grate, candles lit. It looked so cosy, especially with the wild weather howling outside.

Libby couldn't wait to get home. She was always wrecked by Saturday night. The last thing she felt like was going out. She'd go home to her little flat, heat up a casserole, open a bottle of wine, light the fire and have a nice, long soak in the bath . . .

Her mobile phone rang. Uh oh, she thought. Sasha.

It wasn't Sasha, though.

It was a male voice. But the line was so bad it kept breaking up. Oh hell, Libby thought, remembering that she hadn't charged her mobile that morning. They'd been so busy she'd forgotten. She checked the battery. It was right down.

She pulled over. Maybe that would help. She could get this call at least. And then recharge the battery as soon as she got home. 'I'm very sorry, could you say all that again?'

The voice crackled, breaking up now and again. 'Is th– Big Ni– In? The caterers?'

'Yes,' Libby shouted. 'Libby Smith speaking.'

'Hello, Lib–, this is Ned Ra– I'm lookin– aft– er my– bir–day par–y. Ord–ed the foo– you. –t of a prob– can you–'

Libby felt like shaking the mobile. She'd only got a bit of that. But had she heard the word problem? She didn't like that word. Not on her work mobile.

'There's a problem with your order, did you say? Ned, is it? What kind of problem?'

'I –n't qu– know what to –'

This was no good, Libby thought.

'Where are you?'

He had to repeat his address three times before she got it.

'I'm not far from you. I'll be there soon,' she shouted.

Fifteen minutes later she pulled up in front of a small terraced house.

There was a bedraggled bunch of balloons tied to the gate, being buffeted by the gusty wind.

Libby clambered out and ran up the path, ducking her head against the rain.

She knocked at the door.

An agitated orange-haired clown answered.

'Ned?' she said, trying not to laugh.

'Libby? From the caterers?'

She nodded.

He smiled a big, clowny smile. 'Thank you so much for coming by. I'm sorry to sound so stupid, I'm actually just supposed to be helping my sister out. But she works in the emergency services and got called away to help with the storms. So I've been left in charge and, quite frankly, I'm baffled.'

It was a little bit hard to take a man in a frizzy orange wig seriously. She had to ask. 'And your clothes? Are you normally dressed like this?'

He laughed then. 'Believe me, this is the first time. And the last, too. My sister asked me when I was jet-lagged last week and I was in no sound mind to say no. It's her daughter's birthday party.'

Libby followed him inside as they spoke. 'Jetlagged? Where had you flown from?'

'Canada,' he said. 'I've been working over there for the past four years. Just came home last week.'

She nodded. She thought he had a touch of an accent. 'Well, lead me to the kids. And the hamper. What exactly is the problem?'

He looked very embarrassed again. 'I hope you don't think I'm too thick. Debbie, my sister, said she'd ordered a whole lot of kids' food from you. But I'm just not sure how to serve it.'

Libby remembered the order now. It was standard kids' party food. No tricks to serving it. Poor man must still be jetlagged.

Libby walked into the living room. It was like walking into a fairy glen. Eight little girls, all dressed as fairies, were waving their wands and doing trit-trotty dances across the floor.

Music was blaring out of the CD player. Libby winced. It was some sort of modern jazz. All squealing trumpets and snare drums. Very modern kids in this house, by the sound of things.

Libby followed Ned into the kitchen. The hamper Sasha had delivered was on the counter, with a long row of little foil containers lined up beside it.

'It won't take me a moment to sort all this out,' Libby said cheerily. 'Those kids must be getting very hungry.'

'They're like wild animals,' Ned admitted. 'Hyenas. Ready to tear me limb from limb with hunger. It's more like *Dances with Wolves* in there than *Swan Lake*.'

She grinned at him. He was really very sweet. She wondered what he looked like without all that face make-up. And that orange wig. And dressed in something other than a baggy orange all-in-one suit.

'Well, don't worry, I'll have them fed in just a moment.' Libby opened the first container and her stomach gave a flip. She opened the second. Then the third. And the fourth. Faster and faster, until they were all open.

She looked down at them. Then looked up at Ned.

He smiled again, the effect spoilt a little by the mad make-up. 'I'm happy to help serve it to them. I'm just not sure where to start.'

Libby swallowed. She could tell him where to start.

It was quite easy. You started with the sushi and sashimi. Followed by the emu pâté. Then the wattleseed pasta. Then the other six dishes which perfectly demonstrated innovative Australian cuisine.

It was obvious what had happened. Sasha had dropped off the wrong basket. Which meant that she had dropped off the wrong basket to the other address, too.

Which meant that around about now, just a few kilometres away, Hayley Kemp was probably opening her hamper. Opening her little foil containers. And preparing to serve the influential *4C* magazine journalist a fine dinner of Vegemite sandwiches. Mashed potato and sausages. Aeroplane jelly and lolly snakes.

Washed down with hot, milky Milo.

With the *Best of the Wiggles* CD playing in the background.

Libby looked at her watch. There was still time. She could pack this up again. Drive across town. Switch the hampers. Make sure Hayley Kemp's evening wasn't ruined after all. Or . . .

She could turn down the volume on her mobile.

Switch it off, even. Because she'd bet a million dollars it was just about to ring.

She could reassure Ned that everything was just fine. That this was standard Australian children's party fare these days. Tell him a lot had changed while he'd been in Canada.

She looked at him. He looked back at her. She noticed what lovely eyes he had. The blue clown make-up seemed to accentuate the colour.

There was a sudden chant from the living room.

'We want food! We want food! We want food!'

Ned looked really worried. Scared, almost. He touched her arm briefly. 'Libby, if you stay, I owe you. For ever. Lunch, dinner, whatever you like.'

That clinched it.

'Of course I'll stay. And don't worry, this food looks much scarier than it is. It won't take me a minute to show the girls how to use chopsticks. Or eat the pâté. If we need to, we'll tell them it's magical fairy food from a land far, far away . . .'

He smiled in relief. 'Thanks, Libby.'

She smiled back. 'It's my pleasure, really.' She reached into her handbag and turned off her mobile phone. 'Now then, where would we find the plates?'

One hour later, the little girls were having sword fights with the chopsticks Libby had found in the bottom of a kitchen cupboard.

But Libby and Ned hardly noticed them. They were too busy talking, eating and laughing.

Four months later, Libby and Ned were curled up on her sofa, reading the Sunday newspapers and finishing their Thai takeaway.

The afternoon sunshine spilled into their flat. A light breeze ruffled the curtains at the open window behind them.

'More wine, sweetheart?' Ned said.

Libby looked up. 'Oh, great, thanks Ned.' She held up her glass and smiled at him as he poured the wine. She loved their Sunday lunches. Long, leisurely afternoons that usually stretched into long, leisurely nights together.

He grinned at her. His smile still made her heart skip. And his eyes had turned out to be even nicer without the clown make-up. Who'd have thought such a treasure was lurking under that bright orange wig and costume that night?

Ned refilled his own glass, then went back to the newspaper. The room was quiet for a moment.

Then he laughed out loud. 'People really are unbelievable. Listen to this, Lib. *A respected trend-forecasting magazine has predicted a return to childhood food as the next big thing in cuisine, with an Australian food expert playing a major role in the resurgence.*'

Libby looked up. Childhood food? Australian food expert? No, surely not?

Ned read on.

'*In the new issue of* 4C *magazine, Sydney-based food queen Hayley Kemp explains the new theory. "As the world gets faster and more impersonal I believe we will all be looking for safety and a return to the innocence of childhood. It isn't so much a fashion statement as a return to traditional values, in food as well as behaviour."*'

Libby shut her eyes. Hayley could have. Hayley had.

Ned looked at her and smiled. 'Come on now, Lib. Pay attention, your customers will be queuing up for this soon.' He started reading aloud again. '*If Hayley and her fellow futurists have their way, dinner parties of the future will feature simple fare like Vegemite sandwiches, sausages and mashed potato, hot milky Milo to drink and for dessert . . .*'

Libby interrupted. 'Don't tell me, Ned. Jelly and lolly snakes?'

He looked up in surprise. Libby was now lying stretched out on the sofa, the cushion over her face. She seemed to be groaning. Or laughing. He couldn't tell which. 'Yes, jelly and lolly snakes for dessert. Sorry, Libby, have you read this already?'

She looked up at him, shook her head and smiled. 'No. No, I haven't.'

'Then I'm even more impressed with you. You really do have your finger on the catering pulse, don't you?'

She stood up suddenly, came over to him and planted a big kiss right on his lips.

'Yes, I do, don't I?'

Then she took the newspaper out of his hand and threw it out of the window.

The Fortune Teller
Santa Montefiore

'I'll steal away in the dark like a common whore,' she breathed, running a long nail down his torso. Then she laughed. But her laughter was uneasy. It no longer felt appropriate to make light of their affair. It had been too long and her lover was restless for an answer. She watched the smoke of her cigarette mingle with the flamingo light of evening then disappear altogether, taking with it what little remained of their enchanted limbo. It was late, her husband would be home soon and wonder where she was.

'When will you steal away with *me*?' he asked, his poet's eyes searching her features anxiously for her thoughts. After all they had been through she still resisted telling him the truth. She still tormented him with her evasiveness, unless, of course, she was too ashamed to admit the truth even to herself. Finally his impatience overcame his caution and he exclaimed in exasperation, 'You don't want to sacrifice your status and your wealth for the simple love of a man who can give you nothing more than love.'

She stared at him in astonishment and for a moment he thought she would slip out of bed, dress and leave in fury like she had done once before when he had unintentionally caused her offence. But to his relief her expression softened. She no longer looked angry; she just looked sad.

'How can you think so little of me?' she replied, stubbing her cigarette out and sitting up on the edge of his iron bed. 'You're not the only love in my life. I have my children to think about too,' she argued.

'They're almost grown up, you said so yourself. They don't need you like they used to,' he reasoned. Then he too sat up and pulled her into his arms. 'For God's sake, Stella,' he begged, 'I love you.'

'And I love you, with every nerve in my body,' she exclaimed, almost angrily. 'Don't think that when I lie beside my husband at night my thoughts aren't with you, that every moment of the day I'm not calculating when and imagining how. Darling, be patient. I promise you I will leave him. When the time is right.'

She looked about the familiar attic where so many hours of love vibrated in the dull fabric of the curtains, in the plain wooden walls and in the endless piles of poetry and prose that lay unpublished in loose stacks on the desk beneath the skylight. Witnessed only by the pair of pigeons that surveyed the busy street below from the windowsill and the Vietnamese pig that softly grunted on the sofa, their illicit afternoons of pleasure were concealed from the world.

They had met two winters before in the bookshop downstairs. Undetected by the incisive Mrs Schulz, who rarely missed such delicious fodder for gossip, they had talked behind the self-help section where Stella had been searching for a way through her unhappiness. She hadn't expected her search to lead her to such an extreme remedy. She hadn't been looking for an affair. Besides, she knew her husband would kill her if she so much as looked at another man. But nothing could have prepared her for the force of love which, like the blast of a volcano, felled every obstacle in its path, reducing her reservations to ashes. Suddenly nothing else mattered but him. Her husband's rage, her children's sorrow, her mother's disappointment and her own dignity – she would have sacrificed everything for a night of sweet indulgence in the arms of this stranger.

She talked with animation and yet she wasn't aware of anything she said. She watched his lips move and suppressed the ardent desire to kiss him by pulling out a book and flicking through the pages absent-mindedly. But he had recognised her longing, for it reflected his own. 'I live above the shop,' he had said, 'with a pig and a couple of pigeons for company, and I write unpublishable prose and poetry.' Then he had laughed and the lines that creased around his mouth and eyes had enchanted her so that she too had laughed. Mrs Schulz shuffled past, filling the gaps in the shelves, one bulbous eye on the pile of books she was carrying and one on the attractive woman with the expensive coat and handbag. Then he had asked her out for a drink. Aware that she was being watched, she agreed and followed him into the street. But they had walked no more than twenty paces when he had turned and said, 'This is ridiculous. What am I doing taking you to some sterile café when I really want to take you to my attic and introduce you to Gunter? If we buy some milk I'll make you tea myself.' She had laughed at his forwardness but she had accepted his offer without hesitation. Unhappiness makes one reckless and she had suffered enough unhappiness to be prepared to risk anything for a taste of joy.

His attic was cold and damp and the tea too strong for her liking and yet she had found his simple abode pleasantly quaint and refreshingly understated. Gunter the pig had warmed to her immediately, rubbing his snout against her leg, begging to be scratched. Yet with the discretion of a true gentleman he had retreated to his sofa and closed his eyes at the first indication of intimacy. Stella had relished her first act of rebellion against her husband. She had committed adultery with the enthusiasm of the newly converted. With this stranger she could be anyone she wanted to be and with zealous abandon she made up for the years of insensitive lovemaking at the hands of her impassive husband.

But the initial fervour had cooled with time. At the beginning she had been prepared to run away with him, but he hadn't been ready to take her. Later she had grown complacent, for his love was absolute and unconditional. She had become accustomed to her duplicitous life and reaped the benefits of both. Then he had begged her to leave her husband.

Now she pulled away from her recollections and turned to face her lover, whose languid eyes she knew more intimately than her own, and recognised that she could never give him up. He had sustained her through her unhappiness and given her the will to go on. He made her laugh, he made her feel attractive. With her lover she wasn't a wife or a mother, just Stella. But without her husband she was nothing.

Her impulses told her to run away with him, to live simply in a hot place and exist on the rarefied air of their love. After all, money, titles and status were nothing without love. But her vanity clung onto the lifestyle to which she had become so attached; it was only with the thought of relinquishing it that she realised how much she depended on it. She enjoyed the comfort of her large home, the convenience of staff, the pleasures of shopping in designer stores without even looking at the price tags. She took pride in the way she looked, which all depended on regular visits to the beautician and the hairdresser. She was accustomed to travelling first class and to the luxury of the new Mercedes-Benz. At the same time she adored the simple, poetic life of her attic world, which was an uplifting antidote to the other. But she couldn't have both. He was forcing her to choose and she feared that if she hesitated for much longer she might lose him for ever.

'All right,' she conceded wearily. 'I'll go and see your witch, maybe she'll advise me what to do.' He dropped his shoulders with relief.

'I knew you would,' he said happily and gathered her into his arms. 'I want to sail away with you and live on a distant shore, make love to the sounds of the sea and the scents of exotic plants. I want to take you away from the pressures of the city, the cold indifference of your controlling husband and watch you blossom in freedom.' Disarmed by his smile her anxiety faded, and she stretched out beneath the hypnotic sensation of his hands on her skin.

The next day she followed his directions and knocked on the door of Maggie Broom, the clairvoyant whose company he sometimes sought when he needed reassurance which no one else could give. According to him, Maggie had predicted their meeting two years before and she had predicted the baby that Stella had conceived and lost in the small attic above the bookshop. Now she arrived with a suspended heart because she knew, whichever the choice, the half she left behind would torment her for ever.

Maggie lay on a divan, draped in purple robes and surrounded by overfed ginger cats. Her long red hair was piled up on the top of her head like a tidy nest for some unsuspecting bird and her long red nails played with the beads that disappeared into the cushions of her bosom. The room was small and in dire need of repair, with an overpowering smell of cat urine that stuck in Stella's throat and made her retch. 'I've been expecting you,' Maggie breathed in a deep voice, indicating with a wave of her hand that Stella should sit in the armchair opposite.

'So you know why I'm here,' she replied, perching on the edge of the chair and glancing around in the hope of finding a window to open. There was none, just the dim light from a naked bulb that hung from the ceiling. Maggie smiled, an incomplete grin that hung crooked on her sallow face, and nodded slowly.

'I know why you're here,' she replied, in a tone of voice that suggested she could read her innermost thoughts.

'You know everything.' Stella chuckled, in an attempt to conceal her resentment.

'No. I don't know why it took you so long.'

'Because, with respect, I don't believe in people like you,' she retorted, longing to add that if she really did know anything she'd get rid of the stench.

'That's all right,' she laughed, 'I have enough belief in myself for the two of us.'

'So how does this work?' Stella asked, hoping it would be quick. She was finding it hard to breathe without wincing.

'Give me your hand,' she instructed simply.

'So, no cards or crystal balls?'

'I'm not a gypsy,' she replied indignantly. 'I can read your vibrations from here. I don't need a crystal ball.' Stella obediently extended her hand. To her surprise Maggie's hands were cold. She watched as the clairvoyant closed her eyes.

'Ah, I see your lover,' she began. 'He's waiting above the bookshop for your return. He's very anxious. His love for you is genuine.' Stella sighed impatiently. 'But you don't need me to tell you that. Now I can see your husband. My, what a handsome man he is, if you don't mind me saying.'

'Some think so,' Stella replied dryly. She had found him handsome once, before the tedious familiarity of his features had dulled her awareness. She looked about her and noticed the cats were all staring at her with menace. She had never much liked cats, but these were the most disagreeable looking creatures she had ever encountered.

'No, you're disenchanted with him. As well you might be. He's incapable of love because he received none as a child. He doesn't know what it means. Poor man, he's a prisoner, but why should you try to rescue him? You feel nothing for him now but loathing. Yes, I can feel the hatred in your energy as I speak of him. Take a deep breath, my dear, he can only hurt you if you let him.' Stella stopped gazing around the room and began to listen to the witch's words with her full attention. 'You weren't to know what a poor, emotionally crippled man he was when you married him. He was so glamorous and rich, and as a young girl you thought that was all you needed. He dazzled you with material things to make up for the affection he could not give you. He was incapable of giving it. You believed his generosity to be an expression of his devotion, not a gilded collar to control you with. But misery followed as it surely would. You began to dry up like a plant in the desert. It surprised you, but it shouldn't have. Material things are worth nothing without love. You know that now, but it is only due to years of unhappiness that you have learned that valuable lesson. When your children could no longer satisfy your need for love you found it in the arms of a hopeless writer – a poor, hopeless writer. How ironic life is! Can you sacrifice those material comforts for the simple love of a man who has nothing but a big, generous heart?' Maggie laughed with scorn. 'You need your husband more than you know,' she added.

'Like a hole in the head,' Stella replied flippantly. But Maggie didn't laugh. Her eyelids suddenly began to flutter about as if she had lost control of them and her lips trembled before sagging like two dry slugs. Stella watched transfixed as the witch's face imploded like a burst balloon.

'I see a black Porsche,' she continued in a low voice, articulating her words with deliberation. Her large bosom heaved as her breathing became shallow and staggered. Stella straightened up, barely daring to breathe. Her husband's car was a black Porsche. 'I see death,' Maggie declared, then dropped Stella's hand as if it had grown too hot to hold.

'Whose?' Stella whispered urgently. 'Whose death do you see?' But Maggie opened her eyes and shook her head.

'I couldn't see, but I saw a black Porsche and then death. I can tell you no more than that.' Stella sank back into the armchair, not wanting the meeting to finish. In her curiosity to discovery the identity of the corpse she had even ceased to be aware of the stench.

'How can you possibly see death without a face?' she asked in frustration.

'Sometimes death does not wish to be recognised,' Maggie replied darkly.

'Was it my husband?' Stella insisted, without

attempting to hide the hope in her voice.

'Does he drive a black Porsche?'

'Yes.'

'Then it must be your husband.' Maggie conceded, drawing a cat onto her lap and stroking it with a shaking hand. Death always managed to surprise her.

'Then I have the answer I came looking for, although it wasn't the one I expected to hear,' she said brightly, getting up. 'You see, Maggie,' she continued indiscreetly, 'if my husband were to die I could keep my lover *and* my lifestyle.'

'You no longer have a choice to make,' Maggie nodded slowly. 'How fortunate you are that your decision has been taken out of your hands.'

'I must go back to the attic and tell him,' she enthused, 'then I will go home and wait.' She added as an afterthought, 'How soon can I expect it?'

'Imminently,' Maggie replied, still visibly shaken. 'Imminently.'

Maggie watched as Stella left a fifty-pound note on the table and let herself out. The session was only worth twenty.

With a buoyant step she strode down the wet streets towards the bookshop where her lover waited for her, his pen poised above a blank sheet of paper, but in his agitated state he could find nothing to write. She knew she shouldn't be glad that her husband was destined to die in a car crash, it was a gruesome way to die, but she couldn't suppress the joy that rose in her spirit like bubbles and almost lifted her off the ground. She would hold onto her status and his money, mourn with the dignity of a loving wife, then in the fullness of time introduce her lover as the man who had rescued her from the depths of despair and taught her how to love again. It would be a romantic end to a tragic story and be sure to move everyone. She would have their sympathy and their support. She would play each part with the skill of a professional actor. With great relish she envisaged the funeral. She would wear a little black suit with black leather boots to show off her legs to their best advantage. She would wear little jewellery and barely any make-up, just enough to make her look pale and suitably grief-stricken. She then worried about who would make the hat. Should it be large or small, with or without netting, what would be appropriate? Her husband would no longer control the money, she would. He would no longer tell her what to do and when to do it. She would be the master of her own destiny and yes, she would allow her lover to make love to her on a distant shore, to the sound of the sea and the scents of exotic plants. She would blossom under his caress but also with the power her new independence would give her. Finally, she'd have the best of both her worlds.

As her mind hung in a magical tomorrow she saw the orange glow of the skylight above the bookshop where her lover awaited her. She raised her eyes anticipating his delight and stepped out into the road. She was too busy dreaming to look to her left and right. Suddenly she heard the screeching of brakes but she had no time to react. With a dull thud she felt the full force of the car hit her legs and throw her onto the bonnet, where she crashed against the windscreen before rolling off onto the damp pavement. She lay inert, blinking in bewilderment at her own misfortune. She felt no pain, just the rapid draining away of her life as the blood trickled into the gutter.

Before she closed her eyes to the eternal blackness of death she saw a smug ginger cat leap onto the bonnet of the black Porsche and then spring off the other side, disappearing altogether.

No Strings Attached

Alexandra Potter

The tequila slammers had seemed like a good idea at the time. But what wouldn't after four glasses of house white, two vodka tonics and too many Marlboro Lights? A bungee jump? A perm?

'*A blind date?*' Choking back the Jose Cuervo fumes I stared at Kate who was draped across the leather button-backed sofa like a pashmina – aerobics-firmed thighs crossed, Wonderbra cleavage displayed. Whacking her glass on the table, she dived on a bowl of mixed olives and sun-dried tomato ciabatta.

'Oh, c'mon Jess, I wouldn't call it a blind date. You already know the guy you're meeting . . .' She paused from scraping the purple flesh off a Kalamata with her front teeth.

'Hardly . . .'

'You've spoken to him.'

'Only on the mobile . . .'

'So? The only time Jon and I *ever* spoke to each other was on our mobiles.' She dropped the olive-stone into the ashtray, swilled out her mouth with the lukewarm dregs in her wineglass and lit up a cigarette.

'That's probably why you broke up after three months,' I pointed out. In the four years I'd known Kate, she'd met, slept with, and discarded dozens of men. Jon, the accountant who wore novelty cuff links and a pinky ring, had been the most recent to be told 'thanks, but no thanks'.

'I doubt it. To be honest I think that's how we managed to stay together for so long. Whenever we did meet we only ever ended up arguing . . .' Reaching for another piece of ciabatta she dug out the marbled streaks of sun-dried tomato and discarded the bread. After reading an article in *Marie Claire*, she'd self-diagnosed a wheat allergy – it was this, and not McDonald's round the corner, that was responsible for her jeans being too tight. 'Anyway we're not talking about me, we're talking about you and your mystery admirer.'

I felt my cheeks flush and it wasn't the wine. Sometimes telling Kate everything wasn't such a good idea. 'His name's Brodie.'

She pounced on the scrap of information. '*See*, you do know him.'

We were ensconced in our local pub-cum-trendy-eaterie, hogging the table closest to the bar so that Kate could eye up the new shaven-headed barman. Despite being severely short-sighted she was too vain to wear her specs but not, it seemed, vain enough to stop herself screwing her face up like a drawstring bag as she tried to bring him into focus. We'd been there for a couple of hours – in desperate need of advice I'd called her from the office, begging her to cancel her fat-burning class and meet me for a quick drink after work – but as soon as I'd mentioned Brodie, and she'd caught a blurred sighting of the barman, plans for one vodka-tonic had been immediately abandoned. '*Ohmigod*,' she'd gasped, wide-eyed with the promise of gossip. 'I'll get a bottle of wine and you can tell me all about it.'

And so I did.

It had all started a week ago. Rewind to last Thursday. Leeds city centre. Christmas shopping. Well, I was supposed to be Christmas shopping but somehow I'd veered off course, and instead of fighting through the twinsetted scrum at M&S for my dad's annual crimbo jumper, I'd found myself wedged inside a Warehouse changing room, umming and ahhing between a sequined boob-tube-and-black-flares ensemble that screamed CHRISTMAS OFFICE PARTY or a spangly, cleavage-plunging Gucci rip-off that either made me look vampishly sexy à la Cameron Diaz – or a dead ringer for the cruise-liner queen herself, Jane McDonald. I was having trouble deciding which.

Not that I needed any new clothes. It wasn't as if I'd been invited to any fabulous Christmas parties, unlike all my loved-up girlfriends who kept moaning-slash-boasting about how full their diaries were. Every time I suggested meeting up for a drink they'd mumble something about 'free windows' and 'pencilling me in' as if I was a bloody colouring book. My diary, meanwhile, was a ring binder full of blank pages – apart from *smear test, Tuesday a.m.* – an exciting entry at the end of December.

Last year had been completely different. I'd been with Rob, and the run-up to the festivities had meant cuddling up on the sofa eating the miniature Cadbury's chocolate bars out of the advent calendar and watching *Who Wants To Be A Millionaire*, choosing a Christmas tree from the market and then getting so smashed on mulled wine we couldn't carry it home, and leave-it-to-the-very-last-minute shopping for presents for his nieces and nephews. Christmas was for children and couples. Not a single, celibate and seriously skint thirty-year-old.

Feeling myself beginning to sink into the abyss of seasonal self-pity, I began tugging the dress off over my head. What was the point? I might as well brave M&S and buy myself a pair of winceyette pyjamas for all the action I was going to see this Yuletide. Unfortunately, the dress had other ideas. Wedging itself under my armpits, the zip refused to unzip any further. *This was all I needed*. I yanked harder, beginning to get impatient. My squashed arms were beginning to ache, the fluorescent strip-lighting was heating up the changing room like a pressure cooker, 'Now That's What I Call Christmas' was blasting out of the overhead speakers and the wraparound mirrors were making my cellulite look 3D . . .

And then my mobile rang.

Knee-deep in discarded clothes, I scrabbled around trying to find it – now I realised why the ringing tone I'd chosen was called 'Mosquito' – *because it was so bloody annoying*. I could hear its piercing whine getting louder and louder, until finally I discovered it wedged inside one of my trainers. I grabbed it. 'Hello?'

'*How could you?*' A male voice yelled down my Nokia.
'*Did you really think I wouldn't find out?*'

'Scuse me?'

'About Steve. I know you said you'd met someone else, but Jesus Christ, Stacey, he's a fucking friend of mine . . . correction . . . *was* a friend of mine . . .'

I held the phone away from my ear. *Who the hell was this?* As the unidentified male drew breath ready for another onslaught, I butted in. 'Excuse me, but I think you've made a mistake.'

There was a momentary pause. '*Stacey?*' This time the voice didn't sound so sure.

'No, this isn't Stacey.'

'Oh, shit . . . I think I've got the wrong number.'

'I think you must have,' I snapped, cutting him off in case he began shouting any more abuse. I stared at my phone. What the hell had that been all about?

Stuffing his mobile into the pocket of his denim jacket, Brodie crossed the main road. *Christ, he was such an idiot.* Yanking up his collar, he hunched his shoulders against the December drizzle and tried to concentrate on zigzagging in between the hordes of people spewing from the exit of the station. It wasn't easy when his mind was racing. *How could he have just dialled the wrong number and bawled out a complete stranger? Okay, so he was wound up that a so-called mate was sleeping with his ex, but thinking about it, it was more his ego that was hurt. He and Stacey had been over long before that.* Cringing as he remembered his diatribe, which stung like a day-old tattoo, he turned the corner. *And even if he was wound up, it didn't give him the right to shout at some poor girl. Jesus, she must have thought he was some kind of nutter. And who could blame her?*

He swerved to avoid colliding with a mean-looking Christmas shopper who was menacingly brandishing a three-for-two roll of wrapping-paper like a spear.

Maybe he should ring her back and apologise. After all, he'd been such a rude son-of-a-bitch. He glanced at his watch and changed his mind. Maybe not. He was late for work, his boss was going to kill him. He'd only had the job a fortnight and this was the third time he'd overslept. Trying to speed things up he quickened his pace, but it was twelve-thirty and the crowded pavements were already a sea of Christmas shoppers – it was like trying to run in waist-high water. The grey drizzle was steadily turning into sleet, and he was getting soaked through. Even so, thinking about it he really should call her back. Just to say sorry. She could tell him to fuck off, but so what?

Swerving the advancing army of soggy black umbrellas, he sheltered under a newsagent's awning. Dug out his mobile. And pressed redial.

My phone started ringing again. I eyeballed it suspiciously. Nobody's name popped up on the screen. Instead, 'Call' flashed ominously. Don't say it was him again. It couldn't be. Surely not. He wouldn't have the balls to ring back. *Would he?*

He would.

'Hey, I'm sorry . . . I just wanted to call back to apologise; you must think I'm some kind of strange nutter calling you up out of the blue and going on like that . . .'

I was tempted to tell him to sod off but something stopped me. Instead I listened to his apology. Now that he wasn't shouting I realised he had a nice voice with some kind of accent – Geordie? Scottish? No, hang on, it was Irish. Christ I was a sucker for men with Irish accents, always had been, ever since I was about five years old and I used to watch *The Val Doonican Show* with my gran. Feeling my reserves crumbling, I suddenly heard myself saying, 'Oh, don't worry, it's okay . . .'

'You see, I dialled the wrong number. I thought you were my girlfriend.'

'It must be love,' I replied dryly, unable to help my sarcasm.

'I meant ex . . . shit, I know I must sound like a right arsehole, but I just found out she's been sleeping with a mate of mine – well he was a mate of mine . . .'

I softened. Poor bastard. So blokes got cheated on too. 'Sorry to hear it.'

'It's okay, I guess I'm just suffering from hurt pride. We were hardly love's young dream.' He laughed sheepishly. 'Anyway, I didn't mean to freak you out . . .'

'Don't worry about it. You just took me by surprise, that's all.'

There was a pause.

'I'm Brodie by the way.'

For a split-second I considered introducing myself. And then I caught myself. *What was I doing? For christsakes Jess, he could be anyone, a pervert, an axe-murderer, a lunatic . . .*

'Look, I've got to go.' I made an attempt at sounding brusque and business-like. As if I was in the middle of something. An important meeting. An urgent memo. And not a hot sticky Warehouse cubicle.

'Yeh, sure . . . sorry again, by the way.'

'It's okay. Bye.'

'Bye . . .'

So that was it. I was surprised at how disappointed I suddenly felt. Maybe I should have been a bit chattier, friendlier. After all, ever since I'd finished with Rob, Kate had been nagging me to be more sociable. But then again, maybe not. Standing half-naked in Warehouse, chatting to a wrong number on my mobile, probably wasn't exactly what she'd meant when she'd told me to 'get out and meet new men'.

Still, he had sounded nice. Apologetic. Funny. Handsome? Mentally I bit my tongue. I was getting carried away. Who cared what he looked like? It wasn't as if I was ever going to speak to him again, let alone meet him. Switching my attention back to the matter at hand, I finally pulled off the dress and glanced down at the piles of clothes around my ankles. Oh what the hell. So what if I didn't have anywhere to go or anyone to go with to wear them. Throwing on my clothes, I grabbed both outfits and headed towards the cash-register. I could live in hope.

'Where the hell have you been?' flounced Stephan the manager, as Brodie tried to sneak in through the side entrance.

Fuck. He froze in his tracks, wiping away the rain that

was dripping from his hair and forming a rivulet down his forehead. Sniffing apologetically, he affected a hang-dog expression. Hopefully it would do the trick.

It didn't. Rolling up the sleeves of his black Paul Smith shirt, Stephan adjusted his silver identity-bracelet so that it showed off better against his Maldives suntan and, pausing for dramatic effect, fixed Brodie with a managerial glare. 'Do you know what time it is?' He didn't wait for an answer. 'It's nearly one, we're short-staffed . . . Jeff's called in sick, Angie's going to be late as she's got a doctor's appointment, some women's problem no doubt,' he rolled his eyes, 'and I've got a stack-load of paperwork that needs doing.' Getting no reaction from Brodie, who was stood in the middle of the floor forming a puddle, he tutted exasperatedly. 'So what's the excuse this time?'

Clenching his jaw, Brodie pulled off his leather jacket that was clinging to his skin like a wet-suit. He couldn't let Stephan wind him up. He didn't want to lose his tem-per. And his job. 'I had to make a phone call.'

'*A phone call?*' Stephan's Adam's apple shot up and down violently as he jammed his hands on his skinny hips. 'I hope it was urgent.'

Brodie thought about the woman he'd just spoken to. She'd sounded attractive, probably late twenties, it was difficult to tell by her voice. She could be a middle-aged housewife with three kids, for all he knew. Still, whoever she was, she'd sounded pretty cool. Looking up, he stared straight at Stephan and smiled. 'Yeh, actually it was.'

Work was as boring as hell. I stared at my screen, trying to concentrate on the press release I was supposed to be writing. It wasn't easy. My mind kept flicking back to lunch time. Back to the phone call. Back to Brodie. Sad, but true, it was about the most interesting thing that had happened to me in ages. I glanced at my mobile lying on the desk, wishing it would ring.

Suddenly it did.

Shocked by my telekinetic powers, I lunged for it, nearly spilling my lukewarm cup of coffee.

'Hi, I hope you don't mind me calling again. It's Brodie.'

My insides were doing something weird. 'Oh, hi.'

'Sorry, did I disturb you?'

Over the top of my screen I could see Alison, my boss, watching everyone like a CCTV camera. Swivelling around in my chair, I jammed the phone into the crook of my neck. 'No, no.'

'I just wanted to apologise again, for earlier, and . . . well . . . look, I know this is going to sound crazy and I wouldn't blame you if you told me to sod off . . . but I was wondering if you wanted to meet up, just for a coffee, no strings attached.' He gabbled out the last sentence.

My mind raced. A part of me had been hoping he'd say that, but my knee-jerk reaction was to turn him down. Flat. What kind of person called up a stranger and asked them out? *What kind of person wanted a stranger to ask them out?* I mentally flicked through my diary. It wasn't exactly brimming with dates. Suddenly I heard myself saying, 'Yeh, I'd love to.'

'Tomorrow?'

'Tomorrow's fine.' There was no turning back.

'Great . . .' There was a pause. 'Christ, I haven't even asked you where you live . . .'

'Leeds.' Knowing my luck he probably lived in Dublin.

'Hey, me too.'

My heart did a drum-roll.

'What about Starbucks in the station, 7 p.m.?'

'Yeh, fine,' I breezed, trying to be all cool and confident. When I was exactly the opposite. We said goodbye. Looking at my watch, I saw it was five-thirty. I needed a drink and some advice. I speed-dialled Kate.

'I wouldn't worry. You can always leg it after ten minutes if this Brodie person turns out to be an ugly old weirdo.' Kate squinted lustily at the barman who was pouring champagne for a group of thirtysomething women in their Christmas beaded Monsoon outfits. So this was her reassuring advice. 'On the other hand, what if he looks like Robbie Williams?'

'What if he looks like Robbie Coltrane?' I stabbed in an attempt to get her attention.

'I like Robbie Coltrane,' she tutted defensively, swivelling back round to face me. 'He was great in *Cracker*.'

I ignored her.

'Anyway, you said he sounded sexy.'

Admittedly, I had been gushing all evening. He *did* have a lovely voice. An Irish accent that was part Liam Neeson, part James Nesbitt. What more could a girl ask for?

'And that he sounded single and straight.' Digging out her lip-gloss from her itsy-bitsy beaded bag, she began smearing her lips with the wand applicator. Normally she'd go to the ladies but tonight she was too drunk to feel self-conscious. Correction: Kate never felt self-conscious.

'Mmm.' Admittedly, it was very appealing.

'Look, if you're not going to meet him, I bloody will.'

I smiled. 'Okay, okay, you're right.'

'I'm always right.'

We clinked glasses. It was decided. Tomorrow I was going on a date. A blind date. We ordered another bottle of wine to celebrate.

It should have been to commiserate. Fast forward twenty-four hours and I was sat in Starbucks experiencing a drastic change of heart. What the hell had possessed me to go on a date with a guy I'd only ever spoken to on the telephone? *On my mobile, for godsakes?* To chirp 'I'd love to meet up for coffee' to a complete stranger, to shave my legs (just in case), deep-condition my hair, get all dolled up in my new Jane McDonald outfit and then – wait for it – *wear a red carnation*.

I know, it was truly horrific, but last night I'd been so plastered that Kate's idea of wearing a corsage so we'd recognise each other had seemed wonderfully romantic. I'd even left a message on Brodie's mobile telling him so. I cringed at the hazy memory. A flower was bad enough, but a carnation? I felt like an escapee from a wedding.

Burying my nose in a copy of *OK!*, I tried to concentrate on a celebrity's soft furnishings, and not on catching anyone's eye. Why, oh why had I agreed to this humiliation? Why hadn't I called up and cancelled? Made up some excuse? Paperwork . . . a bikini waxing appointment . . . *painful verrucas?* Anything would have done the trick. But I hadn't. God knows why. I had no such qualms about fibbing when it came to telling my local GP how much alcohol I consumed in a week; '*Oohhh, hardly anything, four maybe five,*' I'd breezed, pretending not to realise he was talking units, while I was talking bottles of house white. Or when I threw a sickie by calling up work and groaning, '*Yes, I think it might be broken, in fact I'm in casualty right now,*' while being snuggled up under the duvet with four M&S all-butter croissants, happily watching *Richard and Judy* and trying to get through to play for Midday Money.

But when it came to blokes, especially single, potentially handsome, funny, kind blokes, I couldn't bring myself to do it. I didn't know if it was because I'd have felt too guilty, or because if I didn't go through with it I'd always wonder 'what if?' What if Meg Ryan hadn't gone to the Empire State Building to meet her Sleepless in Seattle? What if Harry had never met Sally? What if Brodie was The One? Okay, so it was a long shot, but I was hardly in the position to take any chances.

Which is why, at 7 p.m. that evening, I had ordered my first of many decaf lattes, perched myself unsteadily on a buttock-numbing stool in Starbucks wearing a bloody stupid carnation and my new glittery togs, and tried not to look – or feel – like one of Cilla's contestants on *Blind Date*. It hadn't been a 'lorra, lorra fun'.

Forty-five minutes later I was still sat there – alone.

'I've been stood up,' I hissed down my mobile to Kate, who'd been calling every five minutes from the pub to check on my progress. 'I can't believe it.'

'Men are such bastards,' she yelled, trying to make herself heard above the happy-hour brigade. 'Don't stay there a minute longer. Come down to Bonaparte's. I'll order you a vodka – in fact I'll order you two vodkas.'

'I'll see you in ten minutes.' I hung up and hailed a cab.

Brodie listened to the voicemail message: '*Hi this is Jess, leave me your name and number and I'll call you back.*' Her phone had been engaged for the last hour, either that or she'd turned it off. He considered leaving a message and then decided against it. If she had gone to meet him she'd no doubt be hating his guts right now, and if she hadn't then he'd feel like a prick. What would he say? The truth? 'Sorry, I can't make it tonight because my wanker of a boss has made me work.' Sighing, he gave up trying to get through and stuffed his phone on the side. What was the point? He'd obviously blown it.

'I always thought he sounded like a bit of a prick,' declared Kate.

If this was her attempt at making me feel better, it wasn't working. 'I'm such an idiot,' I wailed, draining the last of my vodka-tonic.

'He's the idiot.'

I smiled weakly at Kate. Ever the best friend. 'I feel like calling him up and telling him exactly what I think.' I jabbed my ice-cube with a straw as if it was a punch-bag.

'Why don't you?'

'First I need another drink.' I stood up. 'Same again?'

She nodded and then sighed lustfully. 'God, that bar-man's so cute.'

With everything that had happened, I'd forgotten all about Kate's crush on the barman. I glanced across at him. Before, I hadn't paid much attention, but now I saw what all the fuss was about. Kate was right. He was bloody gorgeous. 'Look, just because my love life's a disaster, it doesn't mean yours has to be. Go up and introduce yourself.'

Kate paled. She was being unusually coy. 'I can't do that.'

Knowing what was coming next, I shook my head. 'No way.'

Undeterred, she held up her hands as if they were paws and began whining like a puppy.

I gave in. 'Okay, what do you want?'

Flashing me a broad smile, she fired back, 'Name, address, marital status . . .'

The bar was jam-packed and I found myself jostled behind a suited beer-bellied city boy who was obviously trying to get into *The Guinness Book of Records* by buy-ing the largest round known to mankind. Knowing I was going to be there for ever, I sighed wearily.

Could my day get any worse?

Apparently it could. At that precise moment my mobile chose to ring.

'Jess, it's Brodie.'

'Oh, the invisible man,' I snapped bitterly. Forget trying to play it cool. I was sub-zero; even the Arctic would have seemed positively Caribbean in comparison.

It didn't seem to put him off. 'Look, I'm really sorry, something came up and I had to work tonight . . .'

'What a shame,' I deadpanned. What a bloody liar, I thought. Since when did offices have loud music and people yelling 'two pints and a whisky' in the background? Brodie wasn't at work, he was in the pub.

'I've been trying to get hold of you all night, but your phone was engaged the whole time . . .' He paused, obviously waiting for me to say something. I didn't.

'Jess, are you still there?'

As he'd been speaking a space at the bar had appeared and, squashing myself against the counter, I yelled, 'I've been here ages, are you going to serve me or what?' at the good-looking barman who had his back to me. Sod being subtle, I wasn't in the mood. He turned round. I couldn't believe it. There was I, standing at the bar like a lemon, and *he was on the bloody phone.*

It was the last straw.

'Brodie, can you hang on a minute?' Without waiting for an answer I prepared to launch an attack on the barman. But something stopped me. Something half-hidden by a bottle of Bells. Something that looked suspiciously like a carnation. *A red carnation.*

'I'm really sorry, I'll be with you in a minute.' Covering the mouthpiece with his hand, the barman gave me a gorgeously crooked and apologetic smile. My legs went all newborn-foal-like. *He had an Irish accent.*

The penny dropped.

'Brodie?'

He stared at me for a few seconds, crinkling up his forehead. '*Jess?*'

Still holding my mobile, I heard his voice in stereo. I nodded, and without saying anything we just stared at each other, both grinning like a couple of idiots. Until suddenly I caught sight of Kate giving me a hopeful thumbs up. *Oh shit.* My blind date was *her* barman.

Whatever happened to no strings attached?

Forwards
Mark Powell

Ford's at Dagenham is fixed to the bottom of East London and Essex like a keel. Steadying the load.

Derrick's dad works at Ford's. Driving away each morning in the Escort. In blue overalls.

Derrick doesn't want to work at Ford's. Sleeping away each morning in bed. In boxers.

Derrick, fifteen years old and spending the summer freely – after the June GCSEs. Will think about a proper job when the results come through and the summer ends and the east flank of London settles down. Not that he wants to work. But he will need the income. And Dad will harass. And there doesn't seem to be an alternative.

Glad to be out of school – too much bullying, drugs, skanking, violence, and teachers breaking down in front of class. Derrick rolled with the pack, on the side lines, put up a bit of bravado in the face of conflict but never felt too right with it. Felt sorry for the staff, struggling to control a school that no longer wanted to work.

Felt sorry for the weak kids who got hell. Who got worse than he did.

No longer have to slip into too-tight blazer with ripped seams and torn badge. Into baggy trousers that slipped off hips.

No longer have the daily worry of spots. The acne won't go. Each morning to wake, to bathroom, to mirror to check the night's effect. Then think of facing the girls in his year that had no interest in him. In his tall, skinny frame. Pimpled shoulders. Red face.

No longer.

For Derrick, Sundays are orange; comfortable.

He sits at the kitchen table for Sunday breakfast. With Mum, Dad, and younger brother, Joel. Bacon hissing under the grill. Steaming teapot. Slices of toast being plucked from toaster and thrown on plate for buttering.

Outside, white light parts a curtain of cloud. Another hot day.

Kitchen floats in brightness.

Derrick rips into a bacon sarnie.

– So, what did you say to Uncle Ray? Dad asks.

– You know he said yes, Mum huffs.

– So, what did you say to Uncle Ray? Dad repeats.

– I said yes, Derrick replies, throwing a bemused glance at Mum.

– When's he want you? asks Dad. – Tuesday?

– Tuesday.

– Until when? Friday?

– Friday.

Uncle Ray runs a little electrical and plumbing shop in Seven Kings. Derrick's agreed to hold the fort for four days while Uncle Ray is away. Derrick has worked there before. He knows the ropes. Knows the difference between a fuse and a washer. The various kinds of plugs.

– It'll give you a little bit of cash, Dad says.

– Gonna take me a long time to save up for my moped.

– That's what work's all about.

– I'll be old enough to get a motor by the time I get a ped.

– Cousin Carl saved up for his.

– He's a blooty, man.

– A what?

– A show-off.

– Just been made a Junior Fitter.

– Sounds pretty unimpressive, Derrick sneers.

– Easy to demean those not present.

Cousin Carl is the son of Uncle Ray. He works at Ford's. Not enough custom at the shop to sustain both father and son.

Derrick and Cousin Carl run with The Ilford – a collection of youth, numbering sixty or seventy, who live within the designated perimeter around Ilford that includes Newbury Park, Gants Hill, Barkingside, Redbridge.

The Ilford is one of the five Fords that inhabit the flatlands to the east of the City. The others are: The Romford, The Chelmsford, The Wickford and The Stratford.

Together, they can put out five hundred heads when they leave the lowlands to take on other parts of London. Or Kent.

The Fords act like the ballast of a ship; keep the youth stable.

For Derrick, Mondays are red; alarming.

In the evening, Derrick and Joel play the Scalextric set up in Joel's bedroom. On a sheet of chipboard that lowers from the wall like a drawbridge.

Downstairs, Dad watches the television, breaking his stare with random bursts of laughter. Mum cleans the kitchen and brings the boys cups of tea.

The house is warm, sweet-smelling, from Dad's earlier bath and generous sprinkling of talcum powder.

For Derrick, Tuesdays are yellow; promising.

Woken early for a lift to Seven Kings.

Into the car, the keys to the shop held in his hands, creating metallic sweat.

Onto the tree-lined streets and then the dual carriageways that intersect and bind the vast conurbation lying low for thirty miles. Wide open roads with throngs of traffic lights at every junction, filter lanes, bus stops, gargantuan pubs, signposts, and walls of council flats either side of the highway with waste-water dripping down brickwork.

– This could be the start of things, Dad says.

– I ain't thinking long-term.

– We'll have you down at Dagenham yet.

The shop is tucked awkwardly between an off-licence and barber. A glass door plastered with product stickers, two small windows either side displaying sink units and bath taps, piles of plug sockets and rolls of cable.

First customer is a huge man, with a beard. He stands in the doorway for a moment, looking surprised. He smiles, his eyes don't blink, he walks to the counter.

– Never noticed this shop before, the man says.

– Hope we can help, Derrick says softly.

– I was looking for a light switch.

Derrick reaches below the counter and drags out a cardboard box full of variously sized and shaped switches.

– Marvellous, the man smiles, gazing at Derrick.

The man rummages, finds a suitable piece and pays.

– All I need now is a good screw, the man winks.

– To attach it to the wall, of course.

Derrick grins self-consciously. Never been comfortable around adults or figures of authority. Never understood them. They all seem to know something that he should know but doesn't. They make him feel guilty, inferior, and make him lower his head onto his chest.

The Ilford meet in Valentine's Park. On mopeds, bikes, foot. Sitting on the backs of benches and smoking weed and practising their American accents. No one comes into the park in the evenings except them.

Derrick walks the deserted pathway, his arrival met with an air of apathy. A few faces look over, the odd head nods. Derrick sits on the edge of a bench, saying nothing. His face covered in skin-tinted acne cream.

Most of The Ilford wear US college baseball jackets, with hoods. During the summer they wear bare-chests below to stay cool.

Derrick can't afford a jacket like that and so he wears a bomber jacket with a hooded cagoule underneath. In summer he boils.

Most of The Ilford call him 'The Pikey'. Even Cousin Carl. Who pulls up on his ped and yanks off his lid.

– Wha's happening, rollers? he shouts.

– Wha's kicking, someone says back.

– Another hot mother today, you get me? Cousin Carl says, wiping sweat off his top lip.

– I hear that, comes the reply.

Cousin Carl notices Derrick perched on the bench, across the concrete from where he stands.

– Wha's the tune, Cuz?

– Hey, Derrick smiles.

– You keeping the shop tight?

– You know it.

– Ace. Now get your arse over to the corner for a few Cokes, yeah?

Derrick leaps to feet and jogs away from the group towards the B2 on Cranbrook Road.

He returns with six cans that are quickly distributed.

– Way to go, Pikey, Cousin Carl sniffs, turning away and back to the older boys of the crew.

Back home, the family are waiting in the lounge. The dim light from the television casts them in bronze; statuesque. Mum gets up to make Derrick a hot chocolate, bring him a few biscuits. So nice to be home. And Joel smiles at him. And Dad winks. And Derrick sinks into an armchair.

For Derrick, Wednesdays are blue; cold.

The shop is cool, sheltered from the sun by surrounding buildings.

The man with the beard returns. Wearing extremely tight denim shorts and an open shirt that reveals a bush of chest hair.

– I had to come back, he smiles.

Derrick grins nervously. Says nothing.

– I've got a hole to fill.

Derrick continues the grin.

– I hope you sell bath plugs? the man chuckles.

Derrick manages to raise a false, anxious snigger. Turns to the shelving units behind him and shuffles a stack of shoeboxes.

– Metal or . . .

– Rubber, the man interrupts, with a raised eyebrow. – Lovely rubber.

– Do you know the size?

– Ooh, it's a big one. Show me and I'll tell you whether it'll fit.

After a few attempts they find the right plug.

They exchange paper bag and payment over the till.

– All I need now is someone to share the bath with me, the man says, breathing over the counter into Derrick's face.

The big man scares him.

At home the hassles of the day dissipate. A hot meal. A deep bath. A computer game with Joel. The bearded man becomes smaller.

Derrick thinks of the money, imagines driving the scooter. Looks forward to Saturday night and his sixteenth. Planning a night out. With The Ilford.

When he has got his ped things will be different. He will be more accepted than he is now. He doesn't mind existing on the fringes – better than being alone, being bullied. He knows that you've got to belong to bloom. And, inside his head, he hears his Dad's voice urging him to apply to Ford's. ('We'll have you down at Dagenham yet.')

For Derrick, Thursdays are also yellow; successful.

The bearded man arrives at ten. Topless in the bright sunshine that bakes the streets.

He rubs his hairy arms as he speaks. – How are you this beautiful day?

– What can I get you?

– Do you have a thick one?

– Eh?

– A long, thick one?

Derrick reddens. – I don't know what you mean.

– Electrical wire. Got to be copper.

Derrick has to come out from behind the counter to show the man where the cable is stored. He pulls open a large barrel. The man leans into him, pushing his body against his.

– I'll g-g-get out of your way, Derrick mutters, pushing himself around a rack of extension leads.

The man looks offended, offers a shrug and then dips his head into the barrel. – Just helping. Just helping.

Thursday evenings are still yellow, but cut with streaks of black. Like a wasp.

The Ilford gather in Valentine's after seven. Still warm, after a day up in the eighties. The black skins are darker. The white skins sport tans. Plumes of dope-smoke fall out of tired mouths. Cousin Carl lying on the grass verge with a girl.

– Yo, Pikey! he calls out.

Derrick looks up from his daydream.

– Get your butt in the middle.

Derrick pulls himself up and walks over to his cousin.

– Stand in the centre, muppet.

Ten benches dot the edges of the concrete square. Each filled with crew members.

– Sixteen years old on Saturday, what do you say? Cousin Carl says from his outstretched position.

– Damn right, Derrick nods, turning about slowly to take in all the watching eyes.

– A few questions for you. To see if you're going to grow up, yeah?

– Okay, Derrick shrugs.

Cousin Carl pulls himself up so that he rests on his elbows.

– Any plans for Saturday?

– Maybe hit the town?

– When are you going to stop wearing those ridic-ulous coats?

Derrick smiles uncomfortably.

– When are you going to sort out your goddam pussed-up face?

The smile becomes more strained.

– When are you going to start putting a bit of brawn on that shrivelled, skinny, stick of a body, boy?

His stare goes past Cousin Carl and into the bushes behind.

– Why are you so ugly?

Derrick's face begins to break into pieces.

– Why do you have no personality?

The mouth drops, the eyes glaze.

– Why don't you run and get us some Cokes?

Without thinking, Derrick sets off for the B2.

Running fast, alone with his panting.

Later that evening, the walk home is longer than usual. His legs don't want to carry him. He wants to fold up.

Mum is waiting in the kitchen with a pan of hot milk.

– Are you okay, love?

– I'm fine, Mum.

– You look run down.

– It's been a long old day.

– You really should stay in after work.

– I guess.

– You know how much we don't like you out all evening.

– I wonder myself sometimes.

– And when you get that moped?

– When? More like if.

– It'll be good for getting to and from work.

– It's a strange shop.

– I think Dad's having a word at work for you.

– I don't know, Mum.

– You're coming up sixteen, you should be starting to know.

– Will I fit in?

– You'll be ever so popular. You always have been.

– I thought so.

– You want a Horlicks?

– I'll get to bed.

Gently presses his feet into the stairs as he climbs to his room. How he loves the carpets, the walls, the stairs, the pictures, the doors, the bathroom, the banisters.

Lies in darkness listening to the mellow rhythms of the late-night drum 'n' bass show on *Power FM*. Letting the vibes take away his thoughts. His thoughts on work, The Ilford, on Joel who's fast asleep in the next room. Forgets the events of earlier.

For Derrick, Fridays are black; final.

All the way to the shop Dad whistles and Derrick joins in on the choruses he recognises. Where the tune divides into uncertain melody, the father and son create unintentional harmonies and laugh, before returning to the part of the tune they both know.

All the traffic lights are green. There are no drivers brawling by the side of the road. It must be Friday.

The bearded man arrives early. Earlier than usual. With chubby eyes. Yet with the usual enthusiastic stare. Pushing the door open as if expecting a warm welcome.

Derrick tenses. Offers a lame smile. Determines to

stay behind the counter and deal with the man as quickly as he can.

– Don't look so worried, the man says.

– My last day.

– No?

– My Uncle's coming back.

– Where do you normally work? the man asks, moving into the shop.

– Just finished school.

– Come out here, let's have another look at you.

– I'm okay here.

– Don't be daft, come out, the man says, lowering his head to stare at Derrick from behind his eyebrows.

Derrick pulls at the counter and goes through the hatch.

The man eyes him up and down.

– Tall lad, he nods.

The man moves closer so that he stands directly in front of Derrick. He takes hold of Derrick's shoulders and gives them a squeeze.

– Could do with a bit of muscle, he says.

The man slides his hands down Derrick's sides.

Derrick is taut with panic. He stares past the man at the window.

– What waist are you? the man whispers, folding his fingers around Derrick's hips.

– T-t-twenty-eight.

– Mmmmm.

– I think.

– Thin.

Derrick doesn't know what to do. He can't be rude.

He can't take on the big man. He can't allow the man to continue touching him.

– P-p-please, Derrick mutters.

The man acts surprised. – Am I unnerving you?

– Please.

Slowly the man loosens his hold and moves his hands away from Derrick's body.

– Maybe you'd like to come and model for me? the man says.

– I'll probably go and work at Ford's.

The man sniffs disagreement. – I reckon you've got what it takes to be a model, you know.

– My dad's been at Ford's for years.

– You've got the height, you see.

– My cousin's there, too.

– I run a little company. Swimwear. Trunks, bikinis, Bermudas, that sort of stuff.

– He's just been made a Junior Fitter.

– I always need someone new to model for the packaging. I'd pay, of course. What do you think?

Derrick swallows. The man is still standing too close.

– Maybe you want to come round to mine and try a few things on. See how things develop.

The man's hand gently returns to Derrick's arm.

– To be quite truthful, you'd be doing me a big favour. Times are hard for small businesses. As you've probably found out with this shop.

– It is quiet, Derrick mumbles.

– Over the past few days I reckon I've been pretty generous in the support of this little shop.

– You're the only customer.

– See? I scratch your back.

– I'm saving for a moped.

– Come over to mine. Try on some trunks. I'd love to see you in a pair of my trunks.

The man slips an address card into Derrick's damp grip.

Dad arrives outside the shop at the regular time; just as Derrick turns the last lock on the door.

Pushes the baseball cap onto his head. Jogs towards the car. Turns to have a last look at the little shop. Turns back to see something wrong with Dad. His expression doesn't make sense.

– Dad? Derrick asks, climbing into the passenger seat. No reply.

– Wha's happening, D?

Like an automaton Dad pushes the stick into gear and pulls away from the kerb. Wide-eyed, as if witnessing terror. Clenched jaw, as if being strangled.

Derrick sits uneasily, flicking subtle glances to Dad as they drive. Keeping most of his stares fixed out of the window, at the parades of shabby shop-fronts. Where owners sit on deckchairs and shout across to one another, enjoying the late afternoon sun that still burns. Where trails of broken glass glitter the pavement from the night before.

At home, Dad falls into Mum's arms while the two sons stare at the kitchen floor. His hands claw at her back, tear at her dress. He cannot stop himself from sliding down to his knees and clutching her around the waist.

– Mum? Derrick asks, quietly.

– Your Dad's not going to be working at Ford's any more, she replies.

Derrick can see that this isn't because of any new job.

– Two thousand jobs lost, Mum continues.

– Goddam Yanks, Joel hisses.

– Why Dad?

– What is this going to do to us? says Mum, with closed eyes, her fingers pushing through Dad's hair.

Derrick is sixteen tomorrow.

The collection of The Ilford in the park is subdued. Some have lost their jobs, some of their parents have lost theirs.

Cousin Carl arrives carrying two black eyes – mounds of mauve and yellow.

– Wha's new, he says to the crowd. – Wha's happening, Cuz, he says to Derrick.

– Who've you been fighting? Derrick asks.

– I got hold of my line manager when he told me. A few of his buddies got hold of me afterwards.

– Dad's busted up.

– We gonna get them. You hear me?

A few of the heads look up and nod. A rumble of agreement.

– I ain't out tonight. I'm licking my wounds. But tomorrow, you get me? We're going to visit, says Cousin Carl.

– Damn right, a voice calls out.

– I'm down with that, says another.

– It's my birthday tomorrow, Derrick adds.

– I've had words with The Romford who've had words with The Chelmsford, Cousin Carl growls.

– I was hoping we might hit the town or something?

– There's a lot of shared anger. We'll make our revenge.

For Derrick, Friday night is black on the outside and red inside; a vampire's cape.

The house is quiet. Different. Not just in the silence but in the way Dad is in bed at eight and Mum is crying in the lounge and Joel is locked in his bedroom. This is not what Derrick wants. This is not how it should be.

The thought of tomorrow's birthday loses its thrill, as things around him crumble.

In the middle of the night Derrick jolts awake to the sound of Dad screaming.

For Derrick, Saturday is green; verdant.

Dad is looking a little better, though still mute.

Mum is looking worse; her skin is blotchy.

They take Derrick into the garage and show him his birthday present; a second-hand moped. Joel stands proudly by the side of the machine with a can of polish and a cloth in hand.

You like it? Joel asks.

– We know how much you wanted one, Mum struggles to say.

– Happy birthday, mumbles Dad.

Derrick, Mum, and Joel just stare at the father. Stare at his desperation.

Derrick wipes his eyes and wet nose. – I can't, he says.

– Course you can, Mum urges.

– I know how much these things cost.

– We can still afford it.

– I can't.

– Please. It's yours, insists Mum.

– No, you've got to take it back. I've got to start working. I've got to start doing things round here.

– We wanted to see your face, she smiles, tragically.

Derrick always has fish and chips followed by home-made chocolate cake for his birthday dinner. Today, though, there is only the fish and chips.

The four of them sit at the table staring at the clogged heap of chips and the stodgy fish that has lost most of its batter on the wrapping. Slices of bread and butter lie uneaten to the side of each plate. The tomato-sauce bottle is untouched. Salt unshaken. And no one dares to catch eyes.

The Ilford, combined with elements of the other Fords, fill the top floor of two Number 129 buses that run from Claybury to Becontree. Decided to travel together out of unity. Dressed in bandanas, caps, sneakers, the baseball jackets. Draped in gold chains, bracelets, rings. Sharing twigs of weed. Bottles of vodka.

They walk the extra distance to Ford's main works. A chosen few then walk to the hole in the wire fence that runs alongside the railway tracks.

They start the fire behind a workshop, in an oil drum.

Smash windows to spread it, hurling in clumps of burning rags.

One hundred youths stand the other side of the A13 and watch the sky turn orange.

Back home, Derrick's bedroom stinks of fire. His breath tastes of cannabis and alcohol.

Derrick knows the bearded man is queer. But it is just a pair of trunks. He could pose half-naked for a photograph. He could at least investigate. He has to start pulling his weight for the family. Doing his bit. All hands on deck.

Derrick takes the address card.

Midtown—New York City
The Escape Route

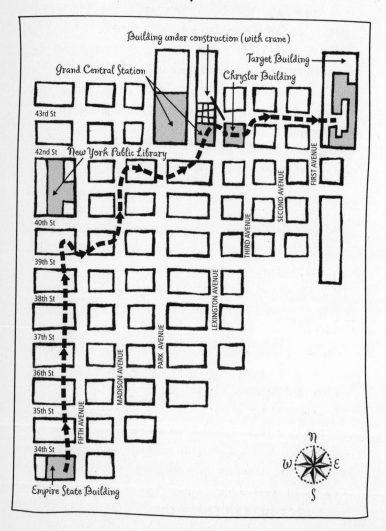

Building under construction (with crane)

Grand Central Station

Target Building

Chrysler Building

43rd St

42nd St

New York Public Library

40th St

39th St

38th St

37th St

36th St

35th St

34th St

Empire State Building

FIFTH AVENUE

MADISON AVENUE

PARK AVENUE

LEXINGTON AVENUE

THIRD AVENUE

SECOND AVENUE

FIRST AVENUE

N
W   E
S

Altitude Rush

Matthew Reilly

Empire State Building
100th Floor
New York City, 6:50 a.m.

There came a shrill electronic *beep* as the masked intruder removed the small rectangular case from its recess beneath the desk's clear-glass top – and suddenly the clock was ticking.

Twenty-five minutes.

The response team would be here in four.

The intruder wasted no time.

As he strode toward the office's corner windows, he slid the rectangular glass case into a small chest-pack hidden underneath the front of his black jacket.

He came to the north-east-facing windows, where he was met by a view of mid-town New York City.

It looked like a mountain range of skyscrapers – all cluttered and crowded. He saw the top of the Chrysler Building, its crystalline pointed peak shimmering in the dawn. The iron lattice Queensboro Bridge and the wide expanse of the East River hovered in the background beyond the Chrysler. In the concrete jungle *in between* the river and the Empire State Building, the keen tourist would find Grand Central Station, fashionable Fifth Avenue, and on the banks of the river itself, the UN building.

Nice view, the intruder thought. As one would expect of a member of the US Federal Reserve Board.

The intruder, however, didn't stop to admire it.

He just drew a silenced Sig-Sauer pistol from his thigh holster and blasted one of the corner windows to smithereens. Then – 100 storeys up, 1000 feet off the ground – he leapt through the hole and the chase began.

```
- - - - - - - - - - - - - - --
OFFICIAL STAMP 046-24 - DOCU-
MENT NOT DELIVERED (7 DECEMBER,
1941) -- DESTROY ALL COPIES --
DESTROY ALL COPIES -- DESTROY
ALL COPIES -- DESTROY ALL
- - - - - - - - - - - - - - --
```

6 December 1941

Dear Herr Hitler,

AERIAL RUN

The flying fox was waiting for the intruder outside the blasted-open window.

After the man – his code name for this mission was, appropriately, Robin Hood – had entered the plush office via an elevator shaft inside the Empire State Building, he had attached a radio transponder to the ceiling over by its corner windows.

It was a homing transponder, sending a signal to his companion – code name Little John – over on the flat-topped roof of Horwicks Tower, an ordinary-looking 45-storey building two blocks to the north.

The rope that now connected the two buildings was very, very steep.

As he'd taken the rectangular case from the desk, Hood had heard a loud *whump!* – the sound of a rocket-propelled concrete-piercing hook slamming into the thick concrete beam above the corner window. Attached to the hook was the rope; attached to the rope was a state-of-the-art flying fox.

Robin Hood grabbed the flying fox's handlebar-like grips and slid like a rocket down its steeply slanted zip-line, soaring clear over 34th and 35th Streets and the low city block in between.

As he approached the roof of Horwicks Tower, Hood applied the handbrakes on the fox and it slowed, bringing him to a sharp swinging halt a couple of feet above the tower's roof.

Little John was waiting for him.

True to his namesake, he towered over Robin Hood. Whereas Hood was small, wiry and compact, Little John was big, barrel-chested and strong. At the moment his bushy black beard was covered by a black ski-mask.

'Thirty-eight seconds,' he said as soon as Hood landed. 'I thought you'd be faster.'

Hood said, 'Sorry, but I didn't want to break my legs on the landing.'

Little John was already hustling towards the other side of the roof. Hood took off after him. Rooftop wind whistled around them as they jogged.

'The Americans are on their way and they're really *really* pissed,' Little John said. 'Their radio networks went berserk as soon as you lifted the pressure case from the desk. They're sending three teams from the *George Washington*. ETA: two-and-a-half minutes.' He turned to Hood meaningfully. 'SEAL teams.'

'Oh, shit.'

'That's what I said. Aren't we supposed to be doing exercises with them next week?'

'Yep,' Hood said, 'which means the Yanks are *not* going to be happy if they catch us today. And what's this about two-and-a-half minutes? I thought we had a four-minute lead time.'

'Intelligence fucked up,' Little John scowled as he ran. 'The *Washington* is in Dock 7 for the weekend, not Dock 46. They're closer.'

They came to the parapet. The roof of another similarly sized building sat across 36th Street from them.

Little John threw a pair of hand-held suction cups to Hood. 'Just in case you turn into an unidentified falling object.'

It was then that Hood saw that John had already connected these two rooftops with another flying fox.

Little John turned to face him. 'So, my friend. You ready to get vertical?'

NOT YOUR AVERAGE DOCUMENT CASE

Hood and Little John's rather irregular form of movement was governed by the pressure case they had stolen from the Empire State Building.

Constructed of super-strong Lexan glass and about the size of a slim laptop computer, the case was manufactured by the W R Grauss Company of Switzerland, and it was unique.

Novelty, however, comes at a price. And with starting prices of $6 million for its custom-designed document containers, the Grauss Company of Switzerland has a rather elite clientele.

Their cases are known to be used by the US and British governments, nearly every major office at the UN, and not a few billionaires who like to accumulate socially *unacceptable* collectibles.

There are two reasons why.

Firstly, Grauss pressure cases are all but impossible to break open. They are protected by four pressure-sealed locks which can only be opened using a high-pressure air-valve release unit – a machine the size of a small refrigerator. Such machines are rare and very expensive.

The second reason, however, is far more intriguing.

You see, Grauss cases are capable of destroying their contents should they fall into the wrong hands.

If a Grauss case is taken too far – or for too long – from its resting place, a small amount of highly corrosive hydrofluoric acid will be released into it, destroying the document that it contains.

Collectors of Nazi memorabilia are known to house them in Grauss cases. US embassy employees carry highly classified messages in them. UN ambassadors are known to use them to safeguard sensitive documents from foreign theft.

Truth be told, the Grauss case that Hood and Little John had stolen held a document – a very old document, written in 1941. Indeed, as he'd taken the case from its home inside the Federal Reserve member's desk, Robin Hood had beheld the document inside it – and gasped.

'Jesus . . .'

This case, however, came with a singular feature, unique even by the Grauss Company's high standards.

Because of its home inside the Empire State Building, this case had an altitude sensor.

A two-way altitude sensor.

If the case detected that it was *higher* than 1000 feet – the height of the Empire State Building – its acid-dissolution system would be triggered. Similarly, if the sensor detected that the case was *lower* than ten feet off the ground, the acid would also be released.

Which meant any would-be thief had to stay both out of the sky *and* off the ground.

As such, the document's owner – a smug proud man who liked the idea of owning a document that could rock the world to its very foundations – lived safe in the knowledge that if anyone stole his precious piece of memorabilia, they could never use it against his country. It would be destroyed as soon as it left the building.

He'd only made one wrong assumption.

The thief who went neither up nor down.

> `It is with grave feelings that`
> `I write to you today.`
>
> `Despite our differences, our`
> `two great nations are, in many`
> `ways, very similar. Ours are`
> `proud nations, strong nations.`

In any event, the case had a fail-safe mechanism.

Its owner liked to show the document to visitors every so often; as he had done recently to a diplomat from Hood's home country. When it was removed from its resting place a timer mechanism was activated, giving the holder twenty-five minutes to return the case to its slot.

That was the twenty-five-minute limit Robin Hood knew of.

The time he had to get the case to a high-pressure lock-release valve.

The only problem: he had to traverse sixteen city blocks to get to a place with a release valve, while staying off the ground.

RUN, RUN, RUN, AS FAST AS YOU CAN

The rest of New York awoke to the usual morning news.

Everybody, it seemed, still hated America: African

warlords did; the British did due to America's refusal to share its oil reserves with petrol-starved England; there was even a cute little protest in Washington by a dozen middle-economy countries like Singapore, India, Sweden and Australia, protesting against America's tendency to protect its home market with high import tariffs. In the meantime, Robin Hood and Little John made their aerial rush across New York City.

Two blocks in thirty-eight seconds was a good start.

The next three went equally quickly because Little John had prepared well. More flying foxes were already in place, allowing them to run across the building tops and whiz down each fox to the next roof.

It also helped that in this part of their journey, each of the buildings was progressively shorter than the last – it was downhill sliding. That was good. Later, they would have to travel uphill, and then things would be different.

They pushed on, following Fifth Avenue northward, crossing the chasms of 37th, 38th and 39th Streets, moving fast.

Between 39th and 40th, they had to cut right. Ahead of them to the north was the New York Public Library but it was too low and irregularly shaped to traverse. Besides, they had to head eastward anyway, which meant crossing the imposing chasm of Fifth Avenue itself.

Little John had pre-laid another flying fox. Its rope soared across Fifth like a long swooping power cable, anchored to the roof of the HSBC Building on the other side.

Hood grabbed the flying fox –

– and then he heard it.

An ominous *thump-thump-thump-thump-thump-thump*.

'They're here,' Little John said as he saw three helicopters thunder down the skyscraper-lined canyonway of Fifth Avenue, booming over the early morning traffic.

They were SH-60B Seahawks. Troop carriers. Flying with their noses down and their asses up. Twelve men per chopper. Thirty-six troops.

Mean motherfuckers all.

'Now it gets interesting,' Hood said as he and Little John propelled themselves off the rooftop and slid in tandem across busy Fifth Avenue, the three Navy helicopters roaring down the glass-walled canyon towards them, bearing down upon them like angry birds of prey.

CHANGE OF PLANS

Robin Hood and Little John hit the roof of the HSBC Building running.

They saw the uneven rooftop landscape spread out before them, the diagonal north-eastern route that they had to traverse in order to get to their destination – a building over on 1st Avenue that backed onto the East River.

Several landmarks stood out: the Chrysler Building and below it, Grand Central Station, both on 42nd Street; plus a building behind Grand Central that was under construction.

A flying fox lay stretched across Madison Avenue on the opposite side of the HSBC Building's roof, waiting for them.

And then the choppers arrived.

They came thumping by overhead, rising up behind the two thieves from the chasm that was Fifth Avenue, showing their sides, revealing armed men seated in their open doorways, guns up and firing.

The roof all around Robin Hood and Little John erupted with bullet impacts, cutting them off from the escape fox on the other side.

Hood and John ran.

Two more lines of bullet holes chased them across the rooftop, catching up to them just as they arrived at a small shack that housed the building's internal stair-well, threw open the door and dived inside, rolling down the stairs an instant before as the shack's thin ply-wood walls were ripped to shreds by the chainsaw-like bombardment of the SEALs' gunfire.

Hood and Little John were on their feet in seconds, racing down the stairwell.

At the same time, the first chopper landed on the roof, disgorging a team of twelve Navy SEALs from its side doors.

The other two choppers split up – one heading north, covering 40th Street; the other heading east, covering the run over Madison Avenue.

The choppers knew where they were going.

```
In times such as these, my
country, like yours, has con-
cerns about the future – about
current alliances, and of
course, the Soviet issue.
```

CROSSING MADISON AVENUE

Hood and Little John bolted down the stairwell, taking the stairs four at a time, swinging around every turn, moving as fast as their legs could carry them.

As they ran, they took off their combat jackets and ski-masks, revealing bulky woollen jumpers and regular trousers. If they ran into someone now, it was better not to look like a terrorist.

They were nine floors down when they heard the SEALs' rapid footfalls booming down the stairwell above them.

'Damn it, *shit!*' Little John yelled. 'They got here too fast! What do we do now?'

'We improvise,' Robin Hood said. 'Where can we pick up the trail again?'

'If you can get us to Grand Central, we'll be back on the escape route.'

'Grand Central it is then.'

They came to the second floor of the building, a bare twenty feet off the ground, and headed east, toward Madison Avenue, hurrying through an empty office area.

They came to the eastern side of the building, to the line of windows overlooking the north–south running Madison Avenue.

A flat steel awning lay directly outside the windows, cover for the pedestrians on the street below.

Hood stole a glance behind him – no SEALs. *Yet.* They'd be here any second, though.

And so he just drew his Sig-Sauer and loosed two crisp shots, shattering one of the windows, and leapt outside.

The sounds of New York met him: honking horns, the clatter of shop shutters, human murmurs; all of it bouncing off the glass walls of the deep Manhattan canyons.

It was close on 7 a.m. and the morning rush was just kicking in.

Buses streamed northward along Madison like migrating cockroaches, taking up all four of its lanes. Yellow cabs filled in the gaps.

And then Hood heard another sound, from somewhere above and behind them – a familiar *thump-thump-thump-thump-thump* . . .

It burst around the corner to the south at phenomenal speed, banking hard and fast – a Navy Seahawk.

Coming right for them.

'*There! Now!*' Hood yelled, indicating a bus that was about to pull to a halt alongside their awning.

The chopper powered up, leapt forward in the air.

Hood and Little John ran out onto the awning, toward the bus's moving roof.

There came a sudden bang as they ran – the sound of a door being kicked open.

Then, suddenly, *every* window looking out onto the awning behind them started exploding, sending glass showering outward.

The SEALs were inside the office and firing hard.

'Go! Go! Go!' Hood yelled, running fast and low, ducking forward.

He and Little John ran step for step along the awning, windows shattering behind them, the chopper roaring above them, before they leapt – together – onto the roof of the bus, just as the long white vehicle lurched forward and continued on its northward journey up Madison.

But it wasn't over yet.

The chopper above them wanted in on the action. Since it didn't have room to turn on its side, it swooped in low above them, trying to get to the next inter-section, Madison and 41st, where it would have room to pivot in mid-air and give the men in its side doors a shot at Hood and Little John.

But the bus, picking up speed now, hit the inter-section first and slipped through it, so the chopper had to power up again and head for the next one up at 42nd Street.

Meanwhile, Hood and Little John were busy crossing Madison Avenue itself – by hopping from one moving bus to another!

A bare twelve feet off the ground, they jumped from bus to bus, slowly making their way across the four lanes of traffic – two tiny figures moving *above* the morn-ing rush, using full-sized buses as stepping stones.

But they had to move fast, for as they crossed the wide avenue laterally, the forward movement of the traffic was bringing them closer and closer to 42nd Street and the big chopper now hovering in the inter-section there, swinging slowly around in the open space . . . .

With one final jump, Hood and Little John landed on the steel pedestrian awning on the eastern side of Madison Avenue, fifteen yards short of the 42nd Street intersection.

No sooner had they landed, however, than the chopper swung around fully in the air above the intersection, showing them its side door: a door packed with machinegun-toting Navy SEALs.

The SEALs opened fire, just as Hood raised his own pistol and blasted another window, causing it to spiderweb with cracks, and with Little John running behind him, he dived through its cracked glass shards into the safety of yet another New York City building.

UPHILL

Up the stairs they ran.

Hearts pumping. Legs pounding.

It was tough going, but Hood and Little John were fit, very fit. After all, they were their country's finest.

They had to keep pushing eastward, paralleling 42nd Street. They were close to Grand Central Station now, separated from it by only two streets: Park Avenue to the east and 42nd Street itself to the north.

'Damn it,' Little John said as they ran. 'I didn't plan on us coming so far north so soon. Any ideas how we get across Park?'

'Not yet,' Hood said.

They hurried up the stairwell, arrived at the roof, threw open the door, burst out into the early morning sunlight.

Hood hurried over to the parapet overlooking Park Avenue. The building directly across from him was the same height as this one, its walls made of sheer glass; the gap between the two structures maybe sixty feet.

'We got any flying foxes left?' he asked Little John.

'All out, I'm afraid.'

Just then, Hood saw one of the Navy helicopters swoosh by beneath him into Park Avenue. The chopper began to hover in front of Hood's building, a few floors *below* the rooftop.

It rose slightly in the air. It looked as if the chopper was trying to peer *inside* the windows of the building, trying to get a glimpse of Hood and Little John inside.

As he watched it check out each floor, Hood saw that this chopper's side doors were open but empty. This Seahawk must have already unloaded its troops.

And then Hood got an idea.

He spun, he'd need a – and he saw it: *the window-cleaners' platform.*

Within a minute, Hood and Little John had opened the guard gates on the window-cleaners' platform and positioned it on the edge of the rooftop in such a way that it was jutting out perpendicularly from the roof, extending about twenty feet out from the edge, like a springboard.

The chopper beneath them kept rising, searching, searching . . .

Hood pulled out his suction cups, held one in each hand. Little John did the same.

'You know what I'm thinking?' Hood asked.

'Uh-huh,' Little John said. 'You know you're crazy, don't you?'

'Just take a good run up and stay with me. It's the only way we're going to get across Park.'

The chopper beneath them rose quickly, checking each floor, until at last it came to the roof.

The Seahawk came level with the extended window-cleaners' platform, rotating laterally as its pilots scanned the area, in the process showing Hood and Little John its open side flank.

Which was just what they wanted.

'Now!' Hood yelled.

He and Little John ran, close together, out onto the window-cleaners' platform.

They hit the platform at a run, shot along its length, their feet clanging on its metal flooring.

And then they jumped . . .

. . . out into the clear open sky . . .

. . . and landed . . .

. . . *inside* the hovering Navy helicopter!

But they didn't stop. In fact, they didn't miss a single step.

The chopper's two pilots spun around in astonishment, but all they saw were two blurs enter their helicopter's rear troop hold from the left, dash across its width, and then dive out through its open right-hand doorway!

Hood and Little John blasted out the doorway of the Seahawk and threw themselves into the air like sky-divers, arms outstretched, suction cups gripped in their hands.

They both flew through the air . . . soaring, flying, falling . . . before – *whack-whack!* – they hit the glass windows of the building on the other side of Park Avenue and engaged their suction cups.

The cups held, and suddenly they were hanging against the outside of this new building!

Two quick gunshots later they were inside it.

```
And although in the past the
United States has preferred to
remain isolated from conflicts
such as the present one, there
comes a time when a country
must make a decision that will
ensure its future, and as such
choose its allies based not on
past allegiances, but on what
is best for the nation in the
cold hard light of reality.
```

INSIDE RUNNING – GRAND CENTRAL STATION
Downhill. To the second level, because this building possessed a glassed-in pedestrian bridge that spanned 42nd Street and opened onto Grand Central.

They reached the second floor, and cut through a small shopping centre and, for the first time that day, encountered people: earlybirds buying breakfast, doughnuts, coffee.

They hit the glass-walled pedestrian bridge and raced across it, just as, without warning, the windows on both sides of the bridge shattered violently under the weight of an incoming team of Navy SEALs.

It was as if someone had set off a chain of fireworks on either side of Hood and Little John.

But they just kept on running as the twin lines of windows on their flanks blasted inwards – *crash! crash! crash!* – the star-shaped explosions of glass closely followed by the bodies of black-clad SEALs swinging into the interior of the bridge on drop-ropes.

Robin Hood and Little John swept out of the bridge a split second before the bullets started flying, and entered Grand Central Station.

They charged into the concourse, careful to stay high up on the mezzanine level, and skirted the main lobby, dodging people, running hard, heading east now.

'This way!' Little John called, back on the plan now.

They hit a 'Staff Only' door and burst into a utility stairwell, storming up it at the same time as the SEALs hustled across the concourse behind them.

More stairs.

More running.

7:06 became 7:07. They had until 7:15 a.m.

They came to the roof, stepped out onto it, and once again found themselves looking at the New York skyline.

Dominating the immediate area was the colossal Chrysler Building. It loomed above them to the east, seventy-seven storeys high, across the wide chasm of Lexington Avenue.

Hood gazed at the top of the Chrysler Building.

That was where they wanted to go, he thought. *It was the only building in this area that was high enough to allow for the final leg of their journey . . . .*

'All right, LJ, we don't have much time,' he said, breathing hard. 'You said you had the route figured out from here.'

'This way,' Little John said.

Behind Grand Central, a new tower was under construction. It was basically just the shell of a building, all scaffolding, gantry elevators and unfinished concrete floors. It didn't even have windows yet, so you could see all the way through.

It also, Hood saw, had a crane mounted up on its roof, from which hung an extra-long cable and hook.

Little John, he noted, had already been here. The crane's cable was stretched out to the west at a steep angle, tied to one of the middle floors of the structure.

They raced for the nearest gantry lift, stepped inside it and whistled up toward the floor where the crane's hook was tied.

The SEALs chasing them must have radioed their companions, because no sooner was the lift moving than the three Seahawk helicopters arrived on the scene and the whole construction site was pummelled with gunfire.

The lift came to the tenth floor and Little John flung open its metal grill and led Hood across the exposed concrete floor to the tied-down hook at its edge. As soon as they stepped out of the lift, the little cage headed straight back down to the SEALs below.

They were coming.

Through the exposed sides of the open-air level, Hood and Little John saw the Navy choppers circling the building, searching for them like bloodhounds. They'd have them in ten seconds . . .

They came to the crane's hook. The way Little John had secured it, it was ready for a big swing – a long pendulum-like arc that would carry them eastward, alongside the unfinished building's southern side, then *over* Lexington, right up to the steel and glass superstructure of the Chrysler Building's eleventh floor.

'I'll hold the hook,' Little John said, 'you hold me. Just make sure you're ready with a suction cup by the time we reach the Chrysler.'

'Got it,' Robin Hood said.

Little John untied the hook. Hood grabbed the bigger man's belt, while keeping a suction cup gripped in one hand.

Then, without any further ceremony – and just as the first SEALs arrived on their level in the gantry elevator – Hood and Little John jumped off the edge of the dusty concrete floor and swung.

THE CHRYSLER

It was a spectacular swing.

Two tiny figures, suspended from a building-mounted crane, flanked by three Navy helicopters, swinging in a beautiful flat arc, high over Lexington Avenue.

They swung fast – swooping downwards, across the face of the ugly unfinished tower – then they shot out into the open air above Lexington, reaching the bottom of their arc . . . and came back up again, up and up and up, zeroing in on the shiny vertical side of the Chrysler Building.

They came to a window, hit it hard – and *stopped*, thanks to the suction cup in Hood's hand, now affixed to the exterior of the great structure.

Within seconds, the adjoining window was broken and they were inside, heading for the nearest lift.

Bing!

A minute later, the lift arrived at the seventy-fifth floor of the Chrysler Building.

Hood and Little John charged out of the lift, blasted a security lock and stepped into a partitioned office area.

'Jumpers off,' Hood said.

They wrenched off their jumpers as they hustled across the floor, heading for the eastern windows.

The removal of their bulky woollen jumpers revealed small packs on their backs – as well as, in Hood's case, the chest-pack containing the coveted document.

They came to the eastern wall of the building, saw the world beyond it: the tops of buildings, the East River and, right next to the East River, their destination . . .

'You ready for the rollercoaster ride?' Hood asked.

'Are you kidding? This is what I've been waiting for,' Little John said.

'Then let's do it.'

Firing as he ran, Hood blasted the eastern windows to hell and then, without so much as a second thought, he and Little John sped up and launched themselves out through the gaping hole where the window had been and plummeted down through the sky.

> Although our two nations have traded indirect blows in this burgeoning conflict, the United States is not yet a formal part of this war. Our entry into it, however, need not occur at all.

THE FINAL LEG

The backpacks, of course, held parachutes.

But these were no ordinary parachutes.

Hood and Little John had known the Americans would send choppers. Likewise, they had known that getting to their final target would require at least one parachute jump.

The only problem: parachutes tend to hang in the air a long time.

And so they were using stunt chutes. High-speed, high-performance chutes that dropped fast due to perforations in their canopies, but which were also capable of tight control. After all, they were still three blocks from their target building, which was why the Chrysler had been the only option: it was high enough to allow them to parachute fast and low, without any hovering through three blocks of street canyons and onto the roof of their target destination.

The choppers saw them as soon as their twin parachutes blossomed. And took off in pursuit.

The stunt chutes worked well. Hood and Little John shot downward through the air like twin bullets, falling fast but flat, in dead-straight trajectories. They swung around onto 43rd Street, banking like race cars, now heading due east.

And for the first time that day, they saw their destination.

It loomed before them at the end of 43rd Street, two blocks away – a medium-sized square-shaped building made of glass and grey concrete, with an endless line of fluttering international flags stretched across its top.

The UN Building.

Fronting onto 1st Avenue.

Hood and Little John were losing altitude every second – *fifty storeys . . . forty-eight . . . forty-six . . .*

The choppers swung into the canyon behind them, rotors thumping, the lead helicopter trying to give the SEALs in its side doors a clear shot.

It was going to be close.

The two thieves shot through an intersection, descending quickly, flying fast.

Forty storeys . . . thirty-eight . . .

Shooting forward, the windows on either side of the street blurred with motion.

They came to 1st Avenue, blasting out of the chasms of New York City, shooting high over the street, soaring over the wide paved forecourt of the UN's head-quarters.

The choppers boomed out of the canyon system a second later, chasing desperately.

But they were too late.

The two parachutes sailed over the top of the UN Building, pulled up sharply, and landed deftly on its roof.

The moment Hood and Little John landed, they jettisoned their stunt chutes and took off at a run, disappearing inside a rooftop elevator shack just as security personnel appeared from the firestairs.

The three choppers lurched to a halt in front of the imposing international structure, stopping in mid-air, their race lost.

The usual bank of TV crews out the front of the

building caught sight of the two parachutes, a couple of them actually raising their cameras in time to get footage of the two daredevils.

Hood didn't mind. In fact, it was exactly what he wanted.

It was the nicest touch of all that they had painted some symbols onto their stunt chutes: anti-nuclear slogans berating the French for their continued nuclear testing in the South Pacific.

It was reported on the news that night as just another publicity stunt by guerilla environmentalists.

Once inside the UN Building, Hood and Little John attached clip-on ties to their collars, and assumed the walk of regular bureaucrats.

Owing to the labyrinth of national offices inside the building, the Americans would never know into which mission the two thieves walked – would never know which country's high-pressure release valve was used to open the mysterious Grauss case.

> In this vein, Herr Fuhrer, I
> propose an alliance between our
> two great nations – between
> Germany and the United States
> of America – that will supersede
> any previous treaties my coun-
> try may be party to.
>
> I await your reply. In the
> meantime, I remain,

```
Yours sincerely,
Franklin Delano Roosevelt
President of the United States
of America


- - - - - - - - - - - - - - -
OFFICIAL STAMP 046-24 -- DOCU-
MENT NOT DELIVERED (7 DECEMBER,
1941) -- DESTROY ALL COPIES --
DESTROY ALL COPIES -- DESTROY
ALL  COPIES  --  DESTROY  ALL
COPIES -- DESTROY ALL
- - - - - - - - - - - - - - -
```

THE BENEFITS OF LEVERAGE

Two days after the theft, the President of the United States gave an impromptu press conference during which he announced that tariffs preventing Australian meat products from entering the United States – tariffs which for years had unfairly protected American farmers from open-market competition – would be abolished.

He also issued a statement saying that aggressive US tactics toward the Euro and the European economy would cease. Some economic commentators noted that several currencies that were 'tied' to the Euro would benefit immensely from such an action, one of which was the beleaguered Australian dollar.

When questioned about the sudden changes of policy, the President denied that it had been the result of a recent meeting at UN Headquarters with top-level Australian diplomats.

In fact, he said, relations between the two nations were stronger than ever. Why, just next week, US SEAL teams were to engage in exercises with crack troops from the elite Australian SAS . . .

The Rat

Allison Rushby

The rat bites me at approximately 3 a.m.

It bites my left big toe.

It bites my left big toe hard.

I sit straight up in bed and scream. Later, when I get to know the people in the area, they will tell me I was heard as far as three streets away.

Without stopping to take a breath after the scream to end all screams, I grab my foot and jump out of bed with the other one onto the polished floorboards. It's freezing. I look wildly around me, not quite grasping what has happened. It takes me a few shakes of my head to get it together. When I do, I work out I know three things for certain:

1. I've been asleep;
2. now I'm not; and
3. my toe is *killing* me.

I thump down and sit cross-legged on the floor between all my still-unpacked moving boxes. I take a closer look at my appendage. It hurts. It's bleeding.

Blood!

I look back up at the bed. Which is when I see the little twitch-and-wiggle dance going on beneath my blue-checked doona.

Releasing my foot I press my hands over my mouth as I gag. Whatever the thing is under there, it's too big to be a mouse and too small to be a cat, a small dog or even a possum.

Which leads me to think there are only a few things in that mid-size there's-an-animal-in-my-bed range.

Like a guinea pig.

Or a rat, for instance. A rat would be about that size.

Right about that size, actually.

I forget about my toe and sit still, very still, on the floor as the realisation hits me: I have moved. I have moved away from my home, away from my family, away from my friends and away from my ex-flatmate, Lyle, who was so brave he used to pick up spiders and *set them down safely outside*.

Now there is only me . . . and the Thing Under the Doona. Which I am thinking is a rat.

Stupid new job.

Stupid new town.

Stupid new *rat-infested* town.

I sit for a while longer before I force myself to stand up and take the edge of the doona between two fingers.

Independence – it's what I wanted, right?

Yeah, sure.

I might have thought I wanted independence, but now I realise what I really wanted was independence plus one of those gadgets you plug in that emit a high-pitched noise to chase the nasties off (they don't work on closet monsters, I checked).

I close my eyes for a second and then open them as, in one movement, I rip the doona off the bed, praying that I'll see a nervous little guinea pig just begging to be fed a carrot or two.

But there's no sweet little brown and white guinea pig waiting to wiggle its nose at me under that doona.

Instead, right there in the centre of the mattress is the rat. It looks up at me, surprised. Then, discovering it is free of its Laura Ashley doona constrictions, it tries to make a run for it. I scream again and dump the doona right back down on top of it. I whip around, looking for something to hit the rat with because I am not, repeat *not*, doing a Lyle and picking it up and setting it down safely outside.

No, I am not, I think as I look down at my toe.

My eyes fall on my Nikes then, sitting on the floor, but as I reach for one I think better of it. It's going to take something bigger than one of my Nikes to kill that rat, even if I *do* have size 10 feet.

Plus, those Nikes – they're rat-sized. The perfect little cubbyhole – the rat might take it as an invitation to move in.

I look around for something else to use, but nothing catches my eye. Which I know means I'm going to have to leave the room. I watch the rat-sized lump moving under the doona for a few seconds to make sure it's not going to disappear. I don't want it to do that fly thing – the thing where you turn away for half a second to grab the fly spray and when you turn back, the fly is miraculously gone, not to re-appear until the fly spray is safely in the cupboard once more.

Okay, it looks like it's going to hang around for a bit.

I run out to the kitchen, dodging more boxes as I go, grab the broom from beside the fridge, then hot-foot it back to my bedroom. Where the rat is still doing the doona hula.

Good.

Kind of.

I take a deep breath and psych myself up a little. You can do it, I tell myself. You can kill this rat. You are an independent woman of the new millennium. You are broomed and dangerous.

I make sure I've got a good grip on the handle before I flick the doona cover off again. The rat, smarter now, doesn't hang around this time. I watch as it scoots across the bed and then hesitates at the edge. Seeing it pause, I push myself into action, knowing that this may be the only decent shot I'll get.

Things start to move in slow motion.

I take aim and swing at the rat with the broom, con-necting with it just as it makes the leap to freedom. My timing is a thing of beauty – something to tell the grand-kiddies about. The rat flies with a strange mammalian grace across the room and thuds against the wallpaper (I was looking for an excuse to change it anyway).

And in that one swift moment, I know I can now proudly tell my parents that all those tennis lessons they forked out for years ago have paid off. And then some.

I admire my handiwork for a moment, then run around to the other side of the bed to take a closer look.

The rat's fat little body lies spread-eagled on the floor. Not sure if it's quite dead, or simply stunned, I poke it with the end of the broom.

It twitches.

Oh.

My.

God.

A rat in pain. What to do? My toe starts to ache again.

And with that, I don't pause to think too hard about the ethics of the situation. Rather, I give the rat a few more good whacks in the general direction of its head. Then, disgusted with myself, I slide my back down the wall and sit on the floor, making sure the bloody view is hidden by another removal box.

I sit for quite a while. Eventually, as I start to gather my wits again, I begin to remember passages from one of the more morbid assignments I'd written at high school. It was on The Plague and I'd researched it extensively. As far as I can remember, it was rats and their flea buddies that carried The Plague. And I reason that rats are still dirty flea-infested little critters to this day – even in nice suburbs where people mow their lawns, and recycle, and know when they're allowed to use their sprinklers and then remember to actually turn them on.

The thought of The Plague stirs me into action. Well, it would, wouldn't it?

I take one more look at my toe, then stand up and grab a jumper, pulling it on. It gets stuck on my head for a moment and I have visions of beady red eyes staring at me – the rat's extended family. But when my head resurfaces (care of a little frenzied grappling), nothing stirs. I bend over and pull a sneaker onto my right foot, leaving the rat-bitten one bare. Then I hop down the hallway towards the front door, stopping only to grab my bag and rummage around in it for my car keys.

It's a long hop to the car. The longest hop in the world. Outside, everything is completely still. Obviously no one else has been bitten by a rat.

This is probably a good thing. A late night rat-bite express bus to the hospital could mean another move.

In the car, I give myself a moment to calm down, remind myself not to bleed on the upholstery, then drive in the direction of the closest hospital.

Making my way through the dark streets, I realise my toe, which had simply ached before, is now really starting to throb. Carefully, I reach down and touch it. It's bleeding again. Ugh. Disgusting. Blood and rat spit. I wipe my hand on my pyjama pants thoroughly, while I wonder just how long I was sharing my bed with the rat *before* it worked up the guts to bite me.

Yuck.

Hitting an 80 kmph zone, I speed up. I want to get to the hospital as fast as possible. Putting my foot down even further, I start to feel sorry for myself, going through all this alone. I am on an empty highway. I am cold. And lonely. And a rat has bitten me. I start to sniffle. Then I sniffle a bit more. Trying not to cry, I reach over and search around with one hand for the elusive tissue box I always keep in the car, but can never find. Eventually I give up on the glove box and try the back seat. The car swerves a little and I right it again. Almost instantly, a blue light flashes on behind me and a siren wails.

Oh shit.

I pull over and stop, taking a quick peek or two in the rear-vision mirror. Where the hell did he come from? I hold my breath as I watch the police officer park his motorcycle, take off his helmet and walk over to my side of the car. He gets out his notebook. The notebook of death.

Waking up to myself, I search frantically for the handle to wind the window down. I fumble. The police officer is waiting at the driver's side window now and motioning for me to wind it down. Clumsily, I do as I'm told.

He bends down to my level. 'You're out late,' he says.

I nod.

'You were swerving around a bit out there.'

I nod again, not being used to this police-pulling-me-over stuff.

He looks at me as if I'm not quite normal, then pulls out a small black machine, fitting a mouthpiece onto one end. He gives me the spiel and I blow into the mouthpiece, watching him as I do so. He isn't very old. My age, probably. His badge says his name is Michael. Michael Bollen. When he tells me to stop blowing, I stop. Then he turns the machine around to show me the reading. It's all zeros.

Michael Bollen the police officer looks surprised. My toe starts to throb a bit more and my bottom lip has a little wobble.

He goes to say something, then hesitates. I notice his expression change. He looks concerned now. He clears his throat, 'Um, is everything all right?'

This is all I need to set me off. I start to bawl. Messily, inelegantly and rather too loudly.

'A rat bit me,' I wail. Then I go straight into the story – or as much as I can between sobs. I have moved. I have moved away from my home, away from my family, away from my friends and away from my ex-flatmate, Lyle, who was so brave he used to pick up spiders and *set them down safely outside.*

When I'm done, Michael Bollen the police officer takes a step back from the car. 'What? I don't understand. A rat bit you so you moved?'

I try to stop myself, but I can't. I'm off again. I gulp and hiccup and cry all at the same time. 'A rat bit me. Now. At home.'

His eyes widen. 'A rat?'

I nod.

'Where?'

'At *home.*'

He gives me a look.

'Oh,' I wipe my nose on my sleeve, not caring if he sees or not. 'On my toe, I mean.'

He begins to laugh and I look up at him indignantly. This is no laughing matter. A rat bit me. On my toe. This is serious business.

'It's not funny,' I gulp again.

He laughs even harder.

Pissed off now, I stick my hand out of the window and punch him in his pale blue-shirted stomach. He stops laughing. It is only then that I realise I've punched a police officer.

'Um, sorry,' I say, surprised at myself because I've never punched a police officer before. Actually, I've never punched *anyone* before, and I realise a police officer probably isn't the best place to start.

He breathes out slowly, one hand covering his stomach, and pauses. Then he shrugs. 'It's okay, I guess I shouldn't have laughed at you. I take it you're on your way to the hospital?'

I nod again. For a moment there I'd started to get a little scared that he'd book me and sling me in the lock-up for the night. If I'd ended up there, I might just have acquired a second, matching, rat bite for my *right* foot.

'Well?' he looks at me, waiting for an answer.

I realise that, busy with my own thoughts, I've missed something he's said.

'Sorry?'

'I asked you if you wanted a police escort to the hospital.'

'Really?' I am surprised he'd do this for me after I've belted him one in the stomach. 'That'd be great.'

I close my window and he walks back to his bike, pulling his helmet on over his short, curly brown hair. I wait until he's pulled out in front, then follow behind. For a moment I am truly pleased with myself. I am smug, thinking about how quickly I'll get to the hospital with a police escort and how this means I've got a better chance of staving off the rabies or whatever it is the rat has given me. It isn't until I'm driving again that

I remember it is 3.45 a.m. – there isn't going to be a lot of traffic around to hold me up.

It takes less than ten minutes to get to the hospital. Michael Bollen the police officer helps me to hop into the emergency room and sits me on a nearby chair while he goes to find a nurse. I look around at the regulation government coloured green and cream walls and up the silent linoleum corridor. I smell the regulation hospital ice-cream, mashed pumpkin, old peas, tough roast and runny, lumpy gravy. I have to admit I am surprised at how quiet it is in Emergency. It's never this quiet on *ER*. Could it be they are lying to me for the hour I sit on the couch and drool all over the remote control each week?

After a few minutes Michael Bollen the police officer comes back and sits down next to me. 'The nurse said a doctor'll be along in a few minutes – you'll need a tetanus injection.'

'Well, that's something to look forward to,' I joke.

Michael Bollen the police officer doesn't say anything.

I feel my face starting to flush as I think about what has happened. 'Look, I'm sorry I was so, um, *emotional* before.' I can't bring myself to look at him.

'Don't worry about it. If I'd been bitten by a rat I'd probably be the same way. What actually happened?'

With the courage to look at him now, I take a deep breath and recount my epic tale of woe. I try not to embellish it too much. Well, maybe I make the rat just a *little* bigger.

I finish with a flourish of my left hand. 'And that's when you pulled me over.'

He looks impressed. 'Well, it's a great story, if you're lucky you might even reach urban-myth status.'

I smile at him, but this time I see the blue of his uniform. As much as I want him to stay, I open my mouth. 'Thanks for all your help and everything, but don't you need to go?'

He glances at his watch and shrugs. 'Doesn't matter – I'm off duty in a bit anyway.'

A door nearby opens and a guy walks out and speaks to the nurse for a few moments. He takes a manila folder from her and turns around. 'Jessica Walters?'

Michael Bollen the police officer and I look up at him, and then at each other. This guy is a doctor? He doesn't look more than eighteen. He isn't even wearing a tie for God's sake. I stand up and limp after him, thinking that, if this were a movie, the doctor would have been about ten years older, gorgeous and we would have had a whirlwind romance, got married and had two beautiful children. End of rat tale. I snort and sneak a look back at the waiting area. Michael Bollen the police officer smiles and shrugs. As I turn away, I realise I am a bit put out that he isn't coming in with me.

A needle and a dressing and it's all over. As the doctor snaps his gloves off he tells me I can make an appointment with my GP to take the dressing off and check up on whether the wound has healed properly.

And that's it.

Dismissed without even a jellybean, I go back outside, closing the door behind me.

'So how was Doogie Howser?' Michael Bollen the police officer asks.

I laugh and the nurse looks at us both with her evil nurse stare. He shuts up and I stop laughing.

We walk back down the corridor in the direction of the car park. Suddenly, I become acutely aware that I am wearing a flannelette fashion ensemble. Complete with teddy-bear pattern.

As Michael talks, I pull down my jumper self-consciously, hoping he hasn't noticed. Then I surreptitiously run a hand through my tangled hair. We pass a vending machine and Michael stops.

'Wait a second,' he says.

He goes over and fishes some loose change out of his pocket, pushes it into the slot and makes his selection. I see a packet of Lifesavers fall. Michael retrieves it and walks back over, holding out his hand.

'Oh, no thanks, I've already eaten,' I say, then kick myself. What do I mean *already eaten*? It's approximately four o'clock in the morning.

Michael shakes his head. 'No, they're all yours. You always get lollies after an injection – in my family anyway.'

I smile and take the packet, thinking that this is corny. But sweet at the same time. Corny *and* sweet. 'Thanks,' I say.

As we get closer and closer to my car, I know I don't want to go home. Well, not new home. I want to go home home and have my mum fuss over me. Have my dad bring the TV into my room so I can lie in bed and watch it, and be brought tea and toast and the occasional Lucozade for sustenance.

But I can't.

I look over at Michael and wonder if I should ask for his phone number. He seems nice. And I know that I've never had the courage to ask a guy for his phone number before, but these are desperate times – I'd give anything for a bit of human company. I have no family in this city, I have no friends in this city. There is just me, my house, my car and the people at work I haven't even met yet, though I now have a great story to get started with. I deliberate about the phone number all the way to the car.

When we get there, I open the driver's side door and lean against it in what might be a seductive fashion if it weren't for my teddy-bear pyjamas.

'So . . .' we both say at the same time, then laugh.

'Don't get bitten by any more rats,' Michael says.

I remember the rat lying bloody and beaten beside my bed and wince. I'll have to clean that up when I get home. And sterilise my doona somehow. I shudder.

'I'd better get going,' I say, sitting down slowly in the driver's seat.

'Okay.'

'Well, I'll see you around I guess. Next time I get bitten . . .'

Michael looks down at the ground, then up at the sky, then down at the ground again. 'Right. Yeah. See you later,' he says, his eyes avoiding me. He turns and walks over to his bike.

I close the door and shrug, watching him walk away. Maybe I've been getting the wrong vibes. Maybe he's already in a relationship. I watch as he keeps walking, turning the tube of Lifesavers over and over in the palm of my hand. Soon enough, I drop them.

As I pick them up off the floor of the car the realisation hits me. What am I thinking? He *must* like me. He's given me a packet of *Lifesavers* for God's sake. In primary school that would have been a lifelong commitment. I open the packet, take the first one out and eat it.

Cherry. My favourite.

Then, before I can change my mind, I open the car door and get out. 'Michael,' I say, 'wait'.

Hit and Myth

David Smiedt

Fiction. Domain of nuance. Realm of insight via intimation. Of bugger all help when it comes to understanding men. Granted, you may see us reflected – either as individuals or a gender – but when was the last time a plot enhanced your own relationship?

So here's to playing it straight when it comes to the greatest myths surrounding men's sexual desires plus the experiences that we genuinely crave. What you are about to read ain't gonna be pretty. There will no literary equivalent of that movie sex euphemism whereby a trail of discarded clothes equals unbridled passion, or a long, slow pan to the fireplace calls to mind the heat being generated elsewhere in the room. We're going to get down. We're going to get dirty. And we're going to uncover new ground in territories of his mind *you* thought you knew, while exploring the shadowy terrain *he*'d prefer you didn't wander around in.

The subject of sex attracts lies and falsehoods like collagen to a fading starlet. The reasons for this are manifold, but the primary cause lies in the rich irony that although sexuality bombards us from every page, billboard and bus stop, we still don't talk about it a great deal.

And when we do, it's more often than not with a trusted friend who has been around for longer than most of our romances combined. In short, the people with whom we are most open about our sex lives are frequently not those with whom we are actually having sex. My theory is that this twenty-first century lull in the carnal conversation stems from the fact that we've gone from being embarrassed about not being able to distinguish our elbows from our areolae to thinking we're more sexually sophisticated than we actually are.

After a couple of seasons of *Sex and the City* with a handful of *Jerry Springer*s thrown in for good measure, it's all become a bit of a bore, right? Everything's passé to our jaded sexual palates. We are so surrounded by a media bonkfest that we believe we have an in-depth knowledge about sexual encounters that we've only ever read about and seen depicted on TV ad nauseam.

How do I know this? When was the last time you orgasmed like Kim Catrell? As frank and open as the depiction of sex is in TV shows, movies and books, it's always still a constructed entity. It's as one-dimensional as the set of *Friends* or, for that matter, the cast. On TV guys don't orgasm while still wearing their underwear, no one's private parts produce air bubbles that need posthaste expurgating and no one ever emits guttural vowel medleys at the point of orgasm. The gulf between reality sex and Hollywood luuurvemaking is vast, but it should be pointed out that all the blame for the continued evolution of sexual myths in the information age cannot be laid at the immaculately pedicured feet of Sarah Jessica Parker et al. Us regular folk play our parts in this charade too.

Believing that we have happened upon a juicy piece of sexual trivia, we eagerly share it with friends. 'Did you know men also have G-spots? It drives them all crazy. It's right behind the . . .' we authoritatively reveal. And so a sexual myth is born.

THE MYTH OF THE MALE G-SPOT

Yes, men have the equivalent of a G-spot but having it stimulated does not drive us *all* crazy. The reason that many of us would prefer to go through life not knowing the joy of our G-spots is that they lie at the end of a road reserved for one-way traffic in the opposite direction.

In addition, referring to this area as a 'G-spot' is both misleading and inaccurate. For a start, it was not actually discovered by one Dr Grafenberg, though he did show great foresight by contracting that part of the locale named after him to just 'G', in so doing avoiding the bedroom use of a name that sounds more like an ill-fated Zeppelin than titillation central. Secondly, the good doctor also dismissed terms like protrusion and membrane in favour of 'spot'. Kinda has a swinging jazz vibe to it, much in the same way that 'niteclubs' once did: 'Cocktails at the G-spot? I'll see you there. Now are you sure you know how to find the place?' And if you think that G-spot has a groovier ring to it, consider the fact that the Italian equivalent is called *Il punto G*.

How exotic is that? It sounds like a resort on the Amalfi Coast. You can just hear Glenn Ridge saying, 'Unfortunately no money behind Kim Kilby but you have won two sun-filled weeks of fun at Il Punto G'.

The male equivalent of the G-spot should really more accurately be known as the 'P-gland'. Yep, it's the old prostate – the very same that your dad presents to his doctor for annual examination And if you still think every man goes wild for a little disappearing digit action, ask Pop how much he looks forward to that check-up. What's more, I believe that any discomfort he might feel at the prospect of discussing this subject with his daughter will pale into insignificance beside that which accompanies the snap of a rubber glove on his doctor's wrist.

Logic dictates, of course, that while there are some men who are not the least bit interested in a new level of sexual fulfilment, there are also some who are. But before you ensconce your pinky in something suitably viscous and go boldly forth, it might be a good idea to experiment a little in the general area before launching your projectile. Catch him unawares and you'll soon have a frightened naked man with eyes like saucers hanging from your light fitting. And if that doesn't kill a mood, nothing will.

One of the greatest myths about the male G-spot is that the stimulating party actually has to make contact with it. Wrong. The whole process can be done externally. This is because the prostate gland is to be found only a wafer-thin piece of skin away from the flesh at the base of his scrotum. Light pressure on this thumb-nail-sized region at the point of orgasm will have him speaking in tongues. I'd like to remind you, however, that the word 'pressure' a sentence back was preceded by 'light'. I beg you to err on the side of restraint should you choose to spice things up some. Push too hard and before you can ask 'Does this feel good?' he'll be crouched on top of the wardrobe wielding a table lamp for protection.

THE FAKING ORGASM MYTH

The next sexual myth is that men never fake orgasm. Of course we do – the difference is that Billy Crystal doesn't look half as cute as Meg Ryan when he moans, flushes and bangs his fists on a dinner table in ecstasy. Where it does differ from female fakery is in its frequency, though I have to admit to not exactly being sure how often women hit the whimper button.

Never believe a man who tells you he can always pick a woman who's faking an orgasm, and try to resist the temptation to point out that if he put the same time and effort into actually providing the real McCoy that he spent on spotting counterfeit orgasms, then he wouldn't need to spend his sex life suspicious of being duped.

I believe I speak for the majority of men when I say that I have no clue when it comes to telling a genuine orgasm from a faked one. This is the reason why while I'm certain that some of my sexual partners have faked orgasm with me, I'm not sure which. They all could have feigned every squirm and exhortation and I would be none the wiser.

The only fake orgasms I can tell from real ones are

mine. And yes, I've had both kinds. Since men can orgasm at the sight of a woman's underwear, it stands to reason that we rarely fake a climax during the first round of action for the evening. The histrionics most often come into play when the couple concerned have re-covered from their initial tryst and decide to re-enact the whole shebang. These sexual sequels hold the promise of enhanced fulfilment for the woman, as most men can generally last longer the second time around. Especially if condoms are being used. The problem is that sometimes Mr Happy can become so desensitised that while turgid is not a problem, sufficient stimulation to prompt orgasm is.

I've spoken to numerous female friends about the subject of faking orgasms and many have pointed out that 'You just know when it's going to happen and you know when it's not'. The same applies to men who are banging away to satisfy their partner but realise that orgasm is as distant a prospect as a politically stable Middle East.

A complex dance then unfolds. Men are ever mindful of the need for stamina under such circumstances. But, believe it or not, it's often not the blessing it may seem. Once our female partner is sated and urging us to abandon our restraint, many of us would like nothing more than to slip up a gear and pump our way to ecstasy. But, as mentioned earlier, if we've already detonated the love rocket within the previous hour or so and are wearing a condom, chances are the orgasm may be less than forth– er . . . imminent. That's when some men may resort to a contrived tempo shift combined with a little groaning before collapsing in a heap of pseudo-satisfaction.

Don't take this to mean that you are a less-than-spectacular lover. Physiology wins out every time and, like many of the most perplexing forms of male behaviour, his dramatic performance comes about as a result of his perceived lack of sexual brilliance. Men like to view themselves as carnal stallions, and the prospect of being thought of as a 'one shot per night' guy is an abomination in the eyes of many. It all comes back to ego, but then so many male quirks do. As if any woman ever left a man because, although he satisfied her, his personal climax rate wasn't up to par.

THE THREESOME MYTH

The overwhelming majority of men *fantasise* about a threesome with two women. Right.

The overwhelming majority of men *want* to engineer a threesome with two women. Wrong.

Before explaining why many of us aren't that interested in turning fantasy into reality, I should point out that if you're squeamish about the bouillabaisse that is the male psyche, hold onto your lunch.

Let's start by examining the esteem in which this fantasy is held by men. From Cape Town to Cairo, Singapore to San José, few erotic scenarios rival this one for pure power. How strong is it? Well, you know how much he wants to do that thing which involves two hours of begging, a lubricating agent and assurances that 'Once you relax, it will feel great'? This turns him on more than that.

Right now, I bet you're shaking your head or rolling your eyes and mumbling 'Not my man. I'm all the woman he needs'. Your man too! And if you're tempted to write this off as a rather clichéd fantasy to treasure so tightly, you have no clue as to your man's take on the two-on-one scenario. You see, as popular as this fantasy is, it's never quite the same for any two men. We all become impressionists when it comes to the way our imagined trysts unfold.

Some of us imagine chancing upon two girls who have succumbed to animalistic passion at, say, a picnic or perhaps at work, and are pleasuring one another senseless. The bearer of this fantasy doesn't make himself known to the girls he's caught in flagrante delicto. Instead . . . he watches. The element of voyeurism is often overlooked when discussing this male fantasy, as it is wrongly assumed that a man with little sexual patience in real life could be restrained in his imagination. Not true. Men find it incredibly arousing simply watching two women have sex.

I don't think as many women would be so entranced by the sight of two guys painting the town red, though some may disagree. I'm not sure why this disparity exists, but I think it has something to do with the fact that we live in a society where the female body is generally more eroticised than the male. As simplistic as it may sound, this means that when there are two naked female bodies together, the combined erotic power is not merely doubled but somehow squared.

Some men take this mathematical element further

by adding three, four or more women to their erotic imaginings. However, for the most part, it's the standard two-on-one affair. Why do most men choose to stop at two? To be honest, deep down most men are thoroughly aware of their limitations and realise they would be hard-pressed to satisfy any more than two women. Many can't even make one happy, right? And the prospect of a partner who found his lovin' underwhelming poses a threat to his ego that is simply too horrible to contemplate and counters the psychological reward of bedding a twosome.

The concept of mutual satisfaction is crucial – men always satisfy the women in our fantasies with a deadly mix of panache, stamina and the type of agility usually reserved for seven-year-old Soviet gymnasts and Shaolin monks.

Aside from the aforementioned man-catching-two-ladies-in-the-act-then-joining-in scenario, many a man would also stake his claim on a fantasy where he and a woman are making love, but unbeknown to them are being watched by another woman who becomes so filled with lust that she can't help but make more than her presence felt. Which brings us to the women involved. Sometimes it's our current partners doin' the do with us and another woman. Often it's not. This is where men's threesome fantasies begin to take on idiosyncratic tendencies. Some go for two girls from the office, while others go for imagined girls who dress like they work in an office. Some think of the neighbour, ex-girlfriends, a nurse who was on duty when he was recovering from having his wisdom teeth extracted. The cast is a veritable collage of our past, our imagination and our subconscious.

There are only three things you can say with any certainty about the phenomenal popularity of this male fantasy. Firstly, while there is definitely a staggering majority of men who relish the idea of doing the horizontal tango with two women, there is an identifiable minority who wouldn't mind trying the two guys and one girl thing. Secondly, I think this fantasy's allure is connected to notions of power. The, ahem, pulling power is heightened because women are still apparently the more sexually demure gender, and the blatant flaunting of such rule-breaking is powerfully erotic. Especially if the guy involved believes that it's because the female participants want him so badly that they are willing to share him – and each other. This is an ego trip. Pathetic? Yes. Fact? Certainly.

And finally, for all the individual manifestations of this fantasy, it remains just that. We don't necessarily want to make it happen. Why? Because we kind of suspect the experience will never match up to a fantasy that only gets stronger and more erotically charged the longer we hold onto it.

THE PURELY PHYSICAL MYTH

While it is widely acknowledged that men become slaves to their own lust more readily than women, it should also be explained that even though sex can be an entirely physical experience for certain males, this is not always the case. The idea that men are only in it to get their rocks off is a myth that ranks with the Loch

Ness Monster and the Pharaoh's Curse. For all the pleasures the flesh can offer, there's a great deal to be said for intimacy – the stroke of an affectionate hand, holding someone you love close and the unspoken reaffirmation of the bond between you. These elements are particularly pertinent for men for whom verbal communication is a challenge, and ridding yourself of this myth may well make your sex life more loving, intimate and rewarding.

THE MALE WISH LIST

Now that we've got over some myths, let's get onto what men really want. As a man who has made a living by betraying my sex, however, I'd like to make a few things clear before detailing the male sexual experience wish list. For a start, a lot of men aren't sat down as a boy by a caring father or teacher who then gently explains the reality of the sexual caper. Instead, we learn about matters of the flesh from sources such as pornographic videos and magazines which show massively endowed men endlessly pleasuring supplicant females who orgasm at the tweak of a nipple and feel that no orifice should be off limits to their talented lover. What's more, these 'actors' never climax until their partner is satisfied and the orgasms are always simultaneous. Consequently, many a man is rather dismayed when his partner displays a reluctance to place her ankles about her neck and moan filth while they're making love. I therefore beg your understanding that many of the desired experiences you are about to encounter are formulated in this netherworld of flesh and fantasy where G-spots are marked out like baseball diamonds – talk about sliding into home – and women are compelled by the same intense hormonal urgings as the men who watch the porn are.

These biological yearnings should not be discounted – they are powerful, pervasive and persistent. A prime indication of their nature can be found in Plato's *Republic*. Someone asked Sophocles, 'How do you feel now about sex? Are you still able to have a woman?' He replied, 'Hush, man. Most gladly indeed am I rid of it all, as though I had escaped from a mad and savage master.' Let me remind you this was Sophocles – one of the most enlightened human beings to ever walk the planet – and he couldn't keep the dog in the kennel.

Combine these testosterone-fuelled yearnings with the aforementioned sources of stimuli, and perhaps some of the items on this libidinous list might begin to make sense. Doubtless you may have read of some before. What can I say, classics are always classics, but I should point out that wish lists often remain just that. It all depends on the man in question, how important sexual fulfilment is to him and what he's willing to risk to get it.

ONE REALLY DOES A SUMMER MAKE

How do I phrase this delicately? In many ways, this is a matter of personal taste, but when it comes to paying lip service to a lover, there is one thing all men long for. If you can stomach it and not bring your lovemaking to a gagging halt at the point of his climax, I have no hesitation in telling you that there's not a man alive who hasn't longed for a woman who will put the icing on the cake, so to speak. If you still don't know what I'm referring to here, I suggest you swallow your pride, admit defeat and head to the next paragraph. The lengths men will go to for this sexual experience are evidenced by the fact that some have actually left their partners for a woman who is less intelligent and less attractive, yet performs this deed with relish. Go figure.

COME HERE OFTEN?

Sex, as I'm sure you know, has consequences on many levels. Most of the time. The exception to this rule is when a man and woman who have little in common cross paths on their respective ways to somewhere else, and act on their attraction fully aware of the purely physical and certainly brief nature of their liaison. This is an erotic adventure without the emotional ramifications that usually accompany the act. No wonder men hope like hell that fate will someday throw this erotic escapade their way and can't believe their luck when it actually happens. Granted men are cursed – or blessed, depending on who you're talking to – with the ability to disassociate themselves from the intimacy that comes with sex. For the most part, however, this trait is kept in check by the individual's code of morality. Stop giggling, I mean it. All that changes when we meet a woman who simply wants us to supply her with muscle contractions all night long. Like most rare events though, as I mentioned earlier, I suspect that even your most phallus-driven man would eventually tire of bumping uglies without an emotional component. Which is not to say he wouldn't do it a few more times just to make sure.

SORRY, THERE'S SOMEONE IN HERE

Sex within a relationship should, in theory, be enriched by facets such as intimacy, emotional communication via physical means, and a desire to make your partner feel loved, sexy and attractive. There is, however, a liaison which is characterised by lust alone and which is carried out in a spirit of pure raunch. Here's the scenario: you and your man are out to dinner. Between your mains and dessert, you are suddenly overcome by the urge to have him right there, right now. You tell him to meet you in the ladies' toilet in five minutes and to make sure no one sees him slipping in. You then claim a cubicle in which you have fast, hard, erotic sex before calmly making your way back to the table for dessert. The reason men so love this type of sex is – surprise, surprise – directly related to their egos. Despite an apparent social evolution, many women are still shackled by the outdated stereotype that only sluts and tramps give in to their carnal desires in the aforementioned manner.

It won't occur to the man in question that a woman who lures him into the washroom for a little pre-dessert treat may just be rebelling against such outdated sexual politics and claiming her right to a little erotic adventure. He will be of the belief that she is so overcome with desire for him that all restraint has been dismissed in the name of lust. 'Yeah,' he's thinking, 'she wants me baaad!' This ego-salving notion is just as enticing as anything that goes on in the cubicle and is rivalled only by the element of danger in being caught.

TEACHER'S PET

As men feel the first sexual rumblings coursing through them, it's most likely that they will become fixated on – and fantasise about – the women they come into contact with in their day-to-day lives. These unfortunates are probably the girls in their school classes and are most definitely those teaching them. While this fantasy rarely becomes reality, the attraction to tutors, team leaders and other female members of authority lingers like an uninvited party guest with a drinking problem. The thought of disarming and disrobing such a woman burns hot and heavy in the psyche of many a man. Again it's an ego thing, with the woman in question willingly relinquishing her position of authority in the name of overwhelming desire.

PENNY PELVIS

Every man wants to bed a porn star/centrefold/table dancer just once. Once more, ego plays a role as she's chosen to grill the sirloin with him even though she must get dozens of daily propositions. Secondly, he'll be able to enjoy the myriad delights of a woman he knows is extroverted and sexually experienced – I mean she's hardly about to insist on having the lights off or gasp 'You want me to suck what?'

AUTOPILOT

It shouldn't surprise you to read that men are, for all

our bravado and posturing, essentially lazy creatures. In fact, most men's idea of roughing it is turning the electric blanket down to medium. W.C. Fields put it better when he said he knew of a candidate who was so lazy he put popcorn on his pancakes so they would turn themselves. Right now the men reading this (and I know you're out there, fellas) are thinking, Top idea. This trait carries over into our sex lives – or at least we wish it would. We'd all take lazy sex if it were on offer.

In case you were wondering what this involves, here's the score. The man in this scenario might better be called the recipient. He remains seated or on his back for the entire event while the unfortunate female vaults about his person as if it were a pummel horse with love handles. He does nothing but feel great, while she gets to enact any domination fantasies she may have. At least, that's what she tells herself when she inevitably begins to suspect her man has the lovemaking skills of a heavily sedated quadriplegic octogenarian.

Now that you know some of the differences between what popular mythology would have you believe are the sexual experiences every man desires and those he genuinely hankers after, it's up to you to turn this information to your advantage – whether you choose to use it merely as a bargaining tool for greater headboard-shuddering satisfaction on your part, or to take the more altruistic root, er route, by making it a working example of the give-and-take principle upon which the most enduring of relationships are founded. I would, however, abstain from utilising this new-found carnal compendium to transform yourself into his custom-made minx. What possible rewards could this 'anything to keep him happy' approach offer the modern woman? In terms of relationship realities, the answer is obviously a resounding SFA. That's why the only women you'll ever encounter who embark on such a campaign and emerge with a successful long-term relationship in which their self-esteem is untarnished and libido sated stem from the world of fiction. Domain of nuance. Realm of insight via intimation. Of bugger all help when it comes to understanding men.

Last Glance Back
Michael Marshall Smith

I was walking up Leighton Road, my mind on something else. Most people who walk up Leighton Road try to have their mind on something else, and with good reason, but there's no other way of getting from Kentish Town tube to my flat. It had been a long day at work, but not a bad one, because Jenny had been there. Though we worked in different parts of the office, we could sense each other through the walls – and had spent a very warm lunch hour wrapped round each other in a pub. After a month I still found it odd being at work with someone who was now also my girlfriend, strange having to be corporate with each other when co-workers and clients were around. My mood tended to vacillate wildly between irritation at having to deal with other people, joy when Jenny walked into the room, and chagrin at not being able to grab hold of her. Previously secular ground had become more complicated, and while in some ways that was magical, it could also be rather tiring.

Jenny was out drinking with girlfriends that evening, and spending the night in her own flat. This left me to my own devices for the first time in what felt like quite a while. I was already missing her, but that wasn't what I was thinking about. We'd snatched a drink together before she headed off towards her mates, and Jenny had mentioned the idea of living together. She'd lofted it very casually, so that the conversation didn't run smack into it, but also in a way that said she'd already done some thinking on the subject. Most of me had leapt at the idea, but I'd found myself saying it needed considering, and that's what I was doing. Considering it.

Leighton Road was sparsely populated with migrating locals, shambling home to their sofas or drifting in the other direction towards the takeaways and pubs. Like most of those who were homeward bound, my head was down. When I raised it in anticipation of a side road, I saw a girl wandering down the street towards me.

The first thing I noticed were her eyes, which were blue and blurred behind tears. The area round them was already reddened with crying, the skin a blotched pink which stood out against the pallor of the rest of her face. Stood out to me, at least. Nobody else seemed to pay her any attention at all, so intent were they on hurrying home to their televisions.

The area round Kentish Town tube is a Mecca for tramps, and you tend to see the same ones again and again: the one who shouts; the one with the cider; the one who didn't look like he should be there a year ago, but now looks as if he should. I hadn't seen this girl before, however, and while she was obviously homeless she didn't quite seem like a derelict. Not yet, anyway. Her hair was ragged blonde and hung in dreadlock rats' tails around her face, but remained fairly presentable, as did the faded pink top and equally tired orange leggings. Her neck was strung with ethnic necklaces, and cheap bangles rattled round her wrists. I was surprised not to see a stud in her nose.

I'll be honest and say I don't usually have a great deal of patience with the type, but this girl appeared in front of me fully formed in grief, and her wordless distress caught my attention, her sense of being completely cut off from the world around her and locked in some inner pain. She could only have been about seventeen, and she looked doomed. She was floating down the pavement so vaguely that I thought she must have only the most shadowy sense of the distinction between it and the road, but as she came closer she held out her hand.

I know I shouldn't feel like this, but after daily acquaintance with people begging, my policy on giving money depends largely on how I'm feeling about my own world. With her it was different. I felt I had to give her something, even though she seemed barely conscious I was there. I rummaged clumsily in my back pocket and pulled out some change. A quick glance told me that there were three, maybe even four, pound coins amongst the shrapnel, but I placed the whole lot in her hand.

She peered vaguely at it as I stepped past her, and then suddenly looked up. For a moment her eyes were clear, and she was someone real, surprised back into the world.

'Hey, thanks,' she said, bewildered. 'Thank you.'

Flushing slightly, I nodded curtly, and then carried on walking up the road towards the flat I paid £270 for each week. After about ten yards I took a quick glance behind me. She was still standing there, still staring into her palm, as people walked either side of her not even noticing she was there.

The flat felt odd without Jenny in it. I'm a card-carrying materialist who needs his quota of consumer goods around him, but the places I've stored them in have never seemed to mean much to me. I get bored with the corner shop, with tramping the same streets and struggling down the same broken escalator in the Underground, and for the last four years I'd moved at least annually. I like places, in general – and as somewhere to be, they're fine. But as a constant, as somewhere to hang your life, they are not to be trusted. They're too impassive, and they don't care about you, not really. They've seen occupants before you, and they will see others once you've gone. I'd always felt that my real home would be in a person, and now I believed I'd found her. In the last month the flat had been changing behind my back, relaxing into shape, becoming a place I cared about, simply because she was there.

After a shower I wandered around it for a while, noticing her shoes, an empty packet of her brand of cigarettes in the bin, flicking through one of her magazines – and in a quiet, warm way thought how marvellous it was to have Jenny in my life. And in my flat. So why this feeling of trepidation at the thought of her moving in, or rather at the thought of us both moving out and finding somewhere to live together?

I could understand part of it: I'd spent the last two years largely by myself. There'd been a few women in that time, but not many, and all had been glancing blows that both parties had been happy to let fade. I'd got used to solitude and independence, to making plans that included only myself, to being the centre of my world.

And I'd hated it, of course. Suddenly I remembered Saturday afternoons pacing around the flat, faster and faster, trying to achieve escape velocity. Sometimes I made it out the door and paced round town instead, trying to think of something I could face doing by myself, again. It was that and evenings in front of the television, or with a book, or spent leafing through the videos in the local store, trying to find one I hadn't seen. I hadn't minded being by myself. What I'd minded was being emotionally homeless, culturally pointless. Now that I had a home, maybe I was worried about losing space to be by myself, of being constrained. Well, I could make sure that I had time, could preserve some backstage areas. Jenny would probably need some space herself, though I hoped not. I wanted to be with her all the time. Why should she want time away from me?

Suddenly realising the circle I'd come in, I shook my head. Silly. All I needed was time to adjust to the idea.

Feeling better, I glanced at the clock. It was only

eight o'clock. A whole evening by myself stretched in front of me.

What was I going to do?

At ten-thirty I woke on the sofa, surprised by darkness outside. My book lay spilled beside me, and a cold cup of coffee sat on the table. I hauled myself upright, yawning massively, and peered querulously around for my cigarettes.

After microwaving the cup of coffee I settled back down by the window, and gazed blearily at the street outside. It was very dark, a belt of cloud obscuring the moon and streetlights either broken by local yobs or shrouded in trees. The street looked strange, perhaps because for once I felt that there was a real difference between it and where I was sitting, that the flat wasn't simply warmer and brighter.

From nowhere an image popped into my mind, like a still photograph. It was of predominantly bright colours in front of variegated grey, and it took me a moment to work out what it was, by which time it was already fading. It was the girl I'd encountered on Leighton Road, from the neck down. The breasts inside her pink top were small, but nicely shaped, her thighs smooth beneath orange cloth.

I blinked, slightly shocked. I hadn't noticed any of this when she'd been in front of me, and wasn't interested in noticing it now. I'm not like that, and with Jenny in my life everyone else was behind a sheet of glass, and I was happy for it to be that way. It must have been a stray image, something left over from the material my mind had been processing while I slept.

I stood up with no real purpose, and wandered across to the other window. It made sense to go to bed, but it seemed too early. Instead I collected up my keys and went for a walk.

It was a little colder than I was expecting, and I decided to just take a turn round the block. The surrounding streets are very quiet at night, apart from occasional shouting lunatics and sudden janglings from public phone booths, as phone calls went un-answered.

As I walked I thought of Jenny, and wondered what she was doing and thinking at that moment. Was she describing me to her friends, and sounding as if she missed me, or was she off in her own world, plugged back into old friendships and past times? Her friends would have known Chris, the man she'd left for me. For a moment I felt a shiver of pure, naked insecurity, a feeling I hadn't had to deal with for several years. When my relationship with Annette had crashed and burned after half a decade of heavy turbulence, I'd done every-thing I could to shield myself from that kind of wound. Yet here I was again. Jenny could hurt me. I'd signed up, and I wasn't entirely safe any more. And presum-ably, neither was she.

When I got back I sat up for a while, and read a little more of my book. Jenny didn't call. I hadn't expected her to.

As I drifted off to sleep later that night I caught a fragment of a dream. My hand reached out towards someone, and in it there was a ten-pound note.

'Would this be any use to you?' I heard a voice ask.

As the girl took the note and looked at me, knowing what I wanted to buy, and not caring, I realised the voice had been my own.

I slept badly, and was in a ragged mood as I trudged through fitful winter sunlight towards the tube. I'd be seeing Jenny, but apart from that the day ahead held little but stress. Not real anxiety, of course, nothing relating to anything that mattered: merely the workaday run-of-the-mill white noise that comes with employ-ment, along with your pay packet, bad coffee and an inexhaustible supply of Post-it notes. I was becoming increasingly convinced that I didn't want to work for a living. Not a very original thought, but strongly felt all the same. I wondered if any of the people walking in the opposite direction felt any better about the whole deal, if they believed they were growing up instead of merely older. Most of them looked as if they didn't feel anything about anything, as if they were deep in mechanical indifference.

With a slight lurch I recognised one of them, a woman walking in the same direction as me, on the other side of the road. I didn't know her at all, had merely noticed her a few times as I dully marched down the road to work in the mornings. I hadn't seen her for a while, in fact: not since Jenny and I had come togeth-er. We tended to leave the flat slightly later than had been my custom, for a variety of reasons.

The woman was tall, and slim, with rich chestnut hair. She appeared very together, like a fully-fledged adult, but also as if she might remember how to smile, given the right incentive. She'd been the focus of a few utterly platonic daydreams in the days when I'd been single: the idea of walking with her, of turning to see her face, of simply sharing a life, had all seemed rather appealing. It was odd to see her again, now that I had someone with whom I could have those things. For a moment I was pulled back to the previous year, and it felt strangely comfortable there, like a broken sofa which you've got used to sitting on, a tangle of stuffing and springs which nonetheless knows your shape better than some plump new divan.

I stopped to light a cigarette, partly because I felt like one, and partly to put more distance between us. In the old days I'd often covertly kept pace behind her to the station, and shuffled along the platform to be closer, so I could think my wistful thoughts. But that was then, and this was now.

The ruse worked, because when I got to the station I had just missed a train and the platform was deserted.

I waited, irritated by the weight of the bag on my shoulder, and stared belligerently at the advertisements on the opposite wall of the tunnel. One proclaimed the charms of California, and as I read it my heart sank unexpectedly. Another of my fantasies of the last few years, a key support mechanism, had been the daydream of moving to America, of quitting my job and finding a life. That wouldn't happen now, of course. I didn't only have a job. I had a girlfriend. I *had* a life. Or would have very soon. A life and a bigger flat and someone with whom to jointly send Christmas cards.

I walked further along the platform so I couldn't see the photographs of the Redwood forests.

The morning went fine, in that I did all the work I was supposed to do. It wasn't especially good in other respects. Not bad, just not good. Jenny and I went out again at lunch, and had a nice time. Things were all right between us.

But the very fact that I considered the question, that I thought of things being all right between us, showed that the day wasn't really jelling. Until now we'd been like one person. Today felt like a step back from that. Not far, but a step. It was the kind of day you have when you're going out with someone: nice, but not special. Another day in a life that was presumably mine.

We talked a little more about the idea of finding a flat, and I was happy to sound interested, but didn't mind too much when the rather frank gropings of a nearby couple turned our attention away from the subject. Almost all of me wanted to turn it back again, but a little frozen piece did not, and so we covertly giggled at the clandestine romping at the next table until we were feeling rather intense ourselves. We held hands as we walked back to the office.

The afternoon was better, not least because I knew I was working from home the next day, which meant a day off from the hysteria which everyone else seemed to enjoy whipping up. Jenny and I could talk on the phone, and there'd be the evening to look forward to. By the time we were walking up Leighton Road towards the flat I was in a reasonably good mood.

When we were passing the spot where I'd seen the girl the previous evening, I remembered the dream from the night before. A feeling of hot, nervous haste, of yielding to impulse, of letting something hidden inside peep out and touch the world. It was a horrible idea, offering a disadvantaged woman money for sex. I was quite prepared to believe it went on, but hated the fact that my dreaming self had remembered it, or thought it. I could imagine the kind of man who might do such a thing, and felt nothing but revulsion.

For him, anyway. Not so much for her. Again I found I could picture her body within her loose cotton clothes, imagine the slightly rough texture of her pale skin and the firmness of her limbs. And her hair, of course, her stringy blonde hair.

Suddenly I realised something. Jenny also had blonde hair.

Glancing across as we walked arm in arm, chatting about the day, I noticed her hair as if for the first time. Before all I'd thought about it was that it was beautiful. Now I realised that while that was true, it was also blonde. Trying to keep my walk casual and my banter smooth, I struggled to incorporate this.

It may not seem important, in fact it seems kind of stupid, but I'd always sort of assumed I'd end up with someone with brown hair. I don't know why, and it's not that I'm obsessed with it, or even find it particularly attractive. It's just that in my mind, in the region where the dream girl lived who'd got me through drab months, I was sort of banking on brown hair.

It was irrelevant, unimportant. As a matter of fact,

Annette had also been blonde, as had most of the girls I'd been out with. The brown-ness wasn't important, but something was. It was almost as if my life had been alternating for years between two possible states, and now it had settled on one, as if a roulette ball had finally come to rest on black. It was a high-scoring number, a jackpot in fact, and I was very happy with it. Jenny was all I had ever wanted in a friend, and far more. She was intelligent, and loveable, and funny and beautiful. She had a clean laugh and a dirty one, and I could be however I wanted to be with her. I felt very seriously about her, and maybe that was it. A realisation that the ball had come to rest, and that winning on red wasn't an option any more, that there had been so many other numbers it could have landed on, and now I had only one.

The flat welcomed us warmly. Jenny gave me a hug and then disappeared into the bathroom to wash the day away.

I had a cigarette by the window and then, in a fit of domesticity, corralled up the rubbish in the kitchen and took the bin bag outside to stow. I'd just finished kicking the bag into the recess by the side of the steps, when I sensed movement on the other side of the street and glanced up. Then I stopped, foot still poised.

It was the girl.

She was ambling down the other side of the road, dressed in the same clothes as the day before. I felt my heart beating as I watched her bend to stroke a cat. Though she wasn't tall her back was long, and flared into an attractive triangle at her buttocks. Her face was covered by her hair hanging down and suddenly I wanted her, wanted her briefly, pornographically and completely.

She straightened as the cat sloped off, and looked across at me. She seemed to smile, though whether in recognition or simple friendliness it was impossible to judge. I gave her a small and distracted nod, and then turned back towards the house.

When I was back in the flat I stood by the window. She was still outside. The cat had returned and she was rubbing its neck, sitting cross-legged on the pavement. She looked lost, and found, in the middle of a moment of contentment.

I went into the bedroom to chat to Jenny through the half-open bathroom door. We didn't talk about flats.

Mid-afternoon the next day I went to the corner shop, to buy some cigarettes and the local paper. As I walked back I was thinking about Jenny, and the puzzled half-grin with which she'd said goodbye when she left for work, standing with me on the step. She'd picked something up from me, from the way I'd been the previous evening. Some smile had been slightly too narrow, some hug too considered. When she'd turned the corner I stomped back into the flat, feeling wild and panicky.

Something was going wrong. I'd tried to calm myself in the shower but it hadn't worked, and I'd achieved next to nothing that morning. I called her before lunch and we chatted, but it seemed hollow to me, though there was no difference in the things we said. I even said I loved her, and meant it as much as ever. But it made me realise something I'd forgotten in the last month: that you could say those same words and not really mean them. That they could become merely sounds, rather than a statement of everything that was true about the world. There was a distance between us which hadn't existed before. Not between us, in fact, but within me. Some part of me was retreating. Some power source had been interrupted for a flicker of a second, and I was falling back from the front of my mind, trying once more the doors to what had gone before. After cruising in glorious automatic for a month, suddenly my mind was back on manual shift, jerking and racing, subtly out of my control.

The more I tried not to think about it, the more the thoughts popped and squirmed into my mind like gleeful and brightly coloured worms. Some part of me was anxiously trying to patch and mend, turn my thoughts back to the front, but even he couldn't ignore the rising panic. I had the chance to have everything I'd ever wanted, had the chance to be happy. And yet instead of staying safely in the present and the future, I wanted to try those doors, to look back again, though I knew what would happen if I did. The past was too recent a neighbourhood for me, and the locals would still recognise my face. It wasn't safe for me there, not yet: if I went back my old friends would come and find me, take me back into darker corners to kick me to pieces once again.

As I neared the flat, completely blind to the world around me, I could almost see those thoughts, those friends, gathering round me like the bullies of childhood.

'You looked back too soon,' they were saying, hearty with affectionate hatred. 'But maybe it would always have been too soon, my son. You like it here. You know you do. So come back. We may hurt you a little, might even cut you up, but at least you'll be at home. And we know how you like it.'

I didn't know how it had all started, why on earth I was reacting this way, and I didn't know how to stop it. I was falling. I was back in my own mind, my old mind, and couldn't remember how I'd ever got out.

When I saw who was sitting outside the flat I literally dropped everything I was carrying.

'Jesus Christ,' I said.

The girl reached down and picked up my cigarettes.

I took them from her. She smiled, and then turned away slightly, to look down the street.

I scrabbled to come up to speed, to react. Against my will my eyes dropped from her face to her pink top. My subconscious had captured her image very accurately: her breasts were indeed small but prominent, stubby nipples discernible against the cloth. With a flush of embarrassment I realised she was looking at me again.

'I'm thirsty,' she said.

Eager to have something to do, some way out, I reached into my back pocket and discovered it was empty. I'd used up all my change in the shop. All I had was a few pence, which was derisory. And I couldn't offer her a note. All I had was ten pounds. I couldn't offer her that.

'Don't you have anything inside?'

'Er, yes, I do actually,' I stammered with wild surprise, as if she'd scored right with a lucky guess. 'You know, tea, Coke, that sort of thing.' I couldn't believe I was answering, and certainly not in that way. I didn't seem to have any choice.

'Fat or thin?' she asked. I didn't understand. 'Regular or Diet Coke,' she explained patiently, with another smile, as she stood up to let me open the door.

She didn't like Diet Coke, so I made her a cup of coffee. Meanwhile she walked round the living room behind me, examining the books. I dithered about whether to make a cup of coffee for myself. It would seem odd to only make one for her, but wasn't there an air of complicity about both having one together? Did I even want a cup of coffee? What was she doing here?

What if Jenny called?

In the end I didn't make a cup for myself, but just handed one to her. By then she was sitting on one end of the sofa, looking comfortable. I cast an anxious glance at the phone and wondered whether I should switch the answerphone on. Not because I didn't want the girl to know about Jenny, but because I didn't want Jenny to hear me sounding strange. And I most certainly would if she called. What on earth did I think was going on? Clearly the girl must have recognised me when I'd been putting the rubbish out the night before, but what was she doing here now? What did she want?

The girl took the coffee and sipped it, smiling at me in an odd way. I tried to smile back, but I couldn't. My eyes kept finding her top. The pink, I saw, wasn't consistent. Some areas were a deeper hue, making it look almost tie-dyed.

'Oh, this is for you,' she said suddenly, and slipped her hand into a small pocket in the top of her trousers. She held out her hand towards me, palm up. She was holding £4.71 in small change. I stared at her.

'That was nice,' she said. 'But I don't need it.'

'I'm sorry,' I said, embarrassed. 'I thought you were begging.'

'I was,' she smiled. 'Old habits die hard. Don't they?'

She moved slightly, and her legs parted a little. They were slim, but powerful, and the feeling they provoked in me was more like fear than anything else. I could sense Jenny, on the other side of town, could almost see her sitting at her desk. Was she thinking of me? Was she thinking of Chris? I stared at the girl's face, wondering what on earth to do.

She looked me in the eyes, and then pulled mine downwards with her own, until I was looking at her chest again. There were streaks of darker colour amongst the pink. I hadn't noticed them before. Perhaps it was a different shirt.

'It's yours if you want it,' she said. I realised suddenly that I didn't, but it was too late. She reached down and took hold of the bottom of her shirt.

'No,' I said, but she was already pulling it up.

For about a couple of inches the skin was white and smooth. I could see it very clearly, the tiny goosebumps and the varying shades of pale. The area from her navel to immediately below her breasts was a churned mass of dogmeat. The flesh had been gashed wide by some massive impact, laying bare the purples and greys of internal organs. A drunken stumble in front of a car, the lost fury of a damaged boyfriend, whatever. Blood ran slowly in the cavity, so dark as to be almost brown. In a way, it was beautiful.

'You can go back if you want to,' she said. 'You can remember what it's like.' Her eyes were dry, their surface like a winter's overcast sky, and her head was held at an abrupt angle. For a moment she was motionless, T-shirt still raised, and I mourned the terrible life that I had lost, the slow and pointless death I could have had, and to which I had become so attached.

Then I shook my head.

Her face moved again, and she almost looked alive.

'Good call,' she said, and disappeared.

I turned to look out of the window, and she was crouched down on the other side of the road, hand held out towards a cat that was no longer there.

Then she was nearer the corner, caught once more in summer light, laughing at something said six months ago, when it was all still an adventure.

And then she was gone.

By the time I'd had a cigarette I was calm again, calm and almost smiling. I called Jenny. She knew why I was calling before I said a word, and I could feel her happiness down the phone.

'About this flat idea,' I said.

The Masturbation Map

Stephanie Theobald

Riding a horse is much better than riding a bike. Swings (riding them sideways), seesaws (when they go bump), piggybacks and space hoppers are also good but nothing beats a horse. The best bit about riding a horse is going up a bank. You have to lengthen the reins and lean forward and it feels all velvety inside your trousers. The front bit of inside your trousers gets knocked against the front of the saddle as the horse scrambles up the slope so that one minute it feels soft as a horse's muzzle in there and the next it's like being mounted on the back of 600 Sunday roasts – hot sirloins of beef, juicy loins of pork, muscly legs of lamb, all straining and writhing and heaving together with the strength of a hundred furry gladiators.

I like the smell of the hay and horse manure and I like the steam horses make when they go to the loo in the grass on cold frosty mornings, but the main reason I keep coming back to Miss Percy's riding school is for the bank feeling.

Unfortunately, after six months at Miss Percy's we have only ever gone up a bank once. The rest of the time we have lessons about keeping our elbows in and heels down and do lots of sitting trot which is very bumpy and doesn't make your trousers feel velvety at all. Plus it makes you look really stupid because you have to wear a stupid hard hat that makes you look like Princess Anne. Jami says that British riding is all pain and no pleasure. 'American-style riding is way more relaxed,' she says. 'You get on and you grab hold of the big knob at the front of the saddle. Gotta watch out though. Once I jumped a hedge and hit my pussy on the knob. Hurt like it had been slammed shut in a car door.'

Jami says 'pussy'. Jami knows a lot of things for an eleven-year-old. She is from New Jersey in America. Not only has she ridden a llama but she also has a waterbed. She says 'kind of' and 'I guess' a lot and she calls jelly 'Jell-O' and Miss Percy 'a freak'. She doesn't like England much although she does like the brown suede settee in the house her parents have rented here. When her parents go out she takes all her clothes off and lies on it naked. We have a goat skin rug in our house in front of the hearth so I know what she is talking about. Sometimes I lie on it when I am watching *Blue Peter* after school. Although I have clothes on, I find that I am thinking more about the rug than *Blue Peter*. At these times I definitely wouldn't want to be sitting on the green settee that is covered with scratchy green curtain material that feels like a maths lesson.

I first met Jami when I was on Madame Ginger Bits having my weekly lesson from Miss Percy. The lesson proceeded as usual: Miss Percy stood in the middle of a field with twelve or thirteen mini Princess Annes slowly circling past her. Every so often she would throw her chest out and snap commands at us in a loud, posh voice: 'Sit upright, girls!' or 'Heels down, elbows in!' or 'Lead with the left foreleg! Good show!' Then she slumped down on the wooden stool she always brings everywhere with her and took out the silver flask she always carries in one of her leather riding boots. She mopped her forehead with an orange handkerchief of shiny material called silk while she drank from the flask.

Madame Ginger Bits was as bored as I was. She didn't want to move and I didn't want to follow Miss Percy's instruction which she soon hollered out from behind the silver flask: 'Kick, Alice. Kick! Naughty Madame Ginger Bits! Crop, Alice! Crop! Good hard thwack do the trick!'

I gave up after a while and looked around the field to see the Princess Annes kicking their legs into the sides of their ponies like they were hammers knocking nails into wood. I wasn't going to do that. Besides, you couldn't blame Madame Ginger Bits for being naughty. Her fourteen-year-old owner, Susan Smithe, used to be devoted to her but then she started coming to the stables less and when she did come she'd be wearing black eyeliner and her walk had changed. When her father arrived in his shiny red Range Rover to pick her up, she would drag the heels of her boots along the ground like she was a prisoner of war. She had discovered boys. Jami says that when you discover boys it means that when someone mentions 'wild stallions' the tingle in your stomach is different from the tingle you get when you're a kid and someone says 'wild stallions'. Then, it makes you think of being a cowboy and eating beans in the open air and having a brawl in a saloon where those cancan girls do dancing and wear a lot of make-up and where the sheriff has to come and calm things down.

Since Jami and I are eleven years old, we are halfway between kids and Susan Smithe. Understanding the different kinds of tingles that exist doesn't come naturally to us but we are going to investigate them. We know that the grown-ups aren't being completely honest about the velvety feeling. We know that some big thing is being hidden from us. Right now, we are crouching under a clump of conifer trees in a donkey paddock because we are going to find out what exactly it is.

After the lesson, as we all trudged out of the field to await Miss Percy's weekly tack test (snaffles: egg butt unjointed, egg butt jointed, egg butt jointed cheek, French link loose ring, D-ring jointed rubber cover), I noticed a tall girl with thick black hair and a huge purple bubble where a face should have been.

When I finally got Madame Ginger Bits back to her stable there was the smell of an unknown bubble gum flavour mixing with the familiar scent of treacly straw. It was the girl with the thick black hair. She was reading a notice nailed to the gate of Madame Ginger Bits' stable. It is called 'Handy Hints on Cantering', part of a series of Handy Horse Hints that Miss Percy likes to stick around her riding school.

'Number one,' came the sarcastic, twangy voice. 'Do not lean forward during transition or the horse will become unbalanced. Two: sit upright and keep your buttocks in the saddle. The hips and pelvis should absorb the motion. Three: remember that speed is not the important factor. The canter should be ridden at an active and controlled pace with the tempo appropriate to the discipline.'

There was the sound of a large bubble popping very loudly followed by a 'Man, you Brits sure know how to ruin a perfectly good vibe'.

I looked closely at the girl. She was wearing a pink T-shirt saying 'Enemy of the State' in big black letters on the front and she had a stripe of thin purple skin stuck to her left cheek. She passed me a green and pink packet. It was watermelon bubble gum. It was the first time I had seen watermelon gum. Or an American. An American in this neck of the woods is as exciting as things get. Apart from the bank.

She leaned over the gate, introduced herself as 'Jami without an e' and started to stroke Madame Ginger Bits' nose.

'I want to do bareback riding,' she declared. 'My dad says you get to feel all the muscle and the blood pump-ing underneath you. It totally rocks, he says.'

As I watched her jaw chew confidently away on her gum I knew she would understand about the bank feeling.

When I told her, she said she knew exactly what I meant.

'I love that feeling too,' she said. 'I love to ride anything.'

'Anything?'

'Sure. I tried a goat once. It was too little though.'

'What happened?'

'Fell over.' Jami turned and spat her piece of gum into the yard like a high-speed cherry stone. 'In general, farmyard animals are too small. And don't even think of trying a cow. Cows are definitely not meant for riding.'

'What happened when you tried?'

'Bucked me off.'

I told her that I was sorry to hear this but she replied that she liked it. 'Feels good,' she said. 'Crashing, bucking, breaking bones. I take whatever I can get.' She added that when she went to ice-skating rinks she didn't stop by turning the back of her skates to the right like you're supposed to. She just crashed right into the barriers.

'Bang!' she whooped and her eyes gleamed. 'Most years I break at least two bones in my body. Last year I broke three. Broke my right tibia – that's the bottom of your leg – plus I broke my right patella and something in my finger called a metacarpal. A patella's in your knee. It makes a big crunchy sound when it goes.'

She took a packet of orange Tic Tacs from her pocket and put them on the flat of her hand for Madame Ginger Bits.

'Ostriches,' she went on knowledgeably. 'Could've ridden an ostrich once. Gotta draw the line somewhere though. Riding a bird. Gross me out. Straddling poultry. No way.'

I blurted out, 'Nice soft feathers though,' and immediately felt embarrassed. Jami just grinned and jumped over the stable gate to join me and Madame Ginger Bits.

'If it's soft you're looking for,' she said standing next to me, 'llamas are your ride. They're real soft. Alpaca belly fur. Imagine that.' She looked me straight in the eye. 'You gotta be careful though,' she smiled. 'They're not very comfortable. They run. Bumpy. Still,' she said, slapping Madame Ginger Bits on the bottom, 'more pain, more pleasure. Get the picture?'

Jami will be a good person to help me investigate the bank feeling. She knows things. She says things like, 'Check out the rack on her,' referring to Miss Percy's large breasts. A rack means breasts in American. Jami's father says it a lot, apparently. I'm sure my father doesn't even know what a rack is. Once I heard him tell my mother, 'But of course I love you darling. You're comfortable as an old sock.'

You can't really tell what my mother is thinking. She doesn't talk about things. She does the washing-up noisily if she's not happy about something. I can't possibly ask her about the feeling. When we talk, it's usually about how pedestrians should always face the oncoming traffic or how you should neither a lender nor a borrower be or what a shame it is that young people are no longer interested in barley sugar. When I told her about the new girl at riding school called Jami, she replied that being called Jami wasn't allowed.

'But that's her name,' I said.

'Jami's not a proper name,' she said. 'It must be short for Jemima or a derivation of Jane.'

'I'm sure it's just plain Jami,' I said. 'J-A-M-I, it's spelt.'

'There you are!' she said with triumph in her voice. 'J-A-M-I spells "jammy". You can't be called jammy.'

'She's American,' I said.

'Exactly,' she replied with one of her annoying smiles. 'An American name. Not a proper name.'

Jami took the brush from my hand and began grooming Madame Ginger Bits in long, firm strokes. After a while she said, 'Alice, you know that feeling you were talking about?'

'The bank feeling?' I said.

'Yes,' she said. 'The bank feeling. We have to get to the bottom of it. There's something big they're hiding from us. I know it.'

'I know of some donkeys,' I mumbled.

'Donkeys?' her left eyebrow rose.

'Three of them. They've just moved into the paddock next to our house. I'm forbidden to go in there.'

Jami's eyebrows both rose in unison.

I'm not allowed to go near the donkeys. My mother thinks that going anywhere near the donkeys would be breaking the law. She worries about breaking laws, my mother. Anyone would think the donkeys were bulls with heads of tarantulas covered with hundreds and thousands of Miss Percy-sized breasts. I wish my mother was not so worried about what is allowed and what isn't because then I would be brave and experienced like Jami. I am not scared of my mother (although I am really) so I have already been in to stroke the donkeys.

They have a dark cross on their backs, just like Sister Angela told us once at school. 'In memory of our Lord Jesus Christ and his triumphant ride on Palm Sunday,' she said. I wonder if Jesus got the bank feeling too when he was bumping up and down on the warm furry back. Probably he wasn't even wearing any underwear beneath his white robe.

And that is how come we are squatting here under the conifer trees in the paddock, next door to my house, deciding which of the donkeys will be best for us to jump on top of.

We have decided that the bank feeling has something to do with the word 'masturbation'. A long word with lots of syllables. We have already looked it up in the *Oxford English Dictionary* but the definition is of little help. 'A noun,' it says. 'Auto-eroticism. To produce sexual arousal through manual stimulation of genitals.'

'I bet it's like being at the top of the bank,' I say.

'I bet it's like suede couches times a hundred,' Jami says.

'I bet it's like sitting on a chair with a canvas bottom and someone from behind putting a ruler under the seat and moving it.'

Jami's left eyebrow rises. She makes me feel clever. She says, 'A canvas chair and a ruler?'

'Yes,' I reply. 'And also, if you want to go to the toilet a lot but you hold it in and then you go on a suede couch or a canvas chair with a ruler, then I bet something even better would happen.'

'I bet it's like the rats,' Jami announces.

'The rats?'

'James Herbert's book *The Rats*. They all gnaw into people's houses and chew people to death and a lot of people are having sexual intercourse when the rats come in.'

Another bubble bursts.

'Yeah, and I bet it's like bombs,' Jami goes on. 'You ever blow up a trash can or a mail box?'

I shake my head.

'You mix straw and manure and you cook it and put it in a tube with a fuse in the middle. 'Course, a proper bomb needs plutonium. I set fire to three acres of hillside once.'

I don't know what to say. I just say, 'At night in bed sometimes it feels like I want to sneeze from between my legs.'

'Your pussy,' she corrects me.

'Yes,' I say. 'My pussy wants to sneeze but it can't sneeze. I don't know why.'

I don't tell her about Jemima. Jemima is my doll whose head I have recently been rocking up and down on, like a horse, at night in my bed. I can't decide if it's frustrating or nice. Probably I think it's nice because Jemima has ended up with a small grey-ringed stain on her forehead that sticks there stubbornly like the Shroud of Turin in spite of my secret washing attempts.

We even have a masturbation map. Except we can't read it very well. It came out of a box of tampons. Jami's mother uses tampons for The Curse. The map shows a diagram of female genitals with arrows pointing to three different holes. Girls and ladies have three different holes. The last time we went to Miss Percy's Jami brought out a pocket mirror when we got back to the stables and when the tack test was over and everyone had left we pulled our trousers down. We giggled. Jami squatted over the mirror first.

'Doesn't look like anything that I've got,' she said after a while, looking from the mirror to the map. 'Maybe I'm reading it wrong.'

She hands me the piece of paper.

'Looks like one of those diagrams you get for telling you how to put up a set of shelves,' I say.

We giggle. There is more silence. We still have our trousers off.

'Pagan,' I mumble, remembering something the nuns at school are always going on about. 'I bet it'll be like a pagan feeling.'

'Pagan,' Jami says, rolling the word slowly round in her mouth like it's a new bubble gum flavour. She smiles at me. Then she does something strange. She crunches the masturbation map up in her hands and hands it out to me. She doesn't just give it to me though. I put my palm out flat and she rubs the sharp points of the paper slowly over it. She stares at me and the look in her eyes is something between spiteful and hungry. When I close my hand to try and take the map from her she quickly lifts the paper ball away so I can't get it and then she comes down with it again and scratches my flat palm. This seems to go on for a while. When she suddenly stops I want her to do it again, I want her to dig the sharp crinkly paper into my damp palm. I'm not sure why I want her to do this.

'Pagan,' says a hot blast of watermelon, and then finally the whole of the map ball digs into my hand, setting a swarm of butterflies loose in my tummy.

In the end, Jami decides that auto-eroticism has something to do with night and rats and pelvises absorbing the motion of horses' backs and also something to do with having a full bladder. Jami says we're never going to discover anything by being at Miss Percy's. Yet if we have a go at donkey bareback riding we're going to have a deluxe masturbation. We'll probably be the first in our class to do it. We feel pleased with ourselves. We are going to the top of the bank.

It is a hot afternoon. Me and Jami are silent under the trees in the paddock. Our bladders are the size of balloons. All that can be heard are donkey mouths pulling up dry grass and the smell of warm conifer trees. Then suddenly, Jami hisses, 'Marks . . . get set . . . GO!' and off she shoots from under the prickly fronds, out towards the donkeys. I know she is going to head for the tall, grey one. Jami only ever goes for the tallest, the fastest, the roughest. She is having trouble though. The tall grey donkey is frisky and fast. Good job that Jami likes a chase. 'I ain't going for no wallflower,' I hear her yell as she scoots off to the far side of the field. 'I'm going as high up that bank as I can!'

So while Jami careers round the paddock, trying to catch the tall grey donkey so that she can leapfrog onto his back and do a much more impressive masturbation than me, I head slowly for the little brown donkey with a chocolate-coloured stripe on his back. I wonder if it will be like riding on Jemima. But when I heave myself up on his back – like climbing a warm, furry wall – I discover that it is much better than Jemima. Better than one of Miss Percy's horses too. There is no saddle, nobody telling me to keep my heels down and elbows in, no hurry. I sit there astride the little brown donkey as he ambles from grass patch to grass patch like he hasn't noticed me. I am riding on warm blood and muscle. My feet dangle loose to the ground.

The sun beats down on the back of my T-shirt. I close my eyes and the little brown donkey's back begins to feel like real chocolate – all soft and melting – like I am melting into his back, soft as butter. Before I know it, I am jigging up against his neck and there is the smell of dry grass and the chirps of crickets and Jami shouting 'Gotcha, asshole!' followed by sounds of American-style whoops. And then I can't hear her or anything any more because I am jigging up and down on a whole sea of white chocolate seahorses. I take one of my hands off the little brown donkey's mane, I put my middle and index finger together – like I have seen Susan Smithe do – and I pretend that they are lips. I close my eyes and start to kiss my bony finger lips. In the hot, fuzzy darkness I see Jami scratching the map against my palm and I am just starting to slip my tongue through the middle of the lips like you are supposed to do, when I see Miss Percy looking stern. I am a bit shocked to see her there behind my closed eyes. Jami never told me about pictures coming – pictures just slipping into your mind without you having a chance to weed them out. I wonder if Jami is seeing things too. And then suddenly, everything is velvet – cantering velvet and then galloping velvet – and all this is going on like a huge funfair on the back of the little brown donkey who stands there with a fat belly, munching at grass and flicking flies from his ears like this is just any old sunny afternoon. I can't stop now. In my trousers I am Miss Percy's silk handkerchief being pulled through the eye of a needle by the suck of a very, very strong breath. It is a sharp intake, a very big wrench, a big purple bubble that soaks into the rest of my body like blotting paper and butter and gooey custard pie slowly oozing down a rumbling wall of Miss Percy and her rack and Jesus and his robe and a cancan girl flashing her petticoats in a saloon full of screeching donkeys.

Later, as I am wondering if what has just happened is allowed and if my set of shelves has been damaged for life, I stumble across Jami. She is lying on her back in the grass.

'Wow,' she croaks, looking up at me. 'You look kind of weird.'

I look down at her. She is looking kind of weird too. Her hair is covered in donkey dung and the purple on her cheeks is not from bubble gum skin but from a big purple bruise where the tall grey donkey has hurled her to the ground.

'Wow,' she croaks, 'You did it, right? You went to the top of the bank. You gotta tell me what it's like up there.' She tries to shrug. 'I guess my donkey was a little frisky.'

As I am wondering if my new experience makes me better than Jami now, I notice a big wet patch down her trouser leg. Jami sees me looking at this. 'Guess my balloon burst, right?' she says weakly. She heaves herself up onto her left elbow. 'Still,' she says, beaming, 'gotta look on the bright side. The good news is that I think I broke my collarbone. You ever did that? You get to wear the coolest bra thing.'

Behaving Badly

Helen Townsend

Sandie Martin. Aged seventeen. Doing first-year Arts at Sydney Uni. From Bango. That was me.

Camille Figaro. Aged twenty-nine. Honours in Fine Arts. Artiste. Curator. Living in a 1930s worker's cottage in Marrickville. Married to Uncle Bob, my mother's youngest brother.

That was really the only possible connection. The only way I could get to meet someone called Camille Figaro. Camille Figaro, curator, graduate. In Bango, you were a graduate if you finished high school. And she was a performance artist. First-class honours.

'First-class wanker,' Dad said.

'She's nice enough,' said Mum. 'You're always down on anyone who's a bit different.'

'Bloody right I am,' said my father, but he wasn't quite serious.

My mother regarded herself as different from my father – that is, better.

When I was seventeen, I thought my parents were the

685

most boring people in the world. 'It's a personality-free zone back home,' I told Camille. Then I was embarrassed when I noticed Bob giving me a slightly ironic, good-humoured look; same as my Dad often did.

'You weren't too impressed with Camille,' Dad said to Mum when they were discussing whether I should take up Uncle Bob's offer of a room when I started uni. 'When you lent her your wedding dress.'

'It's her loss, not taking marriage seriously,' said Mum. 'The only thing I cared about was whether she returned it. And she did – beautifully cleaned in a special box. I want Sandie to wear it one day.' I sighed theatrically, as if her expectation was beyond belief.

'You didn't like Camille wearing your white dress under false pretences.' Dad was persistent if he thought he could wind Mum up.

'Never mind that now,' said Mum. She raised her eyebrows to him to indicate I shouldn't be hearing the conversation. As if I wasn't tall enough to see raised eyebrows. As if I was still a sexual innocent, which I pretty much was. But I did know about the false pretence of wearing white. It was a major talking point in Bango, seeing as most of the younger generation of the town were living under false pretences. 'Anyway, Camille is Bob's wife now,' Mum said. 'It's not my place to judge her.'

Mum prided herself on being non-judgemental, a term she'd learned at the local community college's course on psychology. She looked down on some of the other women who'd done the course because they had remained judgemental. 'Closed minds, that lot,' she'd say.

I hadn't gone to Bob and Camille's wedding because I'd only been fourteen at the time and because I'd been 'down with asthma' all winter. It was a long drive, I was a known car-sickness victim and Nan needed help taking care of my younger brothers, which seemed like far too many reasons to me. I thought there must be another explanation, especially when Mum came back in a mood, saying the marriage would never last and that the whole thing had been a joke.

She had only modified this view recently, after the community college course.

But even so, when Bob came to Bango to visit us, he never brought Camille, even for Christmas, and he gave non-committal replies when Mum asked how Camille was. Which was understandable because you could be pretty sure that Mum either wanted ammunition against Camille or to know whether she was pregnant. Pregnancy or its absence was also a ubiquitous topic of conversation in Bango.

Dad had explained to me about the wedding one night when we were out shooting rabbits. 'Weird. They had it at a car wreckers, in front of this pile of old cars. The bloke operating the crane lifted up this old white Fairlane with two red hearts painted on the side, and dropped it behind them. It made a shocking noise. Bob told me it was because she's an artist. I tell you what, art's changed since my day.'

I worried about going to uni, which people in Bango spoke of both disparagingly and with admiration. 'She went to uni, you know. Clever. But my Nicole earns almost as much at the meatworks with overtime. You can get too much education, you know.'

But Uncle Bob had gone to uni and while no one really understood quite what he did, my parents certainly realised there was no future in Bango. 'If you go to uni you can be a teacher,' said Mum. 'Think of the holidays!'

When you're seventeen, you don't think about what a pain in the neck it must be to have a seventeen-year-old around. Camille and Bob were amazingly tolerant. They had offered me a room in the Marrickville cottage, mostly out of the goodness of their hearts, but maybe because they needed me there for other reasons. Bob helped me get through first-semester Economics with a distinction. Camille helped me with T.S. Eliot, but I barely got a pass in English.

'Don't worry,' said Camille, 'all this academic stuff is bullshit. The important thing is to *feel* poetry.'

The cottage in Marrickville was a revelation to me. Marrickville was a revelation to me. Middle Eastern and Vietnamese. 'Swarming with them,' my mother had said. She was horrified. 'And do you know what Bob *paid* for that house?' she whispered to Dad.

In Bango, my parents had bought an old house and were busy restoring it. My mother was creative and inventive. I was silently proud of our house, because it was different from and better than the houses of my friends. My mother bought books and magazines on Federation houses. She had colours specially mixed. She painted stencils, and scrubbed back timber.

That was what Camille called 'imitation'. Camille had

no such inhibitions. The room I slept in was timber-panelled. Camille painted each of the boards a different 'grass' colour. Camille explained that grass wasn't actually green, and that you didn't need to mask the edge of each board. Then, with a wet rag, she dragged the whole lot horizontally, and painted the wall above it a pale, blotched mauve. When I lay in bed looking at it in the morning, with the sun shining on it, I felt as if I were back in the country, staring over a paddock to the horizon, while Dad looked at the grass, which was what he got paid for as Inspector of Pastures.

On the floor was the most exquisite silk Persian rug, in pale blues, pinks and greens. 'It's been in my family four generations,' Camille explained. 'Our only material possession. Evidently it's worth a mint, but I'd never sell it. Home is where the rug is.'

Camille taught me to cook things other than spag bol, and Chinese beef with blackbean sauce, which Mum had clipped from the *Woman's Weekly* in 1985. Camille took me to op shops and I bought a 1960s evening gown which she cut short to make me a stunning beach frock, to be worn with black hiking boots and floppy grey cotton socks. She went with me when I had my eyebrow pierced, and was sympathetic when it bubbled up into a massive infection and I had to get the ring removed.

Camille called everyone 'honey' and talked endlessly on the phone about the 'mechanics' of her latest performance, and the 'Zen' elements. She said mysterious things like 'Christ, honey, it's so fantastically *Neighbours*'. I wanted to like her performances, and

I felt a warm glow when I did, even if they were hard to understand.

The first one I saw was beautiful. She hung up a disintegrating, translucent nylon curtain and onto it she projected old, faded slides of dreary suburban houses, interspersed with close-up details like plants in the garden, or lovely pieces of patterned laminex. One old man was crying at the end of it and I could see why. Camille talked to him for ages, while he held her hand. Everyone thought he was part of the performance, and wasn't Camille clever to make that happen.

I never understood where Bob fitted in with Camille's performances. He'd stand there, with his ironic, detached look and kiss her afterwards and then let her go to her more ardent admirers, who gushed and made in-depth comments which she repeated to us the next day. Camille loved praise. She needed it, in what seemed to me a childish sort of way. But then, I was from Bango.

'Debus loved the shot of the Mexican poster in the red and green kitchen. He thought it was genius to put in after the shot of the sunbaked succulents. "The exhaustion of the suburbs," he said,' relayed Camille.

'I've got Marrickville exhaustion,' said Bob. 'I've got to get that report in to Ritchie today. I'll be a bit late tonight.'

'Bob's such a rock,' said Camille when he had gone. 'He represents that absolutely fundamental notion of manhood you see in lifesavers. It's really extraordinary to see it so well preserved.'

I grasped at the things she said. I tried to work them

out. I began to see that life was not just a flat picture, but more like a diamond, with many perspectives. I was excited, in the way adolescents get excited and transformed by ideas.

Camille was pretty, but more than that, her face always showed how she felt. It lit up. It showed fierce determination and utter desolation. Not like a Bango face. But she was elusive. Although she was intense and personal with me, she was like that with everyone, even casual acquaintances, or waiters in coffee shops.

'This is my niece. Can you believe I have a niece? Sandira from Bango.' She dubbed me Sandira, which I loved. I wanted to be known as Sandira, but in tutorials or with people I met at uni, I was too shy. 'I'm Sandie,' I'd blurt out, and then curse myself for losing yet another chance to become Sandira, although with a freckled complexion and pale red hair, Sandie was actually the perfect name for me.

Bob was generous. He'd always give me money if he knew I was short and he'd help me with my work and talk to me about what was on the news. He'd also do adult things with me, like take me to the pub for a beer or go to the movies with me. He was a comforting presence in the world of university, because he was like my parents in some ways, but he knew about the world beyond Bango.

Camille was my focus, however, and my life became increasingly entwined with hers. She was a great user of people, so I often found myself helping her install a show – painting walls, lifting crates, working out how strange objects fitted together, taking phone calls from artists. I did all this with dog-like devotion. I ran errands and reminded her of details.

'Nobody can remember everything,' she said. 'It's nuts, this thing about remembering things.'

It wasn't always easy – there was a lot of tension between Camille and Bob. 'Oh fuck *you*!' they'd say angrily to each other and slam doors, and stamp and shout. Camille must have noticed me wince because she told me that they had an expressive relationship, so they said what was on their minds, and I could also say 'Oh fuck you!' if either of them drove me crazy.

They must have realised I was unlikely to take up the offer.

Then there was the time I came in and found them having sex in the hall.

'It's okay,' said Camille. 'You could have walked over us. We were in the heat of passion.'

But Bob said, 'Next time, just knock, and we'll know to roll back into the bedroom.' After that, I always knocked and turned my key slowly before I came into the house.

Camille spent a lot of time planning her mid-year performance, which was part of a festival of performance art. It was her biggest ever, a once in a lifetime opportunity to do a performance in which there would be international interest.

She explained to me that I was not only to help her, but I was to be part of the performance. I was to be ('Not play,' said Camille, 'be!') a bus conductor with a bag and tickets and a uniform specially designed by Camille. Bob was the driver, reluctantly, and also in a uniform. Camille was the tour guide and there was a Japanese translator who had come to Australia just for the festival. There were video cameras, one at the back of the bus, and one at the front.

The bus, a perfectly ordinary tour bus, started off from Marrickville with friends and Arts journalists and some of the Festival people. Camille did a standard parody of a bus tour. 'To your left, you'll see . . .' pausing for the translator to say it in Japanese, although no one in the bus spoke Japanese. Then, just as I was thinking it was pretty dull fare (a pun I longed to repeat to Camille!) we stopped at the Art Gallery and she and the translator got off the bus and spruiked for business. 'Free tour,' she shouted through her megaphone. 'An hour-and-a-half. Sydney like you've never seen it before. The Rocks, the Harbour Bridge, the Opera House. Native animals.' Quickly, the bus filled up with total strangers. The Japanese translator found two Japanese couples, one very old, another young and giggly, on their honeymoon. I handed out tickets, and then lounged against the doors as I'd been instructed.

'Here,' Camille said, producing a basket, 'give them these.' I handed out binoculars to each of the passengers, and Camille instructed them to look out the windows to see the people of Sydney. But the binoculars were children's toys. You pressed a button and they produced images of cartoon characters in the Sydney landscape, as Camille gave a commentary on the nature of reality. It was very funny and I watched the Japanese as it was translated. The young Japanese couple laughed dutifully, but the old Japanese couple roared with delight.

'They must have got the pornographic pictures,' whispered Camille.

We went out to the Gap. Camille said that these were Sydney's famous rocks. A young German man began to argue, saying he had been to the Rocks and these weren't them. The Rocks, he said, were full of houses and shops and proper tourist souvenirs. Camille told the man that he'd been misled. Sydneysiders did not like tourists from overseas to go to *these* rocks because they were a favourite suicide spot. The man kept arguing, citing a pamphlet, and Camille explained it was a government conspiracy and she was giving him a chance few people had. Once he was silent, she told of how local children used to gather to watch the police bring up the bodies. She told a wonderful story of an old woman who spent hours talking to a young man sitting on a ledge. She persuaded him not to jump. The next day, the old lady's body was found on the rocks below.

Then we drove out west to see a replica of the Harbour Bridge at a car dealership. The angry German man threatened to get off at this point, but Camille told him firmly that the main point of icons was that they caused the creation of more icons, and we were seeing the best possible icon of an icon. I was then deputised to give out small models of the Harbour Bridge encased in clear plastic. When you shook them, there was a snowstorm around the Bridge and Camille conducted the song 'Here's the Sydney Harbour Bridge, big as big can be . . .' while everyone shook their snowstorms.

Next was the Opera House, which was a spectacular topiary in the heart of suburbia. 'And this is the *only*

Opera House with wild animals,' she said firmly to the German man, pointing at the topiary emus and kangaroos and a dingo with his tail under attack from caterpillars. By now, the German listened meekly and attentively. At the end of the tour, as the passengers got out, the German asked her for her phone number and both the Japanese couples bowed deeply to her.

It was a wonderful day and Camille was delighted when the event got a spot on the news on TV and made the *Herald* the next day. She edited the video and sold it at a gallery where she was curating an exhibition called 'Objects of almost no interest'. The video sold fantastically well.

She was on a high for weeks, but there seemed more and more 'Fuck you!' and door slamming between her and Bob.

One night Bob sat at the kitchen table, going over accounts and adding up figures on a sheet of paper.

'I've paid over two grand for that bus tour,' he said to her. 'When's the bloody grant money coming in? Or am I supposed to give them free credit for a couple of months like last time?'

'There wasn't a grant,' she said. 'I just did it. It was the biggest thing in my career. You know that.'

He looked at her. 'You told me there was a grant.'

'There was a grant,' she said quickly, 'and I applied. But I didn't get it. You know what the board is like. They're only giving money for pretty picture stuff now. Anything innovative, forget it.'

'You went ahead, knowing there was no money?'

'I thought they'd come good. Or I'd get a fellowship

on the strength of it. Which I still could. I thought it worth the risk of paying for it myself.'

'Oh yeah,' said Bob. 'Yourself. Your *self*, Camille. *I'm* paying for this. I mean it's not two grand that's coming out of your pocket. Like the rent on that fucking gallery last month. And the four grand that went some place last year.'

'And look who's counting,' she said sarcastically. 'Every fucking cent.'

And so it went on, with me retreating up to my grass and morning-light room, and lying on the Persian carpet, hating this, until there was the sound of a slap, a scream from Camille, a door slamming as Bob went out, and then Camille crying. Then silence. Camille emerged from the bedroom, a slash of red lipstick across one cheek.

'It's symbolic,' she said, as if that explained it. 'I can't stay here.'

'I'll take you out for coffee.' I felt sorry for her, but I was a little embarrassed by the slash of red across her face.

'What does it matter if we lose the house?' she said. 'It's only a house. He's so hung up on those things. I know I shouldn't say bad things about your uncle, honey, but I get so frustrated that he's so materialistic.'

From my parents I was very familiar with the counter-argument about houses. A house is sacred. A house is security. Work is sacred. Work makes money to buy the house to create the security.

Irresistibly, I was drawn to Camille's arguments.

'Why does work have to *make* money? Why can't

work be about spending money?' she asked. 'My God, we're living in one of the richest societies in the history of humankind and we're still fucking saving. It's bloody unbelievable. We're still contracting when we should be expanding. You know, people think this is a natural way to live, but it's the most unnatural way in the world. When did we begin to save? When we had agricultural societies and we could store grain. And it's at exactly that time that people began to get slaves, to exploit other people, to create kings and emperors and mass societies. And now, when we've saved enough, we can't see our way out of the prison.'

Having just spent my small allowance from my parents, lost my job at Woolworths and failed to win Lotto, this explanation was a good rationale for my own state, although I was still enough of a Bango girl to know it wasn't actually a way out.

'I cannot stand this,' Camille said. 'I've stuck by him with his boring thesis and his boring job and his boring clothes. I will not stay through this!'

I hoped desperately I wasn't the boring niece from Bango. 'I'll see you again, won't I?' I said timidly.

'Of course you will, Sandira honey,' and she kissed me. But that night when I went back to the house, she'd taken all her clothes, although she'd left the Persian carpet and some paintings, so I was sure she'd be back. She left a note pinned to the rug. *Take care of this, honey. When I find a home, I'll come back for it and then I'll really have a home.* Bob and I had a sad dinner in a down-market Chinese café that night. He didn't know what to say to me, and I didn't know what to say to him.

I didn't see Camille for weeks after that. She disappeared from our lives. Then I got a call. 'Sandira, honey, could you come down the gallery and give me a hand? I've got this enormous installation about the oppression of women, and the bloody artist has gone bush and I can't get anyone to help.'

She still had the slash of red lipstick across her cheek. 'It's symbolic,' she said. 'It reminds me what I have to do in life, despite the pain. Pain just holds us back, so if I can see my way through male oppression, I'm free.' She handed me a glass of wine. 'Honey, you've no idea what it's like to be free. I'm living with friends, pillar to post, some nights I even sleep here. I haven't got a proper home yet, which is why I've left the rug for you to take care of. But finally I'm free in my mind. I'm free in my body. I can do what I like.' And she put on some wild music and did a wild dance to prove it to me.

It was like being enclosed in a warm circle, like finding a lost love. She talked to me, asked me about my life, was enthusiastic and bubbly. She talked in bits about Bob: 'You know he never, ever said he was sorry . . . the thing is, he's so sexually conservative. He equates that with morality. I can't blame him. He's still stuck in that country town you both come from. I mean I know it's a good place, but really, promise me Sandira, honey, that you won't go back to being like that. Promise me, promise me. You'll be free! You must never buy into male morality. They like to think they're the moral majority. Just because they've hijacked not only the means of production, but also the means of communication. Just because they are so totally threatened by freedom!'

Finally, after a lot of drink and a lot of talking and several more wild dances from Camille, we got the installation done. Camille apologised for not having been in touch earlier. 'I don't like it that Bob scares me,' she said, 'but he does. I abhor physical violence. I really value you, honey. You're so innocent, so open.'

I walked back to Bob's house in the early morning, clasping the heady experience of the night, drunk, light-headed, free as Camille.

Bob was sitting at the kitchen table with his laptop.

'Fuck you!' I said. 'How could you do that to her? God, what she's been through because of that. How could you? How could you?'

'Have you been with Camille?' he said coldly.

'I've been with her, I understand her. You men are all the same. You think you own the world. You think you own her.'

'You don't understand,' he said. 'I'm still in love with her. I hope she'll come to her senses and come back. You don't know what happened, Sandie.' He said it calmly, but I knew he was angry with me, angry with Camille. I wondered for a moment if he'd hit me. I was losing it, caught up in something I didn't understand, but it made me more angry with him.

'It's *Sandira*,' I retorted, 'and I do know what happened. I heard that day you hit her. I saw the mark on her face. I saw how devastated she was. And now, even though she's not really well, she feels free, amazingly different, because she's her own person at last.'

He was silent for a moment. '*She* hit *me*,' he said, 'across the cheek. And then she started screaming. She was crazy. Ballistic.' He had tears in his eyes and he wasn't really talking to me, because I think at that moment he knew it was finished between him and Camille.

I knew straight away that what he was saying was true. I felt an enormous sense of betrayal, of being used by Camille. I walked out of the house, up to the coffee shop we'd gone to so many times. I felt like crying, but I sat there, having short black after short black. Camille had introduced me to coffee. Camille, it felt, had introduced me to life. And now, it turned out that Bob had more substance than she did. I'd always known that she used people, that she used me, that in two months she wouldn't even remember my name. I knew that Sandira, which was a bloody stupid name ('up yourself,' Dad would have said) wouldn't exist, and I'd be the same old boring Sandie Martin that I'd always been.

Bob and I stayed in the house. I couldn't bring myself to talk about what had happened. He sat for hours at the kitchen table drinking more than was good for him. At the end of second semester, he put the house on the market, and I went home to Bango for the holidays.

I felt comfortable. It didn't really feel like a personality-free zone. I was pretty down, but Dad made me laugh and Mum made me lamb roast. I worked on the house with Mum and saw she actually had what Camille had called an eye. I went out on pasture inspection with Dad. Sometimes I'd go off in the early evening with my brothers and we'd shoot a few rabbits. It was a way of distancing myself from Camille and Bob.

'Bob's on the phone,' said Mum one afternoon. It startled me. It was as if I'd forgotten that Bob was family, that he and Mum talked every couple of weeks. I'd wanted to get Camille and Bob out of my life. 'He wants to talk to you.'

'Sandie.' He sounded happy, more like Uncle Bob. 'How you going?'

'Good,' I said. 'It's pretty dry up here and the rabbits are breeding like rabbits.'

'See,' he said, 'you can take the girl out of the country, but you can't take the country out of the girl.'

'Well, maybe that's a good thing.'

'I sold the house and bought a unit. I'm hoping you can find a room somewhere when you get back.'

'Fine,' I said. 'There's a girl I do Economics with. She has a room to let.'

'Great. I'm moving this weekend, so I'm packing everything up. I just wondered if you left anything upstairs. It seems like you took it all home.'

'I did pretty much,' I said, 'there was just Camille's rug.'

'I sold that,' he said. 'It was actually worth a fair bit.' He snorted and tried to turn it into a laugh. 'Not that I got anything like the money I'd put in over the years.'

'Her mother left her the rug,' I said. 'It had been in her family four generations.'

'Yeah, yeah, yeah,' he said sarcastically. 'I care.'

'Serves her right,' said Mum when I told her. 'I knew what she was like when I went to the wedding. Now she'll find out what it's like to support yourself, take care of debts.' Being non-judgemental had gone out the door.

A chill of disappointment ran through me. Disappointment in Bob. In life. In my mother.

'You want to come out and shoot a few bunnies?' Dad asked. For him, shooting rabbits was a sacred crusade, but I was sick of dead things, even rabbits.

'I'll come for the drive,' I said.

We went out in the ute, out of town, over the paddocks, up into the hills, me opening and closing the gates. We got to the top of the tallest hill, and Dad stopped the car. We sat on a rock in the twilight, watching for rabbits.

'Do you reckon what Bob did was right?' I asked.

'What's that?' said Dad.

'Selling Camille's rug. He knew it was the one thing her mother left her. It had been in the family four generations.'

'Oh that,' he said. He cocked the gun and took aim. The shot whistled and we saw the rabbit twist up and then fall. We didn't even bother to get the carcass. We were sick of rabbit stew.

'Well, do you?' I asked. 'Do you think it's right?'

He put his arm round my shoulders. 'Everybody behaves badly now and then,' he said. He pulled me close to him. 'Even your Mum, you know.'

Red Letter Day

Fiona Walker

Faye addressed the envelope, carefully closing the o in Olsen, making the two arcs of the s in Street equal before adding the postcode with meticulous care, its numbers so neat that they could have been printed by a computer. It was important to get it right. One slight mistake and it wouldn't work.

She pasted the stamp exactly a millimetre from the edge of the envelope on two sides, pressing down its frilled edges so that it would stay perfect. Then she popped it into her handbag – in the side-pocket to avoid creasing it.

An impatient secretary was waiting behind the small, scruffy brunette as she dithered by the postbox. Faye whispered to herself quietly, the neat red envelope half-inserted into the slot like a lolling tongue.

'What are you waiting for – a magic hand to come out and take it?' snapped the secretary, waggling her big pile of mail-shots offering discount double-glazing.

Faye scowled at her, irritated that her routine had been so rudely interrupted. It was vital that she said her wish first, otherwise it didn't work. She pushed the envelope in and shrugged, too angry to speak. This time it definitely wouldn't work. Drat.

Big Hair was as poisonous and perfumed as usual when Faye got into work that morning. She spiked her way across the shop floor on six-inch needle heels and pointed a varnished coral talon so close to Faye's nose that her eyes crossed.

'You're late again, and you look a mess.' Big Hair was only in the mood to mince her walking, not her words. She reserved her charm for the customers, who always looked 'sensational in that . . .' (overpriced dress in last season's least popular colour) '. . . Madam' or 'a stone lighter . . .' (in satin? Dream on, you fat cow) '. . . Madam.' Faye, as her lowly assistant, got the sharp edge of her tongue, which was as barbed as her heels.

'This is simply unacceptable,' Big Hair seethed. 'I have overlooked your time-keeping one time too often this month, and I don't know *what* you think you're wearing.'

'This?' Faye looked down and then, smiling with relief, pointed at a rail of dusty pink summer dresses scattered with daisies, 'is that. You told me I should wear our stock lines to encourage the customers.' She'd bought the dress at staff discount the week before. Big Hair had told her it made her look, 'Quite pretty for once'. It was her Hot Date dress. Her look-at-me dress for Matt.

Big Hair raised a well-plucked eyebrow (down to ten hairs, Faye noticed) and sniffed. 'Well I've changed my mind. You'll just put the customers off if you make the clothes look like charity shop rejects,' she smiled back nastily and spiked off, ankles wobbling so much that she almost pitched left into Casual Separates.

Faye pulled a face behind her back and went to collect a cloth to dust the display shelving. Big Hair couldn't ruin her letter day, because it had been ruined already by the girl at the postbox. And she no longer cared about the dress because it hadn't worked last week. It hadn't seduced Matt. He hadn't even been there. He'd stood her up again. That's why the cards had to be right. And today's wasn't.

The next morning, Big Hair's eyebrows had been pruned to just five hairs apiece, and her heels were so high that she had to walk with her knees bent to maintain balance. The resulting calf-ache necessitated a long lunch, leaving Faye in sole charge of the shop floor. As soon as her boss had wobbled off towards Pret A Manger for a low-cal, fat-free sandwich, Faye lent over the counter to a red-haired girl who had just been bullied into buying an over-priced party dress.

'Green's much more your colour,' she told her kindly. 'That orange will date very quickly – it's just a fashion shade. We have a beautiful eau de nil silk in The Sale. Look.' Walking to the rack, she pulled it out and sighed dreamily. She'd thought about buying it herself, but it was far too long. It would look sensational on the tall, willowy girl.

Five minutes later Faye watched proudly as the girl pirouetted around in front of the mirror, amazed that a dress could make her feel so instantly sexy, so ravishing – the orange had made her look like she'd been Tangoed. Her hair was actually a wonderful, deep red – what was the name for it? Titian? Faye loved that word. It conjured up images of tragic, muscular Greek heroes, although this girl was more Pre-Raphaelite and simply staggering when she dressed up.

'I'm so grateful,' she laughed. 'I really didn't like the orange much, but your colleague was so insistent that it suited me.'

Faye could imagine. Big Hair would tell a customer she looked good in one of the shop's plastic bags if she thought it would up the day's takings.

'Is it for a special occasion?' she asked.

The girl nodded. 'My engagement party.' She suddenly spotted the chunky amber nestling between two square diamonds on Faye's ring finger. It was unusual and pretty; Matt had drawn a picture of what he wanted for the jewellery designer to work from. 'Wow, that's so gorgeous. When are you getting married?'

Faye was prepared for this. It wasn't the first time it had happened. 'Oh, someday when we get time, and need a new toaster.' Joking made the lies easier somehow.

The girl nodded, 'You must think I'm terribly old-fashioned having an engagement party? It's just my family are so important to me, to both of us. My brother introduced us, you see. You know what he said to me beforehand? "I've met the man you're going to marry.

He's just *so you*." ' It sounded like Big Hair trying to sell a frock, but a great lump still caught in Faye's throat.

'I think an engagement party sounds lovely,' her smile was wobbling, but she fought to hold it steady. 'I wish we'd had one.'

'Really? Well you still can, can't you?' The girl disappeared behind the changing room curtain.

Faye's answer was too quiet to be heard, her voice hoarse with sadness. 'Not now.'

The sale complete, she wandered around the shop. There were no customers and she let her hands trail along the soft fabrics, pulling the occasional hanger from the racks and propping it under her chin as she stood in front of a full-length mirror, wondering whether Matt would find her attractive in this, or that.

She picked up the last remaining piano shawl – this season's must have, and consequently as expensive as a piano itself. Wrapping it around her shoulders, Faye delighted in the heavy, fringed silk. Embroidered with butterflies and dragonflies, it was like standing on the bank of a river during a midsummer's dusk. It made her think of Matt, of walking along the Thames at Henley on one of their first dates, high on lust and happiness, drunk on red wine, and hoarse from talking and laughing so much.

The red letter hadn't arrived with the morning's post, which wasn't really a disappointment. She'd got it wrong this week, after all.

Big Hair returned just as Faye was signing the delivery slip for a new shipment of French designer wear.

'I'll do that!' She spiked precariously across the parquet and grabbed the slip. 'It's the responsibility of management to cross-check the delivery against the order.'

'I've already checked,' Faye sneezed as acetate fumes pinched at her nose. Big Hair had clearly popped into the arcade's nail bar to have her talons re-rendered in coral. 'They've delivered an extra size twelve in some designs by mistake.'

'Have they?' Big Hair pretended to be shocked. 'Honestly these French are so inefficient. Still, no need to return them. Twelve is a popular size.'

Faye let her teeth pinch at her lower lip, but said nothing. She had known for months that Big Hair deliberately over-ordered items in her own size, usually 'losing' them on the stock sheets rather than forking out at staff discount.

'Oooh – how beautiful,' Big Hair was pulling an exquisitely delicate red dress from its cellophane. Licking her lips impatiently, she eyed the empty store. It was always quiet on Tuesday afternoons. 'Start marking those up with prices will you, Faye? I'm just going to check no customers have left possessions in the fitting rooms.'

Faye turned to hide a smile as Big Hair pelted off on her wobbly spikes, still carrying the red dress. Why bother to lie? She wondered. Why not just say, 'Faye, I am going to try on this dress I plan to steal from the company as a personal perk.'

She fetched the price list and started writing on the labels in her flowing, artistic writing – the one thing Big Hair ever complimented her on. She said it had 'class'.

A sudden strangled moan made her look up. It came from the changing rooms and, had Faye not known better, she would say that there was a very constipated goat in there. There it was again, followed by some breathless panting. And then the long, unmistakable noise of fabric ripping.

Big Hair reappeared several minutes later, absolutely puce in the face, carrying the now crumpled and frayed red dress. 'These dresses *all* have to go back. They're sized up wrongly and the design quality is totally shoddy. I'd expect better of Fior.'

Nodding, Faye took the dress and hung it back up, checking the label. It was only a size eight. Chewing her lip, she wondered whether to say nothing and let Big Hair suffer the agony of thinking that her meticulously gym-trimmed, starved body was fat by chichi French standards. Matt would love the story when she told him. But it wasn't worth the bad temper all afternoon and so she tactfully pointed the error out.

Big Hair was all smiles. 'Silly of me! Those continental sizes always get me. This one will have to go on the bargain rail.'

Faye looked at it; the entire seam had given way and the zip was broken.

'It's too damaged,' she ran her fingers down the big split in the scarlet silk. Like my heart, she found herself thinking.

'Well, then it'll have to be thrown out.'

'No!' Faye grabbed the dress back and cradled the fragile, strappy little bundle to her chest like a broken-winged bird. 'I'll have it.'

Alarmed by her assistant's unexpected passion for damaged stock, Big Hair took a step back, twisted her ankle and pitched left into the hair accessory display, head-butting a rack of scrunchies so that they flew in all directions like hoops at a fair. When she straightened up, she was wearing a silver Alice band at a jaunty angle.

'Well, I suppose you may,' she tried to gather her dignity, straightening the hair band as though she'd been wearing it all day. It sat on her backcombed highlights like a bridge over a drought-dried cornfield. 'But you'll still have to pay staff discount.'

That night Faye decided not to write another card to make up for the one which had been ruined by the secretary at the postbox. Two in one week was getting obsessive. To distract herself, she searched through her drawers and cupboards until she found some red cotton and a needle. Sitting down in front of an old Bogart movie, she started to mend the red dress, repeating tiny little stitches with a surgeon's concentration, wanting to leave no scar, no reminder of the savage rip. She stayed up until the early hours.

Faye was so tired the following morning that she hardly noticed the absence of a red envelope in the post. At the shop, Big Hair was in raging spirits as she anticipated a cosy meeting in the stock-room with her favourite rep, blue-eyed Boris. Boris was as camp as a tented Rococo marquee and had been living with an air steward called Lionel for three years, but it didn't stop Big Hair fluttering around him girlishly whenever he paid a visit to show off his under-wired support range. When he arrived, it was difficult to tell who was mincing more – Boris, who always walked as though he was trying to hold several marbles between his buttocks, or Big Hair, who was today sporting shoes that looked like miniature ski jumps. She was in dire need of ski poles.

'*Must* we have this dreary music, Faye?' she wobbled and spiked her way over to the cassette player and flipped out Portishead, turning back to Boris. 'Poor, darling Faye is still terribly distressed after "*what happened*", but we're all trying to cheer her up, and I don't know about you, but I think a bit of Steps is called for.' A moment later she was swivelling on her six-inch ski slopes to 'Tragedy'. Boris jabbed his flat-fronts around a few times to indicate that he was joining in. If anything was guaranteed to make Faye cry, then that was. It was, indeed, tragic.

She managed to escape under the pretext of fetching herself an espresso, Boris a mocha frappe and Big Hair a skinny latte. It still amazed her that her boss always referred to her heartache as 'what happened'. Not only that, but she whispered the words in a theatrical, breathy, eye-rolling gasp. It irritated the hell out of Faye.

Her favourite stationary shop was next door to Starbucks. It sold expensive handmade cards with glitter and macramé and dried flowers glued to the front. On a stand in the doorway was one Faye hadn't seen before: a red satin padded heart. Now preoccupied with her dress, she had vowed that there would be no more letters that week, but Big Hair's crass comments had upset her so much that her resolve crumbled. She needed another fix. Within minutes the card was inside a paper bag and in her pocket.

The dress took just two more hours to finish that evening. It would have taken less, but Faye was watching *It's A Wonderful Life* and it reminded her so vividly of Matt that she cried non-stop, even though she knew it was the happiest film on Earth. Her stitches became clumsier and she pricked her fingers a hundred times, like Snow White's mother.

Sobbing, not thinking, grief-stricken, she wrote the padded heart card. The blood was still dripping from her fingers and splattered around her words like red exclamation marks. Her writing was wild and uncontrolled, not right at all. The flap of the envelope – a course, chunky one made from dark red card – wouldn't stick and she thumped her fist on it in frustration, howling as it just sprang open again. In the end, she tucked it in, ripping it in her haste. She slapped a stamp on and ran to the postbox. There was no whispered wish this time. There was no point. It was already ruined. She leant against the big, red pillar and wept. Not caring about the curious looks from passersby or the worried question from a concerned pensioner, she screamed until her lungs hollowed out and could give no more but a high-pitched, forlorn little squeak.

Big Hair immediately noticed her red eyes the following morning.

'You need Dew Drops – I swear by them,' she said,

reaching into her handbag for some lethal chemical con-
coction that was guaranteed to tighten the bloodshot
capillaries and make you squint like a film baddie all day.

'Thanks,' Faye was touched. It was almost unheard of
for Big Hair to show any compassion. Even straight
after '*what happened*', Big Hair had insisted that any
time off Faye took would be subtracted from her
holiday leave.

For a moment her boss's hard face twitched with
something close to sympathy, the four hairs still left on
each eyebrow clustering together kindly, but then she
said brusquely, 'That myxomatosis look will put off
trade.'

When, twenty minutes later, Faye was still as puffy-
eyed as a new-born puppy, she was sent into the stock-
room with a clip-board to count 'thins and fats', the
excesses of sizes eight and sixteen. From the other
side of the door came a loud blast of plinky-plinky
drumbeat as Big Hair's favourite Steps tape started up.

Sitting on a box in a corner, Faye took the envelope
out of her pocket. It had arrived that morning, much
later than expected. Despite herself, her heart had lifted
when she'd spotted the familiar, ultra-neat handwriting
and the North London post-mark. She'd pressed it first
to her lips, as though imagining she could taste the
sender, and then breathed deeply, chasing a tiny trace of
aftershave, of cigarettes and coffee, croissants and newspaper print. But she hadn't opened it. That she had
saved until now.

Her hands trembled. Christ, why did they still do
that? Why even now when she knew what would be

written inside, when she knew that the love was safe, was eternal, would never . . . say it, Faye . . . never die? But she still ripped into the paper with messy eagerness, pulling out the card and almost dropping it from her shaking grip. On the front was a picture of a big, goofy dog wearing a propeller-head baseball cap. The caption read 'Doggy Fashion'. It was typical of his humour. Faye's puffy eyes filled with tears that squeezed from the corners as she read the message inside and smiled. It never changed.

I love you. I always will. Matt.

She looked at it for a long time. So it had worked after all. Not as well as usual, admittedly, but just enough to keep her going until she saw him again.

'Christ – d'you do a line of charlie in there or something?' Big Hair watched Faye emerge five minutes later.

Bounding towards the counter, Faye shook her head and laughed. 'Another sort of line entirely.'

Big Hair obviously wanted to ask more, but at that moment a hefty middle-aged woman appeared from the changing room wearing a pair of grey linen trousers that gave her an arse like an elephant. 'Oh yes, Madam looks *sensational*. That look is *so* this season, and I have the *perfect* scarf to accessorise.'

While her boss was busy flapping around with the beautiful piano shawl that cost more than a grand piano, Faye noticed that a red-haired man was waiting patiently at the counter. She kept a jealous half-eye on her dancing dragonfly shawl as she turned towards him.

'Can I help?' she asked before remembering that Big Hair had insisted that she should say '*May* I help?'

'Sure,' he grinned, revealing a smile as wide and delicious as a fresh slice of apple. 'I'm looking for something – er – girly.'

This was such a profoundly daft, male and (dare she think it?) such a Matt-like thing to say, that Faye found herself grinning back. 'We do girly. Were you thinking pink, fluffy girly, or skimpy, tassely girly?'

He pretended to ponder this deeply for a moment. 'More blushing bride girly. She's quite old-fashioned, so I'd like to treat her to something for her – what's it called – true soul?'

'Trousseau.' Faye laughed. Not a cross-dresser then, she realised with relief. 'Underwear, outer-wear or something that could pass as either?' Big Hair would freak out if she was listening in, but she was still stalking around Elephant Bum with the piano shawl like a bullfighter. Faye was relieved to see that the customer had clocked the price tag and was shaking her head violently.

'Oh, I was thinking of something more like –' his eyes followed hers. 'That.'

'The shawl?' Faye felt a tiny stranglehold of panic take her throat. She knew that she couldn't afford it – even at staff discount – but she wanted that shawl. It would go with her broken-heart dress. It was perfect. 'I'm afraid that lady was first.'

He politely pretended not to notice that the reluctant customer was now fighting Big Hair off with her handbag. 'Do you have another?'

'No,' she muttered, praying that Big Hair would press it upon Elephant Bum long enough for the redheaded man to leave.

'I see,' he didn't look as though he was about to leave at all. His gaze moved brightly around the shop. 'Amanda said this place was unique – lots of beautiful, unusual things – rather like her. Rather like –' he looked at Faye for a moment, studying her face, on the edge of adding something else, but then he just smiled another huge appley smile. 'The green dress she bought here really suits her. She looked radiant at the engagement party.'

Faye remembered the Titian-haired girl who she'd rescued from being Tangoed. The girl with the eau de nil dress. So this must be her fiancé. Wow. All that red hair, and the same dark blue eyes. They would look ravishing together. They'd have amazing children.

Suddenly Faye didn't mind about the shawl. She wanted the red-haired girl to have it. She wanted this beautiful Titian-haired Greek hero to buy it for his bride. She was so carried away with her reverie that she could already see it wrapped around their first-born – the beautiful Titian family tableau.

In a thrice, she had whipped it away from a startled Big Hair and was reaching for the tissue paper.

'One moment,' the man held up his hand, laughing at her haste.

Faye turned pink. He'd only asked to look at it and she was practically frisking him for an Amex so that he could buy it as a swaddling cloth. 'Sorry – here – take a look. It's handmade. Egyptian silk, Belgian needlework. Beautiful.'

'I'd like you to try it on,' he pushed it back at her.

'Me?'

He nodded, clearing his throat, 'Just so I can see what it looks like, you know – get an idea.'

Faye wanted to point out that his future wife had far more stunning colouring, was at least a foot taller and would consequently look like a graceful leggy starlet in it compared to Faye's Romanian refugee, but she was aware that Big Hair was hovering nearby now, panting for a sale. The piano shawl was by far the most expensive item in the shop. Faye would be expected to jump from the light fittings using it as a parachute if it led to a sale. She wrapped it around her shoulders.

Oh God. She was back on the bank of the Thames at Henley. She was drunk with Matt, and with loving Matt in heady, never-let-it-end free fall. She was kissing him in a haze of evening sun, dragonflies, pollen and lust, realising that she'd met the other side of herself at last, the side that was always in the sun.

She wasn't sure what happened next. All she knew was that one minute she was standing in front of the red-haired man with tears streaming down her face, the next she was running through the arcade, the sound of the shop alarm wailing behind her and Big Hair clacking in screaming pursuit, closely followed by the security guard from the neighbouring leather shop. She lost Big Hair up the cobbled alley between Starbucks and Pizza Express – hearing a scream from behind, she looked around to see a pair of legs sticking out of the pile of cardboard boxes, the six-inch spiked shoes at jaunty angles. The sixty-year-old, sixty-a-day security guard was no match for Faye's adrenaline-pumped broken heart and she shook him off in the car park. At least her house-keys were in her pocket. She ran all the way home, the shawl flapping behind her like wings.

Big Hair limped back into her shop, strappy shoes dangling from one hand, to find the red-haired man standing exactly where they had left him, in front of the counter. He was rubbing his mouth and nodding. 'Amanda was right,' he whispered. 'She promised she'd return the favour and she has.'

Deciding that he was as demented as Faye, Big Hair went straight to the phone.

'Yes, I'd like to report a shoplifting offence – no, the thief has left the premises, but I know where she lives. It's all on security camer –' A warm hand covered hers and pulled the receiver from her mouth before returning it to its cradle.

'There's no need to call the police,' the redheaded man cut through Big Hair's furious squawking. 'I'll pay for the shawl, plus ten per cent on top for any inconvenience.'

It was too good an offer to refuse but, as she swiped the man's credit card, Big Hair still muttered darkly under her breath that Faye no longer had a career in retail, 'And she'd better not ask for a reference. I bet her handbag's still here. I'll murder her when she comes back for it.'

'I'll take it round to her house,' the man offered.

Big Hair's eyes narrowed as she assessed his potential as a mad assistant-stalker. Quite which of them was the madder was debatable. They were welcome to each other. 'I'll fetch it,' she limped into the storeroom.

When she re-emerged she was carrying a small bag from which a red envelope tumbled as soon as she put it on the counter.

'Her address is written on here.' Picking it up, Big Hair noisily pulled out the card and snorted as she registered the picture. Then she opened it up and her eyes stretched so wide that her few remaining eyebrow hairs stood on end. 'This is from her fiancé.'

The man tipped his head back and smiled sadly. 'I knew it. Amanda said that she thought the relationship was in the past, was somehow over. The moment I saw the ring, I guessed –'

'But that's the thing,' Big Hair looked at the envelope again, and turned pale when she saw the postmark. 'It *is* over. This card – this card has been sent by a ghost.'

It was time to look at the cards again. Faye knew that. It had been more than a week. The one that had arrived that morning was still in her handbag at the shop, but it hardly counted compared to the others. It was the early ones she needed to see, the ones that he had sent each week for three years, even when they moved in together, even if they were on holiday in Africa, in the Caribbean, in Europe. A card every week. Always the same message. *I love you. I always will. Matt.*

She called his parents afterwards, carefully keeping the tears from her voice as she asked how they were that week. They told her that they had some good news at last.

When Faye replaced the receiver, she lay back on the scattered cards and stared at the ceiling for a moment, her heart pounding with excitement. Rolling over, she pressed her lips to an envelope. Dropping kisses on post-marks from Paris and Scotland and N1, she started to laugh as she gathered up all the cards and hugged them tightly.

She was going to have to see him. So what if it was a Thursday and not their usual Friday. They were going to have a date. He would be there this time. She was going to dress up for him.

He saw her turn the corner long before she realised that he was waiting in her porch. She wasn't hard to miss in her red silk dress and a piano shawl, quite the most beautiful thing he had ever seen. She walked in a languid, almost directionless way, swinging the ends of the shawl this way and that, stopping to stare at the sky, to smile, to stretch out her arms as though soaking in the last rays of sun, although it was long dark and starting to drizzle. He watched, mesmerised. She jumped when he stepped out to greet her.

'Sorry – here, I brought you this back.' He tried for an easy smile as he held her bag out by way of explanation. 'I was in the shop earlier, remember?'

'It's *so you*,' she laughed, her eyes liquid bright. She seemed to be smiling and crying at the same time.

'Yes – amazing the hot looks you get when you stand in a doorway holding a woman's handbag for half an hour,' he joked nervously. He'd been worried that he would scare her, although right now she was the one doing all the scaring.

'Thank you, that's really kind,' she hung her head, looking up at him through her damp lashes apologetically. 'I'm so sorry I stole the shawl that you wanted to buy. It was horrible of me. But, you see I needed it for a date. It was a very special date. You can have it now.' She started to pull it off her narrow shoulders, but he reached out to stop her.

'No, you keep it. Really, it suits you – I've sorted it out with your manageress. I'll get Amanda something else. Plenty of time.'

'Both your lifetimes,' she nodded.

He winced. Christ, he had to ask it. This was eating him up – it was all getting way too Twilight Zone. 'You say you went on a date?'

She nodded, her eyes dreamy. 'I've been every week since, since . . . but he hasn't been there. That is, he has been there, but not – oh, it's hard to explain. Anyway he was there this evening. I hugged him for hours.'

Seeing his bewildered expression, she suddenly laughed. 'I know. How stupid is that? Hugging a gravestone. I could almost hear him joking to leave off, that I was making a fool of myself, but I knew he'd like me doing it really – just as he'd understand why I send myself cards and pretend they're from him. I've waited long enough to say goodbye, after all.'

He swallowed hard as he realised that she wasn't seeing a ghost at all. It was much simpler than that, and much sadder. 'How long ago did he die?'

She scratched her head nervously, the question still an uneasy trigger to tears that required hasty displacement

721

activity to abate. 'Almost a year. Every week there's been a little more grass on the new turf and nothing to remind me of Matt – no stone and no words. His family couldn't agree over the epitaph, you see. They let me choose in the end – "Always loved and always will be".

'We were about to get married, you know?' the tears were tumbling already. She wiped them with the backs of her hands like a child, talking in a rush of jumbled words. 'Well no, that's a lie, we got engaged almost on a whim, but I think we might have done – given time, but then he died. He just . . . died.' She punched angrily at her nose with her sleeve to stop it streaming.

'And you know what happened on the morning we buried him?' She gazed at him through blind tears. 'A card arrived in the post. From Matt. From Matt who'd died the day he sent it. My Matt, telling me he loved me.

'I've been so sad, so demented with sadness. I mean I'm still sad now, but today . . . it's like I've got a bit of him back, you know? It's like . . .' She suddenly stopped herself, covering her mouth, big brown eyes huge with shock and apology. 'Christ, I'm so sorry! You just came into the shop to buy your fiancée a scarf and here I am blithering on about Matt, and –'

'She's not my fiancée,' he interrupted. 'She's my sister.'

She hardly seemed to hear as she fumbled with her keys, sobbed, laughed and said 'sorry' again. She grabbed her bag and backed hastily towards the door. 'This is so embarrassing. Once I start, I can't stop. Everyone thinks you don't want to talk about dead people, but you do – all the time in fact. It makes up for not talking to them, the dead person that is. But you're just the lovely true soul man and you've brought my handbag back and paid for the scarf I stole so I really can't bore you with all this,' she was almost through the door now.

'Wait! I don't mind being bored,' he said urgently. 'Shit, that sounds awful. I mean you're not boring. You can talk to me. Maybe we can meet for a drink sometime?'

She looked at him for a moment, wet eyes glittering. A tiny smile hit the edges of her mouth before falling away. 'I'm sorry – it's lovely of you, but it's really too soon. I can't.'

'Take my number at least,' he pulled a business card from his pocket and scribbled a home number on the back, cursing as his pen took ages to work.

'Thanks,' she grabbed it without looking at it, disappearing behind her door.

There was a message waiting on Faye's answerphone from Big Hair, telling her in no uncertain terms that her employ was terminated. Wearily, she took a long bath surrounded by scented candles, trying not to see Matt's face in the flames.

As she sat on the sofa drying her hair, she picked up the business card from the coffee table. She tapped it against her teeth before dropping it in the bin.

A dark red envelope was waiting in her hallway the next morning. She knew that it was the one containing the padded heart card because it was odd-shaped. The weird thing was that the flap was stuck down. Good old Royal

Mail – they might deliver late, but they were generous with their glue.

Faye picked it up and wondered whether to throw it straight in the bin. She didn't need the cards any more. She had the message that said it all, one that was ready and waiting every week of the year for the rest of her life, one that every now and again – when no one was looking – she could even hug.

But then something struck her. There was no blood. She had pricked her fingers the evening she wrote it, and yet there was no blood on the envelope.

And then her scalp seemed to shrink as she looked at the address. She distinctly remembered addressing it so hurriedly that she'd made no effort to make the handwriting look like Matt's, but this was so like his neat, meticulous hand it could be for real. It was far better than her self-deluding forgeries.

Sliding down the wall of the hallway, she ripped it open. There was no blood inside the card either. The message was unmistakably in Matt's hand.

I love you. I always will. Love is for life. Don't forget that. Matt.

Propped up on Faye's mantlepiece that night were two cards. One was a padded heart, the other a small, battered business card. She wasn't about to call the number scribbled on the back, but it was there as a reminder that one day – maybe this month, maybe next, she might. If love was for life, she realised, then it was about time she started living again.

Enfemme
Matt Whyman

Without her face on, Missy was a stranger to us. All the girls agreed. Even if it did go unspoken. The open pores. The dreary do. The *pounds* it piled on her. Honestly, when she opened the door, my first thought was to take a Polaroid and tape it to my fridge. Despite everything she had taught us, the hints and tips on application and attitude, subtlety and finish, underneath the hemlines of her own life Missy hid some serious baggage. I had to blink before I believed it. Wished I was looking through a lens rubbed with Vaseline. It was a trick that Missy herself had encouraged us to apply to our own bathroom mirrors. *Anything* to soften the edges.

'Pearls before swine. You know the rules.' That was the first thing she ever said to us at the start of our long hot summer together. Didn't even look round from the mirror on the counter when she put us in our place. Just carried on combing her lashes like we could wait all day for all she cared. Shannon juiced the air between her teeth. Debrella folded her arms and tipped her head to one side, but neither of them took it any further. Which just about summed us up at the time. The fact was we didn't really know the rules at all. Having spent the better part of our lives watching from the sidelines, this was our first outing onto the pitch. I may have been the instigator, but Missy was a formidable presence. Old enough to be our mother, too. Age before beauty was what sprung to mind, but that wasn't strictly true back then.

'Honey,' I said instead, and hoped the words spinning inside my head would come out in the right order. 'You can't fix what's born broken.'

It was a moment right out of the cabaret, when Missy stood tall and came round in a corkscrew. Six foot something in her heels and huge hair. Golden arches for eyebrows. Lips painted likewise and pursed so tight she could've had drawstrings in there. All that was missing was the spotlight. South of her choker, she was wearing a cropped halter neck and hobble skirt, with an azure blue jewel nested in her bellybutton. It left me feeling frumpy, shapeless and wishing I had at least braved the boa.

'Show me your nails.' She batted her gaze between us. 'All of you.'

'Excuse me?' said Shannon, and gasped when Missy grabbed her wrist. '*Hey!*'

'Easy now' I warned them all, anxious not to cause a scene. We just weren't prepared to handle that kind of attention at the time. Unlike Missy, who thrived on it.

We had seen her in all the right places, never less than dressed to kill, and that was what had drawn us to her. Earlier that day, the three of us had stepped out with our brand new names and followed in her footsteps. Only now we had come so close there was no going back. Especially not for poor Shannon. Reluctantly, she straightened her digits, her eyes lifting apprehensively as this figure who had been everywhere before us came in for a closer inspection.

'Oh, please!' Clutching at her own throat, Missy swayed back suddenly as if she had just foreseen the future.

'What is it?' Shannon's voice lifted some now. 'What's *wrong*?'

Debrella and I, we forgot ourselves and closed in for a better look. Forming a circle that wouldn't be broken throughout the season that followed.

'Sisters,' said Missy, working through our hands in turn. 'When it comes to faking it, this just won't do.'

'It won't?'

'Not even close. You want to go places? You gotta give *one hundred* per cent!' She dropped my hand. Almost tossed it away. Then showed us her own perfect ten. 'Compromise in any way, you might as well be dead.'

Meeting Missy was like crossing a bridge. She led us to ourselves. Shannon, Debrella and I, we gathered outside her lobby doors every Saturday. Waiting there on the pavement for Missy to drop down to our level and then guide us from May through to September. The three of us learning to walk and talk all over again. Aspiring to be better than the real thing. But before all that we had to get right back to basics and master the art of shopping. Out went the borrowed blouses. In came the figure formers. According to the woman awaiting our transformation, it was the only way to shape our spirits.

'Well?' I asked sheepishly, the first to zip back my curtain. 'How do I look?'

'Stand proud,' said Missy, touching a finger to her chin. 'Anyone would think you're waiting for a free kick.'

I unclasped my hands as directed, squaring my shoulders until Missy nodded her approval. Shannon joined me from the neighbouring cubicle just then. She looked a little lumpy I thought, even with her belly sucked in, but Missy insisted that a corset would cover the flaws. Shannon kind of died in her own eyes when she said this, but then the girl was disadvantaged from the outset. Built like the plasterer that she was during the week, the poor thing only had to grimace and her face squashed up like a burger in a bap. Where Shannon knew her appearance was something she would have to put up with, Debrella needed putting down. Not because she looked lumpy, bumpy, dumpy or frumpy. Far from it. She looked fabulous, with her long limbs and latte skin, but she knew it too. Parading around us like that, anyone would've thought she had just emerged from a cocoon not a cubicle.

'This is *so* me,' she purred, with one hand on her barely enhanced curve and the other held aloft.

Debrella was always destined to make the greatest

impression. To go further than Shannon or me. Naturally we assumed her genes were responsible. Debrella did so like to flag up the fact that she was quarter Portuguese, on one side or the other. It wasn't until very much later that we learned about the hormones.

'You look *scandalously* good!' declared Missy, and clapped her hands together. 'A million dollars.'

'In used notes,' I muttered bitterly, and watched Shannon bolt a hand to her mouth.

I turned to Missy, hoping she would share the moment, but instead felt the sting of her palm on my cheek.

'*Never* bitch about your own,' she warned, and dragged me to her bosom before I could even think about chinning her. It was suffocating in there, all frilled lace and foam. Momentarily, my instinct to fight back became a fight for life. When Missy relented and I came up for air, I found her expression had softened into a smile. 'You want to sharpen your claws,' she said. 'You go for the girls you aspire to be, understood? Good. Now go dress to impress. I feel a cocktail hour coming on.'

Wig-wise, everyone conceded that Shannon turned the most heads. A honey blonde pile-up with bangs and bows and all sorts. Privately, we all knew it wasn't just the hair that was responsible, but Missy had spoken and Shannon needed more support and encouragement than most. It was Debrella who commanded the kind of attention we grew to crave. As the temperature continued to climb, the girl revealed herself to be all symmetry and slingbacks. Sometimes I wondered whether she slept in a mould at night so her body submitted to the ideal shape. The mane she adopted was as dark and rich as molasses, cut high at the fringe to frame her face and pleated at the back to signpost a piece of ass that moved like she had two *panther* cubs in there. One time, she prowled across to the powder room and the crowded bar just cleaved apart. Nobody pawed her. Nobody mauled her. Nobody whistled or dared disrespect her. Not with Missy holding court in her wake. Seated there in the horseshoe booth at the back. The queen of all she surveyed.

'Finish your drinks,' she declared when Debrella returned. 'It's time to party.'

Girls like us? We weren't designed to queue. All squashed into our Cinderella slippers, we had to keep moving for the sake of our circulation. Fortunately, in the heart of this city on a Saturday night, you could be sure to find a door bitch who was one of our own.

'No trainers or trailer trash, Missy. We got standards to consider.'

We were standing beside Missy this time, not behind her. The three of us dolled up to dazzle, but anxious to be inside. Sequinned side-tie dress for me. A sheer and strappy look for Debrella. Something ruffled for Shannon.

'We're sisters.' Facing up to the clipboard police, Missy reached out and gathered us under her wing. 'Any fool can see the resemblance.'

Enfemme, we were united. Kicking up a midsummer's storm on the dance floors, even the table tops when the drinks flowed freely. Individually, however, we each had our own reasons for coming out like this. Debrella was the kind of girl who liked boys with big bank accounts. Hence the length she went to ensure they got a decent return. Shannon, on the other hand, would for ever have an eye for any lady who would have her. Me? I was on the lookout for nothing more than the next martini. Doing my own thing for myself. We came from very different backgrounds: construction, commerce and law enforcement, but one day a week we lived in a world of our own. Nobody questioned Missy's credentials. She was so much wiser. So much *older*, but so much sharper, too. Everything beyond that remained a mystery. Her inspiration and her direction were all that mattered. The woman we relied upon when things turned ugly. Which was often the case when we paused for breath and refreshments.

'Hey now, sweet babies, that was some show! Do you drink like you dance? You look like you do. Squeeze up now, cos I'm here to pick up the tab.'

The women weren't a problem. Not for Shannon or myself, at any rate. It was guys like this who persistently scored on us. Fat cats from the city with too-tight suits and majority shares in self-assurance. Sometimes I wondered if we looked incomplete without company. More often than not I wondered if they looked at us properly at all.

'Make yourself comfortable,' purred Missy this time,

reaching under the table that had just been our stage. 'If you're man enough.'

It wasn't the question that saw this one's mouth form a perfect circle, but when Missy let go they always made their excuses.

'No balls?' I enquired.

Shannon cackled and lit another fag. I watched her take a drag and then hold it with her palm tipped upwards *à la Missy*.

'No manners.' Missy examined her talons for damage before she returned to her own cigarette. 'Gentlemen are fast becoming history, I fear.'

'Aww, he was cute.' Debrella pouted like the prick we had just dismissed. She twisted round to snatch another glance. Came back blinking dumbly. 'He have a big bonus, I think.'

Shannon rolled her kohl-dark eyes, and I knew why. Ever since our first outing, Debrella had continued to modify her accent like her vital statistics. What was once a hint of ancestral Latino had now crossed the water to become full-blown Brazilian. As if the girl believed she was the one from Ipanema. Tall and tanned and young and lovely she may have been, but there was also a ruthless streak with her. One that didn't rhyme with the rest or scan so well.

'So what if he is loaded?' Missy paused to slip the olive from her cocktail stick. 'Respect doesn't cost a penny.'

Debrella shrugged, said money was a girl's best friend, and fanned a wave for the man anyway.

'You're so cheap,' said Shannon. 'I'm embarrassed.'

'Oh, blow it out your hole,' she spat back, and glanced at Missy for approval.

'Okay,' I said, conscious that Missy was ready to walk right out if the conflict continued between us. 'Who's for another drink?'

I was relieved when autumn approached, and the days began to fold early. The loss of light on a Saturday night did wonders for my appearance, and encouraged me to be even more outgoing. Shannon, meanwhile, was *delighted*. For her, it meant less sweat, less flesh and more finesse. Only Debrella mourned the loss of liberty the sultry nights afforded.

'It's the drugs,' Shannon confided in me. 'Some of the shit she does messes with her mood as well as her mammaries.'

'I knew it!' I said, while trying to make myself more comfortable. We were back at the cocktail bar, waiting for Missy to join us. Usually she was the first to arrive and the last to leave, and her absence filled the booth. It was a space made even more apparent seeing that Debrella had slipped away to powder her nose, though I was beginning to wonder how much went up it not on it. Since making a name for ourselves, the girl had grown to be so self-centred it was a wonder she didn't shut off the lights behind her as she floated into the washroom. The way she always came back with a cold and a story about herself, it made me mad. Not just because she was abusing her body like that, but because she didn't offer to share.

'What do you say we let her go?' said Shannon, who

had just flipped open her compact. She glanced at her reflection as if it might turn her to stone. Snapped it shut again. 'Three is a party. Four is a freak show.'

'Missy won't like it,' I told her.

'Missy isn't here,' said Shannon, just as the bar divided into two and Debrella switched back to her seat. She came in on my other side, sniffing like a blood-hound, and briefly I felt trapped between them.

A cocktail doesn't go far without conversation. For half an hour the three of us sat around the horseshoe booth, turning to our drinks before each other. Without Missy, we were lost for words. Apart from Debrella, that is, who continued to question whether her breasts looked big in the basque she had bought.

'They look fine,' I said finally, sounding as fake and deflated as we both felt in her presence.

Debrella pushed out her chest, and beamed at us both. 'One hell of an upgrade, huh?'

'Even God couldn't do any better,' said Shannon, acidly, and would've had it out with her were it not for the arrival of a beaming face at our table.

'Room for a little one?' The guy's opening line was as bad as his suit. He squeezed in beside Shannon, who immediately looked at me. A silent appeal for some kind of help. I didn't know what to say. Didn't even have time to blink before Debrella found herself in company too. A female this time, for real. With freckles you couldn't count in one night and a figure that put our efforts to shame.

'Is this a party?' she rested her elbow on the seat

behind Debrella, who squeaked into her drink.

This was all wrong. Socially and sexually. Shannon on one side. Debrella on the other. Me in the middle without a partner or a script. Had our guests switched seats their presence might've been welcomed. As it was the three of us froze, and I realised then that Missy wasn't coming.

'We have to go,' was all I could think to say, feeling giddy with drink all of a sudden, and Debrella swiftly backed me up. The trouble was she sounded even more unconvincing, and this time it had nothing to do with her accent. We were all out of excuses, which suddenly made Missy's absence so alarming.

'A friend is expecting us.' Shannon kicked me under the table. I saw a look of panic set in under the pan stick. 'Isn't that right, darlings?'

'Don't you want to party?' the guy beside her asked. He looked to his opposite number, who sneered at us all and vacated the booth. I should've been relieved when he followed behind her. Instead, I looked around and found we were being watched for all the wrong reasons.

'Girls,' I said, and reached for my fake fur stole. 'This party is *over*.'

Shannon busted a nail on Missy's buzzer. It happened on the third attempt. Prompted her to stand back and start yelling her name instead. Hands like brackets round her mouth, head craned back to the boulevard of stars between the buildings on this block. None of us knew which floor Missy lived on, but it seemed right to aim high.

'It's chilly out here.' I turned to Debrella, my arms folded tight under my chest. 'Maybe Missy had the right idea.'

It was this climb down in temperature that had kept our concern in check. Gave us something else to curse on the way over. Debrella was hugging herself as well, only less successfully. Despite the difference in our cleavage, I figured she shared the same chilling sense of insecurity. Shannon too. What we needed was closure. That much was clear. A way to come in from the cold.

Debrella sighed to herself, and for a beat her breath hung in the air. 'When I have enough monies,' she groused, 'I move back to Rio.'

'Back?' I said. 'You've never been!'

'It is my home,' she said, affronted. 'In my heart.' A pack of lads loped past just then. Pressed pastel shirts and fringes gelled to foreheads. The lot of them looking for trouble. Debrella and I, we shrank against the lobby door, while Shannon cut short her shouting and stepped away from the kerb.

'It's no good,' I said, after they had finished with their funny looks. 'We're on our own out here.'

I leaned back against the glass, almost lost my balance when the latch snapped away and the lobby door swung open.

'Correction,' said Shannon, sounding relieved and aggrieved in equal measure. 'She's in!'

Like Missy, the lift failed to respond promptly, so we braced ourselves for a long climb. Debrella even kicked off her heels after the first few steps, though she didn't have to bother. For just as we were swinging round to take on the next flight, a door eased open and there she was. No hair. No slap. No flawless skin or body glitter. Nothing but the same kind of clothes we all wore in the week. Pared down here to a vest and boxers, a little bit of stubble and a lot of extra weight. I felt self-conscious, standing there. Ill-dressed and out of place. Just as I had when we first met at the make-up counter.

'Missy,' whispered Shannon. She paused to clear her throat, and her voice promptly dropped an octave. 'Look at you!'

'Mate, what's happened?' This was Debrella, shorn of her South American accent all of a sudden. Even her poise had gone. 'Are you sick or something?'

'Missy's not coming out any more,' he said quickly, and looked to his bare feet. 'It's Mack, by the way. Real name's Michael, but I never feel comfortable with that.'

'It's Saturday,' I reminded him, and forgot myself as the others had before me. '*Saturday*, man. Our night out!'

A voice called his name from inside the flat just then, asking who was here. My instinct was to flee, but my eyes wouldn't let go when a vision in a snow-white bathrobe appeared behind him and stopped there with a start. She had a towel tied up like a turban and held the tiniest newborn I had ever seen. As one moment spun into the next, all I could think was that they looked so beautiful together. So delicate. Natural. *Genuine*. Mack glanced round, came back with a timid smile.

'My wife and daughter,' he said. 'I'd invite you in, but –'

'It's cool,' I cut in. 'We understand.'

'No sweat,' said Debrella, sounding just as awkward as me. 'Sorry to disturb you.'

'Had we known . . .' Shannon faltered mid-sentence, and blushed brightly. 'Congratulations, by the way.'

Mack seemed lost at first, as unsure how to finish this as we were, but then he looked my way, and I realised it was down to me. I stepped forward, and offered him my hand.

'It's better to burn out, right?'

'Better still to pass on the torch,' he said under his breath, coming back at me with a wink and a hint of Missy. I tried hard to mirror his firm grip, wishing his wife would give us a moment, only to find myself sharing one with him anyway.

'Take care of your family,' I slipped my hand free, loosening up enough now to jab a kid punch at his chest. 'And thanks.'

'No, thank *you*,' he said, to each of us in turn. 'You're gents. You really are.'

Outside on the street, the night air felt sharper than ever. As if a breeze had swept through this city while we were inside. The seasons crossing over. I gathered the stole around my shoulders, and wondered which way to go. The bars and the clubs were west of here, but I lived way out east. I turned to the girls, eyed them both uncertainly.

'So,' I said. 'What do you think?'

'What do I think?' Debrella fired up at this, and her accent returned to the fore. 'A *tramp* is what I think, coming to the door in that terry towel affair and no lipstick.'

'I was embarrassed for the baby.' Shannon flashed a wicked grin. 'Even *I'm* not that much of a minger.'

'And did you see her *nails*?' Debrella linked arms with us both, steered us back into town. It felt good, heading this way. Three girls together. Buzzing without drink or drugs. Preparing now for a party of our own. 'A woman lets herself go like that,' she finished, 'God knows where it'll end.'

Notes on the Contributors

Jessica Adams is the author of two novels, *Single White E-mail* and *Tom, Dick and Debbie Harry* (Pan Macmillan), and two astrology titles, *Handbag Horoscopes* (Penguin) and *The New Astrology For Women* (HarperCollins). She has been the astrologer for *ELLE* for over ten years. Her next project is *The Future Pack* (Penguin) and she recently finished working on the Channel Ten drama, *The Secret Life Of Us*. Jessica is the co-editor of both *Girls' Night In* and *Girls' Night In, Gentlemen By Invitation*. Her website is jessicaadams.net.

Maggie Alderson was born in London, brought up in Staffordshire, and educated at the University of St Andrews. She has worked on nine glossy magazines – as editor on four of them – and two newspapers. She currently contributes to magazines and papers in Australia, Britain and the US. Her first book, *Shoe Money*, was published in 1998 and her bestselling novel, *Pants on Fire*, in 2000. Her second novel will be published in 2002.

Louise Bagshawe was working for Sony Music going on the road with rock bands when she got the news that her first book was to be published. *Career Girls* was an instant bestseller and since then Louise has written five more smash hits; she adapted her book *Venus Envy* for Fox 2000. Her latest, *A Kept Woman*, is out now and she is working on number six. She lives in New York with her husband Anthony and her pug, Friday.

Emily Barr worked for a newspaper for several years, until the day it became too much and she realised she had to go travelling instead. Now she can't imagine why she stayed so long. She went around the world for a year, and wrote a travel column for the *Guardian* as she went. When she came back, she knew she couldn't go back to a proper job so she did the thing she had always wanted to do, and wrote her first novel. *Backpack* was published in February 2001. She now writes a regular travel column in the *Observer*, and is finishing her second book. She lives in Brighton, England, and is getting married this year.

Mark Barrowcliffe has been a full-time writer since the publication of his bestselling first novel *Girlfriend 44* in 2000. *Girlfriend 44* has been translated into ten languages and the film rights have been bought by Universal Pictures. Mark's second novel, *Infidelity For First Time Fathers*, was published this year. Mark is currently living in Paris, where he is poncing about in a rather sophisticated and off-hand manner. He is writing an epic poem which, once he has it out of his system, he intends to throw into the Seine.

The only thing that stopped **Colin Bateman** from being a top journalist was his extreme reluctance to talk to people and his phobia about using phones. He was also completely uninterested in any type of news; luckily he worked on the kind of weekly newspaper in Northern Ireland which had acres of space to fill every week so they could hardly say no when he turned his hand to writing a column which he liked to think was satirical but which was, in fact, just silly. Luckily people liked it, and thus encouraged, he set about writing his first novel, *Divorcing Jack*, which, after being turned down by every agent in London, landed on the slush pile at HarperCollins where it was eventually fished out and published to wide acclaim in 1995. Since then he has written a string of best . . . sorry, quite good sellers, including *Turbulent Priests* and *Shooting Sean*. He has written the screenplays for the movies *Crossmaheart*, *Divorcing Jack* and *Wild About Harry*, and has recently directed his first short film. He fancies himself as the next Spielberg. Sid Spielberg, that is.

Matt Beaumont has worked as a copywriter in advertising but since he wrote *e* and *The e Before Christmas* he hasn't done much of that. He lives in North London with Maria, Sam and Holly. He is working on a new novel and some other stuff.

John Birmingham was born in Liverpool. His parents fled to Australia. He is still here. He lived with nearly one hundred flatmates and kept notes on all of them. Those notes were the basis for his first book, *He Died* *with a Falafel in His Hand*. He has written other books offering gratuitous advice to clueless men and detailing the ugly, untold history of Sydney, where he now lives at Bondi Beach with a wife, a most excellent baby daughter and two unruly cats. John has been a contributing editor at *Rolling Stone* and *Penthouse*. He has written for many pornographic magazines including *Playboy* and *Inside Sport*. He has won a whole bunch of awards, including Business Columnist of the Year for 2000. No one was more surprised than he. Except maybe the businesses he wrote about. He has recently been researching a book about Australian marijuana culture but can't remember the details.

A former stand-up comedian (a real one, not one of these authors who only ever did two open spots), **Marc Blake** is the author of the bestselling comic thrillers *Sunstroke* and *Bigtime*. Also a screenwriter, his movie *Sticks and Stones* is currently in production, while his ITV two-part drama *The Swap* is due to be shown this year in the UK. He has taught comedy writing at London's City University for six years. As Caleb March (a poor anagram of his name), he has also penned *My Computer Hates Me*, *A Boyfriend's Little Instruction Book* and *A Bastard's Bedtime Companion*, all for Boxtree. His third novel, *24 Karat Schmooze* (Flame) is out now in paperback.

Yasmin Boland is a fulltime freelance writer and has contributed to publications around the world, including *ELLE*, *New Woman*, *B*, *The Sunday Telegraph* and *black + white*.

Recently she developed a fiction addiction; this began after she wrote an erotic short story which – to her surprise – was quickly bought by and published in *Australian Women's Forum*. Her less erotic but still quite exotic short story 'Mr Charisma' appeared in the first *Girls' Night In*. Yasmin is also the author of the new age love novel *Carole King Is An Alien* and the spooky romance book *Cosmic Love*, both of which she'd adore you to read. She's currently working on her second novel and her website is www.yasminboland.com.

Like a dodgy wine, **Bruno Bouchet** is the 'product of more than one country of the EU', born in Spain of British and French parents with an Italian grandmother tossed in for good measure. He lives in Sydney writing fiction and magazine articles, and trying to teach business managers to be more creative in their report writing (his most ambitious project to date!). His first novel *The Beauty of Truth* was a bestseller. His next novel, *The Girls*, was released in September 2001. He welcomes any comments or feedback you have via his website www.brunobouchet.com.

Born, bred and still living in Dublin, **Colette Caddle** began her career as a novelist at the tender age of thirty-three. Disillusioned with office life, she had started writing in her lunch breaks. A few months later, when she finally escaped the rat-race, she sent 'the book' off to Kate Cruise O'Brien – late editor of Poolbeg – for a laugh. To her amazement Kate liked what she saw. Colette's first two novels were immediate bestsellers in

Ireland. Her first novel to be published in the UK, *Shaken & Stirred* (Hodder & Stoughton), was a great success. Her next book will be published later this year.

Kaz Cooke is a writer and a cartoonist. Her latest books include *Up the Duff: The Real Guide to Pregnancy* and another in a series of small but perfectly formed satires called *The Little Book of Diet and Exercise*.

Anna Davis is the author of three novels: *Cheet*, *Melting* and *The Dinner*. She also writes short stories and is a frequent contributor to the *Guardian*. Anna grew up in Cardiff and studied at Manchester University, where she now teaches creative writing. She lives in London and works for a literary agency.

Irish writer **Martina Devlin** was born in Omagh, Co. Tyrone. She lives in Dublin, where she works as a reporter and columnist for the *Irish Independent*. Her first novel, *Three Wise Men*, was an instant bestseller in Ireland last year and her second, *Be Careful What You Wish For*, is published by HarperCollins in October. In 1996 she won a Hennessy Cognac Literary Award for her short story, 'Confessions'. Martina Devlin's website is: martinadevlin.com.

Isla Dewar lives in Fife with her husband, a cartoonist. She has published five novels: *Keeping Up With Magda*, *Women Talking Dirty*, *Giving Up On Ordinary*, *It Could Happen to You* and most recently, *Two Kinds of Wonderful*.

Neal Drinnan was born some time in the 1960s in Melbourne, and was dubiously educated at various (now defunct) high schools and Camberwell Boys' Grammar. He has worked in publishing for many years, and writes for a number of magazines. He is the author of three of Australia's most popular gay novels: *Glove Puppet*, *Pussy's Bow* and *Quill*. A seasoned traveller, he is also the editor of *The Rough Guide to Gay & Lesbian Australia*.

This year **Nick Earls** is standing in for Nick(ola) Earls, who was unable to come up with a single new story idea due to the demands placed on her by intensive psychotherapy and deportment classes. Nick(ola) Earls is the author of one (longish) short story, featured in last year's *Girls' Night In*. Nick Earls is the author of several dozen short stories, and the bestselling novels *Zigzag Street*, *Bachelor Kisses*, and *Perfect Skin*. He has also written two award-winning young adult novels, both of which have been adapted for theatre. *Zigzag Street* and *48 Shades of Brown* are currently being developed into feature films. In the UK, a journalist for *The Mirror* described him as 'the first Aussie to make me laugh out loud since Jason Donovan'. He lives in Brisbane and his new novel, *World of Chickens*, is scheduled for publication in Australia in November 2001.

Imogen Edwards-Jones is a journalist and broadcaster. During her ten years in journalism she has written for almost every newspaper and magazine in the UK, with columns in the *Independent* and *The Times*. Her television career includes *This Morning with Richard and Judy* where she pronounced on fashion, and a surreal moment when she had her lips injected on *The Word*. A fluent Russian speaker, she was made an honorary Cossack while researching her first book, *The Taming of Eagles, Exploring the New Russia* (Weidenfeld & Nicolson). She is the author of two novels, *My Canapé Hell* (Hodder & Stoughton), a satire on the celebrity circuit which was published last year; and *Shagpile* (Hodder & Stoughton), a story of swinging in 1970s Solihull published later this year. She is married and lives in West London.

Tim Ferguson is a writer, performer and producer in all media, except interpretive dance. His recent novel *Left, Right & Centre* was allegedly the biggest-selling book in Penguin Australia's entire publishing history. (Remarkably, Ferguson owns the largest collection of that novel in the world.) A tae kwon do black belt, Ferguson dares anyone, and he means *anyone*, to look at him funny. A self-made millionaire by the age of twenty-five, Ferguson deplores arts students, embraces globalisation, is great in bed and writes his own biographies.

Patrick Gale was born in 1962 on the Isle of Wight. He spent his infancy at Wandsworth Prison, which his father governed, then grew up in Winchester. He was educated at Winchester and Oxford, and now lives on a farm near Land's End. He is the author of nine novels including *Little Bits of Baby*, *The Facts of Life*, *Tree Surgery for*

Beginners and most recently, *Rough Music*. As well as writing and reviewing fiction, he has published a biography of Armistead Maupin, a short history of the Dorchester Hotel and chapters on Mozart's piano and mechanical music for H.C. Robbins Landon's *The Mozart Compendium*.

Mike Gayle was born in 1970 in Birmingham, England. After graduating from the University of Salford with a degree in Sociology and Sleeping, Mike undertook a number of jobs before writing novels full-time. These include modelling for a Benetton catalogue (strange but true), being an agony uncle for the teenage girls' magazine *Bliss* (even more strange but even truer) and dyeing his hair bright red for *Just Seventeen* (stranger still). Mike once auditioned to be a presenter on Channel 4's *The Word* and had to interview a fledgling Take That. Both events scarred him for life. He is now the author of three bestsellers, *My Legendary Girlfriend*, *Mr Commitment* and *Turning Thirty*, which have all at various points in time lodged themselves in *The Sunday Times Top Ten*. Mike has also written on various subjects for *FHM*, *Cosmopolitan*, *The Sunday Times*, the *Guardian* and *Girl Talk* (the number-one read for 6- to 11-year-old girls). He is married to his wife, and together they have a small grey rabbit called Pip. He is currently working on a new novel, due out early 2002 and can be contacted via his website: mikegayle.co.uk and . . . er, that's it.

Sarah Harris was born in London, England, in 1967. She has worked as a press officer for the Liberal Democrats, a freelance journalist, and as an assistant producer for BBC *Newsnight*. Her first novel, *Wasting Time*, was published by Fourth Estate in 1998. *Closure* was published in 2000, by HarperCollins. *The Third Time He Left Me* came out in September 2001. Sarah is married with a daughter and son, and lives in London, where she now writes full-time.

John Hegley was born in Islington, London, in 1953. Before the beckoning of show-biz he was a bus conductor, social security clerk, and worked with children excluded from school – carer/educator/gaoler. His first formal performance as writer/performer was in Doggs Troup, London (Children's Theatre) 1978. His first notable media exposure was on John Peel sessions (Radio One) with Popticians – 1983/4: songs about spectacles and the misery of human existence. He was nominated for the Edinburgh Festival Perrier Award in 1989. His first book, *Glad to Wear Glasses*, was published by André Deutsch in 1990. Since then he has been published by Methuen verse/prose/drawings/drama/photographs of potatoes, his most recent publication being *Dog*. Three series of Hearing with Hegley have been broadcast on Radio Four 1997–2000. In 2000 he was awarded an Honorary Arts Doctorate from Luton University. His most notable live engagement was a poetry performance at Medellín, Colombia's women's prison, 2000. He was on tour earlier this year. His dog ran away in 1985.

Linda Jaivin is the author of *Eat Me*; *Rock 'n' Roll Babes from Outer Space*; *Miles Walker, You're Dead*; and *Dead Sexy*, as well as the non-fiction collection *Confessions of an S&M Virgin* and China memoir *The Monkey and the Dragon*. She lives in Sydney. At the time she was asked to write a story for *Girls' Night In, Gentlemen By Invitation*, she was 200 pages into a Chinese kungfu novel and completely obsessed by it. She'd like to be a kungfu heroine in her next life.

Anna Johnson was born in London. She is a freelance writer and journalist and has worked for *Interior Design*, *Sydney Morning Herald*, *Vogue Australia*, *Vogue UK*, *Vanity Fair*, *Conde Nast Traveler*, *ELLE*, *Good Weekend* and *The Australian*. She is the author of *Three Black Skirts: All You Need to Survive*, a life-skills book born in Sydney, published in the United States and due to be translated into German, Spanish, Portugese, Dutch, Norwegian, Russian, Korean and Swedish. Anna's website ThreeBlackSkirts.com welcomes your recipes. She currently lives in New York working on a history of the handbag for Workman publishing.

Gretel Killeen is the author of nineteen books including *Visible Panty Line*. She is published in Australia, Europe and Canada, with many of her books being bestsellers. Having started life as a stand-up comic she still performs as a voice artist in advertising and appears regularly as a humorist on national TV and radio. Gretel recently hit the heights of recognisability while hosting the enormously popular *Big Brother*. She is currently running around like a headless chook raising a son and daughter, preparing several of her works for television, writing a film . . . and having a million affairs of the heart.

Sophie Kinsella is the author of *The Sacred Dreamworld of a Shopaholic*, which has been optioned as a Disney film, and its sequel, *Shopaholic Abroad*, which was published in September. Before becoming a full-time fiction writer she worked as a journalist on a financial magazine, where she wrote many a scintillating article on pension planning. She now divides her time between the computer, the kettle and the shopping mall.

Kathy Lette first achieved *succès de scandale* as a teenager with the novel *Puberty Blues*. After several years as a singer in a rock band and a newspaper columnist in Sydney and New York (collected in her book *Hit and Ms*) she worked as a television sitcom writer for Columbia Pictures in Los Angeles. Her other novels, *Girls' Night Out*, *The Llama Parlour*, *Foetal Attraction*, *Mad Cows* and *Altar Ego*, have all become international bestsellers. Kathy Lette's plays include *Grommits*, *Wet Dreams*, *Perfect Mismatch* and *I'm So Happy For You, Really I Am*. She lives in London with her husband and two children.

Paul Livingston is currently a bi-weekly contributor to the *Australian Weekend* magazine with 'The Flacco Files', an illustrated commentary on the state of being which also appears in book form published by Allen and

Unwin. Paul's acting credits include *Babe – Pig in the City*, *Mr Accident*, *Dark City*, *Children of the Revolution* and *The Navigator* (AFI nomination best supporting actor). His novel *The Dirt Bath* was published in 1998 by Penguin Books. In 1996 Paul was the joint winner of the Sidney Myer Performing Arts Award for outstanding achievement in the performing arts in Australia. In 2001 his play *Emma's Nose* completed a successful season at the Belvoir Street Theatre in Sydney. As Flacco, Paul has toured extensively in Australia and internationally with regular appearances at festivals in Edinburgh and Montreal. Flacco's many television credits include: *Good News Week*, *GNW Nite Lite*, *Sandman and Flacco Special* for the Ten network, *Good News Weekend*, *The Big Gig*, *Daas Kapital* for the ABC, and was a regular on the Triple J Breakfast programme from 1994–97.

Robert Llewellyn is best known for his television appearances on *Red Dwarf* and *Scrapheap Challenge* in the UK. He's had eight books published, written piles of screenplays which have never been made, a handful of stage plays which have been seen, he's been a stand-up comic, a tree surgeon, a bootmaker and a keen amateur intellectual. He lives with Judy Pascoe, also a writer, and their two children, mostly in the Cotswolds. Robert is a closet redneck petrolhead; although he presents himself as a slightly limp liberal male, there is a tattooed, muscle-pumped, mullet-hair-styled thug inside waiting to get out.

Josie Lloyd and **Emlyn Rees** are co-authors of the

bestselling novels *Come Together* and *Come Again*. They first met and became friends in 1996 when they were writing their first novels (Emlyn's *The Book of Dead Authors*, published by Headline, and Josie's *It Could Be You*, published by Orion). They have since written the screenplay for *Come Together* with Working Title films and are currently working on an original screenplay and their next joint novel. They were married in 1999 and live with their baby daughter in London. Their latest book, *The Boy Next Door*, was published by Heinemann in April 2001.

Hector Macdonald grew up on the Kenyan coast, windsurfing instead of playing football and memorising snake names instead of pop groups. This early interest in wildlife led to a biology degree at Oxford, partly under the tutelage of Richard Dawkins. For three years he pursued a career of bar charts, bullet points and international business, writing in the evenings and on weekends, until the completion of *The Mind Game* (Michael Joseph) allowed him to write full-time. *The Mind Game* has been translated into seventeen languages and the film rights have gone to FilmFour and Heyday Films. He is now working on his second book, *The Hunting Ground*. He lives in London, but disappears to the wilds of Africa as often as possible.

Serena Mackesy worked as a temp, English teacher, door-to-door salesperson, lexicographical proofreader, barmaid and crossword editor before stumbling into journalism. After several years producing columns, features, restaurant and television reviews and travel pieces for the *Independent*, her bestselling first novel, *The Temp*, was published by Century/Arrow in 1999. A second novel, *Virtue*, followed last year and a third, *Beyond Belief*, is published in the autumn. She lives in South London and has honed her commute down to leaning out of bed and picking up the laptop off the floor. Her accountant informs her she spends marginally more on taxis than booze.

Chris Manby grew up in Gloucester and published her first short story in *Just Seventeen* at the age of fourteen, whilst still under a parental ban for reading such a racy magazine. Her four wickedly funny romantic comedies, *Flatmates*, *Second Prize*, *Deep Heat* and *Lizzie Jordan's Secret Life*, are available in Coronet paperback. A fifth, *Running Away From Richard*, was published in August 2001. Chris now divides her time between Los Angeles and Cheltenham. Her hobbies include reading in-flight magazines and scandalising her elderly neighbours. She hopes that continually crossing time-zones will help stave off her thirtieth birthday.

Monica McInerney was born in the Clare Valley of South Australia and has lived in Australia, Ireland and England. She has worked in book publishing, public relations, arts marketing, children's television, restaurants, hotels and Irish music pubs. Her first novel *A Taste For It* was a bestseller in Australia and Ireland. Her second novel *Upside Down Inside Out* will be published by Penguin in February 2002.

Santa Montefiore was born in England in 1970. She read Spanish and Italian at Exeter University. After a year teaching English in Argentina, her mother's birthplace, she spent much of the 1990s in Buenos Aires. Her first novel, a sweeping epic of forbidden love based in Argentina, *Meet Me Under the Ombu Tree*, was published by Hodder & Stoughton in March 2001. Her second novel, *The Butterfly Box*, will be published in March 2002. She is currently working on her third title. She is married to the writer Simon Sebag Montefiore. They live in London.

Alexandra Potter was born in Yorkshire, but her itchy feet took her to both Los Angeles and Sydney before she settled in London with her boyfriend Pete. After being made redundant from her job as a features writer, she worked as a freelance sub-editor on various women's magazines until one day she decided to write that novel she was always going on about. Film rights to her first novel *What's New, Pussycat?* have been sold, and the follow-up, *Going La La*, was published by Fourth Estate in March 2001. She's currently working on her third book, *Calling Romeo*.

Mark Powell dropped out of university to travel to New York City when he was nineteen. He spent a dangerous and exciting year in New York (spending most of his time with street gangs) before returning to the UK. The next four years were spent travelling, visiting places such as Israel, Egypt, Spain and Greece. In 1992, Mark completed a law degree and joined the Royal Air Force as an officer. In 1995, he resigned his commission and pursued his writing ambitions, enrolling on Manchester University's MA in Novel Writing and winning the university's Curtis Brown prize. That winning novel, *SNAP*, was published in March 2001. He currently works with excluded students in Brent and is writing his second novel. For more information go to markpowell.co.uk.

Matthew Reilly is the author of the international bestsellers, *Ice Station*, *Temple*, *Contest* and *Area 7*. His novels are published in over a dozen countries in nine languages. He lives in Sydney, hopes to direct a feature film sometime in the next twelve months, and is a big fan of the films of Baz Luhrmann. He also has a tendency to chew on things (pens, his shirt collar) while thinking about creative stuff.

Allison Rushby is a 27-year-old born and bred Brisbane novelist. Her first novel, *allmenarebastards.com*, was published by Random House in 2000. She is addicted to the fake cheese stuff on corn chips, loves her cat Hermione who only has three legs (the dog next door ate one) and gets all her best ideas in the shower. In the past, she has prostituted her writing skills to wedding magazines, having over fifty articles published nationally and internationally. Her next novel will be published by Random House in early 2002. Frankly, all this is a far cry from what she wanted to be when she was five years old – a ballerina with pierced ears. This story is for Barbara and her rat.

David Smiedt is the author of *Boom-Boom: 100 Years of Australian Comedy* (co-written with Rob Johnson) and *Delivering the Male*. He has also contributed to various anthologies and magazines. He recently got in touch with his inner-child, only to discover it has ADD, and is currently enrolled in a support group to cure him of an addicton to twelve-step programmes. He plans to have the words 'I seem to have soiled myself' on his tombstone.

Michael Marshall Smith is a novelist and screenwriter. His first novel *Only Forward* won the August Derleth Award and is nominated for the 2001 Philip K. Dick Award; *Spares* was optioned by Stephen Spielberg's DreamWorks SKG and translated into seventeen languages; *One of Us* is under option by Warner Brothers. His short stories have appeared in anthologies and magazines around the world and in a collection, *What You Make It*. His next novel, *The Straw Men*, will be published in 2002. He lives in North London with his wife Paula and two cats.

As a break from serving double cod, chips and peas to the likes of Bernard Manning in her father's Cornish fish and chip shop, **Stephanie Theobald** used to take weekly horse-riding lessons. There, she discovered that double cod, chips and peas had more to offer on the excitement front so she went to Paris for five years until she had enough sleazy material to write a novel called *Biche*. Meaning 'hello gorgeous' in French, *Biche* was published by Flame in November 2000 and the author describes it as 'existential Jackie Collins'. Her new novel, *Sucking Shrimp*, about sinister food and Spain, is published by Flame in November 2001.

Helen Townsend is the author of twenty books. Recently, she has been exclusively writing fiction. She enjoys writing about contemporary relationships. She lives in Sydney with her family.

Unable to stick to a nine-to-five job, **Fiona Walker** wrote her first novel, *French Relations*, at the age of twenty-one. As well as co-editing this collection and the original *Girls' Night In*, she's the author of six international bestsellers including *Snap Happy*, *Between Males* and most recently *Lucy Talk*. Her unique blend of modern romance, comedy and no-holds-barred sex has earned her the reputation as 'Jilly Cooper for Generation X'. A regular contributor to newspapers and magazines, Fiona is frequently in demand to comment on women and love. She alternates life between homes in North London and Oxfordshire, along with her husband Jon and a menagerie of animals.

Matt Whyman is the author of *Man or Mouse* (Flame), the acclaimed adaptation of Cyrano de Bergerac, and a forthcoming novel, *The Money Shot* (Flame), a tale of sex and Playstation. He is the agony uncle for AOL UK, a 'Love Doctor' for *Bliss* magazine and a regular contributor to *FHM*. A UEA Creative Writing graduate and the author of several advice books, Matt lives in East London with his wife and two daughters. For more info visit www.mattwhyman.com.

ABOUT WAR CHILD

What is War Child?

War Child's mission statement is:

'To provide immediate, effective and sustainable aid to children affected by war to build peace, resolve conflict and empower future generations.'

War Child is an international non-governmental organisation; it works without prejudice of any kind, and champions the right of all children to a happy, healthy and secure childhood. Working together with children, War Child is helping to build a better world for present and future generations.

War Child's work takes it to some of the most difficult, and sometimes dangerous, places in the world, stretching from Europe to Africa, Asia amd Latin America. The focus is always on children, as it is a core belief that they have a fundamental right to care and protection. In a world of plenty no child should go hungry, for food, health care, education or compassion.

War Child receive funds from the public, Government and private donations, and through remarkable initiatives such as *Girls' Night In*. The funds are used to implement a range of projects, for example food and medicine to Sudan, Northern Kenya and Iraq, therapy projects in Sierra Leone and Kosovo, the creation of safe-play areas for children in the Balkans, and radios for child-headed households in Rwanda.

War Child's work is vital if there is to be any hope of a future free from fear, persecution and suffering. If you would like more information, or would like to make a donation contact us at:

Suite 105, 184 Blues Point Road
McMahons Point NSW 2060
info@warchild.globalnet.co.uk

Thank you!